love me always

**J DANIELS • NATASHA MADISON
CARLY PHILLIPS • SHALA BLACK**

Love Me Always

Where I Belong
Copyright @ 2014 J. Daniels. All Rights Reserved

This book is a work of fiction. Names, characters, places, events, and other elements portrayed herein are either the product of the author's imagination or used fictitiously. Any resemblance to real persons or events is coincidental.

No part of this book may be reproduced, storied in a retrieval system, or transmitted in any form, or by any means, electronic, mechanical, photocopying, recording, or otherwise, without prior permission of the author.

Tempting the Boss
© Natasha Madison

ALL RIGHTS RESERVED. This book contains material protected under International and Federal Copyright Laws and Treaties. Any unauthorized reprint or use of the material is prohibited. No part of this book may be reproduced or transmitted in any form or by any means, electronica or mechanical, including photocopying, recording, or by any information storage and retrieval system without express written permission from the author/publisher. The characters and events portrayed in this book are fictitious. Any similarity to real persons, alive or dead, is coincidental and not indented by the author.

This is a work of adult fiction. Names, characters, businesses, places, events, and incidents are either the products of the author's imagination or used in a fictitious manner. Any resemblance to actual persons, living or dead, or actual events is purely coincidental. The author does not endorse or condone any behavior enclosed within. The subject matter is not appropriate for minors. This novel contains profanity and explicit sexual situations.

Dare to Hold
Copyright © Karen Drogin 2015
Working Edition
CP Publishing 2015
Cover Photo and Design: Sara Eirew
www.carlyphillips.com

All rights reserved. No part of this book may be reproduced in any form by any means without the prior written consent of the Publisher, excepting brief quotes used in reviews.

This book is a work of fiction. Names, characters, places, and incidents either are products of the author's imagination or are used fictitiously. Any resemblance to actual events or locales or persons, living or dead, is entirely coincidental.

Wicked as Sin and Wicked Ever After
Copyright @ Shelley Bradley LLC 2020
The characters and events portrayed in this book are fictional. Any similarity to real persons, living or dead, is purely coincidental and not intended by the author. All rights reserved. No part of this book may be reproduced in any form by an electronic or mechanical means—except for brief quotations embedded in critical articles or reviews—without express written permission.
All rights reserved.

where i belong

J DANIELS

I arch my eyebrow. "Oh? And how long have you been watching me to make that observation?"

He chuckles one of the sweetest laughs I've ever heard before replying, "Long enough to see that you're also here by yourself, which surprises me."

I watch as he motions for the bartender, admiring the way the muscles in his arm flex as he reaches into his pocket and pulls out his wallet.

"Why does that surprise you? And are you here by yourself, or is your girlfriend in the ladies room?" My tone is teasing, and I see his lip curl up in the corner as he absorbs my words.

This guy better not have a girlfriend. He'll be wearing my delicious drink if he does.

He turns his body toward me, reaching his hand out to trail down my arm. "You're really fucking hot, that's why it surprises me. And I wouldn't be taking you back to my place if I had a girlfriend."

Old Mia would be shocked by his forwardness, but new Mia is looking up to the heavens, thanking God for putting this gorgeous man who doesn't waste any time on this planet and in this bar tonight.

His finger stops on the top of my hand and he begins rubbing my skin softly there. "That is, if you want to go back to my place. Or we could do yours. It doesn't matter to me. I'm game for any place that'll put me between your legs." His grin spreads and two massive dimples appear in each cheek.

Oh, good God. That's adorable.

"You certainly cut right to the chase."

He shrugs. "I just know what I want, and I've been staring at her for the past twenty minutes."

I like this guy. And not only because he's too good looking for words and blunt as hell. There's something about his playfulness that's drawing me to him. Plus, I feel hotter than I've ever felt; confident even. Which could be because of the one drink I've already downed before this hottie bought me another. Either way, Tessa would be proud of this Mia.

I cross one leg over the other, gaining his attention when the hem of my dress slides higher up my thigh. "Getting between my legs requires changing locations? You don't seem like the type of guy that shies away from public sex."

He definitely doesn't. He looks like the type of guy that would take me anytime, anyplace, and not give a shit what the consequences are. There's an edginess to him that is definitely hitting all my hot spots.

He smiles before he leans in and brushes his lips against my ear. "I'm not, but this bar will eventually close, and I don't plan on stopping what I'm going to do to you until your body can't take anymore."

I shudder at the thought and move my hand to his thigh, flexing my fingers and feeling his muscles contract against me. Turning my head, I put my lips right up to his ear and mimic his position. "Will you be gentle with me? I've never done this before," I whisper. "But God, I want this. I want you to make me come." I lean back and meet his bright eyes, noticing the specks of blue that stand out against the gray. His gaze hypnotizes me. "Do you think you can handle me?"

I swear I hear a growl rumbling in his throat as his hand trails back up my arm and grips the back of my neck underneath my hair. It feels possessive, as if he's claiming me right here in front of everyone. And I know it sounds crazy, but I want to be owned by this man. I want to give myself to him completely and a huge part of me doesn't want gentle. I don't care that it might hurt. I want him to take me and I don't want him to hold back.

He grabs my chin with his other hand and turns my head, bringing our lips together for the slightest bit of contact. I crave more instantly, whimpering when his mouth leaves mine. I see his lip twitch in response to my desperation.

He has me and he knows it.

"I'm going to fucking consume you," he says against my mouth, bringing his other hand around and raking his thumb across my bottom lip. I open my mouth and he slips it inside, his eyes watching with a new heat as I scrape my teeth along his skin and bite down with the smallest amount of pressure. The muscles in his neck twitch and he slides it out, dragging his now wet thumb down my neck. "Your place or mine, baby? I'm close to losing my mind if I don't get inside you soon."

I lick my lips, tasting the trace of whiskey that he left on them from our brief kiss. "Yours. I don't have a place."

"Just passing through?" he asks with raised eyebrows.

We're still sitting so close together, practically on top of each other, and I feel safe. Protected. Something about his looming presence makes me feel like I can trust him completely. It's unexplainable.

"Yeah, you could say that."

I finish off the rest of my drink and stand, indicating that I'm ready to take this where we both want it to go. I can't sit in this bar any longer with him touching me and not lose my mind right along with him.

He gets to his feet and my eyes do a double take.

Damn, he's gorgeous. I couldn't tell from his seated position, but the man has a torso that goes on for days. Broad and built, he definitely works out—and often—with this type of physique. His narrow waist is fitted perfectly in a pair of jeans, and his legs are long and muscular. I can only imagine what the back of him looks like.

I grab my clutch and look up, way up into his face. "I could seriously climb you like an oak tree."

"Oh yeah? I think I'd like to see that." His playful response makes me laugh, and I'm quickly being pulled through the crowd and out the door.

The sweet Alabama air blows my hair off my shoulders.

"You wanna follow me or should I bring you back here to get your car? It's up to you." He stops once we reach the middle of the parking lot, my hand still firmly placed in his.

To my family.

prologue

Mia

BENJAMIN KELLY WAS THE BANE OF MY EXISTENCE. His teasing was relentless, always making sure to point out each and every one of my insecurities whenever I was around him. And because I was best friends with his sister Tessa, I was around him all the time.

"You have food stuck in your braces. That's so disgusting. Maybe you should just stop eating since you're so fat anyway."

"Gross. What is that on your face? It looks like a second head."

"God, can you even see anything out of those glasses, nerd? How many times are you going to run into things?"

"Mia Corelli is the ugliest girl I've ever seen. Oh sorry, Mia. I didn't see you sitting right next to me."

I hated him with a fury. I was convinced that his sole purpose in life was to break me down to nothing. And he succeeded on more than one occasion. I never cried in front of him, though. I never gave him that satisfaction. I just stood there and took it, saving my tears for when I was alone. Tessa was always standing up for me, throwing every insult she could think of at him. And I was grateful for that, because I didn't have it in me to give him what he deserved. My bank of comebacks were pathetic compared to Tessa's. So I'd just sit back and let her handle it.

"You're just jealous that Mia's teeth are going to be straighter than yours, loser. Why don't you go get that giant gap fixed before someone kicks a field goal through it?"

"What's that on your face, Ben? God, it's hideous. Oh, never mind. There's nothing on your face. That's just how you look."

"At least Mia isn't stupid like you, Ben. If you make it out of eighth grade, it'll be a miracle."

"Ben Kelly has the smallest penis in the world. He has to hold it with a pair of tweezers when he pees."

Her comebacks would shut him up temporarily, but when he found his voice again, it was frequently used to take a shot at me. I was his sister's nerdy, awkward best friend who became his favorite punching bag for five grueling years. I grew some thick skin and became used to the torment, but my insecurities were always there. He'd never let me forget about them. He was the spawn of Satan, the biggest jerk on the planet, and I'd hate him for the rest of my life.

Benjamin Kelly was the worst thing to come out of Alabama. And if I never saw him again, that would be fine by me.

chapter one

Mia

"I don't have to go. If this is too much on you, I can stay here. It really isn't a big deal, Aunt Mae." Closing the door to my mother's bedroom, I walk down the hallway into the kitchen behind my aunt. "Really. I mean it. Just because she's doing okay right now doesn't mean it's a good idea for me to leave the state."

My aunt places her hand on my shoulder, squeezing it gently. "You need a break from all of this, sweetie. You've been taking care of her twenty-four hours a day for the past nine months. Everyone needs to take some time for themselves." She tilts her head, her expression softening with a smile. "She wants you to have fun, Mia. Go enjoy your summer and leave all of this to me."

Sighing, I shake my head, not fully committed to the idea of leaving. "What if she gets really sick and I'm not here? What if she needs me?"

The thought of my mother calling out for me while I'm four hours away is enough to cancel this whole trip. She loves my aunt, but I'm the one that's been here. I'm the one that's been doing everything for her since she fell ill. She's used to me, not Mae. I know the look she gets when she's really feeling bad, but won't admit it. I know how to get her to eat when she refuses. Me; I don't need a break, let alone an entire summer off from taking care of my own mother.

"If anything happens, even the slightest change in her condition, I'll call you." Her hand cups my face, her thumb stroking the skin of my cheek. "Promise me you won't let all of your worrying prevent you from having an amazing summer with Tessa."

"I just don't know if this is the best time. She hasn't had her strength back for that long."

Aunt Mae issues me a look, indicating that she's not letting me back out of this. "This is the perfect time. And like I said before, she wants you to go. If you try and stay home now, I'm afraid you won't only be getting an earful from me."

I smile and nod in agreement. My mom does enjoy laying into me when I deserve it. She's stern but sweet at the same time, always following up a punishment with a hug.

"All right, I'll go. But you need to promise you'll call me if there's any change. Even the slightest."

"I promise." She drops her hand and steps around the counter, digging into the pile of dishes that has accumulated in the sink.

I'll be staying with Tessa at her parents' house for the summer while she looks after it. I have a ton of memories at that house, considering the fact that I practically lived there for five years. I'd always go to Tessa's house after school, staying there until my mom would pick me up on her way home. Tessa was like the sister I never had, and when my grandmother got sick and we had to move to Fulton, Georgia the summer before ninth grade, I cried for weeks. We kept in touch over the years, and now I'll be spending the entire summer with her just like we used to. And as long as her pain-in-the-ass brother stays as far away from me as possible, it's going to be the best summer of my life.

Benjamin Kelly. World's biggest dickhead.

I head back to my bedroom, needing to finish up my last bit of packing. Tessa is expecting me tomorrow afternoon sometime, but I'm not waiting until then to get into Alabama. There is something I want to do before I start my summer break. Something I've wanted to do for a long time. If I'm really going to enjoy myself this summer, I need to let go of all my inhibitions. This will not be the summer of hang-ups or shyness. I'm not the same girl that left Ruxton nine years ago. That girl has been gone for a long time. The braces came off first, followed by the weight and the glasses; which were exchanged for contacts. My hair is no longer a wild mess of curls now that I've learned how to manage it. My skin cleared up in tenth grade, and that wasn't the only big change to my appearance that year. My breasts came in overnight it seemed, and they are definitely my best asset, if I do say so myself. And with the help of the volleyball team I joined in high school, my body got tight and stayed that way. The new Mia Corelli is going to let loose and experience everything an Alabama summer had to offer. But in order to do that, I need to handle something first. And that thing is going to be handled tonight.

I grab my phone, falling back onto my pillow after pushing my suitcases to the floor.

Me: All packed up! I'll call you when I'm on the road tomorrow.

Tessa: OMFG I'm so excited! Your ass is mine for the summer! I have so much planned for us already. :)

Me: Yay! I can't wait to get there and relax by the pool for three months.

Tessa: That's not all we're doing. We're finding you a play thing for the summer. I'll surround you with penises if I have to.

Jesus, Tessa.

Me: Well there's an image. Speaking of dicks, any chance your brother will be out of the country for the summer?

Tessa: Don't worry about Ben. I don't even see him that much so you won't have to either. And besides, he's already been warned. If he bothers you, I get to kick him in the nuts.

Me: Only after I get the first shot at him. :)

Tessa: There's my girl. This summer is going to be amazeballs!!! See ya tomorrow!

Me: See ya!

I don't even know the name of the bar I'm currently sitting in. But I doubt it matters. It was the first one I spotted when I got off the Ruxton exit and it looked promising enough. A bar seems like the perfect venue for what I am about to do, or at least attempt to do. I don't want to face another summer as a virgin, especially when my best friend isn't shy about her sexual conquests. If I am going to keep up with her this summer, I have to ditch my virginity, and fast. That's why I picked a bar. This doesn't need to be romantic. I'm not looking for a relationship. This is just sex. Get-it-over-with kind of sex, and hopefully with an orgasm in the process.

Tessa has no idea that I still hold my v-card, and I really don't want to show up tomorrow waving it around like some sort of abstinence banner. So, with the help of my most non-virginal outfit, I'm going to be giving away that card to one of the lucky men in this bar tonight.

"Here ya go, sweetheart," the bartender says, placing a bright purple drink in front of me. "From the guy with the black shirt at the end of the bar."

I wrap my fingers around the glass and glance down the length of the bar, meeting the eyes of the man that bought me the drink.

He's hot. Really hot. Insanely hot. The kind of hot that makes you think, there's no way in hell this guy is looking at me. He has short, dark hair and eyes that are bright enough to see in the dim lighting.

I send him a smile before looking away to take a sip of my drink. It tastes delicious, like raspberry and coconut. I take another sip and glance back down the bar, but the man is no longer there. A surge of disappointment floods my system.

"Crap. Where'd he go?" I utter under my breath as my eyes search the crowded bar. Who buys a girl a drink and then leaves before cashing in on the thank you? Didn't he see the giant florescent arrow pointing to me, flashing *this chick wants to get laid by you?* Damn it. That hottie was definite v-card redeeming material.

"Where'd who go, baby?"

Whipping my head around, I meet the eyes of my sexy little drink buyer as he claims the stool next to me. Gasping softly, I allow myself a moment to take in the hotness that is now brushing up against my arm.

His bright gray eyes are hooded by dark eyebrows, and my attention is drawn down to his lips as they curl up into a smile.

Those. Lips. Holy hell.

Full and way the hell inviting. If I had the nerve, I'd jump all over them.

I look back up into his eyes with a grin. "Oh, um, you actually. I wanted to thank you for my drink. It's really good. What is it?"

"Purple passion. No, purple hurricane?" His eyebrows furrow as he thinks it over. I smile around my straw, taking another sip. "I don't know. Some purple, girly drink. You looked really thirsty from where I was standing, so I thought I'd help you out."

I don't want to pull it out of his to get in my car. I don't want to be away from him for one second, because we'll only have tonight. That's how one-night stands work, or so I've heard. It's not like I know what I'm doing here. But it would make more sense if we drove separately. Besides, if he's some psycho, I'll need a getaway vehicle.

I squeeze his hand, looking up at him from underneath my eyelashes. "I'll follow you, but I'm going to need to feel those lips again first."

He doesn't waste any time. It's as if he's thinking the same thing, because before I can move in, even slightly, to affirm my desires, he's on me. His lips work mine, our tongues stroking against each other's with purpose. These aren't teasing kisses. These are *I want you right now, and if we don't get to a bed soon, you'll be taken right here* kisses. I've never been kissed like this. Never. I could do this for hours. Days even. I feel it radiating throughout my body, pinging off every nerve ending. Our hands are still interlocked; the pressure of his hold intensifies with the kiss. He licks along my bottom lip slowly, ending the passionate embrace our mouths are so happy to be in.

Well, at least my mouth, anyway.

"Coconut," he whispers against my mouth.

"Hmm?"

His lip curls up in the corner. "You taste like coconut. I fucking love coconut." I grin as he flicks his head toward a jacked up truck. "That's me. Follow close behind me, baby. I'd hate to lose you."

"That would be a shame," I tease, walking toward my cherry red Jeep that's parked only a few cars down from his. "I'd hate to have this night end after just one kiss."

His eyes narrow in on my license plate. "One hell of a kiss though, Georgia."

I can't keep the smile off my face as he pulls out of his parking spot and I follow closely behind him.

We are only on the highway momentarily before we hit the Alabama back roads that I used to be so fond of. Tessa and I would go 4-wheeling on back roads like this, and I spent a lot of summers walking up and down the dirt paths, picking wild flowers. But the girl that did those things all those years ago isn't currently following the black truck down these back roads. This is unfamiliar territory, completely new to me, and my stomach is beginning to do flips in anticipation of what is about to happen.

chapter two

Mia

His hand finds mine again as I follow him into his house, and he wastes no time walking straight up the stairs and into the dimly lit bedroom.

I place my clutch down on his dresser, stepping out of my heels.

He isn't far behind me, and I feel him the moment I place my right foot on the carpet. His hands caress down my arms, rough against soft, as I stay turned away from him, feeling his breath in my hair. My pulse begins to thrum in my neck as he takes all of my hair over one shoulder. He presses his lips along the line of my neck and I tilt my head to give him the access we both want him to have.

Oh, God. I close my eyes and feel him. Everywhere. Even though he's barely touching me, I feel him all over my body. The junction where my thighs meet is pulsating and my nipples are so hard they might just rip right through my dress.

Jesus, this is intense.

His lips work up my neck to my ear and he licks it before biting it. I shiver and he does it again.

Who would have thought I'd like a little biting?

He turns me in his arms, latching his mouth onto mine. His tongue sweeps into my mouth and I groan, gripping his head to hold him to me. His hair is soft against my palms, and I run my fingers along the base of his hair line. I feel his desire for me pressing into my stomach, and it isn't a small desire.

Thank you, Jesus.

He moans into my mouth and sucks on my tongue, his hands roaming all over my back. Firmly planting them on my ass, he dips and lifts me off the ground in one quick motion.

My legs instinctively wrap around his waist as he carries me over to the bed, dropping me in the middle of it. I run my tongue along my bottom lip, tasting his mouth on mine. I'm ready. So ready. If he doesn't touch me again soon, I might just resort to begging.

He'd probably like that.

"Christ, you're so sexy. Look at you." He stares down at me, eyes blazing as I stretch out on the bed beneath him. "You've no idea how close I was to pulling over on the side of the road and taking you right there."

That would've been fun. Sex in a truck? A really bad ass looking truck? I'll have to put that on my to-do list.

"Maybe next time," I reply, but I know there won't be a next time. Not with this guy anyway. I'll probably never see him again, and I'm okay with that.

My eyes enlarge as he pulls his T-shirt off with one hand.

Oh, wow. His bare chest is a sight to behold; wide with a bit of dark hair in the middle. He's all man, and I don't feel a bit ashamed about the staring I'm doing. He should be on billboards all over the city.

He's muscular, every cut of him visible from my angle. His right shoulder is completely covered in tattoos, stretching down to his elbow. And trust me when I say that tattoos have never looked this good.

Six, no eight pack, maybe? The V. That freaking glorious V that leads to what I really want that's hiding beneath his pants.

He undoes his belt and his jeans fall to the floor, leaving a very impressive erection pressing against his boxers.

My mouth waters instantly. I want to eat him up.

He drops to his knees at the foot of the bed. and I lean up on my elbows to see him better. I'm about to ask him what he's doing when my feet are grabbed and I'm pulled toward him. And now I'm very aware of what he plans on doing. I yelp and hear a small sound of amusement as my legs are dropped over his shoulders.

"I need to taste this pussy." His hands hike my dress up to reveal my lace panties. My favorite pair, actually. I felt losing my virginity warranted something besides my go-to boy shorts. "You wanna come on my lips, baby?"

Hell fucking yes, I do. Would anyone in their right mind say no to that?

"Uh huh," is all I can give him at the moment. My brain is having difficulty forming a complete thought as I anticipate his mouth on me there.

He groans, deep and guttural, sliding his hand up my thigh until I feel his fingers running up and down the length of the lace.

I'm shaking, fisting the sheets already and he's barely touching me.

"So wet and hot." He presses his face between my thighs and inhales, his moan vibrates against my body. "Damn, you smell good. I bet you taste even better, though."

My panties are removed and that first lick nearly rockets me off the bed.

"Holy shit. That's… oh, wow."

My thighs clamp his head so tightly, I'm surprised he's managing to move his head at all. But he manages, and he's eating me like this is all we're going to do tonight. Like this is the only way he'll get to experience my body. I can't take my eyes off him while he does it, and given the predatory look in his eyes right now, I'm not sure he'll let me look away if I tried. He's all over me, alternating his movements so I don't get used to anything. And he seems to be enjoying it as much as I am, going at it with such gusto and humming against me. The vibration moves through my entire body, pulsing, pulsing, until I'm so close I can't see straight. This is what oral sex is supposed to feel like. Raw. Uninhibited. Thank God, I left my shyness at the door because he's exploring every inch of my pussy. I'm tempted to lock him between my legs and never let him up for air. He's incredible at this, and I know without a doubt that given the chance, I would've never experienced anything even remotely close to this.

This man. Holy fuck. This man right here knows exactly what he's doing.

I don't want to come so quickly, but there's no way I can slow down my body's reaction to him. I arch my back off the bed, groaning loudly as my orgasm barrels through me like a shock wave.

He licks my length once, and then again, making sure to soak up every last drop of what he's earned.

"You're fucking beautiful when you come." He plants gentle kisses between my legs, his eyes glued to mine. "I need to see that again." He kneels in between my legs, dropping his hand to the spot he's just worked like the world was about to end.

I whimper as he teases me with one finger, slipping it inside as he keeps his eyes on me.

"When you get yourself off, do you just focus on your clit or do you fuck your pussy like this?"

Hottest. Question. Ever.

I swallow loudly as he slips in another finger, loosening me, priming me for his cock. "Just my clit. I don't think I can come from," I gasp, "from that."

Holy mother of God.

His eyes sparkle with mischief. "Challenge accepted." He grabs my knee with his free hand and begins fingering me, ignoring my clit completely.

I'd protest if it didn't feel un-fucking-believable. I feel him curl them up inside me, as if he's beckoning me to come closer, to come all together. He's rubbing some glorious spot that I never knew even existed.

"What are you... oh, my God, I've never, is that... are you?" I'm panting and arching into his magical touch. If I begin speaking in tongues, I won't be surprised in the least.

"It's your G-spot, angel. I'll make you come in ways you never thought possible."

He presses up into that spot while his other hand pushes down on the front of my pelvis. I'm not sure if he feels the change that's happening to me or if he sees it. But he knows exactly when it happens.

"That's it. Give me another. I fucking need it," he growls and I obey, giving him exactly what he demands of me.

I lock eyes with him as my orgasm rips through my body, shredding me into post climactic pieces.

"Holy shit. Come up here."

I reach for him, seeing him stand and slip his boxers off as he sucks on the fingers that were just inside me. My eyes wander lower, lower, until I focus in on what might possibly split me in two. He's bigger than I thought. Way bigger.

"Oh, my God," I blurt out, causing him to glance over at me with a puzzled expression. We both laugh together and I cover my face embarrassingly. "Sorry. That was a good *Oh, my God*."

"Christ, I hope so." He slips on a condom and moves between my legs. "Let's see if you have anything for me to *oh, my God* at underneath this dress." His hands grip the hem of my dress and I sit up, granting him access. "I'm betting you're about to blow my fucking mind."

I blush crimson as my dress is removed. Lying back on the bed, I watch his eyes run all over my body, stopping and widening as they land on my chest.

Oh, God. I'm completely naked in front of this man and he's just staring at me.

I should let him stare though, after that mind-blowing orgasm. I should let him do whatever he wants with me. With a tongue like that and fingers I'd give my life for, I can't imagine how good the rest of his body is.

Speaking of the rest of his body.

My eyes drop to his massive erection and the need in me grows to a palpable hunger.

"Umm, is something wrong?" I whisper my fear, seeing his eyes jolt up to mine, finally leaving my breasts.

"Your tits are phenomenal." His hands squeeze them and I arch my back off the mattress, pushing them farther into his palms. "I want to slide my cock right here and come all over them." He trails a finger down the center, his eyes turning roguish. "I bet you'd look beautiful covered in me. I bet you'd like it too."

Jesus. This guy excels in the dirty talking department. And I never thought I'd be into that. But coming out of that mouth, from those lips, I'm way the hell into it. I've never been so turned on in my life.

He leans forward and presses my body into the mattress.

The sensation of him over me is perfect. Every part of his body is touching mine, and I never want him to move. His erection pushes against my clit, and I moan into him as his mouth collides with mine. His tongue twists and dips, licking and swiping into my mouth. God, he's so good at this. I feel like I'm just fumbling around but he isn't complaining. I run along the muscles of his back with my hands, feeling them flex against my touch.

His mouth breaks free of mine, and he slides down slightly. "I gotta suck them, baby." He flicks my nipple once, twice, and then draws it into his mouth.

"Oh, yes." I hold his head to my breast, not ever wanting him to stop this amazing sensation.

He alternates between them, giving each nipple equal attention as he sucks, twists, and bites. The pain is just enough that it blends into pleasure. Intense pleasure. It feels amazing. But I want more. I miss his cock already, now that he's moved down my body.

"Can you, oh…"

His head tilts up. "Can I what?" He keeps his eyes on me as he licks my left nipple. "I'm not doing anything else to this beautiful body unless you beg me to do it." His hands continue their sweet torture on my breasts. "You said back at the bar that you've never done this before. What did you mean exactly? Going home with a stranger? Or what you're about to beg me to do?"

I glance down and meet his smirk.

Christ, he's sexy as hell, and playful. Deadly combination. And he has every right to be cocky. I'm all for begging if it puts him inside me.

"Um, both actually. I've never done anything like this. I've kissed boys and they've touched me a little, but that's about the extent of my experience."

"Are you sure you wanna do this? You don't even know me. I could eat your pussy some more or fuck you again with my fingers. It doesn't have to be my cock getting you off."

I bite my lip playfully. "Tempting. But I want this to be with you." Our eyes stay locked as he sits back between my legs. "I don't want to stop."

"Show me you want this." He holds me with his stare, commanding me to do what he's asking. "Show me you want me to be the one to take it."

I reach for his cock, sliding down the condom and rubbing his length. His groan vibrates through his entire body and I feel it tickling my palm.

"Do you think you can make me come with this?" I whisper my tease. "I'm betting you can. I'm betting you can make me come all night with it."

The biggest, sweetest grin spreads across his face and I swoon. I'm fucking swooning here.

"That's the plan, sweetheart. I'm gonna go slow, but I need you to tell me if it's too much for you."

He braces himself on either side of my face, taking his weight on his forearms. I feel him at my entrance and he gently places kisses to my lips as he slowly slides in with a muted grunt. I inhale sharply and clamp my eyes shut.

Holy shit, he's big. Really fucking big.

He stills, not all the way in, and I let out my air.

"Jesus. So damn tight." He groans and drops his forehead to mine. "Are you okay?" His concerned words blow across my face. "Do you want me to pull out?"

I open my eyes and meet his. I have to keep going. I know the pleasure will come after the pain. "No, don't pull out. I want you to fuck me."

His hand strokes my cheek in the most intimate way. "Baby, I can't fuck you until you're ready for me. It'll hurt if I try to do it right now." He reaches down and grabs my hand, moving it around him. "Grab me and pull me into you. That way you're controlling it."

I nod once, grabbing on to him with both hands and guiding him into me. The pain hits me again and I tense. Every muscle in my body contracts against his. I can't stop. I need to do this. I clamp my eyes shut as I pull him in.

Deeper. Deeper. Fucking hell. My nails dig into his skin and I sharply suck in my breath again.

"Oh, God," I pant.

The pain begins to shift, slowly disappearing into nothing. I lock onto his eyes and bite my lip, seeing his apprehensive expression.

He's just as tense as I am.

He doesn't want to hurt me.

I chose the right guy.

I relax my body completely and become familiar with the sensation. "I'm okay," I reassure him, seeing the tightness in his jaw disappear and his eyes light up.

He slowly pushes in all the way, gauging my reaction closely. Studying my face. His lips are parted slightly and his eyes are so bright, they seem to light up the darkness of his bedroom. A deep, guttural noise escapes his throat as I open up to him, spreading my legs as wide as they'll go.

"I'm all the way in you, baby, and it feels so damn good." He brushes his lips against mine. "Fucking perfect," he whispers.

"I'm ready for you to move," I say, assurance in my tone. I'm more than ready. I tilt my pelvis up and wrap my legs around his waist.

He slowly slides back out, keeping his eyes on mine and watching me closely. The pain is gone and the only thing I feel is pure ecstasy. Elation. Fucking euphoria. I moan and lift my hips, urging him farther.

Oh, yes. That feels good. Amazingly good.

"Holy fuck," he grunts, sliding back in slowly. He bends down and kisses the corner of my mouth. "Does it still hurt?"

I smile against his lips and shake my head.

"Good. I'm gonna really move now, pretty girl. I don't know how long I'll last though. You're squeezing me so God damned tight, angel." And then he picks up rhythm, his hips crashing against mine.

My breasts bob against his muscular chest and I kiss him deeply, exploring every inch of his mouth with my tongue. The room fills with our moans that are in no way muffled. I'm certain people in the next state over can hear us.

Thrust. Thrust. Thrust.

"Oh, my God," I say as he licks and sucks my breast. And I know I'm close. I'm familiar now with what he can do to me and there's no stopping it. The buildup is coming from deep within me, and it's coming quick. Like a wildfire spreading.

"You're right there, baby. Are you ready?"

How fucking hot is it that he knows when I'm about to come? I don't even need to tell him.

"Yes. God, yes," I answer.

He slides his hand between us and rubs against my clit. Thrusting harder and harder, deeper than I thought possible, and my orgasm rolls through me like a current.

"Oh!" I'm coming, clutching his body, and this is even more intense than the first two.

First two. How lucky am I right now?

My entire body trembles against his as I dig my nails into his back and rake them along his skin.

"Do that again," he demands urgently.

I repeat the action and he groans loudly, ramming into me and finding his release.

"Baby. Fuck!"

He twitches inside me and stills, relaxing his body against mine as we both slowly come down.

But I don't want to come down. I like this high. No, I love this high. This high is incredible. Now I understand what appeals to sex addicts. I'm elated and completely spent. I could actually die now and be okay with it. And I would like my tombstone to read the following:

Mia Blaire Corelli

Beloved daughter and friend.

Death by Orgasm. With a capital "O".

I had no intention of falling asleep.

I had planned on surprising Tessa after my amazing night with my stranger, explaining that I was too excited to wait until the next day to leave. But after five orgasms, *five*, a girl can only take so much before she passes out.

After taking a small break to catch our breaths, he took me from behind, bending me over the bed, and then he asked me to ride him. I was embarrassed about that at first.

Me? Take charge?

Then I took him in and realized how deep he was that way. So incredibly deep. I think that's my favorite position now. Plus, it gave him unlimited access to my breasts, which he seemed to enjoy immensely. I believe his words were, "best tits I've ever seen." I'm still glowing from that compliment.

And then, to top off the best experience of my life, he held me. Like it meant just as much to him as it meant to me. Which is where we are now.

His arm is draped across my waist and he's breathing slow, steady breaths in my hair as I glance at the alarm clock on his nightstand. 10:14 a.m.

I can't believe I slept over. At a stranger's house. A complete stranger. Well, not complete. He's the only man that knows my body the way no one else does. And sweet Jesus, does he know it.

Plus, it felt natural to cuddle up next to him and fall asleep on his chest. It was almost intimate, our experience. It was hot as hell but also sweet. He was gentle with each new position, constantly asking if I was okay before he took me to that depth of passion and fucking owning me. And I felt his affection deep within me, but pretended I didn't. This wasn't supposed to mean anything other than a hot fling.

His warm body was pressed up against mine the entire night, our legs a tangled mess under the covers. The intoxicating aroma of his scent filled my lungs, and it was slowly becoming the only air I wanted to breathe. Nothing had ever smelled that divine. Complete manly deliciousness. I wished I could keep him.

I slip out from underneath his arm and scramble around the bed, picking up my dress and panties. After dressing and using the bathroom, I step into my heels and grab my clutch.

"Hey." His sexy morning voice grabs my attention as I'm about to sneak out of his room. "Come here, pretty girl." He props one hand behind his head, holding his other out to me. He looks positively adorable in that just-woken-up way—his hair sticking out a bit and his eyes still sleepy.

I walk over to the bed and take his hand, bringing it up to my lips for a kiss.

He smiles, weakening my knees with his dimples. "That's my move, isn't it?"

"I gotta go." I go to release his hand but he tightens his grip. "You're trouble, you know that? I have places to be."

His cell phone rings from the nightstand, forcing him to release my hand with a disapproving grunt. "Stay with me a little while longer. What's the rush?" The phone continues to ring in his hand as he waits for my response.

"I can't." I lean down and brush my lips against his, the ringtone finally fading out. And then I start toward the door, which is an extremely difficult task. Every ounce of my being wants to stay with this man, if only just to talk to him.

"Wait, damn it. At least tell me your name."

His phone starts ringing again, having been ignored the first time.

I silently contemplate his request, but decide against names. The old Mia would want a name. Not this new Mia that picked up a stranger in a bar and gave him her virginity. I'm a new woman and I'm doing things differently this summer.

I smile. "Thank you for last night. I'll never forget you."

I allow myself one last look before I slip out of his bedroom. His eyes are sad, pleading even, and I can't keep looking or I'm going to crack. I turn and leave before I weaken even more.

And I know I'll never forget him. He was amazing, and exactly what I wanted my first time to be like. A beautiful memory. That's exactly what he'll be.

chapter three

Ben

"Jesus Christ. What?"

My voice gives away my mood, and I'm hoping this phone call is brief. I need to get some sleep. I barely got any last night, but that was well worth it. Really fucking worth it.

"Well good morning to you too," my sister snaps. She's my only sister, but she's all over the place sometimes with her personality, that it feels like there's twenty of her. "What are you doing right now? You busy?" Her voice softens, the snippiness gone and quickly replaced with the tone she uses when she wants something.

"I could've been if you wouldn't have interrupted me." I grab the pillow my nameless angel used last night, bringing it up to my face.

Christ, she smells good. Like berries and cream.

"What do you want, Tessa?"

"Can you come over here and clean the pool? Every time I try to use that stupid vacuum thing, it always jams up on me." I hear her breathy pause, knowing that the begging is about to start. "Please, Ben. It's hot as hell outside and when Mia gets here, I want to be able to spend the rest of the day in the pool with her. Please, please, please."

Mia fucking Corelli. The most annoying girl that's ever lived.

I completely forgot she was spending the summer with Tessa. Last time I saw her, she was an irritating fourteen-year-old. She and Tessa followed me around like damn puppies, always wanting to do what I was doing. And the fact that she practically lived at my house didn't help much. She was always around.

I toss the pillow I've been inhaling to the end of the bed. "Why the hell don't you just stay inside with her? I'm not in the mood to spend an hour cleaning out a damn pool."

"Oh, come on, Ben. You owe me and you know it. Besides, I'd rather have you and Mia get your awkward greeting out of the way so she can relax a little."

"What does that mean?" I get up and start getting dressed, holding the phone between my ear and my shoulder.

I don't know what awkward greeting she's referring to. It won't be awkward. It'll be brief. Really brief. I have no desire to spend any time with that train wreck.

"You know exactly what that means. She's nervous as shit about coming back here because of you." The sound of the sliding glass door opening and closing comes through the phone. "Christ, it's already a thousand degrees out here." Tessa sighs and it's dramatic, even though it doesn't have to be. I know what she's getting at. "If only I had a big brother who did nice things for me. Nice things that are well deserved after all the last minute favors I've done for him over the years."

"All right. Jesus." I zip up my shorts and grab a clean T-shirt from my dresser. "I'll be over there in an hour."

Her shriek causes me to move the phone away to a safer distance. I return it to my ear after her excitement dies down.

"You're the best brother ever. But can you be over sooner? She's on her way over here now."

"An hour. I've got my own shit to do today too, you know."

A particular girl to track down, and hopefully get her name.

I don't miss the slight grunt Tessa gives me before responding, "Fine. Thanks, Ben."

Hanging up the phone, I tuck it into my pocket and grab her pillow one more time.

Wait. *Her pillow?* Christ, get a hold of yourself.

I've had my fair share of one-night stands and never, never, let the girls spend the night. But this one was different. I was prepared to tie her to my bed if she tried to leave last night.

I inhale and let her scent run through me, feeling it hit me deep in my gut.

I've never taken a girl's virginity before. That was intense. I really didn't think she was one, not with a body like that and the way she was flirting with me at the bar. Sucking and biting my thumb like a fucking temptress. But her reaction to the sex we had and the blood stain on my sheets definitely confirms that she was, in fact, a virgin.

Tossing the pillow to the floor, I wrap up my sheets and walk them into the laundry room.

I like the stain. No, I fucking love the stain. It was proof that she gave me something that nobody else will ever have—a part of her I can hold on to since she didn't give me anything else. Not even a fucking name.

I walk back into my room to slip on my shoes.

Why wouldn't she tell me her name? What's the big deal? I get the whole casual hook up thing. No strings. No expectations. But I always know the name of the chick I'm banging, or at least the name they give me. It could be made up for all I know, considering that I've never pursued anything else with them after we've had one night together. But this chick, hell, I'd like multiple nights with her. Weeks even. She wasn't just an amazing lay, the best I've ever had, with a pussy I could eat for hours and tits that'll occupy all my fantasies until the day I die. She was more than that.

She was sweet and funny, with this laugh that I wanted to hear more of. Her whole face lit up when she laughed. I wanted to make her smile again, to see those full lips part and spread across her face. And the way she looked at me with those big brown eyes, so dark I could get lost in them. Plus, she fucking knew what I wanted last night without me having to ask. I need control and she gave it to me, but she also pushed back when I pushed her.

When I bit her body, she cried out for more. When I fucked her until I thought my spine was going to snap in half, she demanded harder.

She met me in the middle and gave as well as she took. It was wild perfection. A beautiful chaos. She was my match in the bedroom and I let her slip away without giving me a name.

The fuck? I should've spanked her and demanded she give it to me.

I inhale the pillow that's been pressed to my face for a good several minutes. Next to her pussy, it's the best thing I've ever smelled. It dulls my senses like a drug. I'm high on her and I'm pissed that it won't last.

I grab my keys and toss the pillow onto the bed.

I'm never washing that pillow case. Never.

The back roads leading away from my house are empty, which disappoints me. I was hoping her car would've broken down or, by some miracle, she would've gotten a flat tire and not known how to change it. Most girls don't, my sister included. But knowing my luck, she can probably change a tire faster than me and went on her way back to Georgia or wherever she was headed. Just passing through were her words. To where? She's obviously from Georgia, and I have to hope she'll be making her way back through Ruxton when she's ready to return there, or if she's already headed that way that she'll want to pass through here again. And if there is a God, I'd see her again. And I will get that fucking name if it kills me.

I pull up around back at my parents' house and park my truck in the hardened mud.

Nobody parks back here besides me, but that's only because my truck is the only vehicle that won't get stuck. Tessa's car has had to be towed out of the muddy terrain back here several times when she's tried to prove that her Rav 4 rallies my truck in off-roading capabilities. She's smartened up and wisely parks on the driveway now.

Walking through the grass, I spot two pairs of legs bent on lawn chairs next to the pool, both forming an upside down V.

My sister's are a dead giveaway, considering she tans out here daily. The other pair contrasts against hers like the dark hair against my sheets last night.

Fuck. Not the time to get a hard on. Don't think about her.

I stroll around the pool and over toward the two girls, stopping next to Tessa. Both girls have their faces covered with beach towels, but that's not what I'm looking at. My eyes are glued to what can't possibly be Mia Corelli's body.

No fucking way. So much for not getting hard.

"Ben! Jesus Christ, you scared the shit outta me." Tessa sits up and drops her towel onto her lap, and I notice Mia's body tense up in her chair. She holds her hands in fists on the towel she's lying on like she's ready to knock my ass out at any second. "I thought you said an hour? I just got off the phone with you twenty minutes ago."

"Yeah, well unfortunately, my plans escaped me." I turn my attention to the tight little body wrapped so perfectly in that yellow bikini. "Mia, it's nice to see you again."

"Humph," she replies.

I chuckle. *Damn. Okay, if that's how she wants to play this.* "You look a lot different since the last time I saw you. Still wear those nerdy glasses?" Tessa's foot connects with my thigh and I grunt. "Ow. What?"

"You're an asshole," Tessa snaps. "Mia, ignore him. He's just mad that he hasn't gotten laid in three months."

I move in front of the chairs, giving myself a better view of Mia but making sure to keep my eyes on my sister's at the moment.

"Fuck you. I just got laid last night for your information. And she was incredible."

"Humph," Mia mumbles again.

I step to the side of her chair, putting her gorgeous body right under my nose.

Her tits are insane, full and barely wrapped up in the tiny piece of fabric. I want to shake the man's hand that created this bikini. It was meant for this body.

"Is my sex life amusing to you, Mia? Because if you'd really like to see what I can do, I'll take you right here on this lawn chair. I'll make you scream until your voice breaks."

"No thanks. I, like you, got laid last night and am good for several months. Years even. My pussy is still humming after getting worked with that mouth of his."

Her response is muffled by the towel but I definitely hear the word pussy. And my cock hears it too.

"Dayyyyum," Tessa chuckles.

I place my hand on her knee, gripping it softly. She tenses. "I bet I can work it better than him." My hand slides down her thigh, painfully slow, barely moving at all. Her skin is smooth and warm. She stops me with hers when I reach mid-thigh. "I'll make you ride my face until you're begging for my cock."

"Jesus Chr..." She sits up mid-sentence, the towel dropping somewhere that I can't seem to focus on. Because I can only focus on the face that can't possibly be Mia Corelli. "You? Ben? Ben! Oh, God. Oh, my God."

"Holy shit." I'm shocked. Completely shocked. It's her. Mia Corelli is *her.* What the fuck are the odds? "Mia, I..." She quickly gets to her feet, her hips swaying as she storms toward the house. "Mia, wait up!" I yell, starting after her until Tessa puts her tiny frame in front of me and blocks me.

"What the hell was that? Did you really just tell Mia that you'd make her ride your face? You're lucky she didn't deck you."

My sister is small, so I can look over the top of her with no problem, and doing so, I see Mia slide the door shut behind her. "It's complicated. Move so I can go after her." Not that I couldn't move her myself, but if that happened, she'd just climb onto my back like she liked to do when I shoved her out of the way, and I needed Mia alone.

Her hands curl up into fists at her hips. "How is it complicated? You made her uncomfortable, like you always do, because you're an asshole."

I'm getting impatient. I grip Tessa's shoulders and firmly plant her in her lawn chair. "Give me a few minutes with her. I'm not going to hurt her, I promise. I just want to talk to her." My voice is sincere and Tessa knows it.

Her shoulders relax and she scoots back on her chair, resuming her favorite tanning position. "Five minutes. And if she's crying when I come in there, I'm keying your precious baby."

Nice threat. Keying my truck would be a way to cut me deep, but there'll be no need for that. Mia won't be crying. I'd never make her cry; if I could fucking find her.

I'm roaming the house, listening for any clues of where she might be, but dead silence fills the space. "Mia? Baby, please let me talk to you."

I hear a door open, and she emerges from the hallway, her eyes reddened and streaked with tears. "Don't call me that. How dare you say those things to me out there?" Our legs bring us together but she pushes against my chest, not liking the closeness our bodies seem to crave. "I can't believe this! I can't believe it was you last night. This can't be happening." Tears run down her face, and I wipe them away before she can reach up and stop me.

"I can't believe it either. But fuck, Mia, if this isn't the luckiest day of my life." I bring my hands up to her face and hold her there, feeling her shudder against me. "I haven't been able to stop thinking about you all morning. Last night was—"

"A mistake," she interrupts curtly. Her hands pry mine from her face and she turns her body, staring out the window. "A huge mistake. If I'd have known it was you, it wouldn't have happened. I'm sure you know that by now."

"It wasn't a mistake." I move closer to her, bending to put my nose into her hair. *Fuck.* Nothing smelled this good. I'll never get enough of it. "Something like that could never be a mistake. What you gave me. What we shared… Mia, I've never…" I pause, needing to choose my words carefully. "I felt it last night. Tell me you felt it too." My hands run down her arms, and the fact that she is still in her tiny bikini is making my dick harder than it's ever been. "Baby, please."

Please back up into me.

Please move my hands to your breasts.

Please turn around and beg me to fuck you right here.

I've never felt so completely geared up and so ready to unravel at the same time. But that's definitely how I am feeling right now. Like I could snap at the slightest crook of her finger.

She moves quickly out of my grasp toward the hallway she just emerged from. "I didn't feel anything. And it was a mistake, Ben. A huge mistake." Her eyes reach mine with regret once more, and I swear that there are tears in them again. "You can't stop ruining my life, can you?"

I watch her disappear, unable to reply.

Ruining her life? Fuck me.

A door slams down the hall just as the sliding glass door opens. Tessa looks at me with raised eyebrows and I motion toward the direction Mia fled to.

"I have a feeling that I'm going to want to punch you, so you might want to leave before your face *and* your truck get mangled."

Instead of responding, I walk past her and make my way back out to my truck.

My mind is scrambled and my heart feels like Mia has taken her keys to it. The girl of my dreams turned out to be Mia fucking Corelli. What the fuck? She's not just passing through. She's here.

My angel is here for the whole summer, and she wants nothing to do with me.

chapter four

Mia

"Well, I did not see this coming. Not in a million years."

Tessa slumps down on the bed I've been curled up on after I shared my naughty little secret with her.

She paced during that run down, her jaw hitting the floor the moment I said I lost my virginity to her brother.

"This. Is. Crazy. I mean, first of all, I had no idea you were still a virgin. Fuck you very much for not telling me. Although, I'm not sure I would've believed you, considering what you look like."

I smile weakly at her compliment. "Yeah, well, I wish I still was. I can't believe I was stupid enough to not ask his name last night. This shit could've been easily avoided."

Because there's no way I would've went through with it if I'd have known that mouth belonged to Ben fucking Kelly.

The boy that made me cry daily for five years.

The boy that made me feel insignificant.

The boy I hated.

"I don't really see what the big deal is here. In fact, I think it's pretty fucking awesome." She moves up the bed and places her head on the pillow next to mine. "How was it anyway? Did you come?"

I roll my eyes at her bluntness. "You're disgusting."

"I'm nosy, and I can pretend it wasn't my brother." She twirls her hair around her finger, smiling at me. "Spill it, Mia. I've shared all my sexcapades with you over the years."

"Without me asking. I'd love to be able to forget some of those horrific details."

"Oh, please. Like you haven't enjoyed living vicariously through my pussy. My very STD free pussy, by the way. You make it sound like I'm a hooker."

I cover my face with my hands, hearing Tessa laugh softly next to me.

If I am going to share how her brother got me off, I don't want her to see how much I enjoyed it. Because I didn't. I'd never enjoy anything involving him. And the tightness in my core that is forming at the very memory of last night has nothing to do with that jerk.

I grunt heavily before confessing, "It was beautiful. He was sweet and playful, but he also knew exactly what he was doing. I definitely came. A lot."

"How much is a lot?" I hold up my hand, hearing her soft gasp. "Holy shit balls. Ben can get it."

Dropping my hands, I roll over and face her. "But I don't want Ben to get it. I don't want him to be the guy that took my virginity. I hate him, Tessa. You know how much I hate him."

It wasn't a secret. I never hid my feelings for him years ago, and I wasn't trying to start now. As long as those feelings stayed familiar. I was used to hating Ben. Those feelings I could deal with. Not, whatever the hell it was that I felt last night. Or didn't feel. 'Cause I didn't feel anything.

"Mia, are you that same girl that used to live here? The girl that wouldn't dare say a cuss word or wear a bikini like the one you're currently rocking the hell out of?" She smiles and playfully wiggles her brows.

"No. I guess not," I reply flatly. I know exactly where she's going with this, and I don't really want to hear it.

"Well, Ben's not that same jerk-face loser that would pick on you every chance he got. He's actually pretty tolerable now." I try to roll away from her but she grabs my arm, keeping my gaze. "He's not that guy, Mia. He hasn't been for a while. And I think you know that deep down." She pauses, her lips turning up into a sassy smile. "There's no way that same guy would've made you feel the way you felt last night."

"Icky? Nauseating? Because that's how I felt."

"Yeah, okay. Tell that to your five orgasms."

She sounds as unconvinced as I feel.

Whatever. Even if he did own my body, I wasn't going to admit it to Tessa. Or myself, for that matter.

"This is so not the way I was hoping to start off my summer."

"I can't imagine starting it off any better. Hot sex that resulted in five glorious orgasms? I'll take, things I'd give my right arm for, for two hundred, Alex." She bumps her shoulder against me and slides off the bed. "I know two men that would help greatly in a situation like this."

"I'm not interested in your vibrators. We're close, but we aren't that close."

I hear her chuckle as she disappears down the hallway.

This is un-freaking-believable. The man I couldn't get out of my head since I laid eyes on him last night, turns out to be the asshole I longed to forget. It was Ben who made me feel hot and wanted for the first time in my life. It was Ben who ignited my skin and made my insides burn, and not in the STD kind of way. It was Ben who I screamed for last night and who I never wanted to leave this morning. Benjamin fucking Kelly. He made fun of my body for years, but last night, he worshipped it. Telling me how good I tasted. How amazing I felt. How he wanted to stay deep in my pussy until the day he died. And I was torn between wanting to take back everything that we'd experienced together not even twenty-four hours ago, and asking him to touch me again. Every time I closed my eyes, I felt his hands on me. His breath on my skin. His tongue on my clit. His cock in my pussy. He claimed me last night, and I hated that I loved it.

Tessa appears in the doorway, two pints of Ben and Jerry's ice cream in her hands. "I say we rent something nonromantic and devour the contents of these containers. You're in desperate need of a girls' night and I'm coming at you hard."

"Is that Half Baked?" *Damn. I haven't had that in years.* She nods and smiles wide. "You're awesome. I'm so in for girls' night."

"That's what I was hoping you'd say. Get changed and plant your perky ass in front of the TV."

She leaves me to do just that, and I don't waste any time. I throw on a sundress and meet her in the living room, diving into my ice cream as she scrolls the movie selections.

"Wolf of Wall Street or Captain Phillips?" she asks as she flips through the On Demand section.

"Wolf of Wall Street. I don't feel like crying, and seeing Tom Hanks held captive by pirates will probably wreck me. You know I love that man." I've been hooked on Tom Hanks' films since I watched Philadelphia. And don't get me started on The Green Mile. I cried like a baby when Tessa and I watched that together. The electrocution scene? I can't even.

She starts up the movie and we sit back, both digging into the meals that will surely ruin any appetite for dinner. We are halfway through the movie and our pints when Tessa's phone rings.

"You're interrupting girls' night, I'll have you know. And the penalty for your crime is death by dick removal."

I giggle around my spoon, my eyes widening as Leonardo DiCaprio snorts coke off some chick's ass.

"Hmm, you're so hilarious. And that's none of your business. I think you've done enough damage to warrant a lifetime of therapy." I meet her eyes briefly before she turns her head. "Just leave her alone. If she wants to talk to you, she'll talk to you."

I don't need two guesses to know who she is talking to. And a part of me that I don't want to acknowledge, wishes she had been on a land line so I could pick up and listen in.

"I have no idea, but whatever it is, it won't be involving you. Now leave us alone so we can watch all this coke get snorted in a way that is definitely heating up everything south of my waist." She tosses her phone onto the coffee table. "Sorry about that. Apparently, you're hard to forget." She smiles coyly at me, and I brace myself for what she's about to say. "But that wouldn't affect you, because it's my brother we're talking about. Right?"

"Right," I affirm without hesitation. I'm not falling into that trap. I keep my attention on Leonardo and far away from thoughts of Benjamin Kelly.

"I mean, it's not like he was sweet and playful with you or anything."

"Nope. Not at all."

"And it's not like he gave you this beautiful experience to treasure for the rest of your life. That so wasn't Ben."

"It so wasn't."

"And he's *definitely* not the guy that, as you so sweetly put it, worked your pussy until you hummed between your legs for hours afterward." I hear her smile through her words, but I don't turn away from the TV. I don't want to crack.

"Definitely not him." I'm struggling, really struggling not to break. I feel keyed up all of a sudden, like my body is fully charged and ready to go. I'm beginning to fidget and it doesn't go unnoticed.

"Quick question. What did Ben call you when he fucked you, since he didn't know your name?"

"Baby. Angel. Pretty girl," I blurt out in the most crushing-on-a-boy sort of way. Even my voice raises an octave. *Fuck.* I turn toward her then. She won and she knows it, and the smile on her face only adds to my irritation. "I hate you."

"You put up an impressive fight, I'll give you that." She chucks a pillow at me, hitting me square in the face. "Just admit that you kind of like the idea of my brother knowing all the intimate details of your body."

"Never." I tuck the pillow she hit me with behind my head, taking a giant spoonful of ice cream into my mouth. I need a gag at the rate she's going with this conversation. I know the more we talk about this, the greater chance of me slipping up and saying something I don't want to reveal.

"This might seem borderline inappropriate…"

"Oh, God. Please spare me." I'm shoveling ice cream into my mouth at an impressive rate now.

Borderline inappropriate for Tessa means cover your ears and please escort all children out of the state.

She turns her body, tucking her legs underneath her ass. "Is he like, really big? Because I've heard rumors." She holds her hands out in front of her, measuring a distance between the two. "Nine inch rumors."

"Jesus Christ."

I shouldn't be surprised. I really shouldn't. This is Tessa Kelly we're talking about. She is comfortable enough talking about sex with anybody. Confessional priests included. I'm sure the number of Hail Marys she's been told to recite is in the hundreds.

I drop my spoon into my empty container and sigh heavily. "Why would you want to know that about your brother? That's incredibly weird."

"So I can high five you. Losing your virginity to someone as massive as he may or may not be is worthy of a damn award." She places her hand lovingly on my knee, but there is nothing tender about this chat. Her tactics are a ploy, a cover to make this conversation seem innocent. "And since your mouth was wrapped around his nine-incher, I'm figuring you'd be able to vouch better than anyone."

I push her dirty hand away. "For your information, my mouth was not wrapped around him. All of his nine inches stayed in between my legs the entire night."

"Ah-ha! So I *can* believe everything I've heard." She holds her hand up to me, and after several long seconds of debating her gesture, I oblige her with a high-five. "Fucking right. I'm jealous. Eight's my biggest number."

"How unfortunate." I grab the remote and turn up the volume. "Can we please watch the rest of the movie? I'm done discussing your brother's anatomy with you."

His damn fine anatomy.

"All right, all right. But answer me one last question before we finish this." I look over hesitantly. Lord knows what she could hit me up with next. She smiles. "How are you, anally speaking? Still virginal?"

"Very."

"Well, that's probably wise considering what he's working with."

The pillow that she used to hit me with is now striking her against the face. "You really should come with a warning label. *Please keep away from small children, the elderly, and anyone with a pacemaker.*"

She chuckles, pulling her long, auburn hair back into a pony. "As should you. *Please keep all dicks less than nine inches away from this pussy, because the bar has been set.*"

I feel my face heat up instantly.

Is it weird to agree with her on that assessment? I mean, surely there aren't many dicks out there that could compare to what Ben was so beautifully graced with. I've seen my fair share of pornos, and even those dicks couldn't hold a candle to his.

I slam my head back onto the sofa and stare at the TV.

Damn it, Ben. Not only have you ruined my life, but you've also ruined all average dick sizes for me. Now I'm going to compare each and every appendage to yours.

Thanks a lot, asshole.

I should be sleeping.

But since I'm not sleeping, I should be reading a book, or watching TV, or doing anything besides what I am currently doing.

This is insane. I've never been pissed off and horny at the same time before, but that's exactly what I'm feeling right now. It's an angry lust and I hate it. I want to punch Ben in the throat and I want to fuck him all over the house. And I know for a fact, and I'm ashamed to admit, that I would thoroughly enjoy doing both.

It's 3:15 a.m., and while the rest of the Alabama population sleeps, my mind and fingers are very busy as I get myself off for the second time tonight with thoughts of Ben.

It doesn't take me long because he was that good and he gave me a variety of memories to work with.

Earlier, I thought of him gripping my hips and slamming into me roughly from behind. He grabbed my hair and smacked my ass, and I came when I pictured his tongue licking up my spine and his teeth biting my back. But right now, he's devouring my pussy with that expert mouth of his. That smart ass mouth that I'd like to smack and then fuck. The one that he suggested I ride when we were out by the pool earlier. My legs are pinned against his head and I'm melting as if he were the sun and I was a popsicle. I come all over my hand, and I can't push aside the feeling of irritation that pours over me as I let Ben Kelly rule my body for the second time in one hour.

And I know without a doubt that he'll be irritating me again tomorrow night.

⌒⌒

The smell of bacon hits me like a Mack truck, pulling me out of the Ben dream that I was annoyingly enjoying.

I'd usually be able to roll over and go back to sleep, but it's bacon, and I could eat my weight in that stuff, so the dreams can wait. I am surprised, though, that Tessa is up and making breakfast. She likes her sleep even more than I do and was usually the last one awake when I used to spend the night with her. Maybe she's just being a really good hostess. Either way, I'm all for getting woken up daily by this delicious smell.

I make my way down the hallway, pulling my wild, bed head hair back out of my face.

"Oh, my Godddd, that smells amazing. I'm so hungry right now."

I stop dead in my tracks as the kitchen comes into view.

Tessa is not the one cooking breakfast, and I suddenly want to hurl myself back into bed and go for round three with my favorite fingers. I bite back the shiver I feel run through me at the thought of doing just that.

Ben turns his head and hits me with a smile. "Good morning. What kind of eggs do you want?"

"What are you doing here?" I ask, crossing my arms over my chest and scowling in his direction.

Damn it. Now I suddenly don't just have a hankering for bacon. He's way too inviting this early in the morning.

Slight stubble. Check.

Hair sticking up a bit. Check.

Vagina awake and ready. Double check.

He's looking very fuckable right now and it irritates me to no end.

He laughs softly and grabs a plate out of the cabinet. "This is my parents' house. I eat breakfast here all the time." He holds the plate of bacon out. "Want some?"

"No."

He stares at me unconvinced. "Did I not just hear you say you're starving? And I know you want this bacon. We used to fight over the last piece all the time when you'd spend the night here." He places the plate on the island, which is already set for two people, and begins whipping up some eggs in a bowl. "Scrambled okay?"

"You don't know anything about me. Just because I used to like bacon, doesn't mean I want it now." I cross the room with an annoying scowl plastered on my face and open the fridge, pulling out the orange juice. "And I don't want any eggs."

"I know a lot about you," he says, his voice dropping to a low rumbled tone. I can't shake the way it ripples through my body, causing all my muscles to contract and my body temperature to spike. "Now sit down and let me feed you."

I take a sip of my orange juice and walk over to the couch. "I told you. I don't want any breakfast." I begin flipping through the TV channels, trying to calm the hunger that is growing more and more persistent. I want that bacon.

And the man making it.

Shut up, vagina.

"Suit yourself," he says. The stool scrapes along the floor before the sound of crunching fills my ears.

And it's crispy bacon. Son of a bitch.

"Mmm. This is really good. Why don't you stop being stubborn and get your sweet ass over here and join me?"

I snap my head around and glare at him. "And why don't you stop being a creeper and eat breakfast at your own house. You can't honestly tell me that you're here just to raid your mom's refrigerator."

His lips curl up into a half smile. That cockiness pouring out of him that I want to not find attractive. "No, I can't. And you can't honestly tell me that you aren't at least a little happy to see me. Especially since I cooked your favorite food." He takes another bite of his bacon strip, smiling arrogantly. "Remember how mad you used to get when I'd steal pieces off your plate?"

I throw the remote down and stalk over toward the island, seeing him lean back in his chair at my irritated expression.

He wants to talk memories? Let's talk memories.

"No, I don't remember that. What I do remember is you calling me a cannibal, since I liked to eat my own kind."

His confidence quickly vanishes from his face, and he seems regretful now. Although, I'm not sure if he is regretting walking down memory lane or coming over here in the first place.

"It was kind of hard to enjoy my favorite food when assholes like you didn't let me forget how heavy I was. I went a couple days without eating one time because of shit you said to me. Did you know that?"

He drops his gaze from my face to the floor. "No, I didn't know that." He looks up again, begging me with his eyes. For forgiveness? For a pass on everything he's ever said to me? Fat chance. "I had no idea I got to you like that. I was a kid, Mia. I didn't really care about hurting your feelings back then. But Christ, it's been nine years. I'm not that guy anymore." He reaches out to stroke my arm but I back away before he can touch me.

I don't want his hands on me. I know exactly how much I'll like it.

His eyes shift and that mischievous glare of his that I am becoming familiar with, hits me. "You seemed to enjoy the guy I am now the other night. If I remember correctly, you enjoyed me five times."

"Wow. You just totally proved my point." I grab a handful of bacon and meet his confused gaze.

"What point is that?"

I glower at him before turning on my heel and walking back toward my bedroom. "That you're still an asshole," I yell over my shoulder.

Upon hearing the sound of the stool scraping again, I slam my door and lock it, backing away as the footsteps in the hallway grow louder.

They stop right outside my room and the doorknob rattles.

"Mia, come on. Just sit and eat some breakfast with me."

I sit on the edge of my bed and begin crunching on a piece of bacon. "Can you not take a hint? I'm not interested in eating or doing anything with you." I take another bite and hear some movement on the other side of the door.

He needs to leave. I really don't want to spend the entire day cooped up in my bedroom. And there is no chance in hell that I am slipping into my bikini in front of him again. Not after the lustful way he looked at me in it yesterday. I can't handle him looking at me like that again. Like he wants to eat me alive. Like he knows exactly what is underneath my bikini and exactly what to do with it.

"I'm persistent."

I look up at the door, imagining him standing on the other side. "What?"

The sound of a throat clearing comes before he speaks. "I'm a persistent guy. If you ask me to leave, I'll leave, but that's not going to stop me from trying to be around you."

Neither of us speaks for what feels like hours.

I don't want to like the idea of being pursued by Ben. My brain wants to hit him with some sort of stalker charge while my vagina wants to put him on lockdown for the summer.

"So, do you want me to leave?" he asks, and I can hear the anxiety in his voice. As if he already knows the answer to his question but is praying, by some miracle, he's way off.

"Yes," I quickly reply, without any indecision. I know if I allow myself time to think it over, my desire for a Ben-style orgasm will overpower any and all rational thought.

He doesn't say anything else before the sound of his footsteps fade into the distance.

After I hear the sliding glass door close, I fall back onto my bed.

Tessa had assured me that I wouldn't have to see much of her brother when I planned this trip, but that guarantee seems to be a distant memory now. I could be waking up every morning to the smell of Ben cooking breakfast if he decided to show me just how persistent he could be. I'm afraid to admit that a part of me doesn't hate the possibility of that type of wake up call.

And it has nothing to do with the bacon.

chapter five

Ben

I'VE NEVER JERKED OFF THIS MUCH IN MY LIFE.

If my dick doesn't fall off soon due to the rough treatment it's been getting, I'll be shocked. I can't get her out of my head. Her lips. Her ass. Her fucking breasts. Every time I think I'm making progress, an image pops into my head or the memory of her noises fill my ears. Those fucking noises she made when I was inside her. When I licked her pussy. When I pulled her hair. I need to hear them again and I need to hear them soon. But she wants nothing to do with me. She hates me, and I can't say I blame her. I was a complete shit to her when we were younger. I made fun of her a lot. All the time, actually. But all guys are dickheads at that age. She has to know that. I'm not that same guy anymore, and she's definitely not that same girl.

And we fucking shared something, God damn it. She had to have felt it.

I had to see her yesterday, if only for a few minutes. I couldn't sleep anyway, so I figured I'd make us both some breakfast. Mia used to eat breakfast with us all the time, so I knew what she liked. I thought I could at least enjoy her company for an hour while she sat and ate next to me, but no. Apparently, I was a bigger asshole to her than I remembered. The thought of her starving herself over some dumbass comment I made, infuriated me. She is holding on to a deeper hatred toward me than I realized. But her pushing me away isn't going to stop me. I'm drawn to her, and not just because I want to be buried deep inside her at all times. It feels right being around her. Just fucking right. I want her. All of her. And I can be one relentless bastard when it comes to getting what I want. At least now, she is aware of that.

My phone beeps on my nightstand and I grab it with my free hand, taking the other off my dick. It's a good thing, actually. I'm about to rub myself raw if I don't get a fucking grip. Other than the one I've had for the last hour.

Luke: *Everyone's going down to Rocky Point today. You in?*

Luke is my best friend and has been since we met in the Academy. I'd usually be all for going to Rocky Point for the day with him. But I'm exhausted from another sleepless night of sexual activity, this time self-inflicted.

Me: *Pass. I'm fucking exhausted.*

Luke: *Are you sure? I hear there's some hot piece of ass staying with your sister and they'll both be there. You know anything about that?*

Fuck sleep.

Me: *I'll meet you there. And don't call her that again.*

Well, now my mind is made up. It really didn't take much persuasion on Luke's part. Or any at all. Where Mia goes, I'm going.

I hop out of bed and begin rummaging through my drawers for my swim trunks. I don't care that she most likely won't want me there. I am fucking going.

My phone beeps again as I'm walking out the door to my truck.

Tessa: I must be delusional for giving you this information, or maybe I just have a soft spot for my big brother. We're headed to Rocky Point today, and I think you should be there. I don't think she'll hate you forever, Ben. But if you make her cry, I'll feed your dick to the gators.

Me: I'm already on my way. Don't tell her I'm coming.

Tessa: Do you think I have a death wish?

She can't hate me forever. I'll spend the rest of my life proving myself to her if I have to. I've made a lot of mistakes. I've done things that I regret. But what Mia and I shared two nights ago, wasn't one of them.

I just need to somehow make her see that for herself.

I don't see Tessa or Mia's car when I park in the grass at Rocky Point. And I'm happy about that. I want to beat them here, that way Mia doesn't get to do anything without me. Even though I probably don't deserve it, I want all of her time. I am a greedy bastard when it comes to her and I'm not ashamed of it. I want everything.

Every smile, every orgasm, every fucking noise that comes out of that pretty mouth. And I'll need as much time as she'll give me if I'm going to make up for being such a shit to her when we were younger. She isn't going to easily let go of all the hate she has stored up for me. That hate runs deep.

Luke is seated at a picnic table with Reed, a friend of Tessa's. I walk over to them, throwing my stuff down on the bench and keeping my eyes out for a familiar vehicle.

"Why do you have two towels, man?" Luke asks as he searches through my stuff. "Oh wait, does this have anything to do with that hot piece of ass?"

I pick up my towels and move them out of his reach. "What the fuck did I say about calling her that? Her name's Mia, and that's what you'll call her. Nothing else. Got it?"

He holds his hand up, leaning away from me. "Sorry. Jesus."

I take a deep breath and let it out slowly.

I need to calm the hell down. I've never felt this anxious about seeing someone before. And for fuck's sake, I just saw her yesterday.

I scan the line of cars that head down the dirt path. No sign of them yet.

"This is the girl that used to live here, right?" Reed asks, moving off the bench to stand.

"Yeah," I reply, not prying my eyes from the vehicles. "She moved to Georgia a while back and is here for the summer."

I still can't believe it myself. This is the same girl that used to have sleepovers every weekend at my house with Tessa. I'd fucking kill for a sleepover with her now.

A red Jeep comes up over the small hill, and I suddenly find it difficult to take in a deep breath.

"I'll be right back," I choke out with a shaky voice. *Get it the fuck together, Kelly.*

"Fuck that. I'm coming with you," Luke states, getting to his feet.

We both walk toward the Jeep as it pulls in between two other cars. As soon as Mia locks on to me through the windshield, her jaw drops open and those chocolate brown eyes widen. I can see her hands tightening on the wheel as she leans over, saying something to Tessa with a tight jaw.

"She looks thrilled to see you." Luke laughs before walking over to Tessa's door.

I ignore him and the look Mia is giving me and open her door for her. "Hey. I'm really glad you came."

I feel calmer now, but my heart is still beating like I've just taken a shot of adrenaline. She is in a tank top, her bikini straps poking out, and tiny white shorts that barely cover the legs I want to be buried between. I pry my eyes off her lap to give her a smile.

"Someone failed to mention that you'd be here." She ignores the hand I hold out for her and steps out of her Jeep, pulling the seat back to get her bag.

I close the door and move to walk next to her. "I warned you of my persistence. This just proves that I'm a man of my word. If I find out you're going to be somewhere, there's a pretty damn good possibility that I'm going to show up."

She tries to ignore my comment, but I don't miss the way her cheeks flush at my vow. That has to mean something. Her mind, and its memories of the guy I used to be, might hate me, but her body doesn't seem to.

I take the duffle bag off her shoulder without a fight, slipping it on my arm. "I brought you a towel in case you needed one."

She stops in her tracks, causing me to double back. "I don't need you to do things for me, Ben. I don't need you bringing me towels and carrying my bags." She reaches for her bag but I step back.

Fuck that. I'm carrying her bag.

"Fine. Whatever. But just know that this nice act doesn't wipe out all the shitty things you've done to me." She steps closer, brushing her body against mine.

I freeze, completely unprepared for this type of contact from her.

She tilts her head up and looks into my eyes while I use every ounce of strength in me to keep myself from getting hard. "That shit is still very raw. And no amount of bag carrying is going to make me forget it."

I watch her ass as she walks away, realizing now that I'm going to need to step up my game to knock down the walls she's building up around her. Which is fine. I'm all for a challenge. Especially one where getting close to Mia is the reward.

By the time I reach the rest of the group, Mia is talking to Reed while Luke and Tessa dive into the reservoir.

I place her bag on the bench, bunching up the beach towel I brought for her and stuffing it into her duffle. I walk up to the two of them, drifting in on their conversation and not giving a shit if I'm interrupting anything.

"You wanna get in the water with me, Mia?" I ask, pulling off my T-shirt and tossing it onto the bench.

I don't miss the way her eyes run down my body, and mine do the same to hers once she pulls off her top and slides down her shorts.

Christ, she is breathtaking. I can't get enough of her long, dark hair and the way it frames the delicate features of her face. That face—I can't get it out of my head. Deep brown eyes and full lips that'll form a knock-you-on-your-ass smile if you're lucky to see it. Then there's the curve of her breasts. Her tiny waist that leads to those hips that sway with each step she takes. Her perky ass and those never ending toned legs I want wrapped around me at all times. I've never seen anything so beautiful in my life.

She glances from Reed to me, not taking nearly as long to look at Reed as he shrugs off his shirt. "I want to get in the water," she replies curtly. She leaves off the "with you" part, but that's fine. I watch as she dives into the reservoir and I don't take long to jump in after her.

The water is warm as it always is, but too cloudy to see her swimming ahead of me. Luke and Tessa have climbed up onto one of the floating piers and are talking closely, but Mia doesn't seem to be headed for the pier. She's headed for the cliffs. I know for a fact that she was always too scared to jump off of them when she was younger. I did it a lot, and it scared the shit out of me every time.

It's high, really high, and I'm not about to let her do it alone.

I swim faster, pushing myself to get up next to her, and within a few strokes, I succeed. We both reach the rock ledge at the same time, and she looks at me once she wipes her eyes. I smile at her and I swear I see the slightest twitch in those perfect lips of hers, but I can't be sure. She struggles to pull herself up onto the rock, slipping every time and falling back into the water.

My girl needs my help and I'm going to give it to her.

I quickly climb up onto the rock, staring down at her and offering my hands. "Come on, pretty girl. Let me help you up."

"I don't need your help." She continues struggling, each attempt making her more exhausted. "There should be a freaking ladder here or something," she scoffs under her breath, and I have to resist the smile that's tugging at my mouth.

"Do you want to jump off the cliffs or not?" She looks up at me and shrugs once. "Give me your hands. I promise I won't bite." I smirk at her and she catches it, rolling her eyes. "Unless you want me to."

"Funny." She grabs my one hand and I motion for her to grab my other. She does, not before giving me an annoyed look, and I easily lift her out of the water and stand her up next to me. "Thank you." Her hands leave mine instantly and she looks up into my eyes. And fuck, I want to kiss her, right here. And I would if I didn't think she'd cut my nuts off if I tried.

"You're welcome." I place my hand on her lower back, moving her toward the rocks ahead. We have a ways to climb to get to the top and she will definitely be making that trek in front of me. "Go on. I'll be right behind you."

"Try not to stare at my ass too much."

Damn. Is she flirting with me?

I catch the smile she is trying to hide from me and I decide to give her one better. "Oh, I don't need to stare, baby. I memorized every inch of your body the other night."

She flicks her head back and spots my grin, her hands braced on the rocks above her. "Where's my birthmark?" she asks, challenging me. There's zero playfulness to her tone. She's testing my knowledge of her body, and by the look on her face right now, she thinks she's got me beat. But I fucking own that body and know it better than she does.

"On the inside of your right thigh. It sort of looks like a peanut."

She opens her mouth to speak, but closes it before turning back around. "Lucky guess."

I laugh and nudge her with a hand on her calf. She begins to move faster. "Luck has nothing to do with it. Fate, maybe. Putting us both in that bar the other night was more than some coincidence. But knowing that you like to watch me eat your pussy, or that you have to be digging your nails into something when you're coming, has absolutely nothing to do with luck." She glances over her shoulder at me with a staggered look. "I pay attention to every little thing about you."

She doesn't linger on my face, nor does she give me a response. But I think I may have impressed her. Maybe. Mia's difficult to read lately. She's definitely not sending me clear signals like she did the other night at the bar.

She turns her attention back to the rocks above her and makes her way up the side of the cliff.

I'm close behind her, keeping an eye on her footing in case she slips and I have to catch her.

We make it to the top and she moves to the edge, apprehensively glancing down. "Holy shit." Her wide eyes blink rapidly and she turns them on me. "This is really high. It didn't look that high from down there."

I stand beside her, brushing my hand against hers. "It is high. I do this all the time and I still get nervous up here." I run my finger down her arm, feeling her skin tingle against mine.

She seems completely unaffected by it and keeps her focus on the water.

How can she ignore that? How can she pretend her body doesn't respond to my touch?

"Want me to jump with you? It isn't so scary if you do it with someone." I try to grab her hand, but she pulls it away from me.

"Jump, you pussies!" Tessa yells, standing on the pier and waving at us. Reed and Luke are watching in amusement and Mia laughs next to me. And it is fucking beautiful. I'd give anything to hear that laugh every day for the rest of my life.

"I love that sound," I say, completely unashamed of my infatuation.

She looks at me with confusion. "What sound?"

"Your laugh. Your voice. Hell, all your sounds." Her lips part slightly, and a shaky hand comes up and tucks some hair behind her ear. "I can't get them out of my head."

She purses her lips, dropping her gaze to the water. "Stop it, Ben." Her voice is an intense plea, like she can't possibly handle another word coming out of my mouth.

Which is too fucking bad, because I have a lot to say right now.

"Stop what?" I bridge the gap between us and grab her hips with such blunt force my fingertips ache. I know she likes it like that, so I don't let her stunned look slow me down. She gasps softly as I turn her toward me. Her body is tense, fearful even, but she doesn't try and get out of my grasp. I hold her gaze, daring her to look away from me as I continue. "Stop telling you that I want you? Stop telling you that I've been going mad since you walked out of my bedroom?"

I reach up and brush my thumb across her bottom lip, wanting more than anything for her to pull me into her mouth like she did the other night. I need some part of me inside her. She allows me to touch her without giving me an inch. I move closer, pulling our bodies together so that they're perfectly aligned.

"Stop telling you that you're so incredibly beautiful, I'm having trouble remembering my own name when you're around me?"

She shoves against my chest, hard, causing me to stumble back a bit. "Stop it! You can't say things like that, Ben. Do you know what that does to me?"

"I know what being around you does to me." I grab her hand and place it against my chest, my other hand reclaiming its spot on her hip. Her eyes dart from my face to where her hand is, and I see her eyes react to the effect she has on me. "Do you feel that? That's what you do to me. Every fucking time I'm near you."

I can hear her heavy breathing while her eyes stay glued to her hand. I don't say anything else. I just let her feel it. *You own this part of me. Take it.* The magnitude behind that admission doesn't faze me. I don't care how crazy it seems to be this obsessed with someone after one night together. I've never felt like this.

She seems hesitant but she stays right there with me, her breathing filling my ears and her fingers moving against my skin. Tentatively. Just the lightest brush of her fingertips, but I swear to Christ, she leaves burn marks on my chest. Scorching me. Branding me with her imprint. And then I see it, the very moment a memory of our past washes over her. Breaking our connection. She blinks several times, her face falling before yanking her hand away from me as if I'm the one burning her. She looks quickly from my worried face to the water, and without a second glance at me, she jumps.

"Mia!"

I move to the edge and see her disappear. I don't waste any time before I jump in after her. My body hits the water hard, my back stinging at the awkward angle I land in. But I wasn't concerned about form when I jumped.

As I come up to the surface, I see Mia wincing in pain as she treads water. I swim over to her and hear her gentle whines.

"Where are you hurt? Let me see." I wrap my arm around her waist to help keep her head above water.

We are chest to chest, and I expect her to push me away but she doesn't. She keeps her eyes down, looking at the way our bodies come together. Her hands are gripping my arms and she slides them higher, grazing my shoulders until settling around my neck. She closes her eyes as I hold her to me, the pain-stricken expression vanishing and replaced with a look of contentment. She moans as I tighten my grip on her waist, bringing us closer.

Fuck me. *Yes, angel. Let your body feel it.*

A minute ago, she jumped off a cliff to get the hell away from me, and now she's making those fucking noises that drive me insane.

She whimpers, raking her teeth along her bottom lip.

I press my lips to her ear and feel her shudder in my arms. "You're killing me, baby. Do you have any idea how badly I want to take you right here?"

I shouldn't have spoken. I should've just enjoyed the moment she was giving me and let her direct what was happening.

Her eyes shoot open, tears filling them instantly, but she doesn't look sad. She looks enraged. And I don't know if it's because of how blunt I was with her just now, or if she is remembering some asshole thing I did to her years ago. Hell, she could be angry at herself for letting her body take over and actually enjoying being in my company. But I don't have time to ask before she pushes against me with the same hands that were just holding on to me like she needed my contact.

I'm frozen in place as she begins frantically swimming toward the pier.

"Mia! Hold up a second."

I start swimming faster than I ever have, wanting, no, *needing* to get to her before she gets to that pier. I want her alone, especially if she is upset. But she beats me to it, and I get to the ladder as she places her feet on the wooden planks.

"Nice choke, Benjamin," Luke jokes as I get up on the pier. "Were you trying to break your back?"

"Fuck off." I move closer to Mia but Tessa once again puts her tiny body in between me and what I want. "Move, or I'll toss you into the water."

She pokes my chest with her finger aggressively. "Once again, you're upsetting my best friend." She leans closer to me. "What the fuck is wrong with you?" she sharply whispers her question, and I know it's because she's secretly pulling for me. My eyes register that no one's heard her but me.

"I didn't mean to." I look down at her and then over her head. "Mia, come on. How long are you going to be pissed at me for shit I did when I was a kid? That's not fair."

Her head snaps in my direction, and I want to jump right in the water myself with the look she is melting me with.

"Not fair? You wanna know what's not fair, Ben?" She steps behind Tessa, bringing us face to face. Mia towers over my sister as well, so it's as if Tessa isn't even between us. "It wasn't fair the last time I came here, when you told me that I couldn't try the rope swing because I would probably snap the branch it was tied to. It wasn't fair the time before that, when you begged me to keep my shirt on because I would blind you if you saw me in my bathing suit." Her eyes well up, and I want more than anything to shove Tessa off the pier and wrap my arms around Mia. "It wasn't fair when you..." she bites her lip to stop the tremors and turns, her shoulders beginning to shake with her cries.

Reed comes up and wraps his arm around her shoulder, doing the consoling that I should be doing.

"Baby, please don't cry. I was the biggest asshole back then." I step sideways to bypass Tessa, but she moves with me like a shadow. I meet Mia's eyes as she finally turns to look at me. "I hate that I said those things to you. I fucking hate how much I've hurt you. I'm so sorry, baby." I grab Tessa and shove her into Luke. She goes willingly with a slight grunt. "Please, just hear me out."

Mia shakes her head as she moves behind Reed, allowing him to put himself between us.

He blocks Mia entirely, and the protective vibe he's giving off blinds me with an overwhelming urge to knock his ass out.

"I think you've said enough, Ben. Why don't you just leave her alone."

I step closer to him and he surprisingly doesn't step back. "Back the fuck off before I beat the shit out of you."

I mean every word of my threat. He is out of his fucking mind if he thinks I'll let him move in on my girl.

Luke grabs my shoulders and pulls me back. "Easy, bro. You need to calm the fuck down. Nobody needs to threaten anyone."

"Jesus, Ben," Tessa shrieks, wrapping her hand around my elbow. "Don't threaten Reed. He didn't do anything."

"She's mine, Reed," I declare, loud enough so there's no disputing what I've just said. Loud enough so everyone at Rocky Point is now aware who Mia belongs to. Everyone on the pier reacts to my words with the biggest eyes I've ever seen.

"Excuse me?" Mia wipes her face and steps in front of me. "I am not yours."

I shrug Luke off my back. "Yes, you are. You just aren't willing to admit it yet."

I move toward the edge of the pier and look over my shoulder at her.

She isn't crying anymore, the expression on her face has shifted into something I can't decipher. I see that familiar struggle in her eyes. The way she tries to ignore how I can make her feel. And that resistance is my fucking motivation to keep pressing her. To keep pushing her to where I need her to be.

Without giving her a chance to argue with me any further, I dive into the water and begin swimming toward the drop off.

Mia is mine. And I don't care if it takes weeks for her to realize it. Not only am I a greedy bastard when it comes to her, but I'm also determined as hell. I'll do anything for her forgiveness. Hell, I'll do anything for her. I see my future with her, and I'll stop at nothing to get her there with me.

chapter six

Mia

I stare up into his eyes as he enters me, so slowly that it is almost unbearable. I want him to take me right now, to use my body for his pleasure, and I don't want him to be gentle about it.

Reaching down, I grab his ass and urge him deeper, harder. But he ignores my request and shakes his head, resting his hand on my cheek.

"No," he says, his word a breathy pant as he drives into me. "If you want me fast and hard, baby, you're going to have to give me what I want."

Anything. I'll give him anything right now.

I pull my legs up, giving him deeper entry. But he doesn't take it. He teases me with his cock and it is the greatest torment of my life.

I feel a brush along my nose, but his hand stays in place on my cheek. Confused, I ignore it and focus on him.

On the way he looks at me, his gray eyes so bright it's almost blinding. On the way his other hand grips my ass, fingers digging into my skin.

I feel another brush and shake my head, needing him to give me what I want. I try to urge him deeper again but his will is stronger than my desire. He keeps up the long, slow drags of his cock. It's a blissful torment that rocks me straight to my core.

"Please. I'll give you anything," I beg, digging my nails into his back. I feel another brush down my nose and grunt it away, not wanting anything to pull me out of this moment.

"You. I want you, pretty girl."

I close my eyes and feel his words run through me.

He wants me, but can I give him that?

"Are you a wheal pwincess?"

Another voice enters my head, along with another brush down my nose.

I shake my head, not wanting to hear anything but the man above me. But I can't hear him anymore. I can't hear his soft moans. I can't feel his skin against mine. Flesh to raw flesh. And when I open my eyes, I realize why.

My eyes focus on a tiny face that is staring at me, with wild brown hair and big gray eyes. He smiles, brushing his finger down my nose, and I don't miss the two massive dimples that appear in his cheeks.

"I woke the pwincess."

His little voice is husky and deep, like he's just had his tonsils removed. He climbs up onto the bed, holding a wooden sword in his tiny grasp.

I rub my eyes and sit up a little, propping myself up on two pillows. Smiling at him, I run my finger down his nose, and he giggles the most infectious laugh I've ever heard. "Hi, cutie. What's your name?"

"Nowwllaann." He drags out his name, jabbing his sword into the bed with three enthusiastic thrusts.

I laugh. "Nolan. That's a cool name." I touch his sword and he holds it up in the air, swinging it around his body. I notice the dragon embroidered shirt and patterned socks he's wearing, sensing an interest. "Did you slay all the dragons for me?"

His eyes go wide and he shifts to his knees before nodding frantically. "Daddy said I had to save the pwincess."

Daddy? Does Ben have a kid?

"Did he? How many dragons did you slay, noble knight?"

"One Fousand!" He jumps to his feet and holds his sword above his head.

I think I've just met the cutest kid that's ever existed.

I hold my hands around him in case he gets too close to the edge of the bed. "My hero. How old are you?"

"This many." He holds up three fingers and falls to his belly, sliding off the bed and swinging his sword all around him. He stops and moves closer to me, running his finger down my nose again. "What's your name?"

"Mia."

"Pwincess Mia," he corrects me with a crooked grin. "Daddy said that you might need to be kissed to wake you up."

"Oh, you're right. How silly of me."

I slump back down in the bed and close my eyes, feeling the weight of a small body next to me. I try not to smile as his lips touch my cheek, prompting me to pop my eyes open.

"I see you found the princess, buddy." Ben leans against the door frame, smiling at me with the same dimpled grin that just saved me from the dragons. "But didn't I say that if she needed to be kissed to come get me so *I* could do it?"

I sit up against the headboard, pulling the covers up to my chest. I slept in a tank top and tiny shorts, and I am definitely not wearing a bra. I smash the covers to my body, suddenly feeling incredibly shy around the only man that's ever seen me naked.

Nolan hops off the bed and walks over to him. "Can I go swinnin now?"

"Yeah, go get your bathing suit from the bag."

"Wait," I say, sitting up and motioning for Nolan to walk over. He quickly scrambles in front of me and smiles. "Your sword, noble knight." I hold out my hand and he gives it to me without question. "Look down at the floor." He does and I place the sword on his left shoulder. "I dub you, Sir Nolan, slayer of all the dragons in the kingdom." I move the sword to the opposite shoulder. "And protector of the realm."

He looks up at me with sheer exhilaration as I hand him back his sword. "Daddy, I'm a wheal knight!" He runs over toward Ben, jumping up and down enthusiastically.

Ben drops his smile from me to Nolan.

"I wanna go swinnin now." He runs out of the room and Ben rustles his hair as he passes by him.

"It looks like another Kelly boy has a crush on you," Ben states, crossing his arms over his chest.

He looks incredible in just a T-shirt and shorts, and my mind is suddenly flooded with images of the dream I was awakened from. Him above me, naked, driving me toward my pleasure at a punishing pace. I shake those thoughts out of my head and focus on him, which doesn't help me in the slightest. The way his muscles stand out, stretching the thin material of his shirt that I want to shred to pieces, is currently making me clamp my legs together underneath the sheet.

I try to keep myself from blushing, but I feel the warmness spread across my face. "He's so cute. I had no idea you had a son."

"I've been told that we look alike, so I guess that means you think *I'm* cute, right?"

I look away from him with a slight smile.

"Yeah, that's what I thought."

I turn back just in time to see his grin turn cocky, and I'd like to say that it doesn't do anything for me, but it does. Damn him and that face.

"Daddy! I wanna go swinnin." Nolan's tiny excited voice comes calling from the hallway.

Ben turns his head to look down the hallway, straightening up before he looks back at me. "The next time you need to be woken up, it won't be my son kissing you, Princess Mia." His words are a promise that I don't want to react to, but I can't deny the shiver that runs through me. He has all the confidence in the world that he'll be the one to wake me up with a kiss. And I want to tell him that I'll never let that happen, but I can't seem to find the words.

I scramble out of bed once Ben leaves. As I'm slipping my favorite summer dress over my head, my mind begins to wander to memories of the old Ben. The boy I remember that never willingly stepped into any room I was in. The same boy that freaked out when he caught me in his.

"*You wanna listen to music while we lay out?*" Tessa asks as she skims the pool for bugs with the net.

"*Yeah, definitely.*" I stretch out on my lawn chair, shielding my eyes with my hand.

"*Well don't just lay there, goof. Go get the stereo.*"

I sit up and smile. "*Where is it?*"

"*Ben's room. I think it's on his desk.*"

I lay back down. "*Forget it. I'll just hum to myself.*"

She giggles softly. "*He's not home. Just go in there and grab it really quick. I wanna listen to my new Justin Timberlake CD.*"

Okay, I can do that. He won't even know I was in there.

"*All right. Be right back.*" I swing my legs off the side and stroll into the house.

I stop outside Ben's room and hesitantly turn the handle, pushing it open. I've never seen the inside of his room. It's off limits, which is fine with me. I don't want to be in here so I'm going to make this quick. I spot the stereo on the desk and run around his bed to get to it.

"Oh!" I trip over something, falling into the desk and rattling everything on it. Including the stereo. "Oh no." I reach for it but it's too late, and I watch with a sick feeling as the stereo hits the hard floor. I clamp my eyes shut, but I hear the damage I've done. "Oh no," I whisper.

"What are you doing?"

My eyes shoot open and I spin around, coming face to face with a very angry Ben. "Uh, I'm sorry. I was just borrowing your stereo. I didn't mean to…"

He pushes me out of the way and bends down, picking up the scattered pieces. "What did you do?" I open my mouth to speak, but he cuts me off. "You broke it. It's ruined. Why are you even in here? I've told you never to come in my room."

I step back, holding my hands out in front of me. "I'm so sorry. Tessa asked me to grab it and I tripped."

He throws the pieces of the stereo against the wall. "Stay away from my stuff! Get out! God, I hate you! I hate you!"

I dart out of the room, through the house, and back outside. Tessa sits up and studies my empty hands, tilting her head.

"Where's the stereo?"

"Your brother's home. I broke it. He's really angry."

Her mouth drops open. "Uh oh."

"Tessa!" Ben's voice booms out the sliding glass door I haven't closed.

We both wince and run for our lives.

I sigh, clearing that God-awful memory from my head. That was the last time I stepped foot in Ben's room. I understood his anger at the time, but it was an accident. And I felt so bad about it; I saved up my allowances and used the money to buy him a new stereo. But that didn't matter. Not to Ben. He still acted like my very existence pissed him off. And that attitude continued until I moved away nine years ago.

My existence doesn't seem to bother him now.

I make myself a cup of coffee, moving to stand in front of the sliding glass door as I stir in my creamer.

Ben is in the pool with Nolan, pushing him around on a boogie board. He seems like a natural father, and seeing him with Nolan does things to me. Things that I try to ignore. He holds on to Nolan's hand so he can stand up on the board and pretend he is surfing. They are both smiling at each other, and watching him share this moment with his son, shows Ben in a completely new light. It distances him from the Ben I remember from years ago even more. I don't want to be intrigued by this Ben, but I am. My brain is screaming at me to stay away from him, but the way my body reacts in his presence is becoming harder to ignore. Hell, I practically came in his arms yesterday at the dam. That would've been slightly embarrassing. He was barely touching me and I was whimpering like I'd actually die if he stopped. Thank God, he spoke and snapped me out of my pathetic state. I really didn't want to fall apart like that. I wanted him to keep his distance from me. Being in his presence felt dangerous. I didn't trust my body around him. It seemed to betray me every chance it got. He didn't even have to work to get me close to orgasm. Just stick him in my general vicinity, and I'm immediately firing on all cylinders and holding the starter pistol in my hand with my finger on the trigger.

Just pathetic.

I don't even resist the urge to stare at him while he's in the pool. It's a battle I know I'd lose anyway, so I might as well save my energy.

The sun beams off his chest, and as he turns in the pool, I watch as the muscles of his back ripple with his movements. The dark ink of his tattoo seems to stand out even more in the sun, and I want to be close to him. Close enough to study the design and read the words that are etched on his skin. His hair is wet and sticking up a bit, reminding me of the way it looked the other morning after our night together. There is no ignoring how attractive Ben is. And Nolan does resemble his dad, but I'd never label Ben as cute. He is ridiculously handsome, almost too good looking to be real. His words to me from yesterday keep playing on loop in my head. *You are mine.* He was so sure of himself, so certain that I found myself considering the possibility of actually being his. But I've hated him for so long, it seems impossible to let go of that emotion. Desiring someone and actually liking them are two completely separate things. And I can't deny that I desire Ben.

It is the whole liking thing that I'm having trouble with.

"Enjoying the morning view?"

I nearly drop my mug as Tessa comes barreling into my inner thoughts.

"Jesus. You scared the crap out of me." I glance over at her teasing smile, ignoring it as I take my first sip of my now cold coffee.

She waves at Nolan who does the same, smiling wide as he does it. Ben seems to only notice me, and I try to ignore that also.

"If I were to ask you how wet you are right now, what would you say?" Tessa inquires.

"My God. Is there any topic that's off limits to you?"

She thinks it over for a moment, twirling her hair around her finger. "Nope."

I step away from the door and sit down on the arm of the sofa. "Why didn't you tell me Ben has a kid?"

She shrugs once. "I told you he isn't the same guy he used to be."

"Just because someone isn't the same guy, doesn't mean they have little dimpled lookalikes running around. Did you really think that was how I'd interpret that?"

She moves to the chair next to me and slumps down in it. "I figured you'd find out eventually, especially if you give Ben a chance and actually hang out with him, Little Miss Unwilling to Let Go of the Past."

I ignore that last dig. "Where's the mom in all this? I'm assuming, considering what's transpired over the past several days, she isn't in the picture?" I take another sip of my coffee, contemplating the idea of Ben being married to someone. My stomach rolls at the thought.

"Ugh, don't get me started on that bitch." Tessa gathers her hair off her neck while I wait for her to elaborate. "She's so bitter about not being with Ben that she uses that against him. They were never together. It was just a drunken hookup that she's tried to make into something more, but because Ben isn't interested, she gives him as little time as possible with Nolan. Shit is fucked up."

"That's horrible. She shouldn't be able to keep his own son from him."

"Yeah, well, tell that to the freaking judge that gave her primary custody. Ben still gets to see him but not nearly as much as she does. And he should definitely get him more. He's the better parent." She pushes to her feet and pulls her phone out of her pocket. "I'm gonna run to the hospital and drop off the transcriptions I did for Doctor Willis this week. Wanna come?"

I stand and glance once more out the sliding glass door. "Nah, I'd better give my mom a call. See how she's doing."

Tessa looks at me knowingly, silently communicating that she is here for me if I need her. I've never kept any of the details about my mom's illness from her, and she and I spent several nights on the phone together, while she just listened to me cry.

I walk back into my room and set my coffee mug on my dresser, swapping it for my phone. After three rings, my aunt's voice comes through the other end.

"Hello?"

"Hi, Aunt Mae. How's everything going? How is she?"

"She's fantastic, Mia. Here, I'll hand her the phone."

I wait anxiously for my mother's voice, and after only a few short seconds, I'm rewarded with it.

"Hi, sweetheart. How are you?" Her voice is strong, and I can hear the smile behind it.

I can't help the tears that fall down my cheeks, but I keep my voice steady. "I'm so good, Mom. I miss you, though."

"I miss you, too. How is everyone there? Are you and Tessa staying out of trouble?"

"Yes, of course. We haven't done anything illegal yet."

My mom's laughter fills the phone, a sound I went several months without hearing when she was at her worst. "And her brother? Is he behaving himself around you?"

I hesitate, not really knowing how to answer that question. "He's... different. I don't know. It's strange getting used to this Ben when I was anticipating the old one."

"Well, time changes people," she states obviously. "It's certainly changed you over the years. My little girl became this beautiful young lady."

I smile and lie back on the bed, playing with the hem of my dress. "You sound really good. How is your strength? Are you eating? Are you having any more of those dizzy spells?"

"Oh, honey, I'm perfect." More tears fill my eyes, and I sniffle quietly away from the phone. "Your aunt and I went for a walk yesterday at the park. It was too nice of a day to stay indoors. I fed some ducks for you."

"Oh, the duck pond. I love that place." I sit up when I hear crying coming from down the hallway. Little, dimpled look-alike crying. "Hey, Mom. Can I call you back?"

"Sweetheart, enjoy yourself. Don't worry about me. I'm feeling great, okay?"

I swing my legs out of bed and stand up. "Okay. I love you."

"I love you, too."

I smile and toss my phone on the bed, walking toward the cries that seem to get more hysterical the closer I get. Nolan is sitting on the kitchen counter, wrapped up in a towel and trying to pull his knee away from Ben.

"Ahhhh stop! No, Daddy!"

"Buddy, let me look at it. I need to clean it out."

I walk over to them, and Nolan's eyes turn toward me. "Oh, no. What happened, Sir Nolan?" I place my hand on his shin, wrapping my fingers around his calf. He tenses a bit but doesn't pull away from me. "Brave knights don't cry when they get boo boos, do they?"

He dries up his tears and shakes his head at me, his tiny lip trembling. His knee is scraped up and a bit of blood is pooling on the wound.

"I fewl." He sniffs. "Daddy's gonna huwrt it."

I look up at Ben, meeting his gaze that I didn't realize was already fixated on me. "Daddy's not gonna hurt it. Are you, Daddy?" I don't mean for my tone to sound seductive, but given the intensified stare that shifts in Ben's eyes, I'm guessing it comes off as that. He blinks rapidly, dropping his gaze to Nolan's. I do the same. "You know, some princesses carry magical powers. And guess what?"

"What?" His eyes go wide and his voice becomes a fascinated whisper.

"I'm one of those princesses."

I disappear down the hallway and retrieve a small medicine bag that I carry with me out of habit. And this medicine bag just so happens to be covered in glitter. Very magical.

"What is that?" Nolan asks, the fear completely wiped from his voice and replaced with wild curiosity.

"This," I open the zipper and begin rummaging through it, "is my magic bag. It's filled with stuff to make knights feel better." I pull out some disinfectant spray, a few pieces of gauze, and a band aid. I place the bag on the counter next to Nolan, seeing his eyes broaden as he tries to see down into it. "Look in the bag and tell me what you see."

He becomes distracted, rattling off the list of items and allowing me to spray the gauze and apply it gently to his knee. Ben watches me intently from the side, my eyes meeting his every few seconds. I want to focus solely on my task, but my eyes betray me, and I allow them to wander. I blow softly on the scrape, but Nolan doesn't notice.

"What's this?" Nolan pulls out an ace bandage, unraveling it to the floor. "Whoa!"

I giggle and apply the band aid to his knee. "That is for brave knights that endure dragon injuries." I raise an eyebrow at him and he grins. "Do you have any dragon injuries?"

He nods anxiously. "I got hit by a tail wight hewre." He points to the invisible injury on his head, and Ben and I chuckle.

"Well, if it's okay with your daddy, I can wrap you up with my magic band."

"Pwease, Daddy?"

Ben picks up the ace bandage and holds it out to me. "Well, I can't have you bleeding all over my truck with that massive head wound." He winks at me, placing the bandage into my hand.

I wrap up Nolan's head as he adorably giggles. "Sir Nolan, you look ready to take on a land of dragons."

Ben picks him up, kissing his cheek before placing him on the ground.

I am about to turn when two tiny arms wrap around my legs. He smiles up at me before running toward the couch, picking up his sword and commencing the battle he seems to be constantly fighting in.

"That was amazing," Ben states, causing me to turn and look up into his eyes. We are standing inches apart, close enough to touch each other if we want to. "I couldn't go anywhere near his scrape, and you cleaned it out and stuck a band aid on it without him even flinching."

"Everyone forgets their fears when they're distracted. And a magic bag to a three-year-old is very distracting."

He moves in closer to me, his eyes flicking toward Nolan momentarily. His hand brushes against mine before he grabs it, interlocking our fingers. I try to pull mine out of his, but he holds it tighter.

"How am I supposed to make you like me if you won't let go of who I used to be?"

I pull harder, but he moves closer, eliminating all space between us. "I'm... not ready to like you yet."

He smiles, and it is so unexpected that I actually giggle like a complete fool. I slap my free hand over my mouth.

"Yet," he echoes. His eyes do a quick sweep down my body. "You look really pretty, by the way."

I swallow loudly, almost uncomfortably, as I drop my hand. "Thanks."

It's suddenly feeling a thousand degrees hotter in here, and I need to back up. I need to put some space between us. I need to pull my hand out of his. But for some stupid reason, I can't. I want to yank my hand away. I want my feet to move. My brain is screaming at me right now to do the right thing here, but my body is overpowering it.

Goddamn it. Why does it have to feel good to be this close to him? Why can't he have halitosis or be all fluffy instead of a mountain of muscle with inviting breath? I may not have control over my body right now, but I still have use of my mouth.

Shit. And now I'm thinking about what I could do with my mouth. Shit!

I take in a deep breath and clamp my eyes shut, needing to at least take away the visual of him. "Ben, please back up."

He laughs softly above me. "Why are your eyes closed?"

"They just are. Can you please back up?"

He laughs again. And damn it, I love his sounds too. "Do you really want me to back up?"

"Ben."

"I'm just making sure." I feel his thumb brush along the skin of my hand. "You look really pretty, Mia."

"You already said that."

"And I'm going to keep saying it."

I open my eyes and stare up into his. There's nothing but kindness in them. No underlining lust. No hidden motives or agendas behind those crazy gray eyes. I suppose they've always been this amazing to look into, but nine years ago, I avoided them at all costs. Of course, nine years ago, he'd never have put himself this close to me. And he definitely wouldn't have given me a compliment.

He smiles, dropping my hand after giving it a light squeeze. "I mean it. I'm going to keep telling you that. You might as well get use to it."

I look down at my feet, concealing my flushed cheeks. "Okay."

He finally steps back and I peek up, seeing him turn away from me. "Come on, buddy. Say goodbye to Princess Mia."

"Bye, Pwincess Mia." Nolan waves, tapping Ben's legs with his sword.

"Bye, Sir Nolan. If I see any dragons, I'll send them your way."

I turn and head toward the bedroom. And I know I shouldn't, I know I've had enough of him today, but I look over my shoulder anyway and lock on to Ben's eyes.

It's as if he is waiting for that last glance, because as soon as he gets it, he's out the door.

chapter seven

Ben

"GOODNIGHT, BUDDY. LOVE YOU."

I squeeze Nolan against my chest, hearing his sleepy yawn. He rubs his face against my shirt before looking up at me, reaching his finger toward my face. I smile as he runs his finger down my nose, and he giggles when I do the same to him.

"Nighty, Daddy." He scrambles down the hallway, Angie following close behind him.

I hate sharing custody of my own kid. I want Nolan with me all the time, not just on days a judge allots. The system isn't fair to fathers. Angie is a mediocre mom, at best, and she gets primary custody just because she gave birth to him. I hate leaving Nolan with her. She isn't very attentive to him and that shit eats away at me. She never takes him anywhere, not even outside. Nolan is an easy kid. It doesn't take much to make him happy. And the thought of her not making him happy nearly kills me.

Now that he's getting older and figuring things out, he's beginning to ask questions. Questions I don't want to answer yet. He wants to know why he can't spend the night at my house every night, or why I don't live with him and his mother. I know I'll eventually have to answer them, but for right now, I am able to get away with changing the subject to something that catches his attention. Like dragons.

And now when I think of dragons, I think of Mia.

She was amazing with him today, and he took to her like she was Tessa, who he also adores. I've never been so completely captivated by someone. She knew exactly how to handle Nolan, and God, she was sexy doing it. The way her tongue rubbed the corner of her mouth while she cleaned out his cut. The way her lips rounded out when she blew on his knee. The way her hair fell past her shoulders, tickling her breasts while she wrapped the bandage around his head. She calmed him down immediately, and she'd only met him an hour before. And the whole knighting thing? Christ, if that wasn't the sweetest thing anyone's ever done for him.

I had to touch her; it was killing me not to. So I took her hand and held it like I had that night at the bar. That slight bit of contact was enough for me. Then she gave me a *yet*, and I felt as if I'd been holding her for years. Pure euphoria washed over me. Adrenaline pumped through my veins, and I finally had hope. Hope that I was slowly tearing down her walls. Hope that she'd eventually come to like me, and maybe even more than that. I could work with a *yet*.

"Who the hell is Princess Mia?" Angie asks, walking into the kitchen with an irritated expression. "Nolan went on and on about some Princess that he killed dragons for today."

I climb off my stool and grab my keys, keeping my smile hidden. "She's Tessa's best friend who's visiting for the summer. Nolan met her today when I took him swimming."

I could've saved my explanation, because Angie doesn't care for it. She's too busy rubbing me through my shorts.

I grab her hand and remove it with a disgusting grunt. "Get the fuck off. I'm not interested."

"Oh no?" She reaches for me again, but I grab her wrist, pressing it against her body. "Jesus. What's your problem?" Her forehead creases as she stares at me, but her face relaxes with her next question. "Does this have anything to do with Princess Mia?"

I don't answer, because Angie doesn't need to know about my personal life. It's not like we are friends and I can share shit with her. We aren't anything. I brush past her and move toward the door. "Tell Nolan I'll see him soon."

"Are you really going to leave with a hard on?"

"What hard on?" I turn, stopping at the front door. "My dick doesn't want you, Angie. Stop kidding yourself."

"Well it wanted me last week, when I sucked you off and swallowed what you gave me. Or what about the week before that when I jerked you off on the couch?" She stands with her arms crossed over her chest, trying to come off as cocky and strong, but her face is giving her away. Angie hates rejection more than anything, and I've been rejecting her for years. "We can make this work, Ben. You know we can."

"There is no *we*. There never was. You've sucked my cock when you wanted to. I've never asked you to do that. I haven't even touched you in three years." I open the door and move out into the hallway of her apartment building.

"What about Nolan? Why can't you at least try for your own son, Ben?"

My blood boils. I grip the doorframe until my hand stings. "Don't ever use Nolan against me. How the fuck would seeing his parents at each other's throats every second benefit him?"

"You won't even give us a chance," she pleads, her eyes glistening over with tears.

"Enough with the bullshit. I won't pretend to have feelings for you just because you're my son's mother. I won't lie to him. Ever." I exhale roughly as her face saddens. "Make sure you tell Nolan I'll see him soon."

And I don't give her a chance to respond before I close the door behind me.

"So, let me make sure I've got this straight," Luke says behind his beer.

We decided to grab a few after our shift ended, and I've just made him fully aware of everything involving Mia. Everything except the fact that I took her virginity.

"You tormented the hell out of this girl eight years ago—"

"Nine," I correct him. Not that one year really matters one way or the other. But I feel putting the most distance between my old asshole self and my current self helps my cause.

He waves me off with his free hand. "Whatever. You used to be a little dickhead, and now you're kicking yourself because she's smoking hot and the lay of your life."

I write her name in the condensation on my glass, but wipe it off before Luke sees it and gives me shit about it. "It's not just about the sex. I could listen to her talk for fucking hours if she'd let me." I sigh heavily, meeting the eyes of my very amused best friend. "Fuck you. Like you aren't completely whipped over my sister."

"I'm not." He is, he'll just never admit it. "And if you ask me—"

"I'm not."

He flips me off before continuing. "I think you're going about this the wrong way. You can't expect Mia to just jump into a relationship with you when she's hated you for years."

"Why not?"

"Because she's hated you for years," he reaffirms. "She'll just keep telling you to fuck off." He states his argument as if it is obvious, which I suppose it is. Even though I have undeniable chemistry with Mia, she isn't going to acknowledge it herself while she still hates me. "Why don't you try to be friends with her first? Let her see that you're interested in more than just fucking her."

I contemplate his advice in silence. That could be a better way to go about this. Winning her friendship means gaining her trust, which would surely grant me forgiveness. And friends do spend a lot of time together, and that definitely appeals to me.

"Nolan's crazy about her, and she's amazing with him. Would I be a complete shit to use my kid as an in?"

"You are a complete shit." He motions for the bartender. "Two Sam Adams, and did you card those fuckers at the end of the bar?" I follow Luke's finger and notice the two kids he is referring to.

And they definitely are kids. No fucking way are they twenty-one.

"Yeah, of course I did. Their ID's said they were twenty-two." The bartender gives us both another beer.

"Grab their ID's for me," Luke insists. The bartender returns seconds later, and I don't miss the uneasiness in the eyes of the two kids. "These are fake. How the hell did you miss this, Ray?" Luke is on his feet and I'm right behind him. He holds the ID's out in front of him, showing them to the kids. "You morons do realize that using a fake ID is a felony, right? How old are you?"

Both of them stand up straighter. "What's it to you?" one asks with snarky confidence.

Luke and I both pull out our badges, flashing it in front of their faces and seeing the panic set into their features. Luke steps closer. "You're making me repeat myself. I don't like doing that. How old are you?"

"We're twenty-two," the one who is apparently doing all the talking states, trying to sound as convincing as possible. His smugness alone makes me want to throw him out on his ass.

I move closer now, no longer in the mood for this kid's shit. "Answer my partner before I make you call your parents and I explain to them that their sons are getting arrested."

"We're nineteen," the meeker one answers urgently. His friend starts sweating, his hands shaking at his sides. "Please don't make me call my dad, officer. Can't you give us a warning or something?"

I narrow in on the honest kid. "Get out now before your friend screws you both."

He moves quickly and his friend tries to follow, but Luke shoots his arm out to stop him.

"Don't lie to a cop, asshole. Especially when you're dumb enough to use your real name on your fake ID, Parker Lance."

"How do you know it's my real name?"

Wow. This kid is asking to get locked up.

"Because you're too stupid to memorize any information that isn't really yours. And no one would willingly pick the name Parker. I'd feel sorry for you if you weren't such a lying piece of shit." The kid opens his mouth to argue but smartly decides to shut it. "Get out."

His now panicked face disappears out the door, and we reclaim our seats at the bar.

"Fucking prick. I should've made him call his parents just for being an asshole," Luke says.

I nod in agreement as I stare at the bottles of alcohol on the shelf in front of me, taking generous sips of my beer. My mind is elsewhere at the moment and Luke notices.

"Damn, man. I've never seen you this obsessed over some chick before. What the hell are you going to do when the summer's over and she goes back home? You know that long distance stuff doesn't work. Ask Reed."

I rub my temples with my fingers. "I don't know. I can't worry about that right now when I'm still trying to get her to tolerate being around me."

"At the rate you're going, you might not have to worry about it."

I ignore him and down my beer.

I can't think about three months from now, and not just because I'm not anywhere near where I want to be with Mia. The thought of her not being five minutes away from me forms a knot in my stomach and a tightness in my chest. I hate the idea of not being able to see her on an impulse. What if I have a sudden urge to kiss her, touch her, talk to her, or breathe the same air as her and she lives four hours away from me? The thought is maddening. I know I'll never survive that kind of distance from her.

The girl I once couldn't get far enough away from has become the woman I can't get close enough to.

Later on that night, I grab my phone and open up a new text message.

I only have three months with Mia, and I want to get the whole friendship thing rolling. The sooner she likes me as a friend, the sooner she'll see me as I see her.

Me: Can I have Mia's phone number?

Tessa: Why? Are you changing it up and trying to make her cry via text message?

Most days I love my sister. Most days.

Me: Look, I fucked up when I was younger and I'm trying to make up for it. You know I care about her, so would you please help me out here? I fucking gave Luke your number.

Tessa: I'll give it to you, but you need to know that Reed got her number too. I don't know if she sees him like that, but heads up. He's a nice guy and he's never made fun of her. He'd be good for her.

Fucking Reed Tennyson. I should've knocked his ass out when I had the chance.

Me: I'd be good for her. Reed can go fuck himself.

Tessa: Easy, tiger. I'm secretly pulling for you if it helps. 205-555-7991

Me: Thanks. I owe you.

Tessa: I know.

I've never been nervous about anything involving women. Never. But right now, a simple text message is terrifying me.

Me: Hey it's Ben. I was wondering if you wanted to hang out sometime this weekend.

Shit. That sounds like I'm asking her out. Which is what I really want to do, but that's not part of this new friendship route I'm trying to establish.

Me: Not like a date or anything.

Damn it. That just sounds shitty, like I need to clarify that I'm definitely not asking her out. Shit.

Me: Just as friends.

I chuck my phone to the end of the bed. I should just throw it outside to keep from making a further ass out of myself. It beeps and I dive for it like my life depends on it.

Mia: I don't know.

I half expected that type of response. And I am locked and loaded.

Me: A certain knight is requesting time with his favorite princess. You wouldn't want to disappoint him, would you? He'll probably cry for days when I break the news to him.

Mia: Wow. Did you really just use your son as bait?

Me: I did. I'm desperate.

One, two minutes go by and I'm starting to sweat.

Me: I just want to spend some time with you. I've made you smile a few times and I think I can do it again if you'll let me. I'm just asking for a chance, Mia. If you hate the guy I am now, then I'll leave you alone. I swear.

Fifty three seconds later, she responds.

Mia: Okay, fine. But I get to pick what we do.

I pump my fist into the air.

Me: Fine with me. What did you have in mind?

Mia: There's this medieval dinner show I passed on my way here the other day. I think it was off two exits before Ruxton. Has Nolan ever been there? He'll get to see knights jousting and stuff.

Holy shit. Nolan's going to lose his mind. Why do I not know about this place?

Me: No, but that sounds awesome. Do I need to make reservations?

Mia: I'll take care of it. Saturday work for you?

Every day works for me. I'll rearrange my entire life at this point.

Me: Yeah. I'll pick you up. Just let me know what time.

Mia: Okay. I'll text you after I book it.

Me: I can't wait.

She doesn't respond to that, but I don't need her to. The only thing I need is the chance she's now willing to give me. I can finally show her the man I am now. I can make up for all the hurt I've caused her. All the pain.

I'll earn her friendship before offering her my life. It's hers anyway. She just needs to take it.

chapter eight

Mia

BEN: *I CAN'T WAIT.*

Me either. I wanted to type, but I didn't. I wasn't just looking forward to spending time with Nolan, who just so happened to be the cutest kid on the planet. I wanted to be around Ben. I didn't want to fight it. I knew I couldn't keep shutting him out. I didn't want to hate him for things he did to me years ago. Not when he definitely wasn't that guy anymore. It'd be different if he was. That hate would be justified. But he's nothing like the old Ben. He doesn't talk to me like that same boy. He doesn't look at me like that same boy. And he definitely doesn't make me feel like that same boy. I'd be a total bitch if I didn't at least give this Ben a chance. So that's what I'm giving him.

Saturday wasn't coming soon enough for me. I've never felt anxious about doing something with a guy just as friends before. But this is Benjamin Kelly we're talking about. He's seen me naked. Completely naked. And now he wants to hang out like we haven't brought each other immense pleasure.

He came just as much as I did that night, so I'm taking credit for that.

How the hell am I supposed to navigate a friendship with a guy that I can't stop fantasizing about? I've had guy friends before. It's doable. But I've never gotten butterflies over those guys. I've never felt like I might actually combust just being in the same room as those guys. And I've definitely never wanted to bang the hell out of those guys.

Speaking of boys that want to be friends with me, I promised Reed that I'd meet him for lunch today. We've talked on the phone a few times since the day at Rocky Point. He was really sweet and funny, and when he asked me to hang out with him, I didn't hesitate to say yes. He picked a sandwich shop in town that I was familiar with. Tessa and I ate there several times with her parents when we were younger. I spent the morning in the pool with her, not being able to sunbathe because the heat was enough to make you pass out. After a quick shower, I drove into town and parked my Jeep next to Reed's truck. He was already seated at a table when I walked through the door.

"Hey, how are you?" I ask, walking around the table as he stands up to greet me. He gives me a hug, which I'm not expecting, but isn't awkward. And it definitely isn't anything other than a hug you'd give a friend, which relieves me. I'm hoping this really is just a lunch between new friends and not anything more. I'm not interested in anything else with Reed, and I don't want this to become uncomfortable.

He ends our one armed hug with a pat on my back. Very non-date like.

"I'm good. I ordered you a shrimp salad sub. I hope that's okay." Reed smiles at me as he takes his seat and I take mine. He has the lightest blond hair I've ever seen, almost white, that falls in his eyes with a bit of curl.

"Yeah, thanks. That sounds delicious." I take a sip of the water he had also ordered for me. "So, you were off work today?"

Reed had mentioned a few days ago that he was a laborer for his father's construction company.

He nods. "Yeah. Business is kind of slow right now. But it should pick up soon. We're usually slammed in the summer time." Our sandwiches are placed in front of us, and we both take a bite, chewing behind our smiles. "What town in Georgia are you from again?"

"Fulton. Smallest town in the world." I swallow my bite and take a drink. "It's a military town. The air base is really the only thing in it besides a Wal-Mart."

"Have you ever been on the air base? I bet they have some really cool planes there."

I shrug. "I've only been on it a few times. They'll show movies there at the theatre for a dollar, but it's always like, three months after their original release date." I take another bite of my sandwich. "I don't think given the choice, I'd choose to live in Fulton. It's mainly a lot of old people that are retired," I pause and grin slyly. "And Marines."

He laughs behind his drink. "I could totally live there. I'm a sucker for girls in uniforms and military planes. My grandfather was a pilot and used to take me to the air shows when I was younger." The chimes on the door ring when it opens, and I watch Reed's eyes react to whoever walks in. "What the hell are the odds," he mumbles before fixating his gaze on me.

I turn in my chair and nearly fall out of it.

Sweet mother of all that's holy. Ben stands frozen just inside the shop door, his eyes shifting between mine and what I'm going to assume are Reed's. But I can't turn around to be sure. I can't do anything besides stare at the glorious sight of him in a cop uniform.

He's a cop? I had no freaking idea. What the hell else is Tessa keeping from me?

My chatterbox best friend seems oddly tight lipped on everything involving her brother.

"Well, look who it is." I'm broken out of my trance and glance up to see Luke's amused grin. "How are you, Mia?"

Movement comes from my left, and I turn to see Ben walking over.

Oh, Good God. He's right next to me. He's right next to me and he's got handcuffs.

I swallow heavily and pry my eyes from his to look at Luke. "I'm good. Great. I'm... I'm good. Or great. Both. I'm both." And I've apparently forgotten how to hold a conversation.

Luke muffles his laugh.

"Hey," Ben greets me with a smile. I'd usually be able to react like a normal human being and say something, anything in response, but considering the fact that he paired that knock-me-on-my-ass grin with the uniform he's rocking, I'm pooling in my chair and unable to do anything but continue breathing. He shoots a glare at Reed, one that I wouldn't ever want directed toward me. "Reed," he practically growls, and I think Reed says something in return, but at the moment, my entire body is completely focused on Ben's, including my ears. He looks back down at me and grips the back of my chair. "Are we still on for Saturday?"

"Hmm?"

His lips move, parting sensually, but I've no idea what words, if any, just came out of them. I know exactly what those lips are capable of and that's the only thing filtering through my mind at the moment.

My God. Those lips are orgasmic.

"I'm sorry, what?"

He laughs and looks over at Luke quickly before returning to my stunned face. "I asked if we're still on for Saturday."

I nod. A lot. My head might have fallen off if I hadn't forced myself to stop. "Yup. I made reservations for the five o'clock show." I clear my throat and take a sip of my water before continuing. *Christ. It feels like I swallowed super glue.* "Um, we have to be there fifteen minutes before showtime. I arranged for Nolan to get his picture taken with the King."

His eyes light up and his cheeks hollow out with his dimples. "Oh man. He's going to freak out over that." We smile at each other. The other two guys could probably catch on fire and I doubt either one of us would notice. I definitely won't notice. "Good idea, Princess Mia."

"Yeah, I can be pretty awesome sometimes."

Luke slaps Ben's back, and the sound snaps me out of my obsessive gazing. "Well, as much as I'd love to stand here and listen to you two not flirt with each other, I'm starving and we need to get back out there." He smirks at me. "You know, bad guys to catch and all. Protect and serve. That whole thing." He turns his head toward Reed. "Sorry to interrupt your date."

"It's not a date," I blurt out, immediately regretting the hidden implication that I'd never actually be on a date with Reed. I look over at him, silently pleading for him to agree with my statement and not make this any more awkward than I've just made it.

Help a girl out. Don't leave me hanging here.

He cocks an eyebrow at me. "Well, that's the last time I service you with my free hand underneath the table. You've broken my heart, Mia."

My jaw hits the table I definitely was not recently serviced under. *Is he nuts?* "What?" I manage to choke out.

"What the fuck did you just say?" Ben questions with a tone that no man in his right mind should challenge. "Say it again, asshole, and see what happens." He moves closer to Reed but Luke steps between the two.

"I'm gonna let him punch you if you say something stupid like that again," Luke states, straining his head over his own shoulder to connect with Reed.

Ben and Luke are roughly the same size, so Luke doesn't have any difficulty in holding him back. Reed, on the other hand, is more leaned out than muscular, and probably wouldn't stand a chance against Ben.

Luke turns back toward Ben, who is still looking ready to kill. "Not a date, man. Just relax." His words are barely audible, but I hear them. And Ben seems to calm down as he processes them himself.

Reed holds up his hands in surrender. "Kidding. Jesus Christ. You used to have a sense of humor, Ben. What the hell happened?"

Ben places his hand on the back of my chair again, hovering over me in a very possessive way. If I'm not mistaken, it's as if he's staking his claim in front of Reed, just like he did the other day on the pier. But this time, I don't object to it. This time, the very thought of being Ben's doesn't infuriate me. It intrigues me. I want to know what that feels like. But he asked me out for Saturday as friends, and friends don't act like that with each other. So that can't possibly be what he's doing right now. He's probably just looking out for me. So I push those thoughts to the back of my mind and watch his eyes shift back to mine. He hasn't said anything else to Reed but I don't think he needs to. His actions and demeanor are speaking loud enough for him.

"I'll pick you up at four o'clock. I figured we'd surprise Nolan so I'm not going to tell him where we're going." His tone is friendly, all edginess and agitation gone, as if he didn't just have a pissing contest with the guy that I am not on a date with.

I tuck my hair back behind my ear. "Make sure he brings his sword. He's gonna need it."

I feel his thumb brush along my back, and that slight bit of contact sends my lower half into a frenzy.

"Ben. Get over here and order," Luke calls out, having moved to the counter. He must have thought it was safe to leave his friend alone with Reed. That or he was too hungry to care anymore.

Ben lets go of my chair with a grin and brushes against my shoulder with his hand. These tiny touches are going to kill me.

"See you Saturday."

"Okay," I choke out with a shaky voice.

He turns and shoots Reed a scowl, before walking over to the counter. And now his back is to me. His shoulders in that shirt. His ass in those pants. Someone may have to scrape me off the floor.

"You're hilarious." I glare at Reed, accomplishing the difficult task of prying my eyes off the glorious body standing no more than fifteen feet away from me. "I think I'd remember getting fingered underneath a table, ass."

"I'd hope so." Reed grins before shrugging. "It's all good. I've never seen Ben get all *I'm caveman, this my woman* before. He's fun to rile up."

I roll my eyes before giving in to the temptation standing at the counter.

I don't want to stare, but given the fact that Ben's back is to me and he'd never know I'm drooling down the front of my shirt, I allow it. I hear Reed's voice as it enters my ear, and it would be rude of me not to answer him. Besides, I'm perfectly capable of answering one person while I'm glued to someone else. I'm a woman for Christ's sake. We can multi-task the shit out of stuff.

"Hmm mmm. Yeah, me too," I reply.

Ben pulls his wallet out of the back of his pants. Where his ass is. That. Ass. It's this perfectly sculpted entity in and of itself. There should be internet sites dedicated to it. Fan clubs. Parades, even.

"Oh wow. That sounds really fun. I'd love to do that," I respond.

Ben reaches over his shoulder and scratches his back, pulling his shirt tight across his muscles.

My God.

"That's crazy. I hate it when that happens." I have no idea what Reed just said to me. No idea. His chuckle catches my attention and I whip my head around. "What?"

His eyes drift from the men at the counter back to me. He grins amusingly. "I just asked you how your sandwich was, and you answered me with 'that's crazy. I hate it when that happens.'" His body shakes with silent laughter.

I slap my hand over my eyes and bow my head in embarrassment. "Oh, my God. I'm so sorry, Reed. That was so rude of me." I drop my hand and turn my body toward him completely, granting him all my focus. "I'm paying attention to you, I swear."

He tilts his head. "So, when should I set us up for sky diving?"

"Huh?" *Sky diving?* Hell no. I'd never agree to something like that.

"You said it sounded really fun and that you'd love to do it. Remember? Just two minutes ago when you were paying attention to me."

I open my mouth to apologize when the door chimes, causing me to whip my head around. Ben smiles at me before he walks out, and I wave like some obnoxious fan girl trying to flag down her favorite celebrity. *Real smooth.* I turn back around and see how much this is entertaining Reed. "Did I mention Ben and I are trying out this whole friends thing? I don't have the slightest idea what I'm doing." I filled Reed in on mine and Ben's history at Rocky Point the other day, leaving out the small detail of the mind blowing five orgasms he gave me. Five!

"Clearly." He smiles and throws his crumpled up napkin at me. "It's not gonna work."

"What?"

"Friends. You and Ben. I'll bet money on it." He crosses his arms over his chest, leaning back in his chair. He is grinning at me like he has it in the bag. Like he is already holding my money and counting it arrogantly in front of me. Oh, the smugness.

"Why are you so sure that it won't work? I can be friends with Ben." I mimic his appearance and lean back in my own chair. "We can totally be friends. It'll work."

"It's not going to work, and I'll tell you why."

"Okay, smart guy. Why?"

Don't ever tell a woman that we can't do something, because we'll die trying to do that very thing that you're so sure we can't do. I think the female race is stubborn as a whole. Maybe it's a design flaw, but whatever. I'm here to prove a point.

"Because—" he sits forward, pulling my half eaten sandwich in front of him before he picks it up "—I don't know about you, but I don't usually eye fuck my friends."

"Who's eye fucking?" I half yell. Thank God, we are the only two people currently in the sandwich shop. But it doesn't save me from getting a stern look from the owner behind the counter. "I was not eye fucking," I harshly whisper.

"And I'm not about to eat the rest of your sandwich." He grins condescendingly before taking a huge bite of my sub.

I roll my eyes, the eyes that were so not eye fucking anyone, before I respond. "What's your opinion on him anyway? Do you think he's a good guy?"

He nods and swallows his bite. "Yeah, when he's not threatening to beat the shit out of me." We both laugh, and I take a sip of my water. "He's really good with his kid. Even when Nolan was a baby, he just knew what to do with him. And he wasn't even nervous about it. I'd be scared shitless if someone threw a baby at me."

I giggle and watch him pop the last bit of my sandwich into his mouth.

I could tell just from being around them once that Ben was amazing with Nolan. They were so sweet together, and Ben seemed like the type of dad that would do anything for his kid, which is exactly how it should be.

"Well, I think anyone would be scared if babies were flying at them," I counter, getting rewarded with a sneer and another crumpled up napkin tossed at my head. We both stand up and push our chairs in. "Thanks for lunch. It was memorable, even without the finger fucking." He winks, unable to form any words with a full mouth. "You're a really good friend, Reed."

He grimaces and swallows his massive bite uncomfortably. "Friend zoned like a boss." I buckle over at his statement, laughing so hard my eyes filled with tears. "No worries. You're not my type, anyway. I prefer really dumb girls with low self-esteem and daddy issues."

I shove him in the direction of the entrance. "Oh that's nice. Daddy issues? Really?"

"Hell yes." He holds the door for me and we both walk to our vehicles. "Girls with daddy issues are always looking for a new daddy." He throws his head back, cracking up at himself and the disgusted look I'm currently giving him. "See ya later, Mia."

I shake my head disapprovingly. Men.

chapter nine

Ben

FUCKING REED TENNYSON.

I didn't know what he was playing at, but I was sure as hell going to find out. And I couldn't waste any time doing it either. Not when he was taking my girl out to lunch and shit. I was not okay with that. I didn't know what his intentions were. If he just wanted a friendship from Mia, fine. Anything more than that? Fuck no. She was mine, and apparently, he might need a reminder.

I know where Reed lives, so I stop by his house later on after work. We never really hang out that much, but I used to pick Tessa up from his house all the time before she could drive.

His truck is parked in the driveway, which is a good thing. I really didn't feel like driving all over the place looking for him, but I would if I had to. This shit needs to be cleared up tonight.

After parking behind him, I knock on his front door and see his head peer out the small window next to it. I hear a soft "fuck" before he swings the door open and greets me with raised eyebrows.

He studies my uniform, keeping his hand on the doorknob. "Are you here to arrest me for taking Mia out to lunch yesterday? Because if I have a choice, I'd much rather have you lock me up than beat the shit out of me."

I lean against the railing, ignoring the smart ass undertone that all of his words seem to be laced with. "What the hell do you want with Mia?"

He chuckles then, and I straighten up, causing him to wipe the smile off his face.

I really don't want to hit him, but he isn't making the decision easy on me. I'll deal with the ramifications later.

"Nothing. I mean, she's a cool chick and I like hanging out with her, but just as friends. Maybe if you hadn't marked your territory, I would've tried something, but I'm not stupid. I don't think she's interested in me like that anyway."

"She's not a fucking fire hydrant for me to piss on, dick. Don't refer to her as territory." I step closer to him, remembering what he said yesterday in the sandwich shop after Mia insisted the two of them weren't on a date. "And if I ever hear you joking around about touching Mia again, it'll take a lot more than Luke to stop me from tearing you apart."

He runs his hands down his face before letting out an exhaustive sigh. Turning around, he starts back into his house.

"Where the hell are you going?" I ask, stepping forward and grabbing the door.

This conversation isn't over until I fucking end it. I follow him inside, stopping at the end of the hallway that dumps out into the kitchen.

He emerges from the fridge with two beers. "Here. I sure as hell need one of these, and maybe if you have one you won't be so inclined to murder me on my porch." He places my beer on the counter and leans against the fridge, taking a swig of his. "Actually, if you are going to kill me, do it outside so I at least have witnesses. And avoid messing up my face too much. I'm sure my mom would prefer an open casket."

"I'm not going to kill you. I might make it so you can't walk for a few days, but you'll still be breathing. And you can't blame me for wanting to find out what the hell your motives are with my girl." I walk over to the counter and grab my beer, keeping my eyes on him as I take a drink.

"Look, man, I'm not moving in on Mia. I swear. But I would like to keep being friends with her, and I don't fucking think I should have to ask your permission to do that."

I grin and take another sip of my beer. I have a good amount of muscle on Reed, so the fact that he has the balls to talk to me like I can't wipe the floor with him, earns my respect. "No, you don't have to ask my permission. I'm fine with you being friends with Mia. I just wanted to make sure that you weren't trying to be anything else with her. I'm fucking crazy over that girl."

He arches his eyebrow at me. "Really? I had no idea." We both laugh, and he pushes off from the fridge and moves across from me. "You're fucking crazy over a girl you're trying to be friends with? That makes a hell of a lot of sense," he states sarcastically.

I grimace. "I'm doing what's necessary. The torture I'm going to endure by not acting on my feelings will be worth it if she lets me in." He looks at me with a perplexed gaze, like I've just explained myself to him in another language. I take another sip of my beer and frown. "When you meet a girl that gets to you the way Mia gets to me, you'll understand. Friends genuinely like each other and I need her to like me. She'll never love me if she doesn't like me first."

He places his beer down with a shake of his head. "I had a girl get to me like that, and she completely fucked me over. I don't see how any of it is worth it. That's why I'm just with girls for one night. They can't rip your heart out if you don't let them anywhere near it." He smiles. "I hope it works out for you though. I think you have a pretty good shot with her from what I've observed."

"Why do you think that? Did she say something to you?"

If Reed and Mia are friends, she could've shared things with him like she does my sister. And I am suddenly all for their friendship if it helps my cause.

He regards me with a smile like he knows things. Things I desperately want to know.

I place my beer down and leer at him. "You're not going to tell me shit, are you?"

He smiles again, more cunning this time, after taking a huge chug of his beer. "I don't have much to tell. But a fucking blind person could've seen the way you two acted around each other yesterday. I could've burned the place down and I doubt either one of you would've noticed. You flustered her so bad she could barely speak, and she definitely wasn't paying attention to a damn thing I was saying once you stepped in the shop. I could've asked her to carry my children and she probably would've agreed without knowing it." He shakes his hair out of his eyes and registers my annoyed expression. "Not that I would've asked her that. I'm sure you've claimed that uterus."

I wave him off dismissively, holding the neck of my beer bottle with my free hand. "I'm glad I make it difficult for her to form a sentence, but I don't need to convince her body that we should be together. I've proven that point already."

He grabs another beer, tossing his empty bottle into the trashcan and offering me one.

I decline it.

"I just need her to see me as the guy I am now and not the shithead I used to be. And being friends and showing her that I'm not just in this for pussy seems like the best option for me."

"Unless she keeps your ass permanently in the friend zone. This whole plan could blow up in your face if you aren't careful." He walks around the counter and sits down on the couch, turning on the TV.

I haven't thought about the possibility of that happening. But I highly doubt Mia can ignore the chemistry we have and only see me as a friend. The spark between us is fucking palpable. The air seems to crackle when we're in the same room. There is an energy to it, a dynamic that you can practically see rippling between us. Drawing us together like charged particles. There's no denying it. And once she only sees me as the man I am now and not the boy I used to be, I'll make it my life's purpose to never again let her feel the type of pain I once caused her.

"Hey, man, I'm gonna head out and go see my kid. Thanks for the beer."

Reed acknowledges me with a nod before I walk out of his house.

I feel better now that I know for sure he isn't trying to get with Mia. And I don't have a problem with him being friends with her. He's a decent guy. He's always been good to my sister.

But if he ever steps out of line with my girl, I won't hesitate to put him back in it.

I park out front at Angie's apartment complex and take the stairs quickly to her floor.

I want to tell Nolan that he'll be spending time with Mia on Saturday night. I know he'll look forward to it as much as I am once I break the news to him.

I knock on the door, hearing his gruff voice singing aloud somewhere in the apartment. The door opens and Angie stands there, looking less than pleased to see me.

"Great. Now I'll never get him to go to sleep." She steps aside and motions for me to walk in. "He's been fighting me for the past hour and my nerves are shot."

I can hear Nolan's voice coming from down the hallway where the bedrooms are. He sounds very animated, but that's pretty standard for him.

"I'll put him to bed. I want to talk to him anyway."

She closes the front door and moves past me toward the couch. "Don't keep him up with another story. I've already read to him four times, and if he doesn't get to bed soon, he'll be cranky as hell in the morning." She begins flipping through a magazine, seemingly done with lecturing me, which is a good thing because I'm fucking done listening to it.

If anyone needs parenting advice between the two of us, it sure as hell isn't me.

I walk down the hallway and stop at Nolan's door, leaning against the doorframe.

He is trying to balance his stuffed dragon on the end of his bed, holding his sword in his free hand. I watch with a smile as he gets his favorite sleeping buddy to stand up on the wooden footboard before he strikes it down with a mighty swing.

"Aren't you supposed to be in bed, buddy?"

His eyes light up and he scrambles off the bed, running toward me. I scoop him up and plant kisses all over his face.

"Daddy! You'wre hewre!"

"Shhh," I say against his hair, carrying him over to the bed. He crawls under the covers and I lie on my side next to him, tucking him in. "Mommy said you were supposed to go to bed a while ago."

He tugs at the buttons on my uniform. "I'm not tiewerd," his voice breaks into a yawn, and I try to hide my laugh. "Can you wead me a storwy?" He looks completely exhausted, and I know I'll never get more than a few pages into it before he passes out. He continues playing with the buttons on my shirt, his sleepy eyes falling closed every couple seconds.

"Not tonight." I lean off the bed and grab his stuffed dragon, handing it to him. He pulls it tightly against him, popping one ear of the dragon into his mouth like he always does. He falls asleep that way every night, and wakes up if the dragon falls off the bed in the middle of the night and he no longer has it in his grasp. I run my finger down his nose and he focuses on my face, repeating the gesture.

"Guess who's going to hang out with us on Saturday night?"

His mouth unlatches from the ear. "Who?"

I smile. "Princess Mia."

His dimpled grin lights his whole face up, and he immediately gets to his knees. "Pwincess Mia! Yayyayayayayay!" He bounces on the bed and I hush him again, tucking him back in. "I wike Pwincess Mia, Daddy," he says in a softer voice before tucking the dragon's ear back into his mouth.

I bend down and kiss him on his forehead. "Me too, buddy."

He closes his eyes and begins humming against his dragon.

I settle down on my side, watching his body relax completely and hearing the low sound he is making get softer and softer. When I know he is asleep, I sneak out of his room, leaving the door cracked open.

Angie is still on the couch looking at her magazine, but throws it onto the coffee table when I enter the room.

"You know, stopping over here during the week and putting him to bed only confuses him."

I'm walking toward the front door but stop and turn after her statement. "What the hell are you talking about?"

She stands, hitting me with her most irritated expression.

I brace myself for whatever bullshit argument she is about to start. It would be nice to go one time seeing Angie and not have it out with her, but she seems determined to bitch me out about something every chance she gets.

"He's going to start expecting it. He already wants us to be a family, and when you come over here and put him to bed, it's just going to make him think that we are one." She steps closer to me, dropping her gaze to her feet. I know this tactic. She does it when she wants me to feel bad about something. It never works and I'm surprised she keeps using it. She looks up at me with only her eyes, keeping her head down. "He'll probably wake up and wonder if you're still here, and then when you're not, it'll just upset him."

"You're wasting your time trying to make me feel guilty. If I wanna come over here and say goodnight to my son on nights that technically aren't mine, I'll do it. He knows that the three of us aren't a family. He has me and he has you, but he'll never have us together."

Her head snaps up, the wounded façade disappearing. "God, you're such an asshole. What the fuck was I thinking hooking up with you in the first place?"

I continue my walk toward the door. "Neither one of us was thinking," I counter. Because I wasn't thinking that night.

If I had been sober, I wouldn't have slept with Angie. After talking with her for a minute, I would've seen what type of person she was. A self-centered, conniving brat. She seems to get joy out of my misery, and I wouldn't have lasted more than a minute in her presence if I wasn't drunk.

I grab the door handle and look behind me where she has fallen back onto the couch, pouting like a kid who has just been reprimanded.

"I'd never take it back."

Her eyes meet mine briefly, before she drops them to the floor, nodding to convey her understanding of what I mean.

I hate Angie, but I love the gift she gave me. Nolan makes me a better man. It pains me to imagine not having him, and I'll always feel indebted to her for not going through with the abortion.

"I'll pick him up after work on Friday," I say.

She acknowledges me with another nod, but her gaze never leaves the spot on the floor she is boring a hole into.

I close her apartment door behind me and make my way out to my truck.

It'll always be like this with Angie. Even giving her what she wants, us, won't change the person she truly is. She's a bitch by nature, and I'm tied to her for the rest of my life. But I don't care how she treats me. She can spew all her poison at me and I'll fucking take it. She gave me my son.

And he's the only thing that matters.

chapter ten

Mia

"What's wrong with what I'm wearing?" I direct toward my best friend who is currently rummaging through my clothes.

For my date, no, friendly hang out with Ben and Nolan, I pick a pair of skinny jeans and a white tank top. I think this is very appropriate for going to a medieval dinner show as friends, but Tessa has other ideas.

Articles of clothing are getting hurled into the air as she stays hidden in the closet I'm occupying for the summer. I step behind her and start grabbing clothes out of the air.

"Do you mind? You're going to be ironing all these after you pick them up." I chuck the handful of clothes I've managed to catch onto my bed.

Tessa emerges from the closet with my teeny tiny jean skirt and a tube top. "Strip. You package yourself up in this hot little number, and I guarantee my brother will be unwrapping you with his teeth later on tonight."

My best friend has a one track mind. A very dirty one track mind.

I snatch the hot little number that I am definitely not wearing out of her hands. "This is not a date, so there won't be any unwrapping going on." I toss the outfit onto the bed and continue brushing my hair in front of the mirror. "I told you, we're hanging out as friends. There's no need for me to be wearing anything revealing."

She plops down on the bed, sighing dramatically, because this is Tessa we're talking about. "Who the hell goes from a night of unbelievable, nine inch, pussy humming sex to hanging out as friends? Did you both hit a large rock when you jumped off those cliffs last weekend? Is your brain currently swelling and causing you to act like a complete idiot?"

I pin half of my hair up before I turn and look at her. "I'm just now getting used to the idea of not hating Ben for the rest of my life. Do you have any idea how dead set I was on that game plan? I was close to having a voodoo doll made of him."

"And now you two have bumped uglies, and you're just going to pretend that you didn't."

I grunt my frustration and shoot her a stern nook. "No one's pretending anything. He asked me to give him a chance and I'm giving it to him. As friends. It would be really shitty of me not to." I turn back around and continue messing with my hair.

There's no way I could ever pretend that Ben and I didn't share that one night together. If it was possible to forget, I would've forgotten about it already. Lord knows I don't want to be reliving it every night alone in my bed. That memory is sticking around permanently. And what a memory.

"I don't see why you can't give him a chance while he's between your legs. You'd at least get some relief if he was fucking you into the friend zone."

"Pwincess Mia!" Nolan's husky voice comes echoing down the hallway.

"Hold on one second!" I snap my head around toward a grinning Tessa. "I really hope your nephew didn't hear that," I scold her, but she merely shrugs her shoulders in response.

I grab my phone and stick it into my pocket, stepping in front of the mirror one last time.

My hair is definitely not behaving, doing this weird curl thing at the bottom that I am so not digging. And of course, the more I mess with it, the worse it gets. I grumble my irritation under my breath.

"Mmm mmm," Tessa teases. "Just friends, my ass."

I ignore her and apply some lip gloss. "What's up with you and Luke? Are you two serious?"

She rolls over onto her back, moaning playfully. "Luke is fun. Really fun. Tie me up and own my body fun."

I should be shocked by that description, but I'm not. Tessa is into anything involving men. Especially when it involves fun stuff.

"But not serious fun?"

"I don't know. I like him and he likes me. I don't need anything more than that."

We meet each other's eyes in the mirror.

She wants to tell me more, I can tell, but decides against it and gives me a sly smile instead. "How many condoms will you be taking with you tonight?"

"You are ridiculous." I flip her off over my shoulder, walking down the hallway and into the living room.

Nolan is swinging his sword in the air behind the sofa, slaying invisible enemies, but my eyes don't linger on him. They can't. Not when *he* is in the room.

All my focus is magnetically pulled in the direction of Ben, who is leaning against the counter. He straightens when he sees me, melting me with his smile that beams like a thousand watt bulb.

If I was wearing heels right now, I definitely would've stumbled.

"Hey," he says, twirling his keys on his finger. It's so casual, like any normal greeting between friends, but his greeting makes my spine tingle and my toes curl.

God, how does he do that? How does he turn a simple *hey* into so much more than that? I feel that hey settle between my legs and root itself there permanently.

"Hey," I reply, trying to sound as sure and steady with this whole friendship thing as he does. However, my hey comes out broken and weak, giving away my anxiety. Although, even if I wouldn't have spoken, I'm sure my body language would be displaying my nervousness for all to see. I am completely rigid, and the conversation with Tessa that just transpired moments ago, is playing on loop in my mind.

Pussy humming sex.

Fucking into the friend zone.

Condoms.

Oh, God, do not get wet right now.

I drop my eyes to Nolan, needing a distraction.

"Pwincess Mia!" He runs over to me and I bend down, bringing myself down to his level. My worries and desires are left above me as I focus in on his cuteness. "Daddy said we're going to a surpwise." He reaches out and runs his finger down my nose, and I do the same to him. His tiny face scrunches up afterwards.

"We are. But I have to ask you a question before we go." His eyes get even larger, grayish blue just like his father's, as he waits for me. "Have you ever been to a real castle, Sir Nolan?" He shakes his head and his mouth drops open. "Would you like to go to one right now?"

I've never seen anyone go from one emotion to another so quickly. If I blinked, I probably would've missed it.

He begins jumping up and down, almost knocking me onto my ass in the process. "A weal castle! Daddy! Pwincess Mia said we can go to a weal castle!"

Ben laughs as I stand up. "You ready to go, buddy?" He picks a squirming Nolan up and smiles sweetly at me. "Are *you* ready, Princess Mia?"

Am I? For friendship with a man that I can't stop thinking about? Pussy humming sex. *Shit*. I force a nod and swallow down my fear.

"Lead the way, noble knights."

Nolan's excitement was infectious, and it grew as the evening played out.

When we pulled up in front of the castle, he couldn't get out of the truck fast enough and practically sprinted toward it. When he got his picture taken with the King, he couldn't take his eyes off him, even when Ben and I told him to look at us so we could take pictures of him with our phones. He stared at him with eyeballs the size of dinner plates, his mouth forming a tiny O. It was the cutest thing I've ever seen. And when the actual show started and Nolan got to see the knights in action, jousting and sword fighting right in front of him, I don't think he blinked even once.

And then there was Ben.

I kept catching glances from him the entire night, meeting his eyes every few minutes when I couldn't keep myself from looking at him. I'm sure my struggle was obvious, considering he caught me each and every time I gave into my temptation. But the look he shot back at me wasn't the one I was used to. It wasn't the look he gave me when I knew he was thinking about doing things to my body. I was familiar with that look. The greedy shift in his eyes, the tightness in his jaw, the way his nostrils flared like he was a caged Pit bull. But I didn't get that look tonight.

Instead of the raw thirst I had seen in his eyes on more than one occasion, I saw tenderness. A friendly affection. He regarded me sweetly, but there was nothing behind it. No underlying hunger.

And God, I wanted to be devoured by him.

"He is completely passed out." I observe, walking next to Ben and focusing on Nolan's exhausted face. I reach up and brush his wild brown hair off his forehead, smiling at his sleepy state. "I don't even think an actual dragon could wake him up right now."

Ben opens up the back door of his truck, laughing softly at the sight of Nolan's face as he peels him off his shoulder. "I figured he'd crash hard after all of this." He buckles Nolan into his car seat, closing the door and grabbing the passenger door handle. "I may have withheld his nap from him today in hopes of getting to talk to you alone on the drive back. My son likes to monopolize the conversation, as you witnessed on the way here."

I smile, climbing up into the truck after my door is opened for me.

Nolan talked nonstop on the drive to the dinner show, and every time Ben tried to talk to me about something other than dragons or knights, Nolan would adorably cut in and change the subject.

I'd be lying if I said I'm not grateful for Nolan's missed nap.

I settle into my seat and buckle up. "I can't say I blame him. Dragons and knights are way more exciting than what Tessa and I did today."

He closes my door and gets in on the driver's side, starting up the truck and pulling away from the castle.

I inhale, taking in Ben's scent that has completely filled the space between us. He smells like pure Ben. No cologne, just him. Like a man that knows exactly how to please a woman.

Shit. Don't go there.

"How's your mom doing? Tessa mentioned a few months back that she was really sick. Is it breast cancer?"

I cross one leg over the other, angling my body toward him.

His one hand stays firmly planted on the wheel while his other relaxes on the console between us. I'm glued to his fingers, the fingers that I moronically doubted that night. I didn't think there was a chance in hell he'd get me off the way he did. And now that I know what those fingers are capable of, I'm fascinated by them. I actually can't stop looking at them.

The length, the thickness, the fucking tips of them that played me like a record. I want him to turn his hand up so I can straddle his fingers and ride out my pent up orgasm right now, but that's not going to happen.

He clears his throat, gaining my attention, and I'm quickly reminded of the question he hit me with before I wandered off into finger fucking la-la land.

I paint on my most convincing I-wasn't-just-fantasizing-about-what-you-could-do-to-me face and answer. "Yeah. She's doing great right now. The treatments aren't making her nearly as sick as they did in the beginning. It was awful when she first started them."

He glances over at me and gives me a sympathetic smile.

"She wouldn't eat anything and she didn't have the strength to get out of bed. I couldn't leave her side for more than a few minutes at a time because she was constantly getting sick."

"But she's doing better now? Does she still have it?" he asks, turning onto the main highway that leads to Ruxton.

I nod once. "Yeah, she still has it, but I guess the treatments are working because she's doing so much better than she was. I think she's gotten most of her strength back." I lean my head back against the seat rest, shifting my eyes from Ben's profile to the road in front of us. "I just, I don't know what I'd do if something happened to her. She's the only family I have left besides my aunt."

The hand that I had longed to mount reaches over and grabs mine. He squeezes it gently, comforting me. "Nothing's going to happen to her. And she's not the only family that you have. Tessa would kick your ass if she heard you say that."

I laugh and he smiles at me. His eyes shift to our conjoined hands. After one gentle squeeze, he lets mine go. I hold in my disappointment and rejoin my own hands together in my lap.

"So, Officer Kelly."

My God, does that have a ring to it or what?

Images of him doing things to me in that uniform flash in front of my eyes too fast to focus on. I blink rapidly as his eyes meet mine and darken. And that look, the look that he's hitting me with is directly connected to the pulsing spot between my legs. I clear my throat and the dirty thoughts from my mind.

"Do you like being a cop?"

Good save.

I hide my heated face behind the strand of hair that fell out of my clip, shifting my attention to the road in front of us. My body goes rigid when his hand brushes my face, tucking my hair back behind my ear.

"I do," he replies coolly, as if he didn't just touch me. As if he's completely unaffected by that touch. His hand returns to his lap before he continues, his eyes returning to the road as mine neglect it completely. I am entirely too focused on him and his smooth voice. "It's never boring, that's for sure. Plus, Nolan gets a kick out of it." His lip curls up into a smile, as if he's thinking of some memory. "What about you? What were you doing back home?"

"I was taking classes at the local community college, but stopped when my mom was diagnosed. I'd like to eventually do something with kids, I think. Be a teacher or guidance counselor or something."

"I can see that," he says. "I'm sure you'd be awesome at it."

I look to the back seat at a very sleepy little boy whose head is slouched against his car seat. "He really is the cutest kid I've ever seen." I pry his wooden sword out of his hand and place it onto the seat next to him. "You've raised this incredible little boy, Ben. If I ever have kids of my own someday, I hope they turn out as awesome as this one."

Our eyes lock.

"If there was any woman that was born to be a mother, it's you."

He means what he says. I can feel it. I settle back into my seat and stare at his profile. "Really?"

I've never given much thought to having children, mainly because I've never pictured the person I would someday have them with. When you've gone twenty-three years without a boyfriend, it's hard to imagine having a husband.

He looks over at me like I've just asked him the most ridiculous question—deep crease in his forehead and a curious frown. "Are you kidding? Look how you are with Nolan."

I shake my head in disagreement. "Nolan's easy, though. He'd probably love anybody that played knights and princesses with him."

"You're not just anybody. You knighted my son, which he hasn't stopped talking about. You gave him this amazing memory tonight, and he does the nose thing with you."

I furrow my brow, confusion setting in. "The nose thing? Oh, you mean when he runs his finger down your nose? That thing?"

"Yeah. Do you know he only does that with me?" He pulls off the highway and onto the back road leading toward the house. I shake my head, and he sees it before continuing. "I've never seen him do that with anybody else. Not Tessa, not my parents, and definitely not his mother. I don't know why he does it, but he's only ever done that with me."

I suddenly feel horrible, like I've barged in on a private Ben and Nolan bonding activity.

"I'm sorry. He did it to me when he woke me up the other day and I did it back out of reflex. I didn't know that was your thing."

"Mia, relax. I like that he does that with you. I like that that's something you and I share with him. He's only known you for a week and he's already formed this special bond with you. You'd be an amazing mom." He pauses, glancing in his rear-view mirror. "You'd be better than the one he has."

"She's not good with him?"

I only have concern in my voice, but the thought of someone not being good to Nolan makes my blood boil. I keep that emotion tucked away though.

Ben shakes his head. "She doesn't spend time with Nolan because she wants to spend time with him. She does it to keep him from spending time with me. She's never been a good mom to him. When he was a baby, she refused to breastfeed him because she was so worried that it would wreck her body. I begged her to do it because I knew it would be good for him, and she still refused." His hand that is gripping the wheel seems to grip tighter. "I hate leaving him with her, knowing that he's probably being neglected. Something could happen to him because she doesn't pay attention and the thought of that…" His voice trails off, and I don't think, I just move.

I push up the flip console and slide across the bench seat, pulling his free hand into mine. "Nothing's going to happen to him. You can't think like that, it'll drive you crazy."

He glances over at me, our bodies pressed up against each other's.

I squeeze his hand the way he did mine when he was comforting me moments ago. "You're going to worry about him because he's your son, but you can't let that worry eat you up. Just focus on your time with Nolan. Focus on making him happy every second you're with him, because that little face back there should always be smiling."

The truck had stopped in front of the house sometime during my speech, but I have no idea when. I am purely focused on easing his troubled mind. Seeing him like this is heartbreaking.

Ben stares at me with fascination. "You've given my son more in one week than his mother has in three years. You have no idea what that means to him. What that means to me." His neck rolls with a deep swallow as he glances down at our hands that are interlocked in my lap. "How did I not see this amazing girl nine years ago?" His thumb grazes the skin of my hand, rubbing it softly.

I don't know how to answer him, so I watch him study our hands instead, admiring his features while he admires our connection—his long, dark lashes and prominent cheek bones. He seems drawn to the very sight of our hands together, but that look of interest doesn't linger.

Exhaling loudly, almost frustratingly, he slides his hand out of mine and bypasses my gaze to look at the dashboard. "It's late. I should probably get Nolan to bed."

Friends don't hold hands. Friends don't sit this close. And Ben knows these things. I don't care what the rules of friendship are because I'm not sure I want Ben as a friend. Not when he makes me feel like this. But that must be how he's seeing me because he's breaking our contact. I slide back over to my side and open my door, jumping out of the truck. I open the back door and lean my head inside, pressing a kiss to Nolan's temple.

"Goodnight, Sir Nolan," I whisper, seeing him stir a bit. I look up front at Ben whose bright gray eyes are studying me. "Goodnight, Ben."

"Goodnight," he says with a smile that seems guarded, unlike his usual halt-me-in-my-place smile that makes me forget how to breathe.

I go to close the door but stop myself, turning back to Ben. "I'm really sorry I broke your stereo."

"What?"

I wince at the memory. "Remember the summer before I moved away? I went to your room to borrow your stereo and I knocked it off your desk, breaking it. I'm really sorry about that."

He shakes his head, his brow furrowing. "What made you think about that?"

I shrug. "I don't know. But, God, I remember how angry you were. You hated me that day."

His gaze drops briefly before returning to mine. "Mia, do me a favor. Don't apologize for stuff that happened between us before. You could've broken everything in my room and it wouldn't have justified the way I treated you back then. You don't owe me an apology. Ever. Okay?"

I smile meekly and nod. "Okay. Goodnight."

"Goodnight."

I walk inside and go straight to my bedroom, collapsing down on my bed.

Tonight was amazing. It was the best non-date I've ever been on. I loved talking and hanging out with Ben, which seems crazy considering how much I used to hate the mere presence of him. The boy I once wished never existed was now the man I wanted to spend every second with. I'm not holding on to that hate I once had for him anymore. I can't. Not when the man he is now makes me feel things I've only read about in books. I'm done trying to forget that I gave him a part of me that no one else will ever touch. I want him to have it. I want him to have every piece of me. Benjamin Kelly is becoming everything I've ever wanted, and I am finally willing to admit that to myself.

At the very moment my eyes shut, Tessa swings my door open and walks over to my bed, lying down next to me. I wait for the interrogation to start, but it doesn't come, which is shocking. Rolling over, I notice her worried expression.

"I'm late," she states, keeping her eyes on the ceiling.

"For…" And then it hits me. Girls only use that wording for one thing when it's paired with the look she's carrying right now. "Oh, my God. What are you going to do?"

She finally looks at me but doesn't respond. But she doesn't have to. Her face is giving away everything she needs to say.

She has no fucking clue.

chapter eleven

Ben

I WANTED TO TELL HER SHE LOOKED BEAUTIFUL THAT NIGHT.
I wanted to wrap my arm around her shoulder and hold her against my chest when she slid next to me in my truck.

I wanted to kiss those soft full lips before she walked into the house.

But I didn't.

I couldn't do any of those things. Not when I was very clear about that night not being a date.

I'm trying to earn Mia's trust, and drilling her into my bench seat isn't the way to go about it. If I act on my impulses, it will fuck up the progress I've somehow managed to make. She's talking to me now instead of brushing me off. She's spending time with me instead of running away. Or jumping off cliffs. I can't lose what I have going with Mia. And my dick can hate me all it wants, but I am adamant about keeping things friendly with her for now.

Four days. That's how long I make it without seeing her before I find myself driving to my parents' house after work. And believe me when I say that those four days were the longest of my life. Thank Christ I have a job, otherwise I'm certain I would've gone completely mental without a distraction. Luke enjoyed my misery immensely, making sure to point out every time I brought Mia's name up in a conversation that had everything to do with work and nothing to do with her. And it was misery. Keeping my thoughts off her tight pussy and focusing on the friendship I was building with her. And if my own mind wasn't hard enough to filter on its own, she started throwing text messages at me that were becoming more and more sexual. Apparently, Mia and I were now the type of friends that joked around about sex. She was so fucking comfortable with me now that nothing was off limits to her.

And she didn't care to ask me if I was okay with that before she shifted us into that category.

Mia: Do you think it's possible to get carpal tunnel from masturbating too much?

This was the first one she threw at me. My brain was immediately flooded with images of her touching herself, and it took every ounce of strength in me not to get off before I replied. I should've answered it with something like this:

Me: Mia, I don't think that's an appropriate friend conversation to have. And we're friends, so let's not go there.

But no, I'm a complete shit with zero willpower. So instead, I answered with this:

Me: If it's possible, I'd already have it.

Yup. Now she knew I was jerking off like a mad man. Which was the God's honest truth. I was hoping that this was a mistake on her part, and she'd realize her error and never tempt me with another text like this again. My dick was throbbing enough without the help from the images she was putting into my head. But apparently, she was just getting started.

Mia: What do you think is my best feature? Tessa says my legs, but I'm thinking my boobs. Thoughts?

Thoughts? Really? I was convinced that she was trying to kill me. She was an angel and a devil wrapped into one package that I couldn't refuse. One that I desperately wanted to bend over my bed and fuck into tomorrow. I couldn't ignore her. We were friends, and if this was the type of friends she wanted to be, then I could be that. I'd be hard constantly, but let's face it, being around her was already making that an issue. So I decided to just go with it and answer honestly.

Me: Tits, mouth, ass, legs. In that order.

I thought I was golden. I thought I was going to be able to handle these sexual texts and not have my dick in my hand twenty-four hours a day. And I would've been, if she didn't up the stakes.

Mia: Do guys prefer a girl that swallows to a girl that spits? I mean, isn't the general act of sucking off a guy enough to make them happy? Does it really matter what I do with your cum?

Motherfucker. This text was reread numerous times, mainly when I was jerking myself off. Especially that last sentence. The implication of it being *my* cum in her mouth was too much for me. I was weak. Weak and hornier than I've ever been in my entire life. Weak enough to give her a response.

Me: It's really fucking hot when a girl swallows. But yes, the act itself is enough to make most guys not care one way or the other.

Not a big deal. I was perfectly capable of handling anything she threw at me. Or so I thought.

Mia: I was so unbelievably horny today. Guys are lucky. They can just tuck their erections away and go on about their day like they aren't sporting wood. Girls can't do that. I had to change my panties twice before lunch.

That does it. I wave my white flag in surrender. I don't give her a response to that, not by text message anyway. No, my response is in the form of me pulling up to my parents' house like a complete dick.

I need to see her, especially after that last text. I should be seeing her to tell her in person that she can't keep sending me messages like that. But the second her body comes into view, lounging on a chair next to the pool, every thought is wiped from my brain. I suddenly can't remember why I am here, but that doesn't stop me from walking around the pool and directly toward her like a man possessed.

Her eyes are closed so she doesn't see me coming. And then she opens her mouth and begins singing along to the song that is playing through her ear buds. I recognize "Crash My Party" by Luke Bryan instantly.

It's an all right song, but hearing Mia sing it makes me really like it.

I stand in front of her, even more enthralled by the sight of her than I usually am as she stays completely oblivious to my presence. My girl can sing. Her voice is as beautiful as she is, and she's belting the tune out and tapping her feet on her beach towel as I enjoy the show.

She hums the final notes of the song before her eyes finally open, meeting the smile that's been plastered on my face since she got in my sight.

"Ben! Jesus Christ!" she yells, sitting up and placing her hand on her heaving chest. Her other hand pulls out her ear buds and discards them in her lap. "How long have you been standing there?"

"Long enough," I reply, thinking back to the night at the bar when I used the same words on her.

Her cheeks react the same way they did that night, the slight flush that causes her gaze to wander from mine temporarily until she regains her composure. But she doesn't have to hide her reaction to me. I like when I knock her off balance. And right now, I can't stop looking at her.

She's all dark hair, slightly tanned skin, and big brown eyes that regard me with curiosity after she collects herself.

"I, uh, didn't know you were stopping by today. Are you here to see Tessa because she ran out for a bit."

For the first time since Mia's arrival in Ruxton, I wish we weren't alone. I wish my sister was sitting out here by the pool. I can't be weak right now, and being alone with Mia in the insanely small bikini she is wearing is making me weak.

No, fuck that. I can do this. I focus on her eyes. Only her eyes.

"I think it's a safe assumption to make that if I ever stop over here while you're in town, I'm not here to see my sister."

Her lips part slightly as she absorbs my words. *Does she really not know that I'm here to see her?*

I glance down at the neglected book in her lap. "What are you reading?"

Her eyes follow mine and her fingers graze the cover. "Oh, um The Giving Tree. I haven't read it since I was little, but I can't really get into it." She peeks up at me slowly, taking her time to reach my face. "You didn't respond to my text."

My breath hitches in my throat uncomfortably. I reach up and rub my neck, suddenly feeling like a shitty friend. But fuck! What the hell kind of response was she expecting out of me? The memory of that text and of her wet pussy has me contemplating nailing her to the lounge chair she's reclining on. Leave it to Mia to cut the shit and just straight up call me out on my neglectfulness. Because if we are friends, why wouldn't I have responded to her? It won't surprise me if her next move is to read the damn message to me out loud and prompt a reply from me that way. And I can't have that happen. There's no way in hell I'd be able to restrain myself if she actually voiced that message. But I gotta give that daunting stare of hers something. She'll never let this go. I know her too well to try and change the subject. So a lie will have to do.

I stuff my hands into my pockets and try to seem unfazed by this. But I'm definitely fucking fazed. "I was really busy this afternoon. Luke and I got called to this domestic violence dispute and it was really intense. I'm sorry. I actually forgot about your text until just now."

I didn't. I could never forget about that text.

"Oh, okay." She begins chewing on the inside of her cheek, her eyes flicking away from mine to the pool. She seems hesitant all of a sudden. The confident girl that was just singing her heart out and ballsy enough to bring this topic up is nowhere in sight. Until I see it, something spreading over her, causing her back to straighten and her eyes to narrow in on mine with a thundering intensity that I've never seen before. "You're going to respond to it, right?"

Fuck. Me.

"I will," I promise without a single thought.

Christ, this woman has the ability to unhinge me like no other. I need to get the subject off that text. I'm going to get hard if I don't. And damn, if her persistence isn't the hottest thing I've ever seen.

She wants me to respond. She needs it. And I hate making her feel like I ignored her.

But I need to focus on something else, so I do.

"Do you know if Tessa's busy this weekend? I need to work on Saturday night and I'm going to have Nolan. I was hoping she'd babysit him for me."

"I don't know. She's got a lot going on right now," she states tensely, avoiding my eyes.

A lot going on? Tessa? Her summer plans consisted of tanning and chasing after Luke. But Mia seems uneasy all of a sudden, so I decide not to pry.

Her eyes return to mine and she smiles. "I can watch him for you if you want."

"Yeah?" I ask, completely stunned by her offer. I shouldn't be surprised at anything involving Mia, though. The girl seems to astonish me with each passing day. "You don't have to do that. I can ask the old lady that lives a few houses down from me. She's watched him before when no one else could."

She smiles wider and cocks her head playfully. "Do you think Nolan would rather spend the evening with a princess that knows her way around a wooden sword, or an old, smelly lady that probably has an absurd amount of cats?"

"An absurd amount of cats?" I arch my brow at her, finding her thought process completely amusing.

She gives me a raised eyebrow in return. "Oh, I'm sure she has them. All old women become crazy cat ladies. My grandmother did. She had eleven roaming through her house." She scrunches up her nose at the memory. "It smelled really bad in her house. You don't want Nolan to make this face, do you, Ben?"

She points to herself, trying to keep the unpleasant look going but cracking into a smile after a few seconds.

I chuckle. "No, I guess not. I'm sure he'd have more fun with you anyway." She nods in agreement, smiling as if she really is looking forward to giving up her Saturday night to babysit. Could this woman get any more perfect? "I'll owe you big time for this, so start thinking of ways I can repay you."

She pulls her bottom lip into her mouth and grabs the sunscreen off the chair next to her. "Oh, I already have a few ideas." She's staring right at me, and the heated look in her eyes is hitting me where I don't need it to. "I think I'm burning. Would you mind?"

Fuuccckkk.

No. I don't mind. Not in the slightest. I'm only a man. I'm not a god. I can't say no to Mia when she's staring up at me like she wants me to do more than just rub sunscreen on her. Because that's exactly how she's staring at me. Ask my cock.

I grab the lotion and clear my throat as she spins around in her chair, offering me her back.

This is a test. A test to see if I can handle touching Mia as a friend. Because friends apply sunscreen to each other, and can do it without it being sexual.

I begin applying the lotion onto the warm skin of her shoulders, feeling the goose bumps pop up against my touch. She drops her head and moans softly, causing my cock to twitch like a fucking traitor. But I ignore it, moving down to her back. She moans again, a bit louder this time as I lift the string of her bikini, making sure to cover the area before I put it back in place. I'm only being thorough. I'd hate for Mia to burn and be in any amount of pain.

Just being thorough.

"That feels so good. I forgot what your hands felt like on my body."

Good God. I don't want to react to that. This is like her text messages, only worse. I can't hide behind the screen of my phone and jerk off with my free hand. And my cock is having difficulty *not* reacting.

I pretend like I don't hear her and run my hands down her lower back, smearing the lotion on. She does that damn whimpering sound, and all the blood in my veins rushes straight to my dick.

That's it. I have to get out of here.

I pick the bottle of sunscreen off the ground and drop it over her shoulder and into her lap.

"I gotta go. I'll drop Nolan off around three on Saturday."

I walk away from her with my hard on, thinking back to her last text message about being able to tuck it away, making it less obvious. I do just that with an agitated shake of my head.

"Oh, okay. See ya!" she yells out, but I don't turn to look at her. I can't.

Christ, the fucking sounds are filling my ears again, and I need a release.

I get in my truck, liking the distance my parking spot gives me from her, and pull out my painful hard on. I stroke it fast, keeping my grip tight to not prolong my climax. I need to do this and get the hell out of here before I fuck everything up.

"Aw, fuck."

I think of her mouth wrapped around me, those full lips teasing the head and pressing softly to my shaft. She'd take me in all the way, I know she would. Her mouth can handle everything I give her and I won't hold anything back. I'd grip her hair and thrust my hips into her eager mouth, and she'd suck me until her cheeks hollowed and her eyes watered.

"Oh, God. Yeah."

She'd swallow because she'd know that I'd love it. She'd love it, too, because she's my dirty girl. My filthy little angel that tells me her panties are soaked. And then she'd ride me, hard and fast, her perfect tits bouncing in my face. I'd suck on them until she screamed like she did the other night. I'd tell her that I'd be coming all over them soon, because I would. She'd get off on my words, my mouth, and my cock, and then she'd come perfectly around me. Her skin would blush across her chest, blooming up toward her neck as she threw her head back. The sight of her orgasm would push me over the edge. I'd come inside her, this time without a condom, because I need to fucking feel her.

I'd bury my face in her tits, my cock in her pussy, and I'd fucking give her everything.

"Fuck." My thighs tense, and I can feel my release surging through me. I open my eyes and grab a few napkins out of my console, holding them against the tip while I come by myself for the countless time this week. I wipe myself clean and then crumple up the napkins, shoving them into my cup holder.

I feel better, but not by much. I can still see her tight little body in the distance, and I want the real thing, not just the fantasy. But that isn't going to happen. It can't happen. Not yet.

I start up my truck and pull out my phone, scrolling to her last text.

Mia: I was so unbelievably horny today. Guys are lucky. They can just tuck their erections away and go on about their day like they aren't sporting wood. Girls can't do that. I had to change my panties twice before lunch.

After I reread it six times, I finally give her the response she wants.

Me: Even a tucked erection is still obvious. Trust me. And you aren't the only one that's been unbelievably horny lately.

I press send and get the fuck out of there before I do something I'll regret. I'm only a man, Goddamn it. She wanted me to respond to her, so I did. I can handle dirty text messages with the girl that I'm falling in love…

Fuck me. That's what's happening. I'm falling in love with Mia Corelli.

chapter twelve

Mia

"Okay, be honest. Tell me if I've completely outdone myself here."

I place my hands on my hips and survey the massive amount of babysitting supplies I picked up at the store.

"I've got chips, cookies, popcorn, ice cream, mini cupcakes that I had to get because they have little shields on them." I stand on my toes to see the rest of my purchases better. "Organic chocolate milk, organic strawberry milk, carrot sticks, grapes, and pita chips."

"He's going to freak out when he sees what you did back there. And did you just say carrot sticks?" Tessa calls out, strolling toward me from the direction of the bedrooms. "Seriously? He's three. He's more likely to use those as mini swords." Her eyes widen at the sight of my purchases. "And he's one kid. Jesus Christ, Mia. Have you ever babysat before? This is enough to feed a small army."

I nudge her with my elbow. "Yes, I've babysat before. But I didn't know what Nolan liked, so I kind of got one of everything. Ooohhh, check it out." I reach over the bags of chips and grab the two Red Box rentals, holding them out for Tessa to grab. "I got Frozen and something called Mike the Knight. I figured that one was right up his alley. The little cartoon knight reminded me of Nolan, minus the dimples."

"Wow." Tessa shakes her head and hands me back the movies. "You're making a serious play, aren't you?" She sits on the edge of the couch, smiling widely at me. My puzzled expression gets across exactly what I'm feeling, prompting her to elaborate. "You love him," she states with a satisfactory smile.

"Sure, yeah, I love Nolan. How could you not love him?"

Tessa had already started to shake her head as soon as I said Nolan's name. "No, that's not who I'm referring to." She pauses, giving me the chance to connect the pieces on my own. It doesn't take me long.

I wave her off with my hand. "I do not love Ben if that's who you're foolishly referring to."

No. I'd know if I loved Ben. I want to bang his back out, but that's not love.

"It is, and you do. Or you're at least open to loving him now. You're not just trying to impress my nephew with all of this." She motions toward my snack pile. "And you're desperately trying to pull him out of the friend zone he so stupidly put you two in. How many slutty text messages have you sent him?" she teases.

Tessa and I never keep secrets from each other. Hell, she was the one who suggested the scandalous text message idea after I told her that I wanted Ben to see me as more than a friend. She predicted he'd drop everything and come at me hard after the first one I sent. But no, I'm either really bad at getting someone hot with my words, or he's completely immune to them.

I cover my eyes with my hand and grunt my frustration. "Not enough, apparently. I threw my best stuff at him and he barely flinched." I drop my hand and look at her. "I'm running out of ways to spell this out for him."

She stands up and walks over toward the sliding glass door. "Get naked. That'll definitely spell it out." She waves and smiles at what I assume is Nolan. "Don't tell my brother about the pregnancy, okay?"

I walk up to her, putting her hand in mine. Nolan is in Ben's arms, swinging his sword in the air as they walk around the pool.

"It's your news to tell, not mine. And the first person that needs to know about it is Luke."

After the initial shock of the possible pregnancy sank in the other night, Tessa and I stayed up for hours talking about it. She was scared, but she was also really happy about having a baby with Luke. The only problem was the two of them weren't supposed to be serious. And throwing a baby into the mix would definitely change that.

She sighs heavily. "I'll tell him. I'm just waiting for the right time."

"Like tonight?" I ask, smiling at Nolan's face as it comes inching closer to the glass. Tessa shrugs her response. "You can do it. You know he cares about you. And if you need me, I'll be right here."

She leans her head on my shoulder as the boys come up to the door, sliding it open.

"Hey," Ben greets me with a smile as he steps inside the house, placing Nolan on his feet.

I am once again stunned into silence from the sight of him in his uniform, unable to give him anything besides a goofy grin at the moment. But my God, he makes that uniform look downright sinful. I'm tempted to go commit a major felony in hopes that he'll pat me down or better yet, strip search me.

Nolan runs right at me, wrapping his arms around my legs and snapping me out of my lustful thoughts.

"He's a little excited. The maniac wouldn't even take a nap today because he was too wound up to come over here."

I laugh and rub Nolan's head, seeing him lift his face to me. "I couldn't take a nap either." I bend down and put us face to face, dropping my smile and trying to stay serious. "I tried to take a nap, but there were all these dragons in my bedroom." His eyes immediately twinkle with interest, doubling in size. "They might still be back there. Can you go check it out for me?"

"Yeah!" he yells with pure excitement, his little legs quickly taking him down the hallway.

Tessa nudges Ben's shoulder, barely moving him an inch. He smirks at her and she smirks right back before looking over at me.

"I'll see you tomorrow sometime." She gives me a knowing look and motions with her head toward Ben without him noticing. *"Get naked,"* she mouths, earning herself a stern look from me before she walks out the door.

I will definitely not be getting naked unless Ben undresses me, and at the rate we're going, I don't see that happening any time soon.

"Here's all his stuff." Ben drops the duffle bag that is on his shoulder onto the couch, opening the zipper. "Pajamas, toothbrush, a few books that he likes me to read to him before he falls asleep, and this." He pulls out a stuffed dragon that looks well loved. It's worn and frayed at the edges. "He can't go to bed without this, but don't give it to him before bedtime because he'll take it everywhere and I'm afraid he'll spill something on it and I won't be able to wash it. If something happens to this thing, I'm completely screwed."

I laugh and watch him stuff it back into the bag. "What time is bedtime?"

"Between 8:00 p.m. and 8:30 p.m. He might pass out before then though, since he's running on no nap." Ben turns his head and glances over at the kitchen counter. "Wow. You are definitely prepared." He smiles at me with a teasing look. "Expecting more children?"

I shove his massive shoulder and move past him. "Oh ha-ha. This isn't all just for Nolan. I've been known to put away a massive amount of snacks when I'm entertaining."

"Take that! Leave Pwincess Mia alone!"

Ben and I both turn our heads. "What is he doing in there?" he asks. I shrug with a sly smile, and he narrows his eyes at me. "Well, now I'm curious."

I follow him down the hallway, knowing exactly what I am going to see when I look into my bedroom. I didn't just go grocery shopping today.

"Daddy. Look at all these dwagons!" Nolan is swinging his sword at the inflatable dragons that surround my bed. They range in size; some are as small as his stuffed animal and others are bigger than him. "I'm gonna kiwl dem all!"

I cover my mouth with my hand and chuckle next to Ben, feeling his eyes on me.

"Where did you get all these?"

"The party store in town. They have everything there." I watch Nolan bop one of the larger dragons in the head. He seems to be enjoying himself immensely. "Totally worth the twenty bucks."

"God, you're incredible."

Our eyes lock, and I see how much he means what he's just said. That is definitely one quality he has that I absolutely love.

Ben is honest, completely authentic when he speaks to me. I never doubt anything he's ever said and I know I never will. Of course, I'm sure he means I'm incredible in a friendly sort of way since he's not pinning me up against a wall.

We stare at each other while Nolan continues slaying the dragons in front of us.

His gray eyes are bright and filled with adoration. It is the look I want Ben to reserve just for me. The look he's given me several times before. At the dam, standing in his parents' living room after we discovered each other by the pool, and in his truck. It's the look that teeters us on the edge of the friend zone, because I've never been looked at by a friend this way before. I want Ben to say something else to me. I want to hear more of his honesty, and for a split second, it looks like he is going to give me what I want. But instead, he breaks our connection and glances down at his watch.

"I gotta go." He looks at me again with the same tender gaze. "I probably won't be back until close to 12:30 a.m., but if you need anything, just call me."

I place my hand on his arm and squeeze it gently. "We'll be fine. Go arrest some bad guys, Officer Kelly."

My voice doesn't waver at his title, but I can't deny the rush of adrenaline that spikes through me when I say it. I wink at him and move into the bedroom, scooping up a few smaller dragons.

Nolan looks at me and beams as I sit on the edge of the bed, watching him slay the biggest dragon in the room. I laugh at him and turn my head, hoping to see Ben standing there, but he is gone. And I know that I shouldn't feel disappointed because I will see him later on tonight, but I can't help it.

At least I have one Kelly boy to keep me company while I think about another one.

Nolan was like this tiny ball of energy that seemed to recharge the more he moved around. I'd never seen a kid go from one activity to another with such gusto. After he had slain dragons for a good hour, he had a snack and wanted to watch his Mike the Knight DVD. But he didn't sit still during that. He jumped around in front of the couch and swung his tiny sword in the air, mimicking the movements on the screen. We colored a few pictures, made a fort out of the extra bed sheets I found in the closet, and blew bubbles on the back patio. I saw his first yawn, the only indication he'd given me all night that he was slowing down, at 8:20 p.m. After changing him into his pajamas, I brushed his teeth and grabbed the books out of the duffle bag.

He settles under the covers in one of the spare bedrooms, holding his stuffed dragon in a death grip. "Wead that one fiwst," he says in a sleepy voice, pointing toward a book about trucks.

I prop against the headboard and hold the book out in my lap, reading in a soft voice. He closes his eyes when I am halfway through it, but I finish it anyway. After giving him a kiss on his forehead, I quietly exit the bedroom and plop down on the couch with my phone.

Me: Little knight is down for the count. Slaying thirty seven dragons takes a lot out of a three-year-old.

I turn off the Mike the Knight DVD that is still playing and change the channel to something I am interested in. My phone beeps as I lie back on the sofa, but it isn't a text from the person I am dying to talk to, and see for that matter. This is the first time I grunt at the sight of this particular name on my screen.

Tessa: I haven't told him yet and I don't know if I'm going to. What if he freaks out and ends it? What if he wants me to abort the baby? I'd never do that, but isn't it his decision as much as mine? We've had sex three times since I got over here and I don't even know if that's good for my current situation.

Me: First of all, why isn't he at work with Ben? Secondly, you freaking out is definitely not good for the baby, so calm down please. And third, do you really think Luke is the type of guy to ditch his pregnant girlfriend? I've only been around him a few times and I know he isn't like that.

Tessa: I'm not his girlfriend! I don't know what the hell I am, but he's never labeled me as that. Fuck buddy seems more appropriate.

Tessa: Ben is riding solo tonight. They don't always patrol together.

I chuckle and prop a pillow under my head.

Me: Just grow a pair and tell him. And I say that in my best Tessa style voice because you know that's exactly what you'd be saying to me. :)

Tessa: Speaking of growing a pair...

Me: Shut up.

Tessa: Just saying, bitch.

I know exactly what she is getting at.

Grow a pair. Please. I told Ben that I'm in danger of causing permanent damage to my hand from excessive masturbation, and I need to grow a pair?

I turn onto my side and tuck one hand underneath my head. My phone beeps again and this time, I can't contain the smile that spreads across my face.

Ben: I can't wait to hear all about it. See ya in a few hours.

I look at the time on my phone. Three hours and forty-three minutes to be exact.

Not that I'm counting.

"Mia? Mia, hey, wake up."

"Hmm?" My eyes slowly open and Ben's face comes into view. "Oh, hey. Sorry. I didn't mean to fall asleep." I roll over onto my back and stretch my arms over my head, seeing Ben's eyes drop to my body and widen before he quickly turns away from me. And I mean quickly, as in, he can't get me out of his sight fast enough. I furrow my brows. "What? What is it?"

He clears his throat as I sit up, still completely oblivious to whatever it is that's making him react to me this way. He stays facing the kitchen, rubbing the back of his neck with one hand. "You might want to put something on. Your...breasts are really noticeable in that top."

Breasts? Oh, how formal.

I glance down quickly, seeing my erect nipples poking through my sheer tank. But I'm not embarrassed at all. I'm irritated. Really irritated all of a sudden.

My boobs are making him uncomfortable? Well, that's just great.

I stand up with a clenched jaw and walk past him, grabbing the hoodie I had taken off earlier and slipping it over my head. "Christ, Ben. You act like you haven't seen them before, or sucked them for that matter." I snap my head in his direction and see the shock on his face. "They're just tits."

"They're *your* tits," he states, his expression toughening and his voice edgy.

The sight of my chest weeks ago would've provoked an entirely different reaction out of him. Now he's desensitized to it. Awesome.

I ignore the stare he is giving me and refuse to let go of my annoyance. This is maddening. "And my tits make you uncomfortable. But I guess they should, considering how *friendly* you and I have become." I grab Nolan's books and shove them into his duffle bag.

"What is that supposed to mean?" he asks, but I ignore him. I'm too focused on getting his shit together so he can leave.

"Here. He was great. Didn't give me a bit of trouble." I thrust the duffle bag into his chest, stalking past him and grabbing my phone. "My tits and I are going to bed before we freak you out even more."

I don't turn back around as I walk toward my bedroom. I don't want to see if my words affect him, especially since my body apparently doesn't anymore. What the fuck? My boobs, that he couldn't get enough of weeks ago, are now being held hostage in his stupid friend zone against their will. And they are not happy about it one bit.

Join the club.

I rip my hoodie off and throw it in the corner of my room with a grunt.

I'm annoyed, hurt, and really horny. Three emotions that are pissing me off at the moment. I grab my phone to respond to Tessa's last text message.

Me: Your brother infuriates me! I'm turned on, pissed off, and sick of this stupid friend zone. I can't be friends with someone that brings me to orgasm in my dreams every night. And I'm tired of getting off on the memory of Ben. Oh, and your get naked idea wouldn't have worked. My tits were just on display for him and he acted offended by them.

I press send and throw my phone down, reaching up and undoing the hair tie that is securing my hair in a loose bun. Just as my hair falls down my back, my bedroom door swings open and Ben stands in the doorway with that blazing look of his that leaves scorch marks on my skin. But right now, it doesn't have that effect on me. Right now, it makes me want to punch him right in the throat.

"I'm really not in the mood to talk right now."

He steps into the room and closes the door behind him. "Did you mean what you just sent me?"

I furrow my brow into a tight line. "What are you talking about? What do you mean *what I just sent you?*" I stand up off the bed and glare at him.

I'm still mad, pissed even, but now I'm confused as hell.

And then I see it, the cell phone he's gripping, and a panic surges through my system. My legs feel weak underneath me and my chest feels so tight it's as if I'm breathing through a straw.

I grab my phone and scroll to the text that I thought I sent to Tessa. But I didn't send it to Tessa.

I lift my eyes and watch as Ben reaches behind him and locks the door, never taking his bright eyes off me. I toss my phone back onto the bed and take a deep breath before responding.

"Yes. I meant it." My answer is firm and definite. This is not the time to half-ass anything. He's giving me an opportunity and I'm taking it.

He smiles that cocky grin that drives me insane. "Do you want me, baby?"

I nod.

"No, I need to hear you say it. I'll give you whatever you want, Mia. But I won't risk misinterpreting what I've just read. Tell me exactly what you want." He stops right in front of me, keeping his body inches from mine. He's so close to me right now it's almost unbearable.

I know exactly what I want. Him. And I'm not above being forward with him right now. I understand his hesitation. He doesn't want to take this somewhere and not be positive that I want to go with him. But he doesn't know I'd follow him anywhere. Anywhere.

I blink heavily before eliminating all space between us, pressing my body against his. He doesn't tense at all, but he doesn't wrap his arms around me either. "I don't want to be just friends. I don't think I ever did." I press my hand to his chest, flattening against his heartbeat and feeling his reaction to me. "I want you, Ben. All of you. Your hands, your mouth, your…" I look down, pausing for the courage I need.

"Say it," he growls. God, I love the authority in his voice.

I don't hesitate at his command. Looking into his eyes, I say exactly what I want with the certainty he needs. "Cock. I've thought of you touching me constantly since we were together that first night. It's all I've thought about."

His hands come up and he cups my face. "I won't be able to hold back."

"I don't want you to."

"It's going to be really fucking intense. I don't think I can be gentle with you right now. It's been too damn long since I've had my hands on you and I'm about to start ripping shit apart."

A small laugh rumbles in my throat. He is just as frustrated as I am.

Thank you, Jesus.

I tease the buttons of his uniform, feeling his muscles clench underneath my fingers. "I don't want gentle right now. I want you to take me."

He nods firmly, understanding exactly what I need. He keeps one hand on my face but brings the other around my neck, gripping it with that possessive hunger of his that riles me up like nothing else. "I was trying to be good, baby. I wanted you to see that I'm not that same guy you once knew. I'll never be that guy. I'll never hurt you, Mia, and I'll fucking kill anyone that does. But this is it. Once I have you again, I'm not letting you go. So you better be damn sure this is what you want, because there's no going back after this."

I snake my hands around his neck, brushing over his hammering pulse. "Good." I tilt my head up and press my lips softly against his. "Fuck me, Ben. Show me that I'm yours." My words blow against his mouth, and they're the only coaxing he needs.

My heart is his and right now, I want him to claim my body.

chapter thirteen

Ben

"Fuck me, Ben. Show me that I'm yours."

When those words escape her perfect mouth, I feel my entire body surge with power. My adrenaline spikes and the commanding need I have for Mia, that I'd dulled out with friendship, comes screaming back to life inside me. There was never any doubt in my mind who she belonged to. And after tonight, there will never be any doubt in hers either.

"If I'm too rough with you, you need to tell me," I say against her lips, backing her body up to the bed.

I'm so geared up right now, so tightly wound that I know the only way I'll be able to hold back is if she can't handle it. I'm feeling speedy, like a racehorse that's been let out of the gate, and I need her to be honest with me. I've never felt out of control before, but Mia has the ability to make me lose my shit completely.

"Baby, promise me you'll tell me if I hurt you." I push her down onto the bed, grabbing her legs and spreading them wide as I settle in between them.

She stares up at me with nothing but trust in her eyes. I'm certain with the look she's giving me, I can do anything to her right now and she won't waver.

She pulls her top over her head before saying, "I will, but I won't have to. I want this just as bad as you do. Please don't hold back, Ben. I'm not fragile."

No, she isn't. I have to remind myself that this isn't the same Mia that used to be afraid of cliff diving at Rocky Point.

I've met my match in this woman, both in and out of the bedroom.

She begins working at her shorts when I stop her, batting her hands away. "Those are mine to take off." I pull them down with her panties, tossing them somewhere behind me. She's naked, completely bare to me, and I almost forget how to fucking breathe. I take a moment to stare at her, appreciating every dip and curve of her body. Her hands drum the sheet at her sides as she allows me to have my moment. I raise my gaze to her face and she wets her lips. "You're the sexiest woman I've ever seen. And you have no idea, do you? You have no clue how stunning you are." I make quick work of my shirt, unbuttoning it halfway and pulling it over my head to get on with it.

Mia laughs softly below me, stretching her body out on the bed. "I thought you said you weren't going to be gentle with me? I don't want sweet, romantic, Benjamin Kelly right now."

I cock my head at her and she smiles. "You'll take what I give you." I pull my belt off and drop my pants and boxers, stepping out of both. "I can fuck you and tell you how crazy I am about you. I'm very capable of making you scream and worshipping you at the same time." I am about to spread my body on top of hers when she sits up unexpectedly and grabs my cock. Her eyes are blazing, filled with a stark need. I groan deep in my throat and stop her hand from moving. "Fuck, baby. I know you want to play right now, but I'm too damn wound up for that. I'm not coming in your hand, and if you touch me anymore, that's exactly what's going to happen."

She arches her brow at me. So playful, yet seductive at the same time. "I was hoping you'd come in my mouth."

Ah hell. My dirty little angel never ceases to amaze me.

I stroke along her bottom lip with my thumb. "Baby, soon, very soon I will fuck this pretty little mouth. But right now, I need to be inside you. I need to feel you around me."

And then my world collapses in on itself.

Fucking motherfucker. I squeeze my eyes tight and step back out of her needy grasp.

"What is it?"

What the fuck? I run my hands down my face and curse under my breath. "I was not at all anticipating this happening between us for a while. I honestly thought it would take a lot longer for you to see that I'm not a complete dickhead anymore, and let me anywhere near your body." I drop my hands and meet her puzzled face. She has no idea what I am getting at. "I don't have any condoms with me. And I'm not searching the house for them because that's just fucking weird. Please tell me you have some."

Her face falls in disappointment. "No, I don't. You don't have any in your truck?"

Her optimism is adorable.

I shake my head and rake my hand through my hair roughly. "No. Nolan likes to snoop around in there and I'm always afraid he's going to find one and think it's a damn balloon or something."

She giggles and pulls her knees up to her chest.

I'm about to tell her that we don't have to have sex tonight, that I'd be completely content with just holding her, because I would, when suddenly she drops the playful demeanor and looks at me with a fierce passion.

"You know I've only been with you," she says, her voice dropping to a soft purring sound. "And I'm on birth control, so there wouldn't be any risk of me getting pregnant. So as long as you're clean, I don't see why this is a problem."

I just died. This has to be what heaven is like. Dirty little angels floating around, tempting you with barrier free sex. Is there any man on the planet that could actually say no to this?

I inhale deeply, trying to calm my painful erection that is all for driving into her wet heat without being wrapped up. "I'm clean." *And I apparently don't need that* much convincing. "I've never done it without a condom. Nolan resulted from one that had a tear in it." I step closer to her and she scoots back on the bed, reaching out for me with an eager hand.

"So I'll be your first this way? I love that."

I move toward the bed, getting up on my knees as she relaxes back onto a pillow. "Are you sure though? Baby, I could just eat your pussy for a good hour, maybe several and be fucking perfect with that. There's no need to rush this."

"But there is." She grabs my hand, and I take her other one so that both our hands are linked together. I'm kneeling between her legs, staring down into those chocolate brown eyes that hold me by the balls and could make me do practically anything right now. "We don't have forever, Ben. I'm only here for the summer. I have two months left to be with you and I don't want to waste another second not being with you the way I want to be. I love that you gave me time to get to know who you are now and I wouldn't take that back. But I don't need any more time. I just need you." She spreads her legs, dropping them on either side of mine. "You're the only man that's ever had me. Take what's yours."

This is heaven. It has to be. And we'll talk about this whole forever thing later. There is no way in hell I'm ending this with her at the end of the summer. I don't care how much distance there'll be between us.

"I don't know what the hell I did to ever deserve you, but you'll never take another breath without knowing how special you are to me." I bend down and bring my mouth to hers, needing to feel her breath in me. Needing to swallow her sounds.

She opens up and my tongue slides across hers, stroking deep into her mouth as she grips my neck with one hand and my shoulder with the other. I break the contact because I need more of her. I've gone almost four weeks without her taste and I want it running through me. I need it coursing through my system.

I scoot my body down on the bed and settle between her legs. She opens up with a soft sigh.

"You want it, don't you? You want my tongue to make you beg before my cock does."

Her hand grabs my head and she pushes me down as her response. I grin against her clit before flicking it with my tongue. She arches her hips up to meet every stroke.

Fuck, the way she tastes. Some pussies just taste better than others, and Mia's pussy is sinful. Addicting.

She pulses against my tongue as I run up her length, lingering on her clit before pulling it into my mouth.

"Oh God, Ben."

I suck hard, then harder, needing her orgasm more than I need to breathe. Getting her off gets me off, and Mia is so responsive that it's hard not to come along with her when she does it so perfectly. My eyes run up her body, over her tits that will be getting my attention very soon, and our eyes lock. I knew she'd be watching me. Her hand tightens in my hair as I move in quick circles. She whispers my name, moaning and barely making any sense as her orgasm builds rapidly. She begs me over and over not to stop. That she's right there. That she's so close. She pins me between her legs, unraveling against me as I grip her thighs and consume all of her. And then she finally relaxes her body, her legs dropping to the sides in complete exhaustion as my angel comes back to earth.

"So, so good. I love your mouth. I mean, really. I love your cock too, but your mouth?" She sighs heavily as I crawl up her body, kissing every inch of her. "It really should come with some sort of warning label."

"Mmm, and what would it say? Multiple orgasms await you if you put this between your legs?" I suck her left nipple into my mouth, pulling another low groan out of her. Releasing it with a smirk, I drop my head between her tits and inhale her scent. That berries and cream scent that completely wrecks me. "I love how you smell. Especially right here." I inhale again and growl against her, feeling her squirm beneath me. I glance up at her with a warning. "Don't you dare try to hurry me along. Next to that gorgeous view between your legs, this is where I'd want to die. Right here." I plant a kiss to her cleavage before moving up her body.

"I need you to fuck me now." She sounds urgent, needy even. As if she didn't just come all over my tongue. "Do you think you could do that?"

I slide straight into her pussy as my answer. "Holy fuck, Mia." She's soaked, her need for me is just as strong as my need for her. I groan as she arches her back and presses her tits against my chest. Nothing has ever felt like this, and I know without a doubt that there is no other woman I want to experience this with besides Mia. And I also know I'm done using condoms with her. I won't take her any other way. This is fucking perfection. I'm all the way in her, but I can't move. Not yet. I am too fucking close to losing it and I want this to last.

She wiggles beneath me, urging me on with her hands gripping my ass.

"Give me a second, baby. You have no idea how good you feel right now and I don't want to come in you just yet." I drop my forehead to hers and steady my breathing.

Her tongue darts out and she licks her bottom lip. "Why not? Can't you get hard again right away? I was hoping this wasn't a one and done deal."

I laugh, brushing against her lips with mine. "Are you challenging me? Do you want to see how hard I can fuck you and how hard I can get again just by looking at you? Just say the words and that's what you'll get."

She doesn't say any words. Instead, she clenches down on me and squeezes me tighter than a vise grip.

I rear up, grabbing her legs and pinning them against the mattress as I drive my hips into her. "Is this what you want? Fuck, baby. Is this how you want me to take you?"

I can barely get my words out before I feel my orgasm building at an impressive rate. I'm fucking her like I haven't had her in years, because that's how I feel.

I'm a man deprived, and I won't stop until she can't imagine not having me between her legs.

The room becomes filled with our moans and the loud slapping sound of our bodies crashing together.

"Yes! Oh God, Ben. Please." She closes her eyes and arches off the bed, thrusting her chest into the air.

"Mia, I'm coming in you, baby. I'm coming in this sweet pussy."

I give her everything and she takes it, coming on my cock as soon as I tell her I'm filling her. Her skin flushes pink, then red, bursting across her chest and up to her neck. She reaches for me and claws down my chest, giving me the pain that she knows I need.

She's perfect when she comes, a beautiful angel underneath me.

I pull out and she sits up on her elbows, staring between my legs at the erection that is fully hard just for her.

"You came, didn't you?" she asks, her eyes full of shock. She doubts my desire for her, which she'll never do again.

I dip my finger into her and draw it to her mouth, coaxing her to taste what I gave her.

She hits me with that seductive stare she mastered the night in the bar, and sucks on my finger, releasing it with a pop.

My cock lengthens even more at the sight of her. My girl likes it.

"Mmm. I guess that answers that question. Wanna go again?"

I grab her, switching places so that I am now lying on the bed and she is kneeling next to me. "Ride me, baby. I want you to drive this time. Show me how much you want this cock that's rock hard just for you."

She straddles me without hesitation, gripping me in her hand and guiding me into her slick pussy. "Oh God." Her head falls back until I get fully inside her. Then she hits me with those big brown eyes again. "I forgot how deep you are this way. It feels like you're hitting my ribs." She moves slowly, rocking her hips in a gentle rhythm. As if I'm the fragile one.

I practically fucked her through the floor and now she's looking at me as if I'm breakable. I'm not, and she needs to know that.

I grab her neck firmly and pull her down, crashing her mouth against mine. "Do I look delicate to you? Or do I look like a man that's been starving for this pussy." I scrap my teeth along her bottom lip and she whimpers. "Fucking ride me, Mia."

Her eyes widen and she nods once, purposely. And then she reaches behind her and digs her nails into my thighs, rearing up and fucking me with wild abandon.

"Yeah, just like that. So good. So fucking tight, baby." I grunt my praise to her as my eyes wander between her mouth and her tits. I lean in and suck on them, making her scream out and ride me harder. She alternates between rocking her hips, first fast then faster, while crashing down on me. White spots blur my vision as she takes me to the edge.

"I need it, Ben. Oh God, I'm so close." She scratches down my arms and I groan loudly, loving the pain that mingles with the pleasure.

Christ, this woman knows exactly what I need and when to give it to me.

"Are you gonna come on my cock, baby?" I grab her hips and begin directing the tempo, needing that last bit of control.

I can never give it up completely, and even though Mia owns me, I need to dominate how we come together.

"Yes," she answers with a soft plea.

"Come now, angel. I'm right there with you."

I grip her tightly and begin thrusting into her with everything I have. Giving her every part of me.

Feel it. This is how I love you.

We come together, loud and wild, and she collapses on top of me. I wrap my arms around her waist and hold her close, feeling her heart hammering against my chest. Her skin is damp, glistening with sweat. We stay like this for several minutes, our breathing mirroring each other's and coming down to a steadier pace.

Being inside Mia, her body completely connected to mine, is all I'll ever need.

"Here, let me get something to clean you up with."

I slide her next to me and slip on my boxers before I disappear down the hallway. I peak in on Nolan, who is still passed out, before grabbing a hand towel from the bathroom and climbing back into bed.

"We didn't wake him, did we?" she asks as I wipe between her legs.

The sight of my cum leaking out of her makes me want to beat on my chest like a damn caveman. *Mine.* I catch a yawn that she tries to muffle as she climbs under the covers.

I toss the towel into the hamper after wiping myself off. "No, he's out cold." She curls up against my chest as I lie back on my pillow. I stroke her arm, feeling the goose bumps form against my touch like they always do. She hums softly against my skin. "Nolan's a pretty deep sleeper. He fell asleep last year at the Fourth of July fireworks display over Canyon Creek. And that shit was loud. Maybe almost as loud as you."

My girl is a screamer. I love that. I want everyone in the entire state to know what I'm doing to her. My chest expands in pride at the thought.

"I think he gets that from me, though. I can pretty much sleep through anything." Her silence has me straining my neck down to catch her closed eyes. "Mia?"

"Hmm?"

I smile. "Did I render you speechless?"

"Hmm." Her arm that's wrapped around my waist tightens as the rest of her body stays completely limp.

She's falling asleep, but she can't let go of me. It's as if she's afraid I'll slip away from her the moment she passes out. Or that I won't be there when she wakes up. She's holding on to me with everything she has, which is how I've always felt around her. Even when I was only holding on to the memory of us together.

I press my lips to her forehead, pulling the covers up over us both. "Sleep, angel. You have me. I'm never letting you go."

And with those words to her, she finally relaxes.

chapter fourteen

Mia

I don't want to open my eyes.
I don't want to wake up and have this not be real.
I want to stay asleep for days, months, years even. Because this dream is different. This isn't just my typical nightly fantasy that stars Benjamin Kelly bringing me to orgasm over and over. Not that those aren't amazing. But this dream is better. Because he stayed. He is holding me like he did the first night we were together. It feels so right. So real. And I'm terrified of opening my eyes and discovering that I'm alone. That we're still only friends. I can feel his skin against my cheek. I can smell his scent, the strong masculine pheromones that are purely Ben. Is my mind completely fucking with me right now? I shouldn't be able to feel or smell anything. Right? My curiosity is piqued and I have to risk the disappointment I am sure to feel when I open my eyes.

I peek one, then both open, and I almost cry at the sight of him. I don't know if I've ever been this happy before. Forget sleeping forever. I never want to pry my eyes away from the man that is asleep right next to me.

He's in my bed.

It wasn't a dream.

His breath blows across my forehead, his legs tangling with mine under the covers. It's real. I reach up and brush my finger down his nose, seeing his lip twitch slightly. I run my finger over the tattoo that covers his shoulder, tracing over the outline of the design. It's beautiful. The way the colors blend together, the way it stretches down his arm and over his muscles. It's a scene of objects and quotes, but certain ones stand out. "Nolan" is etched on his skin in the handwriting of a child. It's the sweetest thing, and I trace over it several times with the tip of my finger. Ben stirs underneath me as my finger runs up and over the police shield that is on his upper arm. The words "Honor The Fallen" in bold ink stands out on his tanned skin. I run over the words several times as my mind drifts.

How many fallen men did Ben know? He doesn't have the safest job, and the thought of him being in danger is enough to make me want to hold on to him forever and not let him out of my sight. If something happened to him... no. I can't go there.

He stirs beneath me again, and the feel of his finger brushing down my nose brings my attention up to his face.

"Hey." I press my lips to his chest and rest my chin on my hand.

His eyes seem brighter in the morning, almost as if there is a light shining behind them. His hair is a bit messy and he's rocking the perfect amount of stubble. I could get used to morning Ben.

I run my finger down his nose and he catches it, bringing it to his lips.

"I like it better when you're not trying to sneak out on me in the morning." He rolls over onto his side, running his hand down my arm. "You looked like you were stuck in that pretty little head. What's going on?"

I glance from his tattoo back to him. "Have you ever been shot at?" He raises his eyebrows, seemingly unprepared for that type of question. I trace over the words underneath his shield again. "I mean, your job is really dangerous, isn't it?"

"Sometimes. But I've never been put in a situation like that. Luke got shot in the leg a couple years ago." My eyes widen, and he shakes his head at my worried stare. "The bullet barely grazed his shin, but when he tells the story, he almost died. I'm pretty sure his version has gotten him laid on more than one occasion." His hand grips my hip tightly and he pulls me against him. His eyes darken to a devious shade as I become aware of his need for me. Very aware. "Is my girl worried about me?" he asks, rolling on top of me and settling his body between my legs.

"Yes." I wrap my legs around his waist, lifting up my pelvis to grant him access.

He enters me slowly, groaning and dropping his forehead to mine. "Don't be." He kisses my lips once, then once more. "Nothing could take me away from you. You've got me, baby. This is where I belong. Right here." He braces himself on his hands, thrusting into me deeply. "Christ, there's nothing like this." His voice is strained, his eyes focused on my face, gently caressing my features as he moves inside me.

"Ben." I reach up and stroke his cheek.

The connection we share is so strong, so undeniable. I never want to break it. He's so familiar to me. Being with Ben feels like being home. And I can't imagine my life without this man in it. But after the summer is over, what will we have? Will it all just be how this thing between us started out? A beautiful memory that was never meant to last? I can't imagine how difficult leaving him is going to be, so I don't think about it. I don't allow unwanted thoughts to pull me out of this moment with him. I just focus on him.

"Oh God. You feel so good," I moan, lifting my mouth to his. My legs grip him tighter; my arms holding our bodies together like a taut rubber band. I need every part of him touching me. I can't get close enough. I'll never get close enough.

His hips crash against mine as his hands brace my ankles on his shoulders, tilting my pelvis to that delicious angle. I reach above me and press my hands flat against the headboard, forcing him deeper. Meeting his every thrust. That familiar pull is already building in my core and I watch, mesmerized by the way the muscles of his upper body contract with each thrust.

He runs his eyes down my body and settles right where he's entering me. "Touch yourself for me," he demands with both his tone and his eyes that are daring me to refuse him.

I slide my hand down my body and stop when my fingertips feel the hard edge of his cock sliding in and out of me. "Oh, my God. I'm so wet."

"Fucking right you are. God, Mia. I've never wanted anything as much as I want this. I'll never get enough, baby."

He continues to drive into me while I rub against my soaked clit. We find a rhythm, my two fingers circling while he fucks me, and I suddenly feel drugged with pleasure. At some point, he wraps my legs back around his waist, but I don't even register it happening. I'm lost. Completely lost in the feel of him. Just him.

"I'm close," I pant, seeing a sly smile form on his wet lips.

"You think I don't know that?" He presses his thumb against my fingers and begins moving with me, directing the tempo. I reach up with my free hand and grip his neck, pulling his face down to mine. Our mouths tangle in a brutal kiss, and I feel his air fill my lungs.

We are in that moment together, so completely in tune with each other that neither one of us hear the door creaking open.

"Daddy. I can't get dis off."

Nolan's husky voice causes me to gasp and Ben to curse under his breath. The orgasm that is about to rip my body apart quickly evaporates.

I look over at Nolan, seeing a cupcake in his hand and his face covered in green icing. His big gray eyes dart between me and his father.

"What arwe you doing wiff Pwincess Mia?"

I cover my face with my hand and try to contain my hysterics while Ben slides off me, keeping his back to Nolan. I pull the sheet up to my neck.

"Buddy, can you go wait for me on the couch? I'll be right there."

But Nolan isn't having that. Instead of leaving the room, he climbs up onto the bed, causing Ben to let out a string of muffled curse words as he tries to keep his erection hidden. My entire body is shaking with my laughter as Nolan holds the cupcake out to me, completely unaffected by his father's struggles.

"Can you take dis paper off?" His dimpled grin hits me, along with his crooked smile.

I smile back at him, taking the cupcake and pulling off the wrapper. "Are you having cupcakes for breakfast, Sir Nolan?"

I guess this is my fault. I completely forgot to put all the treats away that I purchased yesterday before I stormed off to bed. But in my defense, I was more concerned with offending Ben with my tits than putting sugary snacks out of the reach of little hands.

Side note: He's definitely not offended by my tits.

He nods quickly and takes his cupcake back. I anticipate him leaving, but no, Nolan has other plans. He crawls toward me and wiggles between Ben and me, flopping down onto my pillow. "Were you and Daddy kissing?"

I look quickly over at Ben, seeing him sliding on his boxers underneath the covers. He winks at me, giving me the go ahead to answer however I want to. I turn my body toward Nolan and prop up on my hand, making sure to keep myself completely covered.

"I was kissing your daddy. When two people really care about each other, they usually kiss." My eyes meet Ben's again. "A lot."

He chews up his bite and takes another one. "Can we go swinnin today, Daddy? I wanna show Pwincess Mia how I can jump in da pool."

Apparently, Nolan is finished discussing anything involving kissing. My answer was either sufficient enough to satisfy his curiosity, or he is a three-year-old boy who has his priorities straight.

He pops the last bit of cupcake into his mouth and reaches his finger toward Ben, running it down his nose.

Ben smiles and does the same back. "Yeah, we can go swimming. But I need to take you back to Mommy's house before dinner."

Nolan sits up with a protesting grunt and pounds his tiny fist into Ben's chest. "No, Daddy. I wanna stay here wiff you and Pwincess Mia."

I haven't seen Nolan display any emotion besides pure joy, but right now, he is definitely not a happy kid.

"Don't hit me, Nolan." Ben's gentle voice he always uses with him is gone and replaced with a stern fatherly tone. Even I cower a bit at it. He grabs Nolan's fist. "If you throw a fit like that again, you aren't going swimming. Do you understand?"

Nolan nods, his face falling as if Ben had just told him that dragons don't exist.

I reach over and run my finger down his nose. He perks up and does the same to me. "No sad faces allowed. Why don't you go grab me and Daddy a cupcake?"

He grins and scrambles off the bed, the quick tapping of his feet tapering off in the distance.

"Your son just totally cock blocked you. Are you going to be okay down there?" I quickly slide off the bed, brushing over the front of Ben's boxers.

"Not if you keep doing that I won't be," he warns. His hand grabs mine and he pulls the two fingers that I'd been using moments ago into his mouth, sucking on them as I stare with fascination. That has to be one of the hottest things I've ever seen.

I think there are two types of guys. Guys that pretend they're into eating pussy just to please the girl they're with, and guys that crave it like it's their favorite food on the menu. Ben is definitely the latter.

He slips out of the bedroom with a cocky grin and returns moments later in his swimsuit.

I dress as fast as I can, hearing Nolan's feet and animated voice coming down the hallway. I have just secured my bikini top, batting away Ben's naughty fingers, when he comes in, carrying two bright green frosted cupcakes.

"Pwincess Mia! I can jump into da pool without my fwotties!" He practically throws our cupcakes at us, his excitement uncontainable. "I'm gonna go get my bavin suit!"

"Wait a minute, buddy. It's hanging up in the bathroom," Ben yells after him. He turns to me and leans in, kissing my icing covered lips. "I should eat my cupcake off you." He licks his lips, only pulling back an inch. "My girl would look good covered in icing."

"I want to be covered in *your* icing," I tease.

His jaw twitches, along with another body part I'm sure. He growls into my hair, smacking me on my ass before he goes off after Nolan.

I pick my phone up off the floor, laughing softly at the image of it getting flung off the bed in the heat of passion last night. I want to check in on my mom before I spend the day in the pool with my two favorite boys. She answers after the second ring.

"Hello?" She coughs before clearing her throat, the muffled sound coming through the phone.

I sit down on the edge of the bed, my entire body tensing up. "Mom, are you okay?" She can't be sick, not now. Not when things are just starting to fall into place for me.

God, that sounds awful. How selfish is my thinking right now?

She sniffs a few times, clearing her throat once again before replying. "Oh, I'm fine, sweetheart. It's just a little cold." *Cough. Cough.*

A little cold to my mom in her condition isn't something to take lightly. I am suddenly feeling panicky.

"How long have you had it? Do you have a fever? How's your appetite?"

"Sweetheart, please relax. I'm fine, really. My nose started running yesterday and now I have this little tickle in my throat. That's all. No fever. No nausea."

"So you're eating?"

It's very important for my mom to be able to keep her food down. She had lost so much weight when she started her treatments and we had finally gotten it back up to a healthy number a few months ago. I never want to see my mom that thin again.

"Yes, yes I'm eating. Soup mainly, but that's good for a cold, which is what this is, Mia. I don't want you worrying yourself to death over this. Your aunt has everything under control."

"I can't help it that I worry, Mom. You know that."

She sighs, clearing her throat again. "Yes, I know. But I'm still the parent here, and if I say that I don't want you to worry, then you need to listen to me. Now tell me, is the weather as miserable there as it is here? It's so hot outside right now that you can't even breathe. And don't get me started on the damn sand fleas."

Sand fleas. I don't miss those. They are everywhere in Georgia when the weather gets hot. These tiny little nats that will bite you and make your life miserable.

"It is really hot, but you know I've always loved Alabama summers. The air is just better here or something, I don't know. I'm getting ready to get in the pool now."

She sniffs again. "Oh, well, why are you wasting your time talking to me? Go have fun, sweetheart."

"I'm not wasting my time. I just wanted to see how you were doing."

"I'm doing great besides this tiny little cold. So please go swim some laps for me. Maybe by next summer, we'll be able to go to the pool on base together like we used to."

I stand up and smile. "Absolutely. You'll be so strong by then, Mom. I love you."

"Love you, too."

She will be stronger by next summer. I can't wait to see my mom doing everything she used to do.

But with that joy comes the heart wrenching sadness of realizing that I'll be with her in Georgia and not here with Ben.

Life can be a total bitch sometimes.

No, fuck that. I'm not going to let anything ruin my day or the rest of my time here. After brushing my teeth and pulling my hair up into a bun, I walk outside to the pool.

"Pwincess Mia! Watch dis!"

Nolan is standing on the edge at the deep end while Ben stands a few feet in front of him in the water. I walk around and watch him with excitement. He squats down ever so slightly before jumping off the side and splashing into the water. He goes under and pops back up after a few seconds, prompting Ben to grab him.

I clap for him and sit down on the edge. "That was awesome. You're such a big boy doing that without floaties. I don't even know if I'm brave enough to do that."

Ben moves closer to me in the water, holding Nolan out in front of him so he can splash around. He turns his body, putting himself between me and Nolan. His eyes do that shift from sweet to mischievous, that he seems to do better than anyone, as he rakes over my body.

"You better hurry up and put that body of yours under the water before I do very inappropriate things to you in front of my son."

I give him a disapproving smirk. *He wouldn't dare.*

He leans in and nips at my bottom lip, sending a chill up my back in the sweltering heat. "I'm completely serious," he warns with a smolder that I feel in places only he is familiar with.

"Well, I'd hate to see you put those handcuffs to use if I choose to disobey orders, Officer Kelly." I shoot him a teasing look as I slide into the water. It's warm but still cools my body off instantly.

He brushes his lips against my ear. "You'll be in my handcuffs soon enough. Disobeying me has nothing to do with that."

Good God. I was completely kidding, but by the look Ben's currently giving me, he definitely isn't. And I am down with whatever ways he wants to use them on me.

He backs away from me and holds Nolan out in front of him. "Show Princess Mia how you can swim, buddy."

I hold out my hands to him, backing up to the wall. His little legs kick as hard as they can, splashing Ben in the process as he slaps his arms against the water. It takes him a little while, but he finally makes it to me with the biggest dimpled grin on his face.

"You're like a little fish." I wrap him up in my arms and he immediately draws me closer into a hug. He buries his face into my neck, holding on to me with all of his strength. "You give good hugs, Sir Nolan."

"I wove you," his husky little voice declares.

I lock eyes with Ben who is watching us intently. "I love you, too," I vow, never drifting from Ben's eyes. His lips part slightly as he moves closer to us. Strong arms find my waist under the water and he pulls the two of us against his chest. And we stay like that for as long as Nolan allows, Ben and I stealing kisses above Nolan's head. It's the best time I've ever had in that pool.

A perfect day with my two favorite Kelly boys.

chapter fifteen

Ben

I'VE NEVER HEARD MY SON SAY I LOVE YOU TO ANYONE BESIDES ME.
Not even to my family, and I know he loves them. He is crazy about my parents and my sister. And I'm sure he loves his mom because all three-year-olds love their parents no matter how shitty they are to them. But he's never said those words to her in front of me. Like the nose thing, those three words were something that he and I shared. Something that he kept between the two of us.

Until he met Mia.

And I can't blame him for loving her. She is incredibly easy to love. Hearing him say it to her hit me right in my soul. It was the same way I felt when he said it to me. Like I'd just been given this amazing gift. And he meant it. My son is brutally honest with his feelings. He'll tell you exactly how he feels and he won't sugar coat it. He didn't hesitate in the slightest either.

His words were strong and steady, just like I knew mine would be when she eventually heard them.

When she said it back to him, she looked right at me with those eyes that were impossible to look away from. No woman has ever looked at me the way Mia does. It was new, yet familiar at the same time. Like she's been looking at me like that our entire lives. Like she knew me better than anyone. I was use to women staring at me because they wanted me. I was familiar with that look. That desire that was completely superficial and void of any real emotion. I could easily break away from those women. I wasn't completely pulled in by a single fucking glance. Ready to hand over my entire life because of just one look. But that's how it was with Mia.

When she looked at me, she saw me. My hopes, my fears, my future, that for all intents and purposes, belonged to her. She fucking owned me with that stare and I never wanted to look away.

I wanted Mia to come with me to take Nolan to Angie's apartment. She seemed uneasy about it at first, but Nolan turned on that Kelly charm that she'd become completely helpless against. I wasn't sure how Angie was going to take it, but honestly, I didn't give a shit. No matter how much she wanted to deny it, Angie was very aware of my feelings toward her. I've always been straight forward and honest, even when I allowed the occasional blow job. And looking back, I hate that I was weak in those moments of loneliness.

But she knew we didn't have a future, and I wanted to show off mine.

"Oh, um, I figured I would just wait in the truck." Mia looks at me with an anxious expression as I stand outside her side of the truck.

I hadn't mentioned that she would be walking inside with me, but she is well aware of that intention now. She hesitantly puts her hand in mine and allows me to help her down.

"Ben, really, I don't have to go inside."

I close the passenger door, pulling her against me and inhaling her hair. "Baby, relax. There's no reason to be nervous. You're the first woman I've ever introduced to my son's mother."

"That's supposed to make me relax?" she asks with tenseness in her voice. "If anything, that makes me even more nervous."

I gaze down at her, cocking my head to the side. "I've also never introduced any woman I've been with to Nolan before." She seems to ease in my arms, her bottom lip finally releasing from her mouth. "That's how much you mean to me. I want you to be a part of Nolan's life as much as you're a part of mine. He loves you, and Angie's bound to find out about you eventually. We might as well get this over with now."

She shifts on her feet slightly while she stays in my arms, keeping her eyes on mine. "Is her son the only Kelly boy that feels that way?"

Wow. Leave it to Mia to put a guy on the spot. I'm certain there isn't any question that is off limits to her. But that's how she is. She isn't afraid to call you out on anything. And I'd never want her to be any different.

"No." I brush my lips against hers, teasing her with my tongue. "I'm sure my father loves you like a daughter."

She smiles against me before planting quick kisses to my lips. "Oh, is that how you're going to play this? What if I said it first, would you give it up then?" I arch my brow at her, daring her to make the first move. "I..." she kisses my jaw, "love..." her lips move to my ear, "sunflowers." She chuckles against me.

I bit back my smile, narrowing my eyes at her when she leans back.

She wipes the grin off her face and shoots me a flirtatious stare.

"You know, I carry a spare set of handcuffs in my glove compartment that I won't hesitate to use on you." I grab her wrists and pin them behind her back, bringing our chests together. Her breath hitches and she purrs against me. "Mmm, you'd like that, wouldn't you? Not being able to touch me while I have my way with you. Giving yourself up to me completely."

She nods and licks her lips.

Damn parental duties. My dirty girl wants me to take her right here, and the only thing stopping me is currently sitting in the backseat of my truck, swinging his sword around his head like a maniac.

I release her wrists and kiss her once, then once more. "Later, pretty girl."

We walk up to Angie's apartment, Nolan running ahead of us. He knocks lightly on the door and then bangs on it several times with his sword. As Mia and I walk up behind him, the door swings open.

Angie's eyes are immediately drawn to Mia, who is struggling to pull her hand out of mine.

But I'm not having that. I hold on tighter.

Angie crosses her arms over her chest in annoyance. "Let me guess. Princess Mia?" Her eyes shift to mine. "Really, Ben? Did you have to bring your latest hook up to my apartment?"

Nolan runs past her into the living room, which I'm grateful for. If we are going to have it out right now, I don't want him hearing it.

"Don't be a bitch, Angie. I'm doing you a courtesy here. Our son is going to be spending a lot of time with Mia, so I figured you two should meet."

Mia steps forward, as much as my grip on her allows, and holds her free hand out. "Hi, Angie. It's so nice to meet you. You have the sweetest little boy. I'm crazy about him."

Angie glances down at Mia's hand, refusing to take it. She turns her attention back to me instead. "Do you really think it's wise to confuse our son by introducing him to your flavor of the month? And I thought we were trying to work things out between us, Ben." She drops her hands then and wipes the irritation from her face, replacing it with a false hurt. "It really is what's best for Nolan."

"Maybe I should just go wait in the truck," Mia says softly, dropping her hand.

I shake my head at her. "No. You belong where I am."

"Oh, give me a fucking break," Angie barks out in irritation.

I look past her and see Nolan at the kitchen table with a box of crayons. Dropping Mia's hand, I step closer to Angie and she tenses up. "You're lucky he didn't hear that. And don't ever take your bitterness out on Mia. She never did anything to you, and she's amazing with Nolan."

"I'm his mother. And you should be more concerned with fixing our family than who your dick wants to play with."

"Ben, can I please have the keys to the truck?" Mia asks, holding her hand out to me, palm up.

Even though she states it as a question, she isn't asking me. But I don't want her to leave. Fuck Angie. Mia has every right to be where I am.

Unfortunately, I know now that Angie will never calm down as long as Mia is in front of her.

I reluctantly pull my keys out of my pocket and hand them to her. "Thank you." She turns her head toward Angie and offers her a smile. "I hope you realize how lucky you are to have Nolan."

Angie grimaces at her comment. I wait until Mia is out of earshot before I tear into the woman who makes my life a living hell. "Don't ever talk to Mia like that again. She doesn't deserve to be disrespected by you."

"What the hell do I care if I hurt your fling's feelings?"

I step closer to her. "She is not a fling. That woman is it for me. Do you get that? She's not going anywhere, so it would be in your best interest to accept her. Our son sure as hell has."

She inhales sharply. "What does that mean?"

"He told her he loved her today. Does he tell you that?"

Her bottom lip begins to tremble, prompting her to pull at it with her fingers. "I just don't understand why you can't at least try to make this work."

I am over this conversation. If she doesn't understand that the two of us will never work by now, she'll never understand it.

I push past her and walk over to Nolan, kissing the top of his head. "I love you, buddy. I'll see you soon, okay?"

"Wove you, Daddy. Look what I dwawed for you." He holds up the paper he's been working on.

It's three people, all looking like circles with stick limbs coming out of them. Two of them are larger than the third. He's even labeled us in his chicken scratch handwriting.

"Dats you, dats Pwincess Mia, and dats me." He hands it to me with a smile before he runs his finger down my nose.

I repeat the gesture and hold the picture against my chest. "Thanks, buddy." I rustle his hair before I walk toward the doorway.

Angie avoids my eyes, looking down at her feet instead. I don't have anything else to say to her so I walk out of her apartment and close the door behind me.

I had a feeling she wouldn't take meeting Mia very well. Angie still held on to the idea that we were going to wind up together. And considering that I've never introduced her to anyone before, I'm sure that only added to her delusion. But pining after me didn't excuse her behavior toward Mia. And I'll never let her treat my girl like that again.

I climb into my truck after folding up Nolan's drawing and slipping it into my back pocket. "I'm sorry about that. She won't talk to you like that again. I promise." I reach for Mia's hand and she places it in mine with a smile. She seems completely unaffected by the hate she just had directed at her.

"It's okay, I get it." She links her fingers through mine as I pull out of the apartment complex. "She loves you, and she's hurt that the two of you aren't together. I'm sure it isn't easy for her."

Jesus. She doesn't even have a negative thing to say about Angie after that bitchy encounter. She actually feels sorry for her.

"I don't think Angie loves me. I think she's just desperate for attention. We had one night together and neither one of us remembers any of it."

She shakes her head in disagreement. "She definitely loves you. I can tell." Her head rests back on the seat and she turns it toward me. Our eyes meet briefly before I have to put them back on the road. "Did you ever try to make it work with her?"

"Yeah, after Nolan was born. I knew Angie wanted us to be a family and I owed it to Nolan to at least try. They moved in with me after the two of them were released from the hospital. But it only lasted two weeks." Her hand tightens in mine. "We fought constantly about everything and I was fucking miserable all the time. Having a baby at twenty-three was stressful enough, and then throw in the fact that I couldn't stand my son's mother. It wasn't good. When I told her it wasn't going to work, she freaked out, threatening to keep Nolan away from me. I took her to court to make sure I'd at least get my time with him and that only pissed her off even more."

I park the truck in my usual spot at my parents' house. I help Mia out on her side, keeping her hand in mine as we walk toward the pool.

"Sometimes I wish I would've never slept with her that night, but then I wouldn't have Nolan. And I can't imagine not having that little maniac."

She laughs softly against my shoulder as we round the pool. "I can't imagine you not having him either."

I slide the door open, placing my hand on her back and moving her ahead of me into the house. Tessa is sitting on the couch, her lap completely covered in used tissues and her face in her hands.

"Tessa? What's wrong?" Mia goes straight to my sister, sitting down next to her.

"Are you all right?" I ask, moving in front of her. I haven't seen Tessa cry since we were younger, and back then, I was usually the cause of it. The older she gets, the less she lets things get to her.

If she had balls, they'd be made of steel.

She looks up at me and then back to Mia. "Oh, my God. Are you guys together now?" Mia nods and Tessa begins to cry harder. Not the reaction I had been expecting. Tessa was my biggest supporter when it came to winning over Mia. "That makes me so happy. You have no idea." She sobs, prompting Mia to wrap her arms around her.

"Do you need a girls' night?" Mia asks, giving me a knowing look over Tessa's shoulder.

I pick up on the message loud and clear. The two of them don't need me here for this. Nor do I really want to be here for whatever the fuck happens at a girls' night.

I lean down and kiss Mia's forehead. "I'm gonna head out. I'll see you after work tomorrow." She winks at me and nods against Tessa. I place my hand on my sister's shoulder. "If you say this is because of Luke, I'll go find him right now and beat his ass." She whimpers against Mia, and I would've taken that as a yes until she begins shaking her head.

Fucking women and their mixed signals. A simple yes or no would've been nice.

I exhale loudly in annoyance. "Just call me if you need me." I smile once more at Mia and get the hell out of there before I get any more cryptic responses.

chapter sixteen

Mia

"See, it's a good thing I stocked up like I did yesterday," I say, carrying over two bags of chips and the box of cookies that Nolan and I had made a dent in yesterday.

Girls' night can't exist without some sort of junk food.

I drop them onto the coffee table and settle in next to Tessa, turning my body toward her. She isn't crying anymore, but she looks emotionally drained. I tuck my legs underneath me and place my hand on her knee. "What happened with Luke?"

She sniffs, leaning her head so it rests on the back of the couch. Her eyes are puffy and bloodshot and her nose is bright red. I've never seen Tessa cry before. Not even when we were younger. She was always the stronger one out of the two of us.

"I didn't know where Luke stood on the whole kid thing. We've never talked about it and I didn't want to just drop the baby bomb in his lap without being somewhat prepared for his reaction." She reaches up and wipes a tear from her face. "I was anticipating him saying that he'd want to wait a few years to start a family, and then I'd say something like *instead of waiting a few years, how do you feel about waiting a few months?* But he didn't say that." She looks down into her lap and begins picking at her nail polish.

"What did he say?"

"He said he didn't know if he wanted kids. He said that every time he saw Ben and Nolan together, he never once thought that was something he'd want someday." She lifts her head and looks at me. "I got so angry. I pushed him away from me and started screaming at him. I told him I was tired of whatever the hell it was we were doing together and that I didn't want to see him anymore." She starts crying again, and I grab her hand before she continues. "I don't even know if he was fully committed to me. He could've been fucking every girl in Ruxton for all I know, and then the thought of him getting all those girls pregnant pissed me off even more. I was yelling and crying. I don't even know if I was making any sense. He tried to calm me down, but I couldn't even look at him. I told him never to call me again and I left."

I grab a tissue out of the box and hand it to her. "So you didn't tell him you might be pregnant?"

Even if she and Luke weren't together anymore, I still thought he should know about it.

She chuckles softly, which completely throws me off.

Ending things with the father of your unborn child doesn't seem humorous to me.

"The timing of this whole thing couldn't have been more fucked up. After I got home, I went to the bathroom and low and behold, there was my stupid period. That bitch really took her sweet ass time making an appearance." She shakes her head and drops it to the side, leaning it against the couch. "I keep thinking that if I would've just waited a day, that whole conversation wouldn't have happened and we'd still be screwing around. But I'm glad I didn't wait. I want a family someday. I want to get married and have kids and I wouldn't get that with him. I'd just be wasting my time."

Her words are certain, but she seems saddened by the loss of whatever it was that she and Luke shared.

I tighten my grip on her hand. "I'm really sorry things didn't work out. With Luke and the baby. I know you were excited about being a mom."

She shrugs. "It's probably for the best. I see what my brother has to go through raising a baby with somebody he isn't with. And I'm sure Luke would've ended things once I told him that I was keeping it." She grabs a few cookies and rests back on the arm of the couch. "I am going to miss the sex though. My God."

I chuckle and grab a bag of chips. "That good?" She eyes me up humorously. "Well, there's always Reed. Have you two ever gotten together?"

I really had no idea if the two of them had ever hooked up. Reed was a good looking guy, and Tessa was, well, she was Tessa.

She holds her hand up to stop me, grimacing. "Gross. That would be like sleeping with Ben. And he's got a lot of baggage. Didn't he tell you about his last girlfriend?"

I shake my head and dive into my chip bag, preparing myself for some gossip.

"It's really fucked up. He started dating this girl senior year, Molly Mcafferty, and they were like, crazy in love. Everyone thought that they'd end up married with a shit load of babies someday." She gets up off the couch and walks to the fridge, returning with two beers and handing me one before reclaiming her seat. "But that obviously didn't happen." Tessa takes a sip of her beer and licks her lips. "Molly went to college in Virginia and Reed stayed here, getting on at his dad's company. He was determined to make it work though and stayed completely faithful to her. I mean, he acted like they were married already. He wouldn't even look at other girls. He wrote her letters all the time and would take road trips every weekend to go see her, but she never came back here to see him. Not even during holidays. And after a while, she stopped calling him all together."

I have an idea where this story is going and I almost don't want to hear anymore. Reed is a sweet guy, and doesn't deserve what I fear Tessa is about to tell me.

She continues with a heavy sigh. "I voiced my opinion on their seemingly one-sided relationship and he got all pissed at me. I told him that if he was so certain that she wasn't two timing him, that he should go see her during the week when she wasn't expecting him."

"Did he?"

"Yup. He walked right in on her banging some dude in her dorm room."

I have the sudden urge to go find Reed and hug him and beat the shit out of this Molly chick. I despise cheaters. My mom's last boyfriend was one.

"Oh, God. Poor Reed. Has he dated anybody since her?"

She digs into her bag of chips, popping a few in her mouth before answering. "I wouldn't classify hooking up with random chicks as dating. He's like the king of one-night stands around here."

I chuckle softly.

It could've been Reed that night at the bar, buying me purple drinks and telling me he'd lose his mind if he didn't get inside me soon. That thought is quickly pushed out of my head. I don't want to imagine giving myself to anyone but Ben. I belong to him.

"He's just afraid of falling for some chick and then getting crushed again," she continues. "But he's never admitted that to me. He acts as if Molly didn't completely wreck him, but he didn't see what I saw. That boy was destroyed."

We both chew up our mouthfuls, placing our chip bags on the coffee table when we are finished.

I am picking at the label on my beer bottle when I feel a pair of eyes on me. I look up and meet her beaming smile. "What?"

"You got naked in front of him last night, didn't you?"

There's the Tessa I know and love. I chuckle and shake my head. "No. I sent him a text that was meant for you." I pull my phone out of my pocket and show it to her.

She arches her brow, reading over the text several times. "Damn. Well, that's definitely one way to go about getting him out of the friend zone. How did he react to this?"

"How do you think he reacted to it?" I ask playfully. I scoot over next to her so that we can rest our heads against each other's. Our legs are stretched out in front of us with our feet propped up on the edge of the coffee table. "You were right."

"I usually am. But what exactly are you referring to?"

I sigh, pausing for dramatic effect. She bumps her knee against mine, indicating that she isn't having my stalling tactics today.

"I love him."

I actually feel my heart swell inside my chest when I admit it out loud. The butterflies that only Ben can evoke inside my stomach begin fluttering about in there. I feel my love for him streaming through me as if it runs through my veins. And I know without a doubt that I'll love him fiercely and forever.

Her hand squeezes my knee. "Of course you do. And he loves you. It's ridiculously obvious and annoying now that I'm single." She yawns at the end of her observation, prompting me to do the same at the sound of hers.

I want to believe Tessa. I want to believe what my own heart is telling me.

But I'll never be sure until he speaks those words to me himself. A part of me thinks I shouldn't love him, but for completely different reasons than I've ever had before. I know how hard it's going to be to leave him when I have to go back to Georgia. And leaving my heart here isn't going to make it any easier. Maybe that's why Ben hasn't said those words to me, if he even feels them at all. Maybe he's being sensible and keeping his heart out of this.

But I want him to jump off that cliff after me. I want him to feel that rush and risk the pain because I'm willing to.

I'd risk it all.

"You know you're best friends with someone when you're willing to handcuff them, while they're practically naked, and help them get ready for a sex fest with your brother," Tessa says through a smile that I hear rather than see.

I can't see much of anything in the position I am currently in besides the headboard and the comforter.

She fastens the handcuffs to my wrists, securing my arms behind my back. "This is nuts, considering we don't have a key for these. How fucked up would it be if he got held up at work and you had to stay like this for hours? Or days?"

Shit. I hadn't thought about that. God, that would be awful. Not to mention embarrassing. I'm not sure how I'd manage to go to the bathroom like this.

I open my mouth to respond when I hear the sound of the sliding glass door opening.

"Showtime," Tessa says. "I'll be heading out for a few hours. Try not to kill him."

"Thanks," I whisper.

My entire body is buzzing with anticipation as she leaves the room, closing the door behind her. I hear muffled voices in the distance, laughing to myself at the speech Tessa rehearsed with me when I asked her to help me out tonight.

Mia was not acting like herself today. She seemed a bit on edge and a little hostile. I had to restrain her. And then the kicker. *She's been a bad girl, Ben. A very bad girl.*

I would've loved to have seen her face when she delivered that line. And his for that matter.

The floorboards in the hallway creak with his footsteps that inch closer until finally, the door swings open.

I can't see him, but I can hear him clearly with the one ear that is facing the ceiling. I am kneeling on the edge of the bed, my body angled down and my cheek resting on the comforter. My wrists are bound behind my back, and I'm only wearing a very skimpy pair of black panties. They barely cover anything and I might as well be naked right now. And by the sound of Ben's heavy panting, he isn't hating this surprise.

"Dear God. A man should be warned before he walks in on you like this. I almost came at the sight of you, baby." He moves closer and places his hand on my lower back, running it up my spine. I whimper at his touch. It's like fire melting ice. "My dirty girl looks absolutely stunning face down. And I bet you like this, don't you? I bet you're dripping right now."

"Touch me and find out."

His hand moves lower, teasing me between my legs. "Holy fuck," he grunts, sliding my panties down to my knees. His fingers dip inside me, moving in a steady rhythm as I moan against his touch. His lips press against my back, licking and kissing my skin. "What do you want, angel? Tell me and I'll give it to you."

"You, Ben. I want you."

"And you're going to get me, sweetheart. But I want you to be specific right now. Do you want me to make you come like this?"

I groan loudly into the mattress.

Jesus. His fingers are like magic. I am certain he can get me off in two seconds with them if he wants to. But I know what he wants to hear and what I want him to give me.

"I want you to do whatever you want with me. Take what you need and don't hold back. This belongs to you."

"Yes, baby." He removes his fingers, and the sound of him sucking on them nearly pushes me over the edge. And then I hear his belt loosening and I'm reminded of one more very important thing.

This needs to be said before he uses my body for his own pleasure. This is my fantasy as much as it is his.

"Leave your uniform on."

"Fuck yes." The sound of a zipper lowering is the last noise I hear before he enters me. We both moan together, his louder than mine, as his hands grip my forearms. "Christ, you're perfect. I don't think I've ever been this hard."

He moves in and out of me, taking what he needs. His power during sex is immeasurable. The way his grip tightens on me, the way his hips slam against my backside. He is fucking me with such force, such greedy need. And God, I want everything he is giving me. I want him to possess every inch of me. I am certain my body is specifically made for his pleasure and his for mine. Our sounds and his words to me ring out around us. He tells me how badly he wants me. How nothing has ever felt like this. And how he'll never get enough. I feel everything he gives me and every word he speaks. This is what being in love feels like. Raw. Honest. He makes me feel beautiful and wanted, even in this vulnerable position. When he's close to losing it, he presses his lips to my ear and his fingers find my clit. And when he tells me to fucking come, my body answers him immediately.

I'm panting into the comforter, trying to steady my breathing, as he unfastens the handcuffs. But I know we're not done. If I've learned anything from being with Ben, it's that my insatiable hunger for him will always be met by his need for me.

We'll never be easily gratified when it comes to each other. Even after we've given every piece of ourselves, we'll still want more.

His hands massage my wrists, rubbing the life back into them as I turn over onto my back. My panties are finally removed and he tosses them somewhere off the bed. He pushes my one leg close to my body as he enters me again, grinding his hips against mine.

"Keep your eyes on me," he commands as his forehead beads up with sweat. He grips my other knee and pushes it against my chest, leaning his hard body into mine and stroking me deeper.

Even if I wanted to look away, which I don't—let's be clear about that—I doubt I'd be able to. Him fucking me in his uniform has gone way past any expectation I could've conjured up. I watch his eyes and the possessive gleam in them. The fullness of his mouth and how it stays slightly parted. The tease of his tongue as it licks the corner of his lips. My eyes dart up to his hair and I want to grab it, to pull it hard and bring his mouth down to me. To steal that tongue of his and hold it captive in my mouth and between my legs.

But it's his eyes that command the most attention from me. He doesn't just look at me like a man who, as he so eloquently put it, is starved for my pussy. He looks at me like a man who would do anything for it. Who would do anything for *me*. It's a look that would completely throw me off balance if I wasn't prepared for it.

But I'm prepared.

"Talk to me."

His lip twitches with that knowing smile of his and he slides out of me, grabbing me by my neck and sitting me up so we're face to face. I'm pulled into his lap, my legs wrapped around his waist, and he brings his mouth to mine.

"And say what, angel? That I could kiss you for hours. That I love the taste of you on my tongue."

He licks along my bottom lip and I open up for him, allowing him the access we both want. He explores my mouth, breathing his fire into me and setting me ablaze from the inside out. And then he breaks our kiss and presses his lips to my ear, his hands holding me tightly against him.

"You're going to have to be specific. There are a lot of things I could say to you right now." His voice is a low rumble, like thunder in the distance. He leans back and commands my attention with the storm in his eyes.

I shift in his lap so he brushes against my entrance. "I want all your words. I want to be filled with them so that when I go home, I'll never forget how I made you feel." I'm hovering over him, wet and ready when he grips my hips and prevents me from lowering myself onto him.

He brushes his lips along my jaw, nipping at my skin. "You are home," he whispers.

I lower my face into the crook of his neck, biting back the tears that sting my eyes.

He strokes my hair with one hand, his other still firmly holding me above him. "I'll always want this, Mia. I could have you every day for the rest of my life and I'd never get enough of you."

"Me too," I say, finally leaning back and letting him see my face. He reaches up and brushes the tear off my cheek with his thumb. A smile teases my lips and he gives me one in return. "Can I have it now?" I ask, shifting in his arms so he brushes against my clit. A gasp escapes my lips when he applies the slightest amount of pressure to my swollen sex.

"You want it?"

I nod, slowly, emphasizing my desire.

He eases me down onto him, grunting when I'm fully seated. I let him take the lead, moving my hips in the rhythm he wants. He keeps his eyes on my mouth, a constant of his that I love. He isn't ashamed about his obsession with certain parts of my body, and I'll gladly let him stare at me with that wild hunger of his.

His one hand digs into my hip while the other pushes on the center of my back, arching me up so he can take my left breast into his mouth.

"Ben, my God."

I watch him leave bite marks all over my chest, whimpering each time I feel his teeth graze my skin. He tilts my head, giving him access to my neck while his other hand grabs my ass and grinds me into him. I rake down his back through his shirt and he groans against my shoulder.

"Fuck. Get there, baby. I'm not coming without you."

I rock harder into him. "Bite me." His teeth skim over my shoulder and then I feel it. The sharp sting that pulls a gasp out of me, like I've been starving for a breath. "Ben." My orgasm knots in my stomach, radiating up to my chest, and I grab his face to make him look at me. "Coming. Now." I can barely get my words out as my climax takes over, burning me from the inside out.

I fall around him, a pile of embers as he gives me his release.

My eyes are already closing when he positions me on the bed so my head can rest on a pillow. And the sensation of the bed dipping next to me and his lips on my forehead are the last thing I register before I slip into a dream.

··

I know I'm alone before I open my eyes.

His body isn't tangled with mine, his breath isn't blowing on my skin, and I simply feel like a part of me is missing. I rub my face into the pillow before opening my eyes. And there, lying in the spot that belongs to Ben is a bouquet of sunflowers. I could cry right here. And I do.

He remembered.

chapter seventeen

Ben

She was perfect.

No other woman got to me the way Mia did. No other woman will ever know what I need without me having to ask for it. I want control, but I also want her to take what's hers. To tell me what she needs when I might hesitate to give it to her. To demand I fuck her harder, to bite her there, and to bare my soul to her.

And I almost said it.

I love you.

The words were right there on the tip of my tongue, but I swallowed them down.

I know she is waiting for my own admission before she gives me that heart of hers that she so fiercely protects. But once I have that last piece of her, I won't be able to let her go. And how much of an asshole would I be if I asked her to choose between going back to Georgia to take care of her mother and having a life with me? Mia is mine, and she'll be mine forever, but I can't have her two hundred and forty miles away from me. And my only other option is packing up my shit and moving to Georgia with her, but that means leaving Nolan behind. Because of my screwed up situation with Angie, I'll never be able to take him with me. Which means that I am fucked.

Completely fucked.

Leaving her this morning was the hardest thing I've ever done. She was an angel next to me, curling up against my body as if she couldn't get close enough. I loved how our bodies sought each other's even in sleep. We were completely entwined, one entity instead of two. It was hard to tell where my body ended and hers began. And still, I needed her closer. I wanted her with me at all times. Every second I spent with Mia, I fell harder.

And fuck, I wanted to fall. I wanted to risk everything for something so unpredictable. Something I didn't quite understand. Loving her was wild and I wanted more of it. I wanted all of it.

Figure out your shit, Kelly. Then make her yours.

My post Mia mood was tainted by the day I was having. Everything seemed to be going to shit, and to top it off, I had a partner that was suddenly into sharing his feelings with me. By midmorning, I was very aware of the reasoning behind my sister's tears last night. And I couldn't tell what bothered Luke more; the fact that he got dumped or the fact that he had no fucking clue as to why.

"It was completely out of nowhere," he informs me for the hundredth time today as we patrol downtown Ruxton.

No matter what topic I brought up or what the hell we were doing, Tessa crept into the conversation. I can't say anything, though. I did the same shit the other day when I couldn't get my mind off Mia.

"I know you really don't care to know the details of my sex life."

"No, but that's never stopped you from sharing before."

In fact, he over-shared most of the time. Luke didn't have a filter when it came to his sex life, even when it involved my sister.

He exhales exhaustively, dropping his head back to the seat. "I just don't get it. She was insatiable that night and the next morning. I don't think I have any semen left."

"Jesus, man. I don't want to know that shit."

"Sorry. But what the fuck? She goes from not being able to get enough of me one minute, to dumping my ass the next. And she didn't even give me a reason. I could fucking work with a reason."

He starts scrolling through his phone, no doubt debating on sending her another pleading text message. I've had to stop him seven times already today from embarrassing himself.

"Do I need to throw that out the window?"

He shoves it back into his pocket with pure aggravation. "She didn't say anything to you?"

He was in deep. I knew Luke was infatuated with Tessa, but I hadn't realized until today that he was in love with her. I don't think he knows that though, and if he does, I doubt he'll admit it. Especially after getting dumped for the first time in his life.

I turn the receiver volume up on the radio before answering. "No, in the ten minutes it's been since you last asked me that same question, she hasn't said anything to me. The only thing I know is that she looked really upset."

I begin tailing a car that is going twelve over the speed limit. I'd normally let it go if we weren't currently in a school zone and I wasn't in a shit mood. Having a kid has made me stricter on certain things, and the asshole in front of me picked the wrong day to go a little heavy on the gas. We've already ticketed nine people today, all of whom decided it was in their best interest to give me an attitude. And once you argue over a driving violation with me, I'm not giving you a fucking warning.

Luke grips the back of his neck with both hands. "Goddamn it. How the fuck am I supposed to fix this if she won't even talk to me?"

He turns the laptop toward him and begins looking up the license plate information.

I flip on the lights and the driver pulls over onto the shoulder, barely leaving me enough room to get behind him. That just annoys me further.

"I'm not okay with being dumped without knowing what the hell I did wrong. If she doesn't talk to me soon, I'm going to go fucking crazy."

I grab the bottom of the mount that holds the laptop and turn it so I can see it. "Give me the fucking thing. Do you realize you just looked up my sister's information in here, dick?"

Luke leans over, looking at the screen that displays every past address and speeding ticket Tessa's ever had. He flinches before falling back into his seat. "Fuck me. I'm in deep, man."

"No, you're in love, asshole."

And when he doesn't argue with me, I don't feel the need to say anything more. He'll have a hard enough time dealing with that realization himself without me fueling the fire. But I do owe it to him to at least try and get some information out of Tessa. And I silently vow to do that.

I didn't dare mention my sister's name again while we finished patrolling. Luke had dropped all conversation involving her after he looked to see if she had a record accidently. And I wasn't a glutton for punishment, so my conversations with him stayed as far away from that topic as possible. I didn't even mention Mia, because I knew that would just trigger him. And not talking about Mia was more difficult than I had anticipated.

I am mentally exhausted by the end of the day.

The only thing I want to do is hold Mia against me and fall asleep with her. So you can only imagine the surge of disappointment that runs through me when I arrive at my parents' house and she isn't there.

I grab my phone and dial her number, needing to at least hear her after the day I've had.

"Hello?" she answers in that voice that can drop me to my knees.

I smile against my phone and sit down on the couch, aimlessly flipping through the channels. "Baby, I'm at the house and you're not. It kind of sucks here without you."

"Oh, God, is it after six already? I'm so sorry, babe. Tessa wanted to get our hair and nails done today and I completely lost track of time."

Muffled voices come through the phone, and I can tell she's in a crowded place.

"You called me 'babe'," I state.

She's never called me anything besides Ben, except for some profanity that I'm sure she labeled me with when she first discovered who I was. Or multiple profanities.

"Oh, yeah, I guess I did." She laughs softly. "Is that okay? You call me so many different nicknames and I wanted to try one out. I liked babe."

I shift on the couch, resting my feet on the coffee table. "I like it too." My phone beeps, indicating that I'm getting another call. "Oh, hold on a second, angel."

"Okay, babe," she responds, the obvious smile in her voice.

I press a button and answer the incoming call. "Hello?"

"Hey, Ben. It's Rollins." Phil Rollins is another officer that works in my precinct. I don't see him or his partner much, considering that they worked nights. "Listen, man. You're gonna need to come down to the 14th block of Canton Street. I just pulled Angie over for drunk driving and she's got Nolan with her."

I am on my feet and moving toward the door as soon as I hear Nolan's name.

"What? Is he okay? Rollins, fucking tell me if he's hurt!"

My entire body tenses up, and I feel my heart pounding in my head.

"He's fine, man. I'm about to arrest Angie though. She's way over the legal limit and she seems to be on something besides alcohol."

That stupid cunt.

I sprint to my truck, not being able to make my legs move fast enough. "Don't arrest her until I get there. Do you hear me? I wanna see her fucking face before you take her away."

"All right, just promise me you won't be joining her in the back of my car. Keep your shit under control, Kelly. Your son needs you."

"I'm on my way. Tell him Daddy's coming. Don't let him think I'm not coming for him."

I start my truck and hang the phone up, startling at the sound of it ringing again. *Shit. I forgot about Mia.*

"Baby, Angie was just pulled over for drunk driving and Nolan is with her."

My voice cracks at the end. Something could've happened to my son. She could've killed him.

"Oh, my God. Is he all right? Where are you going? I'll meet you there. I'm leaving right now just tell me where to go."

Now it's her voice that is quivering. I hear movement and the sound of a set of keys jingling.

I need her. Nolan will need her. I clear my voice and keep it steady.

"He's okay. He wasn't hurt, thank God. If he was, I wouldn't be responsible for what I might do to that bitch. They're at the 14th block of Canton Street."

"Okay. Tessa and I are on our way. Babe, just try and stay calm, okay? Nolan's probably really scared with all that commotion and he's going to need you to be strong for him."

God, I loved this woman. She knew exactly what to say to keep me composed.

"Just meet me there, angel. I need you."

The sound of a car starting comes through the phone. "I know. I'm coming."

There are three cop cars at the scene, and an ambulance.

People are starting to gather on the street outside their homes, but I don't pay attention to any of that. The only face I see is Nolan's as I scramble out of my truck and run up to the back door of the ambulance. He is in Rollins' arms, getting checked out by the paramedic. As I rush up to them, Rollins takes in my terrified state.

"Just a precaution, man. He's perfectly fine."

I nod in relief, smiling at Nolan who finally registers my presence. My son grins at me the way he always does.

"Daddy! Wook at all da powice carws!"

The paramedic gives me the go ahead to grab him, having finished with the examination. I pull him to my chest and hold him gently. "Are you okay, buddy? You aren't hurt anywhere?"

He looks completely unharmed, but I feel like I am cradling a wounded animal against me. I can hear Angie's hysterical voice in the distance but I try to block it out. I don't want to get angry in front of Nolan. I pull him away from me and look all over his face, his arms, and his legs. I'm scanning every inch of exposed skin for some sign of injury, but I find none.

"Nolan, you don't have any boo-boos?"

He shakes his head and looks past me over my shoulder. His face lights up. "Daddy, Pwincess Mia and Aunt Tessa arwe herwe!"

I turn my body and feel a rush of calmness run through me.

Mia's face is streaked with tears, but she quickly shakes off her sadness when she sees Nolan. She is either relieved or she doesn't want him to see her like this. Tessa, on the other hand, looks murderous.

"Here, can you take him for me while I go handle this?" I hand Nolan over to Mia and he can't seem to get into her arms fast enough. She leans into me and kisses me on my jaw before walking toward my truck, her lips pressed to Nolan's forehead.

Tessa waits until Nolan gets several feet away before saying, "Where the fuck is that stupid bitch? She doesn't deserve jail. She deserves to eat my fist."

"Calm down, Tessa." Luke's voice startles us both, Tessa more than me. He walks past her and joins my side, keeping his eyes on her. "How would you going to jail help out in this situation?"

She glowers at him, crossing her arms over her chest as we walk toward the first cop car behind the red Altima.

I can feel the blood rushing in my ears as Angie's face comes into view, her lower body hanging out of the back of the cop car. Her hands are obviously bound behind her and she is crying hysterically. She seems to cry harder when she senses my presence. And now that Nolan is out of ear shot, I don't have to remain calm.

I push past the officer that is standing right outside the door, not even bothering to register who he is, and bring my face a breath away from hers. I can smell the booze on her and that just fuels my anger. If she was a man, I'd rip her throat out.

"You fucking bitch!" I feel the hands on my shoulders, trying to pry me away from her but they aren't strong enough. I stay right where I am and she feels every ounce of hate I have for her. "You're a fucking disgrace. I hope you've enjoyed your three years with him, because you'll never see my son again." The hands multiply on me, and I am slowly being dragged away from a regretful looking Angie. But I don't care how sorry she is or if she's sorry at all. There is nothing she can say to make me feel a shred of remorse for her. But the dumb bitch speaks anyway.

"I'm sorry. Ben, I'm so sorry. But you gave up on us." Her tears come harder. "You gave up!"

I lunge forward and fill my lungs to the max. "There is no us! And I don't give a shit if you're sorry! You could've killed him! You could've killed *my* son!"

She is delusional if she thinks any amount of apologizing is going to help. And the fact that she thinks it will help only enrages me further.

"You're a fucking piece of shit!"

"Ben, that's enough," Luke strains in my ear.

He has the main hold on me and I am now a good fifteen feet away from the cop car. I see Tessa's wide eyes and realize I need to calm down. I can't be like this when I get back to the truck. I've said all I wanted to say to Angie, and I don't want to see her face again.

"All right. I'm fine." I shrug him off me and walk over to Rollins, who is watching the scene.

"Can't say I blame you for that outburst. I would've reacted the same way."

"What are my chances of getting sole custody of my kid now?" I ask him.

Rollins' wife is an attorney that we work with frequently, and he in turn knows more about the system than I do. He also has an ex-wife that took him to court years ago over a custody battle.

He puts a hand on my shoulder and applies mild pressure. "Pretty damn good, man. Especially if the test results come back with more than just alcohol in her system. That on top of the class E felony she's getting charged with should give you full custody."

I knew under law, she was facing up to four years of jail time for having a minor in the car with her. And I figured I'll have a damn good chance of getting full custody of Nolan. But I wanted to hear it out loud. I needed to hear those words. I wanted certainty.

I nod at Rollins, thanking him before walking back toward Luke and Tessa.

She is watching me while he is watching her. And by the look on both their faces, they still aren't talking.

"I'm going to stay at Mom and Dad's tonight with Nolan. Did you drive here or did Mia?"

"I did. I'll meet you at home." She turns on her heel without giving Luke a glance.

"Tessa, come on. Will you at least talk to me for a minute?" Luke calls out.

She hears him, but she doesn't respond, not even with a look over her shoulder.

He runs his hands down his face and lets out a grunt behind them. "I'll see you tomorrow, man. I'm glad Nolan's okay." He walks away looking defeated, which is not a look he wears often. Especially pertaining to women.

I feel bad for the guy.

I talk to some other officers before finally walking to the truck.

Mia is holding Nolan against her chest in the front seat, both of them asleep. I open her door and pry him out of her hands so that I can put him in his car seat. She stirs at the loss of his weight on her.

"Hey." She places her hand on my cheek after I settle into the driver's seat. "Are you okay?"

I turn my face into her palm and kiss it. "I am now."

She doesn't ask me any questions on the drive back to my parents' house. It's as if she knows I need the silence right now. My brain is working out the possible scenarios that could've transpired tonight. All of them involving Nolan injured somehow. My grip keeps tightening on the wheel, and every time it does, Mia tightens her hold on my hand. She keeps her other hand on the back of my neck, massaging it gently and relieving the tension that is beginning to permanently set in.

When we get to the house, I carry Nolan inside and lay him down in the middle of the bed he sleeps in when he spends the night here. I can't leave him. Not yet. So I sit on the edge of his bed and watch his chest rise and fall.

I could've lost him.

I'd never be able to watch him sleep again. I'd never hear his husky voice ringing throughout the house or see him slaying invisible dragons. I'd have three years of memories to live off of for the rest of my life, and it wouldn't be enough. He is my world, and now because of his mother's reckless decision, he's all mine. I'll never have to miss another moment with him. I'll never have to beg to see my son on days that aren't technically mine. And I feel like a complete shit for feeling slightly grateful for the events that unfolded tonight.

What the fuck is wrong with me?

I have no idea how long I sit there, but when I eventually get up and turn around, Mia is leaning against the doorframe. I walk over to her and she wraps her arms around my waist, pressing her face to my chest.

"You know if you want to talk about it, I'm here." She turns her face up and I kiss her forehead.

"I'm glad it happened. How fucked up is that?"

Her hands grab my face. "You're not glad it happened. You'd never want Nolan to be in any sort of danger. The fact that you'll probably never have to split your time with him again because of Angie's poor judgment is a small silver lining. But Nolan's well-being is the only real thing that matters to you. You'd give up all your time with him if it meant keeping him safe. I know you would."

I love you.

The words burn the back of my throat, aching to be released.

I have no idea how long it will take to get Nolan's custody arrangement sorted out. And I can't take him to Georgia until that happens. The legal system takes its fucking time when you want it to hurry the hell up. And Mia may have to leave me before I can take him out of the state. Plus, I'll need to get a job lined up out there. It could be weeks, months before I'm with her again. And I won't make this harder on her. So I swallow those same three words again, not letting them out. Not yet.

I bend down and lift her by her ass, prompting her to wrap her legs around my waist. "I need you," I whisper against her lips.

"You have me."

I carry her into her bedroom and drop her in the middle of the bed. "Take all of that off." She sits up and pulls her dress over her head, revealing herself to me in only a pair of white panties. "Fuck. I need to be inside you, angel."

She sits back on her hands, pushing her perfect tits out and teasing me with them. "I'm waiting."

I practically rip my shirt off, and when I start loosening my belt, she lies back and slips her hand into the front of her panties.

"Jesus, Mia."

I step out of my pants and move over her, letting my cock drag up the length of her body.

"Get in me," she pleads, her hand still working between us and her eyes rolling closed.

"Not yet. I need to taste you first."

Her eyes shoot open with that flirtatious glint and her hand wraps around my cock. "So do I."

Her panties are torn from her body before I pick her up and position her over me so that she's straddling my face. I feel her warm breath tickling my cock as I nip at the soft skin of her inner thigh. "Those pretty lips of yours better find themselves wrapped around my dick in two seconds."

Her soft laugh fills the room. "And if they don't?"

I lick up her length, not being able to hold out any longer. Her taste fills my mouth and her moan vibrates against my lips. I savor her with my tongue, letting everything fade out around me. I'm a junkie getting his fix. But instead of the hit dulling out my senses, I feel my pulse quicken and my bones begin to vibrate. I'm a fucking king between her legs, and when she finally swallows my cock, I grab onto her hips and bury my face into her pussy.

She releases it with a pop and presses down on my pelvis with her hands, her back bowing in pleasure. "Oh, my God. I'm not going to be able to focus if you keep doing that." Her voice breaks with another moan when I don't let up, and her hand takes over where her mouth was.

I groan against her clit before biting down on it gently. She gasps and I release it. "Bend down and suck my dick, Mia. I'm coming in that mouth tonight."

"Then you're going to have to let up a little."

Yeah, that's not happening.

I smile against her. "Nothing could pull me away from your pussy, angel. Put my dick in your mouth and don't be fucking gentle about it. I want to feel the back of your throat when I'm coming."

I feel her weight shift and her tongue licks the head of my cock. I'm about to tell her not to tease me when she deep throats me like a fucking champion and scraps her teeth along my shaft.

"Mia!" I grunt out, digging my fingers into her ass.

She sucks me like her life depends on it, and I flatten my tongue against her clit, stroking it in a rhythm that makes her lips vibrate against my cock. And then it's about getting her off before me. I alternate between sucking on her clit and fucking her with my tongue, pulling her hips down so hard I'm practically being smothered. I feel her pulse against my tongue, and when she releases my cock and digs her nails into my hip, I know I have her.

She rocks against me, fucking my face and riding out her orgasm while she softly chants my name. I press my lips once more to her clit before she collapses on top of me, her face now resting on my thigh.

"Sorry. Just give me a minute," she pants, sliding off my stomach and settling between my legs. She glances up at the smug face I'm wearing and wraps her hand around my cock. "Still want to come in my mouth?" she questions before pressing her lips to my shaft.

I groan as she slides down. "Stop talking and suck my cock, baby."

Her cheek twitches with a smile. "Yes, Officer Kelly."

chapter eighteen

Mia

The bed is jolting underneath me, bringing me out of my dream. A tiny laugh fills the room and prompts me to open my eyes.

Nolan is jumping on the bed and giggling at himself, and when he sees my eyes on him, he hops over toward me and collapses on my stomach.

I grunt as his elbow connects with a few of my ribs.

Jeez. How can such a tiny body inflict so much pain?

After recovering, I rustle his hair with my hand, rubbing his back with the other. "You are a little ball of energy in the morning. Are you hungry?"

He slides off me and scoots off the bed. "I want pamcakes."

His husky little voice is hoarser in the morning. That and his crazy hair are the only things giving away that he has just woken up. He certainly isn't moving as slow as I know I will be. Even off the bed, he is jumping around like a jack rabbit.

I sit up and rub my eyes with both hands. "Go wake up Aunt Tessa and I'll meet you in the kitchen."

His little feet quickly take him out of the room and down the hallway while I get dressed for the day. My phone beeps on the nightstand just as I am pulling my hair back into a pony.

Ben: Is the maniac awake yet?

Me: Are you kidding? He's running on full speed already. :) We're getting ready to make pancakes.

Ben: He's probably psyched out of his mind getting to spend the day with you. I'm jealous.

Me: You'll get me tonight, don't worry.

Ben: Bet your ass I will. I'll see you around six.

Me: Can't wait.

I tuck my phone into my pocket and walk out into the kitchen. Tessa is rummaging through the cabinets while Nolan is playing with her phone on the couch. I snicker at the sight of him browsing iTunes like he's done it a million times.

"Crapola. We don't have any pancake mix," she says, closing the doors she had opened and turning toward me. "My parents really should have stocked up before they decided to take a six month trip to Europe. I'm extremely disappointed in them."

I chuckle and grab my keys off the counter. "Yes, how dare they not provide you with food for half the year while they go on vacation."

She scowls at me playfully, pulling the orange juice out of the fridge.

"I'll run to the store and get some. Do we need anything else?"

"We'll need some more milk with Nolan here. Other than that, I think we're good." She walks over to the couch and plops down next to him. "Can you not buy apps please? How do you even know my password?" She leans her head into his and monitors his actions on her phone.

I laugh under my breath as I walk toward the door. "All right. I'll be back in a little while. Hold down the fort, Sir Nolan."

He shoots his dimples at me before returning to purchasing apps on Tessa's phone.

I'm waiting in the checkout line at the grocery story after having grabbed the pancake mix, some milk, and a dragon coloring book I found near the greeting cards when my phone starts ringing. I pull it out of my pocket and place my basket at my feet, seeing my aunt's name flashing on the screen.

"Hey, Aunt Mae."

"Mia, sweetie, you need to come home." She sniffs loudly, and my heart immediately drops to the floor next to my basket.

I'm out the door, running across the parking lot within seconds. "What's happened? Is it that stupid cold she had? Does she have a fever now or something?"

I knew it was more than a cold. *Fuck!* My tires screech as I pull out of my parking space and drive toward the exit for the highway.

My aunt sobs through the phone.

"Aunt Mae, tell me what's going on. Can I talk to her?" I hear a faint beeping sound through the phone in between my aunt's cries.

She's in the hospital. That's what that sound is.

"She was fine. I don't know what happened. I went to wake her up this morning and she wouldn't respond to me." Her voice cracks and she starts crying harder. "She won't wake up, Mia. The doctors are waiting for you to get here. Oh, sweetheart. I'm so sorry."

I'm crying now, sobbing uncontrollably. I have to keep wiping my eyes to be able to see the road in front of me. The hand holding the phone to my ear is shaking so badly, my aunt's cries are fading in and out.

I know what she means. My mom has a DNR. The doctors are waiting for me to get there before they take her off the machines. My mom is dying and I'm not there.

I haven't been there for her.

"I'm on my way. Tell her I'm on my way!"

"Honey, she's unconscious."

"Tell her I'm coming!" I hang up the phone and drop it somewhere, anywhere. I don't give a shit about my phone right now.

My attention is on the road and nothing else as I fly down the highway. The speed limit means nothing to me. Nor do the other cars on the road. I swerve in and out of traffic, taking the median occasionally when I can't get around someone. The only thing I care about is getting to her in less than four hours.

Four fucking hours. Why the hell did I leave her?

I knew in my gut that I shouldn't have left for the summer. I was selfish. I was more concerned with having an amazing summer with my best friend than taking care of my own mother. And now she's dying and I'm not there. I wasn't there when she got that fucking cold. I wasn't there last night when she probably started feeling bad, and then the bad turned to worse sometime in the middle of the night. She probably called out for me in her weak voice, too weak to alert my aunt. And now I'm two hundred miles away from her and I can't get to her fast enough.

The world blurs in front of me.

The image of my mother in a hospital bed fills my thoughts as I speed down the highway. I only stop when I absolutely have to, and it's only to pump gas. I don't even run inside the gas station to use the restroom. But I do grab my phone that had slid underneath the back seat. I have a few missed calls from Tessa, but I ignore them for now. I dial Ben's number and it goes straight to voicemail.

"Babe, my mom is dying. I'm on my way to Fulton now." I pause and take in two shaky breaths, wiping underneath my eyes. "I know you can't be here with me, but can you at least call me? I just, I need to hear your voice right now. I'm not ready to say goodbye to her. I don't really know how I'm going to get through this." I blink, sending the tears streaming down my face. "Please call me." I end the call, keeping my eyes on the pump. As soon as the numbers stop rolling over, I yank it out of my car and get back on the road.

How I manage to get to Fulton in two and a half hours, I'll never understand. But I do by some miracle. Of course, I did break the speed limit by a long shot the entire way here. I pull my phone out of my pocket as I run up to the entrance. I need to tell Tessa where I am. She's probably worried sick right now, and I can only imagine how hungry Nolan must be. After four rings, her voicemail picks up and I curse under my breath.

Is nobody answering phones today?

"Hey, it's me. I'm so sorry I missed your calls, but I'm in Fulton at the hospital. It's my mom. She's dying, Tessa." I bit my lip to stop myself from crying. "I got the call from my aunt when I was at the grocery store and I just drove straight here. Can you tell Ben to call me? Or text me or something? I tried calling him but he didn't answer." I remember the groceries I left on the floor by the checkout counter. "Oh, and tell Nolan I'm sorry about the pancakes. I'll make him some the next time I see him."

I tuck my phone away and run into the hospital, stopping at the information desk. I'm directed toward the ICU, and as I run off the elevators, I see my aunt.

She's pacing outside the room, glancing down at her watch repetitively when she turns toward my footsteps. She wraps her arms around me and I cry against her shoulder.

"Oh, sweetheart. I'm so sorry this happened. I swear to God she was fine yesterday. I would've called you if I thought it was serious."

I pull away from her and look into the room. "Do the doctors know what happened? She was doing so well. I just, I don't understand. She was beating it. She was going to beat it."

I watch as the nurse jots something down in my mom's chart, her eyes shifting from the monitor to her clipboard. Just then, a man walks over to where my aunt and I are standing and holds his hand out to me. He's wearing a white lab coat and an apologetic expression.

"Miss Corelli? I'm Dr. Stevens, the attending that's been looking after your mom."

I shake his hand weakly, my eyes straining to look at him because they want to stay glued on my mom. Now that I'm here, she has my full attention.

"I'm sure you're aware of how sick your mom was. The treatments seemed to have been working, but these things can happen. The slightest infection that wouldn't affect a healthy person can really be detrimental to someone with her condition."

I start crying again. "She told me a few days ago that she had a cold, but she said it wasn't a big deal. But I knew it was. I should've been here."

My aunt's arm wraps around my shoulder as I blink heavily, sending the tears streaming down my face.

Dr. Stevens puts his hand on my shoulder. "Darling, there's really nothing you could've done. The cancer was just too strong and your mom couldn't fight it anymore. She's not in any pain now." He looks into her room briefly before turning back to me. "You take as much time as you need, okay?"

I nod and give him a weak smile before walking into the room.

My aunt stays outside, giving me the privacy I need, and the nurse steps out as well. I sit down in the chair and grab my mom's hand. She's pale but her hand is warm, and she looks peaceful. Content. Like she's ready to let go. I bend down and press my lips to her knuckles.

"Hi, Mom."

I stay with her for hours, listening to the monitors and the light chatter of the people out in the hallway. I never once let go of her hand, not even when the nurses come in to take her vitals. I talk to her like she's awake and watching me, listening intently to my voice. I tell her all about Ben and Nolan, and how I've fallen in love with the boy that I'd once hated more than anything. I tell her that I wished she could meet the man he is now, because I know she would love him. And I tell her that I want to have babies just like Nolan with him. Dimpled little versions of Ben with maybe a few of my features, but mostly his. The tears come back when I realize she'll never see me on my wedding day, or meet any of her grandchildren. But I promise her that my children will know all about their grandmother and how beautiful and kind she was.

My aunt joins me after a while and we talk about the last several days she spent with her and what they did. She fills me in on every tiny detail, making me feel like I was there instead of miles away. I keep checking my phone but never hear from Tessa or Ben, and I can't hide the sadness that overwhelms me when neither one of them contact me.

Especially Ben.

I need to hear his voice. I need him with me, but he doesn't call me or text me and I don't understand why. And as time drags on, the hurt in my heart grows to the point of being agonizing.

Maybe I had imagined what we had together. Maybe he didn't love me. Maybe this was all just some game to him, tricking his sister's annoying best friend into loving him. And when Dr. Stevens comes in to ask if we're ready to say our goodbyes, I lose it.

I drop to my knees and cry harder than I ever have before. I cry over losing my mom to this bullshit disease that doesn't care whose life it ruins, I cry over my selfishness and the fact that I chose a summer with Ben over my last summer with my mom, and I cry because the man I love doesn't care enough to comfort me over the phone.

I know he can't be here with me. He has to work. But he could've called. And as I stand outside my mom's room, watching them cover her up with a white sheet, that familiar hate I once reserved just for him comes right back up to the surface.

"You know, I think it's really amazing that your mom wanted to donate her body to science. She could be the reason they find a cure for that fucking disease."

I can't help but laugh at my aunt's use of profanity. She never cusses around me.

Her hand tucks a piece of hair behind my ear that has fallen out of my hair tie. "Are you going to stick around here for a while or are you heading back to Alabama?"

I glance down at my phone again. Still nothing. "I don't have any reason to go back to Alabama."

"Isn't being in love a good enough reason?" she asks.

"Not when it's one-sided." I look down at my phone and squeeze it tightly, willing it to ring. "He didn't even care about me enough to text me. You really can't get more impersonal than a text, and that was still too much for him." I meet my aunt's pitiful gaze. "It's fine. I'm used to hating Ben. It's not very difficult. I can get my stuff mailed to me, that way I don't ever have to go back there."

The thought of never seeing Nolan again makes my stomach churn. But seeing Nolan meant seeing Ben. The Ben that doesn't care enough.

She takes a sip of the coffee she's been nursing for the past hour. "Why don't you step outside and get some air. It'll be good to get out of this stuffy atmosphere for a few minutes. Clear your head a little."

I nod in agreement and take the elevators down to the main level, walking out of the entrance I came sprinting through several hours ago.

As soon as I step onto the sidewalk, my phone starts beeping like crazy in my pocket. Startled, I pull it out and watch as the number of missed calls from Tessa's cell phone rack up. But still nothing from Ben.

How the hell did I miss this many calls?

And then it hits me—there isn't any cell phone reception in the hospital.

I begin listening to the voicemails she left me. The first several are wondering where I am, telling me that Nolan is driving her nuts with his impatience. Then she tells me that Nolan was messing with her phone again and she noticed that he turned the volume down and that's why she missed my call. She tells me she'll call Ben, and I can't help the aggravation I feel at that statement. She cries in the next message, asking me to call her so she can find out what's going on with my mom. As soon as she starts talking about Ben not answering his phone, I delete the message and go on to the next one. If she had any excuses for him, I didn't want to hear them. He obviously didn't love me, because if you loved someone, you'd take five seconds out of your day to send them a text when their mother is dying. One fucking word could've been sent to me. A simple "sorry." But no. I needed him and he didn't care. He doesn't love me. And that realization stings my entire body with a discomfort I've never felt before. But just when I think my world can't crumble anymore, I reach the last voicemail in my inbox.

"Mia, Ben's been shot. He's been fucking shot. I don't know anything except that they're taking him to St. Joseph's hospital. Please call me. Please."

I can hear the restrained panic in Tessa's voice.

I fall to the ground, my knees hitting the sidewalk and causing a shooting pain to ride up my thighs. But that's not the pain that has me struggling to breathe.

"Oh, no, God. Please no." I push myself up and begin running toward my Jeep when I remember my aunt.

"Fuck!"

Running faster than I ever have, I take the stairs because I don't want to wait for the elevator. My aunt is where I left her and she startles when she sees me, meeting me halfway next to the nurse's station. I'm crying and I can barely take in any air, but I manage to speak.

"Ben's been shot. I have to go. Right now. Do I need to do something? Is there anything I need to do here? Please, can I just go?"

My chest is heaving from my run and my legs are burning, but I don't care. And if I have paperwork or anything I have to do, it will have to wait.

She squeezes my hand, shaking her head with concerned eyes. "No, sweetie. Go. I'll take care of everything. Call me when you get there."

I run back down the stairs, nearly falling in my hurried state. Once I get outside, I dial Tessa's number as I sprint to the Jeep. It goes straight to voicemail.

"I'm on my way. Oh, my God, please call me back and tell me he's okay. Tell him I love him, Tessa. Tell him I'm going to say that to him every second for the rest of his life. He'll never go another day without hearing those words from me."

I wipe the tears from my eyes so I can focus on the road in front of me as I whip through the parking lot.

"Please don't take him away from me."

I whimper my plea to God, and to Tessa, not knowing if either one of them will hear me. If Tessa is in the hospital, she probably won't get this message until she walks outside. And if Ben is dying, why would she leave him? I wouldn't leave his side if I was there. The man I spent the last two hours bitterly hating was the man I loved more than anything in the world. He was my life, my family, and my future. I couldn't lose him. I wouldn't lose him. I've never believed in fate before, but I did the moment I saw Ben in that bar. He was always the one for me. We were always meant to end up together.

And the two hundred miles that are separating us now will be the last thing to ever keep us apart. I'll make damn sure of that.

chapter nineteen

Tessa

"I WANT PAMCAKES! I WANT PAMCAKES!" NOLAN YELLS, JUMPING UP AND DOWN ON THE sofa. "Pamcakes, pamcakes, pamcakes!"

I love my nephew, but I'm about to stick him in the dryer.

I grunt my annoyance, looking for any sign of the red Jeep out the window. "Nolan, relax please. Mia should be back any minute."

"It's Pwincess Mia," he corrects me, causing me to narrow my eyes at him.

I snatch my cell phone from his little grubby fingers and dial her number. It rings four times and then her voicemail greeting comes through the phone. I wait for the beep. "Oh, my God. Please tell me you're on your way back. The little monster is getting unbearable to be around. Oh, and if you're still at the store, can you pick me up some mountain dew?" I hang up and watch as Nolan rips all the pillows off the couch and jumps on them like stones in a creek. "How about some Fruit Loops to hold you over?"

He jerks his head up and connects with my eyes. "Gwoss. I hate fwuit woops. I want pamcakes." His little menacing body flies into the air with each leap he takes. "Pwincess Mia pwomised me."

I turn away from him and look out the sliding glass door, praying that Mia's body will come into view any second. But it doesn't. And my impatience begins to grow right along with Nolan's as the time ticks by. I dial her number again.

"Hey. You do remember how to get to my parents' house, right? Nolan's about to start eating the furniture."

And again.

"Which grocery store did you go to? There are some in Alabama. I'm about to start making pancakes out of cornmeal, and I'm not sure how those are going to go over, so you might want to speed it up a little."

And again.

"Sweet Jesus! Would you call me and let me know that you're still alive!"

Nolan's voice grows louder and louder, more urgent as the minutes drag on.

I silence him with my phone when I think my head is going to explode, and raid the fridge myself. I don't need to wait for pancake mix to eat breakfast. I am perfectly happy with Fruit Loops, unlike my hot meal loving nephew.

"Nolan, don't buy any more apps. I will be looting your piggy bank to pay for the seven that you bought already."

He doesn't respond as I clean up my dishes, most likely browsing the hottest games on iTunes. Another hour goes by before I grab my phone and really start to worry. There's no way in hell it should take Mia this long. Not unless she really did go to another state to grocery shop. I notice the missed call from Mia on my screen.

"Nolan, damn it. You turned my volume down."

He gasps softly, and I look up at his wide-eyed stare.

"You said a bad wowrd."

Shit. I hold my phone up to my ear to listen to her voicemail, turning the TV on as a distraction. Hopefully he'll find something amusing and will forget all about my potty mouth. I really don't feel like getting my ass handed to me by Ben for my language usage around his son.

"Hey, it's me. I'm so sorry I missed your calls but I'm in Fulton at the hospital. It's my mom. She's dying, Tessa. I got the call from my aunt when I was at the grocery store and I just drove straight here. Can you tell Ben to call me? Or text me or something? I tried calling him but he didn't answer. Oh, and tell Nolan I'm sorry about the pancakes. I'll make him some the next time I see him."

"Oh, God." I exit my voicemail and quickly dial her number again, cursing under my breath and moving into the kitchen. She doesn't pick up and I begin to cry. "Oh, my God, Mia, I'm so sorry I missed your call. Nolan was playing with my phone and turned down the volume." I try to muffle my cries, but I'm one of those loud criers and it's useless. "Jesus, I should be there with you. I'm going to call Ben right now and let him know what's going on. Just call me when you get a chance, okay? I love you."

I wipe my eyes and dial Ben's number. Nolan jumps around on the couch cushions, completely oblivious to me and anything else that isn't the cartoon he's watching. Thank God, I got his mind off those pancakes.

"Goddamn it."

Ben's voicemail message begins playing. I wait for the beep and slip farther into the kitchen, trying to get out of earshot of Nolan.

"Is nobody answering their phones today? Mia's mom is dying, Ben. She needs you. She's already in Fulton and you better call her or get your ass there. I'll take care of Nolan. And answer your phone when I call you, please."

I dial Mia's number again.

"Hey, it's me. I called Ben but had to leave him a message. God, I wish I was there with you. I hate that you're dealing with this alone. Just call me as soon as you get this and let me know what's going on. I'll keep trying Ben."

I dial his number again.

"Answer your fucking phone. Mia needs you, asshole."

I hang up and walk over to the counter, grabbing the box of cookies that is almost empty. There is no way in hell I am going to inform Nolan that he won't be having pancakes any time soon. I've seen some of his temper tantrums.

I pick up the couch cushions and re-situate them before plopping down on the end.

"I feel like having cookies for breakfast." I take a bite of one of the chocolate chip ones as he scrambles up next to me, his crazy, gray eyes flicking from my mouth to the box. "What about you?"

He nods eagerly and dives for some cookies. He then stretches out, lying sideways on the couch with his head at the other end while he eats and watches his cartoon.

I dial Mia's number several more times, hoping to get a hold of her, but get her voicemail each time. I also call Ben a few more times, and I'm sent straight to his voicemail with each dial. I'm hurting for Mia and want to be there with her. Ms. Corelli was always so sweet to me when I was younger. She would do anything for anybody, a quality my best friend acquired. I think about throwing Nolan into my car and beginning the drive to Fulton, but I'd never do that unless I made Ben aware. And since my dumbass brother isn't liking his phone today, I can't make him aware of that plan.

Nolan and I devour the cookies while watching several of his favorite shows, and just as I'm about to grab us both a drink, my phone finally rings.

I lunge for it, hoping and praying that it's either Mia or Ben, but it isn't. Luke's name flashes on my screen, and I hit ignore with my middle finger before turning it up in front of my phone as if he can see it.

He is the last person I want to talk to.

He calls again, and again, and each time I hit ignore with an irritated grunt. Until I realize, like a complete dumbass, that I need to talk to Luke. Because talking to Luke means getting through to Ben.

"Shit." I frantically hit redial and stand from the couch, walking around the back of it.

Nolan giggles at my choice word before turning back to his cartoon.

"Jesus fucking Christ. Finally!" Luke barks into my ear. I open my mouth to cut him down to size, and to remind him that we're not together, so I don't have to answer his calls, when his voice halts me. "Ben's been shot, Tessa. They're taking him to St. Joseph's hospital."

His words are like a kick to my diaphragm. I feel the air leave my lungs, and I don't register anything else coming through the phone. It's all white noise. Background gibberish from a guy that I don't really want to talk to anyway. The bones in my hand ache as I grip the phone tighter and stare at the back of Nolan's head.

Ben's been shot. Nolan. Mia. I somehow manage to take in a breath and find my voice.

"I'm on my way. I'll meet you there."

I hit end and run down the hall toward my bedroom, dialing Mia's number. I'm not even surprised at this point when it goes to voicemail. I try to keep my voice as calm as I can for her.

"Mia, Ben's been shot. He's been fucking shot. I don't know anything except that they're taking him to St. Joseph's hospital. Please call me. Please."

I hang up and grab my keys before sprinting back into the living room. "Nolan, come on. We gotta go."

He continues jumping on the couch. "I wanna watch dis." I grab him and feel his body tense in protest. "Noooo!" He flails in my arms, but I just hold him tighter as we head out to my car.

"Stop it, Nolan. We need to go see Daddy."

He immediately stops fighting me, and I immediately regret telling him where we are going. If something were to happen to Ben and Nolan doesn't get to see him, I'm not sure how I will handle that. Not only for him, but for me as well. And Mia. God, no. I can't think about that. Nothing was going to happen to him.

I fight back my tears and buckle Nolan in before peeling away from the house.

St. Joseph's hospital is thirty-five minutes away, but I get there in a little under twenty. I wanted to call my parents, but I couldn't inform them of Ben's situation with Nolan and his sonic hearing listening in, so I resorted to a text message. I knew I'd get an earful once they saw that this was the way I'd decided to fill them in, but it was my only option at the moment.

I manage to keep myself calm when I collect Nolan from the car and carry him into the hospital. But once the lady at the reception desk tells me Ben's room number, I sprint toward the elevators.

I don't know what condition I will find him in. He could be unconscious. Unrecognizable. Dead. I have no idea. I don't know the extent of his injuries, and I am willing to risk Nolan seeing his father in whatever state he is in, because I need to see him.

Once the elevator stops on my floor, I clutch Nolan against my side as I maneuver between the people in the hallway.

319. 319.

I'm scanning for Ben's room number as I pass every doorway. Finally, after what feels like a lifetime, I pass room 317 and know his room is next. I stop just before reaching his door, my heart pumping so loud it's causing tremors in my field of vision. I let out an unsteady breath and shift Nolan on my hip before filling the doorway.

I'm prepared for blood.

I'm prepared for the annoying constant beeping of machines and the sight of my brother bandaged up.

But this? I'm not prepared for this. Not after the multitude of emotions I've felt today.

My heart thunders in my chest at the sight of Ben, sitting up in bed while a nurse tends to his shoulder. He looks completely unharmed except for the deep gash that the nurse is stitching up. Luke is sitting next to him in a chair beside the bed, and as I step into the room, both pairs of eyes fixate on me.

"Daddy!" Nolan scrambles out of my arms and runs over to the bed, climbing up on it.

"What the hell is this?" I gesture with my hand toward my brother, getting a bewildered expression in return. "I thought you'd be dying. Or at least severely injured." I snap my head toward Luke who leans back in his chair in response to the anger behind my glare. "Jesus Christ, Luke. You think you could've mentioned that Ben was only suffering from a flesh wound! Do you have any idea how scared I was! How scared I've probably made Mia!"

"Where is Mia?" Ben asks, but his question goes unanswered when I continue contemplating how I'd like to inflict pain on the idiot in the room.

Luke's eyes shift from Ben's to mine. "I told you he was wearing his vest, thank Christ, and only took one to the arm. If he hadn't been wearing it, he'd probably be dead. Look at this thing." He reaches down and lifts Ben's police vest off the ground, numerous holes visible through the chest plate.

I put my hands on my hips. "You didn't say that. You only said he got shot and was en route to the hospital. Thanks for keeping the important details to yourself, asshole."

I don't want to admit to Luke that I had tuned him out sometime during our conversation. He could've told me that Ben was okay, and the thought of me not hearing it instead of him not saying it was maddening. I've freaked everyone out for no reason. This was all me. But he doesn't need to know that.

Ben grabs Nolan's head and covers his ears. "Really, Tessa? Could you not cuss around him? And where the fuck is Mia?" he harshly whispers, keeping Nolan completely oblivious.

Luke stands up and drops the vest on the bed. "God, I'm so sick of this shit from you. You break up with me for no Goddamned reason at all, and now you act like a complete bitch." He bridges the gap between us, bringing his face inches from mine. "Why did you end it? You owe me a reason and you're going to give it to me right fucking now."

"I don't owe you shit."

"Tessa!"

Luke and I both turn toward Ben's frantic voice.

The nurse who is working on him grabs his shoulder and pushes him back so he's reclining on the bed. He's still covering Nolan's ears, which is a good thing.

"Sir, you're going to have to keep still so I can finish this. If you yell like that again, I'm likely to stick this needle straight into your arm."

"Sorry," he says to her before looking back at me. "Where is she? Nothing else comes out of your mouth until you tell me where she is."

I ignore Luke's closeness and feel my stomach drop at the thought of my best friend. "Her mom was dying. She went out to get pancake mix for Nolan and got a call from her aunt. She's in Fulton."

The words come out like rapid fire, and as soon as I finish talking, Ben tries to get up. The nurse firmly pushes against his shoulder again. "Sir, I'm not finished."

He shrugs her off and shifts Nolan in his lap. "I don't care. I need to go."

"Mr. Kelly, you can't leave with an open wound. You're likely to get an infection. A nasty one at that. Let me finish stitching you up and we'll see if the doctor will release you."

He grunts and leans back, both fists clenching on his sheet. "Hurry. Up," he firmly directs her. His eyes pierce into mine. "Why didn't you call me? Why didn't she? She shouldn't be there, going through this, without me. One of us should be with her."

"I know that. I haven't been able to get a hold of her all day. She left me a message and asked me to try and get a hold of you because she couldn't reach you. And then I couldn't reach you. Where the hell is your phone?"

He looks at the vest on the bed and reaches for it, pulling out a barely held together phone. "Shit," he whispers, looking quickly at Nolan, who is now playing with the TV remote at the foot of the bed. He winces while the nurse continues to stitch him up. "Call her. Find out where she is and tell her I'm coming to get her."

I pull my phone out and notice the nonexistent reception I'm currently getting. "I have to step outside. Do you want me to take Nolan?"

"No. But I'll need you to watch him when I leave. I'm getting to Fulton in under four hours." He turns and watches the nurse, undoubtedly willing her to hurry the fuck up.

I nod and exit the room, hearing footsteps behind me. I turn, and Luke runs straight into me, grabbing me before I topple over. "Christ! What? I don't have time for this. I need to call Mia."

He keeps his grip on my arms. "Tell me why you broke up with me."

I'm sick of this. And I know Luke. He won't let this go until he gets what he wants.

Persistent little bastard. Just like when he has to get another orgasm out of me.

The nerve.

I pull my arms out of his grasp and grit my teeth. "I thought I was pregnant, you prick."

He leans back as if I've just slapped him across the face. "What? You did? When? Are you?" His voice is softer, the heat that was in it moments ago completely vanished.

I feel my body remembering that day and the pain I felt when I delivered the blow that broke us. The agony burns like acid in my mouth, coating my words. "No, I'm not. But I thought I was."

He holds his hands out in front of him, still seemingly clueless to why I ended things.

"I asked you if you ever saw yourself having kids someday and you said no. You said you never wanted what Ben had. And I want that." I bite my tongue to distract me from the pain of the memory.

His nostrils flare and he steps closer to me. "You broke up with me thinking you were pregnant? And you didn't think I should know about it? Do you know how fucked up that is?"

"You wouldn't have wanted it. You said…"

He steps into me and brings his face so close to mine; his breath tickles my eyelashes. "Don't tell me what I would've wanted," he growls. "Was there a chance it wasn't mine? Is that why you didn't tell me?"

His words are like venom coming out of his mouth. I gasp, stepping back and putting some distance between us. "No, there wasn't a chance it wouldn't have been yours. But since you're bringing it up, how many other girls were you sleeping with besides me? I should probably go get myself tested while I'm here."

He shakes his head and comes up beside me, stopping when his arm brushes against mine. "You should've told me," he snarls down at me.

He's never looked at me like this before. I can practically feel the revulsion coming off him. And then he's gone, moving down the hallway in the direction I was originally heading.

He chose not to satiate me with an answer to my question, but I suppose his silence answers for him.

I walk outside and quickly dial my parents' number after my phone beeps with a voicemail alert. My mother's casual voice throws me off, until she informs me that she hasn't read my text message due to the fact that they've both been asleep. However, that doesn't prevent the earful she gives me about not feeling the need to call her with that kind of information. She calms down eventually after I tell her Ben's okay, and only keeps me on the phone for a few minutes. After hanging up with her, I dial Mia's number. She picks up on the second ring.

"Oh my God. Is he okay? Please tell me he's okay."

Her panicky tone makes my heart shudder in my chest cavity. It's my fault she's so worried.

"Sweetie, he's fine. He's not really hurt at all. Just a minor cut on his arm."

She cries through the phone, her whimpers mixed with the noise of traffic. "Tessa, I thought… I thought I'd never see him again. I never got to tell him…" Her voice breaks apart in sobs, and it kills me.

"Shhh, Mia, it's okay. He's okay, I swear. He's fucking pissed as hell about not being there with you. And so am I. Are you okay?"

She pauses, taking in a few deep breaths. "I'm okay, I guess. She wasn't in any pain when she died. It was very peaceful, and I got to say goodbye. My last memories of her are of when she was healthy, so I have those to hold on to."

"I'm so sorry I wasn't there. And Ben's torn up about you going through this alone."

"I actually thought that maybe he didn't care about me. That he didn't care enough to call me when I needed him. And then when I got your message telling me he had been shot, God, Tessa, I almost died right there. I've never been that scared before."

I wipe the tear that had worked its way down my cheek. "Oh, sweetie. How could you think he doesn't care? He loves you. Hasn't he told you that?"

"No, not yet. It doesn't matter. I'm telling him as soon as I see him. I can't wait another second." Her voice sounds steady now, full of determination. When my best friend wants something, she goes for it. "I better get off here though before I get pulled over. I'm about two hours out, so tell Ben I'll be there soon."

"He's coming to you, Mia. I'm telling you right now, as soon as he's discharged, he's leaving here."

She sighs heavily. "Well, tell him to stay put."

"You've met him, right? I can't tell him anything when it comes to you."

She laughs slightly, sniffing at the end of her subdued chuckle. "Yeah. Just have him call me when he's leaving. I guess I'll meet him somewhere."

I walk toward the entrance to the hospital, having worked my way along the side during our conversation. "All right. I love you."

"I love you, too."

I end the call and pull up the voicemail, crying again when I hear her voice. And then she says it, "Tell him I love him, Tessa." And I stop the message.

This isn't for me. It's for him.

chapter twenty

Ben

I keep my eyes on Nolan as he fumbles with the TV remote. I need a distraction, and he's the only thing keeping me from jumping out of this bed and not giving a shit about my stitches. Every time I watch this nurse work the needle in and out of my skin, she seems to slow down. So I don't look. Because I need to get the fuck out of here.

I wasn't with her when she needed me.

It kills me to think that Mia couldn't get a hold of me. And worse than that, that there was a moment I considered not putting on my vest before that raid. Something could've happened. One of those bullets could've been fatal, and I'd never hold her again. I'd never see her face light up with her smile or the playful glint in her eye that teetered on seductive. My chest is on fire where the welts are forming, but the pain I'm feeling right now, being without her, is excruciating. I feel like a part of my soul is missing.

She's the best part of me, my entire future, and as soon as I see her, I'm saying it.

Tessa walks into the room, wiping underneath her eyes before giving me a nod. "I talked to her. She knows you're okay. And she seems okay now. Her mom wasn't in any pain when she died. She's on her way here."

Fuck. I wasn't there for her. Her mom died and I wasn't there.

The pressure forming in my chest intensifies. and I scoff at the nurse who seems to be taking her good old fucking time on my arm.

Tessa walks over to the bed, holding out her phone. "Here. You need to listen to this."

I take it from her with apprehension. "What is it?" She doesn't answer me as she walks over toward Nolan, and I place the phone up to my ear. Within seconds, my angel's voice fills me.

"I'm on my way. Oh, my God, please call me back and tell me he's okay. Tell him I love him, Tessa. Tell him I'm going to say that to him every second for the rest of his life. He'll never go another day without hearing those words from me." I hear her quivering breath before she pleads, "Please don't take him away from me."

The desperation in her voice nearly guts me. But those words, the words I've held off saying, have my heart slamming so hard against my sternum I'm certain it'll snap it in half. But I don't care if it does. I never want it to stop beating like this. I'd do fucking anything to keep feeling this way.

I need her. Now.

I start to move off the bed when the nurse slams her hand on my shoulder. "I have one more stitch. And then you'll have to wait to see if the doctor will release you. You have a lot of bruises from those bullets and you'll be in a lot of pain. You might want to think about going home with some medication."

I turn my head and make sure she is looking right into my eyes. I don't want to have to repeat myself.

"I don't care about the pain. I'll endure anything to get to the woman I fucking *breathe for*. She needs me, and as soon as you're finished with that last stitch, I'm going to her."

Her eyes widen slightly, and she steadies the needle against my shoulder. "But the doctor will want—"

"Tell him that I'm not waiting to get discharged. Say I went against orders. I don't give a shit." I look at my shoulder and then back at her. "It doesn't need to be pretty. Just finish it so I can get out of here."

She gets to it, and I hold Tessa's phone out to her.

She waves me off with her hand. "No. Take it. You'll need to call her so you two don't pass each other on the highway." She looks down at Nolan and smiles before looking back at me with a saddened expression. "Her message kind of killed me."

I rest my head back on the bed. "Yeah. It kind of killed me, too."

The nurse stands and pulls off her gloves after placing a bandage over my stitches. "All finished. I'll go grab the paperwork you need to sign."

I'm out of bed before she leaves the room and my speed startles her.

"Uh, you're not going to stick around and sign anything, are you?"

"Nope." I turn to Tessa who is scooping up Nolan as the nurse utters something under her breath while leaving the room. "You got him?"

"Yup. Go to her. But please be careful. I've suffered enough stress today."

I give Nolan a kiss before I sprint out of the room and down the long hallway to the stairwell. I'm out the door and running toward my truck that thankfully, Luke had made sure would be here for me when I was released. But it didn't matter. I'd fucking steal a car at this point to get to her. As soon as the bars register on Tessa's phone, indicating the reception, I dial Mia's number.

"Hey, I'm still like an hour and a half out. This traffic is ridiculous! Does nobody work anymore?"

I start up my truck and pull away from the hospital, the sound of her voice sending an ache throughout my entire body. "Baby," I whisper, my voice a strained plea. I hear her soft gasp, and then her staggered breathing fills my ear.

"Ben," she says through a soft cry.

My name on her lips blankets the pain I'm feeling right now. The pain that I've felt for the past several hours. Hope and pure need flood my senses, and I push my foot down on the gas pedal until it touches the floor.

"Oh, God, babe. I'm so happy to hear your voice. I was so worried."

"Angel, where are you? I'm getting on 215 right now."

"I'm on Route 7. Why don't you just wait there for me? We might pass each other."

I laugh slightly, my first laugh since yesterday. "There's no way I'll let you pass me, baby. Just keep driving to me and I'll find you."

She pauses for a beat, and I can almost see her fidgeting through the phone.

"Ben, I have to say it. I can't go another second without saying it to you."

Christ, I needed to say it, too. But not like this. Not fucking yet.

"Don't say it, Mia. I want to be looking into your eyes when I say it to you. And then you can say it back. Okay? Just hang on for me."

She sniffles several times. "Okay. But you better say it the second you see me or I'm saying it first. I've waited long enough for you, Benjamin Kelly. Don't make me wait anymore."

I shake my free hand out of the fist that is beginning to permanently set in. Knowing Mia is this close to me feels like having an itch I can't scratch.

"No more waiting, baby. I promise you that."

"Good." She pauses and a muted grunt fills the phone. "Shit, babe. My phone's about to die. I should get off here in case we completely miss each other and I need to call you. I'm actually betting on that happening."

"Don't doubt me, Mia. I'd find you anywhere."

The possessive hunger in my blood yearns to prove her wrong on this one. She won't need that phone again. I'm drawn to her like a fucking honing missile.

She laughs slightly. "Yeah, you better."

I knew I'd run into her on Route 7 somewhere.

It's the longest stretch of highway that connects Alabama and Georgia. I'm only looking out for one vehicle across the grass covered median that separates east and west bound. And as soon as that cherry red Jeep comes into my line of sight, I feel like someone plugs me into an outlet.

My entire body stiffens in anticipation as I cross the three lanes and drive my truck across the median. My back end fishtails several times given the speed I take it at, but it doesn't slow me down. I drive toward the direction of the traffic, still in the median, and the red Jeep darts off the highway in between cars and skids to a halt in the grass.

Christ, baby. If you got into an accident right now…

I slam on my emergency brake and jump out of my truck, leaving it on. She swings her legs out of the Jeep and hops down, steadying herself before taking off running in my direction.

Mia. Mia. Mia.

She slams against my chest, a whimpered moan escaping both of us as I cradle her to me. The pain she's causing against my welts is ignored. I can't let her go. Not yet. But I do ease her away from me and take a hold of her delicate face with both my hands.

She looks at me with desperation. To hold me. To talk to me. To fucking hear what I've kept from her. And I don't make her wait.

"I love you. I can't remember a moment when I didn't love you. I'm so sorry that I wasn't there for you when you needed me, but that'll never happen again. I can't be without you, angel. Please tell me you'll stay with me." I drop my forehead to hers and close my eyes. The magnitude of my love for her is crippling. "I can't say goodbye to you."

Her hands grab my wrists with a gentle squeeze. "I love you, too. And you'll never have to say goodbye to me. It was always supposed to be you in the bar that night, Ben. You were always meant to be my first, and my last. I can't imagine giving myself to anyone but you. Not now. Not ever."

I open my eyes when I feel the tears falling down my face.

She reaches up and wipes them away. "This is where I belong. Wherever you are. Always."

Her declaration has me struggling to stay upright. My knees feel weak enough to drop me. But she has me. She wraps her arms around my waist and places her head against my chest. I bury my face in her hair.

"We'll come back for your car. I'm not driving home in separate vehicles when I've been without you for this long."

She giggles against me, her face turning up and knocking me out with that smile. "It hasn't even been a whole day."

"Felt like a whole year. Come on."

I move her along the grass and help her up into my truck after securing her vehicle. There's no space between us, not anymore. And there never will be again.

She's against my side the entire drive home. Her head against my shoulder and my hand in her lap with both of hers holding on to me. I let her scent fill my lungs, feeling it calm me like a damn drug. Pain killers? No. I won't need any pain killers. She has me completely relaxed, every muscle in my body loose, until I feel her lips press against my neck.

She squirms against me, wiggling my hand down so it settles between her legs.

"Remember when you were so close to pulling over and taking me in your truck?" Her breath heats the skin below my ear, sending a jolt straight to my cock. "I want that. Right now." And then her hand is pressing on my massive erection, the one that is threatening to rip through my zipper.

I hiss through a moan as she works me through my shorts. "You want me to throw you in the back and fuck you on the side of the road?" I feel her nod against me as her teeth scrape against my ear. "Fuck. How wet are you right now?"

"Very." She grabs my hand and slips it under her dress, pressing my fingers against her panties. My cock becomes painfully hard at the feel of her arousal, and she moans when I press a finger against her clit. "Ben, please," she pants, digging her nails into my wrist as I twist my hand.

I slide underneath her panties and dip one finger into her. Her head falls back onto the seat with a shuddering gasp.

"Jesus Christ. Hold on, angel."

She protests with a whimper as I slip my finger out of her and pop it in my mouth.

I pull off on a back road that breaks into a secluded wooded area, parking my truck between the trees. I turn the truck off and unbuckle my seatbelt as she does the same.

"Climb over the seat and take that dress off. I want you naked and ready for me."

She complies with a gleeful chuckle, giving me a gorgeous view of her ass as she crawls into the back.

I step out of the truck and glance around. We're completely isolated. Good. Nothing is interrupting this. Opening the back door, I pull my cock out of my shorts before I climb inside. She's slipping off her panties, her dress discarded somewhere. Her hungry eyes focus on my dick that I'm slowly stroking while I watch her.

"You're so hard for me," she states with a fascinated tone. She reaches for me but quickly pulls her hands back. "Do you want me to do that? Or should I touch myself while you watch?"

Christ. That is tempting as hell. My cock jerks in my hand at the thought. But I'm suddenly hectic with the need to feel her around me. Nothing else will suffice right now. I grab her leg and pull her toward me, keeping my other hand on the base of my cock.

"Straddle me. I want those tits in my face."

I guide her over me, sliding my hands up her thighs as she grabs my cock and rubs it against herself, slicking the head. "Fuck, you feel amazing, baby," I grunt through a tense jaw. I lean in and lick her taut nipple, teasing it before drawing it into my mouth.

"Ben," she whispers urgently, shifting her weight forward and guiding me to her entrance. She grabs my face with both her hands, pulling me away from her breast, and locks eyes with me. "Watch me." Her mouth parts slightly as she lowers herself down, taking me to the hilt. "I love you."

I lean my head back and smirk. "Me? Or my cock?" Before she can answer, I grab her hips and lift her up, slamming her down on top of me five times with brute force. "You. Love. This?" I ask with my thrusts.

"Yes. God, yes."

When I finish, she takes the lead and digs her nails into my shoulders as she rocks against me.

"Easy, baby," I warn her when her hand presses against my stitches.

Her eyes go to the spot on my arm, and she raises the sleeve of my shirt. Her brow furrows with pain, maybe guilt. I'm not sure. She leans in, pressing her hand to my chest as she kisses the bandage. I wince at the pressure she puts on me and she notices. Her hands grab the bottom of my shirt. "Take it off."

I stop her from lifting it farther than my upper abs. "I'm fine. Just a little sore."

"I want to see it." She pulls with determination and I comply, shifting so she can lift it over my head. She inhales sharply, her eyes taking in the nine welts and the bruises that have formed around them. Her hand lies gently over the one welt that sits right in the middle of my chest. I see her lip tremble and reach up, cupping the side of her face. Her eyes meet mine with agony. "I could've lost you."

I pull her face toward me. "No. You'll never lose me. I told you that nothing could ever take me away from you." I brush my lips against hers and taste her tears on my tongue. "Don't cry. Not now. Be here with me, Mia."

She kisses me gently after wiping her tears away. "Make love to me. Just like you did that first night."

"You want me to be gentle?" I ask, snaking my arms around her waist. She nods before sliding off my lap and lying out on my back seat, legs spread. I shove my shorts and boxers down to mid-thigh before getting between her legs. "Guide me in, baby."

She smiles and reaches around me, pulling me straight into her.

I thrust my hips slowly, letting her feel every inch of me as I brace myself on my elbows. Her eyes flutter close and she arches against me, brushing her chest against mine with a deep inhale. I can feel her heart knocking against my chest, mimicking my beat. I kiss her jaw, her nose, her cheeks. Every inch of her face is touched by my lips. She lets me worship her body like it's the first time. My hands caress every part of her, my lips sliding along her skin. I commit her to memory. Her scent. Her taste. The way her body shudders against mine. The feel of her right now, beneath me while I drag this out, while I prolong this moment with her, this, fucking *this* is the reason for my existence.

With every breath I take, I take one for her.

She moans loudly and grabs my face, pressing her lips against mine. "I'm so close."

I move in her at the same pace. Not speeding up. Not taking her the way she's become accustomed to.

"Oh, God, Ben," she says against my lips, raking her nails down my back. "Please."

"I know, angel. I've got you." I slide my hand between us and press my thumb against her clit. She answers with a whimpered cry and I get her there. Right there with only a few strokes.

Her eyes open and she wraps her legs around me. "I don't want to come without you." She barely gets her sentence out before her body tightens around me. "Ben…"

I groan loudly and feel my orgasm burning up my spine. "Holy shit." I watch her lips part with a silent cry, eyes closing as the pleasure builds, and push her knees back, needing to get deeper. My breath is stolen from me as I go off inside her, driving into her to the point of exhaustion. Giving her every piece of me. And even though I was tender and unhurried, it rocks me with a blinding intensity.

The kind I've only ever felt with Mia.

I collapse on top of her, resting my head on her chest. Her arms wrap around me and hold me tighter. Closer. Never close enough. I can't imagine loving her any more than I do right now, but I know I will. Because every second I'm with her, I fall harder. It's how it's always been between us. Even when I held myself back. I loved her when she became my best friend. And given the chance, I'd never change the way it happened. I'd never take back those weeks I suffered in silence, wanting more than she was willing to give me. I'd give her that a thousand times over if she needed it. A future with her was more than I'd ever deserve.

And I'll cherish her like the gift she is until I draw my last breath.

chapter twenty-one

Mia

"You know, before this whole thing started between the two of you, you technically were mine for the summer," Tessa says as she helps me pack up my stuff in the bedroom I've occupied for the past two months. "I mean, I don't see the harm in you finishing out your time here with me and then moving in with Ben after the summer's over."

"Because he'd be so quick to agree to that arrangement," I state with a soft chuckle.

I knew there was no way in hell he'd go along with me prolonging my move. It's all he's talked about for the past five days. I'm actually surprised he's given me this long.

"And you act like I won't be right around the corner. You do realize I'm here permanently, right?"

She smiles over her shoulder as she grabs the clothes that are hanging in the closet. "That's not the point. I love that you two are together, but he's a horrible sharer. He always has been."

I take the clothes from her and pull them off the hangers. "Have you talked to him?"

"Who?" I give her a knowing look and she rolls her eyes. "Why would I talk to him? There's nothing to talk about. It's over."

Her words are final, but I know Tessa. She's hurting. She'll never admit it, but she misses him. "Isn't tonight going to be weird? Seeing him at the concert?"

She shrugs once before taking the hangers back to the closet. "There's going to be like, five thousand people there. I can avoid him in a crowd that size. Plus, I plan on getting shitfaced, which is sure to help with the situation." She closes the closet door before dropping her forehead, hitting the wood with a soft thud.

"Tessa…"

"I don't want to talk about it." She lifts her head and turns toward me, her eyes giving away exactly what she's feeling. "Okay?"

I nod. "Okay."

We finish packing up my room in silence. I know when she's ready to talk about it, she'll open up. And she knows that I'm here whenever that time comes.

My aunt is taking care of selling my mom's house for me, allowing me to stay in Alabama during the process. Ben and I will be making a trip to get the rest of my things soon, but to be perfectly honest, I have everything I'll ever need. I never imagined moving back to Ruxton, but now I can't imagine not living here.

This was always my home. Wherever he was.

After loading my stuff into my Jeep so that I can take it straight to Ben's after the concert, Tessa and I head over to the field.

Ben somehow managed to snag tickets to see Luke Bryan. Lawn seats, which allows us to park in the field overlooking the stage and sit in our vehicles while we enjoy the music. I spot Ben's truck after weaving in and out of the crowd and park next to it, watching as he jumps out of the bed and walks over to my door.

"Hey, baby. You all packed up?" He opens my door for me and I hop out, waving to Reed who Tessa is making her way toward.

I take his hand and let him lead me to the back of his truck. "Yup. Everything's in the Jeep. Your sister's not too happy about it."

He stifles a laugh as he drops the tailgate down. "Like that would stop me from moving you in with me. Here. Up you go."

I climb up into the back of his truck, spotting the pillows and the blankets spread out for us. I turn to him with a smile. "Am I getting lucky during this concert?"

He wraps his arms around my waist and kisses my bare shoulder. "I'm always prepared, angel. My girl seems to be a bit insatiable lately."

"You're like a dirty little boy scout," I add, hearing Tessa's laugh get louder behind me. I turn in Ben's arms and spot her walking over toward us with Reed.

"Hey. I'm really glad you guys worked your shit out. You sucked as friends," Reed says through a teasing smile.

I flip him off over Ben's shoulder and he throws his head back with a laugh. Just as Tessa opens her mouth to speak, another truck pulls up alongside Ben's and catches her attention.

"Oh, perfect. He couldn't have gotten lost on the way here?"

Ben's chest shakes with laughter against my back as his hands splay across my abdomen. "We've been here a thousand times. I doubt he'd get lost."

Tessa's body goes rigid suddenly, and I turn my head to see why.

Luke isn't the only one emerging from his truck. A tall, leggy blonde is at his side as he joins the group, stopping just a few feet short of Tessa and Reed.

He shifts his gaze from Tessa to Ben and then to me. "Guys, this is Brandie. Brandie, this is... everyone." She waves her delicate hand, the one that isn't currently roaming freely over his chest. Luke wraps his arm around her waist. "We're going to head closer to the stage. We'll catch up with you guys later."

As he walks away with little Miss Handsy, Tessa slams the tailgate of the truck up and startles the three of us. "Well, she seems lovely. He's really scraping the bottom of the barrel now, isn't he?"

Reed shrugs once. "I don't know. She's pretty hot."

She glares at him and he steps back a bit. "Yeah, she's really got that street corner look down. And could her name be any more whorish?"

"You'd think that if her name was Mary," Ben says. "Stop being jealous, Tessa. You broke up with him."

She waves him off and grabs Reed's hand. "Whatever. Let's go get several hundred beers. You guys want any?" she directs toward us, her face still tense with bitterness.

"I'm good," I say, looking back at Ben who is situating the pillows and spreading the blanket out.

"Me too," he adds.

Tessa and Reed disappear into the crowd.

I turn around just in time to see Ben reach through his back window and pull out a picture frame. He smiles at me and sits down on the blanket with his back against a pillow. He reaches for me with his free hand. "Come here, angel."

"Whatcha got there?"

He pats the spot between his legs. and I sit with my back against his chest, drooping my arms over his legs. He places the frame in my lap. "Don't cry," he whispers against my ear.

I tilt the frame up and look at the drawing. Three figures, undoubtedly drawn by Nolan, depicting our family. My family. He even labeled me as Pwincess Mia Mommy. And the tears come instantly. I can't help it.

"Your artistic skills are horrendous." I reach up and wipe underneath my eyes as Ben laughs against me. "God, he is the sweetest, isn't he? Can we hang it up at your house?"

"Our house," he corrects me. He presses his mouth to my hair again. "Don't cry, baby."

I open my mouth to tell him that I can't not cry at seeing our first family drawing, but he wipes every word from my vocabulary when he places a small box in my lap.

You know, the kind of box that every girl recognizes.

I gasp softly, holding the frame tightly against my chest while my eyes stay glued to the box.

His steady hands open it. "Do you know how much I love you?"

I nod and clutch the frame harder, feeling the tears well up in my eyes. I blink them away and focus on the ring that he's holding between his fingers. "As much as I love you," I choke out.

"No, angel. No one has ever loved anyone as much as I love you. I got you beat there, I'm afraid." He motions for my hand and I place it in his, allowing him to slip the ring on my finger. "You're my best friend, Mia. I want you every day, for the rest of my life. I will always cherish every moment you give me. Marry me, baby."

I'm nodding and whispering "yes" before he even finishes. And then he's turning me and cradling me against his chest, worshipping me with kisses all over my face. "Thank you," I say against his lips.

I feel them curl up into a smile. "For what?"

I kiss along his jaw up to his ear. "For being at the bar that night. For being the guy that you are. For giving me Nolan." I pull back and cradle his face in my hands. "Can we have more babies?"

He brings my hand up to his lips and kisses the back of it. "Can we start right now?"

And then I'm on my back, his body covering mine. I laugh against him as he brushes my hair away from my face. "We're in the middle of a field."

"Don't care. Nobody can see us anyway. Look how high up we are."

"Yes, but I've been told I'm rather noisy," I tease as he kisses my neck. He grunts once and nips at my sensitive skin there. "I love you."

"Love you."

"I want lots of babies."

His head comes up and he smiles widely. "Lots." He shifts his weight and lays his head on the pillow, pulling me so I'm lying against his chest.

And we stay like that long after Tessa and Reed return. Long after the concert starts and ends. Until we're the only vehicle left in the field. He makes love to me under the stars, his tenderness breaking into a wild frenzy when we both need it. It's perfect. And I'm right where I belong.

Where I always will be.

epilogue

Ben

Mia: *Meet me at our spot.*

I stare down at my phone, reading the text message for the second time.

Our spot. What spot? As far as I'm concerned, every spot I've taken Mia to has become our spot. And we've racked up a lot of spots over the past four months.

I go to reread her text again when my phone beeps.

Mia: *The bar, Ben.*

I shake my head with a laugh.

Me: I would've figured it out. What have I told you about doubting me?

Mia: *Just hurry up before one of the other men in here takes me home.*

Me: Mia...

Mia: *Kidding. Hurry though.*

I'm in the parking lot within ten minutes, pulling up next to her Jeep. It's about as crowded as it was the night Mia became mine, but I spot her on that same stool she occupied all those months ago. I don't go to her though. Instead, I go to the side of the bar where she can't see me and watch her without her knowing.

She's tapping the bar anxiously with her fingers, looking over her shoulder every few seconds toward the door. Her hair is down, and she's wearing a shirt that has my eyes going from her chest to her face and back again. I motion for the bartender.

"Can you send one of those purple drinks to that girl right there for me?"

He nods and gets to work on her drink while she pulls her phone out with a scowl. My phone beeps.

Mia: *I mentioned today, right?*

Me: You're so fucking beautiful. Do you know that?

Just as my message goes through, the bartender sits the drink down in front of her. She smiles at him, looking at the drink and then glancing at her phone. Her eyes immediately find mine across the bar, and I make my way to her. My hand brushes along her back, and I claim my spot.

"You looked thirsty from where I was standing. Thought I'd help you out," I say with a smile.

She places her one hand on my knee. "I need to talk to you about something."

I tilt my head and push her drink closer to her. "And what is that?"

"We need to move the wedding up." She grabs the straw between her fingers and dunks it in and out of her drink.

"Why? I thought you wanted a summer wedding? I mean, I'm all for stealing you away right now and making you my wife, but you seemed pretty dead set on the date."

She smiles and pushes her drink away, motioning for the bartender. He stops in front of us and gives me a friendly nod before looking at her. "I'm sorry. Can you make this nonalcoholic? I can't drink this."

"Sure thing," he says, taking her glass away.

She hits me with a smile and grabs my hand, laying it across her stomach. "Ben."

"Hmm?" I'm still trying to piece together why she suddenly doesn't want the drink that she so eagerly consumed our first go-around. It takes me a minute to focus on my hand. My eyes meet hers and she smiles. And then it clicks. "Baby, are you pregnant?" The hope in my voice dominates over the sudden anxiousness that begins to brew in my gut.

"I really don't want to be the size of a house when I'm walking down the aisle to you. So, I was thinking maybe a spring wedding instead? I'd be five months by then."

"Angel." I'm on my knees in the middle of the bar, pressing my face against her stomach. "Please tell me I'm not hearing you wrong."

She giggles against me and turns my face up. "You're not hearing me wrong. Nolan's going to be a big brother."

My senses are flooded with a need to protect this woman and my baby that she's carrying. "We need to get out of here."

"Why? This is our spot."

I shake my head and stand, grabbing some money out of my wallet and paying for the drink she won't be consuming. "There's people smoking. And it's really loud."

She laughs and puts her hand in mine, allowing me to lead her outside. "Babe, I don't think the noise level in here is going to hurt the baby. He's barely the size of a peanut right now."

I stop in the middle of the parking lot, spinning around. "He?"

She smiles up at me and places her hands on my chest. "Just a gut feeling I have. It's too early to tell."

I wrap my arms around her, staring down at the woman that I'll give my life for.

"You're going to put me in a bubble for the next nine months, aren't you?"

I kiss her forehead, pulling her against my chest. "I'll do whatever's necessary," I say.

And she doesn't argue with me. She allows me to hold her right where we stood that night. Before I knew she'd change my life. Before I knew I was holding the woman I was going to marry.

My future. My forever.

All mine.

The End

a message from the author

Hi! Thank you so much for reading *Where I Belong*! I hope you enjoyed Ben and Mia's story as much as I enjoyed writing it. Please consider leaving a review! I'd love to hear what you thought.

#BamaBoysForever

xo, J

acknowledgements

My family, thank you to my family for your continuous support. To my ridiculously amazing husband. You, YOU are my favorite thing in the entire world. I'm a bit crazy about you. Heads up.

To all the amazing blogger friends I've made so far, thank you. SERIOUSLY, I can't even express how much you all mean to me. Beth Cranford, Kylie McDermott, Smexy, Lisa Jayne, Maree Hunter, Karrie Puskas, and countless more. Did I just name drop? Oh, fuck yes I did. You all have showed me so much love ever since I published Sweet Addiction and I will never be able to thank you enough. To Give Me Books for everything you've done for me. I heart you girls. Now, all of you come to Maryland so I can hug you. Now. Do it.

R.J. Lewis, for always being there. Even when I'm stressing out. Even when I'm really stressing out. My cell phone bill has reached a new high due to our international text messages and I love it. However, if I don't get a new book from you soon, I might become hostile. :)

Trish Tess, thank you for showing me so much love. You, my little friend, are the sweetest.

To the best readers a little indie author could ask for, thank you for taking a chance on me and for all your kind words. Your support means the world to me, and I wish I could hug each and every one of you.

Thank you again,
J

also by

J. DANIELS

SWEET ADDICTION SERIES

Sweet Addiction
Sweet Possession
Sweet Obsession

ALABAMA SUMMER SERIES

Where I Belong
All I Want
When I Fall
Where We Belong
What I Need
All We Want

DIRTY DEEDS SERIES

Four Letter Word
Hit the Spot
Bad For You
Down Too Deep

about the author

J. Daniels is the *New York Times* and *USA Today* bestselling author of the Alabama Summer, Dirty Deeds and Sweet Addiction series.

Best known for her sexy, small-town romances, her debut novel, Sweet Addiction, was first published in 2014 and went on to become an international bestseller. Since then, she has published more than ten novels, including the Dirty Deeds series with Forever Romance.

Daniels grew up in Baltimore and currently lives in Maryland with her husband and two kids. A former full-time Radiologic Technologist, she began writing romance after college and quickly discovered a passion for it. You'll still catch her in scrubs every now and then, but most of her time is spent writing these days—a career she is eternally grateful for.

Always an avid reader, Daniels enjoys books of all kinds, but favors Romance (of course) and Fantasy. She loves hiking, traveling, going to the mountains for the weekend, and spending time with her family.

To receive an email when she releases a new book, sign up for her newsletter! bit.ly/jdaniels_newsletter

She loves meeting and interacting with her readers. Visit her website to see where you can find her! www.authorjdaniels.com

SOCIAL MEDIA:

Facebook: bit.ly/jdaniels_facebook

Instagram: bit.ly/jdaniels_instagram

Twitter: bit.ly/jdaniels_twitter

Reader's Group: bit.ly/jdaniels_readersgroup

Goodreads: bit.ly/jdaniels_goodreads

tempting the boss

NATASHA MADISON

chapter one

Lauren

Beep, Beep, Beep. My hand snakes out from underneath the warm cocoon of my blankets. Grabbing my phone from the side table, I shut it off and bring it under the blankets with me. Seven minutes later, I feel it vibrate under my pillow between my hands.

Pulling myself up and swinging my legs out of the bed, I walk downstairs, going straight for the coffee machine. Thank god for this programmed machine, because the coffee is ready for me to drink.

I blink my eyes a couple of times while I turn on the light over the stove. With it lightly dimmed, I lean against the counter and look at the clock. Five thirty on the nose. Smelling the coffee, I slowly take a sip to not burn my tongue. My brain jolts awake as the hot, strong brew rolls over my tongue.

It's the calm before the storm. In thirty minutes, I will have to get the kids up and get them ready for the bus that is always here at exactly seven ten.

I look into the dining room, taking in the hurricane that is my children. Opened backpacks linger on the floor near the chairs, papers are tossed on the table, homework they finished but haven't put away. No matter how much I tell them to clean up the table before they go to sleep, Gabriel, who is ten, and Rachel, who is six and a half going on twenty, always leave it until the last minute. Something they inherited from their father.

I look around the house—the open concept floor plan makes it easy to see into the rooms around me—taking in the changes that the house has gone through in the last six months. No more men's sneakers at the door. No more suit jackets hanging on the back of the chair at the table blending in with the backpacks.

Nope. Nothing. Nada. Taking another sip of the coffee, I let my mind wander to when it all changed.

Walking up to the children's school for the parent/teacher interview, I am running late, of course. I had to pick up Gabriel from soccer practice, while rushing Rachel to gymnastics, then we grabbed McDonald's in the car on the way home. Eating my cheeseburger in the car is why I now have a mustard stain on my shirt. Pulling a scarf that I find in my back seat, I throw it over my neck hoping it covers the stain.

Once in the school, I make my way to the classroom of Gabriel's teacher. I run down a list of things that I need to get done when I get home. Thinking about the birthday parties that the kids are invited to this weekend. The gifts are already sitting in the trunk waiting to be wrapped. I hope that Jake will at least be available on Sunday.

Stay-at-home mom. That is my job, and I love it. Sometimes. Most times. More days than not. My husband, Jake, is an ad executive in the biggest marketing firm in the city. He spent the last eight years working his way up the ladder. His long work hours are our sacrifice until he gets that corner office, then he can cut back a bit. At least that's what he keeps saying. I still stand by my conclusion he is a workaholic.

We met when I was fresh out of college; I had just started working at the same agency he did. Not the one he's with now, but the first agency he worked at after college. I was hired as the office temp assistant. Since it was a small office of only five, it was normal that we spent all day together. Those long hours together resulted in us becoming good friends. Becoming a couple was the natural next step. I don't think it surprised anyone when we walked in on a Monday morning holding hands, both of us looking at each other with our hearts in our eyes.

Getting to Ms. Alvarez's door, I knock once and then walk in. Looking around, I'm shocked to see Jake sitting in one of the chairs in front of the desk, while Ms. Alvarez sits in hers.

Walking up to him, I lean down and kiss him on the lips. "Hey, I didn't know you would be here," *I say, sitting down in the chair next to him.*

He nods at me and then looks down at his shoes. I don't know how to describe what came next, except to say that my world crashed around me. It's like my heart knew it. It's like my body knew it had to go into protection mode.

"Lauren," *he says still looking at his shoes. I look down at them wondering what he is looking at exactly. I will never forget them. Brown, with light brown laces. Stain free, scuff free. Clean.*

It is at this point I start to panic, start to think something is wrong. "What's the matter?" *I ask him and then look over at Ms. Alvarez. She is gorgeous, with beautiful thick, black curly hair that is always styled perfectly. Whether she wears it in a ponytail or loose, you can't help but envy her fantastic hair. She always looks so put together, but right, now she's looking at my husband nervously as she blinks away tears and her hands clasped together in her lap are shaking.*

"I've met someone." *The breath I have been holding rushes from my lungs. My legs go so weak, I feel it so strongly even though I am sitting. My heart is beating so hard and fast, I hear it echo in my ears. My mouth gets dry and my hands start to tremble as I feel that heart starting to break.*

"What?" *I look at him and then at Ms. Alvarez.* "Jake, now is not a good time. Not here." *It's like I'm begging him to not tell me. Like I'm begging him to take it back.*

"I love her," *he says with a whisper, and then all the pieces to the puzzle start coming together. Gabe's tutoring classes that Jake would always pick him up from—the ones they'd always be late getting home from. I look at my son's teacher and see a tear run out of the corner of her eye while she smiles at my husband. My fucking husband—the one who made vows to me. The one who promised to love, honor, and cherish me for the rest of his life.*

"You?" *I say to him and then look at her.* "You slept with my husband?" *I ask her while I feel Jake's hand on top of mine. I shake it off, not wanting to feel his touch right now. Not wanting him to try to comfort me.*

"It was me. I started this. I did this, not Camilla." He tries to reach out and touch me again. Getting up from the chair, I start to pace the room. Thoughts running through my mind. How did I not know? How did I not suspect? Was it because I was too tired for sex? Was it because I still needed to lose the extra ten pounds that I had lingering on me? Was it because I was too tired at the end of the day to even talk to him?

Stopping in my tracks, I look at them. He has now stood up and so has she. A desk still separates them. "We had sex last night," I tell him, and he doesn't continue to look at me; instead, he looks at her.

"It was the last time. Kind of a good-bye kind of thing," he says, now looking at the ground.

"A good-bye thing." I now raise my voice. "A good-bye thing?" I shake my head. "How long? How long has this been going on? How long have you been sleeping with your student's married father?" My voice is firm, anger starting to rush through me.

"Lauren, let's not—" he tries to say, but I don't give him a chance. I yell, and this time loudly, "How long? How long have you been sleeping with her and coming home to me? How long have you been telling me you love me and lying about it? How fucking long, Jake? How much of my life is a lie?"

They both look at each other. "Seven months," he answers right before there is a knock on the door. The principal sticks his head inside "Oh. Mr. and Mrs. Watson, is everything okay?" The poor man doesn't see anything coming.

"Oh, we are totally fine." My voice starts to rise, while my hands start to shake. "I've come to attend my son's parent/teacher conference only to be told his teacher is fucking my husband. Looks like in addition to tutoring her students in math, she also offers sex ed lessons to their fathers! She deserves a raise." I laugh humorlessly. Maybe I'm having a stroke. Maybe, just maybe, this is all a dream. "But other than that, I would say everything is perfect."

I walk to the chair that I have been sitting in, picking up the purse that fell off my shoulder while my life fell apart. Grabbing it, I turn to walk out as Jake grabs my wrist. "Lauren, wait."

I yank my wrist away from him, the force shocking both of us. "Don't fucking touch me," I hiss before I walk past the principal and right into the hallway, where I'm greeted by the president of the PTA, Colleen.

The tears have now started to freely fall down my cheeks. "Oh, honey, I just heard." I look at this woman who I thought was actually my friend. I tilt my head to the side. "You knew?" I don't really need her to answer, since she puts her head down to look at her hands she is wringing together.

I can't stop the angry laugh that bursts from my mouth. I'm that oblivious spouse who everyone makes fun of. I'm that wife who said it would never happen to me. I'm that woman who they all feel sorry for. I'm her. That poor, clueless woman who can't seem to keep her husband from falling dick first into a sexy, twenty-something woman. I look around to see who else is looking at us.

The secretary, the principal, Colleen, and four of her posse, who are there trying to get *parents to join the PTA, Jake, and her. "Does everyone know he was having an affair? Was I the only one who didn't know?" I throw my hands out to the side, turning on my heel as I walk out of the school, vowing never to return.*

I get in my car and make one phone call to Kaleigh, my sister. I don't know how much she understands between the sobs and the yelling, but ten minutes later when I pull up to the curb of my perfect house, she is there throwing Jake's clothes out of our bedroom window. They land right in the front of my house on the lawn.

It takes her a full five minutes to toss everything out. I stand there, still in shock, still in a daze, looking at the mountain of his clothes. Clothes I bought him. Clothes I picked out. Clothes I washed, ironed, and put away. I don't see Kaleigh come from the side of the house with the gasoline container in her hand. I just see her pouring it all over his clothes. She walks over to me, handing me the packet of matches. "Let's burn this motherfucker down."

And we do. Till one of the neighbors calls the fire department, who rush out, three full trucks, lights blaring in the night, an EMT, and one police cruiser. I sit there on my lawn, watching the flames rising up from the pile of everything that he owns before the whole mess is drenched in water.

The second alarm sounds, bringing me out of my trip back into that nightmare.

"Gabe! Rachel! Time to get up, guys! Mommy starts her new job today," I yell up, hoping they hear me. I take another sip of my coffee before I make my way upstairs to get ready for my new job. Yay me.

chapter two

Lauren

I LOOK AT MYSELF IN THE MIRROR, SMOOTHING THE FRONT OF MY SKIRT DOWN. WHAT A difference six months make. Gone is the extra weight that had been lingering on my petite frame for the last six years, thanks to some cardio at the gym and the fact that I stopped eating. You would think that your husband leaving you would have you drowning your sorrows in carbs, ice cream, and cheese, but it was actually quite the opposite for me. On the rare occasion I actually have a little bit of an appetite, the second I put something in my mouth, I feel sick. So, I am getting there slowly but surely. I have grown out my hair, adding layers into it instead of just the 'mom bob' I had been sporting. I also added some golden, honey-colored highlights.

I've dressed in a tight, grey knee-length pencil skirt that I paired with a light pink silk shirt with a ruffled collar and cap sleeves. I've added my very favorite Manolo Blahnik black Mary Janes, a Mother's Day present from three years ago. If nothing else, he left me with two beautiful children and a closet full of designer heels.

I take a deep breath. This is it.

My phone beeps again. "Ten minutes, guys, let's go." I walk out of my room, heading down the stairs while watching my ten-year-old put his cereal bowl in the sink and grab all his papers from the table, shoving them in his backpack. "Rachel, don't forget to pack your reading log that's on the couch."

I look over at my sister, who is nursing her second cup of coffee. She sits with her legs crossed, watching it all. Dressed in her yoga pants that mold perfectly to her thin, five-foot-seven-inch body and a loose sweater that falls off one shoulder. "How do you remember this stuff?" she asks.

"It's magic. Once you become a parent, you'll get a brain," I tell her with a smirk.

"Then what happened to Jake?" She smiles back while taking a sip.

"Okay, I take that back. Once you become *a mother*, you get a brain. I mean, I don't think all men are dicks. Look at Dad," I tell her while I put the milk back in the fridge and pick up the cereal box, putting it back into the cupboard. My phone alarm sounds again. "Two minutes, guys!" I have my phone set to different times so I never run late. It's another thing I got when I became a mom.

I look over at Kaleigh, who is now reading the newspaper. "Aren't you going to be late?" I ask her while I grab the lunch boxes and walk to the door with the kids.

She folds the paper in half. "Nope, I have a client at ten thirty. We are doing yoga in the park today. Become one with the earth and all that." She does the Namaste hands, while I walk out with the kids to go to the bus stop.

I hold Rachel's hand while we walk to the bus stop, her brown hair done in a side ponytail with a huge flower headband. "Don't forget, Auntie Kay will be there when you get off the bus this afternoon, because Mommy has the new job." She looks up and smiles at me, one tooth missing. "I know, Momma, you said it. Twice." I look in front and see that Gabe is talking to another kid who is waiting at the bus stop. Once the kids get on the bus, I wave to them and turn to go home.

Mrs. Flounder, who is my next-door neighbor, comes out with curlers in her hair and a cigarette hanging from her lips. "Hey, there, Lauren, you look fantastic. Is today the day you finally become free of that scum bucket?" she asks while picking up her paper.

The news that Jake cheated on me spread faster than the flames did over the pile of his gasoline-soaked clothes. Of course, once it was confirmed that Camilla slept with a father of one of her students, she was quietly transferred to another school. She is now teaching at another school a town over.

Telling the kids that we were getting a divorce was hard, but they didn't seem surprised by it. I guess half of their friends' parents were divorced, so it wasn't unusual to them. I, on the other hand, didn't have such an easy time with the idea. I honestly thought forever meant forever, not till someone sexier waves their ass in my face and shows me attention. Maybe if he'd come home and done the vacuuming once in a while, I would have showed him some attention. Fuck, maybe if he'd picked up his sweaty socks, I might have felt inclined to do even more for him.

Shaking my head no at Mrs. Flounder, I look at her. "I start my new temp position today."

"Oh, that's nice, dear. Time to earn the bacon." She shakes her hand and goes inside. Once I get back inside, I grab my lunch and my purse. I look at Kaleigh, who is now in the middle of my living room doing some crazy yoga pose. "I'm so fucking nervous. What if I fuck up or cry or, or, or… fuck up?" I look at her while she moves back to standing instead of balancing on her head.

"You are going to go in there and kill it. And if you don't"—she shrugs her shoulders—"then you don't. What's the worst that can happen? You fall face first in your boss' crotch?" I glare at her, throwing my hands in the air.

"Don't forget, the kids are off the bus at two forty-five. Did you set an alarm?" I ask her.

"Yup, on my internal clock." She rolls her eyes at me. "Stop stressing. It's going to be fine. You are going to be late if you don't leave now." She ushers me out the door. "Don't forget to play nice and make friends. Friends who are nice and hot and have big dicks!" She screams after me as I get into my car and close the door. Mrs. Flounder gives me the thumbs up, clearly in agreement with my sister. "Dear God," I mumble to myself as I start the car.

I shouldn't use the word 'car', because this isn't a car, it's a minivan. A big, safe, screams-it's-for-a-family vehicle. I obviously got this in the divorce settlement, while he drives around in his new Mercedes, which is not for families. It's for cheating bastards who only get their kids every other weekend and once during the week.

Making my way to work, I'm stuck in a bit of light traffic. Nothing that is bumper-to-bumper, just flowing slowly. My eyes keep traveling between the clock and the GPS on the center console, as well as the occasional peek at the GPS on my phone, which just so happens to calculate the traffic between where I am and my destination.

I'm singing along to Maroon Five's "Don't Wanna Know" when a call comes in. Penelope's name flashes on the screen. Penelope is my friend from college, the only friend who I kept in touch with. She runs an HR firm that specializes in placing temps. She is the reason I have this job right now.

"Hello," I say while I wait for her voice to fill the car.

"Hey, there, just checking in. You ready?" she asks me. I hear her rustling papers in the background, so I know she is already at her desk.

"Yup, I'm on my way there now. I'm so nervous, I may puke, though. But I'll be on time." I chuckle at the thought of me barfing all over my new boss. I brake for the traffic that is slowing to a crawl in front of me when I feel my van jerk forward slightly. My head flies forward and then snaps back. Looking in my mirror, I see that someone just hit me.

"Oh my god. Someone just ran into me. Fuck me, P. I have to call you back," I say, unlocking my seatbelt and climbing out of the car.

I put my Tory Birch sunglasses on top of my head, walking to the back to see the damage. I don't even have time to get there before I hear a raspy voice ask, "What the hell is wrong with you? You just stopped!" I put a hand over my eyes to block the sun and see him. And boy, do I see him. My heart skips a beat when he whips his aviator sunglasses off his face.

He's about six feet tall, maybe taller, with dark hair that's short on the sides and a bit longer at the top, which almost looks like it was combed back by his hands. His eyes are a mossy green with shimmery gold flecks in them that I can see thanks to the sun hitting them just right. A freshly-shaven face that shows off the strong angles of his jaw and hints at where I'm sure a five-o'clock-shadow of delicious stubble will emerge in a few hours.

He's wearing a suit minus the jacket. His dark blue pants are a perfect fit, molding to him like they were made especially for him, and from the looks of them, they probably were. His crisp, white dress shirt is open at the collar and covers his broad chest and thick biceps. His sleeves are rolled up to his elbows and show off a big, masculine silver Rolex watch.

He throws his hand up as he angrily asks, "Is something wrong with you? Are you drunk?"

I take a step back, putting my hand to my stomach. "Are you talking to me?" I look around wondering if there is someone else he could be talking to. "You hit me. You. Hit. Me." I storm to the back of the car to assess the damage. I see that my bumper is a bit scratched, but his Porsche is going to need some body work.

"I can't believe this. I can't flipping believe this! Now I'm going to be late because you were probably too busy on your phone texting to pay attention to the road." I walk to my car, opening the door and leaning across the seat to grab my purse. Cars pass us slowly, everyone taking a look to see what's going on.

Looking at the clock on the dash, I see that I have to be at my new job in twenty minutes. Grabbing my license, registration, and insurance ID card, I slam the door and walk over to see him leaning on the side of *my* car, watching me.

"I'm going to be late. Is there any way we can just exchange numbers and get all the information after?" I ask, looking through the papers.

I hear him huff. "You probably don't have insurance, which is why you want to call me later so you can get some while I drive around with a missing a light." He walks over to his car, leans down, and grabs his phone from the driver's seat.

I look at him. "So, you weren't on the phone? Riiighhhhttt," I say glaring at him.

"I don't have all day. Some of us have actual work to do. What do you want from me?" His tone is snarky.

"Actually, I don't want anything from you. My car has a scratch, yours is the one that is damaged. Besides, it wasn't even my fault. Maybe we should call the police to make a report so we can get it on the record that you were driving while texting." I lean my head to the side. "I'm not a police officer or anything, but I think that's against the law."

He snarls at me, "Just give me your number." I tell him my number, and when he asks my name, I gladly tell him. "The woman whose car you hit because you were texting while driving." He looks at me and his eyebrows pinch together. "Is that name already taken?" I ask him, waiting for his answer. When I realize he isn't going to reply, I ask him, "Now, what's yours?" He shoots off his number, and I store it in my phone.

I turn around to walk away. "Aren't you going to ask me my name?" He puts his hands on his hips, his biceps bulging and his chest looking impossibly broader.

"Nope, no need. I just put you under 'Asshat who texts while driving and hit my car.'" I smile at him. "Have a fabulous day," I grumble, turning around and getting back in the car.

Fuck. I see that I now have ten minutes to get there. I dial Penelope right after I buckle and take off watching the asshole get into his car. "I think I might still make it," I tell her even before she says hello.

"It's okay. I called and told them there was an accident on the way, and they said not to worry, that Austin was going to be late, too. So, you're still good to go. How's the damage?" she asks.

"Minivan: 1 – Porsche: 0." I laugh and tell her I'll check back in with her at lunch.

When I finally make it to the office building, I check my face and apply lip gloss one more time before walking inside. I look at my phone and notice that I'm only seven minutes late. Not bad all things considered. I walk in and tell the security guard I am there for Barbara at Mackenzie Jacob Associates. When he calls up, he gets the all clear to send me up.

I make my way up to the forty-sixth floor and walk to the receptionist, who is smiling from ear-to-ear. "Hi. I'm here to see Barbara. My name is Lauren. I'm the temp," I explain as she gets up and comes around to shake my hand, introducing herself as Carmen. She then takes me back to meet Barbara.

Barbara is short with white hair, and her glasses are perched on her nose. "Hey, there, Lauren. I'm so happy to finally meet you. I've heard great things from Penelope." She reaches out to shake my hand and motions for me to sit down.

"Thank you so much, and I'm so sorry I'm late. I was in a little fender bender, and I tried to finish as fast as I could," I tell her, sitting down in the chair in front of her desk.

"No worries. I heard Austin was going to be about ten minutes late, but he got here right before you did. Now, if you will fill out these papers here, I will get your elevator pass ready for you," she says while she goes to her cabinet in the corner.

Because this is just a temp job, I don't have to do much. Just an emergency contact form. "Now, I should warn you that this is the tenth temp we have hired for this position… this month," she finishes quickly.

I look at her, confused. "But it's only the seventeenth of November." My heart starts racing. What if he throws me out? What if he laughs at me since I haven't worked in ten years?

"Mr. Mackenzie is, um, well… special to work for," she murmurs while looking down at the papers in front of her and not even trying not make eye contact with me.

"Special? What does that mean?" I ask, my eyebrows pinching together.

"Let's just say that my money is on you." She gets up. "Shall we?" She points to the door. I nod at her, trying to get some saliva going in my mouth. It's dry, and my palms are sweating. I think my armpits are actually starting to sweat, too. Oh boy. I can't do this. I should turn around and run away.

But before I can make my move, we reach a door that is closed. The big brown door is solid, and the windows that look out into the office have their shades drawn. I hear Barbara knock on the door before we enter.

I don't see much in front of her. I just look around the office at the view of the city, since there are wall-to-wall windows affording it an amazing view. I don't have a chance to look much further, because all I hear is a raspy voice asking, "Are you fucking stalking me? Did you follow me here?" I whip my head around to look at him.

Just my luck. It's the asshat from this morning, the one who hit me. Except now, the asshat is sitting behind the desk, the desk that apparently belongs to my new temporary boss.

chapter three

Austin

I'M ALREADY HAVING THE SHITTIEST DAY EVER AND IT'S ONLY FUCKING EIGHT O'CLOCK. My alarm didn't wake me at five a.m. like it does every day, so I didn't have a chance to get my run in before I had to head to work.

Just a quick shower and a coffee before I hurried out. I walked out of my apartment, rushed to the elevator, and ran smack into my ex who, according to her, 'just happened to be in the area.'

It took a lot for me not to roll my eyes at her. She wasn't in the area; she's fucking the dude who lives upstairs. Not that I care. I was the one who let her go. Whatever, I blew her off and headed to my car.

Right as I started up my car, my mother decided it was a great day to call and lay out everything that's wrong with my life. I'm nearing forty; all I have is my career, blah blah blah. Newsflash, Mom, that's all I want.

So, just when I thought it couldn't get any worse, I hit a mini bus, or a van, or whatever the hell it's called.

I expected a frumpy housewife to get out of the car, but instead I was greeted by a woman who could only be described as sex-on-a-stick, or I guess I should say two sticks, because those legs of hers aren't something I'll forget anytime soon. I couldn't even talk I was so stunned. Then she bent over her seat and presented me with the most perfect ass. I think I actually groaned.

My cock was getting ready to salute her right then and there as she walked back to me from her minivan. The thought that she was someone's wife and I was jonesing on her made my skin crawl. I may be an asshole, but I don't fuck with marriages or people in relationships. There are more than enough single people on earth to not get involved with someone who isn't.

I tried to see if she was wearing a ring, but I couldn't see anything. I took her number, and she rushed away.

The whole way to work, I replayed the scene in my head over and over again. I tried to think back on anything that I could have said that would have had her reacting so hostilely.

I got to the office just four minutes late. I absolutely loathe tardiness; people who are late drive me nuts. I built this company from the ground up. I am now the most sought-after commercial contract developer in the city, especially when it comes to entertainment establishments. If you want to open a restaurant or nightclub in this city, let's just say I am known widely as the best choice to make sure it happens.

There is never a dull moment in this business. If I have to get in there and swing a hammer or wash the damn glasses myself, I do it. There is nothing I won't do to protect my and my company's reputation. If you are opening a restaurant or a nightclub and you attach it to the name Mackenzie Jacob, chances are it'll be a hit from day one.

So now, here I am walking into my office a few minutes late. The cute new receptionist, Carmen, is batting her eyes at me as I walk in, dragging out her greeting. "Good Morning, Mr. Mackenzie." She's new here, so she mustn't have heard the news yet, but I don't fuck where I eat. Ever.

"Morning. Is my new temp here yet?" I ask her, getting right to the point as she hands me my messages. A new temp who is yet another thing I didn't need today.

Since my secretary retired last month, I've gone through six or seven temps… okay, maybe ten. But it's not all my fault. I can't take it if they're stupid and I have to sit there and spell things out for them. I need someone who can take direction, get it right the first time, and just do what I ask the first time I ask it. It's simple, really.

When I ask you to get me coffee, I'm not asking you to join me for a cup. When I tell you to scan and email something, I don't need reporting of the task as if you're waiting for a sticker on your paper. When you have a caller on hold, I don't need you announcing them to me through the intercom in a singsong voice. I also don't need you knocking on my door every few minutes to ask me if I need anything. Trust me, when I need something, you'll be the first one to know.

"Can you tell Barbara I'm in now?" I prompt her, walking away while I pull the collar from my neck, making my way down the hall toward my corner office.

I walk into my office, taking in the view of the city. We are on the forty-sixth floor, so I can see the skyline perfectly, and at night, it's even better. I eat, sleep, and breathe my work. There aren't set hours for my work. So, if I have to be at the office for fifteen hours a day, then that's what it takes. Which is why I don't need, or want, a wife at this point. I'd just let them down.

I've lost count of how many relationships I've had that have ended because I wasn't there when I said I would be. I'm married to my work, and she is my first priority.

Sitting in my chair, I start going through the messages. I flip through them, seeing two messages from Vegas. I'm thinking of branching out and opening an office there, but something is stopping me. I like to stay local. I like to show up during construction. I like to pop in when you least expect it, and I wouldn't be able to do that if I branched out to Vegas.

I'm about to call them back when there is a knock on the door. I don't even have to tell them to come in before Barbara opens the door. I look over at her. She's been here from day one, but she isn't what I'm looking at this morning; it's the girl behind her.

Fucking unbelievable! This crazy chick followed me to my work. She is probably coming to sue me. I'll show her. "Are you fucking stalking me? Did you follow me here?" I growl at her while I stand up behind my desk.

Barbara's face pales and her mouth hangs open, but not the sassy one behind her. "Follow you? Are you insane?" She looks at Barbara. "I can't do this. I totally understand why you've gone through so many temps. Who would work for him?" She shakes her head. "Not only did he hit my car"—she looks at me—"while texting. The first thing he asked was if I was drunk!" She looks back at Barbara, who then glares at me. Great, just great, she's on crazy chick's side. "You would think he would ask me if I'm *okay*, right? Nope, not this guy. He wanted to know if I was drunk at eight a.m. Who the hell drinks at eight am anyway?" She folds her arms under her breasts, unnecessarily pushing them up. Fuck. I can't stop the mental image of her standing there, arms crossed under her tits, in nothing but her shoes. I shake that thought from my head.

"Wait." I throw the messages on my desk. "You, you're my temp?"

"No, sir," she says, and fuck me, but does that ever make me want to hold her hands behind her back as I bend her over my desk and pound into her while she calls me sir. "I *was* your temp." She looks at Barbara. "I wish you well." Then she turns and starts walking out the door.

Barbara's raised voice stops her. "Wait a second!" She looks at me. "Austin Montgomery Mackenzie, is Lauren telling me that you hit her car and then asked her if *she* was drunk? I raised you better than that, young man," she chides in that sharp tone I remember from my childhood. Okay, so Barbara was also my nanny growing up. That was to be expected when you're the child of world-renowned doctors who jetted around the globe saving lives. One is a cardiologist, and the other is a brain surgeon. They had very little time to raise a child. So, that's where Barbara came in, and she stayed until I was eighteen. She retired, but when I opened this firm, she was the first one I thought of to handle the HR side of the company, something I knew she would handle far better than me. "Apologize right this second, Austin," she demands, and I scoff at her. I will not do any such thing.

"She braked suddenly for no reason! There was no one in front of her," I defend myself. Barbara's eyebrows pinch together, and she takes her glasses off so they hang on the chain around her neck. I know that if I don't say sorry, this will just end in her quitting again. Last time, it cost me a month-long Mediterranean cruise. "Fine," I huff out, "I'm sorry I accused you of being drunk. I should have just called you what you are—a reckless, clueless female driver."

Lauren stands there glaring at me as Barbara yells, "I quit!" This must shock Lauren, because she immediately goes to Barbara and strokes her back. "Oh no. No, no, no. Please, really, it's fine. It's totally okay. I accept his apology." She aims a glare at me. "I understand now why so many women left, he's a..." She leans in and whispers in Barbara's ear. I don't know what she says, but they both snicker. Great, just great.

"Yup, my money is on Lauren." She looks at me. "You're lucky she saved you this time." She smiles at Lauren. "Let's do lunch tomorrow. Austin's treat."

She leaves the room leaving us all alone. "Fine. I guess I'll try and work with you, for Barbara." She walks out to the desk facing my office. She puts her purse on it. Turning the computer on, she grabs a pen and notepad and comes back in. "No time like the present to get this out of the way, so why don't we start with your expectations of me?"

I look at her while she sits in the chair in front of me, crossing her legs at her ankles. I sit down, leaning back in my chair, and start rocking. "Okay, fine. I expect you to be on time. Every day. No exceptions."

She doesn't write it down. "That isn't a problem. I hate when people are late, so you don't have to worry about that. Unless, of course, irresponsible people hit my car while I'm innocently driving, I'll be here on time."

"There is a list on your desk of routine tasks required of this position that you can read. If it's not clear enough, then come ask me questions. How's that?"

She gets up. "That sounds like a plan." She turns to walk away, and I watch her. Every fucking step she takes she swings her hips; the best thing is, she has no idea she's doing it. She has no idea that I'm sitting here negotiating with myself about my own rule. I'm not sure how I'm going to get anything done, because fucking her on my desk is the only thing I can think of that needs to be done right now.

chapter four

Lauren

I walk out of the office on shaky legs but manage to make it to my desk. I look up, letting out a slow breath.

I look down at the list that sits on my desk of tasks to be done during the day.

Looking over the list, I realize it looks pretty straightforward. Storing my purse under the desk, I take out my phone sending a quick text to Penelope.

Get me the fuck out of this job. STAT.

I turn and start going through the emails. I forward most of them to Austin, since I have no idea which ones are important or not.

When the phone on the desk rings, I look down to see if they wrote down how to answer it. When I notice that there are no instructions on the paper, I just answer with, "Hello."

"Can you tell me why I have fifty extra emails that you forwarded to me?" His snarky voice makes me close my eyes and count to ten. It's like dealing with my children.

"I didn't know which one is important or not, so I forwarded them to you for handling or direction," I respond, looking at the list, checking to see if I missed something.

"It defeats the purpose of having an assistant if I have to answer my own emails," he huffs into the phone. "Come in here. I'll show you how it's done," he growls before he slams the phone down in my ear.

I take the phone from my ear and look at it. Did he just hang up on me? Without saying 'please' or fucking 'thank you?' I put the phone back down in the cradle, slamming it a little forcefully. There are a couple of things I just won't tolerate. Being called a bitch is one of those things, and the other is when you don't say fucking 'please' and 'thank you.' Three words. Very easily said, and they make a world of difference in any interaction.

I get up and walk over to the door, knocking once. I walk in and sit down in front of him. "How are you going to see what to do if you aren't over here so I can explain it to you?" he asks.

"Okay, now, just a minute. We may have started out on the wrong foot here." I watch him watching me. "But I'm not your slave. I'm your assistant. While I am paid to do things for you, I also haven't even been here an hour yet, an hour that we've spent arguing, by the way, and not going over things. I'm learning as I go, and while I'm learning, I'm going to make mistakes. I get you don't know how to socialize with people." He starts to sit up straight, trying to talk, but I hold up my hand. "But I will not tolerate rudeness. You want something done, you say 'please'; I do something for you regardless of whether you pay me or not, you say 'thank you.'"

He nods at me. "Please," he says through his clenched teeth. "Come over here so you can see." He is clenching his teeth together so hard I think they might shatter.

"See, was that hard?" I get up and walk over to his side of the desk. The moment I get close to him, I realize my mistake.

Before, I didn't feel his presence next to me, I couldn't smell the woodsy, spicy scent of him. So, I make a mental note to not get this close to him again.

We go over all the fifty emails I sent him, and I take notes as we go along. It lasts maybe an hour. Right before I walk out the door, I turn and ask him, "How do I answer the phone? There is nothing in the notes." I have one hand on the door knob, ready to walk out.

"What do you mean?" He looks up at me with a raised brow. "I thought you were calling me Asshat?"

"Fine, then, that is exactly how I'll answer," I say walking out of the room, fighting the temptation to slam the door behind me.

I walk over to my desk, drop the pad on it, and throw myself into the chair.

I look at my phone and see that there are five messages from Penelope.

What happened?

Are you still there?

Are you okay?

I don't know what you did, but Barbara just called and extended your contract. What do I say?

Whatever you do, don't kill him!

I answer her right away.

He's an asshat, and he's rude. He's a jerk, and he's a dick.

Her response is immediate.

I've been told, but you are the best person for the job.

I roll my eyes.

How am I the right person? I have killed him a million times in my head since I've gotten here, and it's only been an hour. I want out.

I answer the emails that came in. My stomach rumbles, and I automatically look at the clock, seeing it's almost noon.

I pick my phone back up, and there is a final text from Penelope.

They doubled your salary. Why don't you see how you feel tomorrow?

Ugh, I'll deal with Penelope later. I get up and bend over to grab my purse from under the desk.

"Holy mother of God," I hear said loudly behind me. I go to straighten myself up too fast and knock my head on the desk, the bang echoing in the vast office space.

"Oh my god, are you okay?" I hear behind me as I feel hands trying to help me up. "Are you okay? I'm so sorry. I didn't mean to scare you."

He is holding my hand while my hand is rubbing the back of my head. "It's okay. You startled me," I start to say and then look at him.

Crystal-clear blue eyes crinkled with laugh lines greet me. His blond hair is falling onto his forehead. He is almost on top of me at this point, my back pressed into the desk.

"What the hell is going on here?" The roar comes from behind me. I push this stranger away from me and look over at Austin. He stands there with his hands on his hips, the vein in his neck twitching.

"It's my fault, Austin," the stranger says, dropping my hand. "I came in and was surprised to see her. I startled her, and she knocked her head under the desk. I was just helping her up," he says as he walks around my desk, right up to Austin, and slaps him on the shoulder. "I was wondering if you wanted to get lunch?"

Even though his 'friend' is standing next to me, he hasn't taken his eyes off me. "No, I'm eating in. I have to go over the Grey Stone Park file. Lauren, can you get me lunch? Go to the deli at the corner; we have an account there. Just tell them it's for me. They know what I like."

I put my hand on my hip, glaring at him, waiting for it. When he doesn't say anything, I cross my hands over my chest. "Please," he hisses out.

"Fine." I grab my bag and walk out, holding my breath till I get inside the elevator. I grab my phone and text Kaleigh.

Please get me three bottles of wine for dinner.

I put the phone back in my purse and make my way to the deli on the corner, where I get my boss his lunch, all the while praying that I will actually get through the day without poisoning him.

chapter five

Austin

WHEN I OPENED THE DOOR AND SAW MY CHILDHOOD BEST FRIEND, NOAH'S, hands all over Lauren, I wanted to rip out his jugular and then spit down his throat. I have no fucking idea why. She is my assistant, making her the definition of off limits.

We both watch Lauren walk away, her ass swinging from side to side with each step. I'm so intent on watching her, I don't even notice Noah push me aside and walk into my office.

He throws himself on the couch I have in the office, while I open the shade to see out into the office space.

"Jesus Christ, who was that sex kitten in heels? I nearly had a heart attack when I walked up to find her bending over," he says, looking in the direction of her desk.

"My new stay-away-from-her assistant," I grumble as I sit down on the other side of the couch.

He throws his head back and laughs. "Oh, what happened to the 'don't fuck where you eat, Noah' speech that you always give me?"

Noah and I have been best friends since we were in Kindergarten. His parents were both criminal lawyers, so we were always with our nannies. Of course, no one could top Barbara, while he kept getting different nannies every week. Until he was old enough to fire them himself and hire whoever he wanted. By the ripe old age of fifteen, he had gone through thirty nannies, and at that point, he was hiring them to teach him everything they knew about sex. That was until his parents found him fucking his last nanny bent over the pool table, wearing his mother's shoes. We still laugh about it today; well, at least I do. He just sits there and groans.

"She's crazy," I say. "I hit her car this morning, and then she shows up in the office. I thought she was fucking stalking me."

That just pushes him over the edge, and now he is laughing so hard the couch is shaking. "You hit her car and then thought she was following you? Holy shit. Were you an asshole to her?"

I smirk at him. "She named me Asshat in her phone." That set us both off. I figure if I laugh I'll notice how stupid the idea of getting her under me is. Getting her naked and sweaty and wet under me. Fuck, I need to do something about this.

"You know you're fucked, right?" He finally stops laughing and throws his hand over the couch. "When you saw me touch her, I thought you would charge at me like one of those bulls running toward the red sheet."

"She's nothing more than a crazy chick with a tight ass. Who will get me coffee daily."

"Oh really?" Her voice cuts through the air, and just when I thought I could turn her opinion of me as an asshat into that of a nice guy, I'm caught again. "Well, then, I'm happy I could assist you in your day," she snorts, coming in and dumping the bags on the table in front of us. "I also got something for your friend," she huffs and then walks away. This time slamming the door on her way out.

"Oh fuck, you are in so much fucking trouble. Dude, she is going to fucking string you up by the balls. Remember that chick you played in college? The one you promised to bring home during spring break? She turned around and cancelled all your tickets. Then she put that ad all over Craig's List 'Lonely man searching another lonely man.'" I shake my head thinking about it.

"She was fucking crazy! I had to change my number four times. Four! Then I had to start wearing beanies so she wouldn't recognize me." I shake my head, while Noah laughs so hard he falls over. I look over at him "It was fucking May! I had to take three showers a day. I had no idea the head could sweat so much."

He finally stops laughing and looks in the bag that Lauren just dumped on the table in front of us. "If I were you, I'd enjoy this. It's probably going to be the last meal she hasn't had the time to spit in." I open the box that has my name on it. It's pastrami on rye, touch of mustard and a pickle. The other box has a ham and cheese on brown.

We spend the next thirty minutes eating our lunch while shooting the shit about everything else.

"Are you going out this weekend with Deborah?" he asks me. Deborah is a family friend who I turn to when I have nothing else going on. We both have jobs that keep us busy; she is in real estate law, so we touch base from time to time. I shrug my shoulder. "Not sure what my weekend plans are. What do you have planned?"

He takes out his phone, scrolling. "Andrea, that is who I plan to do. I met her at Starbucks. She has the longest legs I've ever seen. I plan to have them wrapped around my neck, and not in a wrestling move, either." He raises his eyebrows. "If you know what I mean."

I chuckle at him. I don't think I've ever seen him with someone more than twice. He gets up, putting the garbage in the bag. "This has been a hoot, but sadly, I must run."

He takes the bag while he walks out. I follow him out and see him stop at Lauren's desk. She is busy typing something, so she only turns her head. "Thank you so much for lunch, Lauren. You were a life saver." I roll my eyes at the bullshit he's spewing, but it's the sweet smile that Lauren is giving him that really gets to me. I'm about to scoff when he walks away, leaving her with a wink.

"He is so nice," she says while she continues typing. I don't know why I feel like I want to rip the keyboard out from in front of her just so she will look at me, just so I can see her face.

"Yeah, well, looks can be deceiving," I comment while leaning into the door jam.

She finally stops typing and looks over at me. "Don't I know it." Her eyes roam from my head to my toes. It makes my spine stand straight.

"I'll have you know that I'm the nicest guy here." I have no idea why I'm trying to convince her of this. I couldn't care less if she likes me or not. I'm her boss, she is my temp. The fact that I want to see her smile at me is not the point right now. Nor is the fact that I'm also wondering if she is wearing a thong under her skirt or going commando? Does she wax or shave? Landing strip or bare? All these thoughts are running through my mind, so I don't hear her talking to me right away. "I'm sorry, what did you say?" I ask her again.

"I said Denis sent over the files and plans that you asked him about. He said if you want, he can meet you there so you can go over it. He also said the loft that you were asking about has a roof top terrace that would be great for a restaurant during the day and a bar at night."

She has been here less than six hours, and she is a million times better than the last ten temps I threw out of here. "Also, I've gone over your schedule and color coded all your meetings, so that when you click on the color, all files that correspond to that meeting will pop up as well."

She organized my whole schedule in three hours. "I didn't touch Saturday or Sunday, since it's not my job. Unless there was a note in there that said it's a work-related event or meeting."

I run through my schedule in my head and wonder if I wrote anything private down. She must see that I'm thinking this, because she laughs. "Don't worry, I didn't find your little black book notes." She shakes her head, picking up her Starbucks drink that is red with berries in it. "Is there anything else you need from me?" she asks, looking down at the notes in front of her.

I don't say anything; I just walk back to my desk to go through the notes she just sent me. I also check my calendar and see that everything is organized not only by color, but alphabetically. Jesus, where has she been all my life?

I spend the next three hours going over the plans with Denis, making sure everything is set for us to visit the site of the new nightclub that is set to open in a couple of weeks.

When I hear a knock on my door, I yell for whomever it is to come in. Once the door opens, I see Lauren poke her head in.

"I'm heading out. Just thought you should know." I look at my watch and see that it is already four p.m.

I lean back in my chair, putting my hands together. "I guess for the first day, that's okay, but there might be times when you may have to stay late." I don't even finish before she cuts me off. She opens the door and walks inside my office. She stops right in front of my desk, cocks her hips to the side, and places her hands on them.

"No go. I have two kids. My hours are eight to four. Not one minute later. I don't care about eating lunch at my desk, but I made it crystal clear that my hours were non-negotiable when I took this position."

"Why can't your husband get them?" I hold my breath as I wait for her answer. My stomach starts to burn, my chest tightening at the thought of her going home to someone. Then, just like the she-devil she is, she glares at me.

"I'm divorced, and I have full custody of them, so if you can't accommodate my limitations, it's better we find out now and part ways." She starts to turn around and walk away. I clear my throat, watching her fling her hair around. It's almost like she is doing it in slow motion, just like the commercials for shampoo.

"Fine, okay," I concede against my better judgment. "We'll work around it." I tilt my head and smile. "You're welcome."

She nods her head, but I see her pressing her lips together. I'm sure if I weren't her boss, she would tell me to go fuck myself, and I don't know why just the thought that she would fight me on this makes me want to belly laugh. She turns and walks out, closing the door softly behind her, which I know is the opposite of what she really wants to do.

I pick up the phone and dial Barbara, who answers on the second ring. "Yes, Austin."

"What is the story with Lauren?" I ask her, looking out into the office space, watching her pack up her things, pick up her phone, and scroll through it. I see her put the phone to her ear and smile at whoever answers. The thought that it's her boyfriend, or any man for that matter, makes me want to snatch that phone away from her and smash it.

"I don't have a 'story.' She's a temp. All I have is her emergency contact form that she filled out this morning. And I'll have you know, I've already called Penelope and gave her a raise."

"What?" I shout at her, and by the time I look up, Lauren is gone.

"You called her a drunk, and she didn't even kick you in the balls, which is what you deserved, by the way. I raised you better than that."

"I don't even know why I try with you." I slam the phone down, but not before I hear her laughing.

I turn to my computer and try to Google her name, except all I have is her first name. I search the company directory to find her full name: Lauren Harrison. With that, I turn back to Google and go on my search.

I see that she has a Facebook account, but I can't access anything because she has it set to private. The only thing I can see is the profile picture that she has of her two kids. She is in the middle with her son on her side, hugging her, and her daughter on her lap. You can't see her hands, but you know she is holding both of them. Her son looks nothing like her, but her daughter is her clone. I try to look through her friends, but I can't get anything. When a knock on my door startles me, I close down the page and yell out.

My partner, John, comes walking in. "Hey," he says while he makes his way to the chair in front of my desk, throwing himself down in it. "Just saw your new temp." He whistles. "If I weren't married, I think she might be worth bending the rules for." John has been married to his wife, Dani, for twelve years now. 'College sweethearts till the end' is their motto. She works at a big marketing firm downtown. We often use her when promoting our brand.

I shake my head at him and say, "Dani would skin you alive and leave you with nothing but your two balls hanging all the way to the floor. Right before she sets you on fire." I know full well she would do that and so much more.

He laughs out, folding one leg over the other. "She pretty much would leave me with maybe the hair on my head. Other than that, it will all be gone."

"If you're lucky. How was Vegas?" He just got back from Vegas. He went to see if he thought branching out there was doable for us. I'm still unsure about it.

"It was what you expected. It's hard to get your foot in the door anywhere. They all 'have their own people.' Dani and I checked around, but I'm leaning more toward shelving this for a later date." I nod, agreeing with everything he is saying.

We spend about thirty minutes talking about the projects we have going on. He has four restaurants that are opening up in the next three months. All different cuisines and atmospheres, so he's excited for what is to come. We discuss the nightclub/restaurant project that I have taken on. It's more of a challenge, because everything has to work for both purposes.

After that, he tells me he's leaving. I look at the clock, seeing it's only six thirty. I haven't been out of the office this early in forever. I decide I'm going to hit up the gym.

I close up everything, making my way outside. I walk by Lauren's desk, where her scent of berries lingers lightly. I see that she has Post-it's all over her computer screen.

I walk over and can't stop myself from moving a few around. It's childish, I know, but I can't help it. This is what she does to me.

chapter six

Lauren

He asked me to stay late—as if. I was very specific about that when I filled out the form. I pick up the phone right before I head out, dialing Kaleigh. I'm surprised when I hear Rachel's voice "Hiya, Mommasita." I smile just thinking of her standing there in the kitchen with her curls bouncing.

I walk out to the car telling them I'll be home in twenty minutes. I pull into my driveway, put the car in park, and I rest my head on the steering wheel, clearing the stress of the day away by drawing in a few breaths and letting them out. I think it's the first time all day that I finally breathe normally.

I don't have much time to myself before I hear Gabe running out of the house. "Mom, you have to come in quick." The tone of his voice snaps me back to reality.

I sling my seatbelt off, getting ready to run inside "What's the matter?" I look at him.

"Aunt Kay is making supper." He looks at me nervously, his big, brown eyes open wide in dismay.

"Oh crap," I say, and quickly head into the house. The last time she attempted cooking us dinner, we ate sticky peanut cauliflower wings. There was nothing good about that concoction. Hell, it was barely edible. I won't even talk about the aftertaste it left in my mouth, either.

I hurry in the door just as I hear the smoke detector go off. "Oh, dear Christ, Kay, what the hell are you doing?" I grab a broom out of the closet and position myself beneath the smoke detector, using the broom to fan the smoke away. "Jesus, Jesus, Jesus," I chant while looking over to the kitchen in time to see Kayleigh pulling a tray of charred, smoking cauliflower out of the oven.

"Oh my god, oh my god, oh my god! I'm so sorry! We went outside to do some kid yoga, and I totally forgot," she explains while she walks with the pan to the sink, turns on the water, and soaks the smoking remains of what was once cauliflower. The sizzling sound of water hitting a hot metal pan fills the quiet room, along with a burnt, smelly, steamy smoke that has the potential to set off the now silent smoke detector again. I do the only thing I really can do, which is to continue fanning.

"Oh, Auntie Kay, what are we going to eat now?" Rachel asks. She would have been the only one of us to attempt to eat one of Kayleigh's creations.

Kayleigh slaps her hands together. "Oh! I have some tofu we can cut up and…" Before she can even finish that sentence, Gabe and I both yell a combined firm yet panicky, "No!"

I look over the mess that is my kitchen and begin a mental count to ten. "Okay, I'm going to change. Gabe, start your homework. Rachel, go start studying your spelling words. You"—I point at my sister—"clean up this mess. I'll find something to throw together for pasta."

She groans. "I don't have any gluten-free pasta here."

I look at her. "Okay, so you'll be going home. Got it." I point to the kitchen. "Clean this mess up before you leave."

I head upstairs and change out of my work clothes, throwing on some yoga pants and a sweat shirt. I'm in mom mode now. I get back downstairs and see that Gabe is sitting at the table doing his homework, while Rachel is in the living room writing her words, and Kaleigh is putting things in the dishwasher. "Oh, good news," she informs me. "I found some rice, so I'll throw whatever sauce you make on there. Yumm-O."

I shake my head, laughing at her as I start prepping the veggies to go into my pasta primavera. After I've sautéed everything and added the pasta, I toss it with a bit more olive oil and some parmesan. "Kay, set the table," I call over to her.

She looks over my shoulder and complains, "I can't eat that. You put cheese in it."

"It's okay," I whisper to her. "I won't turn you in to the vegan police. We'll pretend it never happened." I serve up some pasta onto plates for the kids.

I hear the fridge open, followed by a squeal from behind me. "Score," she squeals, taking out one of her frozen meals from the freezer. "Look! Tofu ravioli! Saved!" She does a little dance on her way over to the microwave, raising her hands in the air and shaking her ass as she pops it in. "Oh yeah, oh yeah, oh yeah!" She continues dancing till the microwave beeps.

She pulls it out, peeling off the filmy plastic cover, and waves it under my nose. "Smells so good, right?"

I raise my eyebrows and nod yes, but I'm totally lying. Throughout the meal, the kids tell me about their day. Rachel tells me that today someone threw up in class because someone else farted. Apparently, this is hilarious to her, since she is in stiches about it as she retells the story.

By the time eight o'clock rolls around, I've got the kids bathed and tucked into their beds. I'm ready to pass out, but I come down the stairs to lit candles and a full glass of a crisp, perfectly chilled white wine. "Aww, if you weren't my sister—and I were into chicks—I'd make you my woman," I swoon, grabbing my glass and curling up on the couch with my feet under me.

"So, tell me about this boss of yours?" she prompts as she sips her own wine.

"Oh, where do I start?" I close my eyes as I try not to picture him staring at me. Trying even harder to not picture him looming over me. Definitely trying really, *really* hard to not picture him taking off his clothes while he looms over me and stares.

"Good-looking?" she asks.

I nod my head yes and finish off my glass of wine in one long, satisfying drink.

I pick up the bottle, pulling the cork out with a pop, and pour myself another glass. "Too good-looking."

"Fit or chunky?" she asks, and now I know what she's doing. Small questions now, big discussion later.

"Fit," I answer, pausing to sip another glass that's already half drained. "Very fit." I think the wine is hitting me pretty fast, because I look around next before I whisper, "I think he has a six pack." Then I finish the remaining wine in my glass.

"Hair color? Eye color?" She fills up my glass again.

"Brown and hazel-green with gold specks." I drink a little more.

"Facial hair? Would you get a burn from his beard or not?"

I look up and think I blush a bit. "Depends on the time of the day. He was clean-shaven this morning, but he had a good five-o'clock-shadow going by three o'clock." I drop my head back on the back of the couch and close my eyes. Seeing his eyes right away, the smirk he gave me, the way he asked about my husband, not swallowing before I answered. Then his eyes suddenly lighting up with mischief.

"You like him?"

My eyes snap open as I turn to her. "No! No, I don't. Absolutely not. I don't like him at all."

She giggles as she takes another sip. "He hit my freaking car, Kay, and then the asshat asked me if I was drunk," I plead my case. "Drunk at *fucking* eight a.m."

"He's gotten under your skin! There hasn't been anyone who's pushed you this far. Well, there was Pacey from Dawson's Creek…"

"Hey!" I point at her. "Joey went sailing with him all summer! Just because Dawson is there and crying, she thinks she should be with Pacey. He was always her choice." I pour myself another glass, spilling a bit as I do it.

"Do you think he manscapes?" she asks, putting her glass down on the table, while I just down another one.

"I have no idea, but I would guess it's probably manscaped. I mean, who doesn't manscape these days?" I look over and wonder.

"Some like to be free and let things be natural; there is nothing wrong with that. Don't judge. Well, unless you have to suck his dick, then by all means, you put your foot down. You don't need to be choking on long pubic hair. In fact, if you think it isn't, then just run. Run fast, like he's waving a bomb in front of you."

I nod at her. I should probably be taking notes. I feel like I should be taking notes so I can remember this.

"Shoes?"

"Nice. Black ones." I look at her, my eyes opening wide. "And clean. Very nice." I hate when guys don't have clean shoes; it's like having dirty feet. Ewww.

"Teeth? Straight? Crocked? White? Stained? Stinky breath?"

I tilt my head to the side and remember if he smiled today. I saw him smirk, I saw him glare, I saw his jaw muscle tick, but I'm not sure I saw his teeth. "I don't know."

"Big hands?"

"Oh yeah, so big." I open my hands wide to make her see how big, but I shake them a bit "This big." I motion with my hands, making big circles.

"You think he has a big dick?" I stop moving.

"He would have to. You can't be that good-looking and have a small penis. Actually, maybe that's why he's such an asshole! His penis is small. He has small penis syndrome." I look at her, waiting for her input. "I mean, why else would he be smoking hot and an asshole, unless…"—I giggle—"unless it's so big it hurts when he walks." I put my hand over my mouth and laugh out loud. "I can't sleep with him. He's my boss and besides, he doesn't even like me."

I rise from the couch, picking up my glass of wine and spilling whatever was left in it on the floor. "I need a dog, so if I spill something, he can lick it up." I look over at Kaleigh, and she is silently laughing. "You think we can get a dog and train him to bite my boss?"

"Yes, I think you just need to bring a picture and a sweater with you to training school so they can use his scent. They'll train the dog to attack your boss as soon as he gets close."

My mouth forms an O. "Oooh, we need to look into that," I say. And that is the last thing she says to me.

The next thing I know, I'm lying in my bed with her on the other side. "You think he doesn't like me because I'm old? Or ugly? Or is it because I'm fat?"

She leans over and strokes my cheek. "You are not old. You are the opposite of ugly, and you are definitely not fat. He acts like he doesn't like you, because he probably likes you too much. Remember Ricky in the third grade who chased you with a frog because he loved you? This is just the adult version."

"No way would he go for someone like me. He did say I had a tight ass, though. That means he was looking at it, right?"

She tucks a strand of hair behind my ear. "He was definitely checking you out."

I close my eyes. The room is spinning as the day replays in my head. I fall asleep to the sound of Kaleigh talking about a beef vegan soup that she is going to try to make, minus the beef, of course.

Her voice lulls me while I'm brought back to the day, sitting at my desk, knowing he was watching, feeling he was watching me.

chapter seven

Lauren

The next day, I make it to work without incident, clocking in at seven fifty-five. I make my way into the break room, where I get the coffee going.

I'm leaning against the counter, waiting for the coffee to finish brewing, when a tall man with glasses walks in. He is lanky, his tan pants are perfectly ironed with a crease down the front of the legs. His plaid shirt completes the look. I smile at him and say a polite "Hello."

He nods his head at me and goes to the fridge, where he stores his lunch.

"You must be Austin's new PA?" His voice is quiet as he waits for the coffee to finish also.

"I am." I reach out my hand to him to introduce myself. "I'm Lauren." He grips my hand, and his palm is just a tad sweaty, but not enough for me to wipe it on my navy skirt.

Today, I've dressed in almost the same skirt as yesterday's, except that it's a dark navy blue and has some pleating at the side. I've paired it with a plain white cotton button-down. It's simple, but professional. I've gone with my tan peep-toe pumps that give me an extra four inches.

"My name is Steven. I'm in the accounting department," he says while pushing his glasses up on his nose. "Are you enjoying your time so far?" he asks right as the machine lets out a gust of steam, letting us know that it's done brewing.

I grab the handle. "I am. I thought it would be harder at the beginning, since I haven't really worked in over ten years, but it's just like riding a bike." I smile over at him while I pour my coffee. He places his coffee mug on the counter and waits for me to hand him the pot. But I'm going to be friendly. "Please, let me, tell me when to stop." He smiles at me.

"When you're done flirting, you can fix me one, too. And we need to go over a couple of things." Austin's voice bursts into the room, startling me and causing me to spill a bit.

"Jesus, you scared me," I say while I put down the pot in the holder and quickly grab a napkin, cleaning up the spilt coffee. Steven quickly grabs his cup and heads out with a smile to me, a nod to Austin, and a mumbled "Good morning."

"I know you're a temp, and you don't know the company policies, but we have a no-fraternizing policy." He eyes me while putting his hands in his pockets.

I throw the napkin out and turn around to face him. He is dressed in a simple black suit, another crisp white dress shirt, looking sharp and as if they were custom-fit for him.

He didn't shave this morning, so he's got more stubble than he did last night when I left, and I can't help but think to myself that I'd definitely get beard burn from that. "I'll have Barbara send over the policies so you don't get confused."

"I wasn't flirting with him. I just met him. I was merely being polite. Although I'm sure that concept is foreign to you." I pick up my mug and start to walk away.

"I asked for a coffee," he stops me, and my head turns and I snap.

"No. You didn't ask, you demanded. After you insulted me. Again. And for the record, when someone asks another person for something, it is customary that they follow the request with the word 'please.' The coffee's done. Help yourself." I glare at him.

I don't have time to say anything else before Barbara comes into the room. "Good morning, you two. Lauren, I love that skirt. Very, very nice," she compliments me while she grabs two mugs and goes about pouring her coffee.

"Barbara," I address her, "Austin was just going over the company policies that are included in the employee handbook. If it's not too much trouble, would you please send that to me? There is a non-fraternization policy Austin seems to believe I need to check out." I hold my mug in front of my mouth to hide my smile.

Barbara looks up at me with a surprised look on her face and then looks at Austin. "I will send it right over to you. It seems I don't have the right copy, since I don't remember that particular policy. Austin, if you've amended the handbook, perhaps you should send it to me so I can make sure those changes are noted and emailed to everyone," she suggests while she finishes making two cups of coffee, handing Austin one of cups she prepared.

I look at Austin to see that his mouth is closed and he is swallowing, since he hasn't said anything else. "We just finalized it last week. I'll send it over," he says and walks away, leaving me and Barbara by ourselves.

I look at her and see her smiling as she raises her cup to her lips. "I hope you know that I won't be staying here long," I inform her. "I've already informed Penelope to look for a suitable replacement for me here, as well as another position for me somewhere else." I watch her sip her coffee and ask, "Does he always take half a sugar and no milk in coffee?"

She looks at me with a surprised look. "I'm very observant." I smile at her and head to my desk. I turn on my computer, noticing that some of my Post-its have been moved.

I get up, heading into Austin's office. The door isn't closed, so I walk in. I check and see if he's on the phone before I ask him, "Do we have a cleaning crew come in here?"

He looks up from his paper, and his eyes slowly eye me from toe to head. "Excuse me?" he asks.

"My Post-its have been moved." His Adam's apple moves like he's swallowing. "I'm assuming someone was cleaning and moved them. So, my question is, do we have a cleaning crew?"

He leans back in his chair. "How do you know they've been moved? What do you do? Memorize them before you leave?" He laughs, but it comes out shaky.

"I don't have to memorize them. I post them alphabetically, which is why I know they've been moved."

His face turns a nice shade of white. Yup, asshat moved my shit. But instead he says, "Must be the cleaning crew."

I glare at him for a second. "If you could please let them know that I'll be cleaning my own desk from now on. Or you know what, I'll see if I can find their number and get in touch with them my—" I don't have time to finish before he pipes in.

"No"—he shakes his head—"I'll call Hector now and mention it." I nod yes at him. "Now, if that's all, I have a busy schedule and discussing your filing system isn't on it."

I turn around and head out the door, but right before I'm out of the door, he informs me, "I'm having a business lunch in my office with a friend. If you could make sure we both have lunch ready for noon. It will also be a private lunch. She eats light. So, a salad for her is good. I'll have my usual," he says.

My back is still facing him, so he doesn't see me close my eyes slowly and open my mouth in shock. It takes me a second to turn around, putting a mask on my face. "Considering I've been here for twenty-four hours, I don't know what your usual is. If you want me to order your lunch for you and your booty call"—I let out a little forced laugh—"oh sorry, your 'private lunch,' I'm going to need to know exactly what you want for lunch. Send me the details via email." I turn and walk out of the room, not giving him a chance to reply.

I open my email and start a message Penelope.

To: Penelope Barns
From: Lauren Harrison

Subject: GET ME THE FUCK OUT OF HERE

If you don't want to be responsible for my children being raised by Jake and his side slut, you will make sure I'm out of this job by Friday. Or better yet, tomorrow. Because I may kill him.

Sincerely,
Lauren

MY BOSS IS THE MAYOR OF DOUCHEVILLE

I hit send and then continue going through the emails. I forward the necessary ones and start making notes on what has to be done with the ones that I can handle. Within three minutes, there is a reply from Penelope.

To: Lauren Harrison
From: Penelope Barns

Subject: Re: GET ME THE FUCK OUT OF HERE

I'm working on it, but it doesn't help that Barbara is blowing up my phone to get you in there permanently. She's isn't caving. PLEASE DON'T KILL HIM, HE'S MY BIGGEST CLIENT.

Sincerely,
Your friend Penelope, who is so fucking sorry and knows she owes you big time.

Ugh. What the hell am I supposed to do now?

To: Penelope Barns
From: Lauren Harrison

Subject: Re: GET ME THE FUCK OUT OF HERE
I don't know how you are going to repay me for this. There isn't enough wine in all of Italy to call this even.

I won't kill him, but I may poison him slowly.

Sincerely,
Your friend Lauren, who is already plotting how she will be getting you back one day.

I quickly reply and then take out my phone to text Kaleigh.

I've thought about it, he has a pencil dick and doesn't manscape.

She replies right away.

Fuck me, what did he do in ten minutes?

Besides the fact he fucked with my Post-its, he asked me to order lunch for him and his fuck buddy.

Whoa, he touched your Post-its!

Really? That is all you got from the text? Did you not read he wants me to order lunch for him and his date?

I'm sorry, that was rude of him. You should make him pay. I mean, the last time I touched your Post-its, you switched my almond milk for cow's and I drank the whole thing.

I giggle to myself at the reminder. It was really funny watching her drink the whole carton in ten minutes. She was oohing and aahing about how great it tasted.

I continue with my task, trying to organize all the items that have been scanned, placing them in the correct files and relabeling everything so it actually makes sense.

The phone buzzes on my desk. I pick it up, but I don't say hello till I hear his voice bark into the phone.

"We have a conference with Denis and his team at three. I need all documents printed and labeled so we can see what is going on."

"Isn't it better if I just do a slide show with PowerPoint? That way, you can display it bigger instead of on the table," I suggest, smiling to myself.

"I wasn't sure if you knew how to do that, since you haven't been in an office environment in a while. I didn't want to expect anything."

I take the phone from my ear, ready to smash it on the desk. "I think I can manage it. If not, I can always use YouTube; they have tutorials."

I look into the office and see him staring straight at me. All I see is his jaw getting tight. "I hope you can manage that one." And he slams the phone down.

I quickly place it down in its cradle, smiling to myself. Score one for me.

But my mood doesn't last long. He sends me an email.

To: Lauren (Latest PA)
From: Austin Mackenzie
Subject: Lunch Order

Please order me a pastrami on rye and a grilled chicken salad, dressing on the side. I want this by noon. Try not to mess this up. She's expecting it to be perfect.

Austin Mackenzie

My eyes glare at the screen, thinking if she wants it to be perfect, she's starting with the wrong date. I don't have time to answer when another email comes through.

To: Lauren (Latest PA)
From: Austin Mackenzie
Subject: Conference with Denis

Although I don't think you can bring anything to this meeting, you need to be there to take notes.

Try not to flirt, since he is also considered a co-worker.

Austin Mackenzie

My blood is boiling. I want to reply with a simple 'fuck off,' but instead I think of something better. Oh yeah, I'm going to give him something better, alright.

I place the order at the deli on the corner. At eleven thirty, I start to get up, but I'm stopped by a woman walking down the hall.

She is wearing a brown trench coat tied at the waist. The trench coat falls to her mid-thigh. Her short blond bob of loose curls bounces with every step she takes. Her blue eyes shine. Her black Louboutins click-clack against the floor as she approaches.

"May I help you?" I ask while walking around my desk. She gives me the once-over.

"No, thank you," she huffs and continues walking straight into Austin's office. "Darling," I hear her purr. "It's been forever."

I look into the office, seeing her walk around the desk and sit on his lap. I don't know what he says, but I hear giggling that has me rolling my eyes.

I hear my phone ring. "Hello?"

"I'm going to need that lunch later. And would you close my door?" he says and then hangs up before I can answer.

I'll close his fucking door. I walk in and hear them whispering, the bottom half of the desk covering whatever he is doing. So gross. It's the middle of the day! My heart is beating so fast. I try not to look up, but he looks up right before I close the door. Something flashes in his features, but I don't get a chance to figure out what it is before the door closes. I hear the blinds start to shut. I'm not sitting out here while he fucks in his office.

I walk around the desk, grabbing my purse, and leave to go to lunch. I guess I'll be having the grilled chicken salad, dressing on the side.

I pull my phone out of my purse and shoot Kaleigh a text.

He's fucking some woman in his office!

Your boss?

No, the fucking tooth fairy! Who else would I be talking about?

Barf. Make sure you use Lysol wipes on the surfaces you sit on. You don't want to be catching cooties.

Do people still use the word cooties?

Ummm. Yes.

I walk out of the building to the hustle and bustle of lunchtime. Once I make it to the deli, I pick up the order and eat the salad there.

I'm almost done when my phone buzzes. When I pick it up, I see 'Asshat who hit...'

Where are you?

I look at the clock and notice that it's only been twenty minutes since I've been gone. Wow, I guess he's a wham bam thank you ma'am kinda guy.

I'm at the deli having lunch. I didn't think you would be finished so soon. My bad.

I don't pay you to think. Bring me my lunch.

I smash my phone down on the table. That's it. I've fucking had it.

I walk over to the Walgreens across the street. I pick up a bottle of Dulcolax. "You don't pay me to get your lunch either, asshole," I grumble to myself while I walk back to the office. Once I make it there, I go the other route, picking up a water bottle from the kitchen.

I take a quick look around the kitchen, checking to see if anyone is coming this direction. When I see no one is there, I take out the Dulcolax and open the package.

I start reading the dosage instructions on the package when I hear someone coming. I shove the box and the bottle into my purse. When I turn around, I see Steven walking in.

"Hey. Are you having lunch?" he asks, going to the fridge and grabbing his bag.

"Nope, just finished. I'm picking up a water bottle for Austin. I just got his lunch." The fact I'm lying and that I might be caught is too much.

My neck starts to burn, and I'm pretty sure he can hear my heart beating it's so loud.

"Oh, he hates water. Bring him a Coke instead," Steven suggests while he smiles and walks out.

Fuck. I walk back in and grab a Coke can out of the fridge. Looking for a glass, I finally find a red solo cup in one of the cupboards.

I open my purse, scan the package, and see that the dose is five ml. I have no idea how much five ml is, so I use the cap to measure, hoping for the best. What's the worst that can happen? I can't control the snicker that bursts from my mouth.

Pouring the Coke into the cup, I grab a spoon and stir it. There you go, Asshat. Take that!

I walk back to my desk, depositing my purse on it.

His door is open and so are the shades. When I peak my head inside, he is sitting alone on the couch, his jacket still on. Jesus, he had sex and still looks the same.

I dump the bag on top of the table in front of him, placing the cup of laxative-laced Coke next to it.

"What took you so long?" he growls, grabbing the bag and opening it to take out his sandwich.

"How was I supposed to know it would take you ten minutes to seal the deal?" I cross my arms under my boobs while I lean on one leg.

He takes two bites of his sandwich and then drinks a long gulp of Coke. "You going to watch me eat?" He looks at me from the corner of his eye.

I don't reply to him. Instead, I turn on my heel and walk out, taking a seat at my desk as I watch him eat his lunch and drink the Coke. When he's finished, he throws everything out, including the cup.

He doesn't buzz me or talk to me until five minutes to three, when he gets up and walks out of his office.

"Let's go, Denis is here."

I grab everything I need and follow him to the conference room. Right before he opens the door, I hear his stomach start gurgling.

He looks up to see if I heard it, but I keep my head down, pretending I didn't. It's all I can do not to laugh out loud.

I'm introduced to Denis, who is a short, older man with that bald-on-top-hair-wrapped-around-the-sides thing going on.

I don't say anything else to him as I put my things down and start to set up the PowerPoint presentation.

Denis and Austin start talking, but his stomach gurgles again, this time louder.

I look over at him and notice that his forehead is starting to get shiny and beads of sweat are forming on his temples.

He takes off his jacket, unbuttons his cuffs, and rolls up his sleeves. He walks to the end of the table where water bottles are set up.

Opening one, he drinks half of it, then sits down at the head of the table.

I start the presentation and Denis starts speaking. "We have a great setup with the tables for the day crowd and the dinner rush. The good news is that once they're cleared away after the dinner service, the space has a good-sized dance floor." I look at the display, seeing what he is saying.

Austin's stomach grumbles very loudly. So loudly that Denis stops talking and we both look over at him. I see sweat is now pouring down the sides of his face, which is flushed and looks pained.

Denis looks over at him, his eyebrows raised in question. "Are you okay, Austin?"

He doesn't answer, but his stomach lets out another loud grumble before he shoots out of his chair, running for the door.

Denis looks over at me, unsure of what to do. I shrug my shoulders and feign bewilderment. "I guess he got some indigestion."

Denis nods his head in agreement. We wait about twenty minutes before I tell him that I'm going to go check on Austin.

He's been emailing and texting since Austin left. Walking into Austin's office, I hear moaning coming from the corner where the bathroom door is closed.

I walk over and knock on the door. "Are you okay?" I ask. He doesn't say anything, but I hear him groaning.

"I think I'm dying," he moans in between pants. "Call 9-1-1."

I giggle to myself. "I don't think you're dying. Maybe it's food poisoning." I try to keep my voice even so I don't give anything away.

I hear him moan one more time, followed by his pained reply. "No, I'm pretty sure I'm dying."

"I'll reschedule Denis," I say, turning and walking out while I hear him cursing God and everyone else.

Score one for me.

chapter eight

Austin

I WALK OUT OF MY PRIVATE BATHROOM AND SEE THAT NIGHT HAS FALLEN OUTSIDE. THE moon shining its light into my office. The outside office is empty and the lights are off out there, with just the lights in my office on and dimmed.

I walk slightly hunched over to the couch, where I throw myself down and put a hand on my forehead. I have nothing on but my pants, and they're not even buttoned. I ripped my shirt off when I thought I was dying on that toilet. *Dying.*

The minute my stomach started gurgling, I knew something was wrong. Then the cramps started, followed by the sweats. The longer I sat at that conference table, the more certain I was that I might actually shit myself. Literally.

I am not exaggerating when I tell you I was dying. I thought for sure it was God's way of punishing me for calling in Danielle.

The minute she sat in my lap, I knew I made the mistake for two reasons. First, the look on Lauren's face made my stomach clench, and second, at the sight of the woman in my lap, my dick shriveled up. Even when I closed the blinds and she took off her coat, revealing her semi-naked form to me —encased in garters and all—my dick just lay there, not rising to the bait.

I tried to think of something to get him up, but he was just not interested.

I got up from my desk and closed her coat, telling her that it really wasn't the best time, I had a surprise meeting I had to get to.

She pouted and even stomped her foot. I made a mental note to block her number. She tried to claw at my chest, thinking it was sexy. Newsflash, pretending you're a cat is not sexy. At least not to me.

She walked out five minutes after she got here, and I sat there on the couch as I stared out at Lauren's desk. After about half an hour passed and I realized that she wasn't back, I texted her. Okay, so I was a dick, but seriously, where was she? Was she having lunch with Steven? With someone else?

But then she came in and dumped my lunch on the coffee table in front of me and put my Coke down next to it.

I sat up straight at that recollection. She fucking drugged me!

I text Noah right away.

My assistant put a laxative in my Coke.

I don't have to wait long before he sends me back a text filled with nothing but laughing and crying emoticons.

I send him back the middle finger.

She drugged me. I thought I was dying. I almost called 9-1-1.

You almost called 9-1-1 because you had the shits?

Which he follows with a text of shit emojis.

I shake my head, this isn't a joke. I almost died. The stuff that came out of me… I didn't think it was humanly possible to be full of that much shit.

I have to get her back.

Whoa there, you don't even know if she did anything.

I know it in my gut.

BAHAHA!!! Is there anything left in your gut? Maybe what you think you're feeling is just emptiness.

I don't even bother answering him at this point. I throw my phone down and get up slowly. I reach for a bottle of water. I look at it carefully to make sure it wasn't tampered with before I open it up and start drinking it.

I walk over to her desk and see it spotless. I rip all her Post-its down and crumple them up. I pull out her chair and sit down at her computer, then open it up and start going through her emails.

She thinks I'm an asshole. I find emails to Penelope and see she's really thinking about quitting. Over my dead body. I'm going to fire her before she can quit on me.

I then think over last year when I got a virus from a porn site. Oh, don't sit there shaking your head; we all watch porn. I know you do, too.

I open up the porn site and start flipping on all the links that pop up. I click girl porn, anal porn, BBW porn, big tit porn, gay porn, lesbian porn, MILF porn; you name the porn, I open all the links and put her volume to the max. Take that, you little minx.

I close down her screen, rubbing my hands together in evil glee. The minute I do that, my stomach starts up again, and I barely make it to the bathroom, where I am, once again, sitting there thinking I'm dying.

It's almost three a.m. when I finally make it out of the bathroom. I decide to just spend the night in my office. Making sure I set my alarm for seven so I can get up and shower before she comes in.

I fall asleep with a smile on my face and at least five pounds lighter.

By seven thirty, I am showered and changed. I opt for warm water with honey this morning instead of coffee. I rinse out the cup before using it just in case she's tampered with everything in the kitchen. Who knows, maybe she's trying to kill everyone in the office.

I'm sitting at my desk when she walks in. When she walks past my office, I see that her skirt today falls to right above her knees and is not as tight as the others.

Of course, my dick starts to stir right away. I look down and mumble, "Traitor" at him.

She takes off her scarf and jacket, and I see that her shirt is a V-neck today. Finally showing off some skin and a hint of her nice, full C-cups. Her cream sweater molds to her, and my traitorous dick has risen to fully salute her. I give him a firm squeeze as I picture Danielle from yesterday. He shrivels right up in response, leaving me shaking my head.

I watch her sit down and touch the mouse to bring her computer screen to life.

The second her computer fires up, the normally quiet office is filled with the sounds of loud sexual moaning.

"Oh my god! Oh my god! OH MY GOD!" she squeals, getting more and more flustered.

I get up from my chair and walk to my door. I lean against it as I say, "Watching porn at work. Real nice."

She throws a panicky look over her shoulder at me but doesn't have time to reply before she turns back to the screen, where a woman with the biggest tits I have ever seen in my life bounces on a guy reverse-cowgirl style as her voice echoes through the office. "Oh yeah, I like that. Play with my tits, give it to me harder! Ooohhhhh yeah, oh right there! Fuck me like that right there!"

She clicks that screen closed, but another one pops right up in its place. Two guys this time. "I'm going to fuck that ass hard, and you're going to take it all, baby."

When nothing else happens, she starts to freak out. "What the heck is happening?"

She tries to close it down but to no avail. The screen is frozen on the image of one of the guys' dicks entering the other guy's ass. His face looks pained—and not in a good way. The screen may be frozen, but the sound is still coming through loud and clear.

"Fuck that virgin ass, tear it up. I'm going to cream you so good." At this point, people are starting to arrive. They're looking over at Lauren, who now has her hands covering her face.

Barbara comes out of her office, walking with purpose right over to us. The moaning starts again, and the screen flickers to life. The first guy is now pounding into the second guy while ordering him to "jerk that cock while I fuck your ass."

"Lauren, dear, I don't think this is the time or place for this. Perhaps you should do this in your own place." She pushes her glasses up higher on her nose, "Oh, that is some scene, right?" She giggles a little.

Lauren turns around, her cheeks blazing pink with embarrassment. "I don't watch this. It was on my screen when I turned it on, and I can't seem to shut it down. I closed the screen." She clicks the X in the corner, but another screen pops up, titled 'Please Cum On My Face' with a girl on her knees surrounded by ten hard dicks all shooting off their loads at the same time on her face.

"See? I can't shut it down," she says as she places her hands strategically over the computer screen in an effort to block out the video. "It won't stop!" I see some tears in her eyes.

She looks over at me, and for just one second, I feel bad, but then I remember that I almost died yesterday in my bathroom, and I just smirk at her. The tears are blinked away, clearing to show a murderous rage in her eyes that is aimed at me.

"I'm going to call JP in tech support to come over here and get this situation taken care of," Barbara says while she picks up Lauren's phone.

"JP, can you come to Lauren's desk? She seems to have been watching porn, and it's taking over her system."

"I was NOT watching porn! It was already on when I got here," she insists adamantly.

Barbara puts her hand over the phone. "Sure, sure, dear, whatever you say." Then she turns back to her conversation with JP. "Oh, she has tried clicking everything, but it seems she must have stumbled onto the wrong site."

I don't know what JP is saying, but Barbara nods her head and laughs. "See you soon."

She hangs up the phone. "He'll be right over." She looks at me then Lauren. "But for now, he says to not click on anything else."

"I didn't click on anything to begin with," she says, throwing her hands in the air, her tits bouncing with her movements.

She stands up and walks around her desk, and I finally see the full effect of today's outfit. Her skirt isn't tight, it's loose, almost flowing, and whenever she moves, it brushes against her thighs. Her creamy, perfectly toned thighs. *She almost killed me*, I quickly remind myself.

"Well, this is awkward, knowing what your assistant's sexual proclivities are. You really shouldn't view that type of material during working hours, though. I should probably sit down with you and discus this." I shake my head and look down. "I don't think I can let this slide. I'm so sorry, but I'm going to have to let you go." I don't even finish saying what I want to say.

"What the hell are you talking about? You can't fire her for that. It's discrimination! You can't tell her what not to do on her own time," Barbara says.

"It's not her time, she is on the clock." I put my hand on my hips, glaring at her.

"Austin, it's not even eight yet. Technically, you aren't paying her yet."

I look at my watch and see that it is just a couple of minutes before eight. "Oh please, she doesn't even want to be here."

I look at Lauren and see that her head is tilted to the side. She looks back at her computer and then back at me "Where are all my Post-it notes?" She turns and looks me straight in the eyes.

I shrug my shoulders with what I hope is my best 'I don't know what you're talking about' expression. "Maybe the cleaning staff threw them out."

"What are you talking about? You know the cleaning staff only comes in on the weekend, Austin. I mean, they come and empty garbage cans, but they don't do the full cleaning until the weekend," Barbara puts in her two cents.

"Really," I hear Lauren say, putting her own hands on her hips. "Fascinating, since someone touched my desk two days ago."

I don't have time to answer before JP shows up with a briefcase. "Okay, where is the porn monster located?"

Lauren points to her computer, where she goes to tell him that she hasn't touched anything. It takes him a few minutes to get everything cleared up. "There, that should do the trick. It really wasn't that bad." He chuckles and looks at me. "Remember last year when I had to totally reconfigure your hard drive when the same thing happened to you?"

I look at Barbara and Lauren, who are both looking at me now. Barbara is smiling, while Lauren is glaring. "Thank you for all your help, JP. Now that the problem is fixed, perhaps you can start your day," I say to Lauren.

"Oh, I'm going to start my day, alright," she tells me with a twinkle in her eye, and I somehow know that she's just upped the ante.

chapter nine

Lauren

THE REST OF THE DAY GOES BY WITHOUT ANYTHING HAPPENING. THAT NIGHT BEFORE I leave, I take out four pieces of tape, folding them in half, and stick them under my mouse.

Take that, Asshat. I glare at him through his blinds, but he doesn't see me.

I send him an email before I go home, just letting him know I'm leaving.

I'm still so fucking embarrassed. The whole office was talking about the new PA watching porn at her desk before the start of the workday.

Steven didn't even say hello to me when I saw him in the kitchen; he just waved and looked down as he hurried out.

By the time I make it home, I'm almost in tears. The only thing keeping them at bay is the rage I feel. I slam my car door a lot harder than intended. I storm into the house, slamming that door behind me, too.

Kaleigh is the first one to come out of the kitchen to greet me. The look on my face has her rushing back into the kitchen and returning with a full glass of wine. It sloshes over the rim as she hurries it to me.

She quickly hands it over with a smile. "Should I ask?"

I drink half the glass before I answer her. "He gave my computer a porn virus," I say while I walk over to the couch and throw myself down on it.

She sits next to me. "What do you mean, a porn virus?"

"I mean that when I turned on my computer this morning, porn was just popping up on my computer." Kaleigh starts to laugh, but I turn and glare at her. "Don't you dare laugh! I was mortified. As if that wasn't bad enough, the screen was freezing up, but the sound was blasting. Before I could even do anything, all of this moaning and groaning was blaring all through the office. 'Oh, fuck me harder!' Ugh!" I put my empty glass down after I drain it. My arms are flailing around me as I continue my story. "Oh, and let's not forget the gay porn. Yeah, of course that's when the screen froze, just as one of the guys had his dick halfway in the other guy's ass!"

"Was it big?"

I look over at her incredulously. "What the hell does it matter?" I throw my hands up in the air. "And where are my kids?"

Her hand waves through the air. "At a playdate next door. You have soccer in an hour, so go get yourself changed. Unless you want to show up like that, make a statement."

"Fucking porn all over my computer. I can't believe he would do that."

"You did put a laxative in his Coke." I don't let her finish before I point at her and hiss out, "You cannot tell anyone about that. You promised."

She takes her fingers, zipping her lips closed. "Fine. Now, I'm going to go change and head to soccer where I'm hoping nothing else goes wrong."

"What could top your co-workers thinking you are flicking the bean while at work? I hope you washed your hand after."

"I didn't flick the bean at fucking work, jackass! He played with my computer and the asshole threw out all my Post-its."

Kaleigh shakes her head. "That asshat," she agrees just as the door opens and the kids run in.

"Who's an asshat, Auntie Kay?" Rachel asks while she climbs on my lap, rubbing her nose to mine. I grab her tiny face in my hand, kissing her on the nose. "Don't say asshat."

Gabe walks up to me, kissing me on the cheek. "Mom, we have to leave in thirty. Dad says he might make tonight's game," he says, jogging upstairs to change.

"Okay, change of plans, no changing for you," Kaleigh says. "Show him what he's missing."

I'm almost feeling better when my phone bings with a notification.

I see that it's a text from Austin.

Tomorrow when you come in, before you start with your porn surfing, I need you to pick up my dry cleaning. I'll share the address with you. I need those shirts for the conference I'm having with the marketing firm tomorrow afternoon.

I don't watch porn at work.

I beg to differ. Actually, JP begs to differ.

It's times like these when I want to take my phone and run it over. Actually, I want to run *him* over. Front and back. Just for fun.

I don't have a chance to answer, since Gabe runs down the stairs with his shoes slung over his shoulder, his chin pads on but not velcroed on the top. His uniform is almost on.

"We need to go if we are going to be there on time," he urges, going to the fridge and taking a cheese stick and an apple from the counter.

I look at Kaleigh. "Are you coming?" I get up and grab another apple and a cheese stick for Rachel.

"I wouldn't miss his game for the world," Kaleigh says while grabbing her yoga mat. "I could do yoga while he plays." Rachel comes into the room and claps her hands excitedly.

"I'm going to bring my mat, too, Auntie Kay. Can we do it doggie style?" I spew water all over the counter.

Kaleigh laughs at me and bends down, squatting in front of Rachel. "Downward facing dog, honey, not doggie style. That's for when you get older."

I slam the glass down in exasperation. "Kaleigh, I will not only make you drink cow's milk, I'll throw a burger at you."

Rachel giggles. "Gabe, when we get older, we can do it doggie style!" she sing-songs while walking out of the door to go to the car.

I glare at Kaleigh, who is laughing so hard she's hunched over in the corner, holding her stomach. "If she repeats that to Jake, I will kill you." I point at her while I walk out of the door. She follows me to the car still laughing.

When I get in the car, Rachel asks for me to put *Frozen* on, followed by Gabe, who is begging me to put on anything else but *Frozen*. He groans and moans the whole way, which is ten minutes past the point I almost jumped out of the car into oncoming traffic.

When we pull into the parking lot by the field, I see that Jake is already there. I look over at Kaleigh and mutter under my breath that it's a cold, cold day in hell, I suppose. We all get out of the car and Rachel runs over to him, her arms flinging all over the place. "Daddy, Daddy, Daddy," she screeches right before he leans down and swings her in his arms.

Gabe runs over to them, also hugging him on the side. Jake wraps one hand around his shoulder, squeezing him and kissing his forehead.

I don't stand around to hear their conversation; instead, I open the trunk, taking out our two soccer chairs. I walk over to the side of the field where the bleachers are. I say hello to a couple of people but not really making eye contact with anyone. I'm just not in the mood for small talk today.

The phone buzzes in my hand once more while I open the chair, and then one more time when I sit down.

Did you get the address?

Did you get the message?

Where are you? Why haven't you answered?

I don't have time to respond before another one comes in.

Are you watching porn?

I put my head back and type back.

Yes, and you're disturbing me.

I press send and look over to see that Jake is leaning against his car, typing away on his phone. Then my phone buzzes again.

Jesus, do you ever stop?

I roll my eyes, crossing my legs, looking over to see Kaleigh and Rachel bending down.

Nope! Leave me alone. I got the memo. I'll get your clothes. I think I can handle it.

I put the phone in the cup holder once the game starts. I clap when the kids run onto the field, yelling, "Go, Gabe, go!"

I'm not alone for long before Jake sits down in the empty chair beside me.

"You're looking good, Laur," he says, using his nickname for me from when we were married.

"Yup," is all I say, because my phone buzzes again. Three times, then four. I pick it up, reading it quickly.

What time will you be in?

I need it for noon!!!

I have a meeting with the developer from the club that will be opening in three weeks.
Are you there?

I groan and type back.

I'm not on the clock, therefore it doesn't matter where I am or what I'm doing or who I'm doing it with, for that matter. See you tomorrow at 8!

I look at the phone, seeing the bubble come up with the three dots. I wait. It goes off then comes back, then goes off again. Then the text comes through.

Who you're doing? I thought you were divorced?

I turn the phone off, so I won't answer or know if he answers.

"So, how is it being back in the job force?" Jake asks, opening a bottle of water and drinking it.

"Jake, I have to be nice to you in front of the kids so they don't think I'm a bitter bitch. But when it's just the two of us"—I point to him then me—"I don't have to be nice to you. So, if you don't mind, I'll dispense with small talk. I don't want to talk about my day, my job, if I'm doing okay, if I have a date, or really anything at all with you. So, if you'll excuse me, I want to watch Gabe's game." I look to the field. "In peace."

Jake doesn't say anything else to me for the rest of the game. We sit in silence as we watch Gabe's team win. When the three whistles ring at the end, I see Kaleigh roll up her mat and walk over to us.

Jake kisses both kids and promises to see them next weekend. It's his weekend, which means I get very familiar with my wine glass, my Kindle, and my couch. Netflix is also on deck for a big ol' marathon!

I'm so excited to do absolutely nothing that whole weekend, I almost skip to the car.

By the time the baths are over and everyone is tucked in, I turn my phone on to set the alarm. I have five messages, all from Asshat.

Hello???

Did you get my messages?

Why aren't you answering me?

Your professionalism is laughable. I don't even know why I still have you as my PA. Do you even know what PA stands for?

Unbelievable! Just get my clothes.

I want to write him back to go fuck himself, him and his pencil dick, if he can even find it.

I whip the covers off and march to the hall closet, where I take out Gabe's practical joke box he got for his birthday last year.

I open it, tossing aside the moustache glasses, Chinese finger traps, whoopee cushion, squirting ring, nail through finger, and electric shock buzzer, coming up with the itching powder. I take it out and close the box, replacing it on the top shelf.

I'll show that asshat professionalism!

The next day, I get up, shower, and dress in a gorgeous royal blue wrap dress that I pair with a slim-fitting, tailored white blazer, since the dress is sleeveless. I quickly tuck the itching powder into my purse before the kids see it.

I make my way over to his dry cleaners, which is on the other side of town. Once I walk in, I give them his name and phone number, and collect his clothes.

There are about five suit jackets, ten pants, and twenty-five shirts. I have to walk to the car twice.

Once I'm inside the car, I open my purse and climb into the back seat.

I grab all his pants, taking one at a time, unfolding them neatly, and opening and sprinkling some powder in the crotch area, then pressing the legs together to rub it in a bit. I repeat this until all his pants are done.

I smile to myself, but then my phone rings, startling me as the sounds fills the car, causing me to jump as I bobble the bottle. It goes flying, landing on the floor near my foot. I let out a little yelp as I kick it away.

I peek at my phone and see that it's him.

"Hello?"

"Where are you? Why aren't you here?"

"Where am I? Did you not tell me to go get your clothes from the cleaners this morning? The cleaners that, mind you, is half way to Guatemala," I return tartly while climbing back into the front seat and starting up the car. "I'm on my way. What do I do with your clothes?" I ask him as I start making my way to work.

"What do you think you do with them? You bring them up!" he replies smartly.

"Bring them up? It took me two trips to get them all in the car. Are you even dressed?" I ask, merging on the highway. "What do you need for the meeting? I can bring up what you need, and then when I leave later, you can come down and get them from my car."

"Ugh," I hear him groan. "Okay, fine. Bring me up my black suit," he says and hangs up. He doesn't have to say anything, because the car lets me know, "Phone call disconnected."

Asshole.

Once I get to work, I slide open the back door and look for his black suit, except almost all the suits are some shade of black. Fuck. Grabbing what I hope is a matching jacket and pants, I walk into my office building.

Looking at my watch, I see that it's already nine a.m. Once I get to the floor and the door opens, I see Steven at the reception desk talking to Carmen.

"Good morning, guys," I say, smiling to them while I fold Asshat's suit over my arm.

Steven smiles at me shyly. "Morning. You're late this morning. Is everything okay?" he asks.

"Oh yeah." I point to the dry cleaning. "Had to get his laundry."

"Right. Are you staying in for lunch?" Steven asks. I shake my head no.

"I'm actually thinking of going to this restaurant around the corner. They have little tables outside. And it's beautiful today," I say

"That sounds delightful," Steven says "What time are you going?"

"Probably around noonish."

"Would you like some company?" He puts his hands in his pockets. It's the same move that Austin uses, except with Steven it doesn't fit.

"I would love some company. I'll call you when I'm ready," I say to him and then walk down the hall to my desk, dumping my purse on it before I walk to his office.

Seeing that the door is closed, I knock and wait for him to tell me to come in.

I open the door and see him behind his desk, eyes on the computer while he types away.

"Here is your dry cleaning. Where do you want it?" I ask him.

"Just put it over the back of the couch and check your email. There are a couple of things that need scheduling; also, we have the grand opening for the club in three weeks. You need to attend with me."

"Which day?" I ask, trying to pull up my calendar in my head, hoping that I don't have anything.

"You have all of that in your emails. Now, if you're done asking me insignificant questions, you can go," he dismisses me, not once looking at me. "And because you were late today, you are going to have to eat lunch here."

"I wasn't late. I was running an errand for you. Besides, I have plans at lunch."

"Don't care. Change them." I'm about to tell him to suck a dick when Barbara knocks on the door and walks in.

"Good morning, you two. Austin, we are ready for you," she says, and he gets up and walks out.

I'm stuck watching his back while he walks away. He never once makes eye contact with me.

I take in the jeans he's wearing today. They hang low on his hips but are tight on his ass. And what an ass it is. The kind that makes you want to grab it and bite it.

Wait, what?! What the hell was that? I don't like him. I really don't like him! Not at all. Not even a little bit. In my head, he's my sworn enemy. Now, if only someone would send that memo to the rest of my body!

chapter ten

Austin

All night, I tossed and turned. The fact that I texted her and she didn't answer me pissed me off. Again and again, I waited for her answer but got nothing. The thought of her with someone else irked me. I tossed, I turned, I got up, I looked outside.

I kept my phone near me all night, just in case she answered. Finally, around two a.m., I fell asleep, and when my alarm rang, I rushed, thinking the phone was ringing.

So here I am, still pissed off that she didn't answer, mingling with the fact that I'm grumpy because I'm tired. And to top it all off, I have to go into a marketing meeting with Dani about the club that is opening in three weeks.

I also have to talk to John about the Christmas party that is coming up. I walk into the meeting with John and Steven, pissed off, because not only did Lauren just walk in, but she also looks hotter than she ever has. That dress wrapped around her catches every curve she has, and when she walks, you get a glimpse of her inner thigh.

So, now I'm sitting in this meeting with a hard-on. "Are we disturbing you, Austin?" I hear John ask.

I shake my head, leaning back in my chair, rocking. "Nope, I'm all ears." He looks over at me, eyes narrowed speculatively as if he's trying to figure me out.

"I think that's all for now, Steven. You're good to go," John says while still looking at me.

"Perfect. If you guys need me, I'm headed out to lunch with Lauren, so I'll be back after that," he says, gathering his things and getting up from the table.

"No, you're not," I almost shout, and he stops picking his things up to look at me. "She needs to set up for my meeting with Dani." I grab my phone, sending her a meeting, telling her that I need her to set up for my meeting with Dani.

"Oh, okay," he says, turning and walking out of the room.

"Want to tell me how she's going to set up for your meeting with Dani when Dani is the one bringing everything for the meeting?"

I shrug my shoulders. "She needs to make sure we have water and shit."

He slaps his hand down on the table and bursts out laughing. "You have it so bad for her, and you don't even know it yet."

"I don't have anything bad. She almost killed me! I have to make her life a living hell." But he doesn't say anything; he just continues laughing. "She fucking put something in my Coke, and I thought I was shitting out my organs."

He wipes the tears from the corner of his eyes. But just then the door is thrown open, and Noah saunters in. "What are you guys laughing about?" he asks, plopping himself down in the chair that Steven just vacated.

"Austin's PA put something in his Coke, and he had the shits all night long," John says between fits of laughter.

"It wasn't all night long; it was till there was nothing left inside of me," I correct him while Noah chuckles.

"Wow. I thought my PA hated me," Noah says.

"She caught you fucking her mother on your desk," I remind him.

"She didn't knock. It wasn't my fault." He points at me.

"You had sex with her the day before," I also point out.

He shrugs his shoulders, thinking nothing more of it. "At least she didn't try to kill me."

"She put your face on a billboard with your home address and open invitation for free lodging for the homeless," John comments, still laughing.

"We don't know if it was her," I tell him. "I know that Lauren gave me something, that's the difference here."

"And didn't you infect her computer with porn viruses?" John asks. "Barbara says you're paying JP for that visit yourself, by the way."

"You got her computer with porn? Oh, my fuck, you like her!" Noah accuses.

"How can I like someone who almost killed me? She also hates the fact of my very existence on this earth. Not to mention that she didn't even answer my texts last night."

"You texted her after hours?" Noah asks, confused.

"I needed her to pick up my dry cleaning." I'm making excuses right now that are so lame not even I'm buying them. "Besides, you text your PA at night."

"Yes," Noah confirms. "For sex."

I throw my hands up when they both laugh at me, then I look at my watch. "I'm not doing this. I have to get ready for Dani's meeting."

"Oh yes, that's right. The meeting Lauren has to 'prepare' for." John even uses his hands to make air quotations. Noah continues laughing. Those bastards.

"Fuck off, the both of you." I storm out of the conference room and run straight into Lauren. I wrap my arms around her so she doesn't fall; one arm wraps around her waist easily, while the other brings her closer to me.

Her body fits mine perfectly. Her head tilts back, and I look into her eyes. They are startled at first, but then they turn softer. "Sorry," she says, and I get a whiff of her berry sent. If I bent just a bit, my lips would touch hers. I would be able to find out if that shiny, pink lip gloss of hers tastes like strawberries. I'd find out how those plump lips feel against mine and if I could get her to light up for me. Maybe then I'd finally figure out how she really feels.

All these thoughts are running through my mind, and I decide I'm going to go for it, to finally scratch this itch that has been taunting me since the moment she got out of her car on the side of that road. Before I can do it, though, the conference room door opens and Noah and John both come walking out. Their laughter stops the second they take in the scene before them.

"Hey," John says. Lauren pushes herself away from me.

"Hi, John. I wasn't watching where I was going and slammed into Austin. He caught me before I fell." She's babbling so fast and nervously, I don't think she realizes that it just makes us look even guiltier. "I've got to set up for the meeting. Excuse me," she rushes out, walking past them.

"Dude, cover that shit up." Noah points to my crotch, where it's plain to see that I'm, once again, at full mast. They both start laughing at me.

I walk away from them, shaking my head while I attempt to cover my hard-on.

Walking into my office, I slam the door. Fuck me, I can still feel her full tits pressed to my chest. I rub my hands on my face. Shit!

I stay in my office and out of sight until I change into my black suit. I tuck my white shirt in and thread my black leather belt through the belt loops of my pants.

I grab the file and walk to the conference room, where I hear Lauren's laughter.

I open the door and see that she is talking to Dani. "Well, I'm glad I could help," she says then looks at me. "If you need me, you can call me." She gets ready to leave.

"Why don't you stay and take notes?" I ask while I go to the head of the table and take a seat.

"Sure," she replies and takes the seat to my left, leaving Dani to sit on my right.

Dani opens the plans for the restaurant first. "Now, if you look here, you can see that we added some booths upstairs that can be used for lunch or supper."

I look at the plans, but then I feel a prickle in my balls. So I adjust myself in the seat, while she continues. "One thing I was thinking was that for supper, we can do a Tapas menu upstairs and at the bar, and stop serving at eleven. Which is good, since we won't have to move anything. We can also use the booths for a VIP section." She continues talking, but I'm having trouble focusing on her words, because my balls are starting to burn.

So, I pull my pants away from them, thinking that they are squeezing them.

"That sounds like a good plan. Can we also do some couples' booths?" I ask her right before I feel another prickle and then another. Fuck, is there a mosquito stuck in my pants?

"That's a great idea! I'll look into that right away and get back to you with specifics," Dani says.

"I'd love to go out to a club with my friends and not have to deal with drunk, aggressive guys all night," Lauren puts in.

"I hear you. I'd love to do a girls' section," Dani says. "With booths all the way around the perimeter and comfy seating clusters, so you can sit down when your feet hurt."

"Yes! That's a really great idea. I love that!" Lauren answers enthusiastically.

I'm trying to concentrate, but my pants are starting to suffocate my balls. Jesus, did the cleaners shrink my fucking pants? What the hell?

"Excuse me." I get up and walk quickly to the bathroom in my office.

The minute I pull my pants down, I start scratching. It feels like my balls are on fire. I yank down my boxers and gasp out loud.

My balls have ballooned to three times their normal size. Well, one looks like it's twice its normal size, while the other is even bigger than that. Oh my god! What the hell?! I start to panic and pull my phone out of my pocket to call John.

"You need to come to my office right now," I demand and then hang up. I take a picture of my balls with my phone to inspect them closer.

I grimace at what I see. Holy fuck, are they are huge and red, and are those bumps?

I hear John call my name. I open the door just enough to pop my head out. "Come here!"

"Ummm, no way. What the fuck, man? I thought you were in trouble," he says and turns to walk out.

"John! Get the fuck in here," I whisper-yell angrily through my clenched teeth.

He walks in, and I close the door as he looks down and gasps, taking in the state of my balls. "What the fuck, dude?!"

"I don't know what's going on! I was sitting in the meeting when I felt a prickling sensation. I thought my pants were just tight. Dude." I look down. "My balls."

I look up again to see that John is standing there, a hand over his mouth, his eyes wide. "You need to go to the doctor. Jesus, do you think they'll explode?" he wonders as he crouches down—a little too close considering our relationship—to get a better look.

"Get the fuck away from my balls, please," I snap while I take my phone out and call Noah. "If anyone knows anything about this kind of thing, it's Noah. Didn't he get crabs from some chick in the Hamptons once?"

He answers on the first ring, "Yo," and I put him on speaker.

"When you got crabs, did your balls swell?" I ask, closing my eyes. I haven't had sex in about a month, so I have no idea if this is some sort of a delayed reaction.

"You have crabs?" he asks instead of answering my question.

"I have no idea. My balls are on fire and have swelled up to the size of a baseball," I explain while I continue to scratch them.

"Don't touch them," John says from his side on the phone. "I'm Googling this. Can I take a picture?" he asks right before he looks up and sees the glare on my face.

"Oh, send me a picture, too," Noah says, while John continues to mess with his phone.

"It says something might have ruptured or you could have a hernia. Did you lift something heavy?" he asks while continuing to read.

"I was in a fucking meeting! I lifted a goddamn water bottle!" I look down at my balls, which seem to have gotten even bigger. "Oh my god, I think they're getting bigger."

"Can someone please send me a picture?" Noah begs through his laughing.

"I'm not sending you a picture of my balls, man," I say.

"You really need to get that checked out," John says. "I'll call Phil, maybe he's on duty."

"What color are they?" Noah is still chuckling.

"Fuck you." The itch is so bad I can't stop scratching.

"Phil says he's at Mercy Hospital now. If you get there in the next thirty, he can see you," John says while he's on the phone with Phil.

"I'll meet you there," Noah says, and I hang up on him.

"Will they fit back in your pants?" John is now laughing at me, too.

"Fuck you, this isn't funny. What if they exploded inside?" I question as panic sets in and my heart starts to beat faster. Jesus, what if I broke my dick?

I pull up my boxers then my pants, my balls protesting the constriction of my pants.

"Fuck, oh god, it hurts now," I groan as I head out of the bathroom. I'm walking like I'm severely constipated, or worse, like I just had anal sex with a telephone pole. "Someone needs to tell Dani that I'm leaving."

"On it," John says, typing on his phone.

"Let's go before someone else sees you." We walk to the elevator as fast as we can, given my condition. When we get to Mercy, Noah is outside with a wheelchair waiting for us.

"Is this curbside service, or what!" he says, laughing at us. "Come on, big nuts, let's get this taken care of."

I sit down and get wheeled inside, where Phil is waiting for us. When he ushers us to a room, I expect Noah and John to wait outside. But I'm that lucky, and I shouldn't be at all surprised when they follow us into the exam room.

"Seriously? You guys really need to be in here?" I ask them both.

"I've already seen it," John mutters, while Noah says, "I wouldn't miss this for the world. Can I film this? Maybe do a Snap story? Oh! I know, it can be my Instagram story!" I glare at him. "We could do that Facebook Live thing, you know, for medical purposes, of course."

"No one is filming shit," I grumble, while Phil tells me to lower my pants. I pull my pants and boxers off at the same time, and male gasps fill the quiet room.

"Jesus, fuck me, your balls are the size of a miniature poodle's head!" Noah eclaims, and I start scratching again.

"Fuck! They got bigger," John comments. "I didn't think it was possible. Phil, can they explode?"

Phil grabs a pair of exam gloves, pulls them on, and rubs them together. "I'm warming them up," he says and then proceeds to put his ice-cold, latex-covered hands on my poor burning, itching, swollen balls. He starts inspecting them, bringing them up to look at the underside of my scrotum and moving them to the side to inspect the area where my leg meets my groin. "I don't see any puncture marks, so it's not a bite. A small rash is forming on your scrotum, however."

I put my head back and let out a breath I have been holding. "It looks like you're having an allergic reaction to something. Did you eat anything different? Change soaps? Anything at all?"

I shake my head no. "I don't think so. I don't wash my clothes, and my pants just came back from the dry cleaners. Lauren picked them up this morning."

I look at Noah and John, who are now folded over laughing. "Dude! She fucking hates you! And obviously, she hates your dick!" Noah says.

"Good news is that it will be back to normal in about twenty-four hours, maybe forty-eight, tops. I wouldn't put the pants or boxers back on," Phil says. "The swelling should go down, but if it doesn't, call me and I'll give you some meds. I'm going to have the nurse administer some Benadryl, and I'm going to have you stay for a couple of hours to make sure they don't swell any further," Phil says while writing on a paper. "I'll be back." He walks out.

"If you sit down, do you think your balls will crowd your dick?" John asks while he types on the phone.

"Who are you texting?" I ask.

"Dani and Barbara. You want me to text Lauren?" he snickers.

Noah is now sitting in the only chair in the room while he types. "I'm sending flowers to everyone I fucked over as a thank you for not giving me swollen balls."

I have no comeback. I just close my eyes and lie down on the table to wait for the swelling in my balls to go down. It's five hours later when I'm finally discharged. I leave the hospital dressed in a pair of blue scrubs.

When I finally get home and settled, I take my phone out and see that I missed a text from Lauren.

I hope you're okay?

Oh, I'm going to be more than okay. I sit down to plot and plan. The stakes just went up.

chapter eleven

Lauren

Fuck, fuck, fuckity fuck! I fucked up this time and took it too far. I'm headed back to his cleaners where I picked up his pants this morning to have them recleaned.

I saw him shifting in his chair during the meeting, and I laughed inside until I saw his face change a little right before he took off and didn't come back.

I was still discussing with Dani how to place tables when she got the text from John telling her they were taking Austin to the hospital.

When I heard he was going to the hospital, my heart lurched in my chest. I debated whether I should go after him or hide, hoping and praying that he wouldn't find out it was me and one of my pranks. It was supposed to be a harmless joke, like the porn virus on my computer. I never, ever intended to actually hurt him.

By the time I left for the day, the word around the office was that he had an allergic reaction to something.

I practically ran to my car, calling Kaleigh the minute I was inside and the door was closed.

"I think I almost killed my boss!" I yell into the phone as I speed to his dry cleaners.

"What do you mean, almost? Does he know? Did you wear gloves?" She peppers me with questions, and I hear banging in the background.

"Kaleigh, please, just this once, can you try to be fucking normal?" I ask, thumping the steering wheel in exasperation as I start freaking out.

"Okay, fine. What exactly happened?"

"I put fucking itching powder in his pants. And I think his dick or his ass, or I don't fucking know, maybe his balls, was allergic to it, and he had to go the fucking hospital!" I finish on a shrill yell.

"You put what?"

"Itchy powder I took from Gabe's prank box! It was just supposed to be a stupid joke. A payback for the porn bombing he pulled on my computer," I say as my eyes start filling with tears.

"You mean after you put a laxative in his Coke?"

"Kaleigh, not now, for the love of God. You are on my side always. Blood thicker than asshat boss," I remind her. "The minute he ran into me and I almost fell but he caught me instead, I regretted doing it. Oh god. Do you think he's going to know it's me?"

"I don't know. Does anyone else in the office hate him?" she asks me.

"I have no idea if anyone hates him. It's not something I can bring up, you know? I mean, I'm his PA; I can't go around asking people 'Hey, how are you? Isn't Austin an asshole?' Oh my god!" I pull up to the cleaners. "I gotta call you back. I'm at the cleaners. I'm bringing his clothes to be recleaned."

I hang up even though she is still talking. I rush into the cleaners, my arms full of all his clothes.

"Hi, there. I need all of these recleaned, twice please." I put the clothes down on the counter.

"Ma'am, you just picked these up this morning," the lady says while she picks up the clean clothes that are still in the plastic covers.

"Yes, I think something spilt on them and he wants them cleaned again," I say, smiling "Twice."

"Twice?" she asks, confused.

"Yes, just in case. He wants them run through the cleaning process twice," I repeat to her, and she puts my special request on the card. I turn and rush out of there. I climb back into my car, toss my purse onto the passenger seat, and head for home.

While I brake at a stop sign, the empty bottle of itching powder rolls to the front floor board at the same time as my phone rings. I see that it's Kaleigh calling.

"Are you okay?" she whispers.

"No. I'm not okay. I caused my boss to end up in the ER with an allergic reaction and swollen balls because I was trying to get back at him." I feel the sob creeping up my throat.

"Did you get rid of all of the evidence?" she asks me.

"I still have the empty bottle here in the car." I look down at it, and it's almost as if it's taunting me.

"Throw it out of the car right now," she instructs me. "Open the window and toss it as far as you can."

I pick up the bottle and hold it in my hand. "Should I wipe it down?" I look around for a rag.

"Lauren, do you honestly think he is calling CSI to come and find the bottle? Just throw the fucking thing out the window and come home."

Just as I'm about to throw the bottle out of the window, I hear a honk, starling me. "Fuck," I say while the bottle falls into my lap.

"I'm on my way," I say while I drive on, and when I'm all alone on the street, I toss that bottle as far as I can while driving.

Once I park my car in the driveway, I text Austin.

I hope you're okay?

I wait a couple of seconds, but nothing comes in. So, I walk into the house, where I'm greeted with hugs and kisses.

When I finally tumble into bed, my phone beeps with a text from Austin.

I'm not coming in tomorrow, so you can take the day off.

Oh, are you okay? I heard you had an allergic reaction.

You could say that.

Well, I'll be here all weekend if you need anything. I'm hosting my parents and a couple of their friends for their anniversary brunch on Sunday morning, but if you need anything, please let me know.

Sure thing.

This is really weird. He's usually sarcastic and an asshole, but now he's all soft and not at all snarky.

The next couple of days are pretty much the same as usual. On Saturday night, after putting the kids to bed, I start preparing the dishes and everything for tomorrow's brunch.

Mom is having a caterer come in, since I'm hosting their anniversary brunch. We plan to set up outside and have a beautiful outdoor celebration with twenty of their closest friends.

My phone rings, letting me know that it's my mom calling.

"Hey, Mom."

"How did you know it was me?" she asks, all confused.

"Mom, the phone has caller ID." My mom isn't a tech friendly person. Last time she tried to FaceTime the kids, her screen was facing the other way and all we saw was her finger on the camera.

"Are you ready for tomorrow, dear? You didn't really have to do this, but we are so excited about it." Her voice is pitching higher with her excitement.

"It's my pleasure, Mom. You know I would do anything for you two." And I would. Mom and Dad have been married for thirty-nine years.

They met while Dad was visiting a friend from college. All it took was one look, and he was hooked. The minute he finished his residency, he came and proposed to Mom, promising to love, honor, and cherish her, and he actually kept those promises.

Mom stayed home with us girls, while Dad grew his practice. He's retired now, and the practice is in Josh's hands.

"You know, Josh is coming, and he's single again," Mom reminds, interrupting my thoughts.

"Mom, please don't. We went on one date, and that was only because I was guilted into it."

My mother heaves out a huge sigh. "Oh please, he's perfect for you! Single and a doctor."

"Mom, he's shorter than me, by almost a foot, and he's balding," I tell her.

"It's what's inside, Lauren, not what's outside."

"Mom, he's thirty!" I yell out.

"So he aged early, there is nothing wrong with that. He's a total catch," she says. "Oh honey, I have to go. The Robinsons just got here. See you Sunday!" She adds, "Oh, and tell Kaleigh that a bra is mandatory!" I laugh and hang up the phone just as Kaleigh walks in.

"That was Mom." I point to the phone. "She said that a bra is mandatory this time."

She waves her hand like she isn't paying attention. "Oh please, it was one time. How was I supposed to know that you could see my nipples through that pink sundress?" she says while grabbing her almond mild and drinking straight from the carton.

Right when I'm about to scold her to use a glass, the phone rings again. This time I see it's Austin.

"Hello?" I say tentatively, since he's never called me.

"I have an eight-a.m. meeting Monday morning with Dani to finalize things, since I had to leave yesterday."

"Okay, I can get in a bit early and get things set up again," I confirm, looking at Kaleigh, who is looking at me, making the blowjob motion with her tongue poking her cheek.

"I need my dry cleaning. Is it still in your car?" he questions me, and my head snaps up as I wave my arms to get my sister to stop distracting me.

"Um, yeah, I still have it. How about I bring it to you on Monday morning, is that okay?" I'm freaking out and pacing the kitchen floor, while my sister pretends to be humping the counter. I mute the phone and look at her. "Would you be serious? He wants his dry cleaning." I unmute it while he grunts his okay.

"If that's all, I have to go. I have to run errands for my Sunday brunch."

"Yeah, that's all," he says and hangs up.

"Oh my god." I run to my purse, searching for where I put the dry-cleaning bill. Once I find it, I call the number at the top. They answer after one ring.

"Rinse and Clean, how may I help you," the lady says right before I stutter out.

"Hi, hi, I was in a couple of days ago. I don't know if you remember me. I needed an order washed twice." I sit on the stairs. "The number is 076453."

"Oh, the one who brought back the clothes still in the wrapping. Yes, ma'am, I put a rush on it, and they should be ready in about an hour."

I look at my watch and see that it's already almost four. "Okay, thank you. Are you open tomorrow?" I ask her, knowing I won't be able to get there and back before I have to get Gabe to his soccer game.

"We are open until four on Saturday and noon on Sunday," she says and hangs up after we say good-bye.

"Fuck! I have to add a stop to our growing list of things to do tomorrow. Next time I offer to host a brunch, kick me in the ass, please," I tell Kaleigh. The day flies by in a flurry of errands and preparations, and before I know it, it's Sunday morning.

I set my alarm for eight, since the caterers will be arriving at eight thirty.

I make my way downstairs just in time to see Kaleigh walk in the door still wearing last night's outfit.

"Oh, the walk of shame. Nice. Very Nice," I say while I sip my coffee and she sits down at the counter.

"What's a walk of shame?" Rachel asks, and I look over at Kaleigh.

"It's when you are still wearing last night's clothes," Kaleigh discloses to her and then whispers to me, "After they were on the floor of the hot guy whose cock you rode all night." And then she throws her fist, pumping.

I smack her arm and pick up Rachel in my arms. "You get to wear the pretty dress today. Are you excited?" I ask her.

"So excited! We get to go get our hair fixed?" She throws up her hands, mimicking Kaleigh.

The doorbell rings, and I let the caterer in while we go upstairs to get dressed so we can leave the caterers to do their thing while we get pampered.

Even Gabe comes along for the fun. Well, not fun for him, but he pretends.

Once we get home, we all rush upstairs to change with only twenty minutes to spare.

I hurry into my room and pull out my white skirt that is tight to the knees with pleats all the way around. I pair it with a tight brown spaghetti-strapped camisole that molds to my boobs, and my brown strappy wedges.

"Umm, Lauren? I think you should see this," I hear Kaleigh say at the same time the doorbell rings. I spray my perfume on and rush downstairs, where my parents have just walked in with all of their friends arriving at the same time.

"Happy anniversary, Mom and Dad." I greet them with a hug.

"Thank you, dear," Mom says, hugging me in return.

"Please, everyone, come in. I had the backyard set up for our brunch." I point the way to the backyard. Kaleigh, who has changed and is now wearing a pretty, pink sundress—with a bra, I might add—rushes over to me.

"I think you need to see outside before everyone else does." She says talks with her teeth clenched, which confuses me.

"What are you talking about?" I ask and then the doorbell rings again. I go to answer it before Kaleigh does. I open the door to be greeted by a guy holding a huge chocolate bouquet.

I gasp out in shock when I see that all of the chocolates are made of penises and the pail holding them is adorned with a huge pink bow. "I have a delivery for Lauren," he announces, looking at the clipboard in his hand.

"I..." I stutter, while he pushes the pail into my hands. "I didn't order these." I look down and see that there are both white chocolate ones and milk chocolate ones, all on white sticks. I shake my head, my throat getting dry. He walks to his truck that is parked in the driveway and comes back with two more pails. "I don't want this," I say to him, but he's just a delivery guy, so he just smiles and leaves.

"Oh my god," Kaleigh says from beside me. "Don't freak out." She looks at me.

"Why would I freak out?" I ask right when my mother yells from outside.

I walk past the caterers, who are still preparing. When I walk into the backyard, my eyes survey the scene as my mouth hangs open at what I see.

I look at the white tables I ordered that are all set up with the turquoise tablecloths I requested. The little glass vases holding the white flowers in them just like I ordered in the center of each table. Except there are also bouquets of balloons—all white and turquoise, each one stamped with a penis.

Now, as if that isn't bad enough, there are also approximately fifty two-foot tall pink, penis-shaped helium balloons. The penis has a smile on the head and a blue bow around the shaft. They are all floating around the yard.

"Oh my god, oh my god!" I cry, looking over to see that there are penis straws in all the glasses. The table in the corner that I set up for the cake is now filled with cupcakes with little penis cake toppers.

"Dear, what is this?" my mother asks me with a forced smile on her face. My father is holding a glass of scotch, which he is sipping, mind you, through a penis straw.

"I didn't order this. They made a mistake." I look around, making sure everyone hears me.

One of the servers walks by with the chocolate penises. Of course, my mother grabs one before she even realizes what it is.

"Grammy, why are you eating a chocolate willy?" Rachel asks. "Look, Momma! It's just like Gabe's willy!" She grabs a balloon and runs over with it.

I look over at the guests, who are all snickering at this point. "Surprise!" Kaleigh yells. "You guys are in for a treat!"

Mom's best friend, Sarah, comes up to me. "I love it, it's very liberating. And fun," she giggles as she takes a sip of her drink through her own penis straw.

I am completely and utterly humiliated, and I'm about two seconds away from sobbing in the middle of my backyard. The song "It's My Party And I Can Cry If I Want To" is playing on repeat in my head. Tears well up in my eyes.

I'm about to have an epic meltdown, and we didn't even serve the meal yet. I hear a knock on the side gate and in walk, or should I say saunter, Austin and his friend, Noah.

Austin looks like sin on a stick. He's dressed in blue jeans and a linen button-down shirt rolled up at the sleeves. His silver Rolex on his wrist, and his gold aviator glasses on his face. A dusting of two days' worth of stubble gives him an edge. "Oh, I'm sorry. I don't mean to crash your party," he says with a megawatt smile on his face.

I look over at Noah, who is looking around at all the penises, his eyes bulging out of his head. He turns and looks at Austin and covers his mouth with his hand. It is in this moment that I know I've been played.

"You." I point at Austin.

He walks up to me, turning his smile at Mom. "You must be Lauren's sister," he says, kissing her hand. She smiles and throws her head back and laughs.

"Oh, you silly boy. I'm Deidra, Lauren's mother. You can call me Dede," she invites while she smiles at him.

"You can call her nothing, because you're leaving. Now. And"—I turn to him—"how did you know where I live?"

"Lauren, stop being rude to the guests," my mother scolds, while my father walks over and introduces himself. "Hello, son, I'm Frank, Lauren's father."

"No," I say, shaking my head. "He isn't a guest. This is my former boss." I look at him. "I quit. Done. Finished. Finito. I'm out," I snap with my hands on my hips.

"Who is the other one?" Kaleigh asks with a chin lift in Noah's direction.

"That's Noah," I answer. "Gabe, can you go inside and get my car keys? Mr. Mackenzie was coming to get his dry cleaning," I say to Gabe, who runs inside to get my keys.

"Mom, can I have a willy chocolate?" Rachel tugs at my skirt while she asks me the question.

"No, you cannot have a willy chocolate. We are going to eat in a minute." I turn and storm inside, walking past the kitchen to the bathroom, where I try to slam the door shut, but a brown shoe blocks it from closing.

"Seriously, what do you want?" I look at him. He's pushed the glasses to the top of his head. I blink away the tears that have formed in my eyes and look away from him so he doesn't see. "Didn't you get your revenge already?" I throw my hands up. "You penis-bombed my parents' anniversary party!"

He leans against the closed door, folding his arms across his chest. His scent fills the room, making it feel small all of a sudden.

"You made my balls swell to the size of fucking grapefruits. I thought they were going to explode," he fires back at me.

"I did no such thing." I look at my shoes and then look up. "But this, this... You pushed it too far."

"How about we call a truce?" Austin asks. "I don't think I can take any more. I almost died, and my testicles almost exploded."

"Fine," I agree, putting out my hand to shake his. He grabs my hand in his, and the minute he touches me, my breath hitches and I try to pull my hand away, but he holds it firmly.

"Truce," he promises, his thumbs stroking my hand. I look down where our hands meet. The room is getting smaller and smaller.

Right as I start to lean into him, there is a loud knock. "Hey, I don't mean to interrupt, but, um, Jake is here."

chapter twelve

Austin

THE MINUTE SHE TOLD ME SHE WAS HAVING A BRUNCH AT HER HOUSE, I SET A PLAN IN motion. This was after I called the dry cleaners and asked them if they changed soaps.

I was told that my clothes had been brought back with the very odd request that they be recleaned—twice. That little shit.

It took about thirty hours for the swelling in my balls to go down. Thirty hours of praying to every god I could think of that they would return to normal. I just didn't want to have big balls anymore.

So when I finally calmed down, I put my plan in motion. I found her address in the company directory that only HR and higher management can access.

From there, I set out to find local businesses who sold party materials in the shape of a penis. I called in the event planner that I usually use, and she was nothing but professional. I was really surprised that she didn't even bat an eye at my strange requests.

"Isn't this a weird request?"

"Austin, you would be surprised the stuff I have had to find. Penises? Please. That's like trying to find princesses nowadays."

After telling her what I wanted, she set it all up to be delivered before noon. I called Noah and asked if he wanted to do brunch with me, but not telling him anything further in case he tried to talk me out of it.

When we show up in front of Lauren's house, that is when I fill in Noah.

"Where the fuck are we? I thought you said we were going to brunch." He looks over at all the white-picket-fenced houses.

"Yeah, pit stop first. I have to pick up my dry cleaning at Lauren's," I tell him, getting out of the car.

Once I make my way around her house, he asks me. "Why are we at her house?"

"She's having a brunch." I shrug. "I may have sent her some penis decorations," I say before walking to the side of the gate.

The first thing I see are all the balloons. Fuck, the event planner wasn't kidding when she said she could get anything.

"Holy shit, she is going to cut your dick off with dental floss," I hear Noah say before I knock and walk into the backyard.

I stop in my tracks, mid-step, when I see that it isn't just her parents, but there are about fifteen or so people scattered around the yard. Noah, of course, bumps into me, his mouth flopping open and closed in shock.

"Holy shit," he whispers. "Dude, I think she's going to cry," he says, and my eyes snap straight to Lauren.

When I put this plan into motion, I assumed she would probably intercept the decorations before her guests saw them. I thought she would spend her morning trying to hide and/or dispose of them before they arrived, and then spend the party looking over her shoulder, fearful of another delivery.

I head over to her and the women who are obviously her sister and her mother. Her mother, who is right then biting into a chocolate penis. I'm introduced to Lauren's mother and father, and I'm pulling out all the charm. I'm not exactly sure why. I usually run away from parents.

I know she is seconds from slipping into meltdown mode, because she abruptly turns her back on her daughter and her mother and hurries toward the house.

"Excuse me," I tell her parents, walking right into her house after her. She walks into the bathroom, slamming the door behind her, but not before I can wedge my shoe in there to block it from closing.

"Seriously, what do you want?" She looks straight at me. I move the sunglasses that I'm still wearing off my face to the top of my head. I stare at her valiantly trying to hold it together, noticing the tears that are welling in her eyes. She blinks repeatedly and stands tall to face me down.

"Didn't you get your revenge already?" She throws up her hands, and that's when I notice how what she is wearing hugs all of her curves. The tank top that molds to her full breasts perfectly, and the skirt that skims her body in all the right places.

""You penis-bombed my parents' anniversary party!"

I lean against the closed door, folding my arms across my chest. "You made my balls swell to the size of fucking grapefruits. I thought they were going to explode," I fire at her.

"I did no such thing," she tries to deny weakly. She breaks eye contact, looking down at her shoes for a moment, before she squares her shoulders and looks me in the eye. "But this, this... You pushed it too far."

"How about we call a truce?" I ask. I have no idea why I'm even trying to get on her good side. "I don't think I can take any more. I almost died, and my testicles almost exploded," I tell her the truth.

"Fine," she complies, putting out her hand to shake mine. I raise my hand to grab hers. The fit is perfect. As I take in the feeling of her hand in mine, I notice that they are soft, delicate yet strong. As soon as her hand slipped against mine, I felt my heart rate kick up. I rub my thumb along the soft skin of her hand, trying to find a reason why I shouldn't just pull her into me and plant my lips on hers. The memory of her body pressed against mine at work the other day still lingers in my mind.

"Truce," I whisper, my thumb still stroking her hand. She looks down at our hands that are still connected. It looks like she's not even breathing.

I can feel her getting closer and closer to me. Then, right before I feel her start to lean into me, there is a loud knock. "Hey, I don't mean to interrupt, but, um, Jake is here."

She drops my hand like it's a hot potato, pushing me aside and opening the door. Her sister greets us with a huge smile, Noah standing right behind her. "What do you mean, Jake is here? Why is Jake here?" I hear her asking, her voice rising with each question.

"Hi"—the sister pushes Lauren aside—"I'm Kaleigh, her favorite sister," she introduces herself.

"She's my *only* sister, and she will be homeless in a second if she doesn't get out of my way." Lauren's voice is angry.

I hear Noah chuckle behind her. Lauren turns and points at him. "You, if I find out you helped him, it's going to be on," she hisses and leans in closer to him when she continues, "like Donkey Kong." And then she walks away.

"What the fuck does she mean, like Donkey Kong?" Noah turns to Kaleigh, looking for an answer.

"Oh, I was only on that list once"—she leans in closer to Noah—"and I begged and cried to get off of it." She looks at me then back at Noah. "It was like living in that movie *The Shining*, but worse." Noah's face pales at that little tidbit of information. Yeah, welcome to my world, buddy.

He points at me. "If I get it like Donkey Kong, I'm going to put the pictures of your swollen, abnormally large testicles on a billboard in Times Square," he threatens, while Kaleigh just watches us.

"Who the fuck is Jake?" I ask her.

"Her ex. This should be fun," she claims, walking away from us.

"You took a picture of my nuts?" I ask him.

He shakes his head at me. "No, I took a burst of shots of your nuts." Then he walks out, following Kaleigh.

"What are you doing here?" I hear Lauren ask a guy who I assume is Jake.

"I forgot that today was going to be the brunch. I was going to see if Gabe wanted to hang out at the park." He looks over at a boy who is standing in the corner of the yard, taking a picture of a penis balloon. That must be Lauren's son.

"Why didn't you call first?" she questions then shakes her head. "You know what, it doesn't matter. He can't go with you, so—"

"Daddy, look at all the willies," Lauren's miniature clone says as she walks over to him, two chocolate penises in her little hands. "You want to eat a willy?" She extends her hand to offer him one.

"No, honey, that's okay, you can have them." He looks around. "I should go," he adds, nodding at everyone and then leaving the backyard.

"Hey, Mister." The little girl looks up at me. "Who are you?" She is biting off the tip of the chocolate penis in her little hand.

"I'm your mom's boss," I explain to her, squatting down in front of her.

"Oh, you the Asshat?" she wonders, and Lauren's hand flies to cover her daughter's mouth in an effort to muffle whatever else she was going to say.

I look up at Lauren to see her shrug her shoulders. "This is Rachel and that is my son, Gabe." She points back to the kid in the corner, who just raises his hand in a little wave.

"Are we eating or not?" Frank asks.

"Yes," Lauren answers. "Everyone, please grab a seat wherever you feel comfortable. I'm going to tell Edward we are ready."

"You two can sit at my table," Kaleigh invites, while Lauren walks away.

She doesn't make it inside before she turns around. "They aren't staying."

"Oh, come now, Lauren. That would be rude," Dede chides. "You can sit at our table." She turns to Frank. "Let's go sit down, honey."

Once everyone is seated, I look around at our table. Noah, Kaleigh, Frank, Dede, Lauren, and Josh, who I found out is a doctor and bears a striking resemblance to Newman from *Seinfeld*.

He sits next to Lauren, standing up when she gets to the table and pushing her chair in. She looks over at him and smiles.

What the fuck is that smile all about? I wonder as I grab my glass of wine and down it in one gulp. "Slow down there, slugger. We don't want you flying off on one of those penis balloons," Noah whispers in my ear.

"So," Josh starts, looking at Lauren. "I hear congratulations are in order. You're back in the work force now." He continues in that annoyingly nasal voice of his, "How does this weekend sound?" He blushes and looks down to his hands. What a putz.

"Oh, um, she can't do it this weekend," Kaleigh answers for Lauren. "She's having her bikini area waxed and styled," she explains, nodding her head.

"What?" He looks confused.

"Well,"—Kaleigh leans in and whispers—"it's like the Amazon down there."

Noah spits water from his mouth, while their mother puts her hand to her mouth and Lauren throws her fork down on the plate, the clatter hushing the whispers at our table. "Kaleigh," she grates out, her jaw ticking.

"What?" she asks. "Was it a secret?" She shrugs. "So sorry." She brings her glass of wine to her mouth in an attempt to hide her smirk.

"Dear," Lauren's mother questions, "are you okay? Is this procedure normal?" She gives her daughter a look filled with concern.

"Mom—" Lauren starts before she is cut off by her father.

"Lauren, it's been a while since Jake left. Maybe if you—" he gestures with his hand in a circle and his finger sliding in and out—"you won't be so stressed."

I look over at Lauren, whose face is red with embarrassment and looks like she is going to lunge right over the table and throttle Kaleigh. She slams her hands on the table, the glasses clinking and rocking with the force of it. "I'm not having any hair removal procedures done, because it is not necessary. Can we please just—" This time, she is cut off by her mother.

"So, you've had sex since Jake?" Dede asks her, a smile on her face. "This is so good to hear." She claps her hands together then leans over and puts her hand on Lauren's. "I thought you had that glow about you."

"I'm going to the bathroom," Lauren excuses herself as she gets up and points to Kaleigh. "You"—she growls—"come with me."

"Oh," Kaleigh replies, completely unperturbed, "I'm good. I don't need to go. I'll just wait here. Keep the guests entertained."

"Not a word. Or else Donkey Kong," she promises before she storms off.

"So," Dede starts, turning to me. "How long have you two been dating?" She looks at me and then at the door that Lauren just walked through.

Kaleigh laughs. "Oh, they aren't dating, Mom. He's her boss," she helpfully points out. "He sent all these penis balloons."

Frank looks over at me. "You sent all these balloons and ruined all her hard work?" he asks.

"Um, sir, if I could just explain?" I start as my heart beats fast. Before I can say anything else, he puts up his hand to stop me.

"I like you," he declares right before someone clinks their glass and the speeches start.

I look around at the yard, taking in Lauren's family and friends. I sip my glass of wine and look over at Noah, who has his arm draped around Kaleigh's chair and is whispering in her ear. Whatever he's saying is causing her cheeks to turn pink.

The seat next to me gets pulled out when Lauren's daughter sits down next to me. "Hey, Asshat, can I have your strawberries?" I look over her head to the door where Lauren disappeared a few moments before and see her walking back outside. With an angry scowl on her face. Oh shit, the naked strippers must have arrived.

chapter thirteen

Lauren

I AM IN HELL. SOMETHING OR SOMEONE OUT THERE IS DRIVING THE KARMA BUS right into me. What I want to know is, what the fuck did I do wrong and to whom?

Not only is my boss, the bane of my existence, sitting at a table in my backyard with my parents at their anniversary brunch—after he sent me a yard-full of penis balloons, every single penis-themed party decoration known to man, and more penis-shaped chocolates on a stick than one woman could ever possibly eat— but as if that weren't enough, I'm now face-to-face with what appears to be the entire cast of the Australian all-male revue *Thunder From Down Under*.

"Hey, there, mate, we are here to party," he taunts with a thrust of his hips.

"Please, you obviously aren't even from Australia. That accent sounds Jamaican." I put my hands on my hips, and I'm pretty sure that this is the straw that broke the camel's back. Visions of me picking up a knife and stabbing him in the fucking heart in a fit of rage dance through my head.

"Party was cancelled. But you can charge the card twice for your trouble," I tell them before slamming the door. I head back out to the backyard and look right at the man who has set this particular nightmare in motion.

I see Rachel in the chair next to him, and watch as his head lifts, eyes seeking mine. I see it, the moment his eyes recognize the fury in mine and he realizes that I'm onto him.

"Okay, folks,"—he gets up—"I hate to cut out early, but..." he stammers, "but, but..." He looks to Noah for help, but Noah is too focused on whatever Kaleigh is saying. Austin kicks Noah's chair to get his attention.

His eyebrows shoot up when Austin says urgently, "Gotta go," then glances over at me and continues, "Now would be good."

I don't know if Noah knows what is happening or not, but he throws his napkin on the plate in front of him "This has been fun," he murmurs, trying to escape while keeping an eye on me at the same time.

"Running off so early, guys?" I sing-song as I come up behind them.

"We intruded," Austin says. "Thank you for having us. Dede, Frank, I wish you many more years of happiness," he rushes out on a wave as he hurries out the side gate.

Kaleigh gets up. "What did I miss?"

"The entire cast of *Thunder From Down Under* just arrived." I look around to see if the guests are okay. I can't wait for this party to be over.

She looks around excitedly, pulling her skirt up a bit. "Where? Are they inside? Shit, do I look okay?" She fluffs her hair.

"Kaleigh," I whisper-hiss, "they aren't here anymore. I sent them away."

She groans. "Why? Why would you do that?" She runs to the side gate to see if they're still in the driveway. "Buzz kill." She calls me as she picks up Rachel. "Can you protect me from Mommy?" she whispers in her ear before blowing kisses in her neck.

I sit down in my chair and immediately start drinking another glass of wine as I try to calm myself by counting down from ten. It takes four times before I no longer feel like I am a danger to myself or others.

The rest of the afternoon goes by without any further penis-related incidents. All cupcakes have been consumed, minus the penis cake toppers that I removed before serving them.

Once everyone has left, I plop down into my chair and throw my feet up on the one Austin sat in. "That was fun, right?" Kaleigh asks.

"You told people I had a strange excessive hair issue on my hoo-ha that required a complicated bikini wax and styling." I glare at her.

"I was trying to get Josh to imagine that you're a woman with a hairy bush so he doesn't ask you out again!" She drinks from the wine glass she is holding in her hand. "You're welcome." She smirks.

"What the hell are we going to do with all those penis balloons?" I look around, hoping to see that some of them are deflating. Sadly, they are all still fully erect and happily smiling at me. "Asshole," I grumble under my breath.

"What's the story with Noah?" Kaleigh tries to be casual so I don't pick up on her curiosity over him.

"No idea. He's Austin's best friend from what I gathered today," I tell her while looking at Rachel, who is running in circles with, unfortunately, a penis balloon in her hand. "Ten minutes to bath time!" I call out, hoping she acknowledges me, but she just continues her one-girl—with a penis balloon—parade.

"Mom," I hear Gabe call from behind me. "Can I go to Jesse's house to kick around the ball?"

I check my watch and see it's almost seven. "Only for thirty minutes, okay?" I know he'll be forty-five minutes.

"So, what are you going to do to Austin for all of this?" Kaleigh asks, pointing to the balloons.

"Nothing." I smirk. "We called a truce."

"I know that smirk. I've been on the receiving end of that smirk!" She sits up.

"I mean, we called truce today, right? We didn't call truce on Wednesday when he made me run back out for a fucking crisp kosher pickle, because the one that came with his sandwich was limp, right?" I ask her with a perplexed smile on my face.

"What did you do now? From the pictures, his balls were almost the size of Gabe's soccer ball."

I slap the table. "You saw pictures?" My mouth hangs open.

She nods her head yes. "I did. Not the actual frank, though, just the beans. But they were ginormous." She motions with her hands, forming them into huge round objects in the air. "Now, what did you do!"

"Nothing that will make any part of him swell. I will never, ever do something like that again." The guilt still runs through me. "I may have shred one of his parking tickets that had to be paid by yesterday so he could avoid his car getting booted," I confess quietly, looking into the glass I picked up from the table.

"Holy shit. I hope you kept the photocopies, because you can't not pay that. He is going to know it was you," Kaleigh warns

"I know, I know. I kept them, so just relax." I put my hands on my hips and state defensively, "I'm going to pay them."

"When?" she asks, earning her an eye roll from me.

"Next week," I reply as I get up and ignore any further commentary from her. "Rach, bath time." I walk to the back door. "Don't you dare sit there and judge me, missy." I point at Kaleigh. "By the way, the potatoes had butter in them. That's for the bikini wax," I say before I turn my back to her and walk inside with the sound of her curses filling my ears.

The next week goes by without any more incidents. It seems we are both on our best behavior. Well, I am. He's still a Neanderthal, and I'm almost tempted to not pay his tickets, but I promised Kaleigh I'd be the better person. Apparently though, I was one day too late on that, because at around one o'clock, he storms out of the office without a word, running down the stairs instead of taking the elevator.

Twenty minutes later, he comes storming back in, huffing and puffing as he stops at my desk.

"Did you pay my tickets?" he asks as I pretend I'm shuffling around papers and hope that he can't see my heart practically beating out of my chest.

"Um, yeah, I did. I have it here somewhere. Why?" I glance up and see the vein in his forehead is twitching and some sweat is gathering at the side of his face, obviously from running down the stairs.

He puts his hands on my desk, leaning into me as I lean back in my chair. I know I should be pissed that he's in my space, but I only feel a trickle of excitement. "Why, you ask? Because Trent just called from downstairs. They booted my car and towed it."

"No!" I say, trying to force a look of shock onto my face instead of laughing in his and saying, 'HA, in your face, sukkah!'

"Yes, Lauren, they towed me." He is leaning even further into me. "Now, you are going to lend me your car for the meeting I have to go to downtown."

"Um, I can't lend you my car. What if my kids get sick at school and I have to leave? What if—" I start but think the better of it as I take in the murderous look on his face. "Okay, fine." I duck under his arm to reach into my purse and grab the keys. "But if anything happens to it, you'll pay for it," I warn, dangling the keys in front of him.

He snatches the keys from my hand and turns to head into his office, slamming the door behind him, causing the shades to rattle on his side of the room. I pick up my phone to send Kaleigh a text.

Oopsie. I waited too long to pay the tickets.

I wait for her reply, hoping for some words of wisdom, which is not at all what I get.

Play with the devil, you're gonna get burned.

I look at my phone in confusion, because really, what the hell does that even mean? Before I can question her, Austin's door opens and he comes back out. He has changed out of his suit, which was probably all sweaty anyway.

The suit he's wearing now is navy blue and molds to him perfectly. He swings the jacket around, putting it on in one fluid motion, then grabs his cuffs, pulling them out of the sleeves of the jacket. He's not wearing a tie, but the top two buttons of his bright white shirt are undone, giving me a slight peek at his bronzed chest. The image of my fingers playing with that third button pops into my head, and I have to blink to clear it.

Having inappropriate thoughts about my boss is the biggest no-no in my life; that and there's the fact that I hate him. Well, maybe not hate, hate is a strong word. But I do dislike him, like a lot.

"You think Kaleigh can come get you if I don't get back on time?" he asks almost like he's worried about how I'm going to get home.

I nod my head yes and then tell him, "Listen, there are a couple of things you should know about the car," I try to explain, but I'm quickly hushed by him instead.

"Seriously, I think I got it. It's a minivan. How different can it possibly be from any other vehicle?" He heads to the elevator.

"Okay, but just so you know how t—" I continue from right behind him.

"Lauren, I got it. It's not brain surgery. I'm good." Then he gets onto the elevator and the doors close.

I look to Carmen. "Oh well, I tried to warn him that *Frozen* is stuck in the DVD player and "Let it Go" is on repeat." I give a little shrug before I turn and walk back to my desk. Oh, to be a fly in that car right now!

chapter fourteen

Austin

The minute I got that phone call, I knew this had to do with Lauren. Ever since she came into my life, it's been one crazy, fucked-up episode after another. There has never been a time when I've frowned more than I have lately, but I can also admit that I've laughed more than I ever have as well. She brings out not only this insane, absurd awfulness in me, but also a fun, silly, playful side I didn't even know I had.

A month ago, I would have had her fired without a second thought, but now, she quits pretty much every day, smiling each time she gives me her notice.

But her not paying my tickets was a low blow. My car—my baby—was impounded, and I have an important meeting with Denis on site at the restaurant so we can finalize a couple of things.

Now, I'm walking out of the office with the keys to her bus in my hands. Okay, so it isn't an actual bus, but it's damn close to one.

I click 'unlock' on the key fob and get in. My knees are pressed against the dash, and the steering wheel is so close it's practically cutting off the air to my fucking throat. I fumble around on the side for the buttons to change the seat's position and give me some leg room.

Once I'm situated and circulation returns to my legs, I touch the keyless starter button, and the car starts right up.

I buckle in and am on my way. Soft music plays in the background when all of a sudden, a girl's voice starts filling the car.

Soft at first, and a bit annoying, so I push the button on the touch screen to switch to radio. After clicking it once, nothing happens, so I try it again. And again, nothing happens.

I'm too busy trying to weave my way through traffic in this huge behemoth of a vehicle, so I try to block it out. And I'm somewhat successful, that is, until the shouting starts and scares the shit out of me. Someone yelling about letting it go

What the fuck is this? I press the button again, this time for the satellite radio, and still the fucking song about letting it go is playing. The voice gets higher and higher. The music gets louder and louder as I desperately try to turn it down.

Unable to silence this current Lauren-induced nightmare, I grab my phone, dialing her number, still trying to turn down the volume but having no luck.

She picks up after one ring.

"Yes," she answers, obviously annoyed that I'm bothering her if the tone of her voice is any indication. Well, good, I'm annoyed, too.

"Something is wrong with the car," I yell into the phone that I'm holding in my hand as I tab the screen, putting her on speaker.

"Well, whatever you did, undo it," she advises then continues, "I told you before you took it that if you break it, you pay for it."

I breathe out an aggravated sigh. "I didn't break anything. I can't get the radio to shut off." Meanwhile, the song has started—*again*—the voice breaking in with the fucking letting go.

"Oh that, yeah, I know. I have to get it checked. It's like it's frozen," she says and immediate starts laughing at herself. "Get it? Frozen?"

I look at the phone, wondering if this is really happening, if I'm really having this conversation. "I don't get it," I huff while the lady sings about the cold never bothering her anyway. "How the fuck do I get her to shut up?" I shout over the music.

"Oh yeah, I don't know. I tried to Google it, but nothing came up." I hear her typing like this conversation isn't even bothering her.

"You 'Googled' it," I deadpan and then repeat because surely, I heard wrong. "You Googled it?"

I can practically hear her eyes rolling. "Yes, I Googled it. What else would I do? Google knows everything."

"Lauren, I'm about to puncture my eardrums if I have to keep listening to this girl go on and on AND ON about letting go and the fucking cold never bothering her. How do I turn this shit off?" I touch every single button on the screen

"You aren't the only one. I just don't know what to do. I guess I have to call the dealer." Her voice is flat.

"You should call them the minute you call impound and find out how the fuck to get my car back," I snap right before the radio yells 'let it go' again.

"Yeah, yeah. I'm on it. Is that all you called for?" She is brushing me off. Just when the piano drift starts again.

"That's all," I grumble. "Thank god, I just got to my meeting. This fucking song is the soundtrack from hell, I'm sure of it," I state before disconnecting and turning off the car. Of course, I'm shocked and dismayed that I can still hear it playing. It isn't until I open the door that the radio finally shuts off. I'm hoping—praying, really—that it resets itself. Grabbing the keys and my phone, I shut the door and don't even bother to lock it, thinking Lauren would be lucky if someone stole it.

When I open the door to the restaurant, the smell of wood and paint hits me. This is my favorite part of my job. Creating something. I may not be good with my hands, but I have the gift of vision and conceptualization, which is what I get paid for.

Denis walks up to me, wearing his regular cargo pants and construction boots. "Hey, you look much better than you did last time." He holds out his hand to shake mine. No kidding, I almost died the last time he saw me. I just nod to him and head over to the bar area where the plans are spread out.

I look up seeing the staircase coming along nicely. I notice that the glass blocks are installed exactly as I intended them to be, so that when patrons head up the stairs, they can see through them to the downstairs area. The rounded booths will be great for a group of friends who want some privacy; each booth can be seen from downstairs as well. I can't wait until the draping comes and is installed, completing the look that I was going for—like a cozy fort. A sexy high class but still cozy fort, obviously.

I look around to see the tables that will be scattered throughout the middle of the vast space are all stacked up in the corner. "You also got some high-top tables, right?" I ask as I look around for them.

"I did, yes. Those are coming in next week along with the stool version of those chairs." He motions toward the chairs stacked next to the table. I run my hand along the bar top, a heavy mahogany wood that is smooth and shiny, sexy. It's the only rustic touch in the space; the base of the bar is a frosted glass with lights that appear to be embedded in its panes. The barstools look like they're made of thin metal rods, giving them a sleek, modern appearance. The whole back wall of the bar area is mirrored, causing the space to look bigger. The shelves, which will be made from the same frosted glass as the base of the bar, have yet to be installed.

I see Serena heading toward me. Oh, Serena, with the glossy brown hair that flows down to her waist and those long, lean, toned legs that she's flashed at me enough times in her efforts to entice me. Her eyes never wavering from mine, she saunters over to me like a huntress tracking her kill.

I smile as I take in the red suit that pours over her curves like it was made just for her. With the money she has, it probably was.

Serena is one of the backers of this venture. It's one of her 'side jobs' as she calls them. She made the bulk of her money from the style app she created.

"Austin," she sings in her Southern accent. "I didn't know when I got here that my day was about to get a million times better with a visit from you." She walks right up to me, hugging me close as she tilts her head and kisses the underside of my jaw.

I move away from her and her bloodred-stained lips. "Serena, I didn't know you would be here," I say over her head and mostly to Denis.

As hot and gorgeous as Serena is, my dick knows that if I go there with her, she'd do whatever she could to sink those bright-red talons into me. Plus, she sucked off Noah and swallowed. So yeah, I know it's crazy, but my mouth is never getting near hers. Ever. For those reasons, I haven't taken even a little sip of what she's constantly offering.

I disentangle myself from her clutches and look around. "This is going to be a huge success, I can feel it," Serena states as she continues to eye me up and down with blatant carnal interest.

"I think so, too. Denis, you said you had something to discuss with me, something in the kitchen?" I look at him pointedly, seeing a look of surprise before he finally gets it.

"Right, right." He nods. "I think the plumber said something about…" He stops talking once we get inside the kitchen and the door slides closed behind me.

"Fuck me, she's like a vulture." I try to shake her touch off of me.

"Opening night will be interesting." Denis knows she'll probably plaster herself to my side and never let go.

I shake my head, not wanting to even think about it. "What else do we need before the final touches come together?" I ask him as my phone beeps in my pocket. I take it out, looking at the screen and seeing a text from Lauren.

Car will be out of impound as soon as you head down there and fill out a form. Sorry, I can't do it, because the car is in your name.

I shake my head.

You have to drive me there. This is your fault after all.

She answers in a matter of seconds.

Great, I can't wait. Good news, I can sing along to the song!

Fuck me, that goddamn song starts up in my head again.

Forget it. I'll ask Noah.

I text Noah next, asking him to pick me up at my office in an hour. Looking at my watch, I notice that I have to get back or I'll have to drive the car to Lauren's house.

"Okay, so when are we doing the photos?" I ask Denis as we walk back out of the kitchen. I scan the area and see that Serena has either left the building or is hiding somewhere, probably ready to pounce.

"I have to talk to Jake at the PR firm, but I'm thinking the night of the opening before everyone comes in would be best." Denis replies while taking his own phone out to take some notes.

"Perfect." I say good-bye and head back out into the hot sun. My good mood is short-lived when I see what is sitting there, awaiting me, in front of the restaurant. What I begin thinking of as the vessel to hell, aka Lauren's minivan, waits to transport me back to the office on a ride filled with the song that will surely haunt my nightmares for a long time to come. Fuck my life.

chapter fifteen

Lauren

I'M TYPING UP THE NOTES FOR TOMORROW'S MEETING WHEN MY KEYS DROP ON MY DESK with a big clank.

"Never a-fucking-gain." I look up at him with a smile on my face, which is wiped away the minute I see red lipstick on his shirt collar.

"You better not have had sex in my car," I snap at him, getting up from my chair. "You are having my whole car shampooed." I wag my finger at him and hope that he can't see how fast my heart is beating. The pit of my stomach burns at the mere thought of him having sex in my car.

He looks at me as if I have two heads, his brows furrowed in confusion. "Seriously, don't you ever have sex at night?" I ask him. "It's what normal people do."

"I don't even know what the fuck you're talking about right now." He puts his hands on his hips.

"You have skank all over your collar." I point to the lipstick.

"Oh, that." He reaches to exactly that spot before smirking at me.

"I thought you were at a meeting. Or does a booty call qualify as your meeting these days?" I ask, glaring at him. "Good times."

"You wouldn't know a good time if it hit you in the face."

I roll my eyes and scoff at him as I cross my arms over my chest. "Ok, whatever you say." I look past him to see that our fighting has drawn a bit of a crowd. Peeking around the corner is Carmen, along with Steven and Barbara, who is standing there watching us over the glasses perched on the tip of her nose. "You had sex in your office and now my car. Jesus. Can't you control yourself?" I grab my keys off my desk while I lean down to grab my purse.

"Are you always this uptight?" My body stills while he continues, "Maybe if you loosened up a little, you would still be married."

The minute the words leave his mouth, I hear a gasp from Barbara, but that isn't what gets me. What gets me is the fact that he is right. Maybe if I weren't so uptight, I would still be married. Maybe if I lived a little, Jake wouldn't have cheated. I don't know what hurts me more, the fact that I'm questioning myself or that he thinks these things of me. All I know is that my heart just hurts.

I place my purse on my desk as I gather my things. I do not make eye contact with him or acknowledge him in any way.

My coffee cup, my Post-it notes, the picture of my kids that I put next to the computer all get tossed into my purse, overfilling it.

I grab my keys off the desk and walk away from him, never once looking at him. Not once giving him the satisfaction of knowing that he hit his mark and hurt me. All the pranks in the world couldn't have come close to hurting me as much as the words he just spoke did.

"Lauren," he says softly right when I'm about to turn the corner. "I didn't—"

I turn around, the hurt now mixed with anger. "You didn't, what, Austin? You didn't mean to insinuate that I'm uptight and that's the reason my husband had an affair and left me? Well, good job, Austin, you guessed it in one," I hiss at him, trying to keep my voice from cracking.

"Lauren, I didn't mean—" He walks up to me and reaches out with one hand to touch me.

"No, no, it's fine. And you're right, that's what happened." I side-step him and use my hands to block him from touching me. I hear the elevator ping and turn to hurry around the corner to slip inside the open door right before it slides shut.

The last thing I see before the elevator door closes is Austin turning the corner quickly, racing up to the door. He's too late, though; it closes in his face, right before I hear what I assume is his hand slapping the closed door.

I press the button for the lobby repeatedly, ridiculously hoping it will make the elevator go faster than it is. I know it won't work, I know this, everyone knows this, but I keep pressing the button anyway.

The door opens to the lobby, and I'm thankful that it is empty. I run toward my car and don't look back. Austin parked it exactly where I left it this morning. Thank god for small favors.

Opening the door, I throw everything inside as I rush to get in the car, get going, get the hell out of there before I can allow the first tear to fall. Because it will. It's just a matter of time.

My eyes fill with tears, blurring my vision. Starting the car and making my way out of the parking lot, I pull up Penelope's number on my phone.

If I'm on Bluetooth and on my phone, thankfully that overrides the music.

"Hey," she answers cheerily.

"Hey." I angrily wipe away the tear that has made its way over my lashes and onto my cheek. "I'm not going back. I'm sorry. I really tried to tough it out. I hate to put you in this position, but I…I just can't go back," I finish as my voice cracks.

"Hey, now," she whispers, her voice softening. "I don't give a fuck about the job. Are you okay?" I shake my head no while more tears fall freely.

"I'm going to hang up now. I'll grab a couple of bottles of wine and head to your place. Is this a case for Alanis Morissette?" She asks, because everyone knows Alanis Morissette is the wronged, hurt woman's anthem, no matter how old they are.

"I already have the CD in my player at home," I sniffle.

The phone beeps and I see it's Austin calling me on the other line. I quickly decline his ass.

"Okay, I'm going to go call Barbara and let her know that you aren't coming back," she assures me. "See you in an hour."

"I think she probably knows. There was a scene." I'm not sure how much of a scene it actually was, but to me, it felt like all of my co-workers were there to witness my humiliation.

"Oh fuck. No worries, hon, I'll take care of it." And she clicks off just in time for the fucking "Let it Go" chorus to ring, loud and clear, through my car.

I make it home in record time, climbing out and thanking the powers that be that the kids are staying with Jake tonight. Every second week, he gets a mid-week sleepover, and tonight is that night.

I open the door, letting myself in, dumping everything down by the door. I walk straight to the kitchen, open the fridge, and grab the open bottle of wine from the door.

Ripping the cork out of the bottle and not bothering with a glass, I bring the bottle to my lips, gulping down enough wine to begin the process of soothing my jagged little edges. Somewhat.

I'm about to go for a second big swig when the back door opens and Kaleigh walks in. She looks at me and drops her yoga mat.

"What happened?" She rushes over to me.

I take that swig before answering her. "I'm uptight, apparently." I allow those hurt feelings along with the tears I've tried to keep at bay to consume me. "According to Austin, it's why my husband left me," I whimper before bringing the bottle back to my lips and finishing it off in one long pull.

"What are you talking about? Explain, please." She goes to the wine fridge in the living room and comes back with another bottle. She looks for the cork screw, slamming drawers in effort to find it quickly.

I pull off the jacket that I was wearing today and climb up onto a stool, while she pours two glasses of wine. Handing one to me, she offers a toast. "To assholes, and to the women who think they're fucking the prize."

I nod in agreement and finish the glass off. I don't think I even stop to breathe.

My phone rings from over by the front door. I don't even move to get it, but Kaleigh does. "It's Austin. I'm assuming this"—she points to the bottles of wine—"has to do with him?"

I don't answer verbally; instead, I just offer her a jerky nod yes. She presses decline, and I see her fingers move over the screen. "Don't bother," I tell her. "I already quit."

Her eyes snap up. "What did he do?"

"Well, he borrowed my car, possibly had sex in it, and when I called him out on it, he called me uptight. Me. ME, MEEE!" I shriek while pulling the bottle of wine closer to me. "We need to play Alanis." I start pouring myself another glass.

"Fuck, I'm going to hide the sharp knives," she murmurs as she heads into the living room and plugs in my phone. Her fingers move across the screen, and in no time, Alanis' angry, raspy, knowing voice is serenading us in commiseration.

"After he said I'm uptight, which I totally am not. Remember that time I gave Jake car head in the driveway?" I ask her.

"Yes, I was very proud of you." She comes around the counter to sit on another stool and listen to the rest of my story.

"Well, after that, he said that maybe if I loosened up a little, I'd still be married." I look at her, letting the pain I felt at that moment show. "I'll admit, maybe he's onto something, but it's not the whole reason. It's because that skanky whore waved her non-saggy tits in my husband's face, and he made the decision to sample what she was offering." I look up at her with tear-filled eyes. "Right, Kay? I mean, you don't think Austin is right, do you?"

"Abso-fucking-lutely not," she says vehemently. "There is no fucking excuse whatso-fucking-ever for a married man to cheat on his wife. None. Not even if Gisele Fucking Bündchen comes in and sits on his dick while wearing goddamn angel wings."

"I'm totally in agreement," I mumble to myself as I get up and try to walk away, but my spinning head stops me before I can even take a step. I reach out to steady my woozy self with a hand on the counter. "We need pizza," I tell Kaleigh as I let go of the counter, mentally crossing my fingers that I don't fall.

Once the spinning stops, I make my way up the stairs, taking my tight skirt off when I reach my bedroom, and face planting on my bed. "He's such an asshole. Right, Kay?" My voice comes out a bit muffled seeing as I'm facedown on the bed.

"I took my Post-it notes. Haha, take that." I turn my head to the side, away from her. "I think I really liked him," I admit quietly, while Kaleigh gets on the bed next to me. "I should have known better, right? No happy for me." My eyes get heavier and heavier as I continue blinking. "I need a little nap," I whisper right before I drift off to sleep.

chapter sixteen

Austin

"**M**AYBE IF YOU LOOSENED UP A LITTLE, YOU WOULD STILL BE MARRIED."

As soon as the words left my mouth, I wished I could call them back. I didn't even have to see her face to know I hurt her. Her body went rigid, and for a moment, I thought she was going to let me have it. Hell, I wish now that she had, because what she gave me instead of the dressing down I deserved was a million times worse. Despite her best efforts to mask it, I don't think I will ever forget the wounded look on her face. I immediately wanted to pull her into my arms.

I wanted to tell her that I really was an asshat. But instead, I just stood there, watching her pack up all her things, even the fucking Post-its.

When I realized what she was doing, I tried to reach out to her, but she just dodged me and blocked my hands like she was protecting herself—from me—before she turned and practically ran away. And I fucking let her.

As if that were not bad enough, of course, Carmen, Steven, and—even worse—Barbara were all watching and heard the whole thing. Carmen and Steven refused to look at me and quickly dispersed, while Barbara just stood there shaking her head at me in disappointment. "That is going to cost you more than you realize, Austin." Leaving me with that bit of wisdom, she walked around me and went back to her office.

"Fuck, don't I know it," I mutter under my breath as I head into my office, pick up my phone, and try calling Lauren.

No surprise, she must have declined the call, because it goes right to voicemail after two rings. "Motherfucker."

I try calling her again right away, and as expected, it goes straight to voicemail. "Lauren, please call me back. I want to apologize. I was way out of line," I say before I finish with a plea. "Please, Lauren, just call me back."

I end the call and decide to text her.

Call me, please!

I sit at my desk, watching the phone for the grey bubble with those three blinking dots, but they don't appear. Nothing at all happens. The message isn't even marked as read. I don't know how long I stare at my phone willing her to call back or reply, but the next thing I know, Noah comes waltzing in. "Woah, dude, who killed your dog?" He throws himself into the chair in front of my desk.

"I fucked up," I confess, looking back down at my phone.

"Nothing new there. What happened now?"

"I may have told Lauren that if she weren't so uptight and she loosened up a little, that maybe her husband wouldn't have left her and she would still be married." I don't even finish getting the words out before he's pulling out his phone. "What the fuck are you doing?"

"I'm making sure I clear my schedule for your funeral," he says, earning himself a glare from me.

"Fuck off, asshole." It's the only thing I can say right now. "Let's go get my car, and then I'll pass by her house. She has no choice but to answer the door, right?" I ask him as we walk out to the elevator.

I see Barbara come out of her office and head straight for me. Her mouth is pressed together in a tight line. I cut off whatever she's going to say by holding up my hand and stating, "Not now, Barbara." I press the elevator button.

"I think my balls just crawled back into my body, and that look wasn't even directed at me," Noah murmurs from beside me as we watch Barbara turn and storm away. "If I were you, I wouldn't drink or eat anything that anyone else, especially someone who is a female or an employee here, offers you," he advises as he follows me into the elevator.

We make it down to the impound lot, where I fill out all the forms and show all my documents in order to get my car out. It takes about forty-five minutes, and the whole time we're there, I've got my phone in my hand. I've tried to call Lauren about fifteen times now, and each time, the call goes straight to voicemail.

Once I get my car out, I make my way over to Lauren's, parking my car at the curb. I take a deep breath, but my door is whipped open. I look up and see Noah.

"As your friend, I'm going to try to talk you out of this." I shake my head, ignoring him. I get out of the car and walk to her door. "This is a really, really bad idea. Women who are pissed can do evil things. I mean, she wasn't even that pissed at you when she almost made your balls explode."

"I have to see her," I say and then knock on the door. When I hear the locks click open, my heart literally skips a beat and a smile starts to creep across my face. It's quickly replaced with a frown when I see that it's Kaleigh who opens the door—with what appears to be a machete in her hand. Okay, so maybe not a real machete, but it sure as hell is a knife that looks like it can easily debone a chicken and probably take off a man's—hopefully not this man's—hand. She comes outside, closing the door behind her as the sound of Alanis Morissette is playing in the background.

"You have some nerve showing your face here," she spits out at me.

"Is Lauren home?" I sound like a dork. Obviously, she's there, her car is here.

"She is," she confirms as she sways a little. I look a little closer and can tell that she is totally blitzed.

"Whoa, there, little lady." Noah wraps an arm around her shoulders to avoid the knife to the dick.

"I need to talk to her," I say.

"Not going to happen. Not now, not ever." She continues, "You fucked up bad." She is now pointing the knife at me and her voice is rising. "Really, really bad."

"Babe, can we put the knife down?" Noah pleads with a smile, and she smiles at him while bashfully giggling.

"Can I please just talk to Lauren for two minutes? Then I'll leave, I promise," I practically beg.

"Nope," she replies and then turns around, grabbing the door handle and talking to us over her shoulder. "If you're not gone in two minutes, I'm calling the cops and telling them you're stalking me." I scoff at that, and she glares at me. "And show them the inappropriate dick pics you sent me."

I turn to look at Noah, who says, "I may have showed them to her and she might have forwarded a couple of them to herself."

"Can you please tell her that I was here and ask her to call me? Please, Kaleigh?" I beg as she slams the door in my face and flips the locks with loud clicking sounds.

I hang my head, while Noah pats me on the back. "She'll call." He assures me. "Or send someone to kill you. I mean, she did say Donkey Kong."

I shrug his hand off me and walk back to my car, wishing I could just start this day over or at least go back to the moment when I walked back into the office after my meeting.

Noah gets in his car and goes home, while I head to my condo. I go straight into my bedroom and throw myself onto my bed. I scrub a hand down my face as my mind runs back over my day. Fuck! This is a such mess.

I get up, tossing my jacket onto the chair in the corner and pulling my shirt out and unbuttoning it. I shrug it off and see the red lipstick on the collar. The same damn lipstick that started this whole fucking nightmare. I wad up the shirt and throw it straight into the fucking trash.

The next day, I get to work earlier than normal. I wait anxiously for eight o'clock to roll around, so I can see her the minute she comes in.

When it hits eight ten, my hands start to get sweaty, and my shirt starts feeling a bit tight around my neck, so I undo the collar. An email ping comes from my computer, and I turn to look at it when I see Carmen sit down at Lauren's desk.

I get up and go over to ask her, "What are you doing?"

She smiles at me. "I'm your new PA. Isn't this exciting?"

I don't say a word to her. Instead, I march right over to Barbara's office. The door is open, so I just walk in. "What the fuck is Carmen doing?"

"She's your new PA. Not only did Lauren quit, but Penelope also cancelled her contract with us, leaving me without a reputable temp agency to rely on, so I did the only thing I could do under the circumstances." She takes off her glasses and leans back in her chair, steepling her hands together in front of her as she taps her pointer fingers on her lips. She looks at me with disappointment radiating off of her. "You fucked up so bad here, Austin. I'm not even sure if you actually realize the depth of what you've lost."

"I know. I know I did. I called her to apologize, but she didn't take any of my calls. I even went by her house, but her sister wouldn't let me see her," I tell her, hoping it will soften the blow I know she's about to deliver to me.

She sits up straight in her chair, looks me dead in the eyes, and starts to speak to me in that soft but angry, firm, and concise tone she used on me when I seriously messed up as a kid. "You told that beautiful, vivacious young woman that she is undesirable and that's why her husband left her. And you have the audacity to think that because you say sorry she is going to forgive you? I must have dropped you on your head when you were younger." She shakes her head.

"Austin, you have to know that she had feelings for you, just as you have them for her. It sure as hell was obvious to all of us who were thoroughly enjoying that dance the two of you were doing. Hell, we were getting ready to start a pool for when you two would finally get it together and *get* together. What you're not getting is that it was going to take a lot of bravery and trust and faith on her part to take that step. The last man she had feelings for wounded her, Austin. And the next man she thought she might possibly open up to just wounded her, too. Men wonder why women turn into raging bitches? Think about what SHE has been through at the hands of men she's cared about, and there's your answer." She waits a beat for that to sink in before continuing.

"You needed an assistant, I did the best I could. Carmen was available, and even after that display yesterday, was still willing. You need to understand that Lauren will never come back here, Austin, and it is highly unlikely that she will ever give you the time of day to deliver that apology," she finishes as if she didn't just gut me with that speech. Fuck, what have I done?

I'm so mad at myself, I can't help the glare I aim at her as I ask, "Aren't you the one who says never say never?"

"I also taught you how to be sensitive and kind-hearted. What happened there?" She raises an eyebrow at me.

I turn and practically storm out of her office, coming face-to-face with John. "Hey, there, buddy. You're looking a bit uptight today," he remarks as he puts his hands in his pockets.

"Fuck you." I walk away from him, hoping he doesn't follow me, but hearing his breathing beside me, I know that I'm not that lucky.

"Did you really call her out in front of everyone?" I look over at him when he finishes asking the question.

"I didn't do it in front of anybody. They were just there," I say as I walk back into my office. "Close the door."

"Oh, now you want privacy?" he asks, chuckling. "All kidding aside, I heard that it was brutal. You're lucky no one caught that on video. That shit can go viral, and the next thing you know, you're all over the Internet as the World's Worst Boss."

I tolerate him until he walks out and then start my day. My emails come in all fucked up. Nothing is entered in my calendar. My meetings aren't even entered. I have no idea where I'm going. I pick up my phone and call Carmen.

"Hiyeah," she greets. And, really, is that even a word?

"Have you sent me the emails that came in today? Did put all the meetings that I have next week in my calendar?" I look at my computer screen.

"No, I assumed you would do it," she replies.

"No, I don't do it. You do it," I bark and then hang up. It just gets worse from there. The notes she enters make no sense. She is confusing projects and entering things in the wrong places. She can't even get my coffee order right.

For the next two days, I text Lauren, begging her to call me. I've even driven by her house a couple of times to try and catch her or the kids outside, but so far nothing.

Finally, it's Friday night. I shut down my computer and text Barbara.

Go see Lauren. Double her salary. I promise, I won't even talk to her. We can do everything by email. Do whatever it takes, but just get her back.

Her reply comes right away. It's a picture of Lauren sitting on her couch, laughing. There's not a stich of makeup on her face. She's wearing a pair of black yoga pants and a tight tank top, and she's holding a glass of wine. Her hair is piled on top of her head. I've only ever seen her dressed professionally, and she always looked hot, but she looks comfortable and effortlessly pretty now. That isn't what really gets my attention, though. No, it's Barbara, who is sitting right there next to Lauren, a glass of wine in her hand, and they are both laughing.

I reply with one word.

Traitor.

I send Noah a text.

Tomorrow night. You, me, drinks, women, good times.

He answers right away.

It's on like Donkey Kong.

Fuck me. She's left her mark all over my life and on everyone in it.

chapter seventeen

Lauren

It's been four days since I've spoken to Austin. Four very long, very boring days. I called Penelope and begged her to find me something, anything. So far, she has nothing.

I've rearranged furniture and reorganized closets and cabinets. I've done a big deep cleaning of all the bathrooms. I've gone through the kids' toys, closets, and drawers. I've stripped the beds and washed all the bedding. I forced myself to stop when I found myself eyeing up the windows.

Tonight, the kids left to go to Jake's until Monday night. Leaving Kaleigh and me to entertain ourselves. I had great plans to Netflix and chill, but she came in with Barbara, of all people, following right behind her after the kids left. Barbara came bearing gifts, and by gifts I mean wine, so I wasn't about to tell her to leave. That would be rude, plus, I like Barbara and I missed her.

We laughed over wine about everything and nothing at all. Neither of us bringing up Austin, which made me happy and sad all at the same time.

It was when she was getting up to leave that Kaleigh left us alone to talk.

"You have to know that we all miss you," she says, emphasizing the 'all' as she reaches for the empty pizza box in the center of the table.

I shake my head a bit sadly, hoping I don't start tearing up again.

"We do. He does especially." The way she refers to him makes my heart beat just a tad faster. Makes it hurt, too.

"He humiliated me," I tell her, taking the box out of her hands so she can see me. "And he didn't even know it. My husband had an affair with our son's teacher." I drop the box back on the table.

"He would never—" she starts, but I hold up my hand.

"I know he wouldn't, and I understand that he didn't know, but what he said hit close to home. Very, very close to home."

"He's miserable. I replaced you with Carmen." She laughs a bit evilly. "She barely knows how to email at all, so forget it if there's an attachment. And let's just say that she and Excel are a big, fat no-go."

"Good. He deserves it. Asshat," I grumble as I sit down. "I know you have your loyalties, I understand that." I grab a Kleenex from the side table and dab at my eyes. "I will never, ever put you in the middle. I like you, and I'd like to continue our friendship."

"Please come back," she pleads. "I'm begging. I'll give you whatever you want, just name it."

"I don't know," I say, but I'm thinking about it. Who am I kidding, I'm so, so, so, close to saying yes.

"Just think about it. Go out tomorrow night with your sister. Get dressed up. Drink, flirt with hot guys, have fun. Then call me on Sunday, and we'll talk," she says as I walk her to the door. "Flirt a little for me, too." She winks at me, gives me a quick squeeze, and walks out the door.

"So, are you going to go back?" Kaleigh asks from the stairs where she is sitting.

"I don't know."

"I think you should. Don't let him chase you away from a job you genuinely liked." She gets up and makes her way down the rest of the stairs. "Now, let's discuss outfits. Are we doing slutty maids or slutty school girls?"

I look at her like the crazy person she is and ask, "Why do we have to do slutty anything?"

"Because sluts have more fun." She shrugs. "Or so I've been told."

I stare at her and wonder, not for the first time, how the hell I'm related to this woman.

The next day, we spend the afternoon lounging in the backyard. At three, I go up to my room to take a nap, because let's be honest here, I'm a single mom of two who thinks that eleven p.m. is a late night.

My nap lasts a solid two hours, and when I wake up, I'm almost tempted to cancel this debacle that Kaleigh is planning. I'm about to tell her that we should just stay home when the door flies open and she comes through it, telling me, "Don't even fucking think about it. Get your dusty vagina in that shower. You will exfoliate and shave—*everywhere.*"

"Jesus, Kal, it's not dusty." I storm into my bathroom and slam the door. I lean back against it, thinking to myself that she might be right. It's probably a little bit dusty.

I walk over to the sink and look at myself in the mirror. I'm hot, I'm young, and I'm single. Tonight, I'm going to go out, drink some cocktails, flirt with men, and maybe, just maybe, have sex. Hot, no-name sex. Okay, well, maybe not sex, sex. Maybe just some kissing and I'll give him my number. And if he's really hot, maybe my real number. Definitely not my real name, because you know, he could be a stalker. Oh, for Christ's sakes, I'll most likely just have some drinks and come home drunk.

I wash and dry my hair, setting it in big curlers so it will be wavy. I do my makeup darker than usual, with a smoky eye in dark brown and gold tones.

I walk out of the bathroom and stare at the outfit I picked out this morning. A tight peach high-waisted dress that goes to mid-thigh. In case that isn't short enough, the is a V-notch in the center that shows off my inner thigh spectacularly, especially when I walk. I've paired it with a black strapless bustier. It's tight, too, holding the girls in place and making them appear firmer than they really are. I put on a chunky black necklace. The whole outfit is put together with black strappy heels. My feet will be screaming in about an hour, but the shoes are sexy as fuck. Well, at least that is what Kaleigh says.

I grab my Michael Kors black wristlet and put the essentials in it. "Are you ready?" I yell down the hall.

Kaleigh walks out of her room, and I'm left speechless. Her outfit consists of a pair of white lace looser-fitting short shorts with a small, shiny black belt. Her top is a black tube top. I know for a fact that she isn't wearing a bra, mainly because her breasts don't need it. She finishes this look with a seriously sexy pair of black open-toe, lace-up stiletto boots. "Let's go get us some dick!" She raises her hands in the air, and I can't help but laugh.

Before I can answer her, I hear a honk outside. "CAB'S HERE!" she yells in her best Jersey shore accent.

I shake my head and say a prayer to whomever is listening at this point that I come home tonight, safe and sound, and with both shoes.

Two hours later, I'm finally sitting down after dancing my ass off. When we got to the club, Kaleigh, of course, knew the bouncer, so we walked right in and were given a booth. The booths sit in a section that is a bit higher than the dance floor. You can get to this area by using the set of six stairs leading up here around the dance floor.

Bottle service is a whole different ball game. The club that we're at is called Light Night, which is weird, because it's almost pitch black with soft light moving around the room.

I'm finally drinking my vodka and cranberry when the Drake song "One Dance" comes on.

I stand up, throwing my hair back, putting my hands in the air as I yell how much I love this song. I grab Kaleigh, and we run back out onto the packed dance floor.

I sway my hips to the beat of the song, singing out loud with Drake.

I feel a pair of hands land on my hips, and I slowly turn around to smile at the guy who put his hands on me. He's cute. Tall with shaggy hair. He smiles at me and pulls me to him. I go with it and live in the moment. Singing the song and moving my hips, I'm having fun taking in the scene all around me.

As I scan the room, my eyes land on a familiar pair of green eyes that I haven't seen in almost a week. I don't have time to think, let alone escape, before I see him making a beeline right to me. My hands fall from my dance partner when I feel his heat against my back.

"Get lost," he demands, using a tone of voice that unmistakably conveys the message not to test him on this.

I whirl around to face him, pissed off that he thinks he can come here, interrupt my dance, and try to ruin my night. I'm about to tell him to go fuck off when he grabs my hand and drags me across the dance floor and out the side door into the cool night.

I try to yank my hand out of his once we get outside, but I'm suddenly pushed up against the wall. I'm about to say something when I see the look he is giving me and snap my mouth shut.

"Don't push me, Lauren, not now," he warns me, and I look at him.

He is dressed in low-slung, tight blue jeans that mold to him. A baby blue button-down, tight-fit, tailored shirt has two buttons open at his neck. His sleeves are rolled halfway up to his elbows, and his silver Rolex is on his wrist.

"Don't push you?" I question, pushing off the wall and squaring my shoulders. "Don't push you? You have some nerve, Austin." The alcohol is giving me a little bit more courage. "You called me uptight, and I was in there enjoying my night when you charged over there like…like…I don't even know what the hell that was all about, except for the fact that I wasn't the uptight one in that scenario. Hmm, who needs to loosen up now, Austin?" I taunt.

"You drive me nuts! I can't sleep! I can't think! I can't even fucking get anything done at work without thinking about you!" He roughly runs his hand through his hair, his shirt tightening across his chest with the movement.

"So, I come out tonight. I'm going to kick back, have a few drinks and not think about you. But of all the places, you're here, looking like this." He gestures to my outfit, his eyes running up my body from my shoes to my face.

"What's wrong with how I look? I look good!" I cross my arms under my breasts and cock my hip to the side.

"No, Lauren. No, you don't look good. You look fucking amazing. As usual. I tried to ignore you. I turned my back. I wasn't going to pay you any attention at all. But when I turn around, there you are on the dance floor, swinging your ass with that douche all over you," he grates out angrily.

"So? I'm here to have fun, too, Austin. And I was! Until you marched over there like some crazy man and dragged me out here. What the hell was that, huh?" My voice rises as my anger ratchets up a few notches.

He steps further into my space, and I'm now sandwiched between the wall and Austin. He tips his face down so we are nose-to-nose. I can't see the rest of his expression, but his eyes are blazing.

"I didn't like it, Lauren," he rumbles in a quietly angry voice.

"Why, Austin? Why did it bother you?" I whisper, completely mesmerized by that look in his eyes. I should have paid attention, though, because instead of answering me, his lips come crashing down on mine.

chapter eighteen

Austin

I SPEND THE WHOLE DAY SATURDAY RUNNING A 5K THROUGH THE PARK AND REARRANGING my emails in alphabetical order. Fucking Carmen.

Noah picks me up at seven, when we hit up a pub and watch the Yankees kill it again. At the end of the ninth inning, he suggests going to Light Night Club.

Shaking the doorman's hand, I make my way over to the corner bar. We have spent many nights closing this place down. This is one of the first clubs to hold our names. I look around taking in the beauty of it.

The minute I scan the booths, I see her. The woman who has been a thorn in my side. Tonight, she looks like she just walked off the red carpet. Her hands rise to the sky, taking her skirt up to dangerous levels.

I stand up straight, draining the bourbon in my glass in one gulp. I make eye contact with the bartender and raise my glass to get another shot.

He pours my shot and passes it to me, and I shoot it down in one gulp, signaling for another. When I look back over to the dance floor, I see some douche with his hands all over Lauren, while she shakes her ass.

She turns around to put her back to his front and her eyes scan the area around her. The minute they land on me, it's like I've been lit up from the inside.

I take the last shot and make my way over to her. I know exactly when she feels me, because her body goes stiff.

I look at the idiot she's dancing with and motion with my head for him to move on.

"Get lost." My voice is tight, my mouth doesn't even move, since I'm talking through my clenched teeth.

The douche doesn't even try to fight for her. He just puts his hands up in defeat and walks away.

She turns around, all pissed off, but before she can say a word, I grab her hand and drag her across the dance floor, through the throngs of sweaty bodies dancing, and out the side door into the cool night.

I don't stop till I'm in the middle of the alley. She tries to yank her hand out of mine, but I push her against the side of the wall.

"Don't push me, Lauren, not now," I warn her.

She looks me up and down before she squares her shoulders and opens her mouth to let me have it. "Don't push you? Don't push you? You have some nerve, Austin. You called me uptight, and I was in there enjoying my night when you charged over there like…like…I don't even know what the hell that was all about, except for the fact that I wasn't the uptight one in that scenario. Hmm, who needs to loosen up now, Austin?" She finishes her rant with her hands on her hips and her breasts heaving with her anger.

"You drive me nuts! I can't sleep! I can't think! I can't even fucking get anything done at work without thinking about you!" I snarl at her as I rake my fingers through my hair, half tempted to pull it out of my head. That's how crazy she makes me.

"So, I come out tonight. I'm going to kick back, have a few drinks and not think about you. But of all the places, you're here, looking like this." I don't even attempt to hide the fact that I let my eyes run up the length of her body.

"What's wrong with how I look? I look good!" she huffs in outrage as she crosses her arms under those luscious tits and throws her hip out to the side.

"No, Lauren. No, you don't look good. You look fucking amazing. As usual. I tried to ignore you. I turned my back. I wasn't going to pay you any attention at all. But when I turn around, there you are on the dance floor, swinging your ass with that douche all over you," I grit out as I lean even further into her space.

"So? I'm here to have fun, too, Austin. And I was! Until you marched over there like some crazy man and dragged me out here. What the hell was that, huh?" Her voice rises as her anger climbs. Well, so what? I'm getting angrier, too.

I step even further into her space, backing her right up against the wall. My chest is heaving against hers, and she tips her angry face up to mine so we are nose-to-nose. "I didn't like it, Lauren," I hiss out.

That seems to take the wind out of her sails a bit. "Why, Austin? Why did it bother you?" she whispers.

I'm still feeling anger, but now it's mixed with lust and confusion. I don't know why I didn't like it. So instead of answering her, I do the only thing I can in the moment.

My mouth crashes down on hers, and I run my tongue along her plump lips. She whimpers, and I use that opening to slip my tongue into her mouth, sliding it against hers. She kisses me right back, meeting my ferocity with a hunger of her own. The taste of her invades my mouth. A small moan escapes her, and the lust I'm feeling kicks up. I move my hand up and into her hair, where I pull it, tilting her head back to look into her eyes.

She watches me with a stunned but way-turned-on expression. Her breathing is erratic, her lips are swollen from kissing me, and her eyes are hooded with desire. I don't move. She does. She pushes up onto her toes and fastens her lips to mine, nipping on my bottom lip and then soothing the sting away with her tongue before slipping it into my mouth. She twirls it in a circle, dancing with mine in the hottest kiss I've ever had.

Her hands slide from my chest around to my back and down to my ass, where she presses me into her.

I let go of her mouth, trailing my lips across her cheek to her chin and down her neck, licking, nipping, and sucking as I go. She is panting, and the hand on my ass squeezes it, while the other one claws at my back.

I go back to her mouth to get another taste of her. She's the drug and I'm the addict. I've never wanted someone so much in my life.

Not just her body, though her body is meant to be worshipped, but her head, her heart. I want it all.

My tongue moves with hers, deeper into her mouth. She wraps her arms around my shoulders and gives a little hop, telling me what she wants. I lift her legs and wraps them around my waist, lining her pussy right up to my cock. I groan from the sheer pleasure of feeling her against me.

I was trying to hold myself back, not sure how fast or far she wants to go, but that last move pushes me to the brink of my control.

I let go of her lips, and she whimpers and attempts to chase my mouth with hers in an effort to get them back together.

I look to the right and left and see that there is a gate locked on the side so no one can come in that way. The dumpster a couple of feet from us shields us on the other side.

"I can only be a gentleman for so long, baby," I whisper roughly in her ear and then roll the lobe between my lips. Her head falls back, hitting the wall.

Her legs are locked around my hips, and I pin her in place against them with my body as I grab her hands, moving them above her head and holding them there with one hand wrapped around her wrists. "I've dreamt about this moment since I watched you get out of your car." I grind my cock into her. She replies with a moan that echoes through the alley.

She tries to push off the wall, but my body holds her in place. "Hold on tight, baby. Lock your legs around me." I order as I feel her ankles shift against the small of my back, securing her to me. I run the hand that was holding her at her ass over her hip and up her side.

My hand is open on her side, and I use my thumb to lightly stroke the swell of her full breast as I tell her, "I used to sit at my desk, watching you bend over yours, hoping to get a look at this." I glide my hand between us to cup her tit and give it a light squeeze as my thumb moves over her hardened nipple. Her lips part as her head drops back against the wall and her eyes drift closed.

"Don't close your eyes now, Lauren," I whisper as I push her top and the cup of her bra to the side. I look down to see creamy flesh and her hard, pink nipple springing free. I don't even wait or take a breath before I lean down and run my tongue over it. I suck the whole thing into my mouth and then give it a light bite before I roll my tongue around it and go back to sucking. "Fuck me," she hisses.

I look up at her, while she looks down at me. "Don't mind if I do," I reply, planning to do just that.

chapter nineteen

Lauren

The minute his lips touched mine, my knees buckled. Totally turned to Jell-O. I've never experienced anything like that in my life.

You always hear about that kind of kiss, the one that will totally rock your world. You wait for it to happen, hoping with each kiss that it will be the one, that it's *that kiss*.

Well, if the fluttering stomach, sweaty palms, and panting are anything to go by, it appears that I just had the best kiss of my life. Right here in the middle of an alley with the Asshat I hate. Okay, maybe I don't hate him, but I thought I did. So, while my brain may not have liked him, I can admit that my heart and vagina lusted after him.

Not only am I now dry humping him, I'm pretty sure I'm going to fuck his brains out. Or he is going to fuck my brains out. Doesn't matter, because either way, I'm getting laid.

As soon as my legs let go of his hips, I pull my bustier back into place and smooth my skirt down. He grabs my hand and pulls me back inside the club. We don't stop; we just head straight to the front door and back outside, where he flags down a cab.

"My place or yours?" he asks as I look up at him.

"Mine." I wasn't going to do this in a place I wasn't comfortable.

"Oh shit. Kaleigh?" I look back to the club door that is still letting in the people who are waiting in line.

"She's with Noah. She's good." He pushes me gently into the back of the cab. My knees are still weak and not totally functional, so of course, my heel gets stuck in the pavement and I dive into the cab, sprawling across the seat on my stomach. I lie there giggling at the display of my sexiness. I sit up and move my legs so Austin can get in.

He gets in, closes the door, and gives the driver my address. "Come here." He pulls me into his lap to straddle him, my knees coming to rest on the seat by his hips.

His hands go straight to my ass, squeezing it, before they roam up my back to the base of my neck, where one makes its way into my hair, the other locked around the small of my back holding me in place.

He closes his fist around my hair, giving it a little tug as he thrusts his cock up against my center.

My head drops back as a groan leaves me.

"No sex in the cab," the driver admonishes from the front.

"No worries," Austin assures him.

His fisted hand in my hair guides my mouth to his, where I open for him immediately as his tongue darts in and out of my mouth. Our kiss is frantic, leaving us both breathless.

He pulls my hair, my head rolling back and to the side as his mouth starts working my neck. "I can't wait to be inside you," he whispers. "Can't wait to fuck you." His words shoot straight through me, and my clit throbs in response. "If I slid your panties to the side, would your pussy be wet for me, Lauren?"

I look at him innocently, a small smirk playing on my lips. "Why don't you find out for yourself?" I will hold nothing back with this. I've held back for too long. His hand releases my hair, skating down my neck, then my arm, until they finally land on my hips. He stops for a second, and I grind down on him. "Don't stop." I lean forward and nip at his neck and then suck on it.

"Oh, I'm not stopping, baby, not at all," he promises right before his hands rub down my thighs and then back up. Once, twice, making me shiver with anticipation each time. On the third pass, he brings the front of my skirt up with his hands.

The tips of his thumbs rest against the soaked black lace of the panties I'm wearing under my skirt. "Next time, don't wear panties. I'll finger fuck you in the restaurant. Got it?" I can barely focus on what he's saying, my body is so keyed up waiting for him to touch me.

Using his left thumb, he hooks the lace to the side, grazing through my wetness as he drags the material over.

"Next time? Next time, I'll suck your dick in the car before we even get to the restaurant," I whisper in his ear before I rise up on my knees a bit, giving him space to enter me. He groans out his reply just as the car breaks suddenly.

"Okay, Romeo and Juliet, it's twenty-eight fifty. Is that cash or credit?"

I get off his hips, while he grabs his wallet from the back and swipes his card. "Keep the receipt." He grabs my hand and exits the cab. He waits for me to get out before slamming the door closed.

"Let's go, Mr. Mackenzie. I have plans for you," I tease him as I walk ahead of him, adding a bit more swing to my strut. "You made some promises back there. You're planning on keeping them, right?" I ask coyly.

"Oh, I'll be fucking keeping those promises, alright. Tonight, tomorrow morning, tomorrow afternoon, and then again tomorrow night. The question is, do you think you can handle me?" He comes at me, picking me up, my legs wrapping around his waist, my hands around his neck as I lean down and kiss him hard. I lightly lick across his lower lip before I drag it back across and push it inside his mouth. Our tongues tangle as my back hits the door. My stomach flip-flops and my heart jack-hammers in my chest. "Open the door, Lauren. Now," he roughly demands, and my core quivers in response to the tone of his voice.

"I don't have my purse," I tell him but snap my fingers. "Wait! I have a spare!"

I tell him as I rush over to the potted plant on my front porch, pushing it over and bending to pick up the key. Okay, fine, I may wiggle my hips a bit in the hopes that he is watching. And from the groan that comes out of him, it seems he is.

I head back to the door and feel his chest at my back as I push the key into the lock. His arm snakes around my waist and he slides his hand down from my belly to cup my pussy. "Not so fast," he says right at my ear. I whimper as I wait to see what he'll do next. "I didn't check if you're wet yet."

My head falls back on his chest, and the hand not holding the key still in the lock latches on to the forearm banded around my waist. I tilt my face up so he can kiss me. He presses his lips to mine and against them, he whispers, "I'm going to finger fuck you right here, and you're going to cum for me, and cum hard, right now, Lauren." I moan my agreement, to which he replies, "But you can't make a noise. Can you be quiet, Lauren?" I shake my head no.

"Fuck, no. I've been quiet for ten years, Austin. This time, I'm yelling. Shouting. Groaning." I widen my stance to give him more access. "Touch me, Austin. Please," I beg.

It's his turn to groan as the hand that was cupping me moves quickly to join the other in hiking my skirt up to my hips. The cool night air skates across my now exposed skin, but with him pressing what feels like a very sizeable erection into my ass, my overheated body barely notices the temperature.

"You know what I'm going to like more than finger fucking you?" He moves my panties to the side, gliding two fingers over my sensitive clit and right into me. "Eating your pussy."

"Yes," I hiss, the small of my back curving into an arch that forces my ass to press into his hard cock. My nipples tighten, almost to the point of discomfort. My hips move with his hand as he fucks me, hard and fast, with his fingers. I'm soaked and hot and throbbing, which is clearly evidenced by the ease with which he's able to enter me. I grind my ass on his hardness as my hips continue rocking with his hand. "I'm going to come," I tell him, knowing it's coming.

"I know. Your pussy is squeezing my fingers. God, so fucking tight," he groans as he moves them faster, rougher. My hand moves from where it was clutching onto his forearm, snaking around me and then between us to palm his cock. I rub him through his jeans, up and down. His cock is huge, and I can't wait to have him inside of me. It's been so long, so, so very long. "Come on, Lauren, come on my fingers so we can go inside and I can eat this pussy." He pumps them in and out of me. My wetness is now leaking down his hand and my inner thighs. "So fucking wet. So fucking tight. So fucking hot. You're going to come on my fingers, then you're going to come on my tongue. And then you're going to come on my cock. *Over and over and over again.*"

And that's it, that's when I come, and come hard. I moan out my orgasm with a barely coherent "Oh my god, so good." My hips move with his fingers to draw out the orgasm that has been lingering since the moment I set eyes on him tonight.

I'm not completely sure my legs can hold me up right now. Thankfully, he still has one arm around my waist, while the other hand is still in me. He slowly removes his fingers, and I turn around, grabbing the hand that was just inside of me.

"That was so good," I purr, looking him right in the eye as I bring it to my mouth. "Got me all excited." I suck one of his fingers into my mouth. One of his fingers that's coated in my cum. I suck it deep into my mouth, twirling my tongue around it. "You know what gets me even wetter, hotter, hornier?" I ask, drawing another finger in my mouth. "Sucking cock," I tell him, and before he can reply, I'm on my knees in front of him, wrestling with his belt. The need to get him out is intense for both of us.

I get his belt undone, open the button with both hands, and slowly pull the zipper down. I open the front of his pants, slide my hands along his abs into the waist band of his jeans, and carefully push them down his hips. When I move the material over his impressive cock, my eyes take in their first unhindered glimpse of him—long, hard, and thick, and all mine.

chapter twenty

Austin

WHEN SHE SANK TO HER KNEES AFTER SUCKING HERSELF OFF MY FINGERS, MY cock jerked painfully against my zipper. Jesus fuck.

Her hands fumble with my belt and then the button. She starts sliding the zipper down slowly. I put both hands against the door over her head and look down to watch, more than ready to enjoy the show.

My dick pops right out, since I didn't bother with boxers tonight. I see her eye my dick, and from her expression, it seems that she likes what she sees. Good. She licks her lips before her tongue darts over the head of my cock in a slow, wet swipe, licking up all of the pre-cum that coats the tip. She pulls her tongue back in, almost like she's savoring it. Then she runs it back over it, a little "hmmm" sounding in her throat.

I use one of my hands to push her hair off her face and hold it to the side, so I can watch her take me in her mouth. She looks up at me, our eyes connecting as she takes the tip in her mouth. Sucking in a little more each time she bobs her head. My pants move further down my hips when I start thrusting shallowly into her warm mouth.

She curls her tongue around the head again and then takes in more of my length into her mouth. Her hot, slick tongue slides along my shaft, while her mouth covers me as she takes me deeper into her mouth.

The need to grab her head and fuck her face is strong. I grab her hair with both my hands and thrust my hips forward. When she groans, I pull her hair a little harder, and she sucks me harder in response. It seems that my girl likes to have her hair pulled. No problem there. I make a mental note to grab her by the hair when I take her from behind.

That mental image has me thrusting into her more forcefully. I take stock of her face, scared I'm going too deep, but she's lost in what she's doing and uses her hands to pull my hips into her.

"Can you take me in all the way to my balls?" I ask her, watching as she starts to do just that. Taking her time as she takes me in deeper each time. She moves one of her hands and wraps it around my shaft, taking her mouth off me to run it over my balls. Her tongue moves from one ball to the other, while her hand continues to work my dick.

She lifts her eyes to mine and warns, "Get ready, Austin. I'm going to take in your whole cock, right down to your balls. It's big, bigger than I've ever had"—she gives me a sexy little smirk—"but I like a challenge." She runs her flattened tongue up my shaft from root to tip right before she slips her mouth over the crown and takes me all the way the back of her throat.

Swear to god, my knees go weak and my head falls back in ecstasy. "Fuck," I hiss out. I pull one hand from her hair to brace myself against the door as I tip my head down to watch her.

I hear—and feel—her humming while she moves up and down my cock with her mouth, hollowing out her cheeks as she goes. I see her hand on my shaft, while the other is buried in between her legs. "Where is your other hand?" I pull her hair, so she takes her mouth off my cock. My cock cries in protest.

"Buried in my pussy," she says with a smile as she closes her eyes to enjoy the pleasure she's giving herself. I stand there watching, still gripping her hair in one fist, as she continues to stroke my cock with her other hand.

"Okay. Play time is over, Lauren. Open the door." I pull up my pants before I bend down to lift her to her feet. She looks a little stunned at the sudden change in plans and surprised when I pull the hand that was playing with her pussy to my mouth, sucking her fingers clean. I groan as her taste explodes on my tongue. Sweet and tangy, like a ripe peach on a hot summer fucking day.

One taste isn't even close to being enough. I let her open the door, but once we're through it, I slam it behind me and yank her back into my front. Her ass is still bared, and my cock is still wet from her mouth. I know if lift her up right now, I'll slide right into her to the hilt in one smooth stroke.

She must be thinking the same thing, because she pushes back, grinding her ass against my crotch. My hand wraps around her front, going straight to her pussy, her panties still moved aside, as my fingers move on her clit.

"Wet," I tell her as I apply a bit of pressure and make tight circles. "Fucking wet, and hot," I groan, easing up to a gentle tease as I switch to bigger circles. "Know what's going to make this pussy wetter?" I whisper into her ear while I remove my hand from her pussy with one last flick to her clit.

I turn her around, almost roughly, pushing her back against the door. No lights are on in the house, but the lights from the street glow outside, streaming through the windows and softly illuminating the foyer.

She's is panting, her eyes are hooded, and she looks at me in question. I smirk at her as I move to my knees in front of her. It's my turn to devour her now. I press my face against her pussy, inhaling deeply. She smells as good as she tastes, and I can't help the groan that escapes as my tongue darts out to lick her wet, slick slit from bottom to top. I use my hand to part her lips, revealing her swollen clit just waiting to be sucked.

Her pussy isn't bald; it's got a neatly trimmed landing strip that runs all the way down. My tongue flutters against her clit, teasing her. Her back arches, causing her hips to jerk forward. "Now, now. Patience," I admonish her while I lick her again, slower this time, my tongue buried between her parted lips as it travels up and back down the length of her, purposely avoiding her clit.

She whimpers and squirms as her pants become almost jagged. My tongue dips into her opening, in and out, mimicking what my cock will be doing shortly. I'm the one looking up now, watching her. Her head rolls against the door. One hand is at her side, resting flush against the door, while the other has found its way into my hair.

"Do you want to come on my tongue or my fingers?" I watch her go crazy with need.

"Cock," she breathes, pushing my face into her pussy. I close my mouth over her clit, sucking it into my mouth while tormenting it with my tongue at the same time. Her head thrashes, the hand not in my hair is now fisted at her side, and her moans are interrupted by words as she says, "Fuck, I'm going to come." She never once lets go of my head as she works her hips against my face. "So good." I continue to focus on her clit as I use my finger to fuck her, moving it in and out as I nibble and suck her clit until she begs me to make her come. "Make me come, Austin, please. I need to come."

I suck harder and then bite down on her clit once before I start sucking again. My finger is moving inside her, and I hook it to find her G-spot. When I do, I make sure to pass over it with a little tap each time my finger enters her. I feel her walls tightening around my fingers and then fluttering. I let go of her clit while still massaging her G-spot, and tell her roughly, "Come, Lauren. Come all over my finger. Come for me now, baby." I go back to sucking her clit, and I feel her legs start to shake as her orgasm starts to rush through her. She comes on my hand with a scream, and I continue to lick her slowly as I bring her down. My hand is now planted against her belly, holding her up as I feel her start to slump.

I stand and pick her up, her body pliant, loose, and sated. Her limbs wrap around my neck and my hips. She starts kissing up my neck to my ear, where she whispers, "Please tell me we aren't finished."

"Not even fucking close," I promise as I head up the stairs to her room. Tossing her on the bed, I palm my aching cock and tell her, "We're just getting started."

I look down at her, legs spread, arms raised over her head. She looks at me looking at her and then lets her eyes drift closed for a brief second as she gives her body a little stretch before she gets up on her elbows.

"What are you waiting for?" she asks me. "You said we were just getting started." Sitting up now, she reaches behind her to take off her chunky necklace and throws it on her nightstand, where it lands with a clump. "Do you want me to undress myself or would you like the honors?" She tilts her head to the side, her hair rumpled. She looks fucking perfect.

Her bedroom has a huge picture window, and the light from the street lamps flows into the space, illuminating her with a backlit glow. "You're taking too long." She rises up onto her knees. Her skirt is still shoved up around her waist, and she reaches to her side to lower the zipper of her top. A quick shuffle of the garment, and it falls to the bed silently. The only sounds in the room are my breathing and my gasp when I finally see her tits in all their glory. Perfect round globes that are plump and topped with tight pink nipples that call out to be sucked, to be played with, to be teased.

"Jesus." She pulls the skirt from around her waist and brings it up and over her head, her tits bouncing with her movements. I'm staring to the point of gawking when I notice that she is about to take her panties off. "No, not yet. That's for me to do."

She nods her head, watching me from her bed, on her knees, wearing her fuck-me shoes and a black lace thong.

I kick off my shoes, pull off my socks, and unbutton my shirt all the way down, shrugging it off my shoulders. Now, it's her turn to gasp and gawk. My body is lean, with no fat. The time at the gym and running keeps everything off. My six-pack abs are key to everything. "Jesus right back at you," she whispers, moving forward on her knees, getting closer to me at the end of the bed.

Her hand fists me, slowly working my cock up and down, as she asks, "Condom?" I reach into my back pocket for my wallet and pull out three. "Only three? We'll have to make them count, then." She leans down and bites my nipple then sucks the sting away.

I move my hands to her tits, cupping them in both hands as I squeeze both nipples between my thumbs and forefingers, lightly at first to gauge her reaction. When she moans, I roll them between my fingers more firmly, and she moans louder. When I pinch them hard, she throws her head back and moans out a curse. I let one nipple go as I lean down, taking the peak into my mouth as I continue pinching the other. Her hands work almost frantically on my cock at this point, and if she continues at that pace, I'm going to come like some teenage boy in her hand.

I move her hand off me and continue palming both breasts with my hands, squeezing, kneading, massaging. "Cover me," I demand of her, motioning to the condoms lying next to her on the bed. "Cover me now."

She puts the corner of the wrapper in her mouth, tearing the top off and pulling the condom out of the package. "I haven't done this in a really, really long time," she confesses as she rolls it all the way down my cock, squeezing the tip to get the air out. "Just like riding a bike," she chuckles while she starts to stroke me again.

"How much do you love your panties?" I ask her, fully prepared to replace them, several times over if she wants me to.

"Not as much as I love the thought that you're going to rip them off me," she groans, nipping at my jaw as my hand grips one side of her panties, ripping them clean off her.

"On your back, middle of the bed, legs spread wide for me." I don't have to ask her twice, because she turns right around and crawls to the middle of the bed, showing me her perfect, heart-shaped ass as she goes. She looks over her shoulder at me as she eggs me on. "This is a position I look forward to—*later.*" Then she moves to her back and lies down with her head on a pillow.

She cocks her knees, placing her shoes flat on the bed as she slowly spreads her legs, wide enough that they fall to the side. She's quite the sight, there in the middle of the bed, open and ready and wet for me, just for me.

I put my knee on the bed and move to her, my cock harder than it's ever been, knowing without a doubt that it's about to sink into pure heaven.

I pull her knees up, pushing them back and causing her pussy to tilt. Holding her legs in place, I tell her, "Guide me in, Lauren." She takes my condom-covered cock in her hand and rubs me through her slick slit to the opening of her pussy. Slowly, she pushes the head in and removes her hand for me to take over. I watch as I sink all the way into her.

Her pussy grips my cock so tight, it's being strangled in the best possible way. I hiss out a breath at the pleasure at the same time she moans, "So good." Tightening my hold on her knees, I pull out and then slam back in with a little snap of my hips. Her pussy is getting impossibly tighter with each stroke. "Oh god," she moans as one of her hands land on her nipple, while the other slowly trails down her body to her clit. She runs her fingers through her slit and around me as I tunnel in and out of her, getting them wet then bringing them back to her clit to circle. I plant myself all the way in her, balls deep, afraid to move for fear that I'm going to come before her. I just need a second to gain some control, but she's got other ideas. "Move, Austin, please!" she begs as she squirms beneath me, tilting her hips and taking my cock deeper into her heat.

I start to move in earnest, pulling out and then slamming back into her so hard the headboard bounces off the wall a few times. "Yes, yes, yes!" she chants, the finger on her clit rubbing faster and faster as her pussy pulses and tightens around me.

I don't stop. I just keep pounding into her, the sounds of our heavy breathing and skin slapping together filling the air.

The harder I pound, the tighter she becomes. "I'm going to come," she breathes. Her hand is now rubbing back and forth, almost violently, over her engorged clit. "Harder," she begs, pulling her legs back further as she tilts her hips up to meet my thrusts as she moans out her orgasm. Her pussy clamps down on my cock, pulsing and rippling around it as I move. The hand between her legs never stops, and the sensation of her climax coupled with watching her let go is the last straw for me. I continue to pound into her, bottoming out with each stroke, as lightning shoots down my spine into my balls, and I follow her over the edge. I come harder than I ever have in my life, so hard that I vaguely wonder if it might break the condom. Her orgasm hasn't stopped yet, either, and her pussy is milking me, squeezing every single drop out of me.

With my cock still buried inside her to the root, I let go of her legs, wrapping them around my waist as I fall onto my elbows by her head. "That was…" I pant out, trying to catch my breath and gather my scattered wits about me, while she wraps her arms around my neck, bringing my weight down on top of her.

"It was," she agrees, kissing my chin and then my lips between her own heavy breaths. "Definitely something we need to do again." I don't get a chance to agree with her, because her mouth has covered mine and all thoughts are gone as I lose myself in Lauren.

chapter twenty-one

Lauren

THE LIGHT STREAMS INTO MY ROOM, LANDING RIGHT ON MY FACE LIKE THE BEAM OF a flashlight. I groan, trying to grab something to block it out. I reach for the covers, trying to bring them up to shield my face, but they won't budge.

Soft butterfly kisses landing on my shoulder make me smile. *Austin.* Best. Fucking. Night. Of. My. Life. Well, besides having my children. Okay, best fucking *sex* of my life.

I don't respond to the kisses. His finger pluck at my nipple, rolling it between them, waking my body up and making it ache for him. "I know you're awake," he says between kisses.

"I need food," I reply. "No sex until we have food." I move deeper into his embrace. His hard cock pushes against my ass.

After the first time, we took a nap, and he woke me for round two with his mouth between my legs before I wound up riding him like a rodeo queen. I think I shocked his ass when I suddenly swung off him, mid-ride, and remounted him, reverse-cowgirl style. I wasn't surprised that when presented with my ass, Austin spanked it. No, what surprised me was how much I liked it. With his back to the headboard, me facing forward and looking at us in the mirror over my dresser was like watching my own personal porn. It was one of the hottest moments of my life.

Jake and I had what I always thought was an exciting and active sex life, but one night with Austin had me thinking that maybe it wasn't quite adventurous as I'd thought. Despite the years we'd had together and the level of comfort I'd felt with him, I've never let go like that during sex before. But after my divorce, I knew the next time I brought a man into my bed, I would be asking for and taking what I wanted. That wasn't something I did with Jake; with him, I followed his lead and took what he gave. It wasn't bad per se, but I think I knew deep down that something had been missing in it for me.

"Food," I repeat when his hand moves down my stomach to cup me. I ignore his hand and stretch my body. Muscles hurt in places that I didn't know could hurt from having sex.

"Okay, I'll go start the coffee." He's still trying to play with me. I slide out of bed and head into the en-suite bathroom in my bedroom. "I'm going to have fun playing with that ass later," I hear him say right before I close the door.

After using the bathroom, I look in the mirror. My makeup is still half on; the mascara isn't that bad, though a bit smeared. I take the time to remove it and wash my face. Tying my hair high up on my head in a messy bun, I brush my teeth. Once I make my way out, I immediately smell coffee.

Grabbing the shirt he wore last night, I put it on. It's huge on me, but I leave the top three buttons undone and button the rest, leaving him plenty of room to reach in if he wants to. I head downstairs and into the kitchen.

He's there, jeans on and buttoned, leaning against my counter, his feet crossed in front of him, drinking a cup of coffee.

His hair is tousled from sex and sleep, and a five-o'clock shadow has crept over his handsome face. I go straight to the coffee machine and reach up to grab a cup but see that he has made me a cup already. "I didn't poison it," he says, the mug shielding his smirk but not the smile in his eyes.

Before I can reply, I hear the front door open. He looks at me with a surprised look. "It's probably Kaleigh." I shrug and see his face start to relax. "Or my parents," I add, giggling into my coffee mug when he looks close to panicking.

Kaleigh comes into the kitchen dressed in a man's dress shirt and boxers, her purse hanging off her arm while her other hand holds her shoes.

"Look what the slut dragged in," I say, leaning against the counter next to Austin.

"Funny, funny, ha ha. I take it the cobwebs have been cleared out?" she fires back.

"Oh, there are definitely no cobwebs in there," Austin murmurs with a little smirk as he throws one arm over my shoulder. "Isn't that Noah's shirt?" he asks.

"I hope you told him you were leaving, Kaleigh." I look at Austin. "She isn't exactly known for sticking around the morning after. She, um, likes to leave before it can get awkward," I explain as I taking a sip of my coffee.

"He's going to lose his shit," Austin states.

"Did you use my almond milk?" Kaleigh asks while he continues to drink his coffee and shakes his head no. "Oh. So, you used the breast milk, then?" Austin spits his coffee out of his mouth all over the counter.

"What?" he questions, looking into his cup and then looking at me.

"She's just messing with you." I laugh. "You are going to clean up that mess." I point to the counter that now has his coffee splattered all over it.

"I'm not messing with him. I ordered frozen breast milk this week and switched it out." Kaleigh looks at me, while I look inside my coffee cup. "You put butter in my potatoes, remember?"

"You let me drink someone's breast milk?" I throw the coffee down the drain along with the rest of the milk. "That's sick, Kal."

"Where the fuck do you even order breast milk from?" Austin is looking under the sink for cleaning products. "Do we need to get, like, a hepatitis shot or something?" he asks, coming up with some Windex in his hand.

"I ordered it online." She shrugs her shoulder. "I switched it yesterday morning after the kids left." She nonchalantly studies her nails, while Austin and I start to freak out.

"What if the woman has a disease? Jesus! Could we catch it?" Austin turns to me. "I feel a little funny." He puts his hand to his stomach, making me roll my eyes.

"Relax, it was from a reputable website for mothers who can't produce enough milk," she assures us right before someone starts banging on the front door.

"Kaleigh! Are you in there?" Noah yells from outside.

Austin smirks at her and walks to the door to open it. "Hey, man." He steps aside for him to walk in. "Come in. Can I get you some coffee? With or without breast milk?" Noah just looks at him like he's crazy.

"What are you doing here?" He walks into the kitchen and eyes me in Austin's now buttoned-up shirt before shifting his gaze to Kaleigh.

"You took my shirt? And then you just fucking left?"

"She's not good with the whole morning-after thing," I add helpfully, while Kaleigh shoots me a glare and the middle finger.

He turns her around on the stool as he cages her in between his arms with his hands braced against the counter. "I thought we said we were doing yoga this morning?" He leans into her.

Austin laughs from beside me, where he stands after closing the front door. "You couldn't do yoga if you tried." He continues laughing while Noah glares at him.

"Plus, you said we could do the down-dog thing," he whispers to her.

"What's the down dog?" Austin asks me in a whisper that is not at all quiet. I shrug my shoulders as I shush him and continue to watch the scene in front of me.

"Don't you two have to be somewhere?" Kaleigh looks back at us.

"Nope," Austin and I answer at the same time and then look at each other and smile. His smile melts me, so I wrap my arms around his waist as he throws his over my shoulders, bringing me closer to him.

"Come back home with me," Noah asks her, leaning in and tracing her jaw with the tip of his nose. "Please."

"Okay," she replies, and I gasp at her in surprise. She never lets her guard down with men, *ever*. "Besides, I think Austin is going to kill me for making him drink breast milk." She tries to make it seem like this isn't a big deal, but I know better.

Noah looks at Austin as he stands back, making room for Kaleigh to get up and gather her stuff. "You drank breast milk, dude? Can you die from that?" He slips his hands in his pockets.

Austin stills next to me. "No, you can't. Now, go away before he goes nuts," I order before turning to Austin. "You can't die from drinking breast milk," I reassure him. "Well, unless the mother had like HIV or something."

Noah bursts out laughing, grabbing Kaleigh's hand and dragging her back out the door.

"We need to get tested," he states.

"I was just kidding. She wouldn't really try to kill me. Anyway, I was thinking maybe we could shower. I'm feeling very, very dirty," I whisper to him.

He grabs me around the waist, my body molding to his like it was made for him. We walk upstairs, where we make good use of our hands and mouths—and that third condom.

When nighttime comes, he gets dressed to go home. I'm a little down. We haven't talked about where this is going, but I'm not stupid enough to think that it's going anywhere. So, I tuck it down, bury it, and try to just live in the moment.

Later that night, he texts me.

Missing you.

I'm not sure what to say to him, so I send a casual reply.

Me too ☺

I don't hear from him the rest of the evening, and then the next day, I make my way to work. I messaged Barbara last night, telling her I would give it another chance. She was very excited. I dressed in a tight black pencil skirt that I paired with a white fitted, button-down shirt with three-quarter length sleeves that has a faux rolled cuff, making it appear as if the sleeves are rolled up to my elbows. I finished the outfit off with a smoking hot pair of Ferragamo patent-leather, pointy-toe stiletto pumps.

I walk in and see Carmen at the reception desk. Her reaction to seeing me is less than friendly. I don't bother questioning her on it, I just walk back to my desk.

I put my purse on the desk as I look into Austin's office and notice he isn't in yet. I walk to Barbara's office to tell her I'm here, but she isn't in yet, either. Looking at my watch, I see it's almost eight, so they both should be in soon.

Walking back to my desk, I come face-to-face with a furious Austin, who is just walking out of his office.

"What are you doing here?" he asks with his hands on his hips, and my heart sinks a bit at his reaction.

"I work here. Barbara asked me to come back, and I agreed." I put my hands on my hips now, too.

He grabs my arm, bringing me into his office and slamming the door.

"You can't work here. I don't sleep with women I work with." I look at him in confusion.

"What?" I ask, not sure I understand.

"I don't sleep with women I work with. I think it's pretty straight-forward," he barks.

"So, you're saying that you won't be with me if I work for you?" I ask him, now folding my arms over my chest.

"I'm telling you that you aren't working here, so we can continue sleeping with each other."

"Well, then that settles it. We won't sleep with each other," I bait him. He drove me out once, he won't do it again. "When we slept together, I hadn't agreed to start working for you again, so that doesn't count," I tell him right before there is a knock at the door.

"Go away!" Austin yells, but the door opens anyway with Barbara peeking in.

"Oh, good, you're here. I see you've found out that Lauren decided to come back. You're welcome." She takes in the tension in the room and looks at her watch. "It's been two minutes. How can you guys be fighting already?"

"It's nothing," Austin says as I stare him down.

"He's trying to fire me, because, apparently, he doesn't work with women he has slept with." I look over at Barbara, who closes the door behind her.

Then I look at Austin, who throws his hands in the air. "Why did you tell her?" he asks.

"Oh, please, she changed your diapers." I look at Barbara and then back to him. "Besides, if she hasn't already, Kaleigh would have told her."

He looks at the ceiling in his office, pinching his nose. "How did this happen?"

"Well, you had sex with Lauren, that's how," Barbara cuts in. "Which isn't that bad, Austin. I might have to change the employee handbook back now that it appears that fraternizing with a co-worker is okay," she teases.

"No, it's not okay," Austin snaps. "I don't shit where I eat." He looks at me. "Not now, not ever."

"Fine, no big deal. We forget it happened and move forward since it won't be happening again." I shrug my shoulders in an attempt to make light of it, while, in truth, my heart is breaking. "It wasn't that great anyways."

"Liar," he snaps as I turn to walk out.

"Now, if you guys will excuse me, I have work to catch up on." I turn and walk out before I break down.

I close the door behind me as Austin calls my name. I ignore the desire to go to him, ignore my aching heart and hurt feelings, and ignore the thoughts that we could have been starting something amazing.

chapter twenty-two

Austin

I HAD THE BEST SEX OF MY LIFE. I WAS WALKING ON CLOUD NINE. I WAS SMILING AT nothing. Then I walked in, saw her in the office, and I snapped.

I promised myself that I would never let my dick get involved with my work. Then there she was, in a tight skirt and a white shirt, and all I thought about was making those buttons scatter as I ripped that shirt off and fucked her tits.

My cock saw her and immediately stood up to salute her. Then she said the words I dreaded. "I work here."

Now, here I am, three days later, sulking in my office. While she comes in smiling every day like nothing happened. I see her bend down and have to stifle a groan. I see her chewing on her pen and think about her sucking my cock. I can't think straight. I can't even walk next to her without fighting the urge to push her up against the wall and fuck her so hard she can't walk afterwards.

I'm watching her while she talks to Steven, her arms crossed over her chest and leaning back. Today, she's wearing one of those tuxedo shirts for women, with rows of pleated material down the center. I wonder if she's wearing a lace bra underneath? All I know is, if I see her laugh one more time at something he says, I'm firing him. I pick up the phone to call her.

"Yes," she answers, and I swear my cock knows when she's close, because he twitches.

"I need the specs for my meeting with Dani." I look over at my screen, knowing she sent it twenty minutes ago.

"I sent it to you already," she huffs and then turns back to her screen. "Yep, it says 'sent.' Did you refresh your screen?"

"Obviously, Lauren," I grate out. "Can you just bring me in the hard copies so I can go over them?"

"Sure." She hangs up and prints out the pages, then gets up to bring them to me right as Steven steps in her way, causing the papers to drop to the floor. She bends over to pick them up, her ass pointing straight at my office window. Steven doesn't even notice that ass; he just helps her pick up the papers.

I groan and throw my pen down, trying to get my thoughts together so when she comes in, it doesn't show that I'm affected by her.

I adjust my cock and mentally tell him to knock it off.

The door opens and she walks in, handing me the papers. "Here you go. Do you need me to attend the meeting?" she asks, and I can't say anything. Today, she has her hair tied up in a ponytail, and I want nothing more than to untie it so I can run my fingers through it. I just nod, pretending to review the plans.

"Fine. I'll meet you in there. I'm going to get myself a coffee. Would you like one?" she asks me over her shoulder as she walks out of my office.

"Sure, no laxatives or breast milk, please." I watch as she rolls her eyes. I continue to watch her as she walks past my office, a little swing in her hips and a small smile playing across her beautiful face. Like me, I know she's thinking of that morning, that incredible morning. It feels like it was ages ago, but it's been only four days.

Every night on my way home, I go out of my way to pass by her house just see if she is there, hoping to catch another glimpse of her. Each and every night, I wish I could text her, call her, go to see her. But I can't.

The knock at the door jolts me out of my thoughts, and I look up to see Carmen standing there, leaning against the door jamb. "Hiyeah. I called, but you didn't answer. Dani is here," she informs me, and I nod as I get up, grabbing my jacket and making my way to the conference room.

Dani and Lauren are in there gabbing away about new recipes. I can't help but notice how everyone has taken to Lauren. She gets along with everyone.

She looks over at me, feeling me staring at her. She smiles at me, her smile different than the smile she gives anyone else. It takes over her whole face, her eyes, her cheeks, and her body relaxes.

"Hey." She points to the table. "Your coffee is there."

Dani sees me and walks over to me, hugging me, and kisses my cheek. "Hey, there, we missed you on Sunday." My eyes fly right to Lauren's.

"Yeah, sorry, I was…" I don't finish. I just look down at the pictures on the table. The restaurant is almost done. "Oh, wow, these are beautiful. I love the booths." I look and see that the booths are exactly like I wanted them to be, but now each also has a chandelier that hangs over the center of the table that gives it the appearance of falling rain.

"Yes, that was Lauren's idea. When she described it, I thought right away about the booths, so I told Chris. We are having a soft opening this weekend to make sure everything goes as planned, and then next weekend, it's go-time. I have a couple of celebrities coming. I even hit up your friend, Cooper Stone, and he's bringing his wife, Parker, with him."

I sit in the chair, looking at the pictures, while she talks, only half listening. "So, do you have a date for this or not? I can set you up with this girl I go to Pilates with. She is very detail oriented, and she just wants a good time."

My head snaps up, shooting straight to Lauren. "Um, no." I see her looking down at the pad in front of her. "I'm not bringing a date."

Dani laughs at me. "Serena will be there anyways." My eyes leave Lauren and shoot to Dani.

"Excuse me." Lauren pushes off from the table and walks out.

I look at Dani. "Is that all? Did we need to go over anything else?"

"No." She looks at me then at the door that Lauren just went through. "Jesus, are you and Lauren..." She motions with her fingers.

"She works for me, so that answers your question."

"Right." She gathers all her papers. "I'm going to hit up John before I leave. I'll see you Sunday?" Every Sunday, we all get together for dinner.

"I'm not sure," I reply, because I'm hoping that Lauren quits tonight.

I walk back to my office, expecting Lauren to be there, but her computer is shut off. I check my watch and see it's only two thirty.

I pick up my phone and call her on her cell. She picks up after the first ring. "Sorry, I'm so sorry I had to leave," she says, almost frantically, without even greeting me.

"Is everything okay?" I'm ready to run out if she needs me.

"Yes," she sighs. "Well, not really. I might have to call in sick tomorrow. Kaleigh has strep throat. She has a fever, and she's at my parents' house now, because the last thing I need is for anyone else to get sick."

"What?" I'm trying to follow her, but she is rambling.

"Kaleigh had fever, so she went to the doctor. She has a throat infection. She is the one who watches my kids after school while I'm at work. Except, tomorrow is a staff development day, and she's sick, so I have no other backup."

"Okay, don't worry about it." I go to my computer to check my calendar, seeing that there's nothing on my schedule till Monday. "What are you going to do with the kids tomorrow?" I ask her, not exactly sure why, but I do it anyway.

"I have no clue. Hopefully keep them from killing each other. Listen, I'm just getting home, so I need to go. Sorry about just taking off like that," she apologizes softly.

"It's fine. I'll call you later to check in," I tell her and then hang up.

I block out my day tomorrow, sending a message to Barbara that I'm going to be working from home.

I have no idea what the fuck I'm doing. But the next morning at nine a.m., I'm standing on Lauren's porch, hoping she doesn't turn me away.

I hear the door locks turning and hold my breath. Rachel opens the door, still in her pajamas. I squat down to talk to her, asking, "Hey, there, is Mommy home?"

She smiles at me, showing me a missing tooth, her lips shiny with what I'm assuming is syrup. "Mommy!" she yells loudly. "Asshat is at the door."

I put my head down, laughing at the nickname. "What?" I hear her voice from somewhere inside the house as she makes her way to the door. She is wearing a short pink cotton robe, loosely tied at the waist, the front a bit open on top so you see her camisole. Her hair piled up on her head, she places her hands on Rachel's shoulders. "What are you doing here?" She looks down at me.

I rise up from the squat position. "I came to see if you and the kids would like to go ice skating?" I ask her, and not waiting for her to invite me, I walk past her, kissing her on the head.

I shrug off my jacket, throwing it on the pile next to the door with the other jackets. Then I turn and look at her. "Is that bacon I smell?"

"Real bacon," Rachel says, turning to run back into the kitchen.

I look at Lauren questioningly. "Kaleigh makes them eat vegan bacon, but I picked up the real deal yesterday, so it's like Christmas morning." She laughs as she pulls her robe together at the top of her neck. "Austin, what are you doing here?" She asks me again, and before I have a chance to answer her, Gabe runs into the room.

"Are we really going skating?" His eyes are wide with anticipation. "Mom, can I bring my stick so we can shoot some pucks?" He then turns to me. "Is it okay if I bring my stick?"

"You play hockey?" I ask him.

"Yeah, I want to, but Mom says I have to choose one sport, so I chose soccer." Gabe looks at his mom.

"I used to play college hockey with Cooper Stone. Have you heard of him? He's retired now, but he was a big deal when he was playing."

"You used to play with Cooper Stone? Matthew Grant is my favorite player of all time! He's still a rookie, but he's awesome."

I smile at him. This kid obviously wants to play hockey. "How about next Sunday, if it's okay with your mom, I ask Cooper to join us on the ice?"

"Mom, please? I'll do all my chores." Gabe turns to his mom and begs.

"First off, you're at your dad's next weekend. And second, you don't have any equipment, and this isn't the right time for me to be buying stuff," she answers him.

"I have extra gear," I pipe in. I totally don't, but I'll buy whatever he needs me to buy.

She looks at me. "How about we go do the skating thing and see how you like it. You've never really been on skates, Gabe," she proposes gently, and he must see it as a win in his favor, because he jumps up and hugs her, repeating 'thank you' over and over again.

"Rachel, we're going skating!" Gabe yells, running out of the room.

"You look cute," I tell her because she does look cute, but it's more than that.

"We aren't dating, Austin. You can't talk to me like that." She shakes her head. "Please, don't make this harder for me." She keeps her voice low, and I advance on her, but she quickly brushes past me and heads into the kitchen, picking up the kids' breakfast plates on her way to the sink.

"What do we call you if we can't call you Asshat?" Rachel turns and to me on her way up the stairs.

"His name is Austin, so no more of that language, young lady. Now, go get dressed," her mother instructs from the kitchen. Gabe grabs her hand to hurry her upstairs to get dressed.

I head into the kitchen, finding Lauren bent over, loading the breakfast dishes in the dishwasher. Her ass taunts me, and my cock is hard and ready to slide into her.

Looking over my shoulder to make sure we're alone, I walk over to her, placing my hands on her hips.

Her body stills and then stiffens once my hands land on her. I press my hips forward so she feels me. The warmth of her body penetrates right through me. She snaps up straight, keeping her back to me. "I can't seem to forget you," I whisper in her ear as I sweep her hair to the side and kiss her neck. "I can't think." I run small kisses up the side of her neck as she tilts her head to the side to give me better access. I'm about to slip my hand inside her robe when I hear someone barreling down the stairs.

My hands leave her hips and I back away from her, while Lauren slams the dishwasher closed. "I'm not quitting my job just so you can have your way," she hisses as she walks past me. "Get ready, because there are more games to play, Austin."

She walks upstairs as I watch her, and I swear there's a distinct swing to her hips.

chapter
twenty-three

Lauren

He showed up like he just walked off a fucking catwalk modeling casual men's fashion. His faded blue jeans fit him perfectly, hugging him in all the right places and making his package look huge. Okay, fine. He's very well endowed, but fuck, those jeans just emphasize that fact. His blue Henley molds to his chest, shoulders, and arms, highlighting all his muscles right down to his trim waist, where the hem is tucked in at the sides in way that's obviously just his style. Topped off with his black leather jacket, the whole outfit looks like he should be riding a bike instead of driving a Porsche.

Then he sweet-talked my kids, mostly Gabe, with the hockey bullshit. And then, the crème de la crème was him grinding his fucking cock into me while I was bending over. I swear I almost raised myself up on my tippy toes to get him to slide in.

Since Sunday, I've masturbated every single night with him starring in all my dreams. He wants me to quit. Well, fuck that! I'm going to make him regret he made this stupid rule, even if I give myself blue balls, or a blue vagina, or whatever.

I grab my yoga pants, because nothing molds to a woman's body quite like yoga pants. I pair them with my blue off-the-shoulder sweater that stops just above my waist and gives a little peek of my stomach, but not too much. I wear a blue lace bra underneath it, which is the same color as the sweater. It's a mom outfit, but a sexy mom outfit, or at least I hope it is.

I text Kaleigh right before I go downstairs.

Hope you're feeling better and that Mom isn't making you want to commit suicide.

She responds right away.

It's Noah, she's with me. I'll take good care of her.

I look down at my phone, confused.

I thought she was staying with my parents?

She was until she walked in on them playing Tarzan and Jane. Your mom looks hot in a loincloth, BTW.

Ewwww! You're a sick man. Off to the arena with Austin. Tell her to text me later.

He finally got over that 'don't shit where you eat' bullshit?

No. I answer him right away and then throw out, *Know anyone hiring?*

You can come work for me. I definitely won't want to have sex with you.

Funny guy. Okay, well, if you have a real suggestion, let me know.

I'm serious. I need a PA to keep my shit in order, and I heard you're the best. Think about it. Let me know. That way, Austin's balls won't get swollen again. BTW I will never ask you to get me coffee or food.

"Mom! Come on, let's go!" Gabe yells from the bottom of the stairs. I take in my appearance. Yup, sexy yet still conservative.

"Coming," I shout as I start walking down the stairs. I see Austin taking me in from my feet to my shoulders, his eyes lingering on the lace bra strap. "Okay, are we all ready to go?" I smile big at him, while he tries to adjust himself discreetly. Score one for me.

We all pile into the minivan, and I throw the keys to Austin, since I have no idea where I'm going.

We pull into an otherwise empty parking lot. "Maybe it's closed," I contemplate, looking around.

"No, I have the key." I've practiced here since I was three, so the owner just gave me a key when I turned sixteen. I called Craig to let him know I was going to be here so he knew. He only uses it on Saturdays and Sundays at this point.

We walk in, and Austin turns on the light. The cement walls are lined with pictures of kids. I walk along the wall, while Austin walks behind the counter, getting a key out of the drawer.

Walking to another door, he opens it up. "Okay, let's see what we got. Rachel, what size do you wear?" he asks her.

"Twenty-eight," she replies, having no idea and just throwing any number out. He comes out of the room and looks down at her with a grin and his hands on his hips.

"She's a three, Gabe is a five, and I'm a six and a half," I tell him.

He comes back with three pairs of skates. Handing Gabe his first, then me mine, and then Rachel hers. "There are no girl skates, sorry, kiddo," he apologizes to Rachel as she sits down and he starts to tie her skates. I'm surprised when I see that Gabe has already tied his skates. "I'm ready," he informs us.

Austin looks at him. "Go into that room. There are some helmets and gloves." He motions over his shoulder to the room he just came out of.

Gabe goes in and comes back out with helmets for him and Rachel. "Can I get on the ice?" Gabe asks, and Austin nods his head while he finishes tying Rachel's skates and then calls me over.

"I think I can tie my own skates, Austin." I sit in front of him, while he is on his knees, readying the skate for my foot as I lean forward a bit, shifting my shoulder so my shirt slips a little, giving him a glimpse of the sheer lace bra under my shirt. I know right away that he's seen it when he groans loudly. I smile innocently at him. "Oops! Sorry about that." I hold my shirt up.

When my skates are tied, he takes his out of his bag and puts them on. It takes him a couple of minutes until he's done.

We make our way to the ice. Rachel, who ran to join Gabe as soon as she was ready, isn't skating. She is attempting to make snow angels on the ice.

Gabe, on the other hand, is skating like he was born to do it.

"I thought you said he hasn't skated," Austin says.

"He hasn't, really, just maybe once or twice." I watch him zig-zag from one end of the rink to the other.

"Kid's a natural," he comments, getting onto the ice, holding out his hand for me. "Let's play," he invites.

I grab his hand, put one foot on the ice, and slip right away. I grab onto Austin with my other hand so I don't fall. He doesn't even budge, while I flail around a bit.

"So, you hold on to the wall with one hand and my hand with the other, okay?" he instructs, skating to the side of the rink.

I'm holding on to the wall for dear life while I've got my other hand around Austin's in a death grip "This isn't fun," I deadpan, concentrating on not falling on the slippery ice. "Nothing about this is fun."

I look over at Gabe, watching him shoot a puck into the empty net. "Where did he get the stick?" I ask, attempting to skate.

"From the back room. Focus on your feet. Glide from left to right." I just glare at him. "Go away," I tell him, letting his hand go and clinging to the wall with both hands. I watch him skate away backwards, smiling at me before he turns around and skates to Gabe. The two of them are shooting pucks while Austin gives him tips.

The rest of the day is spent at the rink. Rachel gave up on skating but figured out how the intercom worked, so she gave us a play-by-play of nothing. By the time we walk out of there, Gabe looks at me and asks if he can join hockey next season instead of soccer. I look over his head at Austin and see him smirk.

"Um, we'll see, Gabe. I need to speak to your father first. Okay?" I say as I get in the car, watching Austin open the door for Rachel and picking her up so she can get in her booster seat.

He gets in on the driver's side, and I'm momentarily shocked by how it looks, as if we've been doing this forever.

"What do you guys think about grabbing burgers for dinner?" He adjusts the mirror so he can look to the backseat at the kids.

We all agree to get burgers at Five Guys before we head home. By the time we finally do get home, it's past seven and Rachel is dragging her feet.

"Okay, Rachel, bath and bed," I urge her when we get inside. Gabe asks if he can call his father, and I nod yes. He runs upstairs with my phone in his hand, leaving me and Austin alone.

"I think I'm going to head home," he says to me.

I look at him standing at the front door, "Thank you for today. You didn't have to do that." I walk toward him. When I'm finally in front of him, I lean up on my toes, wrapping my arms around his shoulders. "You looked pretty hot out there." I whisper, pressing my chest to his, watching his Adam's apple bob up and down as he swallows. "Really hot, so hot." I kiss his jaw.

"Are you quitting?" His voice is almost cracking.

"Nope." I smile. "I love my job, I'm good at my job." I press deeper into him, his cock resting on my stomach.

"Okay. I should go." He's seemingly unsure of what to do. I let him go, watching as he turns the handle of the door. "I really, really wish you would quit," he says before stepping outside.

"I really, really wish you would get over it." I hold the door in my hand, leaning against the jamb. "So I could show you that I'm not wearing panties," I tease him, watching his mouth drop, right before I close the door on him and collapse against it.

Gabe comes back downstairs with my phone. "I had so much fun today. Thanks, Mom." He hugs me and then runs back upstairs.

I look at my phone and see that Austin has already texted me.

Were you serious?

I don't joke about panties. Ever.

What if I fire you?

You wouldn't dare.

After that, he doesn't text me back. I bring up my recent texts and text Kaleigh.

Tell Noah to call me after nine to discuss his proposition.

I really hope your proposition isn't about sex.

Are you still high?

No. Maybe. Yes. I'm so sick. I hope you catch it.

Gee, thanks.

He said the job is yours and to tell him when you want to start.

How does next Monday sound?

It sounds like I need to have sex with him. He's so hot taking care of me. I should give him a blowjob.

With a throat infection? He might catch it!!!

In his dick?

No, dumbass, in his throat. Gotta go.

I start to make the plans in my head. Taking a huge leap of faith by switching jobs, just so I can have sex. Really, really good sex, awesome sex, the-best-sex-I've-ever-had sex. Yep, decision made. Now, I just have to get through the week and that stupid club opening, and we are in the home stretch.

The week went by faster than I thought. I've already spoken with Barbara about leaving. She is sad to see me go but excited that Austin will finally be in a better mood.

It seems blue balls don't suit him.

I also didn't help matters by coming in all week wearing tight clothing. One day at lunch, I left my panties in his drawer. I watched him open the drawer and take them out while looking at me. I smiled at him and waved. He got up and slammed the door and then closed his blinds. I can only imagine what he did, but I don't think I'll ever get the panties back.

Then there was the day my shirt accidently unbuttoned when I went to bring him files. It gapped opened so much, he could clearly see the sheer, cream-colored bra I was wearing, along with my nipples that were standing up to greet him. Oops, my bad. He actually snapped a pencil in half that time.

But nothing—nothing—beats my last day. I'm wearing a tight black skirt that clings to my body from my waist to right below my ass, where it then flares out with a ruffle. I wear lace-topped, thigh-high stockings.

Before I leave for the day, I walk into his office to ask him a few questions about the party we are attending tomorrow.

"So, what time should I get there?" I ask him, propping myself on the arm of the chair.

"I told everyone to get there at six. We have to be out front to do the red-carpet thing by eight, so I want to make sure everyone is on time." He tilts back in his chair.

"Perfect. I guess I'll see you there, then." I turn to leave and then stop. "Oh no, I think I have a tear in my stocking!" I say, looking over my shoulder at him watching me. "Right on the knee." I bend over, knowing full well that my skirt will rise just enough for him to see the border of lace stretched across the center of my thigh. He lets out a tortured groan and then a string of curses as I walk out the door. "See you tomorrow, Austin."

chapter twenty-four

Austin

I'M ABOUT TO CONSULT GOOGLE TO FIND OUT IF A MAN CAN DIE FROM BLUE BALLS when Lauren struts into my office asking questions about tomorrow. I'm almost tempted to close the door and fuck her on my desk.

All week, she has been torturing me. One day, she left her panties in my drawer. I slammed my door, drew the shades, and I sat at my desk picturing her sitting on it, legs spread, in front of me, as I jerked off with them. I came all over them. Hard, too.

The next day, her shirt popped open, accidently, giving me a perfect view of her tits in that sexy-as-fuck bra, her nipples hard and ready for me to bite and suck. That just reminded me of how incredibly responsive she is when I play with them. *Fuck me.*

Then the straw that broke the camel's back was right after she finished asking me the questions about the party. As she was walking out of my office, she bent over, and that fucking hot-as-hell skirt she had on rode up. She was wearing a fucking pair of thigh-highs and the tiniest pair of sheer panties. So tiny and sheer, I could see her pussy lips. *Motherfucker.*

I'm about to throw something across the room when John comes in, heading over to sit on the couch. "Hey, there, man. I heard that someone got their period this week." He jokes with me just as Noah walks in.

"Jesus, did this week go slow, or what? I didn't think it would ever end." He slaps John on the back and sits next to him on the couch. He looks over at me, then tilts his head and asks, "Are you sick?"

"He isn't sick. Lauren is holding her vagina hostage till he lets go of this whole 'I don't shit where I eat' bullshit," John explains.

"It's not bullshit," I snap at them both. "What if we have a good run and then she gets mad at me, we break up, and she sues me for sexual harassment?" I look at them both.

"What if you spend the rest of your life banging the best pussy of your life?" Noah fires back. "Listen, if you want, she can come work for me."

I sit up in my chair right away. "Not a fucking chance in hell. You've fucked every PA you've ever had."

"That was before. I'm a changed man. I went to the strip club yesterday to meet a client, and my dick didn't even twitch. In fact, he was bored. I think he might have even yawned." Noah looks down at his crotch.

John studies him. "No shit, you got the bug?"

Noah just shakes his head. "I did. By the way, I'm bringing her tomorrow." He leans back "She's so fucking hot. She can put her legs behind her head, man."

"I don't want to know that shit!" I yell. "That's Lauren's sister."

"She's not your sister." Noah turns to look back at John. "And she can hold them there." He raises his hand for a high five. Both of them have shit-eating grins stretched across their faces.

"Is Lauren bringing a date tomorrow?" John asks me.

"No," I snap, then think to myself that she fucking better not be bringing a date. But if she is, I have to know.

I pick up my phone and text her.

Are you coming alone tomorrow?

I'm hoping I'll be coming with you, but I'm not sure.

I throw my phone down. "Jesus, she's making my life impossible."

"Poor baby. Just fucking get over it. Have sex with her, work with her, and then I'll have a lot fewer complaints in my email." John gets up. "Now, if you bozos will excuse me, I'm going home to have sex with my wife. On the couch, because we can."

"You liar," Noah says. "Married people only fuck in a bed. Google it." He winks at John as he walks out.

"Let's go to the gym. You can work out your frustration there." Noah gets up. I do the same and follow him out. I spend the next three hours beating the shit out of a punching bag and working my body to near exhaustion.

Now, I'm in the car on the way to the party. I get there right before six, leaving my car at the valet. Walking the red carpet, I see the media setting up and wave at a couple of reporters I know. Opening the door, I walk in, and I'm speechless.

I see Scarlett, the event planner, walking up to me.

"So, what do you think?" she asks as I take in the room. There are dimly-lit chandeliers everywhere, casting the room in a sexy glow. White roses are placed around the entire space in mirrored vases. All the tables have a little lamp that looks like a martini glass is filled with little fake diamonds that are the lights. Once the overhead lights are turned off, they'll give an almost intimate lighting effect.

"It's really sexy." I watch the wait staff getting into their position.

Chris walks over to me, wearing a suit without a tie. "Didn't Scarlett do good?" he asks.

"She did." I look at the door and see John coming in. He's wearing a custom-made black suit with a black tie. Dani walks in wearing a black dress, followed by Barbara and Steven, who are both dressed to the nines.

"It's so beautiful," Barbara says. "This is my favorite one yet."

I look around taking in the booths. There are buckets set up at each one for bottle service. "You guys go reserve a booth now so we don't go crazy later."

When I turn back around, my heart skips a beat as I see Lauren walking in. She looks breathtaking.

She is wearing a coral-colored jumpsuit. It dips down dangerously low in the front and comes up to wrap around her neck, leaving her shoulders exposed. I'm watching her look around when I see the valet guy running back in, calling her name, and she turns around to greet him. With her hair tied up on top of her head, I can see that her back is bare all the way down to her waist. As if that isn't sexy enough, there is a slit on the side of each leg running up from her ankles to the tops of her thighs, giving a good view of her toned legs. She's got on a sexy-as-fuck pair of gold stilettos with fake diamonds on them that I would kill to have digging into my back later. A simple pair of diamond earrings finish her look.

When she walks over to us, I can see her pant legs swish around her with each step, giving me a peek of her legs. "Sorry I'm late, I took an Uber," she explains, and I rake my eyes over all of that exposed, silky skin.

I just stand there, taking her in. The need to grab her hand and claim her as mine is a war I'm internally waging with myself.

"Holy shit, Lauren, you look amazing," Dani exclaims when she comes back over to us after reserving a booth. "I love this color on you."

"Thank you so much. Oh, look, there's Barbara. I'm going to go say hello." She walks away, and we all watch her go. And we aren't the only ones, either. The wait staff has all taken notice of her. The bartender spots her saying hello to Barbara, and he makes a beeline over there, giving her a fake smile and talking to her. She tosses her head back and laughs at whatever he said, and my blood boils.

I make my way over to her side just in time to hear her order herself a lemon drop martini. "I'll have whiskey, on ice," I tell him right before he walks away.

"Can I have a word please, Lauren?" I ask her.

"Sure, but I didn't get my drink yet. How about later?" she says while she talks to Barbara and ignores me. She stands next to Barbara, talking, so I lean on the bar next to her, hoping that me being this close is throwing her off her game.

The bartender puts the drinks on the bar in front of us.

"Shall we toast?" Lauren asks. "To new beginnings and to letting go." She smiles at Barbara, who winks at her and clinks her glass. Both of them sipping and smiling as I take my whiskey and down it in one shot.

"Picture time," Scarlett announces.

"Picture time?" Lauren asks next to me.

"We always take a group picture before the opening of the club for the wall," Barbara explains.

I grab her hand in mine, our fingers intertwining as I walk us over to the red carpet where the photographer is waiting.

She tries to shake her hand free, but I don't let her. I take my place in the middle, next to John. I let go of her hand, bending down to whisper in her ear, "Don't fucking move," I tell her through clenched teeth. "Not one fucking inch. Don't test me." She rolls her eyes at me.

We spend the next forty minutes snapping pictures. Finally done, we walk back inside and each grab a champagne glass, with which we toast our hard work.

I drink my glass watching Lauren watching me. I smile at her, watching her eyes dilate, knowing she wants me just as bad as I want her.

I walk over to her. "You look beautiful." I rub her cheek with my thumb. "Come home with me."

Her eyes on me are smiling. She steps closer to me, then her eyes go over my shoulder and she stills. Her face changes, her smile is gone, her spine is straight. "Jake?"

chapter twenty-five

Lauren

I KNEW SHOWING UP TONIGHT DRESSED LIKE THIS WAS GOING TO CUT HIM AT HIS KNEES. I've never felt as sexy as I do in this outfit.

But I'm not the only one dressed to kill. Austin is in a custom-tailored navy blue suit and a crisp, stark white dress shirt with the top two buttons undone and no tie. Silver cufflinks rest at his wrists next to where his name is monogrammed and his silver Patek Philippe watch peeks out. Polished brown Ferragamos—what can I say, I'm a shoe girl—complete the whole package, and what a package he is.

I tried not to watch him from my spot at the bar, but I saw him heading my way out of the corner of my eye. When he grabbed my hand, intertwining our fingers, I knew I would be going home with him. Well, that and when he told me not to fucking move. I was almost tempted to move just to see what he would do.

Looking at him while we toasted, I was so proud of everything he did. I watch as he walks over to me. "You look beautiful," he tells me while he rubs my cheek with his thumb. "Come home with me." I step closer to him, ready to tell him I'd go anywhere with him. Smiling at him, I glance over his shoulder for one second, and that one second changes my night.

My smile fades and my spines stiffens as anger rushes through me. "Jake?"

Jake walking in with Camilla on his arm brings me back a bit. I didn't attend many of his functions when we were married, because there was always something going on at home.

Austin turns to see what I'm staring at, watching Jake and Camilla walk toward us, his hand holding hers. "What the fuck?" he says under his breath.

I don't have a chance to tell him everything I need to.

"Hey, Lauren, what are you doing here?" Jake asks when they stop in front of me.

"Um…" The words stay lodge in my throat.

"She helped make tonight happen," Austin answers for me, putting his hand on the exposed skin at my lower back. "Austin Mackenzie." He offers his hand to shake Jake's.

"Jake Watson, Lauren's husband." He shakes Austin's hand.

"Ex," I say, gulping down the rest of my champagne. "Ex-husband." I look to Jake and then to Camilla. "Gabe's former teacher. Lots of exes in the room." I laugh nervously.

"Oh, wait." Jakes snaps his finger. "Are you the Austin who took the kids skating?"

Austin grabs champagne from a passing waiter and hands it to me before he places my empty glass back on the tray. "That would be me. We took the kids out last Friday. They had no school."

"Are you two dating?" Jake asks, surprised, his eyebrow going up.

I don't know how to answer this. We've never really discussed the status of our relationship. Having sex, yes, driving each other insane, yes. Dating, um… it's complicated. "We are," Austin states. "If you'll excuse us, I see someone we need to say hello to." When he grabs my hand, I nod at them and follow him wherever he takes me.

He walks over to a couple who just walked in the door. From the shouting that wafts in and the flashing cameras, I know it's someone important. "Cooper," Austin greets, raising his hand to him.

The couple walks over to us, and I can't help but stare at them. The man is huge and gorgeous, obviously not as gorgeous as Austin, but still mouth-droppingly handsome. Austin lets go of my hand to shake his friend's and bringing him in to hug him. "Asshole," Austin says. "Good to see you," Cooper replies with an easy smile at him.

"Thanks for coming."

"Wouldn't miss it for the world. Plus, we get to spend the night in the hotel, where I plan to take full advantage of Parker." I look to the woman at his side who just rolls her eyes.

"Please, he's all talk. Lately, he falls asleep before the twins." She laughs at her husband.

"I'll show you falling asleep," he tells her, then turns to look at me. "This man has no manners. Cooper Stone." He reaches out for my hand. "This is my wife, Parker Stone."

Austin laughs at him. "This is the guy I used to play with in college. He's now retired and playing Mr. Mom."

"And loving every fucking second of it." He leans down to kiss Parker's lips.

"So, how did you too meet?" Parker looks at me.

"I'm his PA." I take another sip from the champagne.

"Are you the one who turned his testicles the size of boulders?" she asks me, laughing. "I saw the picture."

I grab the glass with both my hands, laughing as well. "How is it everyone saw this picture but me?"

"Oh, I can send it to you. I think it's Cooper's screen saver." She laughs at Austin, who is groaning next to me.

"I'm going to fucking kill Noah." He puts his hands in his pockets. I don't get a chance to say anything else, because there is more yelling coming in from outside and the camera flashes are going crazy again.

"I guess Matthew has arrived," Parker says to the group, and we don't have to wait long before the door opens and in comes Matthew.

He's got black hair that is parted on the side, a bit longer on top and shorter on the sides. His slim-cut black suit is cut perfectly for his frame. His dark gray shirt is paired with a shiny black tie. With the way his jacket hangs open, showing of his muscular chest, it's plain to see that he spends a fair amount of time in the gym. "Matthew!" Parker shouts, waving him over. He looks over his shoulder and sees Parker waving. He gives her a big smile and turns to guide himself and the woman who is by his side over to us.

They start to head this way, zig-zagging through the crowd, which has grown, and occasionally stopping to say hello to people on the way.

"Hey, Mom, Coop," he greets them both with a hug and kiss for Parker. "Where is Karrie?" He looks around for whom I assume is the woman he walked in with.

The blond woman is talking to a man who is kissing her hand and laughing with her. She looks amazing in her figure-skimming white dress. The top is off-the-shoulders with sexy little sleeves that cling to her biceps, and the dress hugs her in all the right places as it tapers down her thighs to stop just above her knees. Her thick hair hangs loose around her bare shoulders. Matthew spots her and walks right up to her, grabbing her hand, completely unfazed that the other guy is still holding her other hand.

Right before they get to us, she pulls him to a stop and says something to him. He leans down and kisses her on the mouth, and it's not just a peck either. No, that's a kiss one gives their lover, the kind of kiss that you feel all the way down to your soul. When he finally lets her go, he takes her hand and closes the distance to us.

"Well, that settles that," Cooper murmurs as he sips the beer that the waiter just delivered to him.

When they make it to us, Parker smiles at the girl and greets her. "Karrie, you look beautiful."

Cooper looks her up and down and smiles at Matthew. "Good luck, son." Matthew glares at him.

"Austin, this is my girlfriend, Karrie." Matthew pulls her into his side with a hand around her waist.

"I'm not his girlfriend. I'm his chaperone." She holds out a hand to Austin and then to me. Austin and Cooper both bust out laughing at Matthew's glare at her.

"I'll show you a chaperone." Matthew stares at her, and she glares back at him.

"Good luck finding me," she quips. "I don't have to be with you until next week." She tries to pry his fingers off her hip.

With that, he laughs and grabs a beer off the tray from the waiter who is walking past us. "Try to run. I dare you," he challenges her. "Remember the last time you tried that." He takes a pull of his beer. The memory must be something, because her cheeks turn pink.

"Lauren, do you dance?" Parker asks when Rihanna's "This is What You Came For" comes on. I nod my head and then down the rest of my champagne, handing the empty glass to Austin.

"I love to dance," I say, while the guys all groan.

"Let's go get a booth," Matthew says. "The dance floor looks cramped."

"I'm going to dance. Who is coming with?" Karrie heads for the dance floor, not even acknowledging Matthew's comment. Parker follows her, and I follow Parker.

The three of us find a spot of the dance floor, where we are joined by Dani. The four of us are moving to the beat of the music, hands in the air, hips shaking. Singing along with the music as it changes from one song to another.

I don't know how long we are out there, but I can't help but notice that a group of guys has circled us and are trying to cut into our group. The lights dim, with the glow of the chandeliers softly lighting the room.

I look around to see where Austin is, and I don't have to look far. He's standing at the railing, looking down at us with Cooper on his left and a woman hanging on his right side. She is wearing a red one-sleeved lace dress that is very tight and very short. Her hands are wrapped around his arm, while she whispers in his ear.

"I'm going to get something to drink," I inform the girls and then head over to the bar. I stand at the side of the bar, trying to get the bartender's attention, but there are so many people.

"What do you think you're doing?" I hear from my side. I turn to see Jake there, alone. I look left to right and try to find Camilla.

"I'm getting myself a drink." I lean one arm on the bar to take the weight off my shoes.

"I meant, what do you think you're doing with that guy?" His hands go to his pockets, and it's then I see that he's gained weight around his stomach.

"I really don't understand your question, which is none of your business for that matter." The bartender finally comes over.

"What can I get you?" he asks.

"Two shots of tequila." I look to Jake. "What are you having?" He shakes his head no to the bartender.

"You can't possibly be serious about this guy. He has player written all over him," Jake chides, while the bartender puts the shots down in front of me.

I down a shot, pressing my lips together as the liquid burns all the way down. I look back at Jake. "You can't judge a book by its cover, Jake. After all, you didn't look like a cheater, yet that is what you are." His mouth tightens into an angry, grim line. I take the next shot and tell him, "You don't get a say about who I date. Not now, not ever." I look back at the railing and see that Austin isn't there anymore, and neither is the woman who was hanging all over him. My heart sinks, and my stomach is burning with devastation.

Camilla choses that moment to find him. "I couldn't find you anywhere." She leans into him and kisses him, putting her hand on his face. The big round diamond can't be missed.

I look at them both, while the bartender places another shot in front of me. I quickly down that one before looking back at them. "Congratulations on the engagement." I point to her hand. "Excuse me," I say, trying to walk past them, but Jake stops me by grabbing my arm. I raise a brow in question as my eyes look from his hand on my arm to his face.

I don't get a chance to say anything further before we hear a roar from behind me. "Get your fucking hand off her before I break every single bone in it." I look over my shoulder to see Austin's angry face glaring at Jake.

Jake loosens his grip on my arm, and I snatch it back. "Good luck, Camilla. You know what they say, once a cheater, always a cheater."

And with that parting shot, I walk away from the three of them to make my way to the bathroom.

chapter twenty-six

Austin

We stand upstairs, above our booth, looking down at the four women dancing, the four of us watching closely.

What the women don't realize is that they are attracting attention—a lot of attention. Cooper is next to me, his arms crossed over his chest and his eyes narrowed practically to slits. Matthew stands next to him, growling every ten seconds, and I wouldn't be surprised if steam started pouring out of his ears. The only one calm about all this is John, who is leaning against the railing, looking at us. "Suckers." We all turn to glare at him.

Cooper leans forward. "Um, you mind explaining what you're doing with Karrie?" He asks, turning his head to Matthew.

"Nope. She's mine." He sips his water. "She's just fighting the inevitable."

"She left you once. What makes you think she won't try it again?" Cooper asks.

"I handcuffed her to my bed for four days." He smiles at the memory. "I dare her to try it again."

"You know that's kidnapping, right?" Cooper grins.

"Would you let Mom leave?" he asks him, knowing full well that he wouldn't even let Parker leave for four hours. "Just get on a plane and take off for God knows where?"

"I hope you used comfortable cuffs." Cooper laughs as he looks back down at his woman.

"Exactly," Matthew states. "Now, I'm going back down there, because I've given her enough space." He walks down the stairs and onto the dance floor, going straight to her. He moves in right behind her, his hands landing on her hips as he brings her closer to him. She doesn't move until he whispers something in her ear, then her arms move up his chest and around his neck.

"Austin." I look to the right and see Serena coming up the stairs. "I've been looking everywhere for you." She kisses me on the cheek and holds on to my arm.

"I've been here all night." I look down at the dance floor. The girls are still going at it, but Matthew has taken off with Karrie.

"Isn't it fabulous? We did it, we've got another hit." She digs her claws into my arm, while I try to shake them loose. "We could rule the world, in and out of bed," she purrs. "Don't you think?"

I shake my head at her audacity and huff out an annoyed laugh as I firmly peel her hand from my arm. "Serena, that's never going to happen. Ever." I look down and see that Lauren is heading to the bar.

I walk away from Serena and down the stairs. I head in the direction of the bar, talking to different people on the way down, thanking those who have showed up. I see Noah and Kaleigh walking in.

"This place is insane." Noah looks around. "Congrats, man." He shakes my hand.

"Your shirt isn't even buttoned properly," I point out to him.

Kayleigh shrugs her shoulders. "I can't help it if he dresses like a guy on GQ. Where is Lauren?" She looks over my head.

"Oh, shit. Is that Jake and the home wrecker?" She looks toward the bar.

I don't even wait to hear what she says next. I turn to make my way over to Jake and Lauren when I see her try to walk away as he stops her by grabbing her arm. My blood boils, my hands clench into fists at my side. "Get your fucking hand off her before I break every single bone in it," I growl at him, my voice loud and angry, causing the people around us to turn and look.

Lauren jerks her arm away from him. She looks at Camilla and says, "Good luck, Camilla. You know what they say, once a cheater, always a cheater." Then she turns and moves through the crowd toward the bathroom.

"I know you're just playing around with her," Jake states as he steps in front of me.

"I knew you were stupid. I just didn't think you were a fucking idiot, too." I look from him to his girlfriend, who holds his one hand in both of hers. "You not only down-graded, but you got the cheapest knock-off on the shelf." I turn to Camilla. "I was waiting to see if you remembered me, Camilla. I wasn't sure if you would. But I'm sure you remember Max?" Her face pales the minute I mention my good friend's name. "He's doing well. You know, after you fucked him out of house and home. Made him lose everything, and for what?" I snarl at her and then look back to Jake. "If you think you're the first student's father she's fucked, think again. You're just this year's model." I glance at her in disgust. "I bet she's already fucking someone else right now. After all, the game is over for her. You gave up everything. The thrill is gone."

I scan the room, my eyes going to the last place I saw Lauren. "She hides a second cell phone. Max found it in her tampon box." I leave the fool with that tidbit and head to the bathroom.

I wait outside the bathroom for two minutes, or maybe it is two seconds, before I knock on the door. "Coming in," I shout, walking in and nodding hello at the girl handing out paper towels. Lauren is at the sink washing her hands. "We need to talk," I tell her while she looks at me in the mirror, her mouth hanging open.

She shakes the water off her hands and then grabs the towels from the attendant. "I'm not really in the mood to talk right now." She wipes her hands, throws the towels away, and then walks out.

She gets out the door, and I snap into action. I grab her hand and drag her the other way toward the office. "Austin, really," she says as I hear her heels clicking against the floor behind me.

I open the door to the office I have used in the past to discuss the floor plans, then close the door behind us and lock it.

She walks into the room and to the window that overlooks the whole club. "I'm really not in the mood right now, Austin." I stare at her. "I honestly just want to go home." I walk over to the window, standing next to her while she looks out.

I spot Jake and Camilla fighting right where I left them. "She is called 'Camilla the Cunt' in my circle of friends. One of my best friends, Max, married to a great woman, a father of three. She taught their oldest son." I see her look at me, so I turn to look at her. "He's an idiot."

"It doesn't matter." She shrugs her shoulders. "It really doesn't matter. If it wasn't Camilla, it could have been someone else. Who knows? And with you"—she laughs out—"I am so out of my league with you. I have kids, I'm a mom. I'm not cut out for this." She points to the dance floor. "This is your world. That blonde is your world." She laughs humorlessly and turns to walk away. "I guess that policy was the right call after all." She starts to walk away as my hand snaps out to hold hers, my fingers folding into hers. We both look down at our hands, but she slowly pulls hers away. "I can't do this."

"Are you about done now?" I ask her. "I'm a lot of things, Lauren, but I'm not a liar or a fucking cheat. I want you." I close the distance between us, running the back of my fingers from her shoulder to her elbow. "Only you. You drive me absolutely fucking crazy, and you keep me on my fucking toes. You make me want everything, and I've never wanted everything. I've only wanted me. Now, I want you and everything that comes with you. I want the dinners at the table. I want laughter. I want the kids' banter. Fuck, I even want Rachel calling me Asshat, but not all the time." I chuckle as I see her smile. "I want more Sundays like the one we had when we woke up together."

I pull her to me as I wrap my arms around her, placing a kiss where her shoulder meets her neck. I feel the shiver that runs through her in response. "Austin," she whispers, her chest rising and falling with her nerves. "I would really hate to cut off your dick," she says quietly, "but I will. If that doesn't work, Kaleigh will finish the job."

I push her against the door, taking her mouth before she says anything else. The need to taste her more powerful than my next breath. My mouth devours hers, while her mouth matches my need with her own.

Our tongues are tangling together when her hands go straight to my belt, my hands going for her ass.

I leave her mouth, running my lips down her neck to the plunging V at her chest. Pushing the material off her breast, I bend to take her nipple into my mouth. I suck on it deeply, and her head falls back against the door, her hands stopping their assault of my belt.

"Austin," she moans, lifting a leg to my hip, my hand holding her leg then roaming up it and dipping into the slit to slide along the back of her thigh. I glide my hand all the way up to cup her bare ass.

"You better be wearing panties," I warn her before giving her nipple a soft bite. Releasing her leg, I squat down in front of her, both hands roaming up the backs of her legs until they get to her ass.

"Oops, my bad. I guess I forgot to put panties on." Her breathing turns a little deeper as my hands squeeze her ass.

"Fuck," I hiss, realizing that this whole time, she has had nothing on under this hot-as-hell outfit. I stand up just as she reaches behind her neck, unclips the top, and in one swoosh, the material glides down her body until she's standing in front of me, gloriously naked, except for her gold shoes.

She cups her breasts in her hands and asks, "You ready to drop the whole 'don't shit where you eat' bullshit?" Her eyes close as she rolls her nipples between her fingers. I would give away my soul right now to touch her. Her tongue darts out to lick her lips, and one hand moves down her body as she buries it in herself.

My hands are in my hair, pulling at the strands, as my cock jerks against my pants as if to question why he's not already buried in her. "Fuck. Fine," I give in as I start undoing my pants.

"You would do that for me? For us?" she asks.

"Anything," I tell her then place my forehead on hers. "Anything for you," I whisper, knowing I would give her the fucking moon if I could.

"Good, I quit." She smiles. "Now, how about you show me how much you've missed me?" I pull my pants down to my thighs, reaching into my pocket to grab my wallet and a condom. I cover myself quickly, but it still takes longer than I want it to.

I pick her up. "Really sorry, but this is going to be fast. I promise you I'll make it up to you," I tell her as I plunge my cock into her and fuck her, hard and fast, against the door. No talking is necessary as our bodies, heaving with our need for each other, do the talking for us.

I pound into her over and over again until her pussy finally clamps down on me and she yells out my name. I stroke into her roughly before I plant myself all the way in her and follow her over the edge into orgasm. She's wrapped around me with her arms around my neck and her legs around my waist. My head is resting on her shoulder as I catch my breath. "Tell me you'll come home with me."

She giggles. "Can I say no?"

"Try it, I dare you," I challenge her right before there is knocking at the door.

"Austin, are you in there?" The whiny voice calls from the other side.

"Fucking Serena," I mumble. I place Lauren down on her feet, where she picks up her outfit, sliding herself into it, and fastens it at the neck. I take care of the condom and buckle up. I drop a kiss on her lips right before the door swings open and Serena stands there. "Hey, the door must have been stuck. Serena, this is my girlfriend, Lauren." I grab her and bring her close to me. "Lauren, this is the owner of this place, Serena."

chapter twenty-seven

Lauren

The door swings open, and the blonde from earlier comes in. "Hey, the door must have been stuck. Serena, this is my girlfriend, Lauren," Austin introduces, curling an arm around me and bringing me in close to him. "Lauren, this is the owner of this place, Serena."

I smile at her. "It's a pleasure to meet you."

She looks me up and down, the disdain obvious in her expression. "Hmmm, likewise." She turns her attention to Austin. "We haven't chatted or taken pictures yet."

"Sorry, Serena, but we have to go. We took pictures earlier, and I'll make sure that Scarlett sends them to you," Austin says as he takes my hand and leads us out.

We make our way back to the booth that was reserved for us. Cooper is sitting there with Parker on his lap, John and Dani are sitting next to each other on one side, and Noah and Kaleigh are seated opposite them on the other side of the booth.

"Hey," Kaleigh greets when she sees me. "Where have you been?" she asks, leaning over Noah to look at me. They slide over in the booth, giving us space to sit down. Austin sits first and then pulls me down on his lap. Kaleigh leans in and whispers conspiratorially in my ear, "You totally just had sex!"

I gasp loudly and look at her, denying it by shaking my head no. "Oh yes, you did. You are glowing and have the 'I've just been fucked' face. Trust me, I know that look."

Everyone is talking amongst themselves and the music is loud so no one is really paying attention to our conversation. "You're crazy," I tell her.

"I'm starving," I say loudly and everyone agrees.

"Pizza?" Dani suggests, standing up. "Let's go." We all get up to make our way outside.

I hold Austin's hand as we leave the club. Some fans have spotted Cooper, and he goes over to them to take some pictures. While he's doing that, the rest of us climb into a huge black party bus that Scarlett has ordered for guest who drank and don't want to drive home.

"I can't wait to take off these shoes," Parker whines, propping her feet up in Cooper's lap.

"You can wear flip flops tomorrow when we go skating with Austin," he tells her.

"Skating?" I ask.

"Oh yeah. I was telling them about Gabe, and since Matthew is in town and wants to run drills with Cooper, we are all meeting at the rink at noon."

"Oh, that sounds like fun. Can I come?" John asks from his side of the bus.

"Can you skate?" Austin asks.

"Well, not like you guys, but I can keep up," he states as Dani laughs out loud.

"Honey, I love you dearly, but you can't skate." Dani leans over and kisses his cheek.

"I'm coming," Noah announces from his seat.

They talk and make plans for the next day, while I take it all in. We spend two hours at the pizza place, laughing over their stories from the 'old days.'

Austin asks me, "Your place or mine?"

"I'm going to Noah's. So you can go home and have loud monkey sex without me hearing it." Kaleigh runs up behind Noah, who has already flagged down a cab.

"Let's swing by my house and grab some clothes for tomorrow," Austin suggests, yelling at Noah to wait for us.

We wave good-bye to everyone as we cram into the cab. "You live near each other?" I ask.

"I couldn't leave my boo," Noah jokes.

We pull up on their street, a chic, modern neighborhood, where all the houses are three stories high.

We get out of the cab. I look at Austin's house. It's white with a brown, wooden door. There is a huge window above the door, trimmed in black, and narrow, long rectangular windows are on either side of it.

When he pushes the door open and the lights come on, I take in the modern, masculine space that looks like it could be in a magazine. "You live here?" I ask him, walking into the all-white sunken living room. The back wall is the showpiece of the room with its floor-to-ceiling windows.

"I live here." He laughs. "Want to come see the upstairs?" He holds his hand out for me to take it.

We head up the stairs, which are black and look like they are held together with wire. "Should I take off my shoes?" I ask him when we make it to his room and I see the plush white carpet. His bed sits in the middle of the room, overlooking a wall of windows. He walks in, touching something on the wall so that the lights turn on. Walking further into the room, he opens the door to his walk-in closet, except it's the size of a bedroom. "Jesus, how many suits can one person own?"

"Should I ask about your shoe collection now?" He turns to me while grabbing his bag from the shelf, throwing in a couple of pairs of pants, then going to the wall that has drawers, where he opens a couple and pulls out socks, shirts. "Should I pack boxers?" he asks with a smirk.

"I don't know. Should I go to work on Monday without panties?" I smile back at him and yawn.

"You know, we could stay here and then go back to your place tomorrow." He shrugs off his jacket and kicks off his shoes, pulling his shirt out of his pants and unbuttoning it from top to bottom before shrugging the shirt off and throwing it in the basket in the corner. His pants are next to go. "Sleep with me in my bed?" I look back at the huge bed with its thick, white covers and think that it looks like a cloud. "I want you in my bed. I want to roll over when you're not here and still smell you on the pillow." I take the pins out of my hair, letting it fall down to my shoulders.

"Are you going to do dirty, dirty things to me?" I ask him, unclipping my outfit so it falls to the floor. I kick it over to join his pants. "I just need to take off my shoes." I walk out of the closet to the bed, bending down at the waist to unclip my shoes when I hear him groan behind me. "Like the view?"

"Change of plans." He picks me up and throws me on the bed. "I want to feel those heels digging into my back when I fuck you hard."

"Well, since you asked so nicely"—I spread my legs wide—"let's put those marks on you."

By the time we finish, I think I see the sun coming up, my body is well used, aching in places that I will feel all day. My shoes are gone, long ago thrown somewhere in the room.

I turn to look out the window, Austin curling around me, where we both fall into a deep sleep.

The alarm next to his bed wakes us up, both of us snuggled under his blankets that really do feel like a cloud.

"We need to get to your house." Austin kisses my neck while he cups my breast.

"I need to call Jake and ask him to bring Gabe early." I yawn, blinking my eyes to stay awake.

I get up from bed to call Jake, who sounds as tired as I am, and he doesn't argue with me about dropping the kids off early.

I borrow a pair of his basketball shorts that are so big they go down to the middle of my calf, even rolled at the waist, and a blue Hugo Boss t-shirt. My shoes dangle in my hands as I make my way from his car to my front door.

Thinking that this is what they call the walk of shame, I look over my shoulder at Austin. He is dressed in blue jeans, a tight t-shirt, and his aviator glasses. He didn't shave this morning, so his face is covered in light stubbles. The thought that there is nothing shameful about spending the night with him crosses my mind.

"Remember the last time we were at this door?" Austin asks while gripping my hips. I, of course, move fast before my neighbors get the chance to experience a replay.

I unlock the door, walking straight up the stairs to my room. "I need a shower so bad." I dump the clothes in my hands on the bed. Austin is already without his shirt by the time I turn around. "What are you doing?"

"Conserving energy," he answers while he picks me up and tosses me over his shoulder.

The shower lasts until the water coming out feels like ice pellets hitting our skin, my legs are limp, and I need a nap. Having awesome sex is freaking exhausting.

We are both now dressed and downstairs having coffee together. He sits at my table, reading the Sunday paper, while I flip through the living section. Every now and again, he takes my hand and kisses it.

It's almost as if we have been doing this forever. The doorbell rings, and I get up to answer it. "I think the kids are home," I tell him, getting up to answer the door.

Opening the door, I'm tackled by Gabe and Rachel, who run to me.

"Mom, is it true we are skating with the Cooper Stone and his son, Matthew?" Gabe rushes out without taking a breath.

"It is. Austin is friends with him." I ruffle his hair and kiss him "He's in the kitchen. You can go say thank you."

"Sweet!" He runs into the kitchen, yelling.

Rachel has her head on my stomach and her hand around my hips. "I need a nap," she says.

I look up at Jake, who looks like death. He's wearing a baseball hat, and his face is a greenish pale and unshaven. He looks ragged. "Why are you so tired?" I ask her.

"The babysitter put her to bed at one a.m." Jake takes off his hat to scratch his head then puts it back on.

"Okay." I look over at him standing there. "Go put your things away while I talk to Dad."

I watch as she heads into the kitchen and then hear her greet Austin in her special way. "Hey, Asshat, you're here." I laugh quietly when I hear giggling coming from Rachel and then Austin telling her he's going to tickle her till she gets his name right.

I look back at Jake, who I'm assuming has heard that Austin is here. "You okay?" I ask him, my hand on the doorknob as I lean on it.

"Camilla and I have ended our engagement." He looks at me and then to the side.

I don't say anything, because what can I say at this point?

"I'm so sorry, Lauren, for everything. I ruined it." He looks back at me. "I ruined everything, and for what? For a woman who collects fathers."

"I don't know what you want me to tell you, Jake." I cross my arms over my chest.

"I was a fool. She played me." He takes his hat off again to scratch his head.

"You wouldn't be the first," Austin says from behind me. "Sorry to interrupt." He puts his hand around the back of my neck and kisses my temple. "The kids are getting ready."

"I should go," Jake says. "Tell the kids to call me later." He walks away from us with his head hanging down.

I wrap my hands around Austin's waist, while he uses his foot to close the door. "Do I have anything to worry about?" he asks while hugging me. My face rests against his chest, listening to his heart beating faster than normal.

"Not in this lifetime," I tell him honestly. "No matter what happens between us, Jake and I are over."

"Okay." He squeezes me.

"Asshat, can I do snow angels again?" Rachel yells from upstairs, her voice coming closer.

I hide my face so she doesn't see me laughing, then I turn around. "Rachel, it's Austin."

"I know dat, Mom." She's coming down the stairs, chanting, "Asstin, Asstin Asstin."

I continue laughing and so does Austin. "Well, it's better than Asshat."

Half an hour later, we walk into the arena and see Cooper standing in workout clothes and chatting with a bald man, laughing at whatever they are talking about.

"Look what the cat dragged in," Austin says to Craig as he moves in to hug the old man.

"I couldn't miss my two best boys on the ice again." He looks at both Cooper and Austin.

"Hey," Cooper greets Gabe, who is standing next to me, gawking shamelessly. "You must be Gabe. I heard you're really good." He ruffles his hair. Gabe continues to stare and has still not said anything.

I nudge him with my hip. "Um. You're Cooper Stone," he whispers, and everyone laughs.

Cooper laughs, too, and is about to reply when he looks over at Rachel. "Do you skate, too, or are you just a princess?"

"I'm a princess, and I only skate if I can make snow angels." Rachel smiles.

Parker walks in with Matthew and Karrie following her.

"Hey, guys," she greets us as she goes to Cooper's side. "Who are these guys?" She asks me.

"These are my children," I say, smiling at her. "This is Gabe, who, believe or not, never stops talking." I hug him sideways. "And this is my girl, Rachel."

"She's a beauty." Parker smiles at me in return. Rachel leaves my side to go tap Matthew's leg. He stops talking to Karrie and smiles at her before squatting down in front of her. "Hey, there, Princess."

"Will you be my boyfriend?" Rachel asks, while I gasp out loud and Austin groans beside me.

"Um," Matthew mumbles.

"Rachel, what are you doing?" I question, going to her.

"Well, Auntie Kay has Noah as her boyfriend, and you have Asshat." Cooper bursts out laughing. She looks at Austin and smiles. "Sorry, Asstin. So, I want one, too, and I want him." Rachel points her thumb at Matthew, who is in stitches.

"I would really, really like to be your boyfriend, but Karrie is my girlfriend, and it wouldn't be fair to her."

"Oh, that's totally okay. I give him to you," Karrie says to Rachel. "No takebacks, either." Cooper and Parker are now laughing even harder.

Matthew stands up and glares at Karrie. "I'll show you no takebacks later." His tone is fierce, but Karrie looks at him and then down at her nails. "Can't. I'm busy."

"You're busy, huh?" he mocks. "Really? With no phone, no car, no purse, no wallet?" He smiles at her.

"Matthew," Parker whispers. "You didn't."

"He must have lost the handcuffs," Cooper chimes in. "Okay, why don't we go get ready to skate?"

"How about the girls go out for cupcakes and coffee?" I ask them.

"Is Noah coming?" Cooper asks while walking to the rooms in the back.

"I would love to go for coffee," Karrie says. "You guys can be my getaway."

"You can run, but know that I'll always catch your ass and drag you back," Matthew warns with a wink, then turns and jogs into the back.

"That man is a…" Karrie stutters. "He's a…he's a…"

"He's an asshat," Rachel helps her out, smiling at me and then Parker and Karrie, making everyone laugh.

"Okay, babe." Austin kisses my lips. "Come back, and for the love of god, whatever you do, make sure you bring Karrie back with you."

I look at Karrie, who looks like she is about to blow steam out of her ears, just like in the cartoons. Before she can explode, Parker goes up to her seemingly averting that crisis. "Honey, I'm so, so sorry." With that, we all head out to go have chocolate cupcakes and coffee.

chapter twenty-eight

Austin

WE SPEND THREE HOURS DOING DRILLS AND PRACTICING STICK HANDLING. We play a two-on-two game, since Noah never showed up.

Matthew shows Gabe little tricks, and I have to give it to him; he soaks in every word, following up Matthew's instructions to a T and getting into it right away, hungry for more. When we call it a day, he actually groans and moans.

Craig is there when we skate off the ice. "That boy, with a little bit of coaching, could be out of this world. He's a natural." He looks at Gabe. "I got one more left in me." He looks from Gabe to me.

"What does that mean?" Gabe asks, taking off his helmet and spitting out his mouth guard.

"He coached Cooper and me. Now he wants to get his hands on you." I watch his face turn from confusion to awe.

"Can I?" he asks me. "You think you can talk to Mom?"

"I think we could talk to her about it," I say to him while I whip my jersey off, throwing it into the bag that holds all my equipment.

Gabe finishes before us and goes back to help Craig clean the ice on the Zamboni.

"Kid has the itch," Cooper says, unwrapping the tape from his legs. "Where is the father in all this?" Cooper knows all about being a stepfather.

"He's around." I shrug. "He cheated on her with the kid's teacher. Found out she's Camilla the Cunt." I unwrap my legs also.

"Holy shit, no way!" Cooper shouts. "You think you're ready for this?" He knows I don't have any experience with kids.

"I know that with her come them; they're a package deal. The kids are easy. It's the ex I'm not sure I can deal with," I finally voice my fear. "He broke up with Camilla, so now he's free. What's to say he won't try to get her back? They don't just have a past, they have kids. Can I even compete with that?"

Cooper throws his ball of tape in the garbage. "Oh, I know what you mean. When I met Parker, her ex was always away. The minute he spotted us together, all of a sudden he had second thoughts." He looks at Matthew to see if he is listening. Matthew is listening, and he just nods his heads and agrees with him. "But I knew that the minute I found out she had kids, I didn't give a shit. I wanted her, all of her."

"How do you compete, though?"

"You don't, you be you," Matthew adds from his side. "As long as Gabe sees that you treat his mom well, you make her laugh, and she isn't sad anymore, well, that's all you really need to do." He smiles at Cooper.

I nod my head and think about everything while I get undressed and check my phone, seeing Noah texted me.

Sorry I missed today! Two words, my mother and Kaleigh.

Oh Jesus! Is everyone okay?

Let's just say no more naked yoga in the living room.

I don't even know what to say to that.

There's nothing to say.

We get dressed, each of us grabbing our bags to head out. "Okay, buddy, let's go," I tell Gabe as he walks out in front of me.

"Shit," Matthew says. "They took the car."

"It's okay. I have Lauren's, and I can drive you guys back to the hotel." I open the trunk. "It really is a bus." I wink at Gabe, and he just smiles and drinks the chocolate milk he got from Craig.

The minute I turn on the ignition, the sounds of "Let it Go" fill the car, and Cooper and Matthew both groan. "I take it you guys know this song?"

"Why is it playing?" Matthew yells from the back, putting his hands over his ears.

"Because it's jammed inside the player and Mom didn't have it checked out yet," Gabe explains, his head moving to the beat of the music. "Dad used to do all that."

I look at Cooper, who raises his eyebrows at me. My eyes go from him to the road, letting everything sink in.

We drop Matthew and Cooper off at their hotel, and a couple of fans notice them and come up to ask them to take pictures. We say good-bye with promise to see each other soon.

Once I turn onto the street and pull into the driveway, I jump out, grabbing my bag, while Gabe grabs his. I dump my bag into my truck, then inside the house.

Music and the smells of something delicious cooking flow through the house, greeting us as we walk in. Pink's song "So What" is playing, and whatever is cooking smells amazing. I walk into the kitchen and see that Rachel is at the table doing some sort of homework, while Lauren is at the stove cooking.

"Hey," I greet, coming up behind her and wrapping my arms around her waist.

"Hey, there. How was hockey?" She asks, stirring the tomato sauce she is making.

"Good. Great, actually. Craig wants to coach him," I tell her while she tastes it and lowers the temperature to let it simmer.

"Really?" She turns to drape her arms around my neck. "That's exciting," she says as she kisses my chin.

"Mooommm, I need help with math," Rachel groans.

"Coming," she answers. "I have to do homework. Are you going to stay for dinner?" She smiles. I think back to the bag I packed this morning and left on my bed.

"No." I smile. "I'm pretty beat."

Her smile slowly falls, but she replaces it right away with a forced one. "Oh yeah, of course."

She lets go of me and moves to the table, my body missing her touch instantly. I watch her at the table, sitting down, explaining the math to Rachel. I watch her and think to myself, *Can I do this?*

"Okay, I'm going to head out," I say to her. She nods her head, getting up to walk me to the door.

"Are you okay?" I sense that her demeanor has changed.

"Yeah, I'm good. Just busy. It's Sunday, so we have to finish the homework and stuff. Nothing you would know." Her last comment hits me straight in the gut. I lean down, kissing her on the lips, a soft kiss, a fast one. Totally different than I wanted.

"Mom, I got it!" Rachel yells again.

"I have to get back to her." She opens the door, and I walk out. I get in the car and pull out, looking back at the door, hoping to see her there, but instead finding it closed. I don't know why that pisses me off so much.

I take the long way home, trying to clear my mind.

I see that Noah's car isn't there, so I go straight to my door, opening it and letting myself in. There is nothing there to greet me. No noise, no music, nothing but silence.

It was something I used to crave. Now, I don't know what the fuck it is.

I throw my keys on the table by the door, taking off my shoes and walking to the fridge. It's empty. I slam it shut and grab the take-out menus from the drawer. I go through them, wondering what I want to eat. I know what I want to eat. I want to eat pasta at the table with Lauren and her kids.

Throwing the menus back into the drawer, I open the freezer and take out a frozen pizza, throwing it into the oven.

I walk over to the couch, grabbing the remote and turning the television on for some background noise. This is my life, the empty, the quiet. This is what I wanted, right? I never had ties, because I didn't want them. But two days with her and her kids, and it's something I'm rethinking.

The oven beeps, letting me know my pizza is ready. Getting up, I walk into the kitchen, my breathing and the low noise of the television the only sounds in the house. I eat the pizza alone, in the kitchen, leaning against the counter by myself.

I throw half the pizza away, thoughts of Lauren and how her dinner was so totally different than mine crowding my mind.

Turning off all the lights downstairs, I walk upstairs straight for my bedroom, where the unmade bed greets me. The pillow she slept on still has her indent. I throw my shirt in the basket next to the bathroom door and head to the shower.

By the time I've showered and shaved, it's almost eight thirty. Grabbing my phone, I send her a text.

Hey

I sit in bed waiting for her to answer. Laying my head on the pillow next to hers, I hold it close to me. Her smell surrounds me, the memories of last night playing in my head.

After ten minutes of waiting, I text her again.

I miss you!

I'm giving her ten minutes, and then I'm just going to call her. I close my eyes waiting for her, resting my eyes, but I fall asleep. The next thing I know, my alarm is ringing for me to get up.

I look at my phone and see that Lauren texted me back.

Hey, sorry, I was giving Rachel a bath.

I miss you too!

Okay, I guess you fell asleep. I'll call you tomorrow from work. Eek! I'm working with Noah.

I blink my eyes a couple of times and then text her back.

Good morning. Fell asleep waiting for your text. Are you really going to work for Noah?

I toss my phone aside while I go into the bathroom and splash my face with water. Grabbing the phone again, I go downstairs, where I start my morning routine. It's still as silent as it was last night, so I turn on the television. The voices of the CNN anchors fill the silence while the coffee brews.

The phone rings in my hand, and I look down to see Lauren's number.

"Hey," I answer, smiling.

"Hey. I thought it would be faster if I called you," she says, and I hear her moving around in the background.

"Did you sleep well?" I ask her, thinking about how much I would have loved to wake her up with my face between her legs.

"Yeah, I was exhausted." I hear her call out a five-minutes warning to the kids. "Sorry, it's hectic in the morning."

"I can imagine. Are you really going to work with Noah?"

"Um, well, seeing as I'm due there in an hour, the answer to that would be yes." She chuckles.

"You don't need to do this," I tell her while I pour myself a cup of coffee and take a sip. I can hear Gabe in the background asking where his lunch is.

"I'm doing this, so we don't kill each other." She moves the phone from her mouth to tell Gabe she already packed his lunch in his bag. "Sorry. I have to go. Rachel is not dressed yet. The bus is due in seven minutes, and Kaleigh didn't come home again."

I smile thinking of Rachel running around naked, calling me Asshat. "Okay, call me later."

She doesn't say good-bye, I just hear her yelling as the phone disconnects. The rest of the morning routine is uneventful.

Walking into the office, I groan thinking about training a new temp. God, I hope it's not Carmen.

I see a man sitting at Lauren's desk. "Good Morning, Mr. Mackenzie." He gets up to greet me.

His hair is perfect, his suit is perfect, and he follows me into my office with a small pad and pen in hand. "I've taken the liberty of going through all the emails to familiarize myself with the routine you have. I also see you like your meetings alphabetically arranged, which is perfect, since it's also how I like to file things," he continues as I shrug off my jacket and put it on the back of my chair.

"What is your name?" I ask him.

"Bruce." He folds his hands in front of himself. "I can't wait to get started."

"Can you tell Barbara I'm in, and that I would like to see her? Also, if a woman named Lauren calls, she always gets put through right away. No matter when she calls."

"Right away." He heads back to his desk and calls Barbara. She walks into my office five minutes later with a cup of coffee for me.

"Okay, what has your panties in a twist this morning?" She sets my coffee down and takes a seat in front of me.

I glare at her. "Nothing has me in a twist. I'm just wondering how long this has been in the works?"

"Since the second day, maybe, when she knew that you wouldn't cave and she couldn't fight her feelings for you anymore."

I smile thinking over the last month and all the shit we went through. "Is he the best they got?" I motion to Bruce.

"The best they've got is Lauren. He's the second best," she replies, getting up to leave. "Now, I have lots to do. You let me know if you need anything," she says as she walks out.

Looking over my emails and schedule, I get lost in my work. There is a new space I've had my eye on that I'm itching to get into. Denis just sent me the plans. It looks like a lot of work, but it will be amazing if we can get everything done. My phone buzzes on my desk with a text from Noah and a picture.

I swipe across it, opening up his text.

My PA is better than yours! Under the message is a picture of Lauren, with four guys around her desk as she smiles at the screen.

Fuck off! Is my only reply, but I go back and zoom in on the picture. She's wearing a peach-colored sweater today.

Dude, she is the shit, these chumps are eating her up.

I squeeze my cell phone in my hands and call out to Bruce.

"Yes, sir?" He sticks his head in.

"I need you to send two dozen roses to Lauren at Noah's law firm. The address is in my box." I turn down to see another text came in.

All jokes aside, she just cleared my schedule in ten minutes.

I pick up my desk phone, calling Noah's office, knowing she'll answer, and when she does, I smile. "Hey, there, beautiful. How's your day?"

"Hey," I hear her say, hoping she's smiling, too. "It's going well. I haven't had to poison him yet. So, I call that a success." She laughs.

"What time is lunch?" I ask her.

"I have to meet with HR at lunch today and tomorrow."

"Really, what about dinner?"

"It's Monday, which means gymnastics for Rachel and a soccer game for Gabe. Rain check?" she asks. "The kids are with Jake on Wednesday. How about I make dinner, and we can eat in bed?" she whispers, and my cock springs to attention.

"That sounds like a plan. I'll bring dessert."

"Is that what you're calling it now?" She giggles. "Okay, I've got to go. I just got called into the conference room."

"Talk to you later," I say and hang up. Why didn't she ask if I wanted to go with her? For that matter, why didn't I offer to meet her?

The rest of the day flies by, and by the time I finish my meeting with Denis, it's almost six thirty.

There is a text from Lauren and one from Noah.

I read Lauren's first.

Thank you for the flowers, they are beautiful ;) She also sent a picture of her smelling the roses with a sly smile.

I smile at her face, missing her like crazy.

The next is from Noah.

Way to piss on her leg. We get it, she's taken. Thank god you didn't send a barber shop quartet to serenade her.

I laugh at him and answer with the middle finger emoji.

Closing up my computer, I head down to my car, wondering what field they're at and thinking about going to join them.

I call her cell phone, but there is no answer, so I go home, where I grab my stuff and go for a run.

I run for six miles, getting home soaking wet. Looking over at Noah's house, I see the lights are all off, so I go straight home, where I shower.

I pick up my phone and see that Lauren hasn't called me yet, so I call her back.

"Hey," she answers, out of breath, "sorry I missed your call before. We were at the park."

I hear moving around on her end.

"Yeah, I know, I was going to meet you." I slam the door of the fridge that is still fucking empty.

"Oh, really?" She sounds sad. "I didn't know. I forgot about Rachel's play date with Emma. So they met us at the park."

I smile drinking my water. "Hot moms at the park," I kid with her.

"It was actually Emma's dad with us. Mom left them last year," she explains, while I hear things slamming from her end.

"Is this father hot?" I ask, anger shooting out of me.

"Um, I don't really look at him like that." I hear a door close. "Why would you ask that?"

"No reason, just wanted to know who you were spending time with, since it wasn't with me." Holy fuck, am I sulking? Is this me sulking?

"I wasn't with anyone. I was with Rachel, who was playing with a friend. I didn't go there on a date with him. What is this really about?"

"Nothing," I breathe out my frustration. "I just missed you today."

"I missed you, too. A lot," she whispers. "Like to the moon and back." I hear a smile in her voice.

We continue talking till we drift off to sleep. I haven't done this since high school, but smile when she sends me a text before I wake up.

Have a great day! Kisses in special areas!

I laugh to myself while I get ready and start another day that flies by. I won't say that Bruce is better than Lauren, but he is filling her shoes better than anyone else.

I try calling Lauren during the day, but the conversations are all short. Then after she gets home to the kids, it's almost impossible to get through to her.

I sit in my living room that night, holding my phone, wondering what she's doing. Wondering if Rachel brought home more math homework. Wondering if Gabe is thinking hockey or soccer. I even wonder if Kaleigh is driving them crazy with tofu.

By the time she gets back to me, she's yawning and on her way to bed.

I toss and turn all night as sleep evades me. My mind plays through different scenarios in my head. What if I'm not good enough? What if she doesn't want me in her life with her kids? What if I fuck up and we fight about it?

The questions are endless, the answers never coming. I'm about to throw my phone out the window when Noah comes waltzing into my office.

"Hey, there, stranger." He goes to my couch, unbuttoning his jacket and sitting down. I look at him looking at Bruce. "Well, at least you won't try to bang your new PA, right?" He laughs, brushing his hands into his hair. I notice that he has pink nail polish on.

"That really isn't your color." I point to his hand.

"Rachel painted my nails yesterday." He inspects his nails. "You should see what she did to my feet."

I throw my pen down and sit up straighter. "You saw Rachel yesterday?"

"Well, we had to babysit Rachel and Gabe so Lauren could bring her car in to get the radio fixed." He says it as if it's no big deal, and I'm suddenly pissed off.

"What?" I yell.

"A CD of *Frozen* was jammed in her player and was stuck on repeat, so it played it all the time. You know this," he reminds me as if I'm dumb.

"I know what you mean. What I don't understand is why you were babysitting."

"She needed help," he says with a pointed look at me.

"Why didn't she ask me?"

"I don't know, maybe because you hightailed it right out of there the minute family shit started happening on Sunday night?" He stands up.

"Fuck off!" I yell back at him. Bruce sits up in his chair a little straighter. "She was busy, so I left."

He glares at me. "You left or you took off, it's the same thing."

"Is that what she said?" I look at him, waiting for the answers. Did she think I didn't want to be around her kids?

"She didn't say anything. I just found it weird that she would ask us and not you. Kaleigh said to drop it, so I figured you didn't want to."

"I wasn't asked." I hold out my hands to the side. "I didn't even know."

I grab my jacket, ready to run out of the office, when Noah grabs my arm. "Where the fuck do you think you're going?"

"I'm going to tell her that I'm not scared of her kids.".

"Think about what you're doing. You are planning to go barge into her workplace to profess this to her. Dude." He shakes his head. He grabs his phone and dials someone. "Babycakes, are you home?" He smiles and nods his head. "Okay. Austin needs to come over and do something. Can you go to my place? Pack a bag, or better yet, just bring everything with you." He smiles and then hangs up. "Okay, Kaleigh is leaving the door open for you. Go woo your girl."

"Woo?" I ask him.

"A meal, rose petals, champagne, lingerie, vibrators, cuffs. You know, romance."

"This, I can do." I make a list of everything I need to get. "I'm going to woo the fuck out of her."

I rush out of the office, the sound of Noah's laughter trailing behind me as the elevator doors close.

chapter twenty-nine

Lauren

It's been a long two days, made even more hectic because I was on edge. Ever since Austin hightailed it out of my house like his pants were on fire, I've been a mess.

Does he want to be with me? Does he just want a casual relationship, to be me when I don't have the kids? Can I even be in that type of relationship? I'm not sure. I have my kids all the time. To top it all off, I can't seem to get in touch with him about tonight.

I huff out a breath as I get out of my car and walk up to my front door. Opening the door, I'm hit with thick white smoke and the fire alarm going off.

"What the fuck, Kaleigh?" I storm into the kitchen and come to a complete stop.

Austin is in my kitchen, wearing white Calvin Klein boxers and an apron. My mouth waters right away, but then I see the fire coming from the pot on the stove and notice that he is using the sprayer from the sink to douse the flame with water. "What in the world?" I run to the back of the house, opening the door so the smoke will clear out of the kitchen. I grab what I think is a kitchen towel that is sitting on the table. I pick it up and see what is underneath.

I gasp out in shock, because under the cloth is a mini sex store. I'm talking cuffs, a whip, butt plugs, balls, nipple clamps, bullets, cock rings, four different vibrators. He looks over at me. "Oh, that is for dessert."

I run to the smoke detector and start waving the cloth under it, trying to get it to turn off. "What is going on here?" I look at him and ask. "Why are you burning down my house?"

He looks at me, the water spraying across my whole kitchen when he turns around. "I'm trying to woo you." He turns back around and finally puts out the fire. "I'm cooking for you—flambéed steak—but I guess I put too much alcohol in the pan. It pouffed up too fast and got a little bit out of control." He reaches for a small rag to wipe up the water.

The alarm finally stops ringing and I run up the stairs to get towels. Throwing one at him, I put mine on the floor and start to walk on it across the floor in an attempt to soak up the water before throwing another one down.

"You went to work like that?" I look down at my outfit. I'm wearing tailored trousers, a white fitted shirt, and a matching jacket.

"First you try to burn down my house. Now you're insulting my wardrobe!" I throw my hands up.

He drops his towel by his feet and storms over to me. He grabs me by my ass and hoists me up as his mouth crashes down on mine. His tongue slides against mine, and I pull him closer. I've missed him so much. The feel of him, the sound of his voice, even the annoying pen-tapping thing he does on the desk when he's thinking.

I moan into his mouth while the kiss turns frantic, almost desperate. Neither of us interested in stopping, he puts me down on the counter, right in a puddle of water. *Cold* water. "Fuck," I squeak out.

"Oh shit. We should get you out of those pants." He quickly whips off my shoes. "Lift up," he urges, and I try to lift myself up on my hands, but they slip off the counter because of the water. I fall backwards, and Austin face-plants into my stomach.

"Ouch," I whine, while he just laughs against my stomach.

"I'm supposed to be wooing you," he mumbles into my stomach while placing little kisses on it. "Romancing you."

"Ahh, I see. Nothing says romance or wooing quite like anal beads do." I chuckle, running my hand through his hair and looking around at my house. It looks like a bomb went off in here, but looking down at him with his lopsided grin, I can't be upset.

"The anal beads were for after the wooing." He smiles at me. "I missed you." He gets up and pulls me to a sitting position.

He puts my hair behind my ears, cupping my face in his hands. "This was supposed to be romantic." He kisses my lips softly.

"It is." I smile as I stroke my thumb across his cheek. "No one has ever tried to romance me."

"I was a dick," he says, and my eyebrows shoot up in surprise.

"Which time?" I ask him.

"When I left on Sunday." I look down, not ready for him to see how much it bothered me.

"It's okay." I smile up at him after a minute.

"It isn't okay. This is your life, and it's now my life."

I take his hands from my face and push him off me as I jump off the counter. "No." I grab the towels off the floor. "It's not your life. It's mine."

He grabs the towels from my hand, throwing them back down. "I worded it wrong. I want this, Lauren. I want to be there for you. To be the one who helps you. I mean, I'm pretty sure you can run the world from your phone"—he smiles—"but when you have too many balls in the air, I want to be who you call. I want you to know that I'm there for you not because I have to be, but because I want to be." Then his smile disappears as he continues, "And when you need your car serviced, I want it to be me who you call to help you, not Noah, not Kaleigh—but me." He motions to himself with a thumb at his chest.

"Austin," I whisper, "I'm not going to force my kids and my responsibilities on you."

He places his finger on my lips, stopping me from talking. "You aren't forcing anything on me. If anything, I'm forcing myself on you." He takes a breath and continues. "I want to be there with you when you go to soccer games, if I can. I want to be here with you when Rachel is running around naked. I mean, not to see her naked, that's weird, but I want to be here to throw you her clothes." He reaches for me. "And I really want to drive Gabe to hockey; it's our thing." He shrugs and gives me a smile. "I want to cook for you guys." My eyebrows shoot up. "Okay, I want to be here to order out for you guys. Let me be that person for you." His arms wrap around me, bringing me flush against him.

"Austin, what if you resent this whole thing and then feel like you can't leave?" I question him. "What if you have a headache and the kids yelling just makes it worse? I'm okay with this thing between us not having a title."

"I'm not." His voice is firm. "The last two days, I realized that this is where I want to be. In the middle of the chaos. Ask me," he whispers.

"Will you come to Gabe's soccer game tomorrow night?"

"Yes," he answers, smiling. "Now, can we have dessert?"

"What type of dessert were you thinking about?" I look back at the table of titillation and torture.

"I was thinking bullet, anal beads, and whip."

"Really? I was thinking nipple clamps, cuffs, and vibrator," I counter.

"Who wears the cuffs?"

I wiggle my eyebrows at him, while he looks at me with hooded eyes. "Oh, you are definitely wearing the cuffs this time." His evil laugh comes out. "Let's go upstairs. I want you laid out."

He jogs up the stairs after he collects the whip, cuffs, bullet, vibrator, nipple clamps, and anal beads. "Just in case." He winks.

I follow him up, shrugging off my jacket and shirt as I go. "You're lucky your junk didn't burn off in the fire." I enjoy the view of his ass in those white Calvins.

"That would have been a bigger disaster than your house burning down." He throws his toys down on the bed.

I slip my wet pants off, leaving me in my matching white lace bra and panties that are both sexy and delicate.

"Leave those on," he demands, his erection tenting his Calvins as his hand rubs it. The sight makes my knees weak and my pussy wet.

I get on the bed, moving to the middle and crossing my legs. "Okay, what next, sir?" I laugh.

"On your stomach for now," he orders me. "But first," he states as he reaches for the cuffs, then cuffs my wrists together in front of me. "On second thought, on your hands and knees, head to the wall." I get in position, looking over my shoulder to see what he is doing.

He has the whip handle in his hand while he tests it on his other hand. "You trust me?"

"It's kind of difficult to answer now that I have the cuffs on," I tell him, "but I wouldn't have these cuffs on if I didn't."

"Good, now, eyes facing forward," he demands. "Should have got the blindfold, too," he murmurs to himself.

I'm facing the headboard. The anticipation of what's to come has all my senses on high alert. I feel the bed move and then his heat hitting the back of me.

He opens my knees wider with his hands, sliding them softly up my inner thighs ever so slowly until they get to my pussy, where he starts rubbing me through the lace with two fingers. "Wet," he groans, and I hang my head. "I bet we can make this pussy wetter. What do you think?" he challenges me. His fingers are now gone but are quickly replaced with the tip of the whip, the square leather tip grazing me. His hand goes to my ass, which is only partially covered since I'm wearing a thong.

"So soft," he says, caressing it gently. my back arches, making my ass stick out more. Moving from one cheek to the other, he strokes me in a circular pattern. "Creamy white," he breathes. "Let's see how it looks pink." And then his open-palm hand comes down on my ass with a smack. It stings at first, like a pinch, but he soothes the sting with his hand, and the pain dissipates, leaving a warm sensation in its place. I wait for the next smack, but it doesn't come, and my heartbeat picks up the longer I wait.

Instead, he takes the whip and smacks the other cheek, and I moan. It's a different kind of sting than the one from his palm, more isolated, less painful, but it leaves my skin feeling warmer.

The next thing I hear is the buzz of the vibrator as he turns it on. He runs the vibrator along my lower back, the vibrations pulsing through me. He moves to my side, continuing to slide the vibrator against my back. He then moves it to my nipple, which hardens in response as he circles it. He slides the vibrator under the lace of my bra, pressing it down on the hard peak. The sensation shoots straight through me to my belly before it slowly spreads to my core.

"Austin," I moan as my hips buck from side-to-side. I hear him chuckle as he moves back behind me. He reaches between my legs with the vibrator, landing it straight on my throbbing clit. "Please," I beg, for what I'm not even sure.

"Not yet," he says, and I pull at my hands, the need to take care of myself great.

He moves my panties to the side, slipping the vibrator in between my lips and coating it with my wetness. My hips move on their own, and he smacks my ass to make me stop. "Not yet, Lauren." He smoothes his hand over the spot he smacked. "If I stuck my cock into you now, would you be wet for me?"

"Yes," I groan, closing my eyes to focus on the way the vibrator is rubbing up and down through my slit, the tip hitting my clit with each pass.

"What do you want?" he asks me, teasing me further by pushing just the tip inside my waiting cunt.

"To come," I tell him, exhaling slowly. "So much." My arms begin to wobble in their efforts to hold me up. "Please, Austin."

He pushes the vibrator all the way in, filling me up. My ass pushes back against him, the whip coming down on my ass, delivering a sting that runs straight to my clit. He leaves the vibrator all the way inside of me but turns up the speed, and my eyes roll back, my lids fluttering closed.

I feel him moving around my body to position himself in front of my face. With his boxers riding low on his hips, he taps my cheek and says, "Open." I immediately comply and take him inside my mouth, twirling my tongue around his head as the salty taste of his pre-cum floods my tongue. I take his head fully inside and bob my head, taking him deeper each time until the base of his cock is in my mouth and the head hits the back of my throat.

He drops the whip and uses both hands to pinch my nipples hard enough for the pain to turn to pleasure as it shoots right to my clit. He fucks my face while the vibrator buzzes inside me. I rotate my hips to get something moving, but he stops me with a smack to my ass. He moves one hand to hold my head in place by my hair at the back of my head, while the other hand holds the whip he brings down on my ass twice with a smack to each cheek. My hands fight against the cuffs now, the need to come so overwhelming I can barely breathe. I attack his cock with a vengeance, as the need to make him come so he can make me come drives me.

"I could fuck your face all night long," he groans as he brings the whip down on my ass a little harder this time. "Come down your throat," he moans as his hips thrust forward. "Over and over again." The vibrator continues working its magic on me, making me wetter than I've ever been as my juices run down my thighs.

He pulls his cock out of my mouth, and my arms give out as I fall to my elbows, my ass still in the air. He moves behind me, removing the vibrator from my pussy as it clenches to keep it in place.

I hear crinkling coming from behind me right before the wet vibrator moves from my pussy to my clit, where he uses it to apply pressure to my aching clit. My hips jerk in response, and he smacks my ass again.

"Fuck," I whimper into my hands. "Please."

The vibrations stop as he strokes into me in one long, smooth thrust. We both moan loudly as his cock stretches me, my wetness easing the way for him to plant it in me all the way to the root.

"Harder!" I push back against him, and he gives me what I ask for and fucks me harder. The sounds of our skin slapping together echoes throughout the room. My orgasm hovers right there, sparking beneath the surface, on the cusp of breaking free. My hands ball into fists around my sheet as I try not to move forward every time he thrusts himself roughly into me.

"So fucking tight. So fucking wet. So, so fucking hot," he grits out as he pounds into me even harder and faster. Finally—*finally*—as I'm right about to come, he smacks my ass, the sting exploding across my skin as the burn lights me up and I come all over his cock. He pumps into me twice more before he follows me and comes with a roar.

chapter thirty

Austin

Our bodies press together as our chests heave for a minute, while we both try to catch our breath. I lean over and grab the key from the side table to unlock the cuffs.

Once they are unlocked, I see little red marks where she must have pulled the cuffs. I rub the marks with my thumbs, looking up at her. "Fuck, I didn't think this would hurt."

"It didn't." She smiles and closes her eyes. "Relax, Austin, you didn't go all Christian Grey on me. I'm fine." She laughs, while I continue to rub the marks. "Next time, though, it's my turn to torture you. Did you buy a ball gag by any chance?" Her body shakes with her laughter. She turns herself around and lies down in her bed.

I laugh as I get off the bed to go into the bathroom to dispose of the condom. Washing my hands, I return with a warm washcloth. Gently opening her legs, I am about to wipe her when she snatches it from my hand. "What the hell are you doing?"

"I was going to clean you up." I look at her in confusion. "What's the big deal?"

"I just…" She starts and then stops. "It's weird." She stutters, and I snatch the washcloth back from her and open her legs again.

"You know, I've already been intimately acquainted with it. My fingers have felt it, my mouth has tasted it, and my cock has fucked it," I say as I gently clean her.

"Ok then, when you put it that way, please proceed," she gives in a little shyly. "Um, is this going to be an everyday thing?" She points between me and her as her voice softens with her question.

"You mean us having hot sex? That would be a yes. I would do that daily." I throw myself down on the bed next to her.

"And, um, we won't be doing this with, um, anyone else?" she asks a little nervously.

"Fuck no. I don't plan on fucking anyone else, and I sure as hell hope you don't plan on it, either," I answer firmly.

"Ok, then. Well, I'm on the shot," she informs me. "And I haven't been with anyone since Jake left. I'm clean. I don't know the protocol on this whole sex-without-a-condom thing or how it works." She tries to sound casual, but the slight tremor in her voice betrays her nerves. That, and she closes her eyes to avoid my stare.

"I've never gone without one," I say honestly. I'm never with anyone long enough for it to get that serious. "I'm clean, but I got tested recently. You remember, it was during that time you made my balls swell up to the size of an elephant's." I try to alleviate her nerves by lightening up the moment with a reminder of our not-so-distant past shenanigans. It works and she snorts at the memory.

"So maybe"—she gets closer to me and throws her leg over my hip—"we should try it without one to see if it works?"

"If what works? My cock?" I grip her hip with my hand before I slide it up her back to find the hooks to her bra.

"It's in the front." She unclips the bra so her tits spring free. Her pink pebbled nipples are begging to be sucked, so I do just that and take one into my mouth.

Her head pushes back further into the pillow as her neck arches. My cock is hard and ready for round two. She lifts her hips, pushing me to my back with her thigh as she follows me over and climbs on top of me. On her knees, bent over my torso, hands planted in the bed at either side of my head, she positions herself on top of my cock, and slowly, so fucking slowly, she lowers herself onto me. I know in that moment that this woman was made for me.

Holy fuck, the way her pussy grips me, I feel everything so much more intensely being in her bare. She's hotter, wetter, tighter than ever, and so much softer than I imagined. I moan at how good it feels.

"We are doing this again. At least twice more before tomorrow." I thrust up hard as she meets me with a downward thrust of her own.

And that is exactly what we do. After we clean the mess in the kitchen, that is, and I put away all the toys I bought. They're now in a box in her linen closet, up high under a pile of sheets.

The next day, I walk into work with a lighter step. I woke up with her in my arms. I had her this morning when we woke up and then again in the shower. It's going to be a good day.

Bruce is there with my messages as soon as I walk in, and I greet him with a smile. I don't say much more to him.

I get a text from Noah.

So, how did the wooing go? Did she set your balls on fire?

I laugh, thinking of the fire I started cooking.

The wooing was fine, minus me setting fire to dinner. My balls were not involved. Next time, it's pizza.

I don't know what you did, but she is in a fine mood, she even brought me coffee. I won't drink it. Because there is the chance that she may have poisoned it after I told her she had that just-freshly-fucked face.

How have you not been sued for sexual harassment yet?

Your guess is as good as mine.

I laugh at that last text and by the time I look up again, it's almost six thirty. I stand up and stretch as my phone rings and I see that it's Noah.

"What is it?" I say in place of a greeting.

"I'm not making this phone call right now," he whispers into the phone. "But I thought you should know that Jake the Snake has showed up to talk to Lauren, and she asked Kaleigh and me to take the kids to the park."

"What park?" I ask, grabbing my jacket and keys, rushing out.

"The park at the corner by her house."

"Why are you whispering?"

"I'm playing hide and seek. Fucking hurry." He disconnects the phone call.

I run out to my car not knowing whether I should head straight to Lauren's or go to the park. My mind says go to the park, so that is where I head first.

I see Rachel running around with Noah chasing after her like a monkey. Parking the car, I head over toward them. Gabe sees me and starts running to me. "Austin, my mom says I can play hockey!" He holds his hand up for a high five. I high five him, then pull him in to hug him, happy that I was able to make this happen for him.

"Asstin, you came to play?" Rachel asks as she runs to me with Noah and Kaleigh following behind her, holding hands and looking at each other.

"I came to see if you guys wanted to go out for ice cream?" I suggest the first thing that comes to mind. "How about we go see if Mom wants to come with us?"

"Ice cream!" Rachel jumps into my arms and surprises me so much I almost drop her.

"Let's go get Mom." I walk to my truck, an upgrade from the Porsche I made last week.

I pull into her driveway and see that Jake the Snake's car is still there.

So, I make the kids walk in first and then follow them in. "Mommy, Asstin came to have ice cream!" Rachel shouts as soon as she gets into the house.

We find them in the kitchen sitting at the table. Lauren sees me, and her eyes light up with a smile to match. "Hey, you," she says as I walk to her and lean down to kiss her softly.

"Hey. I thought I would surprise you and the kids." I look at Jake and nod. "But if you're busy—" I stop talking, because she holds up her hands.

"No, that sounds like a great idea. Jake was just leaving anyway." She looks at him, giving him a smile that he has to recognize is fake.

Jake slaps the table and gets up. "Yeah, I was just leaving. Gabe, Rachel, come give Dad a hug and kiss!" he calls for them.

They come back into the room and give him hugs and kisses, and he asks if they want to come over that weekend. "I know it's not my weekend, but I can take them if you guys have plans," he addresses us both. Lauren has now stood up and is standing next to me, and I've got my arm around her shoulder.

"Gabe has hockey on Saturday afternoon," Lauren says to him, "so maybe after that."

"I have hockey!" Gabe shouts with glee.

"That's right, dude. I didn't get a chance to tell you, but I spoke with Craig and he can start you on Saturday."

"Yes!" he cheers. "Mom, I'm going to go and tell Jesse." He runs out of the house.

"Well," Jake says, "I guess I'll just be going."

Rachel runs over and jumps into his arms and kisses his cheek. "Bye, Daddy."

He says a quick good-bye to both of us and walks out the front door.

Rachel looks at Lauren. "Are we still going for ice cream?"

"Sure, go grab a sweater." She doesn't have to ask her twice. Rachel rushes out of the room looking for her sweater.

"Are we going to discuss what happened here?" I look at her, asking about the elephant in the room.

"There really is nothing to discuss. He came crawling back. Telling me how him leaving was a mistake." She shrugs her shoulders, while my heart stops, my stomach drops.

"What does that mean?" I try not to freak out.

"It means exactly what you think it means. He fucked up. I mean, did it hurt me? Yes. Did I want to go all Beyonce on his ass? Fuck yeah. But it's over. I've moved on." She comes over to me. "I'm hoping that you are on the same page as me?" She kisses me on my neck.

"We are exactly on the same page. I will say," I tell her while I look down on her, "he gets a pass for today, because he got fucked over. But"—I push her hair behind her ears—"this is the last pass he gets. Next time, I'm going to tell him exactly where to go fly his kite." I smile at her. "If you know what I mean." I kiss her nose watching her smile.

"I know what you mean. Now, can I have some ice cream?" She puts her hands on her hips. "It's Thursday, it's spin class day."

"Really?" I'm surprised I didn't know this.

"Really. I take spin classes on Mondays, Tuesdays, Thursdays, and sometimes on Saturdays. Usually, I drop Gabe off at soccer practice and then hit up the gym where Rachel goes to the play area."

"Baby, if you want to work out, all you have to do is tell me. You can ride me all night long," I whisper to her while taking her in my arms.

Her hands curl around my arm while she picks off invisible lint. "Oh, I'm going to ride you all night long"—she moves her hands around my neck, pulling my ear to her lips—"as soon as you buy that ball gag." I feel the huff of her laughter across my cheek as I turn my face to kiss her lips.

"I found my sweater!" Rachel yells from somewhere in the house, her footsteps coming closer. I wait to see if Lauren will drop her hands, but she doesn't, so I bask in this second victory tonight. The first being her obviously negative reaction to Jake's presence there and whatever it was he wanted to talk to her about. "Asstin, can you carry me on your shoulders?" She comes into the kitchen as she tries to pull on her sweater. "Are you strong like Noah?" She pets her sweater.

Lauren puts her hand in front of her mouth to stop the laugh from escaping, while I glare at her. "I'm a thousand times stronger than Noah." I grab her and toss her in the air and then catch her and flip her upside down while she giggles.

I finally put her on my shoulders, and we start walking toward the ice cream parlor. Gabe sees us walking down the street and runs to catch up to us after saying good-bye to his friend Jesse.

The four of us walk down the street, me holding Lauren's hand, while Rachel sits on my shoulders, her feet tucked under my arms, and Gabe holds Lauren's other hand as he talks non-stop about hockey.

We eat the ice cream and then make our way back home, almost the same way we came, except now Rachel is telling us all about how she needs a cat, because everyone has a cat, *everyone*.

When we walk back into the house, Lauren starts issuing orders for bath and homework. They both go to their respective rooms, while Lauren looks over at me and says, "I have to do the dishes. Come sit and talk to me." She walks to the kitchen, rolling up her sleeves as she starts cleaning the dinner dishes and putting them in the dishwasher. I don't sit on that stool; instead, I get up and move to stand next to her. When I lean my hip against the counter, we start talking about our days. I undo the top button on my dress shirt. "I need to bring over clothes for when I come here after work."

Her hands stop moving in the water. "Um, is that what you want?" Her eyes avoid me, and I grab her chin with my fingers to bring them to mine.

"I want that very much," I tell her honestly before I lean forward, kissing her lips. I lick across her bottom lip, and she opens for me to slide my tongue in. I grab her waist to bring her closer to me while my tongue plays with hers. My hands roam to her ass, cupping her to bring her even closer. I almost forget where we are, until I hear Rachel's voice calling from upstairs. "Mom, the bubbles are finished." We both groan as our lips separate.

"Coming!" Lauren yells. "Why don't you sit on the couch and watch television?" She suggests before she walks upstairs. I'm about to go sit down when Gabe comes downstairs with his notebook.

"Austin, can you help me study for my spelling test?"

I toss the remote on the table. "Sure," I'm surprised at how excited I am that he asked me. "Where do you want to do this?" I look around.

"I'll just sit on the floor, and you can tell me the words." He lies down on his stomach, a piece of paper and a pencil in front of him.

I go through the list of words, while he gets all but two of them right. "You know what I used to do when I got my words wrong? I'd write it out ten times," I tell him, and he inwardly groans. "I know it sucks, trust me, but it worked. And you know what else? That's going to be something you'll be doing in hockey. Well, not the writing, but the repeating stuff over and over. It's how you'll train your muscles to memorize the movements of your plays. It's the same idea with your spelling words, except instead of training your muscles, you're helping your brain memorize the words through the repetition of writing them over and over."

The comparison to hockey does the trick, and he nods his head as he starts writing the words. When he finishes, he says, "Okay, let's try it again." He grabs another piece of paper, and by the time we're done, he has all the words memorized. He is so happy, he gives me a high five before running upstairs to tell his mom. Truth be told, I'm happy, too. It felt good that he asked for my help, and it felt even better when I saw how my efforts actually did help him.

I finally turn the television on and see that it's almost nine p.m. I stretch out on the couch, waiting for Lauren to come down. When I hear her footsteps, I look up and what I see has me sitting straight up.

She is walking to me wearing a short, pink satin robe, which falls to just over her ass. Tied loosely at the waist, the middle gapes open, showing me that she isn't wearing anything under it. She doesn't say a word, just comes right to me, pushes me back against the couch cushions, and straddles me before she crushes her lips on mine. She slides her tongue into my mouth, her taste filling it.

She slowly starts to rock herself on me. My cock sprung to attention the minute she sat down and is now starting to throb. She finally peels her lips from mine. "You know what really turns me on?" She starts to unbutton my shirt. I'm looking inside her robe, which has fallen open further, showing me her bare breasts. My hand reaches in to cup one of her plump breasts as my thumb grazes over the peaked nipple.

"No fucking clue, but whatever I did, I'm going to do it again," I say, leaning down, taking her other nipple in my mouth as she grinds down hard on my cock.

"You. Doing homework with Gabe, carrying Rachel on your shoulders. It was so hot, my pussy got wet just watching you." She leans down to bite my nipple as a hiss comes out of my mouth.

I don't have a chance to do anything else before she is off me, grabbing my hand and leading me upstairs to her room. I'm barely through the door when she closes and then locks it. She brings me to the bed, positioning me in front of it. Kneeling in front of me, she quickly undoes my belt and works my pants and boxers down as my rock-hard cock slaps up against my belly. She gives my hips a little push so that I sit down and spread my legs as she moves in between them. "The whole time, all I could think about was your cock in my mouth and taking it to the back of my throat. I'm not sure you know this about me, Austin, but I love giving head." I'm panting as her hand wraps around my cock, giving it a few quick strokes. Pre-cum pools in the slit, and she licks her lips. "Mmmm," she hums right before she moves her mouth over me and swallows me down.

My head falls forward as I release a groaning breath and my hands find their way into her hair. She moves her mouth up and down my cock, her tongue twirling around the head with each pass. "That's so fucking good, baby," I moan as she takes me deeper each time.

Her mouth releases me and is replaced by her hand, gripping me firmly and twisting as she strokes me up and down. "I love your cock, babe," she breathes as her mouth moves back to it again. She flattens her tongue against the base of my shaft, running it all the way up the underside of it to the head, where she looks up at me through hooded eyes as she curls her tongue around me. It's a good fucking look. "I want you to come in my mouth," she says, taking me in again, hollowing her cheeks to suck hard, while she bobs her head. Overwhelmed by how incredibly good this feels, I can't help the moans that escape me. Hell, I'm surprised I'm not whimpering.

Her hand reaches to cup my balls, where she rolls and squeezes them as her mouth continues to work my cock. I look down and see a woman who is really into what she's doing, so much so, that my eyes follow the curve of her other arm when I realize that hand isn't on me. I look closer and see that her hand has snaked in to the opening of her robe and is stroking her pussy. "Fuck," I grit out through clenched teeth as my hips surge up into her mouth when it comes down on me. The heat of her mouth and the feel of her throat surrounding me almost take me over the edge. As tempting as it is to shoot off in her mouth, I've missed her and I need more.

I grab her under her arms, picking her up and dragging her onto me as I lie back, and she whines in protest. "In your pussy," I pant, "I need to be in your pussy." I untie the sash of her robe and move my hands to her hips to rock her wet pussy over my cock.

She rises up on her knees, positioning my cock at her entrance, and then slowly slides herself down on me. The movement makes us both moan loudly. I grab her hair with my hand and pull her to me. Our mouths collide, which helps to keep the moaning down. She rides me hard and fast, gliding all the way up until just the tip is inside before she slams back down on me with a grind and twist of her hips.

My hands leave her hair to grip her hips, my fingertips digging into her flesh, our tongues still tangled with one another's.

I feel her hand moving between us, and I let go of her mouth to look at her. Her hair is sticking up all over the place from my rough hold on it, and her tits bounce each time she moves. Her eyes are half closed in bliss, but what makes my cock pulse inside of her is the sight of her hand between her legs.

She has one hand planted in the bed next to me while she strokes her clit with the other. "Fuck me," I groan right as I feel her pussy tighten around my cock.

"I'm coming," she whispers with a sexy little hitch in her voice as her eyes slide all the way closed and her hand continues to rub her clit furiously from side to side, never slowing her ride on my cock. When her orgasm winds down, she starts to slow her thrusts, but I don't let her. Instead, I tighten my grip on her hips and use them to move her up and down on my cock. Her clit and my dick glisten with her wetness, and my balls pull up tight at the sight.

"Give me one more, Lauren, and then I'm going to come." I continue to pound her down onto me by her hips.

"I can't," she says breathlessly, now moving with me to grind down against my pubic bone.

"You can and you will. I can feel your pussy getting tighter, wetter, hotter." I keep slamming into her. My balls are so tight with the need to come, it's almost painful. "Fingers to your clit. Now, Lauren," I command as I lean forward and bite her nipple. "Come on my cock like a good girl, and I'll come in your pussy." It seems that my woman likes a bossy, dirty mouth, because she whimpers at my words and her pussy clamps down even tighter on my cock.

I thrust up a few more times until she comes again. This time biting her lips to keep from screaming. It's the last straw for me. I pull her all the way down onto me and explode inside her. I see stars, hell, I may even black out a little as I come harder than I ever have in my life.

chapter thirty-one

Lauren

The alarm starts to buzz, waking me up. I go to stretch, but I'm wrapped up tight in Austin's arms. Every morning, we set the alarm for five a.m., so he can leave before the kids get up.

It's been over two weeks since he made his declaration. In those two weeks, he's been here every single time I went to spin class to watch the kids. Proving how much he meant what he said, he sticks to our routine, following it to a T. It's crazy how well he just fits in. It's like he was always meant to be here.

We end every night by starting out on the couch before slowly making our way upstairs. Every single night, I fall asleep with a smile on my face, and every single morning, I wake up feeling happy. I'm happy.

He's about to get up and out of bed when Rachel comes running into the room and jumps onto the bed. "Momma, there's a monster under the bed," she whispers as she crawls in between Austin and me. My eyes are wide open as I take them in, trying to gauge both of their reactions to this surprise development. I know the kids are used to having Austin around now; it's just that we haven't done the whole sleepover thing yet. "Asstin, you the man, go kill it." Rachel gets under the covers with us. Thank god, we got dressed last night after we finished. When Austin doesn't move, Rachel looks back at him. "Are you scared, too? Momma, call Noah," she whispers, and it's then that Austin snaps.

"I'm going to go get that monster and kick him out." He walks out of the room, his basketball shorts hanging on his hips. Just one look at him, and my mouth waters. Another thing that has changed is that he has changes of clothes here. When he comes in after work, he changes into something more comfortable and always leaves those clothes here.

I hear some banging coming from Rachel's room and then a swoosh of something. Rachel curls up tightly into me, and I pull her into my arms to hold her. "Honey, there is nothing to be scared of."

"All gone." Austin comes back into the room scratching his side.

Rachel pulls the cover from her face watching Austin. "Are you sure?" she asks, while he nods yes.

She gets up and stars jumping on the bed till she jumps into his arms. "You killed the monster? For me?"

"Anything for you, princess," he replies with a kiss to her head.

"I love you, Asstin," she says, and my mouth just opens and closes as I stumble to formulate a response. But Austin doesn't skip a beat.

"Well, that's good, because I love you, too." He climbs back into bed with her held close to his chest.

"Are you going to do sleepovers like Ms. Camilla does with Dad?"

Austin looks over at me as if to ask for the right words to say. When I just shrug my shoulders, he once again proves his words from two weeks ago when he does his own thing and tells her, "I would like that a lot, and maybe sometime we could have a sleepover at my house. Would you like that?"

"Are there monsters at your house?" She asks him with all the seriousness of a scared six-year-old little girl.

"Nope, none. I think Noah has some at his house, though." He smiles over her head at me.

"We are never sleeping at Noah's house, Mommy." She turns to me. "But maybe we could try sleeping at Asstin's?"

"Yes, baby." I kiss her head. "Maybe we can." I return his smile over her head.

"Do you love my mommy, Asstin?" Her question has my breath stopping in my chest. My heart is beating so fast and loud in my ears, I'm pretty sure that people on the moon can hear it, so obviously the two other people in this bed with me surely can, too.

"Rachel, honey, how about we make some pancakes?" I try to get out of bed in an attempt to forget the question, trying to bail Austin out from having been put on the spot. As I whip the covers off me and Rachel to get us out of bed, Austin's arm reaches out and latches around mine to halt my movements. I look at his hand on my arm, but I'm too afraid to look up at him.

I don't know if I want to know the answer. I mean, I do want to know, but I don't know if this is the way I want to learn it. What if he is feeling forced into telling me? What if he just doesn't want to say it?

"I love your mom more than you know," he answers her, and me as well. His words bring tears to my eyes. There's a softness, almost a reverence to his voice as if he's talking to me, only me, as if we were alone. "I've never loved anyone the way I love your mom." One tear slips out, landing on my arm and rolling onto his hand that grips me. "To the moon and back," he says, quoting one of the books he's read to Rachel when he was putting her to bed while I was out one night last week.

"That's a lot." Rachel stretches out her arms as wide as she can. "It's big, really big, like this, right?"

He squeezes my arm again. "Bigger."

"Do you want pancakes?" Rachel asks Austin, then whispers to him, "If you want, you can ask for chocolate and bananas. Those are the bestest ones that Mommy makes," she informs him as she climbs over him to get up. "Mommy puts chocolate spread on them and then she cuts bananas in a smile." She nods her head to convince him as if it is something unbelievable. "Ask her."

"Will you make me pancakes, Lauren?" He's almost whispering.

I nod my head, the lump in my throat threatening to dislodge and let loose the sob it's holding back. "I need the washroom," I say, rushing into the bathroom and locking the door behind me. I slide down the door, listening to Austin tell Rachel that she could go downstairs and start taking out the bowls. Once I hear her running out of the room and then downstairs, I listen for Austin's steps.

I don't hear anything until I there's a soft knock at the door. "Baby, open the door," he urges softly.

"Um, I'll meet you downstairs," I say, trying to get my voice to come out without cracking.

"Baby, open the door, please," he whispers into the crack of the door.

I get up and slowly unlock the door, opening it slightly. "I'm okay."

"I didn't want to tell you like that." He pushes the door open and grabs me around the waist to carry me over to the vanity, where he sets me down. He pushes the hair from around my face, tucking it behind my ears. "I wanted to tell you in some romantic way." He opens my legs, stepping in between them, while I put my hands on his waist. "But this is our normal now." He smirks at me. "And I wouldn't have it any other way. I love you. I love how much you love your children. I love how much you put up with from your sister, who is crazy, by the way." I smile at that comment, thinking of last week when she made tofu burgers and didn't tell him, and they were half raw inside. "I love how selfless you are, always putting everyone before yourself." He kisses my lips softly, his lips lingering on mine.

"I love you," I whisper. "I love how much you love my kids. I love how you took us all on. I love that you don't actually kill Kaleigh every day, even though I'm sure you want to." I smile. "But most of all, I love how you love me. I love how safe you make me feel. How you make me feel so sexy and, most of all, so loved that it's overwhelming." I give him a smile that I'm sure lights my eyes, because my heart is soaring and I feel like the happiest person in the world.

"Now, wasn't that romantic?" he whispers to me, and I can feel him smiling while he kisses my lips.

"Very. Much better than when you tried to woo me." I nip his lip.

"None of that now. We have Rachel searching for bowls." His hands cup my face. "Now, let's go make pancakes."

"You are totally getting the best blowjob of the year as soon as the kids go to school and I call in sick."

"Oh, and we're totally playing hooky today and having sex all day long," he informs me.

"That we are, Mr. Mackenzie, that we are," I agree as I get down from the vanity and walk out of the bathroom to head downstairs. Once there, I see that Rachel has started by getting the mixing bowl out as well as the box of pancake mix, which must have fallen on the floor, because there is power all over the place with little footprints in it.

"I'm ready!" she shouts excitedly, standing on a chair that she pushed to the counter.

"What is all the noise for?" Gabe says, dragging his feet as he comes downstairs, rubbing the sleep from his eyes that are squinting as they adjust to the light.

"We are making pancakes with chocolate and bananas!" Rachel yells at him, far too loudly for this hour of the morning.

"Hey, Austin." He looks right at him. "You didn't leave yet?"

"Leave?" Austin questions him right back.

He smirks at him. "I know you sleep here and sneak out." He smiles at both of us. I'm too busy with my mouth hanging open to answer. "I got up early last week, and you guys were sleeping, but then he was gone in the morning."

"Um… ahh… well, um…" Austin stutters, not sure what to say.

"It's cool," Gabe says. "If Ms. Camilla can sleep over naked at Dad's, it's ok that you sleep here." He shrugs before going over to the refrigerator and grabbing the orange juice.

"Yeah, she's naked a lot," Rachel agrees from her chair at the counter.

"Rach," Gabe says to her in warning.

"And she says 'oh God' a lot, too," Rachel continues. "I don't want to pray like that at night, Mommy. Once is good."

I look at Austin, who is trying to hide his smile, then I look at Gabe, who is pretending he doesn't hear anything.

"Let's make pancakes. How many do you want, Gabe?"

I mix the pancake batter while we change the subject and chat about what we should make for supper. By the time the kids leave for school, the conversations of the morning are long behind us.

I finally close the door and lock it. I look at Austin in the kitchen, putting the dishes in the dishwasher. "That is almost like watching porn," I tell him. "You doing stuff like washing dishes, vacuuming, homework with Gabe. It's mom porn."

His eyebrows shoot up. "Are you checking me out?" he questions with a smile.

"I'm doing more than checking you out. I'm undressing you in my mind," I tease him as I lean against the counter.

He shakes the water from his hands. "Really? Well, in that case, where the fuck is the vacuum?"

"How about we do that after. I believe I owe you a world-class blowjob." I turn around and head out of the kitchen. I turn my head to look at him over my shoulder. "You coming?"

I don't have to ask him twice. He storms over to me and lifts me up and over his shoulder with a slap to my ass. "Your mouth on my dick, and there's no doubt about it, I'll be coming, alright. Maybe all over you," he states as he walks us up the stairs and throws me onto the bed. "How long are they in school?" he asks, stripping his pants off.

"They get home at three." I watch him strip down and his cock spring free.

"Good. We have all day." He fists his cock, giving it a few rough jerks.

"How will we fill the time?" I ask him, taking off my shirt now.

"Oh, we'll think of something." He meets me on the bed.

And do we ever. We find ways to fill the time in the bed, on the kitchen counter, on the kitchen table, and finally, in the shower.

The rest of the week goes off without a hitch. Austin runs home and brings back some suits, since he doesn't have to leave at five a.m. anymore.

Now, here we are on Sunday morning, getting ready for my parents to come over for brunch, when Kaleigh and Noah walk in.

Another thing that has changed is that she is never home anymore. She comes to get the kids off the bus in the afternoons, but when it's time for dinner, she leaves. I've never seen her looking happier. Except this morning, she looks a little pale, with circles under her eyes.

"Are you okay?" I ask her while readying the roast for the oven. I set the alarm to make sure we put it in on time.

"I just feel tired, and I think I caught a bug." She sits on the stool at the counter.

She is beautiful, her hair curled at the ends, in tight blue jeans and a pink long-sleeved sweater that's tight at the top and flares out at the bottom.

"She was up all night barfing. You know it's love when you get someone water while they are yacking," Noah says, grabbing a coffee cup and filling it up.

"That is really nice of you, pal," Austin comments from his side of the counter while he looks at them. Both Austin and Noah are dressed down in jeans and button-down shirts.

"I can do a lot of things. I just can't do the whole vomit thing. But I was proud of myself." He reaches over and rubs Kaleigh's head.

We don't have a chance to say anything before we hear my mother. "Knock, knock, knock!" she calls out before walking into the house.

"Mom, it defeats the purpose if you just walk in," Kaleigh says. "What if we were all naked?"

My mother gasps. "It's noon, why would you be naked at noon?"

"Oh, dear God," I say under my breath. The kids come barreling downstairs, yelling for grandma and grandpa.

"Hey, Austin," my father greets him, hitting him on the back. "How are you, son? Should we be expecting any penises today?" He laughs as he goes to Kaleigh to give her a side hug.

"Kaleigh, you look like death," my mother remarks while she comes to hug her and then me. "Austin, it's good to see you, without, you know." She motions her hands into the shape of a penis in the air.

"That was a fun time," Noah says into his cup, smiling, while Austin and I just glare at him.

"I don't feel good." Kaleigh gets up to go to the bathroom.

"What can I do to help?" My mother comes into the kitchen and opens the oven to check out the roast. "That looks delish."

"I made it," Noah pops up, winking at my mom while she blushes.

"Yeah, right," Austin says. "Come on and help me set the table." He orders Noah as he grabs the tablecloth and shows him where the plates are.

When they are out of the room, my mother and father both look at me, but it's my mother who speaks first. "He really knows his way around the house."

"Um, yeah, he usually stays for dinner." I don't make eye contact while I move around the kitchen, looking for nothing in particular.

"Does he do this every night?" My father asks, sitting down.

"Most nights, yes." I put the cloth that I have in my hands down. "I like him. A lot."

He nods his head, while my mother clasps her hands together. "You love him?"

"Um, yes. Yes, I do," I finally admit. "I'm happy. Like really happy. So, please, let's just drop the third degree."

"My lips are sealed." She pretends to zip her lips shut. "Is he good in bed?"

"Mom!" I exclaim at the same time my dad warns, "Dede."

She looks at both of us. "Oh, please, she is in the peak of her life. She should be having sex daily." She shrugs. "I read it in Cosmo."

"Oh, dear God," I say again just louder.

"There is a quiz you can take to show you what kind of lover Austin will be."

"What?" I ask the same time Austin and Noah come back into the kitchen.

"It asks you questions." She looks at Austin. "Are you a selfish lover?"

Noah snickers behind Austin, while Austin's face turns from white to red. "Um…"

"Don't answer that," I tell him.

"Do you wait for her to go first, or do you just think of yourself?" My mother continues, actually trying to recall the questions in the survey.

Austin just stands there like a deer caught in headlights. "Um…"

"Well, that isn't good if you have to think about it. I'll send you the quiz, too. You can both take it and see."

"Can you send it to me, too?" Noah asks, grabbing a grape from the fruit bowl. "Frank, did you take this quiz?" he turns to my father.

"Don't need to. I'm a bull in the sack," My father deadpans, fist pumping in the air.

"Gross, I think I'm going to be sick." I put my hand on my stomach.

"Maybe you caught Kaleigh's bug." My mother is not catching on.

"I think lunch is ready." Austin heads to the stove at the same time Kaleigh comes back into the room. "Kaleigh, we made you some tofu stuff that Lauren found in the freezer. I made sure to put it in another pan."

"Awww, so you forgive me for tricking you into drinking breast milk?" she asks him with a smile.

I grab the side dishes that have been warming in the oven with the roast, while Austin grabs the roast. My father grabs drinks from the fridge, and my mother calls the kids. Noah walks over to the wine fridge, grabbing two bottles.

We make our way to the dining room. Gabe runs in, while Austin puts the roast down. Rachel comes into the room banging two white things together. "Tap, tap, tap!" she shouts. "Click, click, click."

"What is that?" I look at the white sticks in her hand.

"They're drum sticks. I found them in the bathroom." She is still tapping them together. "Like a wand. Bippity boppity bo."

"Oh my God," I hear Kaleigh whisper as my mother grabs one of the sticks from Rachel's hand.

"Oh my god." She looks at me. "You're pregnant!" She sits down at the table.

My head snaps back and I grab the other stick from Rachel. Sure enough, it's another positive pregnancy test.

I look at Austin, who has gone paler than a ghost. "Lauren?" he questions, holding the table with one hand, while he looks like he is going to fall over.

"You have to marry her," my mother announces with tears in her eyes. "A child out of wedlock is a no-no." She shakes her head no over and over again

"Lauren," I hear Austin again, this time his voice quivering.

I look around the faces at the table. My heart beating fast in my ears, my throat going dry, my palms getting sweaty.

"It's mine," I hear from Kaleigh, who then looks at Noah. "I'm pregnant."

Noah places the bottles of wine on the table. "What do you mean?"

"I mean, I'm pregnant," Kaleigh repeats, throwing her hands in the air.

"But... but... but," Noah stutters.

"This is worse than Lauren being pregnant," My mother groans with tears running down her face.

"Mom," I snap at her, walking over to Kaleigh and hugging her. "It's going to be okay," I whisper in her ear.

"Holy shit," Austin breathes, finally sitting down.

Noah walks over to us, grabbing Kaleigh's face in both his hands. "I love you. So, so much. More than I love me." He smiles at her and rubs away the tears that are rolling down her cheeks. "Marry me? Be my wife?"

"Are you sure?" Kaleigh asks him while she puts her hands on his.

"More sure than anything I've ever done in my whole life." He pulls her close to him.

"Yes," she agrees right before her hands leave his and she throws them around his neck, kissing him.

"This is wonderful," my mother squeals. "Frank, we are planning a wedding."

"Great!" My father looks at Austin. "Open that wine."

"I'm getting married!" Kaleigh shouts.

"Um," Noah murmurs as we all turn to look at him. "I just need to get divorced first."

epilogue

My heels click on the cement pavement as I walk down the street. I'm going to meet Austin at his 'new adventure,' as he calls it. Kaleigh was supposed to come with me, but the baby is throwing up, so she opted out of it.

It's been over a year since he smashed into my car. One year of pure happiness, really; well, minus that week I kicked him out after he bought both kids a drum set. That they played together. We also made the decision that we should keep it at his house, for when we go there.

The cream peep-toe slingback shoes I'm wearing are starting to pinch my feet, but they were the only shoes I had that go with this outfit. I'm wearing a baby pink high-waisted pencil skirt that stops at the knee and a long-sleeved, lace turtleneck crop top to match. My hair is pinned up in a bun at the base of my neck. To show off the lace back, a gold zipper is holding it together.

I make my way up the stairs to the address he gave me. I check my phone and make sure I'm in the right place. Once I confirm that I am, I pull open the huge mahogany door.

Opening the door, I step inside and stop. The whole room is filled with white candles, accentuating the dark mahogany color of the interior. The thick bar sits in the middle of the room, open on both sides. Bouquets of white roses fill all four corners of it. Three crystal chandeliers hang above the bar. Shimmering pieces of crystal drip down from it, looking like diamonds falling.

The whole place has low tables, all with white roses in the center and candles around them. The flickering candlelight throughout the bar casts a dim yellow glow through the space. There, standing in the middle of the room, leaning against the bar, is my man. Dressed in one of his black suits, this one with a slight sheen to it. One arm cocked on the bar, with his feet crossed in front of him. "Hey, there, beautiful," he says, coming to meet me.

"What is this?" I look around, noticing that no one else is here.

"You look fantastic." He moves down to kiss my neck.

"You look pretty fantastic yourself." I hold on to his jacket lapels. "What is this?"

"This," he tells me, "is my new adventure called Crazy Days. It's mine and John's and Noah's. God forbid, we leave him out."

"So, this is all yours?" I look around to see that it is very him. Dark mahogany everywhere, low tables, elegant.

"It's ours," he says as I see his hands fidget at his side. "I sold my house."

He rubs them together. "I'm never there. It was silly to keep it. But…" His voice trails off.

"But?" I walk to him and take his hand, which is cold in mine. "What is going on?" I kiss his hand to try and make him feel better.

"I want us to buy a house together. I want us to have something together that is just ours," he whispers and then lifts our hands to kiss mine.

"Okay," I tell him.

"Okay? Just like that, okay?" He is surprised by my answer.

"Honey, we live together. We haven't spent a night apart in a year." I smile at him, while he looks down at me. "I would like to stay in the same neighborhood for the kids and school, but yeah, just like that."

He smiles at me, his eyes lighting up. "That was easy." He drops to one knee in front of me. The hand that he isn't holding moves to cover my mouth, and the purse that was in it falls to the floor. "The day I ran into you changed my life. You came into the office with all that sass, and you almost killed me. Twice." He laughs, his eyes never leaving mine, while I smile at the memory.

"Oh, please, how was I to know you were allergic to that powder?" I roll my eyes at him. "I saw the pictures. It wasn't that bad."

He just glares at me, obviously disagreeing. "Needless to say, I fell in love with you. I fell in love with Gabe and Rachel, and even Kaleigh." He continues, "I want us to be together forever. I want to wake up every morning and see my ring on your finger. I want to go out and hold your hand for everyone to know that you're mine." He shakes his head. "I know it sounds silly, but my ring on your finger, the world knowing that you're all mine, it's important to me."

The tear that I blinked back now makes its way down my cheek. "You want me to be yours?" I ask him as he nods his head yes. "Good, because I want you to be mine. I want to see *my* ring on your finger every morning. I want to see *my* ring glisten in the sun when you drink coffee at work. I want to see *my* ring on your finger when we go to hockey games and the other moms all drool over you." I smile at him. "So, I guess that would be a yes. Yes, I'll be yours. I'll be your wife. I'll be yours forever." I tell him and in one second, he is off his knee and twirling me in his arms. I laugh out loud while I wrap my arms around his neck, my head leaning against his. He stops and puts me down, taking a blue ring box from his pocket. When he opens the box, the round diamond solitaire sparkles in the candlelight. He grabs my left hand, slipping the ring on my finger. It is a perfect fit.

"She said yes!" he calls out, and I laugh at him before, seemingly out of nowhere, Gabe and Rachel run to us, followed by my mother and father. Noah, Kaleigh, Barbara, and all of our closest friends and family follow them.

I hear congratulations being shouted out while a waiter comes around with glasses of champagne. Austin makes his way back to me with Gabe next to him and Rachel holding his hand, and he raises his glass to toast. "Thank you, everyone, for coming. I would like to toast to my future wife, and to Gabe and Rachel for giving me their permission. Cheers."

"To tempting the boss," I say as I raise my glass with a smile for the man who started off as my boss and ended up being the man of my dreams. He leans down and kisses my lips, sealing the deal.

And they lived happily ever after.

dare to hold

CARLY PHILLIPS

NY Times Bestselling Author Carly Phillips turns up the heat in her newest sexy contemporary romance series, and introduces you to the Dare family... siblings shaped by a father's secrets and betrayal.

Some women always get it right. Kindergarten teacher, Meg Thompson, on the other hand, consistently makes the wrong decisions—and she is currently single, pregnant and alone. Meg is determined to make changes in her life, to be a better mother than her own had been. No revolving door of men. No man, period. Just a single-minded focus on her baby. Her resolution would be easier to keep if not for hot cop, Scott Dare. He insinuates himself in her life, making Meg want to believe in happily ever after, even if history has taught her to know better.

When Scott Dare hears Meg's friends are determined she have a night of hot sex, before her life changes forever, he decides that man must be him. Their one night is mind blowing and life altering. And Scott, a man already burned by his ex-wife, finds himself all in anyway. While protecting Meg from her violent ex and becoming part of her increasingly complicated life, he's falling hard and he can't seem to find distance. Not when their bodies respond to each other with such heated intensity and he's drawn to her unique combination of strength and vulnerability.

But Meg's future is one Scott has accepted he'll never have, even if his growing feelings say otherwise...

dedication

As always, there are people without whom, my books could not get written.

To Janelle Denison . . . for everything.

To Chasity Jenkins Patrick for knowing what I need before I need it . . . and for everything else.

To Shannon Short for listening and sharing your business smarts with me.

To Julie Leto and Leslie Kelly for plotting, daily help answers and more.

To Marquita Valentine for reading, cheerleading and being my daily texting buddy.

And to my Skype sprinting pals, Carrie Ann Ryan, Shayla Black, Stacey Kennedy, Kennedy Layne, Angel Payne, Lexi Blake and Jenna Jacobs for being there to sprint when I need a push—and a chat—and a pick me up. And to Mari Carr who's supposed to be there sprinting but mostly just hooked me up with this wonderful group!

You all rock and I couldn't do what I do without you. At the very least it wouldn't be as much fun! xo

chapter one

Some women always managed to get it right. To make the right choices, to pick the right man, to nail this crazy thing called life. Meg Thompson, on the other hand, managed to end up single and pregnant. But she couldn't regret the baby growing inside her, and from now on, she was determined to get things right.

She pulled on her favorite pair of jeans, tugged them up over her hips, and unsuccessfully attempted to close the button. She grunted and laid down on the bed, pulling the sides closer together, but no luck. She wriggled, sucked in a deep breath, and tried again, only to end up huffing out a stream of air in frustration.

"Didn't these fit just last weekend?" she asked herself, peeling the denim off her legs and tossing them onto the floor with a groan.

She glanced down at her still-flat stomach, placing her hand over her belly. "How can something I can't see or feel cause so much upheaval in my life?" And how could she love the baby growing inside her so much already?

A vibrating buzz told her someone was sending her a message. She checked her phone.

Lizzy: *Almost ready?*

Meg sighed. Her best friend, Elizabeth Cooper, was due to pick her up in ten minutes. Girls' night out. Or, in Lizzy's words, hookup night and Meg's last chance for a hot, no-holds-barred fling before she started to show and her sole focus became being a new mom. Meg was up for girls' night, but no way would she be picking up a stranger for a one-night stand. Her days of choosing the wrong men were over. Mike was the last in a long line of sucky choices. So not only did she not trust her judgment when it came to the opposite sex, but it no longer mattered. She was finished relying on men to define her or make her happy.

"Right, baby?" She patted her belly and headed to her closet for a pair of elastic-waist leggings.

Meg and her friends settled into their seats at Mel's, a popular spot for casual drinks after work and on the weekends. Mel's was a dimly lit bistro with a wood-fired oven and grill in the back, dark mahogany-looking tables throughout, and a funky bar where people gathered. Meg loved it here.

She waved to the waiter, who stepped over to their table.

"What can I get you ladies?"

The girls ordered alcoholic drinks, and the good-looking waiter turned to Meg.

"I'll have a club soda. With a lime."

"Going for the hard stuff, I see." He winked and scribbled down her order.

Meg smiled. "Designated driver." Which wasn't a lie. Lizzy might have picked her up, but Meg would be the one driving home.

She glanced around at the women she'd ignored for a long time in favor of her asshole ex and, unfortunately, her baby daddy. She was grateful these women were here for her now, because Meg had a bad habit of dropping friends in favor of men. Men she looked to for the love and acceptance she'd never received from a father she barely remembered. Meg sighed and rested her chin on her hands. Her childhood memories included a string of her mother's boyfriends who came and went from her young life.

Her mother had set a pattern Meg unconsciously followed. First she'd latched on to Dylan Rhodes, the one and only good guy in her life. He'd been her high school boyfriend and her rock until they broke up before going to college, and then Meg began emulating her mother's taste by choosing men who always took advantage one way or another.

Luckily, she and Dylan had reconnected when they'd moved back to Miami years later, but Meg had overrelied on Dylan instead of standing on her own two feet. It took Dylan falling hard for another woman to wake Meg up to her too-needy ways. Dylan was her friend, but he was now Olivia Dare's husband. And Meg was determined to be independent. Everything the way it should be.

"Earth to Meg." Lizzy waved a hand in front of her eyes.

Meg blinked, startled. "Sorry. Just got lost there for a minute."

"Nowhere good, from the look on your face." Lizzy tilted her head to one side, her long blonde curls falling over her shoulder. "Everything okay?" Her friend studied her, her brown eyes soft and concerned.

Meg smiled. "Couldn't be better. I was actually thinking about the changes I've made—that I'm determined to keep making in my life. And it's really good to be out with you guys," Meg said, meaning it.

"It's great to be out with you too," Lizzy said.

The waiter stopped by the table and passed out their beverages. Meg took a long sip of her cold soda, appreciating the way it eased her dry throat.

"Well, you must be doing something right because you're glowing," Lizzy said.

"It's the pregnancy hormones," Meg muttered.

"No, seriously. You look beautiful," her friend insisted.

Meg smiled at her. "Thank you."

Allie Mendez, the office secretary at Meg's school, and the third woman in their posse, slipped her cell into her purse and leaned closer to join the conversation. "Maybe I should get myself pregnant, because Lizzy's right. You're gorgeous."

Meg blushed. "And you two need glasses."

"Not if the guys at the next table are any indication. Look. The blond one can't take his eyes off you!" Lizzy said, her voice rising in excitement.

Oh no. All Lizzy needed was a target and she'd be aiming Meg his way all night. "I'm sure he's looking at one of you. Not the pregnant woman in the elastic-waist pants." Lizzy with her blonde beauty or Allie and her olive skin and luscious curves attracted men wherever they went.

"You must not have looked in a mirror before leaving the house," Allie told her, a frown on her pretty face.

"Oh, look! He's coming this way. Now remember. There's nothing wrong with getting yourself some before your life gets serious." Lizzy nudged her arm.

"I don't want some," Meg muttered. "If he's so hot, you should—"

"Hi, ladies," the man said, bracing an arm on the back of Meg's chair.

"Hi!" Lizzy said too brightly.

"My friends and I would like to buy you all a drink." He spoke to the table, but his eyes were on Meg.

She shook her head. "We were just having a private convers—"

"We'd like that," Allie chimed in.

"Mind if we join you then?" he asked, making Meg wonder if he was dense, oblivious, or just that ego-driven.

In response, Lizzy slid her chair away from Meg, making room for the other man to sit. Which, after grabbing his chair and pulling it over to the table, he did. His pals joined them too.

Meg shot her friend an annoyed look.

"Give him a chance," Lizzy mouthed behind the man's back.

Rob, Mark, and Ken, they said their names as conversation began to flow. Ken was the one closest to Meg, and with his light hair and coloring, he definitely resembled his Barbie-doll namesake. Even if she were interested in a hookup, a preppy man who liked to talk about himself wouldn't be her choice. She disliked his wandering hands even more.

He brushed her back.

She stiffened.

He sat forward so their shoulders touched. She shoved her chair in the opposite direction.

Somehow he ended up close beside her again, his thigh touching hers.

She was all too ready to go home, but her friends seemed to like the guys they were talking to, and she didn't want to ruin their time by being rude to Ken. She wouldn't leave with him, but she'd be pleasant while they were here.

"So what do you do for a living?" he asked.

"I'm a kindergarten teacher."

He blinked, long lashes framing green eyes. "That's . . . brave."

"Don't like kids?" she asked none too sweetly.

He fake-shuddered. "Not for a good long while. But you must have a decent pension plan?" he asked, back on the subject he liked best. Ken was a stockbroker and investor, and soon she found herself listening to all the ways she could save more money by investing with the best of the best. Him, of course.

She hid a yawn behind her hand, and when her bladder informed her she needed a trip to the restroom, she nearly groaned out loud in relief.

"If you'll excuse me, I need to go . . . freshen up. I'll be back in a few minutes." Meg rose, and Ken followed, helping her pull out her chair.

Allie met her gaze. "Gentleman," she mouthed in approval.

Meg swallowed a groan.

"I'll be waiting," Ken said as she walked away.

"Oh, please don't be," she said to herself, making her way to the bathroom at the far back of the restaurant.

She spent a long time in the restroom, checking her phone, swiping some gloss on her dry lips, and washing her hands, twice, in her effort to stall returning to the table.

When she did, she paused by Lizzy's chair and whispered in her friend's ear, "I'm going to bail. I'm not up to this. I'm really sorry. Will you be okay driving?"

"Of course. I barely had a sip. But I can leave and take you home."

She shook her head. "No need. You seem to be hitting it off with Mark. I can get Uber," she said.

"I'd be happy to drive you," Ken said.

She hadn't realized he'd left his seat and had overheard them.

"No, really. Stay and have fun. I'm just not feeling too well." Which was a lie, but it was nicer than *Go away, I'm not interested*.

Which was ironic since, not too long ago, Meg would have been all too willing to see where things went with a guy who showed her any interest at all. Maybe the baby really was changing her, making her more self-reliant and aware as well as giving her better taste in men.

"Then you really shouldn't go home alone," Ken said, grasping her forearm.

Oh no he didn't. She pinned him with an annoyed glare. "Let. Go." And what was it about her that attracted assholes anyway? she asked herself as she tried to extricate herself without resorting to insults or calling management.

Lizzy jumped up from her seat just as the jerk released her arm and a familiar voice reverberated in her ear.

"Touch her again and you'll answer to me."

Scott Dare arrived at Mel's and found his brother Tyler waiting for him at the bar. He and Tyler often hung out at Mel's on Scott's rare nights off duty. He was a cop, and after disobeying a direct order by going into a situation without backup, he was currently enjoying administrative leave. He was chafing under the rules and no longer finding the same satisfaction in the job as he once had. Meeting with his brother was the highlight of his week so far.

Scott tipped his beer back and took a long pull.

"So seriously, what's up your ass other than boredom?" Tyler asked.

"Boredom isn't enough?" Scott scanned the room, his gaze landing on a table of women he hadn't noticed before that included one very familiar face. His boredom instantly vanished.

Any time he saw Meg Thompson, every part of him took notice, and tonight was no exception. He didn't know what it was about her. Her brown hair was just that. Brown silk that hung just below her shoulders, but there were highlights that turned some parts a sexy reddish-blonde under the right light. Brown eyes the color of his morning coffee framed by thick lashes that too often showed a vulnerability she tried hard to hide. It was that forced strength that got to him. She was alone, dealing with a difficult situation that would break most women.

But she wasn't like any other woman he'd met. And completely unlike Scott's ex-wife.

"Do you know them?" Tyler tipped his head toward the table of women.

"I know the brunette." Scott rose . . . only to find a blond guy had beat him to it. The man leaned closer to Meg, and Scott stiffened, forcing himself to sit down and watch.

"Who is she?" his brother asked.

"She's Dylan's friend, Meg Thompson."

"Aah. Liv told me about her. She thought Meg would be a problem when she got involved with Dylan, but they ended up being friends."

Scott nodded. "That's her."

"And I'm guessing you two have history since you can't take your eyes off of her?" Tyler nudged him in the side.

"Yes. No. Shit," he muttered, wondering how to explain his reaction to Meg.

From the minute Scott had seen her, looking small and defenseless in a hospital bed after nearly losing her baby thanks to her angry ex-boyfriend, Scott had been invested. Not even her pregnancy had put him off. Which, all things considered, should scare the shit out of him. Since Leah, he didn't get seriously involved.

He'd questioned Meg, taken her statement, and guided her through the restraining-order process. And he'd been dumb enough to try to help. To be there for her afterward, but she wasn't interested. Not in a helping hand.

Not in him.

He'd been forced to see her at occasional get-togethers at Olivia and Dylan's over the last month, had run into her in the supermarket. He'd offered to take her to dinner, to be her friend. Despite the undeniable chemistry between them, she'd declined.

Two other men joined the first, and soon the women at Meg's table were paired off. And Scott was pissed. A low growl escaped his throat.

"Easy, bro." Instead of giving him a hard time, Tyler placed a hand on his shoulder.

Scott blew out a long breath. Logically, he knew he didn't have a say in what Meg did. Or with whom.

He ordered a Patrón. Neat. And settled in to do what he did best. Keep an eye on her from a distance. To his relief, as time passed, she didn't look at all interested in the guy. Her body language screamed *don't touch*, and the asshole didn't appear to be listening.

"I'm going to bash his head in if this keeps up," Scott muttered.

Tyler raised an eyebrow. "First Ian, now you. Are you really going to leave me as the only single Dare guy in the family?"

"She's made it clear she's not interested in me, and besides, marriage? Been there, have the divorce papers to show for it. Not happening again," Scott reminded his brother. At twenty-nine, he was finished with that stupid dream. Leah had screwed with his head on so many levels he was lucky he wasn't still dizzy two years later.

He had no intention of letting his brother in on the fact that Meg was pregnant. His sibling would have a field day with Scott's interest based on that alone. He'd be wrong. But it wasn't worth the hassle or discussion.

"Sorry," Tyler muttered, obviously uncomfortable.

Scott wasn't sure if he was referring to the divorce, the reason behind it, or Meg's lack of interest. All were enough to shit on his ego.

Meg shoved her chair back and headed for the back of the restaurant, where the restrooms were located, and Scott breathed easily for the first time since realizing she was there.

"You going after her?" Tyler asked.

"No."

"It's not like you to give up when you want something."

Good point, Scott thought, but he remained seated. Watching but wary.

Meg returned and stopped by one of her friends, whispering something in her ear. The women spoke, and suddenly the guy who'd been inching closer to her all evening walked up to them. They talked. Looked more like an argument.

And then he grabbed Meg's arm. Scott bolted out of his seat and came up behind Meg. Her soft scent invaded his senses, but his focus was on the asshole who hadn't released her.

"Let. Go," Meg said through clenched teeth.

Scott's hands fisted at his sides. "Touch her again and you'll answer to me."

Meg didn't know where Scott Dare had come from. She hadn't noticed him in the bar earlier, and she was always aware when he was near. How could she not be? He was everything that appealed to her in a man. Tall, with jet-black hair that always looked as if he'd just run his hand through the inky strands. Full lips. Straight nose. So damned handsome.

Though he had a dominant streak a mile wide, one she couldn't miss during their few encounters, he'd been warm and caring when taking her statement in the hospital. And he was a cop, which meant he wasn't her typical bad boy, but he gave off a masculine vibe that just did it for her.

"Who the hell are you?" Ken asked Scott, interrupting her blatant perusal.

"A friend who heard her tell you to get lost." If Scott's pissed-off tone and much bigger build wasn't enough to make his point, he pushed his jacket back, revealing his holstered gun. "I'm off duty, but it still works."

Ken raised both hands and took a step back. "Easy, man. It's not my fault she gave off the wrong signals." He shook his head and stormed off, his friends pushing their chairs back and quickly following.

"Are you okay?" Lizzy asked, her hand protectively on Meg's arm.

"I'm fine."

"And who is this?" Allie asked, coming up on Meg's other side.

She tipped her head toward Scott, still not meeting his gaze. She wasn't ready. "Liz, Allie, this is Scott Dare."

"Holy hell, girl," Allie whispered none too softly. "I can see why you weren't interested in the Ken doll."

Meg's cheeks burned.

"Nice to meet you both," Scott said in that voice that Meg heard in her dreams.

He turned toward her, giving her no choice but to look into those sexy navy—almost violet—eyes, made more vibrant by his light-blue shirt. "Meg, a word?"

She shook her head. She'd managed to put him out of her thoughts, which hadn't been easy, and here he was, coming to her rescue and making demands. If she wasn't so determined to turn over a new leaf, be independent, she'd respond to his sexy tone and probably do anything he asked. Her damp panties were proof of that.

"I was just telling my friends I'm going home." She kissed Lizzy on the cheek and squeezed Allie's hand, reassuring them both she was fine.

She strode past Scott, knowing full well he'd follow. He waited until they were on the street away from the crowds before he grasped her hand and turned her to face him. "Meg."

"Thank you for getting rid of the creep." She pulled her phone from her bag and scrolled for the app that would let her call for a car.

"I'll drive you home."

"Was that an offer or an order?" she asked, unable to help her sarcastic mouth. He brought that out in her.

He shot her a look. One that had her quivering inside. And giving in to his demand. "Okay, you can drive me home."

And then she planned to walk herself inside, close her front door, and forget about Scott Dare.

Without a word, he grasped her elbow and led her to a parking lot where his Range Rover was parked.

"I can't believe what a mess tonight turned out to be," she muttered once they were settled in the plush leather seats.

"What were you doing there in the first place?"

She swung around to face him. "I can't go out to a restaurant with friends?"

"Of course you can."

He wanted to say more. She could tell from the tense set of his jaw.

She sighed and decided to save him the trouble. "No, you're right. Lizzy and Allie had this idea of taking me out so I could pick up a guy and have one last fling before I start to show." She slid her hands over her stomach. "And before I'm busy being a mom."

His grip on the steering wheel tightened. "You were going to hook up with some stranger?" he asked through gritted teeth.

"What? No! I said they thought I should. I just went out to see my friends. Then that guy sat down and—Why am I explaining myself to you?" she asked, trailing off.

But it had been this way with Scott from the first time they'd met. She found him easy to talk to. Understanding. Like he heard what she said and cared, unlike her ex. Or any of the men in her past.

She watched the palm trees and scenery as he drove. She'd already told him where she lived when she'd explained how she'd ended up in the hospital a little over a month ago. She just couldn't believe he remembered. All too soon, they reached their destination. He pulled into a parking spot at her apartment complex.

He put the truck in park, cut the engine, and turned to face her. "You talk to me because you know that you can trust me."

Point proven. He remembered what she'd said at least five minutes ago.

"But I hardly know you."

"Instinct."

She shook her head at that. "Mine's failed me many times before." And miserably, at that, she thought.

"Not this time." He let himself out of the truck and started to walk around to her side.

Realizing his intent, she opened the door and hopped out just as he reached her. He shut the door behind her. "Let's go."

"I can see myself up."

"You could. But since I took you home, I'll get you safely to your door."

He slid a hand to the small of her back, and she felt his heated palm through the fabric of her top. Goose bumps prickled along her skin.

She lived in a first-floor apartment, and they reached her door. He turned her around to face him. "Your friends want you to have one last fling? Is that what you want too?"

She hadn't given a fling any thought. Not until Scott said the word, a husky bent to his voice and determined intent behind his words. "I don't want sex with some random stranger."

She glanced up and found herself pinned by his stare. His lips lifted in a sexy grin. "I'm not a stranger."

She opened then closed her mouth as she processed his words and the meaning behind them. He wasn't a stranger. Not really. He knew more about her than most people, and her best friends could vouch for him.

She ran her tongue over her dry lips. His darkening gaze deliberately followed the movement, and her body responded, nipples puckering beneath the cotton of her shirt. He wanted a fling. Sex. With her.

And she wanted him, every rock-hard inch of his toned, muscled body. Had from the very first moment she'd seen him and every time since. She'd evaded him, certain that was the right thing to do for herself and for her baby, because she had new standards and rules she had to follow for her own sanity and for her future. But this *thing* between them wasn't going away. If anything, it was becoming more intense, growing more heated, and she couldn't deny it or walk away from him again.

"I'm not interested in a relationship," she reminded him.

He inclined his head. "And I'm not asking for one. Not even asking for a date this time."

"Just a fling?" she repeated, thinking he had to be kidding. Just like she'd thought he was kidding when he'd asked her out before. Because what would a hot, good-looking man like Scott Dare want with a woman who'd gotten herself knocked up and then pushed around by her ex-boyfriend?

Even when she'd realized Scott was serious about dating, she couldn't accept. Because she could so easily see herself repeating old patterns with him. Falling hard and fast. Giving in. Losing herself. And now there was more at stake than just Meg.

But this time, Scott was offering something she could handle. A night with a beginning and an end, no expectations. No disturbing her resolution to stand on her own. To be a better mother than her own had been, no revolving door of men. No man, period. Just a hot night and a memory to keep her warm when she was alone.

"One night." He reached out and rubbed his thumb across her lower lip.

His touch made her tremble, and her nipples tightened into hardened points, and the intensity in his gorgeous eyes had need building even stronger inside her.

"Is that what you want too?" he asked again, his gaze hot on hers.

His distinctive scent, a hint of musk she associated with Scott alone, filled her nostrils. Her stomach fluttered, and the desire to wrap herself around him and take what he offered built until it was a tangible thing, living and breathing inside her tightly strung body.

She nodded, unable to speak. Her throat had grown too dry.

"I need you to say it."

Say what? She didn't remember his question. Only the thought of letting him into her apartment . . . into her body filled her mind and her senses.

A low rumble sounded from deep inside his chest. "Say *I want you, Scott*. I need the words, or I'll send you inside alone."

"I want you, Scott." The words tumbled out, an easy capitulation that had been anything but. Another Meg Thompson decision she feared would alter the course of her life. And she was powerless to stop it.

chapter two

MEG SAID THE WORDS, AND SCOTT'S HEAD BUZZED WITH HER HEADY ADMISSION. He'd been holding on by a thread since she'd admitted that her friends wanted her to have a one-night stand. If anyone was going to put hands on her, it was going to be him. Problem was, once he touched her . . . once he *had* her, one time wouldn't be enough. But that was an issue he'd deal with later.

She opened the door to her apartment. They stepped inside, and he immediately pressed her up against the wall, his hips bracing against hers. "I want you too. And if this is what you'll give me, I'm taking it."

He leaned close, intending to kiss her, but her scent beckoned, and he breathed in the warm, sensual fragrance that made him hard and kept him up at night.

He dragged his lips from her jaw to her cheek. "You smell so fucking good."

A small whimper escaped from the back of her throat, and his dick hardened against the teeth of his zipper.

"I need to taste you." He settled his mouth over hers, finding her lips soft, her flavor sweet. Better than he'd imagined, and he wanted more. He nipped at her lower lip and slid his tongue inside, turning things hot quickly.

He discovered Meg was an equal partner in the glide and tangle of their tongues, in the click of his teeth against hers.

She threaded her hands through his hair and tugged, and he knew if she kept touching him, it'd be over before things got started. He pulled her arms above her head and clasped her wrists in one hand. "I call the shots."

He watched her carefully, and her eyes dilated. He grinned, liking her response. He'd always preferred control, more so after his marriage and life had fallen apart, and his older brother Ian had taught him not to apologize for who he was or what he needed. His cousin Decklan had introduced him to Scott's favorite club in New York, and Scott had begun to understand himself even more.

"I'm not sure I like that," she said, her mind obviously at war with what her needy body craved.

"When I make you come over and over, you will."

Her eyes opened wide. And then she laughed. Damned woman actually laughed at him. He raised an eyebrow.

"What?" she asked, her eyes lighting up. "Experience tells me that was a cocky claim."

"You did not just call my skill into question."

She met his gaze, a combination of mirth and seriousness in her chocolate-brown eyes. "Maybe it's the skill of all those men in my past I'm talking about," she murmured, her voice dropping, honesty and embarrassment forcing her gaze down.

Olivia had told him Meg had a history of picking the wrong guys. A pattern that went far beyond the asshole who'd laid a hand on her this last time. Now Scott understood just how bad her prior relationships had been, and he intended to make up for each and every jerk in her past. Something that would take way more than one night.

But he'd start now. "Okay, baby, I'm going to lay down a few rules."

Her mouth opened and closed.

So damned cute, but he wouldn't tell her that.

"I am not your baby," she said, but the gleam in her eyes told him otherwise. She liked when he called her that.

He grinned. "We'll see."

She narrowed her gaze. "And did you say *rules?*" Meg asked, unable to believe his nerve.

He nodded. "Rules. As in, you do as I say, and you get to come. Often."

How could she argue with that? Before she could even respond, he picked her up and into his arms, enjoying the warmth of her body against his. "Direct me to the bedroom."

"Are you always this bossy?" she asked. And why, oh, why did her pussy spasm when he acted like this? A normal woman would be turned off, but not Meg. A guy took control, and she wanted more.

"Yes. Get used to it. Back there?" he tilted his head toward the open doorway and, without waiting for an answer, strode to her room.

He paused by the bed, dipped his head, and kissed her hard. This was no first-date kiss, but then this wasn't a date. This was sex, and she already knew it was going to be the best she'd ever had.

It might also be the last, so she'd better enjoy it. She wrapped her arms around his neck, her fingers gliding over the hard muscles in his upper back, which she could feel through his clothing, then up through his silky hair. She inhaled, and his masculine scent raced through her, a heady reminder that she really was doing this. With Scott, a man she'd wanted since meeting him, she thought, and her belly twisted with need.

He laid her down on the center of the bed, his movements sure and gentler than she'd expected. Then he rose. He removed his jacket and tossed it onto the floor, took care of the holstered gun, placing it on the dresser—and boy, did she find a man with a weapon hot. Especially this man. She couldn't stop staring as he yanked his shirt up and off, revealing tanned skin and a light sprinkling of dark hair across his chest that ran down his abs and tapered into the waistband of his jeans.

He was a sculpted work of art, and she watched him greedily. Ran her tongue over her lips.

"I want that tongue on me, baby."

She couldn't believe the calm, collected, always-in-control Scott Dare was a dirty talker during sex, and her stomach flipped in excitement at his words. She wanted her tongue on him too. She, who could normally care less about oral sex, wanted to take him in her mouth and lick him all over.

"So come here and let me," she said, shocked at the gravelly tone of her voice.

His gaze narrowed. "Who calls the shots?" he asked, unbuttoning his jeans and pulling them down over narrow hips. He'd hooked his thumbs into his boxers or briefs; she didn't know which because they were gone along with his jeans, and she couldn't tear her gaze away from his thick, hard cock.

Jesus.

"Was that an answer?" he asked.

Had he asked a question? Her breasts were heavy, her nipples hard and hurting, and her panties now soaked with the evidence of her desire for him. And she was lying in bed, fully dressed, while this gorgeous specimen of a man stood aroused before her. She couldn't focus on anything but getting naked too.

She reached for the hem of her shirt, and suddenly he was over her, pinning her to the bed. "You can't deny me the pleasure of peeling those clothes off you. I want to see every inch of your skin."

He lifted the shirt and eased it upward, his calloused thumbs trailing over her sensitive flesh. He pulled it off, leaving her in just a flimsy bra—one that would have to be replaced soon, because it did little to conceal the now-larger swells of her breasts.

His gaze never left her body, his eyes darkening as he drank her in. "You're gorgeous."

He swiped his thumbs over her already-aching nipples, and she moaned, his words arousing her as much as his touch. He trailed his fingertips down, then slid his hand into the waistband of her leggings and soon removed those too. Of course, he took her panties along with them in one smooth move.

As he continued to stare, she wanted to crawl beneath the covers, suddenly aware of herself in ways she hadn't been when focused on him. Her breasts were bigger now, and although she figured that was okay, her stomach wasn't flat and tight. She'd always had a slight belly, but everything had shifted lately, making her overly focused on her flaws.

No way he hadn't noticed them too. She slid her hands over her stomach, and he swore, grasping her wrists and pinning them over her head.

"Let's get something straight, okay? I'm here because I want you. All of you. From what's inside that pretty head of yours to the sexy body spread out for me now."

Her eyes widened at the force and sincerity of his words.

"Know what that means?" he asked.

She shook her head. She didn't know anything. This man had her so off-balance she was spinning. She'd agreed to one night of hot sex. Instead, she was getting a lot of dirty talking from an attentive man. She didn't know what to do with either.

"That means while I have you in bed, you're mine." He nipped her jaw, then kissed her hard on the lips. "Keep your hands above your head, and let me give you what you need."

"Again, you seem awfully sure of yourself," she said, falling back on sarcasm. Because what could she say? She was so out of her depth.

A knowing grin pulled at his lips. "Guess you're going to make me prove myself, huh?"

Her mouth grew dry. "Guess so."

He proceeded to do just that. He kissed, licked, and nipped his way down her neck, pausing to nuzzle at her collarbone, an erogenous spot she hadn't known she possessed, before licking around the lace edges of her bra. Her nerves tingled, the rest of her becoming increasingly aroused, and she writhed and twisted on the bed, arms above her head, with him effectively holding her hostage. She didn't care as long as he continued to pay homage to her body.

He unhooked the front catch of her bra with way too much skill and peeled the cups off her heavy breasts. "I need to taste you, baby."

Her sex clenched. Her nipples peaked even tighter. And when he latched on to one sensitive tip, she felt the tug deep in her core. "Scott, God." She arched up, inadvertently pushing her breast deeper into his mouth.

He cupped one big hand around her other breast and began to pluck and play with the nipple, pulling and pinching with his fingers, his mouth continuing to do the same with the other tip. Sensations pummeled her and she rocked her hips back and forth, her pussy seeking the same rough, hard contact he was giving to her breasts.

He pinched a nipple harder, and she whimpered.

"You're sensitive, aren't you?"

She nodded. "That's sort of . . . new. I never—" But she was so close. Could she really come from him playing with her breasts alone?

"You will now." He followed that comment by lavishing her with the most wonderful tugs, pulls, and twists of his fingers and wet laps of his tongue.

As if he'd tapped into a powder keg, sparks flew from her nipples to her clit, a dull roar filled her head, and suddenly he slid his fingers over her sex, adding to the maelstrom. The sounds surrounding her were unfamiliar, loud, and she realized, coming from her. He slid two fingers back and forth over her clit, the pressure building and making her ready to detonate.

"Come, baby."

His words triggered the explosion, and her body began to pulse and fly, her orgasm a living, breathing thing that consumed her, body and soul. The waves of pleasure went on and on with Scott in control, his rough voice and slick fingers taking her on a glorious ride.

She came back to herself as he braced his hands on either side of her shoulders, his large body over hers. "Good?" he asked.

Her lips lifted in what had to be a loopy grin. "Yes, hotshot. You proved you're a man of your word."

"Not yet, I haven't." His gaze met hers, that penetrating stare zeroing in. "I promised you'd come often. That was just once." He slid his erection back and forth over her sex, and what little breath she'd regained left in a whoosh. "Condom."

She swallowed hard. "I think there are some left in my drawer." She looked away.

He pressed a hard kiss to her lips, retrieved protection, ripped the foil open, and slid it on. "I need to feel you wet and hot around my cock." He rocked his thick member lower, nudging at her entrance, gliding in, pulling out with short thrusts and rough groans. Back and forth with obvious care.

She had the distinct feeling he was going slowly in deference to her, and that was the last thing she wanted. "I'm not going to break," she told him.

He studied her as if searching for answers, his need obvious in his taut expression. He was holding back.

"The doctor didn't give me any restrictions." She arched her hips and clasped him more tightly inside her, drawing her knees up and pulling him in deeper.

With a groan, he broke and thrust hard, filling her up completely. He was so big, and she reveled in the fullness. She wrapped her arms around him, and he didn't stop her from touching him this time, so she took the time to memorize the moment. The way his hard body molded to hers, the thickness of him inside her, and his heady, arousing scent. She didn't want to forget a second of this moment and knew she never would.

"Can't not move," he muttered and began a steady pounding inside her, giving her everything, holding nothing back.

His body felt glorious inside hers, and to her shock, pleasure began to tease her again, another climax building quickly. He took her hard, his thrusts culminating with a grind of his hips, the angle of his penetration hitting a spot she'd never known existed but that was sheer bliss. Sweat broke out on his body, and his rough groans sounded in her ear.

"Fuck, you feel good," he said as his lips came down on hers, his deliberate thrusts never ceasing. "Meg!" He groaned and slammed into her over and over, his release obvious and so hot it triggered her own. Soaring again, she came, her entire being narrowing to the epic sensations pouring over her and the man atop her who'd rocked her world.

She was still breathing hard when Scott pulled out and headed for the bathroom. He returned seconds later, wasting no time in gathering her into his arms and throwing one big leg over hers.

Was he planning on *staying*? she wondered, panicked. That wasn't what they'd agreed on. She'd enjoyed him too much and would come to want so much more if he didn't get up and leave now. So she lay stiff in his arms, unsure of what to say or do next.

Scott apparently had no such qualms. He kissed her neck—soft, sexy slides of his mouth that had her squirming because she liked them so much.

"Relax, baby," he said drowsily. "The world won't end if I fall asleep here." And from the lazy drawl of his words, she knew he intended to do just that.

Scott awoke in a strange bed, loud sounds coming from the other room. He was in Meg's bedroom. He grinned and stretched, feeling too damned pleased considering that, without a doubt, she wanted him gone. He understood the sentiment. They'd agreed on hot sex and nothing more. Of course he'd had a hunch he wouldn't be satisfied with just one night, and in the bright light of day, he'd been right. He didn't understand why he wanted to get entangled with a woman whose life was damned complicated. Given his history, it made little sense. But right now, he was in. He'd figure out his own issues later.

He headed for the bathroom, discovering it steamy. Meg had obviously already showered and dressed, no doubt steeling herself for the confrontation ahead. He shrugged. He'd just have to keep her off-balance if he wanted to break through her walls.

He took a quick shower of his own, lathering in her soap, using her shampoo. Both smells made him hard, but he was well aware he wasn't getting any this morning. He just needed to assess the lay of the land for the future before heading out.

Dressed in his clothes from yesterday, he found her in the kitchen, her back to the door. She wore a pair of sweats and a pale-green T-shirt, her damp hair hanging long in the back, curling as it dried.

"Good morning."

She jumped and turned toward him. "You startled me."

"Is that breakfast?" He pointed to a pink smoothie she drank from a straw.

She nodded. "Protein. It's good for me."

"And the baby. I didn't forget." One of her many complications. He pushed the reality away.

A light blush stained her cheeks. "Right. So you understand why we shouldn't draw out this awkward morning-after thing any longer."

He raised an eyebrow. So she really was eager to get rid of him, and it rankled. "No breakfast?" he asked, teasing her.

"Sorry. Nothing but healthy shakes, and I really need to get my day going so . . ." She gestured toward the front of her apartment.

He strode toward her, leaning one hip against the kitchen counter. "About last night." He slid one hand behind her neck in a possessive hold.

"What about it?" she asked, voice shaking. She didn't know what to expect from him, but he affected her. Her body and voice couldn't lie about that.

"It was great," he told her honestly. "*You* were great." He touched his nose to hers in a soft gesture, one he knew was at odds with the man he was in the bedroom. But she brought this side out in him too. Something else to ponder, as nobody ever had before. "So thank you."

"Oh. You're welcome." She blushed harder. "I mean . . . never mind." She waved a shaking hand through the air.

There it was. Cute again. He shook his head, remembering his cool, icy, sophisticated ex-wife. So. Not. Cute.

He grinned at a flustered Meg. "I know what you meant."

"Oh," Meg said softly, and she slid her tongue across her lip in that nervous gesture he found so endearing.

This morning it reminded him of the things they hadn't done together. His mouth on her pussy. Her lips on his cock. Yeah, there was a lot left undone. And he wasn't just talking about sex, though that had been a good start. It would make it that much more difficult for her to keep him at arm's length now that she knew what he did. Together, they were explosive.

How they came together? That would be the next step. One that would determine just what they could mean to each other outside of the bedroom.

He pulled back and rose to his full height. "Take care of yourself." Knowing she'd say no and get defensive, he didn't ask her for anything. Didn't offer her dinner. Didn't ask her questions. Nothing.

Keep her frustrated and guessing. Missing him, if he was lucky. That was his game plan, and he was looking forward to the challenge. Because he fully expected Meg to make him work for her. And after last night, he was okay with that.

Meg wasn't sure how she made it through the rest of the weekend. She was jumpy and nervous. She kept checking her phone, hoping, expecting to hear from Scott. She didn't. Apparently he was a man of his word. One night meant just that.

Wasn't that what she'd wanted? Why was she so . . . hurt, then, over his silence?

Monday at school dragged. The kids were extra cranky, little Billy Miller spilled paint on Lilah Devlin's shoes, and one kid had a fever. By the time the day ended, Meg was so grateful she wanted to cry. Tomorrow she had an appointment with the principal to tell him she was pregnant. She was due in early September, when school would have just restarted for the new year, and he'd need to plan ahead. She didn't think being unmarried and pregnant would be an issue, but she was nervous anyway because she worked in a private school. That meant she was subject to the school board's decisions, and she had no doubt the principal would share her new status with them.

On Wednesday, she was having dinner with Olivia. Dylan was out of town on business, and the other woman wanted to compare pregnancy notes. Since Olivia was due two months later than Meg—they had that in common. She hoped it wasn't awkward that Olivia was Scott's sister.

Because there was no way she could hide her reaction if somehow his name came up. Just thinking about him set her on fire. She hadn't washed her sheets because she liked the musky smell of him, and *them*, that lingered. She'd like to say it was the sex she couldn't get out of her head, but it was more than that. The little things. How he'd jumped out to open the car door. How he'd leaned in and brushed his nose against hers when he was saying good-bye. And how he'd thanked her, as if her sleeping with him was something special and meant something to him.

When was the last time she'd been treated well? When the person she'd been with had put her first? She shook her head hard, the answer too painful to contemplate. True, Scott had been nice, but he wasn't anything to her but a one-night stand. His silence merely reinforced that. Meanwhile, she had a busy week, a full life, and she had to remember that she did not need a man to make her complete.

At the end of a long week, Scott met his brother Tyler at the gym of the Thunder football stadium. The whole family gravitated here, to the everlasting irritation of their father, who had given them all free gym passes at his luxury hotel downtown. Scott, like the others, didn't want much to do with the old man. In fact, his becoming a cop had been a big FU to his dad and his offer to work in his hotel business. Scott couldn't be in business with a man he didn't respect, and from the minute he'd realized the truth about his father's cheating and other family, any respect he'd hung on to for a man who was rarely around when he was growing up had disappeared.

His grandparents had left each kid a trust fund, so money hadn't been an issue. He was luckier than most in that he could do what he wanted in life. So he'd gravitated toward law enforcement, because there were rules, laws, and things were black and white. He knew what to expect. He'd never envisioned feeling constrained by those same rules, because after the personal upheaval his father had caused, his career choice had made sense to him at the time. Unfortunately, those restrictions chafed, and he was miserable.

He and Tyler worked out in silence for over an hour, then showered and were finishing up in the locker room. As it was March, the team wasn't around, and they pretty much had the place to themselves.

"I wanted to ask you something," Tyler said. "Couldn't do it the other night. Mel's is too crowded. And you were too busy looking at that brunette. What did you say her name was?"

"Meg." Scott's brain immediately filled with memories of the night with her, causing his cock to swell. Shit. Good thing he'd put his jeans on.

"Right. Meg Thompson. You get her home okay?" Tyler asked.

Scott nodded, unwilling to get into more about his relationship—or lack thereof—with Meg. Knowing how completely freaked out she'd been the morning after, he'd given her space this week . . . but he couldn't let the silence go on much longer. He didn't want her thinking he wasn't interested any more than he wanted to crowd her and send her running. Not to mention he couldn't stop thinking about her and that hot night.

He and Tyler headed out to the hallway, pausing by a set of oversized couches in the lounge area.

"What's on your mind?" Scott asked his brother.

"I got a call from someone in the music business looking to hire us for the whole nine yards. Updated alarm systems, personal protection, you name it. Apparently a big band is considering breaking up, and someone leaked the information to the press, and they're getting angry threats from fans."

Tyler ran a security company named Double Down, specializing in various areas of protection, including investigations, electronics, and personal protection. He had a group of ex-military men working for him, and he'd done well for himself.

Scott glanced at his brother. "Well, they came to the right place," he said, as always proud of what Tyler had accomplished.

"Who is the client?"

Tyler eyed him warily. "Lola Corbin called. She's the lead singer of Tangled Royal," he said of the huge band currently rocking the music scene.

"Son of a bitch. Grey Kingston's bandmate is looking to hire you?" he asked, referring to the band's lead guitarist.

Tyler clenched his jaw and nodded.

Now Scott understood the problem. Avery, their youngest sister, and Grey Kingston had been hot and heavy back in high school . . . until Grey had left town to make it big, leaving Avery heartbroken. To this day, Scott wasn't sure she'd ever gotten over it. His hands curled into fists at the thought of dealing with the man.

"At least it's not Kingston who wants your services, but that's too close for comfort."

Tyler ran a hand through his dark hair and nodded. "Agreed. I don't want to upset Avery, but I can't turn down the biggest rock star on the planet. Not to mention Lola Corbin is engaged to Rep Grissom Jr., one of the Thunder's hottest stars."

"Shit," Scott muttered.

"You got that right."

"Hey, guys," Olivia said, joining her brothers. Her office was nearby. "I couldn't help but overhear. You should know, Avery's seen Grey recently. He sent her tickets to the last concert."

Tyler glanced at his sister. "Seriously? What the hell? Why didn't I know about this?"

Scott wanted to know the same thing.

"Because of your reactions right now. She knew you'd go all big-brother-caveman on his ass." Olivia patted Tyler's cheek. "She asked me to go with her to the concert. We went, but then Dylan and I got the call about Meg being in the hospital. I offered to stay, but Avery swore she was fine to go backstage alone."

"What happened between them?" Scott asked.

"She won't talk about it," Olivia said, her tone indicating how unhappy that made her.

Scott didn't like it either. Avery and Olivia were close. If she wasn't confiding in her sister, something big was going on.

"Do you think the bastard is pushing Lola toward my business to get back into Avery's life somehow?" Tyler asked, shaking his head in disgust.

Olivia narrowed her eyes, remaining silent while she considered. Then she shook her head. "You're the best there is. I honestly doubt it. She probably really does need your services."

Tyler blew out a frustrated breath. "That's what I wanted to talk about," he said to Scott. "I need a second-in-command. Someone who can oversee everything that goes on. Actually, I need a partner. I need you," he said.

"What?"

"You're a damned good cop, and the beat is a waste of your talents. Not to mention you're bored as shit. I want you to sign on as my partner." Tyler pinned Scott with a look he'd never seen before. One that held admiration and something more.

"Cool!" Olivia said, clapping her hands. "That's great for you, Scott, and he's right. You need something more challenging, and this is it."

"We all know you aren't happy doing the cop thing. This will give you a chance to use your people skills and your training. Plus you can set your own hours, which has to be better than those night shifts you've been assigned."

He couldn't deny they were right. He wasn't happy, and the thought of doing something different definitely appealed to him, as did working with his brother.

Scott ran a hand over his eyes. He'd never considered leaving the force. Never thought his older brother—by only two years, but still older—would want him on board. "You built your business yourself. Are you sure—"

"One hundred percent certain. You can buy in, and we can work out the details . . . I'd have asked you before, but I wanted you to get hands-on experience first. You deserved to follow your dream and see if it was for you before I asked you to leave it behind."

Scott nodded slowly. "Let me give it some thought. But I'm interested."

"Not too long. I'm going to take this job and with the business growing, I need you. As far as Greyson . . . If he shows up around Lola, we can tag-team him," Tyler said, tacking it on as added incentive.

"Oh, you two better stay out of Avery's business," Olivia warned them.

They both shot her a look. If someone hurt either woman, they'd have to answer to a Dare brother.

"I've got to get going. Call me," Tyler said to Scott. He paused to kiss Olivia on the cheek. "You feeling okay?" he asked their pregnant sister.

That was something Scott hadn't wrapped his head around. His little sister married and expecting a baby. At least her husband, Dylan Rhodes, treated her right. Now to get someone decent for Avery.

Olivia poked Scott in the arm. "You and I need to talk. Come to my office?" she asked.

He rose and grinned. "Am I in trouble?"

She pinned him with a warning look. *Uh-oh.*

She waited until they were settled in her private office, she in the chair behind her desk, he in the one in front. "What's up, Liv?"

"That's what I want to know. I had dinner with Meg. I mentioned your name, and she said she ran into you at Mel's this weekend."

"And?" He stared at his sister, not knowing where she was going and not jumping in with anything more before he knew what had her so on edge.

"You spent the night with her!" Olivia said it like an accusation.

Scott folded his arms across his chest. "She told you that?" Because Meg didn't strike him as the gossipy type.

Olivia blew out a long breath. "Not in so many words. But I could tell from the hemming and hawing she did . . . from the way she blushed and couldn't look me in the eye, then asked selective questions . . . I just knew."

He inclined his head. "And?" he asked his nosey sister.

"And what were you thinking? I know there were sparks when you met her, but she's coming off a really shitty relationship, she's pregnant and vulnerable, and you're . . ." She trailed off, her gaze darting away from his.

He stiffened. "Don't stop now," he told her.

"You're *you*! All controlling and alpha."

"So you think I'd hurt her?" he asked, offended.

Olivia wrinkled her nose. "Of course not. Well, not on purpose, anyway."

He frowned. "Thanks for the vote of confidence."

She rose from her seat and came around her desk, sitting in the chair next to him and leaning in close. "Scott, do you remember what happened with Leah? She gutted you when she had that abortion. You haven't had any kind of relationship with a woman since." Olivia held up a hand to make sure he didn't interrupt. "And I'm not talking about sex."

"Me neither, and not with you," Scott muttered. Nor did he need the reminder of how wrong he'd chosen when he'd married Leah Jerome.

Having seen firsthand what his father's cheating had done—not only to his mother, but to him and his siblings—Scott hadn't believed he wanted a family. Leah definitely hadn't. And then she'd gotten pregnant . . . and the reality of a baby had changed his mind. He'd thought he could change hers. He'd been wrong. And Olivia was correct. He hadn't trusted another woman since.

Then he'd met Meg. "I'm not going to hurt her. You know me better than that."

"Of course I do." Olivia laid a hand on his arm. "But all your women lately have been one-night stands or close to it. I don't understand how you can cavalierly sleep with a pregnant woman and walk away. Or think it's okay to have a casual affair with her like she's just a woman you picked up in a bar."

"Whoa." This time he held up his hand. "I'm not sure where you're getting these ideas, but trust me, Liv, you have no clue what I'm thinking, feeling, or planning." Unfortunately, neither did he. But it was the early days . . . They'd slept together once. And he wasn't going to let his sister convince him to walk away.

His sister narrowed her gaze. "Care to share?"

"Not particularly. Just understand, you know who I am. That should count for something."

"I know," Olivia said, her voice softening. "You're a good man. But Meg is different than the women you're used to."

He knew that. She was everything his ex wasn't. He sensed it at a glance. All those differences—the softness beneath the prickly exterior, the outward fragility that he knew belied a strong core, and the beauty that shone from her inside and out all called to a part of him he'd never known before.

"She has a history of picking bad boys who aren't good to her, and she's just promised herself she'll change."

"And you think I'm going to stop her from doing that?"

"I know you *could*."

He ran a hand over his face. Yeah . . . he could. It was in his nature to take over, to control. He wanted to help her, take care of her, and get to know her better. But contrary to what his sister believed, he wouldn't hurt her. He meant to see what could be between them. If that meant pushing her past her limits . . . he'd do just that.

chapter three

Meg had a rough week. The meeting with the principal hadn't gone as she'd hoped. Although she had a morals clause in her contract, it didn't include having a child out of wedlock, and she'd counted on her abilities as a teacher and how much the kids loved her to hold sway. So she'd be a single parent. Women handled it all the time due to divorce or death. They also, occasionally, got pregnant.

Unfortunately, Mr. Ryan Hansen hadn't been happy. Meg wasn't sure if his censure was more because he'd tried to date her before or because he really did have an issue with her teaching children and having to explain to young, impressionable minds why there was no baby daddy in her life. As if a kindergartener would even know about her personal life, let alone think to ask.

Luckily, he couldn't get rid of her. She had just signed a new contract, and she knew her job was secure . . . if no longer comfortable. She blew out a breath, knowing she had to get used to people having opinions and making comments about her situation.

Meg settled into the couch in her apartment, laptop on her thighs, the television providing background noise. She drew a deep breath and began looking for baby items at online stores, making notes on a pad at her side. Budget was important, but safety was first. If she needed to deal with credit card debt to purchase what she needed for her baby, so be it. She had things she could easily give up to free up money. Professional haircuts, eyebrow waxing, mani-pedis—all things she could manage on her own.

A crib would be the biggest hit for now. She jotted down a few possibilities and prices. She didn't want to go into stores until she had a good idea of what she could afford.

Her doorbell rang, taking her by surprise. It was Friday night, and her friends had gone out for drinks. They'd invited her, but she'd begged off, wanting a quiet night at home.

She walked to the door, placed her hand on the knob. "Who is it?"

She was just about to look through the peephole when she heard, "Open the fucking door, Meg."

Her heart skipped a beat.

Mike?

How could he dare to show up here? She had a restraining order in effect. She didn't plan on answering him or letting him inside, but she couldn't stop the tremors that took hold. Shaking, she went back to the couch and picked up her cell.

She returned to the door and leaned against it, hoping he would go away.

He banged hard again. No doorbell this time. "Meg! We need to talk."

She drew a deep breath. He could talk to her lawyer, and he knew it. All she wanted was for him to sign away rights to the baby. For whatever reason, he refused to do it. She didn't have any illusions that he wanted the baby. He just didn't want the child to exist, period.

She placed a protective hand over her stomach. "Go away or I'll call the police." What the hell had she seen in him? How had she missed this side of him? Oh, he'd been fun and exciting . . . at first. Until she'd let him move in and he hadn't paid rent. He hadn't contributed to food. And he'd done what he wanted, when he wanted. And she'd still tried to make things work because it was easier than getting him out of the apartment. Easier than fighting all the time. Just like her mother's relationships.

Ugh.

"Come on, I just want to talk." He banged harder on the door.

"I'm dialing 911!"

She lifted the phone to her ear.

"You stupid bitch!" He slammed his hand against the door, and then she heard the sound of footsteps storming down the hall. She wondered what her neighbors thought. It wasn't the first time they'd heard screaming coming from her apartment. She cringed in embarrassment.

She was still shaking, and there was nothing she could do to calm down. She couldn't pour herself a glass of wine. She couldn't take a Xanax. She just had to deal.

She lowered herself back to the couch and drew in a deep breath. She wasn't sure how long she remained motionless, seeing nothing, doing nothing but shivering. The last time she'd seen Mike, she'd told him she was pregnant . . . and he'd been angry. She still didn't think he'd deliberately pushed her, but who knew?

She'd tripped and fallen back into the curio cabinet with all her glass items. She'd ended up bleeding between her legs and almost losing the baby. The doctor couldn't say for sure if stress or the jarring from the fall had caused the bleeding. She'd been on bed rest for a few days and had had no problems in the two weeks since. She didn't need Mike returning and causing problems. And she didn't want to be afraid whenever she went out.

The sound of the doorbell jarred her, and she jumped. God, not again. She rose and tiptoed to the peephole and looked out.

Scott.

Thank God. She didn't stop to think, just unhooked the chain she'd installed after Mike had moved out and let Scott inside.

After his sister had ripped into him, Scott had actually felt bad, wondering if he'd pushed Meg into something she wasn't ready for. He decided to call her . . . but his car just happened to pull off at her exit. Yeah. He'd keep telling himself that.

He rang her doorbell, not even knowing if she was home. The door swung open wide, and he found himself facing a pale, wide-eyed Meg.

His protective instincts swung into high gear. "What's wrong?" He stepped inside and shut the door behind him.

"I . . . My ex was here," she said, her big brown eyes damp.

Rage at the thought of anyone scaring her, hurting her, filled him. "Here? As in inside?"

She shook her head. "No. I didn't open the door."

He breathed out a relieved breath. "Good girl."

"But he kept banging and yelling, cursing, saying we needed to talk."

"Not happening," Scott said through clenched teeth.

"Not if I have anything to say about it," she agreed. "I didn't answer him. But he's not going to just go away. Restraining order or not."

Her hands shook, and he clasped both his palms around her cold extremities and held on. Despite the serious situation, he couldn't help but notice how soft her skin was, how delicate she felt beneath his fingers.

"I don't understand. I don't want anything from him. Not a dime, even though his family can more than afford it. I just want him to sign away his parental rights. Why won't he just do that?" she asked, her voice trembling.

Scott filed the information about his family's money away for later. "People have strange reasons for doing things." He'd have to figure out Mike's. But right now, Meg was his only concern, and she needed to calm down.

He led her to the couch, where she'd obviously been sitting with her open laptop and notepad. He sat down, pulled her onto his lap, and she immediately curled into him, seeking comfort he was only too happy to give.

"It'll be fine," he assured her, wrapping his arms around her smaller frame. She felt so delicate, so perfect in his arms.

"I hope so." She curled her fingers into his shirt and rested her head against his chest with a small quivering sigh.

"I won't let him hurt you." He stroked the back of her hair, inhaling the fragrant scent of her shampoo. Memories of sliding into her wet heat hit him without warning, and his body responded.

He swallowed a curse, reminding himself she sought reassurance, not sex, but his stiff cock wasn't listening. It didn't help when she wriggled deeper into him, her face tucked against his neck, her breath hot on his skin.

He needed to think with his head. The one with common sense that knew she was frightened. "Hey." He brushed her hair out of her face. "You're safe now."

"I know. I just feel so stupid, thinking a piece of paper would keep him away. And I don't know what to do now."

"Well, first thing, let's get this visit documented by the police. You want everything on record." In case something else happened, which Scott wouldn't say to her out loud. For one thing, he didn't want to frighten her further. And for another, he wouldn't let that bastard near her.

She eased back to meet his gaze. "I can't prove Mike was here."

"I'll talk to your neighbors. See if anyone heard him yelling or recognized his voice. Okay?"

She remained silent, not looking at him. Clearly he wasn't helping. "What's wrong?"

"Everything." She pushed off him, sliding into her own space on the sofa.

He immediately missed the warmth and heat of her body, but she obviously needed distance. "Tell me."

She blinked her thick lashes. "I promised myself I'd stand on my own, and at the first sign of a crisis, I curled up in your lap and let you take over. How's that for falling back into old patterns?" she said, frustration and annoyance in her tone.

"Listen to me." Needing to touch her, to maintain the contact they'd been sharing, he placed a hand beneath her chin and tilted her head.

She met his gaze with wide brown eyes, and he was struck with a connection, a sense of *knowing* he'd felt from the first time they'd met. This woman tied him up in knots, made him want to fix things so he could see her smile and light up just for him.

Shit. He shook his head, not understanding how the hell he'd gone from *never again* to *invested* so quickly.

"What is it?" she asked, breaking into his too-serious thoughts.

He swallowed hard. Forced himself to concentrate on the thread of their conversation and not his emotions. "There is a huge difference between accepting help from a friend who is experienced in these things and falling back into bad patterns," he explained. "Do you trust me?" he asked.

She nodded slowly. "I realize I barely know you, my judgment sucks, but that said, yes, I do."

The notion was humbling. "Good. So go make yourself a cup of tea or get some water. I'll talk to the neighbors and be right back."

"I wish I could do something useful," she muttered, but she rose and walked into the kitchen.

He couldn't tear his gaze from the sexy sway of her hips or the way her hair swung against her back. He bit the inside of his cheek and spent the next few minutes getting his dick to calm down so he could to talk to her neighbors.

His canvass of the two next-door apartments yielded only one result, but at least it was a good one. A middle-aged woman had heard the whole thing. And, she informed Scott, she was the same person who'd found Meg's phone and called her friend after Meg had ended up in the hospital because of her ex the last time. Scott told her the police would be by to interview her and returned to Meg's to find her sitting at the kitchen table with a glass of juice in her hand.

"Good news. Mrs. Booth heard Mike, and she recognized his voice. I put a call into the station and asked them to send someone to take her statement. And yours."

She blew out a long breath and stared at her glass. "Thank you."

He didn't like seeing her so down. He eased into the chair beside her and tucked a strand of hair behind her ear, just so he could touch her again.

Her cheeks flushed, and a flicker of awareness lit her gaze. *There she was.* The passionate woman he knew had returned. "So what were you doing before Mike showed up?" he asked, changing the subject while they waited for the cops.

"Online shopping. Browsing, really. Making lists of what I need for the baby, comparing costs on the big items. Things like that."

"Sounds fun."

A smile lifted her lips, and damned if his gaze didn't zero in on that sweet mouth. The desire to kiss her sucker-punched him, but he remained in his chair, one hand clenched in frustration.

"It is. I don't know the baby's sex, but it's been fun to look at all the cute little baby clothes and think about how I want to decorate for him. Or her."

"Is this a two-bedroom?" he asked, because he wanted to say screw it, throw her over his shoulder, and haul her back to bed, to hell with any damned statements.

All he wanted to do was bury himself inside her while making her come hard and often. Then spend the rest of the night curled around her, keeping her safe and protected.

"No, just one bedroom," she said, oblivious to his sexual frustration and X-rated thoughts.

How the hell he maintained a thread of normal conversation was beyond him.

"I'll put the crib in my room for now. The bedroom is big enough."

He thought about his large house, the one he'd bought as a surprise for his soon-to-be-growing family *before* he'd discovered his wife had had an abortion without asking him. But he'd loved the house and moved in anyway. Four bedrooms, three and a half baths, plenty big for . . . *Shit.*

He was not going there.

"And since my room decor is neutral, I can do whatever I want in the baby area . . ." Meg trailed off, realizing she was rambling, and a hot flush rushed to her cheeks. "I'm really sorry. You can't possibly be interested in decorating talk." She could barely meet his gaze.

"Meg?"

"Yes?" She glanced up at the sound of her name, a rumbling caress coming from his sexy mouth.

His navy eyes were focused on her, and she felt his gaze as if he were physically stroking her skin. Goose bumps lifted on her bare arms.

"Take my word for it. If you're speaking, I'm interested."

And that interest showed in his intent stare and focus. Not to mention she'd felt his erection pressing against her when she'd sat on his lap earlier. She'd done her best not to squirm in her seat.

"Look, I'm sure this can't be easy for you, but life has a way of throwing you curve balls. The important thing is how you roll with them. Have you eaten?" he asked, surprising her with the subject change.

"I was going to make myself a sandwich when I got hungry."

Her stomach chose that moment to grumble, loudly. God, could things get any more embarrassing? She had a hot guy she wanted to jump in her living room, and she was going on about baby furniture while her stomach made unattractive noises.

She'd just have to roll with it, as he'd said. "If you're hungry, I could make you one too? Unless you didn't plan on staying . . ."

"What's wrong?"

"I just realized . . . Why are you here? Don't get me wrong, I'm glad you showed up when you did, but . . . why?" She'd been so thrown by Mike, so relieved to see Scott on the other side of the door, she hadn't thought to ask.

"I came to see how you were doing. And—" He slipped a hand behind her neck, his touch a hot brand on her skin. "I didn't like not speaking to you all week."

Her stomach flipped delightfully at the admission. "I felt the same way," she said, unable to not tell him the truth.

"Now that's good to hear." He spoke in a low, husky voice. Then he moved in, his lips *this* close to hers, his breath warm against her mouth. "Because staying away was fucking hard."

His thumb swiped over her lower lip. A hot, aching feeling settled between her thighs along with dampness and a deep yearning for fulfillment. "Scott—" She didn't know what she wanted to say, just that she wanted—no, needed him.

His eyes darkened with serious intent. She wanted his hot mouth on hers desperately, and barely breathing, she waited for what he'd do next.

But the doorbell rang, jarring them both. She jumped, he swore, and the moment was broken.

"That'll be a cop to take your statement." Scott shot her a look of regret before he rose. He paused and drew a long breath.

His hands, she noted, were clenched in tight fists. At least she wasn't the only one frustrated.

He strode across the room to answer the door, giving Meg a chance to breathe. Stunned, she leaned back against the couch. What the hell had just happened? One minute they'd been talking about restraining orders and baby furniture and the next she'd thought he was going to fuck her right here.

Jesus. She rubbed her eyes and groaned before glancing over to where Scott spoke to a very young-looking uniformed officer.

She studied Scott, pleasure suffusing her as she took him in. In his faded jeans that molded to his hard thighs and taut ass and his navy T-shirt, he was *hot*. Well built, dark hair, and much more clean-cut-looking than the type of guy she usually went for. But everything about Scott was different, from his looks to his commanding air. Meg had been bossed around by men before, but Scott's brand of control made her feel safe and cared for, not put down and concerned.

He affected her emotionally and sexually, tying her in knots of confusion and need. For the last week, thoughts of him had distracted her during the day. She'd sit in her classroom and recall his big hands on her breasts, his mouth on her nipples . . . and then she'd hear a noise and she'd come back to herself, realize she was sitting alone, tingling and aware.

And the nights? He'd consumed her dreams, turning them hot and erotic. She'd actually feel his thick cock pounding into her, going so far as to cause her to orgasm in her sleep. She groaned and squeezed her thighs tightly together, aware and aroused even now.

But because she hadn't been able to stop thinking about him, his silence for the last week had left her thinking she was distinctly forgettable. Meg didn't sleep around often or randomly. That she'd had sex with Scott meant something, no matter how hard she fought the notion. She'd wanted to be memorable in return. Now he was here . . .

"Meg? Ready to talk to Officer Jenkins about what happened with Mike?" Scott called over to her.

At the mention of her ex, all hot, sexy thoughts vanished. She spent the next thirty minutes recounting the visit from her ex, providing a copy of the restraining order, and listening as the cop spoke to her neighbor. By the time the woman finished, Meg was surprised she hadn't complained to the landlord about the problems and noise Meg's issues had caused. But Mrs. Booth seemed sympathetic and understanding. She promised to keep an eye and ear out for her ex while Meg was at work.

Meg thanked her.

The officer jotted down some notes, then flipped the pad closed. "Okay, got it."

"You'll pay Mike Ashton a visit?" Scott asked, although from his tone, it came out as more of a demand.

"We're busy tonight," Officer Jenkins explained, though he didn't sound too upset about it. "And since nothing really happened here other than some noise and disturbance, I'll file the report, and it'll be on record. Meanwhile, keep your door locked."

Scott shook his head and muttered a curse as Meg walked the officer out and locked up behind him.

"He's new and not on my shift." Clearly agitated, he raked his fingers through his hair. "Don't worry, I'll have a talk with your asshole ex and remind him what the fuck a restraining order means."

"No, please don't." The thought of Scott confronting Mike turned her stomach. "It's fine. You don't need to get involved. The officer said if he bothered me again, they'd talk to him. I don't want to get you in any trouble with your superiors."

"Baby?"

She blinked, shocked at how *that* word, the one he used when he was in seduction mode, affected her. Suddenly her body burned hot, desire pulsing inside her again.

"Yes?" she managed to ask, her mouth dry.

"Don't kid yourself," he murmured huskily. "I'm already involved."

Oh. *Oh.* She swiped her tongue across her lips, and his hot gaze followed the gesture. "I . . . Umm . . ."

He grinned at how flustered she'd gotten. "Now I don't know about you, but I'm *starving*," he said in a tone that indicated the word could have two very different meanings.

She shivered, her nipples hardening at the various possibilities.

His gaze fell to the two points sticking out from her shirt, and a low growl sounded from inside his chest. "We'll get to that later," he promised, and her sex clenched at the possibility. "I don't expect you to cook for me, so let's go out and get something to eat. I want to make sure you have strength for later."

And this time, she knew exactly what he was referring to, and she was in complete agreement. She couldn't resist this man and was finished trying. He'd see her get big, and the reality of a baby would send him running soon enough. She pushed that sobering thought away.

He obviously wouldn't let her get away with anything less than a full meal. "I like to cook. Think of it as my way of thanking you for showing up when you did." If not for Scott, she wouldn't have thought to call the police once Mike had left on his own.

"You don't need to thank me, but if you're sure, I'd love to have you *cook* for me." He said the word cook in a rumbling tone.

So hot and gravelly was his voice, he might as well have said, *I'd love to have you fuck me.* She didn't know how she'd make it through the next hour of cooking, dinner, and anticipation.

She turned away, needing to focus on dinner. "I hope you like grilled cheese. I have bakery bread and some really delicious kinds of cheese."

"I'll *eat* anything."

She shivered. God, everything he said made her think of sex.

But he kept her company in the kitchen while she pulled out her frying pan, cover, and other ingredients, and eventually she calmed down while preparing dinner. She was surprised to find herself comfortable with Scott in her personal space. Although . . . comfortable might not be the right word considering how intently he watched her.

And how, beneath his heated gaze, her body buzzed in all the right places. Places she'd been reminding all week to get used to nonuse for the foreseeable future.

Soon the sandwiches began to sizzle. A quick check told her they were ready, and the delicious smell permeated the small kitchen. She served and was beyond pleased when he bit into the sandwich and moaned out loud, the sound too seductive to her ears considering where her thoughts had been.

"This is so good. Where'd you learn to cook? Because I gotta tell you, the most my sisters can manage is to slap cheese on bread in the toaster oven."

She laughed at that. "Well, my mother was similar. I took over meals at a really young age."

"Where was your father?"

She shrugged. "I don't remember him. He left us when I was four. And then it was just me and my mom. She didn't like being alone, and there was a revolving door of men after that."

"That sucks."

She nodded. "I couldn't agree more."

"I wonder what's worse. Not having a father or having one who preferred his other family." He paused, sandwich halfway to his mouth. "I didn't mean to say that out loud."

She reached out and touched his arm, too aware of the muscles beneath her fingers and his hair-roughened skin. "I'm glad you did. It's easier to share if you're not alone when you're doing it."

She'd come late to knowing the Dare family, having just met Olivia through Dylan a few months ago. But of course she'd heard of Robert Dare, hotel mogul, with two families . . . There'd been stories. Whispers around Miami. But she'd never thought about how that had affected his kids.

"What happened?" she asked.

"He wasn't around, and I grew up thinking he was a father who worked really hard for his family. That's what he'd tell us, that he had business trips and he had to visit his various hotels. He'd come home for short periods, spoil us with gifts, and take off again."

Meg watched his face, noting the hard lines visible now. This wasn't an easy subject, yet he was opening up to her. "That's really rough," she murmured.

"It was. And it wasn't. My mom is amazing. You'd really like her—and she'd like you," he said, as if thinking about it had been a revelation. He smiled. "And I had my brothers and sisters. We were cool. But then one day, Dad came home, and there was a big *discussion*." He frowned at the word. "I heard Mom crying, and then they told us we had to go the hospital for tests. Christ."

He wiped a hand over his eyes, and her heart clenched at his visible pain. "They said that Dad had another kid who was sick with cancer and needed bone marrow. He wanted all of us to get tested."

"Oh my God."

"Yeah, except that wasn't the worst part. That came at the hospital when we met his *three* other kids. And that's when the illusion of Dad working hard for his family blew up in all of our faces." Scott rose and took his plate with him to the sink.

She followed, placing her dish on the counter. "What happened to his sick child?"

"My sister Avery was a match. She donated bone marrow, and Sienna's healthy now. Thank God. But I hate him," Scott said tightly, the raw anguish in his eyes as stark as his voice. "For what he did to my mother, to us. For the lies. I don't hate them though. The others."

"That's because they didn't do anything except be born, and you understand that." Although it couldn't have been easy, and she admired the man he'd become, one who was compassionate and understanding despite the curve ball life had thrown at *him*.

"Ian took forever to come around and accept the others," he said of his oldest brother.

"Not everyone handles things the same way."

Scott stood at the sink, head dipped, shoulders tight, arms braced on the counter. It was obvious he didn't repeat this story often and he hated the telling. Yet he'd opened up for her. She wanted to ease his pain. To take him in her arms and soothe him, the way he'd done for her.

On impulse, she stepped behind him and wrapped her arms around his waist, resting her head against his back. "I'm sorry."

He accepted the gesture with a low groan. Then, taking her off guard, he spun around, and she found her back against the counter, his arms bracketing her body, closing her in. He cornered her with his big frame, and her heart rate picked up speed, the serious conversation at odds with the heat passing back and forth between them.

"But you like your other . . . siblings?" she asked, managing to hang on to the thread of conversation although his heat and delicious scent were distracting her. Consuming her.

His lips turned up. "Yeah. They're okay."

She shook her head and laughed. "You're a good guy, Scott Dare."

His smile slipped, and that sexy mouth turned downward in a frown. "That presents a problem then."

She wrinkled her nose, confused. "Why?"

"Because rumor has it you're attracted to bad boys." He braced his hands on her hips, lifted her up, and placed her on the counter, sliding his big body between her legs.

A low hum of anticipation took up residence in her belly—and other places.

"And I want you attracted to only me."

"Not much of a problem there," Meg said, her sex-starved gaze meeting his. "Even after promising myself I'm not going to get involved with any man, I can't stop wanting you."

chapter four

"Well, I want you too, baby." Relief and blinding arousal assaulted Scott at the same time. The wanting was mutual.

Talking about his family always got him wired, and his discussion with Meg had been no different, except now he had a willing, gorgeous woman he could lose himself in. And she gazed up at him expectantly, waiting for his next move. She needed release from her own rioting emotions too, and he was only too happy to provide it.

"Wrap your legs around my waist," he instructed her.

She did as told, and he lifted her into his arms and headed back to the bedroom. His pulse pounded hard, increasing with each step. Once inside, he placed her on the bed. From the minute he'd seen her wide-eyed and panicked earlier, he'd felt a primal need to protect. And when she'd turned to him for comfort, he'd wanted to own her and make sure nobody could hurt her again.

He kicked off his sneakers, removed his socks, then reached down and pulled his shirt over his head, tossing it aside. "I don't know if I can take it slow," he warned her.

Her darkened eyes followed his every movement. "And I don't want you to. I told you once before, I'm not fragile."

She lifted her shirt and threw it the way his had gone, leaving her bare on top, no bra, revealing plump breasts, pink nipples taut and ripe, begging for his lips, his mouth. His teeth.

He hissed out a slow breath, unbuttoning his jeans and shucking them quickly. When he glanced back, she was shimmying out of her sweats, pulling her panties off along with them. She added them to the pile on the floor.

Then he glanced down and took her in—beautiful woman, all glowing skin and flushed cheeks.

"Look what you do to me." He took himself in hand and ran his palm up and down the painfully hard length.

"I am." She pushed herself backward and leaned against the headboard. Her legs were parted, giving him a good look at her glistening pussy. He groaned and pumped his shaft harder.

With an intoxicating smile, she crooked a finger his way. "Come here and let me take care of you."

He shook his head. Much as he wanted those gorgeous lips around his cock, he needed his mouth on her, needed to taste her.

"Not this time." He wrapped his hands around her ankles and pulled her toward the edge of the mattress.

"Aaah!" She shrieked in shock. As she realized his plan, she glanced up at him with dark eyes full of desire and need.

He grasped her thighs and pushed her legs apart, kneeling between them.

"Oh my God."

He chuckled, deliberately blowing warm breath on her soft, damp folds.

"Scott—"

He cut off her words with a long swipe of his tongue, and a shuddering moan escaped her throat, causing him to begin teasing her pussy in earnest. He licked her bare outer lips, working his way inward, sliding his tongue up and down, all over her sex, everywhere except the tight bud that needed his attention the most.

She bucked beneath him, writhing, groaning, cursing, and begging him to make her come. He enjoyed her like this, open to him, vocal, and willing to express what she needed. Because that was his mission, to satisfy her in every possible way.

But before he slid inside her tight, hot sex and found his own release—something that would happen way too fast once he felt her slick walls cushioning his cock—he wanted her mindless and crazy, so he kept up his sensual assault now.

He eased her down from the peak, turning his hard licks and nibbles to softer strokes, not wanting her to come just yet. He soothed her with soft flickers that didn't do anything except arouse and tease. Only when he was sure she'd lost that edge did he begin again, nuzzling her with his nose, inhaling her feminine scent, and sliding his tongue into her hot, wet channel.

Her hips began to buck beneath him, and he fucked her this way, tormenting her and again bringing her higher and higher with his mouth.

"God, Scott, please, I need to come." She arched and pushed herself up against his lips, her pleading voice so sweet to his ears, he was ready to give her what she needed.

He licked his way to her clit, easing up one side, then down the other. Her thighs trembled, and her entire body drew taut and poised. He flattened his tongue over the tiny bud at the same time he slid one long finger inside her.

"Yes, so close, so, so . . ." Her words were nearly incoherent, and he hooked his finger forward, gliding the pad along her inner walls, hoping to hit just the right spot.

She screamed and shattered around his finger, her pussy contracting in deep, damp spasms, as she ground herself against him to ride out the assault.

Damn, but the sound of her coming, the feel of her suctioning his finger, had his balls drawn up painfully tight. When he was certain she'd finished, he rubbed his mouth along her thigh, and she collapsed against the mattress.

He opened her drawer, found a condom, and sheathed himself in record time. He stood over her, hands on her thighs.

Heavy-lidded eyes looked up at him, a satisfied expression on her face that made him damn proud.

"You still with me, baby?"

Was she still with him? Barely, Meg thought, her body still spasming with delicious aftershocks. She managed a small nod, then took a second to study his too-handsome face, the sexy mouth that had just taken her to heaven, and the hard set of his jaw, so at odds with the caring man who'd been here for her earlier. She didn't know how she'd be up for anything, but she wanted to please him too.

He poised himself at her entrance. "You're so fucking amazing," he said, his words tugging at emotions she was having little success tamping down.

He slid into her slowly, letting her become accustomed to him, first the tip, then, inch by excruciatingly slow inch, the rest of his length. There was no need to take it easy. Her body opened for him, just as she feared her heart could, easily and gladly, taking him inside. He aroused nerve endings she'd thought had passed out from his earlier onslaught.

Warmth spread through her veins, and a quickening began deep inside her, sending out delicious tingles to the rest of her system. He pulled out and thrust in on a slow, exquisite glide. She arched her back and tried to suck him in farther. He groaned and picked up rhythm, and so did her body, another orgasm shockingly not too far out of reach.

He leaned over and braced his arms on either side of her head, his gaze hot and steady on hers. "Feel me, baby?" he asked on a hard plunge that took him deep.

"Yes," she moaned, and he began to pound into her in earnest.

She arched against him, which had the effect of rubbing her clit against his hair-roughened skin. She whimpered, shocked by the needy sound, but it felt so good she couldn't breathe. She closed her eyes and focused on the sensations pummeling at her from inside and out. Lights and flashes sparkled behind her eyelids as another orgasm loomed closer.

"That's it, let it build," he said thickly. Every time their bodies crashed together, he ground his hips and pelvis harder against her sex.

Her entire body was on fire as he rocked into her, their joined bodies doing the work, taking her higher than she'd ever been before. The tremors didn't start small; they washed over her in a tidal wave of bliss. Nothing had ever felt so perfect or right.

He thrust a few more times, coming inside her as he shouted her name. He collapsed on top of her, and she accepted his weight, wrapping her arms around his sweat-dampened skin.

A little while later, they'd climbed beneath the covers. Scott lay propped up against the pillows, one well-muscled arm beneath his head. "You okay?" he asked.

She nodded. "More than okay."

Too okay, too sated, too happy for the situation she was in, but she wasn't going to dwell. Things would end on their own soon enough. She didn't have to do anything to push it along. She'd already learned she couldn't deny this man, nor did she want to.

"So . . . you really came here tonight because you missed me?" She lifted herself up on her side and met his gaze.

"I really did." His lips turned upward in a sexy grin.

"Good timing."

That ended his smile. "Yeah, about that. My brother runs a security company, and I'm going to have him start digging into your ex and his background. We'll figure out why the hell he won't just leave you alone without you having to talk to him again."

At the thought of having another conversation with Mike, she shivered, more out of dread that there would be very little talking done if he ever got near her.

"Hey." Scott pulled her against him, tucking her firmly beneath his arm and against his chest. His heat not only warmed her body but also took away the chill caused by fear.

"I can't afford to pay him," she said of Tyler.

"Yeah, well, here's the thing." As he spoke, Scott ran his hand up and down her bare arm, his touch arousing her despite the topic of conversation. Her nipples tightened, and she knew they were now poking into his skin. He kept up the light caress and continued talking. "Tyler offered me a job."

"Don't you already have a job? You're a cop."

"And I'm bored as shit. Not to mention I'm on administrative leave," he muttered.

Oh, this was interesting. "Really? Why? What happened?"

He let out a low chuckle. "Apparently I don't follow the rules too well."

She shook her head. "You mean you'd rather make them? Who would have thunk it!" she teased.

Before she could blink, he flipped her onto her back and straddled her with his large body. "Are you making fun of me, Ms. Thompson?"

She wanted to laugh, but the stern look in his gaze had that giggle catching in the back of her throat. "No, I would never do that." She bit the inside of her cheek and tried not to let any sound escape. He looked like he was just itching for a chance to torment her if she did. She wasn't sure she could handle any of his sensual teasing.

He skimmed his fingers up the sides of her body, pausing as he came to the swells of her breasts and tracing beneath the sensitive mounds.

She stifled a long moan.

"As I was saying," he continued, "my brother offered me a job. Actually he wants me to buy into his company and partner with him," Scott said, sounding surprised. But as he spoke to her, he kept touching her, skimming her breasts with his knuckles, tracing a circle around her areolas with his fingers.

"Ooh." She let out a moan.

He narrowed his gaze. "We're talking," he reminded her.

She wanted to pout but knew better. For some reason, he wanted to mix up conversation and foreplay. Bad man. Somehow she had to focus, because she sensed this was an important topic to him. Very important, and he was choosing her to confide in.

She drew a deep breath to steady herself. "Why do you sound shocked that he'd ask you to be his partner?" she asked.

He paused, his hands stilling. "I'm impressed you picked up on that," he said. "Tyler's just two years older than me, but I always looked up to him. Especially after he joined the army. He's successful now that he's home too. That he'd want me to join him means a lot."

She reached up and traced his jaw with her fingertips, the stubble prickling her skin in a delightful way. "You're smart and successful. Why wouldn't he want you?"

He shrugged. "It's just not something I ever thought was on his radar."

"Are you considering leaving the force?" she asked.

"Yes." He appeared startled at his admission. "I was considering it after he asked, and then I came here . . . You'd been traumatized and I realized, hell yes, this is what I would rather do. Protect people on my own terms."

She smiled up at him, pleased she'd been able to help him decide things, even if she hated what was going on in her own life at the moment. "I think you'll be fantastic at whatever you put your mind to."

He stared down at her, mouth parted as he studied her.

"That means a lot."

Her heart fluttered at his words, but before she could start dissecting his meaning, Scott grasped her wrists in his hands and pinned them back against the mattress.

"I need to fuck you," he said. "We can finish talking later."

She blinked up at him, her gaze settling on his darkening eyes, the razor stubble marking his jaw and his messed hair. Need and want poured through her at the sight of him poised over her. Wanting her.

"Umm . . . okay?" Who was she to argue?

He tipped his head back and chuckled. "I can't remember the last time I laughed during sex. You're the whole package," he said as he settled his cock at her entrance, then swore. "Shit. Condom."

She bit her lip, wondering if she should do this. "Pregnancy isn't an issue, obviously." The words escaped, deciding for her. "And after my asshole ex got me pregnant and bailed, I got tested . . . just in case. So unless you—"

"I'm clean. Tested for work. And I really want to feel you bare, baby." He raised his hips and drove forward, impaling her in one smooth thrust.

"Oh God." She felt him everywhere. So hard and thick, smooth yet not, it was an exquisite difference, and she reveled in the increased friction and sensation.

"I hear you." He slid out and back, his eyes a hazy dark blue, filled with desire as he picked up rhythm. No slow and easy this time, and she was grateful for it. She didn't want time to think or, even worse, feel.

He tightened his grip on her wrists and took her with unrelenting drives that had her coming without buildup or warning.

"Scott!" She screamed his name. Fought to free her hands, to grab on to him as she shattered, but he held on tight. The firm binding merely heightened the experience, intensified her orgasm, and she might even have blacked out for a second. She barely remembered him coming too.

Later, as he slept beside her, Meg's thoughts worked in a frenzied panic as she tried to make sense of his sudden intrusion into her life. She'd been so determined to make a go of it alone. So sure she could easily hang on to her resolve not to get involved or rely on any man. Then Scott Dare bulldozed his way into her life and her bed.

She listened to his deep, even breathing and felt the heavy press of his arm curled around her waist. He was so strong and solid, so . . . reliable. He reminded her of Dylan, her high school boyfriend and, later in life, her best friend.

She blew out a deep breath. Dylan had been her one and only decent choice. A really great guy, and though their initial breakup had been mutual when they'd gone off to college, when they'd met up again later, she'd fallen again hard. He hadn't. And when he'd said they were better as just friends, she'd swallowed her feelings and pride and agreed, telling him she felt the same way. Better to have him in her life as a friend than to lose him because her feelings made him uncomfortable.

At this point, all she felt for Dylan was a brotherly friendship. But back then? His unwitting rejection had reinforced the truth. Good guys didn't find Meg worthy of sticking around. No guy did. First her father, who wasn't a good guy. Then Dylan, who really was. Point made. And she'd chosen accordingly after that, picking the worst, hoping for the best, and never, ever getting it.

Scott was a challenge because Meg knew herself. She had a horrible tendency to fall hard and fast, and this man, with his protective tendencies and bossy air, would make it way too easy.

But soon enough, he'd realize he didn't want to stick around as she grew big with another man's baby. Why would he want to raise someone else's kid?

A sharp pain sliced through her chest, but she relished the warning. The pain would help her remember and stay strong. Like Dylan, Scott would get tired of her needy ways. He'd turn away from Meg and the ready-made family she came with. No matter how nicely he handled it, if she wasn't prepared, his rejection would break her, like Dylan's nearly had.

She'd just have to be aware and stronger than her heart. She would enjoy him now, but she wouldn't allow herself to get attached. Either she'd walk away first or she'd be prepared when he decided the time came.

Scott woke up in Meg's bed, the sun streaming through the windows, feeling one hundred percent different about this morning after than the last one. He'd pushed past her reserve and her walls, and with a little luck, she wouldn't grow cold and distant this morning. They had places to go and people to see. And he wanted to spend time with her outside of bed.

Last night had been phenomenal. Not just the sex, although Jesus . . . He'd never been with a woman without using a condom. Neither he nor Leah had wanted kids, and he'd always used protection. True, it had failed, but he'd used it. So Meg? Feeling her hot walls clasping around him, knowing there was nothing between them, it was heaven times a fucking thousand. Not to mention she could read him well. She'd figured out immediately there was more to his feelings about Tyler's offer than just whether or not he should leave his job. The brother he admired and looked up to found him worthy of joining him as an equal. That also rocked.

Life was looking up, he thought, heading for the bathroom. He showered, once again using Meg's soap and shampoo and getting hard as he inhaled the familiar scent. It reminded him of Meg, how she looked in bed, dark hair splayed around her, big brown eyes looking up at him with trust and arousal twinkling in the chocolate depths.

Fuck. He gripped his cock and began pumping with his hand, using the soap that smelled like her to lubricate his hand as he pretended it was her tight pussy tugging at him and milking him to completion. It didn't take long for him to come in long spurts, giving him a shot at getting through the day without dragging her into a secluded place somewhere to ease the constant ache.

He dressed in yesterday's clothes and decided a stop at his place was in order. He strode into the kitchen to find Meg standing at the counter, drinking the same pink protein shake as last time.

"Morning."

She turned toward him and grinned. "Morning to you too."

Muscles he hadn't realized he'd been clenching released at her easy greeting. He strode over, determined to set the tone not just for the day but for how he wanted things to be between them from now on.

He slid a hand behind her neck and pulled her in for a long, deep, strawberry-tasting kiss. He made sure to taste her completely, his tongue stroking the inner recesses of her mouth, before he ended it with a quick swipe of her lower lip.

"Delicious," he murmured, meeting her gaze and amused by the dazed look in her pretty brown eyes.

"What's on your agenda today?" he asked.

"Nothing exciting," she said, turning away and heading for the sink, where she busied herself rinsing her glass.

He narrowed his gaze. "Remember what I said? Everything about you interests me. What's up today?" he asked again.

"I need to go maternity clothes shopping," she muttered, not turning around.

He walked over and surrounded her, wrapping his arms around her waist. "I can manage a stop by the mall."

She shook her head. "No. You do not want to come while I try on fat clothes."

She set the glass in the sink and attempted to wrench away from him, but he held her in place. "What the hell, Meg?" He turned her around and lifted her chin. Tears burned in her eyes, and he narrowed his gaze. "Fat clothes?" he asked, trying not to get angry and to understand instead.

She remained stubbornly silent.

He shook his head, totally at a loss. Sometimes women fucking confounded him. "What's with the embarrassment?"

"Men," she muttered. She sniffed and shook her head. "Sure, you're here now. My body is reasonably fit. I'm not stupid enough to think you'll still be here when I'm big like a whale, so can we skip the embarrassment of you seeing me shopping for stretchy pants with a pouch in front? I'm sure you have better things to do, and besides, I already have plans with my friend Lizzy."

He blew out a long breath, finally understanding. Or he thought he did. "I realize we're getting to know each other, but can you give me a little credit? It's not like I didn't know you were pregnant going into this." He was still attracted to her. And that was that.

"Whatever," Meg said.

He had sisters, which meant he knew she was going to believe what she wanted to, his words be damned. Fine. He'd just go along with the program.

"I need to stop home and change into clean clothes. Then I thought we'd go by my brother's and give him information to start digging into your ex. After that?" He'd concede defeat on this one. "You can go to the mall while I head over to work and talk to my boss."

"I wasn't aware I needed permission," she said, trying to remain sweet but make her point. She caught his *look*. "Are you giving notice?"

"Something like that," he muttered.

She wouldn't like the next part of his plan, so he intended to put off explaining it to her until her mood and feelings about him improved. He fully expected the fireworks to start again when she found out he wasn't leaving her alone to deal with her lurking ex.

The ride to Scott's took longer than Meg expected, and by the time he pulled off an exit on I-95, she had a throbbing headache. And when he turned onto a tree-lined street with set-back houses—big Spanish-style houses in the adobe coloring she loved, with gates around each—the dull ache turned to a searing pain. "You live here?"

"Sure do."

"On a cop's salary? Not that it's my business," she quickly said, realizing how rude and uncalled-for her remark had been. "I'm sorry. I'm just surprised."

He turned, his gaze hidden behind really sexy aviators. "I get it. And for the record, I want you to feel like you can ask me anything." He turned into a long driveway and parked by a two-car garage. He pulled off the sunglasses and left them on the dashboard.

"Okay . . . Then how do you live here?" she asked, feeling a bit braver but still overwhelmed by the upscale neighborhood.

"My mother's parents passed away, and when my grandfather died, he left us kids each a very nice trust fund. For me, it was a way to separate myself from my father's money."

She studied him without interrupting, wanting to understand this enigmatic, complicated man.

He shut off the ignition and twisted to face her. "When I was married, we lived in an apartment in South Beach."

"Married?" This was the first she'd heard of it, and she couldn't believe the uncomfortable twisting in her belly. She had to remind herself that he'd said he *had been* married. He wasn't currently. And he'd been understanding of her past, so she could do no less for him.

He let out a groan. "It was a couple of years ago," he said, gripping the steering wheel hard. "And in truth, Leah, my ex-wife, was more interested in my family name and status than me. But at the time, I didn't really care. I thought I loved her, and I wanted her to be happy. What I didn't realize was that she hated me being a cop and thought I'd eventually give it up because she wanted me to." He shook his head. "I wouldn't, and we had many arguments over my hours and my job."

Meg let out a relieved breath. Because he'd only *thought* he'd loved his ex and because he was giving up being a cop *now* and his ex had nothing to do with why.

He reached out and toyed with a long strand of her hair. "What's going on in that beautiful head of yours?"

She glanced up at him and smiled. "That's a secret." And she wasn't about to reveal she'd been jealous.

His frown and the warning in his dark gaze promised retribution of the most sensual kind, and she squirmed in her seat.

"The house?" she reminded him.

"Right. Umm, things changed between us, and I decided we needed more space."

"Changed how?" Meg asked.

He grasped her hand and ran his thumb over the pulse point in her wrist. Her sex spasmed, and she swallowed a moan.

"I want to tell you," he said. "I just don't think this is the right time. Can you trust me and will you wait?"

She drew a deep breath. Now she was even more curious, but if he wanted time, she'd give it to him. "Okay. Yes. I can wait. Can I see the house though?"

His expression lightened, and he nodded. "Let's go."

He opened the garage with a remote in his vehicle and came around to her side of the car, helping her out. He clasped her hand and led her through the garage. They walked directly into a laundry room that doubled as a mud room, with hooks for jackets and a high-end washer and dryer along the far wall.

She still used the laundry room in her building, pumping money in to do her clothes, and this setup made her mouth water. Especially since she'd be trudging up and down with a baby in her arms . . . somehow, anyway. She preferred not to think about the details, which were still seven months away and completely overwhelming.

They stepped into a white ceramic-tiled hallway, passed a powder room, and ended up in a massive great room that led to a backyard with a pool, protected by gates that surrounded the glistening water, and a gorgeous patio with padded furniture and a built-in stone grill.

"Scott, this is beautiful."

He strode up behind her and wrapped his arms around her, his body hot. "You really like it?"

What's not to like? she wondered. "I love it. Really."

She spun around, taking in the furniture: a deep-maroon sectional L-shaped couch meant more for comfort than show with a huge table in front of it and a recliner nearby. A fireplace with a large-screen TV sat in front of the sofa, and the décor was simple and tasteful.

"Did your ex decorate?" she asked.

He placed a soft kiss on her neck, causing her to shiver. "No. I didn't move in until after the divorce."

Her breath left her in a rush. That mattered, she realized, although she wasn't certain why.

"Someday, we're going to christen this place," he said, his husky tone a promise that turned her body to liquid desire. "But not today, unfortunately. Make yourself comfortable; look around. I'll run up, change, and be right back."

She knew he'd showered at her place. His hair had been damp when he'd come into the kitchen. "Go ahead. I'm fine." He kissed her again and headed toward a staircase on the far side of the house.

She drew in a deep breath and took in this beautifully decorated, expensive home. More than ever, she was certain she needed to watch her heart. Because a man like Scott, who had everything going for him, was way out of her league.

chapter five

Scott returned from the bedroom with a small duffel bag in his hand to leave in his car. He didn't want to get stuck at Meg's place again without clean clothes, and he wasn't leaving her alone unless he was sure she was protected. He was just grateful she didn't ask about the bag because he doubted she'd appreciate the answer. Her independent streak would kick in, and he'd rather save the argument for another time.

When they arrived at Tyler's office, he took in the atmosphere as if for the first time, knowing his life was about to take a drastic turn. Double Down Security was located in a high-end building meant to impress big-name clients. Scott knew his brother didn't give a shit about appearances, but he did know how to play the game. He gave clients the perception they wanted and the protection they paid for. It was a win-win.

Scott had given his brother a heads-up that he'd be bringing Meg by, and Tyler stepped out of his office to greet them. He slapped Scott on the back and turned to Meg. "I'm Tyler Dare," he said by way of introduction.

"Meg Thompson." She held out her hand, which Tyler engulfed in his larger one. "I can see the family resemblance," she said, her gaze going back and forth between them.

"Just a resemblance though. I'm the better-looking brother." Tyler winked.

Scott rolled his eyes. "Ignore him. He's a pain in the ass."

Meg laughed, the sound warming Scott inside.

"My little brother just can't handle the competition," Tyler said, his gaze never leaving Meg as he assessed her for the first time.

"Little, my ass," Scott muttered.

"And I hate to break it to you, but I don't see any competition," Meg replied, teasing Tyler right back.

A small smirk kicked up the corners of her mouth, and Scott burst out laughing. "She told you," he said to his brother, inwardly pleased she'd stood up for him.

Tyler chuckled. "I like her," he said to Scott. "Okay, so what can I do for you two?"

Scott turned to Meg. "I called Tyler earlier and explained the situation with Mike." He glanced at Tyler. "I'd like to set Meg up with Luke. I want all the information I can get on her ex and his family. There has to be a reason a guy who doesn't want anything to do with a baby is still harassing her. She just wants him to sign away his rights. You'd think he'd be happy to do it."

Tyler's gaze darkened as he listened. Like Scott and Ian, the Dare men were protective of women. And once the woman meant something to one of them? Things got personal.

"Okay, I'll introduce you to Luke Williams. He'll open a case file and take information from you. Don't worry," he said to Meg. "We'll get to the bottom of things and get him off your back."

"Thank you," she said.

"Baby, are you comfortable talking to Luke alone? I need five minutes with my brother, and then I'll join you."

"Of course." Meg straightened her shoulders. "This is my problem. Take all the time you need."

"I think my brother considers it his problem too," Tyler said, wrapping an arm around Meg's shoulders and leading her toward the back rooms. "Meet me in my office," he called over his shoulder to Scott.

A few minutes later, Tyler rejoined Scott in his office. The space was large, with a wall of windows overlooking the city. Because Tyler didn't have a woman in his life, their mother, Emma, had taken over decorating. The office proclaimed elegance and class, from the mahogany desk with intricate carvings and detail to the glass and brass accents and live plants, which Scott knew Tyler's assistant watered for him. In frames on the desk, there were pictures of Tyler and the family, their mother and their siblings. The office was professional.

"She's very different than your ex," Tyler said, cutting to the chase as usual. He didn't bother with small talk when he had a point to make.

"Yes, she is. I take it you think that's a good thing?"

"Rhetorical question." Tyler met his gaze with similar navy-violet eyes. "I don't like it that she's walking around looking over her shoulder."

"Me neither, obviously. I showed up last night, and she was freaked out. The bastard had been by, banging on her door, yelling, and demanding to see her. The restraining order doesn't mean a damned thing to him."

Tyler rolled a pen between his palms. "Let's see what Luke comes up with."

"I made a decision," Scott said, also getting right to the point. He wanted to get back to Meg as soon as possible. "I accept your offer. I'm in."

Tyler rose to his feet and strode around the desk, pulling Scott in for a brotherly hug. "That's fucking good news."

"Hope your military employee pals agree."

"No worries. You know most of them. These guys take orders like they were born to it. They know I've wanted to bring you in for a while now."

"Way to share that with me."

Tyler shrugged. "I needed you to be ready and willing to say yes."

Scott inclined his head, understanding. "I am. In fact, I'm heading over to the station after this."

"Giving notice?"

"If I were on active duty, yeah. Given how shitty things have been? My captain will be happy to have me gone." And Scott would relish telling his boss he was leaving. "Besides, I need to free up my time to make sure that asshole doesn't get anywhere near Meg."

Tyler nodded approvingly. "She know you're about to be around twenty-four seven?"

"Not yet." Scott braced his hands on the chair and pushed himself up. "Let's go see what's going on."

Tyler eyed him with his assessing gaze. "You've got it bad."

Scott didn't deny it.

"Pretty damned fast."

He shrugged. "When you know, you know."

"And I wouldn't." Tyler shook his head and started for the door.

"Someday you will . . . and I can't wait to watch you fall."

"Fuck you," his brother muttered.

Tyler chuckled, and they headed to find Meg.

Meg liked Luke Williams. Blond, big, and imposing-looking, he was pure military, from his commanding posture to the crew cut of his hair. But he was warm and understanding when he listened to her story and wrote down the information on Mike and his family. Not that Meg knew much.

"When I met him, he was estranged from his parents. He said they were wealthy and demanding and expected more of him than he could possibly give." She shrugged. "I felt bad. He seemed like a nice, if misunderstood, guy."

It wasn't like she deliberately went after losers. It seemed like they became that way later on. Or, more likely, they didn't show her their true natures until after she'd been drawn in and had opened her heart to them . . . and, in Mike's case, her home as well. But she was finished putting up with shit from men. Done feeling used and taken advantage of.

"I just want to know what the hell he wants from me. Why he won't just sign away his rights and go away. I know my lawyer's sent the forms."

Luke looked up from the computer, where he'd been tapping away, taking notes. He spun his chair around and placed a comforting hand on her shoulder. "We'll get to the bottom of this. And we'll keep you safe."

She appreciated his words of assurance.

"Hey, Williams! Hands off the clients," Scott barked from the doorway.

Meg jumped at the unexpected angry tone in his voice.

Luke merely glanced up, met Scott's annoyed gaze, and grinned, slowly removing his hand, as if he had all the time in the world. "Nice to see you too, little Dare."

Meg stiffened, her eyes opening wider at the snarky, condescending comment.

Was Luke looking for a fight? If so, from the furious expression on Scott's face, he wouldn't mind obliging him.

Jaw clenched, he started forward, but Tyler placed a firm hand on his brother's arm, stopping him. "Luke, Scott's agreed to join me here. Which makes him your boss."

Luke rose from his seat and strode toward the two men, and Meg held her breath. She wasn't thrilled with Scott staking a claim on her in front of his brother and Luke, yet at the same time, she couldn't deny a part of her liked his possessiveness. Rather, she liked the *thoughts* behind the possessiveness, if not the behavior itself.

"You're joining us," Luke repeated. "That is great fucking news, man. Welcome aboard." Luke slapped Scott hard on the back.

The hit, which would have sent most other men reeling, didn't have an impact. Scott merely grinned and clasped the other man's hand in return.

"Thanks." Scott's voice deepened, the meaning in that one word clear. "And I meant what I said. Hands off *this* client."

Meg rose to her feet, determined to stop this ridiculous display. "Scott—"

"No worries," Luke said, both hands raised in the air in deferral. "I had no idea she was yours."

"I'm not anyone's!" she said. "And besides, do I look like a piece of meat for you two to fight over?"

Tyler burst out laughing. "I don't think you want either one of them to answer that," he said. "Have you made any progress?" he asked Luke.

Luke nodded. "She's given me enough to start."

"Great. I need to go meet with my captain. And Meg has plans with a friend."

"You two go on. We have everything under control and in place," Tyler assured him.

Meg hoped he was right. Because her safety was at stake.

Meg didn't bring up Scott and Luke's pissing contest on the way back to her place to pick up her car. She didn't know what to do with the events of the morning, and she put aside thoughts of Scott, his beautiful home, and how she suddenly had a security firm she couldn't afford digging into Mike's life. It was easier to focus on maternity clothes than the sudden one-eighty her life had taken.

When she checked her cell phone, Meg found Lizzy had left a message canceling their afternoon shopping trip because she'd come down with a nasty stomach bug. Determined to get this shopping excursion over with, Meg called Olivia. Luckily, the other woman was up for a mall trip.

She had to admit she was surprised Scott had given in so easily on not accompanying her, but she was grateful. She needed a break from his intensity and his protective nature. She liked it. Too much. So maybe it was her own surprising desires she needed a break from.

She parked and headed inside to the food court, where she'd agreed to meet up with Olivia. The other woman was waiting, but to Meg's surprise, she wasn't alone.

"Hi," Meg said, joining Olivia and a petite, dark-haired woman at a small table with three chairs.

"Hi!" Olivia rose and pulled her into a hug. "I brought my sister-in-law, Riley, along. Riley, meet Meg. I figured you and I could use an expert for our first maternity expedition."

Riley raised a hand and waved. "Hi, Meg. Hope you don't mind me intruding."

Meg shook her head. "Of course not. If you have advice, I'm happy to hear it. When my jeans wouldn't close the other night, I nearly burst into tears. They fit a few days ago. I'm a little overwhelmed," she admitted.

"I'm the mother of an eighteen-month-old. I now have expertise on things I never thought I could handle. Mind if I finish my coffee before we walk around?" Riley asked.

"Of course not."

"Want to get anything?" Olivia offered.

"No, I'm fine." Meg settled into a chair at the table, and the other women took their seats again.

"So speaking of your eighteen-month-old, where is your . . ." Meg trailed off, not knowing if Riley had a boy or a girl.

"Daughter," Riley supplied. "Her name is Rainey. She's with my mother-in-law." Like any good mom, Riley pulled out her phone and showed off a picture of her baby.

"Isn't she the cutest?" Olivia asked. "She has Ian's eyes."

Meg leaned over the table and glanced at the screen on the phone. Actually, the baby had Scott's eyes, Meg realized, staring into the cherubic face with dark-navy eyes and pudgy cheeks.

"She's absolutely gorgeous," Meg said, unable to keep from grinning at the adorable baby with the cute smile.

"Thank you. She also has her father's . . . shall we say *dominant* personality? Stubborn as heck already," Riley said with affection in her tone.

"You don't say? That controlling personality runs in the family?" Meg met Olivia's gaze just as her friend burst out laughing.

"What am I missing?" Riley asked.

"Oh. Nothing," Meg said. "I just meant—"

"Meg is . . . involved with Scott," Olivia chimed in before Meg could formulate an explanation.

"Your *brother* Scott?" Riley asked.

Meg shook her head and swallowed a groan. "We're not really involved, we're just . . . I mean, Scott is helping me out with a situation." Meg liked her interpretation. Better than telling Riley she was sleeping with the other woman's brother-in-law.

"Is that how you want to play it?" Olivia asked, an amused smile touching her lips.

Meg blew out a long breath. Obviously nothing was sacred among these women, and the truth was, Meg needed female input. Especially from women who knew the Dare men firsthand. "Fine. We're involved. I think."

Olivia grinned, making it obvious to Meg that she approved.

"And I take it from your comment about my daughter's personality that you find Scott controlling?" Riley asked, laughter twinkling in her eyes.

"You could say that. But I'm not trying to insult him or your family," Meg rushed to add.

Riley shook her head. "Oh, honey. You think Scott's controlling? Ian is Scott on steroids. Times fifty."

Meg stared at the petite woman in awe. "How do you handle him?"

"Don't let her fool you. She has my brother wrapped around her finger." Olivia propped an arm on the table and waved her fingers in the air.

"Except it isn't always easy," Riley said. "And in the beginning, it nearly broke us apart more than once." She bit down on her lip. "I really had an issue with controlling men because of my past, and I wasn't used to turning to anyone for help. Especially when that help came in the form of being told what to do."

Like Meg had an issue with leaning on Scott. "I get that," she murmured. "I feel the same way. Scott took me over to Tyler's security firm this morning. I can't afford to hire them, but he has them helping me anyway." She shook her head. "I'm grateful but . . . I'd just promised myself I would stop relying on other people. Men in particular."

"But it's a different kind of reliance, isn't it?" Olivia asked.

Meg thought about the answer. "Yes. Very different. Before, I just wanted any man in my life, and I'd accept almost anyone to not be alone," she said, ducking her head in embarrassment. "Can we go shopping now? I don't think you two together women need to listen to my problems."

She rose from her seat and pushed her chair in so no one would trip. Olivia and Meg joined her, and together they walked toward the stores.

"I wasn't all that together when Ian and I met," Riley said, surprising Meg by continuing their talk.

She glanced at the pretty brunette.

"I fought everything Ian did for me to the point where I ended up in the hospital because I was so insistent on meeting up with my father and handling things alone." Riley placed a hand on Meg's arm, and they slowed to a stop. "My point is, we all have problems and issues, but please don't think you have to go through it alone."

To Meg's horror, tears filled her eyes at Riley's openness and generosity. She pulled a tissue from her bag and wiped her eyes. "Thank you," she said.

Olivia tapped her shoulder. "Do you think *I* had it together when Dylan and I started seeing each other?"

Meg shrugged. "I don't know. He didn't confide in me about you." Which had been her first clue that her best friend had fallen in love.

"Well, I was a mess. So wrapped up in my past I didn't want to trust any man. So listen to Riley. She's smart. And just know we've both been there."

"Except I'm pregnant," Meg said, pointing out the obvious. "And I honestly don't think your brother has dealt with what that means. So while I'm really grateful to have his support and help now, I don't expect him to stick around for too long."

She blew out a long breath, not wanting to dwell on that thought or the tears would return, and they wouldn't be happy or grateful ones. "Now can we go shopping?"

"In a second." Olivia pursed her lips and hesitated before she spoke. "I also understand how you feel. And I'm not saying you shouldn't be wary. Be smart. Protect yourself if you feel you need to."

For some reason, hearing her friend say the things she'd already been telling herself about Scott really hurt. Because it validated her fear that he would eventually realize she came with too many burdens and he wouldn't stick around.

"Don't worry, I'll be careful. Besides, I have more to worry about than myself and my feelings." She patted her belly. "And I wouldn't burden Scott with my—"

"Whoa. That is not what I was saying," Olivia rushed to assure her, sounding horrified. "I just meant I think it's always smart to prepare for the worst. But Meg, it's okay to hope for the best too."

That's what she'd always done, with each new guy, only to be disappointed every time. But every instinct she had told her Scott was different. She knew for certain he desired her. In bed, they were explosive. She enjoyed talking to him, spending time with him. Getting to know more about what made him tick. And she had to admit it was a relief not dealing with Mike on her own.

"You need to start believing that things are going to turn around for you. And I think you should trust Scott. If nothing else, he's a man of his word. If he says he's in, he means it. If he changes his mind, he'll be honest about that too. But if he does, he'd be an idiot. And even though he drives me insane, my brother is not stupid," Olivia said.

Meg nodded. "You're right. I'm going to look at things differently." For right now, Scott wasn't going anywhere. And she should enjoy every minute for as long as she could.

"Now that that's settled, let's go buy out the store for you two pregnant women," Riley said.

With the heavy subjects out of the way, Meg had a blast shopping with Riley and Olivia. Riley did know what clothing was comfortable and what wasn't, directing them away from certain styles and brands and toward others. Meg and Olivia took turns trying on the padded bellies, making sure the clothes they bought would last longer than a few weeks. They laughed over what they'd look like down the road and ignored the more graphic things Riley tried to warn them about. Meg wasn't ready to purchase moisturizer for dry nipples quite yet.

From the store, they went to a late lunch. By the time they finished, Meg felt happier and more relaxed than she had in a long while.

She stretched her legs beneath the table. "This meal . . . this whole shopping trip was amazing."

"I think we should make it weekly," Olivia said.

"My mother-in-law would love to have Rainey once a week. I'm in," Riley said. "I need girl time."

"Hey," Olivia said, leaning on the round table and speaking in what sounded like a conspiratorial whisper. "Do you think we should tell the waiter it's Rick's birthday? They make a whole big deal. All the waiters clap and sing, and everyone in the restaurant usually joins in."

"Who's Rick?" Meg and Riley asked at the same time.

"Rick Devlin. Your security guy." Olivia tipped her head to the right.

"What are you talking about? I don't have security." Meg followed the direction to see a guy with military bearing sitting at a table alone. Her stomach churned uneasily as realization dawned. "He looks exactly like the guys wandering around Tyler's office. But nobody said anything about someone *watching* me."

"Okay, I think I misspoke," Riley said. "Ian is Scott on steroids. Times twenty-five, not fifty. I think he's got more of that dominant gene in him than I realized." She sighed and took a long sip of her iced tea.

"Are you telling me Scott is having someone follow me?" Meg asked, horrified.

"I thought you knew!" Olivia muttered. "You said you were at Tyler's this morning and that Scott has them helping you."

"He's got a computer guy digging for information on my ex and his family!"

Olivia shifted uncomfortably in her chair. "When I recognized Rick, I just assumed you knew. He works personal security for Tyler. That makes him your bodyguard, for lack of a better word. He's had an eye on us all day."

"I'm going to kill Scott." Meg ripped a paper napkin apart in frustration.

"He obviously wants you safe. If you think about it, it's kind of sweet," Olivia said, obviously trying to dig her brother—and herself by extension—out of trouble. Because she'd called Meg's attention to the man.

"R-i-g-h-t," Meg said, drawing out the word. "Because if Dylan had a man assigned to guard you and follow you around without your permission, you'd find it sweet. Good to know."

Riley giggled out loud. "She's got you there," she told Olivia.

"Shut up," Olivia muttered. "I'm so screwed. Scott is going to kill me when he realizes I pointed Rick out to you."

"No, he won't. Because I'm going to kill him first. Besides, I would have figured it out sooner or later," Meg muttered.

Olivia blew out a defeated breath. "Well, if I'm going to get in trouble, and I will, I might as well go all the way. What I was going to say when I started all this was, I can't think of a better way to end the day than embarrassing one military man with a stick up his ass. Let's wish him a happy birthday."

Meg grinned and called for the waiter. Olivia was right. Watching her bodyguard turn bright red with embarrassment and glare at them over his big hot fudge brownie sundae with a candle was the perfect way to end the day.

Scott was on his way to Meg's apartment, a large bottle of Perrier in hand, to celebrate his new job. He couldn't bring champagne to a pregnant woman, so he'd opted for something else that was bubbly. He figured he'd get there around the same time she returned from shopping, and they could *celebrate*.

His cell rang while he was driving. The dashboard indicated it was Rick, the guy Tyler had chosen for Meg's security.

He frowned. The more Scott thought about it—and he'd given his actions a lot of consideration as the day had worn on—the more he realized he needed to tell Meg she had a tail. On the off chance she realized someone was watching her, she'd assume it was her ex, and Scott didn't want to scare her. He also didn't like lying to her, even by omission. He should have been up front, and he would be now.

He hit the play button and used his speakerphone. "Talk to me," Scott said.

"Fucking women," Rick muttered.

Scott had known Rick for a while. The man had served with Tyler during his stint in the army, and they'd been friends ever since.

"What's wrong?" Scott asked.

"I was made. You didn't tell me your girl was meeting up with your sister."

Scott swore. "That's because I didn't know. I thought she was going with a friend." And Olivia knew Rick as well as Scott did.

"They treated me to a big-ass happy birthday sundae including singing waiters."

Scott shook his head, trying not to laugh at the women's antics because he was so fucking screwed. "Sorry, man. And thanks for the heads-up. I'm almost at her place. I'll deal with it."

"Want me to stick around?"

"No, wait for me to get there and then take a break. I'll call you if I leave tonight. You can cover me then."

Scott disconnected the call and shot a wry glance at his makeshift celebratory bottle. He'd hoped he'd be spending the night with Meg, but now he wasn't so sure he'd make it past the front door.

A few minutes later, Scott knocked warily.

Meg opened the door, a surprised expression on her face. Obviously she hadn't expected him, and that was fine. They hadn't made plans, but he was happy to see her. Hell, his entire body lit up at the sight of her pretty face and dark-brown eyes.

"Before you lecture me, I looked through the security hole," she said, as if expecting him to reprimand her first thing.

"I figured." He held out the green bottle of sparkling water. "Care to celebrate my new job with me?" he asked.

She eyed the bottle, a pleased expression on her makeup-free face. "That's a considerate choice. Come on in."

He stepped inside, and she locked the door behind him. He couldn't gauge her mood, and that, more than anything, made him edgy. He wasn't sure whether or not to bring up the subject of Rick, then decided to take her lead.

He turned to face her. She definitely hadn't been expecting company. She wore a pair of pale-blue silk shorts and a matching silk tank top, no bra. His gaze zeroed in on the pointy tips of her nipples poking through the light material, and desire swelled inside him. But he didn't kid himself that she'd be interested in fucking him, and he braced himself for the fight to come.

She took the bottle out of his hand and headed for the kitchen. He followed, watching her ass, the faintest hint of rounded skin showing beneath the edge of her shorts.

His mouth grew dry, and he could have used a sip of that water.

She collected two glasses from the cabinet and opened the top. "So how did your boss take you leaving?"

"He wished me well. He knew how much I hated the rules . . . When I thought I could handle something, I resented having my hands tied by regulations." Scott shrugged. "He said I was better off being someone else's problem. I let him know I'd be my own boss, and we parted ways on somewhat good terms."

She finished pouring the drinks and handed him one. "To new beginnings." She touched his glass with hers, then, keeping her gaze trained on his, she took a sip.

He did the same, completely off-balance at her unexpected good mood. Actually, it was more than good. Her entire demeanor had shifted into a happy space, and he narrowed his gaze, unable to figure her out.

"Okay, dammit, why aren't you yelling at me?" he asked, unable to wait for her to slam him for placing Rick on her tail.

A sexy smile lifted her lips, and she laughed. "Am I making you sweat?" she asked cheekily.

He liked this sassy Meg. "Yes. Care to explain?"

She lifted one delicate shoulder. "When I realized I had someone following me—"

"You mean when Olivia pointed Rick out," Scott corrected.

Meg raised her hand. "In her defense, I had already mentioned we'd been to Tyler's and that he was helping me out. She assumed I knew about the bodyguard."

He inclined his head, less interested in his sister's role than Meg's feelings on the subject. "Go on."

"When I realized you had someone following me, I was furious."

Her eyes flashed with emotion, and he braced himself. "Here it comes."

"No. Because as I drove home, I realized that, thanks to you, I could get out of my car and walk to my door without looking over my shoulder or fearing Mike would pop out of the bushes to attack me. And I realized how lucky I was to have someone in my life who wanted to look out for me." She took another sip of her drink and looked at him over the rim of the glass, a light blush covering her cheeks.

"So you aren't angry."

"I'm not happy you didn't talk to me first. Or warn me. But no, I'm not angry."

He stepped closer, drawn to this softer, more open Meg. "I'd already decided that I'd made a mistake. I would have filled you in tonight."

She ran her tongue over her lips, and his gut tightened as he followed the sexy movement. "Is that why you're here? To discuss security?" she asked.

He placed his drink on the kitchen counter. Took hers from her hand and set it down beside his. "No, I'm here because I can't stay away from you. But I'd much rather get the lecture out of the way so we can move on to more pleasurable things." He stroked his knuckles over her cheek, around her jaw, and down the soft skin on her neck.

She visibly swallowed hard. "Are you going to ask me before you make decisions that involve me from now on?"

"Yes. Unless you're not around, in which case I'll run them by you as soon as possible afterward."

She nodded. "And if I don't agree, we'll reach a compromise?" she pressed on.

Now she was pushing him to make promises he couldn't keep. "I won't compromise on your safety, but we will talk." It was the best he could offer.

As he spoke, he trailed his fingertips along the loose edge of her tank top. Goose bumps prickled along her chest, her skin there flushed, and her nipples became harder peaks. He was dying to take one into his mouth, but they needed to finish up this conversation, and he shifted positions to accommodate his thickening length. The hard denim of his jeans was damned uncomfortable.

She let out a long sigh. Tipped her head, her hair trailing along the top of his hand. He actually fucking shivered at the soft tickle.

"I'll accept that for now," she finally agreed.

He narrowed his gaze. "Can I ask what's making you so . . . accommodating?"

And that was the change, he realized. She was suddenly more accepting of him in her life. More of a willing participant in wherever things between them might go.

"I spent the afternoon with someone who knows how to handle a domineering Dare man." And on that note, Meg wrapped her arms around his neck and settled her soft lips on his.

chapter
six

On the way home from shopping, Meg had thought over everything Riley and Olivia said. Olivia especially. Meg understood she could keep fighting this thing between herself and Scott or she could enjoy what he offered and move on when he was ready. Once she let go of her fear, it was surprisingly easy to let him in.

Especially when he showed up that night with sparkling water and in an obvious panic because he'd been caught being high-handed. How could she resist the man when, beneath the control freak, he was so amazingly sweet? Not to mention drop-dead sexy. She'd looked through the security hole to find him on her doorstep wearing a pair of dark jeans that accentuated his hard thighs and a navy T-shirt that brought out the blue in his eyes and showed off the defined muscles in his forearms.

Making the first move was easier than she would have thought, and she'd clearly taken him by surprise, which she had to admit, she liked doing. But the minute her mouth touched his, he groaned, cupped the back of her head in his big hand, and took over. He slid his tongue across her lips once, twice, then plundered. He kissed her over and over, long, drugging kisses that weakened her in the knees. He tugged at her hair, a gesture that she somehow felt in her core. He kissed her like he couldn't get enough.

She knew she couldn't. She wanted to feel his hot skin on hers. She grasped his shirt and pulled up at the hem, sliding her hands up his abdomen, feeling the hard muscles beneath her fingertips.

He broke the kiss and pulled in a ragged breath, giving Meg the opportunity to take over. She reached for the button on his jeans, popping it open and yanking down. He attempted to grasp her wrists and stop her, but she was faster, and she wriggled the denim over his lean hips. With a grunt of acceptance, he helped, and the denim pooled around his ankles. His cock sprang up before her, thick and hard, ready for anything.

She grinned and lowered herself to her knees. This wasn't an act she normally enjoyed, but something about Scott and how well he treated her made her want to give to him in return. And shockingly, the idea of going down on him made her mouth water and her sex ache with need.

"Damn, baby. Do you have any idea what it does to me to see you on your knees like that?"

She glanced up at him, suddenly shy. But if she had any reservations, they disappeared when she caught a glimpse of the heat in his gaze and the look of reverence in his expression as he gazed down at her. Leaning forward, she licked his erection gently at first, a long, teasing stroke of her tongue over his thickening shaft. He pulled her hair into one hand behind her and tugged hard.

The small hint of pain caused a surprising shock of arousal to spread from her scalp to her pussy. She moaned and grasped his erection in her hand. She eased her mouth around him, taking him as far as she could before sliding back the other direction. She wasn't an expert, didn't know what he liked, but she did recognize his growl as one of approval. And the hip thrust that pushed him deeper into her mouth definitely told her she was doing things right.

She slid her hand up and down, using the lubrication from her mouth to ease her way. Being Scott, he soon was driving the action, pumping into her mouth with long, fluid strokes. To her surprise, giving him pleasure provided her with even greater satisfaction than she'd ever imagined.

He grunted above her, his hand a steady presence in her hair, every tug causing a wave of desire to wash over her. She moaned, the sound reverberating around him, and he thrust hard, the head of his cock hitting the back of her throat.

She fought not to gag and managed to breathe through, taking him even deeper.

"Damn, Meg, you feel so good."

So did he. She loved the taste of him, slightly musky, a little salty, and so very male. The idea of taking him all the way was a heady thing.

She worked him with her hand and mouth until suddenly he pulled himself out completely. "Not coming in your mouth, baby."

He stripped her out of her shorts and panties, leaving them in a pile on the living room floor. And wasn't that hot, she thought, as he picked her up and carried her to the bedroom with long, deliberate strides.

By the time he set her on the bed, she was panting with need.

"As much as I want to taste you," he said, positioning her on the center of the mattress, "I need to be inside you more."

He eased his hips back and pushed into her with ease. She was so wet and ready he filled her completely in one long thrust, hitting her sweet spot immediately.

She arched her back and moaned, feeling the thickness of him everywhere, and her climb toward climax began almost instantly. She wondered if it was the hormones running through her body or whether it was being with Scott, but either way, she'd never been so sensitive or felt so much so quickly. And she wasn't talking just physically. Pushing those terrifying thoughts aside, she focused on the here and now, on the large man who owned her body when he was buried inside her.

"I love being inside you, baby." Scott groaned as she clasped him tighter in her hot body.

From the minute she'd wrapped her sweet mouth around his cock, Scott had needed more, and coming in her mouth hadn't been an option.

"Lift your legs," he instructed in a rough voice.

She complied, her long legs wrapping around his waist, and she pulled him farther into her heat. Using his upper body for leverage, he took a long glide out before plunging back in, hard and fast. Her slick walls gripped him tighter, her heels dug into his back, and he fucking felt her everywhere.

Sweat broke out on his forehead and back as desire and the primal need to own her washed over him. He took her hard, knowing she could handle it, understanding that she wanted him as much and as badly as he needed her.

They strove toward climax together, her nails digging into his back as she arched and ground against him. Physically, it was fast and furious, but at the core, there was something stronger pushing at him from his subconscious, an emotional connection he'd never experienced before, during or outside of sex. He knew what it was, even as he understood it was too soon, too fast. Even as it scared him.

And then her climax hit, and she screamed his name, shuddering around him, her sex clasping his cock in warmth and heat, and he came hard, emptying himself inside her and thankfully shutting down every other part of him, especially the emotions rampaging through his brain.

He became aware of her heavy breathing beneath him and rolled over so as not to crush her.

She turned her head and met his gaze, a flush staining her cheeks. "That was . . . hot," she said, a grin on her face.

"That you are, baby."

She closed her eyes and obviously focused on slowing her breathing. "I don't, that is . . ." She stammered over her words. "It has to be the pregnancy hormones," she muttered finally.

He knew exactly what she was referring to. "It's not the hormones," he said, disgruntled. He'd had enough sex—he'd even had sex with his pregnant ex—to know better. Nothing he'd ever experienced came close to Scott and Meg together.

He reached for her, pulling her on top of him. "This," he said, punctuating the word by rolling his cock against her sex, "isn't just random fucking hormones."

Her eyes opened wide. She was surprised, either by his harsh tone or his body's already thickening response. *That* sure as hell shocked him.

"I didn't mean—"

"Yeah, you did." He crushed his mouth against hers, plowing his tongue inside and claiming her in the most primitive way possible. When he pulled back, he pressed her head into his shoulder and closed his eyes, both startled and alarmed by his primitive response to her trying to brush off something he'd never ever felt before.

They lay in silence, her breasts crushed to his chest and her warm breath on his cheek.

"Scott?" She wriggled free, and he let her roll off him.

"Hmm?"

"This is really scary," she whispered.

His heart cracked a little bit at her admission.

"One minute I was pregnant and alone, dealing with a huge upcoming life change and an asshole ex, knowing I had to step up as the sole adult and take charge. And the next I have you barging in like some white knight, taking over."

He met her gaze, keeping one arm around her waist. "It's overwhelming for me too."

Surprise flickered in her dark eyes.

"But us—we're a good thing. You're not in this alone anymore." And he meant it. He was falling hard and fast for her, and he wasn't going to fight something that felt so right.

A tear fell, and he caught it with his fingertip. "Hey. What is it?"

She met his gaze. "I don't understand what you're doing with me," she said honestly. "And that's not putting myself down or even shortchanging myself. It's a fact. But it's also a fact that I'm grateful you're here, and I'm not strong enough to turn you away."

"Good. Because you'd have a real fight on your hands. Some things are just meant to be."

"And in my experience, fairy tales don't come true."

He pressed a kiss to her forehead. "Don't think too hard, okay?" Lord knew he was trying not to.

She sniffed and nodded. "I'll try."

"Good. Are you tired?" he asked.

"Beyond."

"Then let's get some sleep."

Monday morning came way too fast. Scott had stayed the weekend, and Meg couldn't remember the last time she'd enjoyed just hanging around and relaxing quite so much. He liked action movies and so did she, which meant they were able to agree on what to watch. They viewed *The Expendables* on Netflix, so he got his action and she got her fill of Jason Statham, and then moved on to the *Taken* series, which she'd missed in theaters. Liam Neeson certainly wasn't hard on the eyes either.

Before she left for work, Scott reminded her that Rick would be following her to school and waiting in the parking lot just in case her ex decided to make an appearance. Scott was heading over to his brother's so they could hammer out business details and talk to a lawyer to make their partnership and joint ownership of Double Down Security official.

He left her with a kiss and, "Have a good day, baby."

Her heart fluttered at that, and she set out for work. Maybe because her mood was good, the kids were on their best behavior and the morning flew by. When she sent them off to the music teacher for half an hour, she headed back to her classroom for a brief break but didn't get much time before the intercom sounded in her room. Allie asked her to come to the office, and Meg headed down the long hallway lined with children's artwork on various class bulletin boards before arriving at the office.

Allie's desk was directly in front of the doorway. "Hi," Meg said to her friend.

"Hi." Allie smiled but it didn't reach her eyes. "Meg, these people would like to speak with you." She gestured to an elegant blonde with a classic bob hairstyle and light makeup wearing a dressy pantsuit. By her side was a gentleman with graying hair and a well-fitting suit.

Meg didn't know them, and if they'd been the parents of her students, she would have. In a shocking change of pace, they'd all shown up for parent-teacher night. She didn't recognize either of these people.

"Ms. Thompson?" the man asked.

Meg nodded warily. "How can I help you?"

The woman stepped closer and spoke in a low tone. "I'm Lydia Ashton and this is my husband, Walter."

"Ashton? As in Mike Ashton?" Meg asked as lights began to flicker in front of her eyes. She was suddenly dizzy. She reached for the wall behind her, seeking support.

The woman gave her a slight nod. "We're Mike's parents."

Meg drew a forced breath. She wasn't about to have a conversation with them here, where, heaven forbid, the principal could overhear. He was already upset with her pregnant-single-mother status. She had no desire for him to find her having personal meetings during school time.

Meg pulled herself up to her full height. "Let's go talk somewhere private. I only have another twenty minutes before my students return." She led them away from Allie's curious stare to a quiet part of the hallway where no classrooms were located. "Why are you here? What do you want?" Meg asked.

"Mike tells us you refuse to see him," his mother said.

Meg knew that Rick, her bodyguard, was sitting in his car, watching for Mike, who, thanks to online photos, he'd recognize on sight. Were his parents here because he couldn't show up himself?

Meg curled her hands into fists. "I have a restraining order against him, which means I don't *have* to see him. And he's already violated that order once. If the police catch him near me, they'll arrest him." Meg's legs shook, and she leaned against the wall to steady herself.

"Yes, that is unfortunate. My son is . . . a disappointment, to say the least."

Meg's eyes opened wide at that unexpected statement.

"That's why we're here. We"—the older woman pointed between herself and her husband—"want to know we'll be able to see our grandchild."

Meg shook her head in disbelief. "You do realize that when I told your son he was going to be a father, he questioned his paternity," she said, still offended by his insinuation. "I'm happy to take any damned test. It's his. He was furious, and he pushed me, hard. I fell and nearly lost the baby." She swallowed hard. "Your son is an abuser." Her voice cracked, and she rested her hands on her stomach. "All I want is for Mike to sign away his parental rights. My lawyer sent him the papers, and based on his initial reaction, I don't understand why he hasn't done it already."

A terrifying thought occurred to her as she stared at the couple. "Has he changed his mind? Because I don't want him anywhere near me or my child."

A surprising look of regret and compassion passed over the other woman's face. "As I said, Mike is a disappointment. He isn't interested in being a father."

"Then why won't he sign the papers?" Meg asked.

Lydia Ashton turned, and a look passed between her and her husband, one Meg couldn't begin to decipher. "We don't know why Mike behaves the way he does," she said when she turned back to Meg. "He was always a trying child. He tested us at every turn, and when he found alcohol, we lost all semblance of control."

"You threw him out," Meg said, repeating what Mike had told her.

The other woman winced. "More than once, hoping he'd hit rock bottom and want help."

"But he kept finding unwitting people to see the best in him and take him in," Walter said, speaking up for the first time.

"Like me." Meg shook her head.

"Don't be hard on yourself. We know how charming he can be."

Meg swallowed hard. "Well, I'm sorry you drove over here for nothing. Mike knows what I want from him, and this is between him and my lawyer."

Lydia reached out a hand to touch Meg's shoulder, then reconsidered. "You do realize we're going to be this child's family."

"Not if your son signs those papers." Meg hung on to the slim hope that her ex would act on common sense. He didn't want anything to do with her or the baby.

"We don't want to lose access," Lydia warned her. "Family is very important to us."

And look what a wonderful job they'd done with their own son, Meg thought bitterly, but she wasn't cruel enough to say so.

Lydia shook her perfectly coiffed head. "We just want you to agree to let us see the baby, our *grandchild*. If you do, perhaps we can persuade Mike to do as you asked and sign away his rights . . . not ours."

Meg narrowed her gaze. Would they really help her cut their son out? Or was this a game of some sort?

On the one hand, she understood where these people were coming from. She didn't have much in the way of family, and if her baby could have good, decent people in its life besides Meg . . . But that was the issue, wasn't it? She didn't know the Ashtons at all. Except for what Mike had told her about them being too controlling. Though Mike's word wasn't to be trusted.

"We just want to be close to the baby. My hope is that you and I can work something out," Lydia said softly, her tone pleading. She reached into her purse and pulled out a piece of paper with a phone number on it. "Here. Please think about it."

Meg accepted the paper, knowing she'd do nothing *but* think.

Lydia studied her for a long moment, then inclined her head. "Thank you for seeing us."

If she'd had a choice, she wouldn't have, Meg thought. But then this woman had known the element of surprise would work in her favor.

Meg waited until she'd returned to her classroom to let her emotions free. Her shoulders dropped, and she fell into her chair, shaking. Although the Ashtons hadn't threatened her, they'd made it clear they wanted access to *her* baby. She covered her stomach protectively, wondering how she could gauge the truth about them.

Maybe Tyler's man would uncover information that would help her decide. Her own knowledge was limited. From her early days with Mike, she knew that controlling him via the purse strings was his parents' favorite sport. Although Meg had come to learn Mike did nothing to support himself financially, and so he relied on his parents, making himself subject to their whims. It was a messy family dynamic. Meg didn't want to be a pawn in their schemes. If there was a scheme. Maybe they were being honest.

Her head began to pound. She just didn't want her child to be drawn into an abusive or unstable environment. Meg had had enough of that herself growing up.

Of course, after the Ashtons' visit, the rest of the day dragged on. Meg was preoccupied, so the whining and complaints of the children seemed exacerbated and more annoying. She kept a smile on her face and focused on the kids and her work, finally making it through to the release bell.

She always waited until her young children's parents came to get them. Today, two were late. She didn't want the kids to be scared or feel lost or unwanted. By the time Meg walked out of the building, most teachers had left for the day.

She exited and caught sight of Rick sitting in his car, watching. Just the sight of him made her feel safer.

She blew out a breath and was about to head for her own car when her cell rang. Hoping it was Scott, she answered without looking at the caller ID.

"Hello?"

"You stupid bitch! What are you doing talking to my parents?" Mike's scratchy yell caught her off guard.

At the sound of his voice, she dropped her bag. How did he know she'd seen his parents?

Oh God. He'd obviously been watching her somehow. She swung around, searching for any sign of him in the few vehicles remaining in the parking lot without luck.

She refocused on the call. "Mike! Just sign the papers, and I'll be out of your life!"

"I can't. If I do, my parents will cut me off for good."

Meg closed her eyes and groaned, things becoming clearer. This was about money. Wasn't everything in Mike's life? Hadn't he moved in with her when his parents had cut him off the last time?

Meg pressed the phone to her head, trying to think things through. She was already considering granting his parents their request, assuming they turned out to be decent people. Would that satisfy Mike? Would he sign away his rights and disappear from her life?

"What if I promised your parents *they* could see the baby? Without you," she made clear.

"No!" he hissed. "They'll try to take over its life."

"He or she!" Meg spat into the phone. "Don't call my child an 'it.'" Stupid, selfish bastard.

"What the fuck ever, Meg. Doesn't matter. They can't have a relationship with *him*," he sneered. "They'll make the baby their heir, and I'll lose everything."

Oh, boohoo, she thought. How had she ever thought he was charming? He had been though. Before the alcohol. Or before he'd let her see this side of him anyway.

"What do I have to do to get you out of my life?" she asked as she picked up the items that had fallen out of her open purse.

"What I told you to do from the beginning. Get rid of the fucking baby. I'll go back to being the perfect son, and my parents won't have another heir to threaten me with."

Horrified, she was just about ready to hit disconnect when Mike spoke again. "You do it or I'll do it for you."

Meg dropped her phone and forced a gulp of humid Florida air into her lungs. She remained on her knees, unable to believe what she'd just heard.

"Meg!" An unfamiliar male voice called her name. She swung her head around to see Rick coming toward her.

He knelt and tossed the remaining items on the ground into her purse, then helped her to her feet. "What happened?"

She looked into steady green eyes and drew a calming breath. "I had a visit from my ex's parents at school earlier today. And Mike called just now."

Rick swore. "Phone," he demanded, holding out his hand.

She pulled her cell from her bag, unlocked it, and handed it to him. He checked the last call and redialed.

"Probably a burner phone," he muttered. "Fuck. Let's go." He grasped her elbow and led her toward his car.

She dug in her heels. "Wait, my car."

"We'll get it back to you later."

"But—"

"Do you want to call Scott and tell him why you won't get in the car with me and let me keep you safe? Or would you rather I did it for you? Or you could do what I say." With the push of his thumb, he unlocked his black Ford.

She narrowed her gaze at him. "What is with you bossy men?" she asked as she let him open the passenger door.

"We get the job done," he muttered.

She pulled on her seat belt and leaned her head against the seat, exhaustion suddenly overwhelming her. When had her life become so complicated, and *why*?

Scott spent the day familiarizing himself with his brother's place of business. Now his business as well. Or it would be once they made it official with paperwork.

He couldn't remember the last time he'd felt so right about a decision. Like he was finally in a place where he belonged. He could push boundaries and rules when necessary without someone coming down on him for violating department policy. He breathed out a slow breath, grateful that the guys here had welcomed him too. They'd given him shit for not being able to hack it on the force, slapped him on the back, and that was that.

Scott took over a small office across the way from Tyler, refusing any offer to exchange with someone for a larger one. He didn't need the space or status of a big room. He just needed to breathe, and he could do that here.

As for Meg's ex, he now had a file on the man and his family, and it appeared Mike was the black sheep son, whom they had unsuccessfully tried to place in rehab for alcohol abuse. He had also been adopted as a baby. And that was all he knew. For now. Luke was still digging. He groaned and looked out the window at his glorious view of the parking lot.

An incongruous dark sedan pulled into the lot and parked. Scott blinked against the glare of the sun as Rick climbed out, met Meg on her side, and escorted her toward the building, a hand beneath her arm. Tension radiated from the man who was assigned to look out for her, while she looked subdued and upset.

"Shit." Scott rose and headed to meet them out front, wondering what the hell had happened now.

chapter seven

"I WANT TO GO HOME," SCOTT HEARD MEG TELL RICK AS HE MET THEM IN THE front area.

Scott joined them by reception. "What happened?" He glanced at Meg, who, up close, was pale and completely disheveled, dust marks on her black leggings, her hair falling out of her clip in disarray. She was still beautiful.

"I'll let her tell you. I'll be getting a trace on that number," Rick said, striding away, Meg's cell phone in hand.

Scott narrowed his gaze. Needing answers, he grasped Meg's hand and pulled her into his office. By the time he closed the door behind him, his heart was pounding hard in his chest.

He turned to her, immediately cupping her face in his hands. "Are you okay?" he asked first.

She nodded. "I'm fine. A little shaken up, but I'm okay. I told Rick to take me home so I could pull myself together, but he insisted on coming here."

"What happened?" he asked again. "From the beginning."

"I had a visit from Mike's parents. They came by school to talk to me about visitation with the baby. And believe it or not, that wasn't what has me rattled. Well, it does, but not in an *I'm scared* sort of way."

Scott tried to keep up with the flow of conversation and rambling. "Okay, we'll deal with the parents in a few minutes." He settled himself on his mostly empty desk and slid his arms around her, easing her down beside him. "What else went on?"

"I was leaving school for the day when my phone rang. It was Mike, and he knew I'd been with his parents, which means he's watching them. Or me. Or both. I don't know." She brushed her hair off her face with a shaking hand.

"Slow down. Tell me what he said."

Big brown eyes turned his way. "I told him to sign the papers and I'd be gone from his life. He said if he did, his parents would cut him off financially. I figured that was because they want to see the baby, like they told me. So I offered to give them that right—but not him."

He opened his mouth to ask what the hell she was thinking, but she held up a hand in front of him.

"I was just feeling out the situation for information, that's all. I wouldn't do something like that without more facts. Anyway, I figured he'd jump on the chance to give his parents what they wanted, right?"

"I'd think so, but I'm guessing not?"

She shook her head. "He said if I did that, they'd just make the baby their heir, and he'd lose everything."

"So now we know it's about money." Scott clasped her hands in his, hating how cold and clammy they felt. He rubbed them between his palms in an attempt to warm her, succeeding in warming himself up too, in all the wrong ways.

"I asked him what I had to do to get him out of my life, and he said I should do what he told me from the beginning. Get rid of the baby—"

Those words triggered something primal and still raw inside Scott, and he let out a low, angry growl.

Meg's shocked gaze darted up, meeting his. "What's that all about?"

"He threatened you," Scott hedged, not wanting to reveal his personal shit here and now.

"But—"

"Later," he promised. "I will tell you everything when we get home later."

She nodded. "It's the second time you've put off telling me something. I'm holding you to that promise," she said, her voice strong.

"Okay." He'd suck it up and explain everything about Leah and the baby. Later.

Her shoulders relaxed at his promise.

Right now, though, this was about Meg, and she wanted to keep her baby.

"Back to you. And Mike," Scott said.

A defiant expression crossed her pretty face. "If I wasn't going to get rid of the baby when I found out about it and was in shock, what makes him think I'll do it now?" She pulled her hands free, wrapping them around her stomach.

As a man who'd had everything ripped away from him suddenly and without warning by a selfish bitch who'd never given his feelings a thought, Scott eyed this protective woman with wonder and awe.

"Is that everything?" he asked gruffly.

She shook her head, her eyes damp. "He told me to get rid of it or he'd do it for me," she whispered.

Scott swore, possessive feelings rushing through him. "He won't get near you," he promised. He'd protect Meg and her unborn baby, but more than that, he'd make her feel safe. "I've got you."

She threw herself into his arms, wrapping herself around him and holding on tight. "I don't know why you're with me, but I'm so glad you are."

She fit against him, and he buried his face in her hair, breathing in her sexy scent. "It'll be okay."

She eased back, glancing up. "I believe you." Her gaze intense, she moved her head until her lips touched his, a soft press of her mouth, and he was lost. He skimmed his tongue back and forth over the seam of her lips, coaxing her open, sliding inside.

She welcomed him eagerly, the kiss going on, a long stroking tangle of tongues. He loved tasting her, could kiss her forever. Even with his cock begging to be freed, he could get lost in her mouth for hours. He lifted her shirt, gliding his knuckles up her sides and cupping her breasts through the lace bra.

"I may keep my desk empty just for this alone," he muttered before burying his mouth against her neck.

He suckled lightly, knowing she wouldn't be happy if he left a mark. His inner beast wanted to claim her that way, but he respected her too much to cause trouble for his hot, sexy kindergarten teacher.

She wriggled closer, and he pulled her astride him, her knees on either side of his thighs. His cock jumped in eagerness, but it wasn't getting any real action. She shifted, settling her sex over the hard swell of his erection, and as he rocked her against him, she curled her fingers around his shirt and moaned.

"I know what you need, baby. Let me take the edge off of your stress." He braced his hands on her hips and moved her back and forth, heeding her soft sighs and increasingly rapid breathing.

He gritted his teeth at the heated press of her mound against his confined cock, promising himself release later. This wasn't about him. Since he'd met Meg, nothing he did was about anyone or anything other than her.

"Oh, Scott. This feels so good." Her hips shifted restlessly, her lower body gyrating hard against him.

"Pretend I'm inside you. Hard. Big. Hot. Fucking you and giving you what you need."

She tipped her head back, which thrust her pelvis forward, and she let out a shuddering scream.

Somehow he silenced her, slamming his mouth down on hers, capturing the sound of her orgasm at the same time her body seized over and around his. As she rode out her release, the steady grind of their bodies nearly killed him. He held back somehow, trying to focus on counting in his head and not on the sexy-as-fuck woman coming apart in his arms.

She finally collapsed against him, and even he needed a minute or two to catch his breath. He wasn't sure how much time had passed when he heard the knock on his door.

Meg tried to push off him, but he held on. "Come in."

"Rick's guess was right. It was a burner," Tyler said as he stepped inside. His gaze locked on Scott's before glancing at the embarrassed female bundle in his arms. Tyler grinned. "Want me to come back later?"

"No, go on," Scott said.

Meg pinched his side hard.

He managed not to grunt in surprise.

Tyler leaned against the doorframe. "Like I said, dickhead called from a disposable. No trace. And Rick filled me in on the rest of what went down today. Your best bet is to try talking to the parents. See what influence they have on their kid."

Scott ran a hand over Meg's back, still very aware of the soft woman in his arms. "We'll figure it out," he said to his sibling.

Tyler nodded, grinned, and stepped out, shutting the door loudly behind him.

"Oh my God, that was mortifying!" Meg pushed off his lap and adjusted her clothing, smoothing wrinkles from her leggings and fixing her shirt, which was hanging askew. "I was straddling you, and we'd just, I'd just . . ."

Scott knew well what they'd just done. His dick still stood at alert, and his balls were probably blue. "Relax, it's my office. And Tyler doesn't care."

"Well, I do." She pulled her clip out and tried to fix her hair. "I need to go home and pull myself together. Relax. But I need my car, and that's at the school, so you can just take me there now."

She was so adorably flustered, and he hated to stress her out more, but it couldn't be helped. "Okay, first, yes, you need to go home. But not to shower and relax. I want you to pack up your things and come home with me."

"What?" she squeaked.

"Mike is following you. He's threatened you. Your apartment doesn't have security, you have no alarm, and it's not safe. I want you where I can keep an eye—and other body parts—on you," he said, trying to ease the whole dominant thing with a wink and a tease.

She narrowed her gaze. "I know what you're doing."

"I'd be disappointed if you didn't."

Meg blew out a long breath and paced back and forth in the small office. She might have just had an awesome orgasm, but her stress had returned the minute Tyler Dare had walked in on them. "I promised myself I'd think things through. When it came to dealing with you, to coping with Mike, I swore I'd be smart."

Smart as in not falling hard for this incredible man who was doing his utmost to protect her and keep her safe. Who was insinuating himself in her life and making himself welcome and needed. She shook her head in denial. Nobody was indispensable, and she would be fine on her own. But she also knew better than to put pride, ego, or past mistakes ahead of keeping her and the baby out of harm's way.

"Staying with you until this Mike situation is resolved is the smart, safe thing to do," she conceded, though not easily. To that end, and only that end, Scott's solution made sense. To everything but her heart.

Surprise etched itself out across his handsome face. "Thank you for making it easy."

"Thank you for offering your house." She turned away, not wanting to look into those dark-navy eyes for too long. She could drown in them.

"I'll arrange to have your car brought there."

"Thank you," she said softly. "Can we go now?"

"Yes."

"Good." Because not only did she want to shower and rest, but she wanted the answers Scott had promised her earlier. And she intended to get them.

Scott was grateful Meg needed to unwind when they returned to his house and she didn't insist on talking. Oh, he knew he'd have to come clean eventually, but he appreciated the time to grill steaks, have a beer, and listen to her humming to the music she played through her cell phone while she prepared a tossed salad. He liked the sounds of her moving around in his kitchen, making herself at home. Normalcy wasn't something he had much of, and being with Meg brought him a shocking kind of peace.

She'd taken a long shower first, and now she walked around his kitchen in one of those silky short outfits she preferred, this one in soft beige. The kind that showed everything and gave him a permanent hard-on. If he hadn't caught her wearing something similar when she'd believed she'd be alone, he'd have thought she was deliberately torturing him.

After dinner, they moved out to the patio, relaxing on adjacent lounge chairs. He stared out at the pool, enclosed by a fence for baby and child safety, remembering the time and effort he'd put into designing the yard after he'd bought the house. The yard had been a priority, and he'd started on the back immediately because suddenly he'd been looking forward to a whole different kind of life. Leah hadn't been.

He tilted his head and glanced at Meg. She studied him in silence, serious brown eyes taking him in. Waiting.

"I guess it's time," he said.

She lifted her shoulder, which had the bonus effect of raising her breasts beneath the flimsy top. Her nipples, tight from the slightly cooler night air, peaked against the sheer tank, and Scott bit back a groan. There was way too much to come for his mind or body to consider that kind of detour.

"Only if you want to. I'm not going to force you to bare your soul," she said. Her little tongue darted out, moistening her bottom lip, and he was tempted to say fuck it, straddle her on the recliner, and forget all about his past.

But she'd hold it against him if he didn't talk or tried to distract her. He got it. Her life was an open book for him. He'd made himself a part of hers. Fair was fair. No matter how much he hated revisiting that time in his past, he would.

He leaned his head back against the cushioned headrest but kept his gaze on hers. "You know about my family. My father never being home, finding out about his other kids and his mistress. I guess you could say it left a very sour taste in my mouth about marriage."

She lay on her side and curled her knees in, getting comfortable. "I guess a crappy childhood leads you to go one of two ways. You search for something better, or you decide never again."

Meg wanted better. Scott knew that without asking. For all her talk about standing on her own—and he believed that's what she wanted—deep down inside, she also desired the happily ever after you only read about in books.

Which begged the question: What was he doing getting so involved with her now? Any way he sliced it, she'd be having a baby and settling into a domesticity he'd never envisioned for himself before or after Leah.

"Go on," Meg said into his extended silence.

He blinked, her voice bringing him back to the present. He cleared his throat. "You're right. I had no intention of getting married."

"So what happened?"

He shrugged. "Hurricane Leah. I met her at a Thunder Christmas party. She was a model and had come with one of the players, but they weren't getting along and broke up before the night even ended. He left her there; she was stranded . . ."

"And you stepped up. Scott Dare, to the rescue." She waved her hand through the air.

He heard the bitter irony in her tone, but he couldn't deny it. Apparently he had a pattern, or at least he'd done the same thing twice. Seen a woman in trouble and stepped in to save her.

Instead of addressing Meg's comment, he merely went on. "We seemed to want the same thing out of life, which, back then, was a good time. And I liked having someone to come home to. We moved in together pretty quickly. I won't deny that I knew she liked the status of being with a Dare. She wanted the perks that came along with having my brother as president of the Thunder and my father as the owner of a string of luxury hotels. To be honest, it didn't bother me at the time." He glanced at Meg.

"That's almost as sad as me dating men, hoping they'd change, and keeping them around long past their expiration date so I wouldn't be alone," she said.

Wow. That hurt, he thought, letting her words bounce around his brain. But . . . "You have a point there. And if I'd had my brain in the right place, I might have realized it was inevitable that the relationship would go south. Instead, I listened to my—"

Meg laughed before he could finish the sentence. "I get the point."

"Right. But I really did think I loved her at the time. I knew she wanted to get married, what we had was fine, fun . . . so I agreed. And it remained fun until about a week after the honeymoon when she started pressuring me to leave the force and take a job with Ian or my father."

Meg's nose wrinkled in distaste. "First of all, you would never work for your father. I got that about you pretty quickly. And second, sitting behind a desk with nothing to stimulate you would kill you. You need the excitement of some kind of investigative work. Surveillance, digging into facts, reading motives, going after bad guys, and helping people." She shot him a look filled with pure disappointment. "I can't believe you married someone who didn't understand that about you."

Scott shook his head, a mixture of emotions filling him as he listened to Meg's succinct summary. In a couple of weeks, she knew him better than Leah, who he'd been with for a year before they'd married. Meg not only understood who he was, but she innately knew what he needed. And holy shit, that blew him away.

"Okay, well, yes, you're right. I like to chalk it all up to me being young, horny, and stupid."

"Your words, not mine." She grinned, and the smile reached inside her, lighting up her eyes with a sparkling twinkle. "I think there's more though?"

He ran a hand through his hair. "Yeah, there's more. Leah and I had agreed neither one of us wanted children."

Meg's expression dimmed at that, and Scott felt the loss of that megawatt smile.

Might as well get it over with, he thought. "But then Leah got pregnant, and it was a shock because we'd both been careful."

"The unexpected does happen," Meg said dryly.

The sun began to set behind her, the fading rays hitting her hair, burnished-auburn and red highlights capturing his attention.

He wished he were free to wrap himself up in her, but this story was having an impact on them both, and he felt her curling into herself. He hated it, but he had to finish and then deal with the fallout.

"It started as shock, but like you, I wrapped my head around the reality pretty quickly, and I started thinking about a life beyond just myself and Leah. And I could see it. The family I never thought I wanted, kids I didn't think I'd have . . . I got excited. And invested."

"You bought this house." Meg's gaze fell on the structure behind him.

He nodded. "But Leah wasn't as fired up as I was. In fact, she was depressed. I wanted to show her how good things could be. So yeah, I bought it as a surprise and started the renovations immediately. Eventually, I brought her out here. I figured if she could look at things through my eyes, she'd see what I saw and want the same thing."

"Except she didn't?" Meg asked.

Scott shook his head, and Meg wondered what in the world was wrong with the woman Scott had married. Meg's baby's father had thrown her against the nearest wall when he'd found out she was pregnant. Scott had bought a fricking McMansion. And his ex-wife still hadn't been happy.

"What happened?" Meg asked, needing to hear the rest.

"She looked around, asked me why in the hell I'd think she wanted to live anywhere but South Beach, where the parties and the action were. At which point she informed me she'd already had an abortion and had just been waiting for the right time to tell me."

Meg sucked in a shallow breath and nearly choked on her own saliva. "Oh my God."

"Yep. Didn't even ask me how I felt about it ahead of time. She didn't give me a choice. Hell, she didn't give my feelings any thought at all. And I'd already made it perfectly clear that, while I might be surprised, her pregnancy was a gift in disguise. I wanted that baby."

He pushed himself up and paced in front of Meg's chair, his agitation clear.

Meg's stomach suddenly hurt, and she eased back against the soft cushion and wrapped her arms around her knees. "That's awful."

He nodded. "It sucked."

"So you divorced her."

"Yep. Her behavior and selfish actions mocked my change of heart. I should have gone with my gut instinct after all. My father had taught me a hard-won lesson."

"What lesson was that?" Meg asked softly, almost afraid to hear.

He let out a harsh sound she couldn't interpret. "That the whole family thing is for suckers and happily ever after only happens in fairy tales."

Meg ducked her head, not wanting him to see how much she hurt for him . . . and for herself. Because like Scott, she'd seen the worst in relationships, but unlike him, she kept wanting to believe in the fairy tale. Even now. And she obviously wouldn't be finding it with him.

Her eyes filled, and she blinked back the tears. Despite having promised herself she wouldn't hold out any hope for something more with Scott, she knew now that she had. Having him around, so caring and invested in her safety, looking at her like he wanted to eat her up and come back for seconds . . . A tiny kernel of hope had taken up residence in her heart. Thank God he'd revealed his past and his feelings about marriage and family now and not down the road when Meg would really have begun to delude herself into seeing what she wanted to see. After all, she was good at that.

"I'm really sorry," she whispered.

"At least now you know why I reacted the way I did when you told me Mike demanded you terminate the pregnancy." His tone softened, as it always did when he spoke to her. "I know how much you want this baby." He stood in front of her chair, so big, handsome, and at the moment, self-contained.

He'd pulled into himself much the way she had. And that was a good thing, she told herself. Perspective was something she desperately needed.

"I do want it." Meg pressed a hand to her belly. "And I appreciate you telling me everything. I know it wasn't easy."

He rolled his shoulders, stretching as he rotated his muscles. She watched the flex and bend, swallowing hard at the perfect specimen of masculinity he presented.

"It's in the past," he finally said.

Not so much, she wanted to tell him. But she didn't. Perspective, she reminded herself. She eased herself to a standing position, rubbing her arms, suddenly a little chilled now that the sun had set . . . and reality had dawned with it. Facing the truth was a gift she was determined to give herself from now on.

"I'm going to head inside. I'm cold," she told him.

And where normally he'd wrap his arms around her and chase away the chill, he merely nodded. "I'll be up soon."

"I'll probably be asleep. It's been a really long day."

He didn't answer, and she wasn't surprised. He was lost in thought, probably somewhere in the pain of his past. She wasn't as keen on thinking deeply or dwelling on what she couldn't change. She'd do as she'd told him. She'd turn in and hope she fell asleep. Tomorrow was a new day, and the way things were going, it would bring new challenges. Meg had to be ready to face them.

Scott headed indoors shortly after Meg went upstairs and popped open a cold beer. *What the hell are you doing?* he asked himself. Why had he let Meg go to bed alone when he knew how upset she had to be after his story? *Not the story, asshole,* but his gut reaction to what Leah had done.

That family thing is for suckers, and happily ever after only happens in fairy tales. What the fuck had possessed him to dump all that on her and in those words?

He rubbed his burning eyes with the heels of his hands. Meg had asked for honesty, and once he'd gotten rolling on what Leah had done, his lingering anger had burst through. He hadn't been talking to Meg. Sensitive, caring Meg. He'd been furious and still feeling betrayed by his ex-wife.

Scott put down the full bottle of beer. Drinking wasn't going to help. Neither was attempting to sort through his feelings for Meg, though he couldn't contain his thoughts.

He'd been unable to stay away from her, attraction and desire overcoming any rational thought. To be honest, he hadn't had a single rational moment since laying eyes on Meg in that hospital bed. As a result, he'd talked her into a one-night stand, though admittedly, he hadn't had to try too hard to convince her. She'd been right there with him. Except he'd known going in that one night wouldn't be enough.

And now he found himself acting like her white knight and protector, and he had no regrets about it. None at all. The desire he'd felt for her from the beginning was still going strong, but now he *knew* her. Liked her even more.

Meg was everything Leah wasn't. Warm, caring, nurturing yet strong. Beautiful and real, inside and out. And she was more independent than she wanted to believe herself. He admired everything about her. But as much as he'd told himself he'd known she was pregnant going in, that it didn't matter, suddenly it did. She was creating a life for herself that he'd never believed he desired. And the one time he'd allowed himself to want it, everything had been ripped away from him in an instant, leaving him raw and back where he'd started. Convinced marriage, babies, and family weren't for him.

Except with Meg, a part of him was starting to envision just that, and it scared him to death. He couldn't pull away from her if he wanted to—and he didn't. Nor could he tell himself he was staying because she needed protection. He was sticking around because he needed her. Wanted her. But Meg made it perfectly clear she preferred to be independent and not lean on any man. Which put him back in the same position he'd unwittingly found himself in with his ex. When this mess with her stalker baby daddy was over, Meg might just decide she no longer needed *Scott* in her life. At all.

chapter eight

Meg woke up the next morning to find Scott wrapped around her, his big body curled around her back, one hand cupping her breast. Someone had put last night behind them, and she wished it were as easy for her. Still, nothing had changed between them, at least overtly. She was here until the threat was over, and neither of them had made any promises. If anything, his story and beliefs about the future merely reinforced her need to keep on as she had been. Planning an independent life on her own. But that didn't mean she couldn't enjoy the here and now.

His lips nuzzled at her neck, his breath warm, his touch electric. He pulled her closer and plucked at her nipple with one hand, turning her insides to liquid and making everything inside her melt with need.

She purred at the sensations pulsing straight to her core.

"You were asleep when I came in last night."

"I told you I probably would be."

He pinched her nipple tighter, and the current caused a trickle of dampness to settle between her thighs. "I'm making up for it this morning," he said, the head of his erection nudging at her opening.

"I can tell," she murmured, the last word falling off as he slid inside her body, which opened and eagerly accepted him. He was hot and hard, filling her up slowly and completely. "Ahh," she whispered, the sheer thickness of him pulsing inside her.

He rocked his hips back and forth, sheathing himself deeper, only to pull out and glide back in. "God, you feel good, Meg."

She closed her eyes, unable to fight the truth. "So do you."

He dipped his finger lower, moving from her breast to her clit, lubricating her with her own juices, his deft touch masterful. He always knew just how to play her to bring her to orgasm, but this wasn't the fast, furious sexual connection they normally shared.

His cock glided in and out of her almost reverently, his breathing growing ever rougher against her neck. Even the occasional talk was more intense and less dirty than usual, and she fell headlong into a glorious climax that was even more beautiful for the way he coaxed her through. Words like *so fucking beautiful, keep coming, baby*, and *it's my turn* echoing in her ears as his thrusts grew harder, his grip on her tighter as he came hard and fast inside her.

By the time their breathing had returned to normal, a big old lump had risen in her throat, and getting up to go to work hadn't been easy. Maybe Scott had recognized the intensity, because he, too, had rolled away and said they should get ready for work.

For the rest of the week, they fell into a too-comfortable routine. Most times, Scott would leave first, knowing his brother made a habit of getting into work early. Meg would leave soon after for school. When she left Scott's house, Rick would be waiting in his car and followed her. She was comforted knowing he was around and could handle Mike if he tried something or got violent. And with her thoughts and life in turmoil, she appreciated this little peace of mind.

Meg would get back to the house first, and because she was a guest, she wanted to help out. She'd had Rick accompany her to the grocery store so she could fill Scott's cabinets and fridge with food she could cook, and she had dinner waiting when he came home. Although she kept her mental dialogue going strong, reminding herself this situation was temporary, she couldn't deny how much she enjoyed being with him. It seemed like they fit into each other's lives well, from what they ate and when to watch television shows and bedtime.

Unlike Mike and past boyfriends, Scott had no issues with the time she spent in the evenings preparing her lessons for the kids. He was surprised that kindergarten wasn't just painting and crayons and seemed interested in what she planned for her class.

She couldn't deny not only that they lived together easily but that sex got better each time. She didn't understand it. Her prior relationships had been about making sure he got off or a quickie before bed. Scott's focus was solely on Meg's pleasure. If nothing else, he would be a hard act to follow when things ended.

He'd said as much himself that fateful night on the patio. If he'd been thinking with his brain, he'd have recognized his relationship with his ex wouldn't last. Instead, he'd thought with his . . . libido. And Scott had a healthy sex drive, as he'd proven over and over. What if Scott was thinking that way now, with Meg? What would happen when she started to show? She'd be popping soon if the *What to Expect When You're Expecting* book was right. In fact, she could see the swell in her belly, even if he hadn't said a word. She'd only be getting bigger. No way would she be able to hold his interest sexually then.

Another depressing thought. But reality was her new friend, she reminded herself as she strode into school on Friday morning. After a morning teaching the letter *K*, Meg took her little charges to the art teacher, where they'd stay for the next forty minutes.

Before heading to the break room for coffee, she stopped at the office to check her mailbox and talk to Allie.

Meg hadn't had time with her friend since their girls' night, which felt like a lifetime ago, and she wanted to rectify that. She paused at the wall of small mailboxes and pulled out a few colored papers, notices, and other items before turning to her friend.

"Hi."

"Hi, yourself." Allie sat behind a metal desk and always greeted everyone with a warm smile.

"How are you feeling?" Allie gestured to Meg's stomach.

Meg blushed and grinned. "Pretty good, thanks. You?"

Allie shrugged. "Not bad. Listen, I need to talk to you," she said, lowering her voice.

"And I'd love to grab lunch sometime soon," Meg said. Allie was aware of the situation with Mike but not that Meg was living with Scott. They definitely had catching up to do.

"Great! I'll text you. I'm going to visit my parents this weekend, so maybe the next. But that's not what I wanted to talk about . . ."

"What is it?" Meg asked, concerned.

"Parents have been calling about a sedan in the parking lot with a driver sitting behind the wheel. Mr. Hansen went out to speak to the driver." Allie glanced over her shoulder at the partially open door, as if assuring they wouldn't be caught talking.

Meg's stomach cramped. "What happened?"

"The guy showed him an ID card from a protection agency and explained he was on the job for someone inside the school. He didn't mention names but . . ." Because Mr. Hansen, as well as Allie, knew Meg no longer wanted Mike allowed into the school . . .

"He put two and two together and came up with me as the person who needed protection," Meg said.

Allie inclined her head. "I'm so sorry."

"It's not your fault." Meg drew a deep gulp of air. "Does he want to see me?"

"Right away."

"Okay." Meg straightened her shoulders, ignored the nerves bouncing in her stomach, and strode around her friend's desk to the principal's office, knocking with her knuckles.

"Come in," he called.

She stepped in to find Mr. Hansen sitting behind his desk. He was a bland man in personality and appearance. With his thinning black hair and plaid suits that had seen better days, it was obvious to Meg why she hadn't wanted to date him. There was zero attraction between them. The sun streamed in from behind him, the bright Florida sunshine in stark contrast to Meg's darkening mood.

"Good morning, Meg," he said, as always using her first name instead of the formality most principals preferred. "Please have a seat," he said in a serious tone.

She chose one of the two uncomfortable hard-backed chairs across from him.

"I'll get right to the point. I've had some phone calls from concerned parents about the man sitting outside the school in an unmarked car."

Meg gripped the edge of her chair harder. Of course she could comprehend why parents wouldn't be comfortable with a large man sitting in a black car, parked in the school lot for the entire day.

"I can explain."

"Then it does involve you?"

She closed her eyes and nodded.

"It was only conjecture until now."

Meg had known that, but she believed in owning up to her issues when confronted. "You already know I put my ex-boyfriend on a list of people I don't want to be allowed inside the school. The truth is, I have a restraining order against him," she admitted. She glanced down, noticed that her hands had begun to shake, and shoved them beneath her legs on the chair.

"Is the man dangerous?" Mr. Hansen asked. "Do I need to be concerned about the children?"

"Umm, he's only interested in me."

The other man narrowed his gaze. "What if the kids get in the way of him getting to you?"

Meg's mouth grew dry. "I didn't think . . . I wouldn't put the kids at risk." She couldn't vouch for Mike's stability if he was drinking.

"I know you wouldn't do it deliberately, but that may be the end result. One of the parents who called is on the school board. She wants to call a meeting. She feels you should be suspended without pay, and frankly, given the situation, that's very likely how the board will vote."

Meg dipped her head, knowing what Mr. Hansen was getting at. She could go through with the farce of the board hearing, but the result was almost a given. If Meg was in their situation and had children in the school, knowing what she did about her ex, she'd vote to suspend her. What if Mike did become totally unhinged and was drinking and made a scene outside school? What if he went after her and the children were there? She shook her head, surprised she hadn't thought of this before. But she'd been so overwhelmed with things, she hadn't thought beyond her own problems.

"I understand," she whispered, her fear folding in on her because she knew what was coming.

"Then we're in agreement. You'll take a voluntary suspension, and I'll explain things to the board."

Meg managed a nod as tears sprung to her eyes. Now she wasn't just an unwed mother, she was an unemployed, unwed mother with no income coming in. She'd counted on saving her money between now and when this school year ended for the new and unexpected baby-related expenses.

Somehow she rose to her feet on shaking legs and started for the door.

"Meg."

She turned and glanced over her shoulder. The sympathetic look on his face surprised her. "I really am sorry. I know how you feel about the children and they about you."

"Thank you."

She turned and headed out, walking past Allie with a half wave, unable to find the words to speak. Not without bursting into tears.

Scott spent the morning with Tyler, in a meeting with Lola Corbin. She came alone, no handlers or other band members with her. She was a pop star and music phenom, a woman who'd recently been voted sexiest woman alive by a men's magazine, yet she was clearly down-to-earth and ... normal, despite her party-girl image. Most men would be salivating over her long dark hair, blue eyes, and killer body, but Scott preferred the brown-haired, brown-eyed schoolteacher he'd woken up to this morning.

He looked across the table at Lola, and after hashing out the security plans they'd implement if she hired them, Scott came to the conclusion that she knew how to handle her life. She didn't take shit from her bandmates, nor did she plan to let angry fans ruin her life. She was engaged to Peter Grissom Jr., a Miami Thunder all-star player and another reason Tyler and Scott couldn't turn down the job. No matter how they felt about Grey Kingston.

They wrapped up the meeting with a firm commitment from Lola to hire them.

Scott's cell rang, and the screen showed Rick. "Talk to me."

"She just walked out of school, ignored me, got into her car, and drove off."

He glanced at his watch. They were barely halfway through the day. Was she sick? "Where is she headed?"

"Looks like your place."

"Okay, stick close to her. I'll be there soon. Thanks, man." Scott disconnected the call and dialed Meg, but it went straight to voice mail.

After a quick check-in with Tyler, Scott headed home, making the trip in record time. He acknowledged Rick, who sat in his vehicle on the street in front of the house, and pulled into his driveway, not surprised to find Meg's car already parked there.

He headed inside, not sure what to expect. "Meg?" He tossed his keys on the credenza by the front door.

When she didn't reply, he checked the kitchen and, finding it empty, headed for the bedroom. He found her lying on the bed, fully dressed, curled up on her side.

As much as he liked the sight of her on his bed, his stomach cramped with worry. "Hey." He sat down beside her on the mattress. "Are you sick?"

"Did Rick call and tattle on me?" she asked.

"He let me know you left work unexpectedly. You didn't answer your phone, so I came home to check on you."

She sniffed and pushed herself upright, then settled back against the pillows, her hair falling messily around her shoulders, makeup-streaked tears on her face. His stomach clenched at the sight.

"I'm not sick," she said, and he breathed freely for the first time since Rick's call.

She bit down on her lip, looking up at him with those big brown eyes. "But I am unemployed."

"Excuse me?"

"Parents called school to complain about the strange man in an unmarked car sitting on school property. The principal talked to Rick. He didn't give my name, but considering I'd put Mike on a list of people not to be allowed into the school, it wasn't difficult to figure out who he was guarding. One of the parents who complained is a board member, and she wanted to have a meeting." Meg rubbed her hands up and down her bare arms.

Scott was dying to pull her against him, but she didn't appear at all receptive at the moment. Unlike the time she'd thrown herself against him, she was stiff and unyielding, her body language screaming *don't touch*. She clearly didn't want to rely on him, and damn, but that hurt.

"How did that lead to you being fired?" he asked, sticking to facts.

"Unpaid leave," she said, enunciating each syllable. "The principal didn't force things. But when he asked me if Mike was a danger to the kids, I just didn't know. What if he showed up and was drinking? What if he got past Rick and the kids were in the way . . . I couldn't say for sure it was safe. And if it were my child, I'd want me gone." She shrugged in defeat. "There was no point in letting a board meeting happen, so I just accepted the inevitable."

Scott swore loudly. "I wish we could find the bastard, but according to Luke, Mike is MIA. We can't locate him, and Luke's spoken to friends and last-known coworkers. All the calls you've gotten have been on burner phones and are untraceable. But the Ashtons seem different." Scott needed to tell her more about what Luke had uncovered about the couple, but now wasn't the time.

"It doesn't matter. Mike's got the upper hand, just like he wants."

"Let's see if we can't tilt things in your favor. I think it's time to talk to Mike's parents. Let's see if they have any sway over their son."

"It didn't seem like it when I spoke to them, but it's worth a shot. I need this job," she said, her voice breaking. "I tried to think of alternatives. I can't tutor older kids to make money for the same reason I've basically been asked to leave. And I have savings, but I counted on my income to buy a crib and baby furniture, clothing, formula, diapers . . . I can't afford to let this situation go on."

Needing to touch her, hoping she needed contact with him too, he grasped her hands, threading their fingers together, the act meaning something to him. He pushed back the rush of panic and focused on the now. On Meg.

"We'll figure this out."

She glanced at him, her eyes glassy, her jaw set and determined. "*I* will."

He absolutely noticed her use of the word *I*. Knew he'd caused it with his callous comment about family being for suckers and happily ever after happening only in fairy tales. A lump swelled in his throat, and everything inside him screamed at him to reassure her. To promise he'd be there for her no matter what. But rehashing his past had reminded him all too well of how much pain he'd been in when he'd lost his own baby. Which led to the horrible realization that if he allowed himself to think of Meg and the baby as *his*, and she walked away when the danger was over, he'd lose a lot more than he ever had with Leah.

And he didn't know if he could come back from that.

He glanced at Meg, noting both her fragility and the strength he admired. Damn, but he wished he'd thought this through earlier . . . like when he'd pushed for more than one night. But he hadn't. He'd let his desire for her win out, and as Meg had pointed out, his white-knight complex to come out to play.

Fuck. Now neither one of them would escape this thing unscathed.

"Do you have the Ashtons' phone number?" he asked, focusing on her issues and not the emotions he couldn't control.

She nodded.

"Let's set up a meeting."

"Okay."

A phone call later and Meg had a plan to meet Mike's parents for brunch at their Palm Beach country club on Wednesday. He'd have preferred an immediate get-together, but they were out of town this weekend. Scott didn't know what, if anything, they could do to get their son under control, but assuming they cared about the baby the way they claimed to, he hoped they'd become Meg's allies. She deserved to have something in her life go right for once.

Meg woke up and slipped out of bed, leaving Scott fast asleep. After the craziness of yesterday, she'd barely remembered she had an OB-GYN appointment this morning. Her doctor worked one Saturday a month, and because Meg didn't want to miss a day of school, she'd taken a Saturday appointment. Now, of course, it didn't matter. But no matter how tired she was, she didn't want to skip something so important.

She took a quick shower, dressed, and slipped out of the bedroom, surprised Scott still slept soundly. She left him a note explaining where she went and propped it against the coffee machine, where he was most likely to see it first thing. She'd learned Scott liked his morning caffeine fix as soon as he woke up.

She had a hunch he wouldn't be happy she hadn't woken him and let him know she was headed out, but this was something she needed to do on her own. A doctor's appointment and sonogram of her baby was the most personal, intimate thing she could imagine, and though she longed to have someone to share it with—and that wasn't being needy, just honest—she understood she had to draw boundaries with Scott. No matter how much she wished otherwise, and there was no point denying that she did.

A quick glance told her that her friendly bodyguard sat outside the house, watching over her. Although Scott could handle things inside, Rick was making sure Mike didn't lurk or cause trouble outside. She pulled out of the driveway, slowed, and waved, giving him time to put the car in gear and follow. She wasn't stupid, nor would she take unnecessary chances. Mike was out there somewhere, not happy that she was still carrying his baby. Protection made sense.

A little while later, Meg lay on the table in a flimsy gown, and Dr. Taylor, a middle-aged woman whom Meg trusted and liked a lot, spread warm gel over her belly.

"So we're going to find the heartbeat." The doctor moved the wand around while Meg held her breath. She vividly remembered the hospital visit after Mike had shoved her . . . She'd been bleeding, and the wait while the doctor searched for the heartbeat had been excruciating.

She felt that way now and found herself saying a little prayer until finally, she heard the *whoosh, whoosh* from the machine. She expelled a long breath of relief.

"There we go," the doctor said cheerfully. "Nice and fast. Good job." She smiled and clicked on the screen, printing out the view. "Any questions for me this visit?" she asked.

Meg shook her head.

"You're taking your vitamins?"

"I am. They make me nauseous, but I try to do it after a meal."

"And that is normal." Dr. Taylor hooked her wand back into a holder and met Meg's gaze. "You look tired. Are you getting enough sleep?"

Meg swallowed hard. "Trying. I'm having some issues with the baby's father." She didn't want to go into detail. No point mentioning she was out of work for the moment as well.

"Well, stress isn't good for you or the baby," the doctor said, as if Meg needed the reminder. She wasn't asking for the nightmare her life had become.

"I know. There are just so many things that are out of my control right now."

"Well, I recommend you rest. You're healthy, but you did have that bleeding early on, and we don't want a repeat, right?"

"Right." Meg shifted uncomfortably on the hard examining table.

Dr. Taylor rose to her feet. "Everything looks good. Just try to take it easy," she said. "I'll see you next month. By then we should be able to see the sex of the baby, if you want to know ahead of time." She treated Meg to a warm smile. "Take care."

"Thank you," Meg murmured. She waited for the other woman to shut the door behind her before pulling herself up to a sitting position, clutching the paper gown around her.

Did she want to know the sex of the baby? She wasn't sure, but she had time to think about it. Her heart sped up at the thought of a little girl. Of course, she wanted a healthy baby and would adore a boy, but in her heart of hearts, she hoped she had a girl she could dress up and be there for. More than her own mom had been there for her, Meg thought sadly.

When she'd called her mother and told her about the pregnancy, Alicia's response had been a succinct *Well, that'll kill your chances of finding a good man.* Meg winced at the memory she'd tried hard to push far, far away. Was that how her mother felt about her? That once her dad had left, Meg had been a burden and in the way of her finding her prince? Heaven knew she never had.

Meg dressed and drove home, trying her best not to dwell on sad or negative thoughts. As the doctor had pointed out, she didn't need added stress in her life.

It helped when Luke called to fill her in on his search on Mike's parents. On paper, at least, they weren't the monsters Mike had painted them out to be. Although Meg needed to know more, along with needing time to digest what she'd learned, she calmed a bit about meeting them.

She walked into the house and headed straight for the kitchen where she found Scott sitting with her note and a cup of coffee in front of him. Razor stubble covered his handsome face.

He wore a T-shirt, a pair of track pants, and his feet were bare. Her mouth watered at the sexy picture he presented.

"Good morning," she said, setting her purse, keys, and the sonogram photograph on the table.

"How was your appointment?" he asked.

She shrugged. "Everything's fine."

"Are you sure?" he asked gruffly.

"Why wouldn't it be? Can I get you more coffee?" she asked, changing the subject.

"No thanks." He stared into the mug, his expression unreadable. "I'm fine."

He didn't sound fine, but she couldn't read what was bugging him. Surely he hadn't wanted to go with her to the doctor. That thought was ridiculous in the extreme.

He picked up the picture and stared at the small black-and-white photo.

She wrapped her hand around the top of the nearest chair and gripped it hard. "It's hard to really see anything," she said, suddenly uncomfortable.

Scott stared at the sonogram picture. He'd seen one before, when one of the guys at the station was passing it around like a proud dad. His ex had never brought one home to show him.

Looking at Meg's baby had his insides twisting with so many conflicting emotions it was hard to name them all. But the one that stuck out, the most surprising one, was longing.

He placed the picture back on the table. "You didn't have to go alone."

She pinned him with a surprisingly steady, certain gaze. "Yes, I did." She paused, as if waiting for him to say more. When he didn't, she straightened her shoulders. "Look, I really appreciate everything you're doing for me. And I'm . . . enjoying what we have."

She sounded so blasé. Words like *enjoy* and *appreciate* didn't come close to the feelings she churned up inside of him. When he'd woken up to find her side of the bed empty, no Meg to wrap himself around, he'd been thrown. Which showed him how quickly he'd gotten used to having her in his life. And when he'd found her note in the kitchen, he'd been . . . hurt that she'd gone to her appointment alone. He didn't understand these feelings, couldn't figure out what to do with them, but there they were.

"Scott, are you listening?" she asked.

"Yes." He didn't like what he was hearing, but he was definitely listening.

"Okay." She licked her lips nervously. "Well, I was saying, I really think it's better if we keep the personal separate from—"

"From what?" He rose and stepped into her *personal* space, deliberately crowding her.

He needed to be close, to touch her, to inhale her scent and feel that his world was set right again. Dammit, she tied him in knots.

The minute he crowded her, her words trailed off. Her eyes dilated, her breathing slowed, and she swallowed hard, the action causing her throat to move up and down. He had the sudden desire to kiss her there, to run his teeth along her silken skin.

But she was making a point. One he didn't like. She'd put him on edge, and there was only one outlet that would make him feel better. But first, they had to get a few things straight.

"You'd like to separate the personal from the . . . what?" he asked, his voice dark. He heard the warning in his tone.

"Sex," she said on a rush. "You couldn't possibly have wanted to go with me to the doctor this morning, so I didn't wake you. Now you're acting all hurt and pissed off, and I don't get it."

"Join the club, baby. I don't get it either. But you make me crazy. You make me want things I shouldn't, things that will come back and bite me in the ass in the end. But it doesn't stop me from wanting."

He grasped her arms and hauled her against him, sealing his lips over hers. Her hands came to his shoulders, and for a brief second, he thought she'd push him away. Then her hands curled into his shirt, her lips softened, and she gave herself over to the kiss and to him.

chapter nine

Not only could Meg not resist Scott, she couldn't resist how much he wanted her. His torment called to hers. They might not know what they were doing relationship-wise, but *this* they knew how to do well.

The kiss was hard and demanding, full of the same frustration she'd sensed in him when she'd walked in, but he tasted so good, a hint of coffee and all Scott, as he plundered her mouth.

His hand went for the waistband of her pants, and he yanked them down, his big hand cupping her sex. "So fucking hot and wet," he groaned.

She arched into his touch, and he pushed her panties aside and immediately thrust one finger deep inside, curling into her and finding her sweet spot immediately. Small tremors kicked in without warning, and a low, vibrating moan escaped her throat.

"I love how responsive you are." He buried his face in her neck and sucked along her collarbone, all the while pumping one finger in and out until she was a writhing mess of need.

Oh God. She was *this* close to coming, and when he pressed his thumb over her clit, rubbing her as his finger did its thing, she shattered into pieces, warm, beautiful waves of bliss pulling her under. Only Scott's strong arm around her back kept her on her feet.

As she came back to herself, he was shoving his pants down and kicking them away. Before she could remove her panties, he slid them down her shaking legs. She could barely process where they were or what was happening, some small part of her knowing this wasn't a bedroom. But he picked her up, and she wrapped her legs around him, and he strode to the couch in the next room and stood her on her feet.

"Turn around," he said in a gruff but oh-so-sexy voice.

She spun immediately, allowing him to bend her over the arm of the sofa. Her full breasts pressed against the cushioned material as he grasped her hips and maneuvered her legs where he wanted them.

Excitement pulsed through her veins as the head of his erection nudged her already-slick opening, gliding partway into her with ease. He teased her with his cock, little pumps in and out, never quite embedding himself all the way in. Her sex clenched and squeezed around him, trying to capture and pull him all the way home so she could feel him, thick and pulsing, deep inside. But he maintained the arousing thrusts, and her desire built with crazy speed.

He rested one hand on her lower back and suddenly slowed his hips, tracing her vertebrae slowly with his calloused but gentle hand. "So pretty," he said, almost to himself, but the words, spoken in awe, wrapped around her heart.

She dipped her head forward and moaned, wondering how she was supposed to resist falling for this man. If he was all gruff, demanding, alpha, she could keep her walls high, but the tender, unexpected gestures caused her to trip further over that forbidden line, and a lump formed in her throat.

"You ready, baby?" He gripped her hips with both hands, his tight hold causing a painful rush of arousal in her sex.

"Beyond," she managed to choke out, her empty body craving his. Her heart needing him even more.

No. She pushed that awful, scary thought aside.

And when he thrust deep inside her, deeper than she'd ever felt him before, she stopped thinking at all. He groaned, low and deep, and she felt it everywhere in the best possible ways.

"Are you okay?" he asked, surprising her. "The last thing I want to do is hurt you." He smoothed his hand over her backside, and she turned to meet his gaze.

"You wouldn't hurt me intentionally, Scott. And you aren't hurting me now." Later was probably another story, but she couldn't do anything to stop it. "But if you don't move . . . *now*, I'm going to hurt you." And with that, she thrust her hips back against him.

With a low chuckle, he proceeded to do as she asked, taking her hard while still holding back, she could tell. It didn't matter when he knew just how to make love to her, to find that right spot and send her soaring. He followed after her, and the hot feel of him coming inside her, her name on his lips, echoing in her ears, was something she'd never forget.

A little while later, Meg had showered and was making lunch in the kitchen. Scott had retreated to his office, a masculine room with wooden shelves and a large-screen computer set up at his desk. Meg wasn't stupid; she was well aware something between them had shifted from easy to hard, sex being the one thing they seemed to get right. He was obviously fighting feelings that he didn't want to deal with, either because he was just against marriage and a family in his future or the fact of her pregnancy had finally set in.

She chopped up lettuce and vegetables for a salad, tossed in some grilled chicken, and added dressing.

She was about to call Scott in for lunch when her phone rang.

She glanced down, happy to see Olivia's name on the screen, and answered immediately. "Hi!" she said.

"Hi yourself. How was your appointment today?" Olivia asked.

"Everything's status quo. The doctor asked if I wanted to know the sex of the baby," she said as she washed her hands and put the big bowl of salad on the table.

"Do you want to know what you're having?" Olivia asked. "Because I want to be surprised."

Meg sighed. "I'm so torn. On the one hand, knowing will make the buying easier. On the other, I want to experience the newness and surprise."

Olivia laughed. "I hear you. I have so many things on order, I'm afraid to figure out how to get it all home."

Meg tried to ignore the pang of envy at how easy it seemed for Olivia. The man who loved her, the money to do what she needed for her child. The grass always looked greener, but that wasn't necessarily the case. Although for Olivia and Dylan, Meg truly hoped it was. They deserved every bit of happiness.

So do you, a little voice in her head told her, but she pushed it aside. What you deserved and what life threw at you were often vastly different. "I'm just about to eat lunch. Can I call you back?" Meg asked.

"Sure. But I'll see you tonight?" Olivia asked.

"What's tonight?"

An awkward silence followed, and then Olivia said, "My mom asked all the kids to come for dinner. I just thought . . . Never mind. Call me later." Olivia rushed off the phone, and Meg didn't blame her.

She turned and caught sight of Scott standing in the doorway, watching her. "You scared me!"

"Sorry. I didn't want to interrupt your call."

"No problem. I was just going to get you anyway. Lunch is ready."

"Thank you. Looks good. And I appreciate it."

"It's fine."

He stepped into the kitchen. "Listen, my mother called a few minutes ago. She wants us all at the house for dinner tonight at six. She has an announcement of some sort."

"That's fine. I can keep busy here." She stepped over to one of the cabinets and pulled out glasses.

"Actually, I was hoping you'd come with me."

She met his serious gaze. "It sounds like it's a family thing." Not only didn't she belong there, but she didn't want anyone getting the wrong idea of what was going on between her and Scott.

"My mom's been with this guy, Michael Brooks, for a few years. I just have an uneasy feeling. I don't know what she has to say, and I'd like you there when I hear it," he said, his gaze softening as he looked at her. "Her boyfriend's a decent guy, but it'll be weird to hear if she's going to remarry. She's been through enough."

"You think marrying him would be bad for her?" Meg asked, wondering if this was more of Scott's negative views on family and marriage or if he had a legitimate issue with his mother's boyfriend.

He rolled his shoulders, obviously uncomfortable with the question.

"Probably not. It's still just weird having another guy with my mother," he said. "I hate what my father did to her but . . ."

Taking her by surprise, he slid his fingers into hers, clasping them tightly together. "Like I said, it's awkward, and I'd really like you with me."

Her heart swelled, her throat feeling full at his admission. It was the admission of the young boy inside him, not the man he was now, and she was touched he'd let her in. He'd done so much for her. How could she be selfish and fight him on this?

Even if meeting his mother and the rest of his family felt too intimate and a lot awkward for her, she could put her own feelings aside and be there for him for a change.

"Okay," she said softly. "I'll come with you."

"Thank you." The look he gave her was enough to send her running far and fast, but she was in this.

Until he no longer was.

Meg's heart was in her throat as Scott pulled up to his mother's house in Weston and parked the truck. It was an imposing yet gorgeous structure, with tropical shrubbery, a circular driveway, and acreage, which was unusual in Florida. A variety of luxury cars filled the drive, letting her know that many of his siblings had already arrived.

"Relax." He placed his hand over her own, which were entwined together, as she'd been twisting them nervously in her lap.

"I really don't belong here."

"Hey," he said, his voice strong and sure. Calming even. "I want you here. That means you belong."

She knew that in her head, but her heart was beating way too fast inside her chest.

"You're doing this for me, and I appreciate it." He slid his hand behind her neck, pulled her close, and sealed his mouth over hers, effectively shutting her up. He kissed her hard and long, until the pounding inside her body had nothing to do with nerves and everything to do with the heat and desire he generated. He nibbled on her lower lip before releasing her with a strangled groan, pausing to catch his breath by resting his forehead against hers.

"Better?" he asked.

She couldn't stop the smile curving her lips. "Much."

He shook his head and laughed. "Stick with me. I know what you need."

She pulled down the visor to check her makeup. Not much she could do about her puffy lips, but the rest of her was okay.

"You're beautiful, Meg."

He spoke so softly and reverently that she believed he meant it. "Thank you." Blowing out a puff of air, she picked up the pie she'd insisted they stop and buy. "I'm ready."

A chic-looking woman met them at the door, her dark hair with soft highlights falling around her face. From their similar features, Meg knew immediately she was Scott's mother.

"Scott, honey, it's so good to see you." She pulled him into a warm hug.

"Hey, Mom."

"And you must be Meg! I'm so glad you could join us." Her warmth was genuine. The sparkle in her eyes could be mistaken for nothing except happiness.

"Thank you. I hope I'm not intruding."

"Nonsense. I was thrilled when Scott told me he was bringing a guest." Emma accepted the bakery box from Meg. "Thank you so much. You didn't need to bring anything, but extra sweets are always welcome." She ushered them into the house, and Scott shot Meg an *I told you it would all be okay* look.

Yes, fine. The man had been right again.

He placed a strong hand on her back and led her toward the sound coming from inside the house. The gesture was meant to be reassuring, but every time he touched her, he lit Meg's body on fire. The chemistry between them was that potent and hot.

She smoothed her hand over the dress she'd chosen, glad she'd been able to fit into her favorite one, though barely. No need to break out the maternity wear for tonight.

They stepped into a large state-of-the-art kitchen that was open and led to a great room, where the rest of the family had gathered.

"Meg!" Olivia's familiar voice sounded above the others. Meg walked toward her friend, while Scott stopped to talk to Ian and Riley, who Meg greeted with a wave. She'd catch up with her later.

Olivia greeted Meg with a big hug. "So glad you're here too!"

Meg hugged her back but didn't reply.

She glanced up and saw Dylan, waiting for his hello, a smile on his face. "Hey, Meggie."

"Dylan! It's been a long time." They embraced as old friends do.

It had been a while since she'd spoken to Dylan. These days, when she needed an ear, she was more likely to call one of her girlfriends or Olivia than her old friend. And that seemed to work fine for them both.

"Oh! Avery's here. I'll be back in a few," Olivia said, rushing off to talk to her sister.

"You look good," Dylan said, holding on to her hand. "And Olivia keeps me up on how you're doing."

"It's been . . . interesting, to say the least."

"You're handling everything, just like I knew you would."

"Well, I have help . . ." She trailed off, afraid Dylan would think she was falling back into old patterns, relying on a man when she should be handling things herself. "It's not the same this time," she rushed to tell him. "Scott's helping me professionally. I really don't know how I'd handle Mike practically stalking me if not for him."

And she didn't feel like she was latching on to him the same way she had with men in her past. Whatever her feelings for him were, they were more solid and real. Even if he'd made it clear they couldn't go anywhere.

"Relax, Meg. I'm not judging you," Dylan assured her.

As her one-time boyfriend, later best friend, Dylan knew her insecurities and tendencies better than most. He was the one who'd called her out on her behavior when warranted. He was also the one who would never abandon her if she really needed him. The amazing thing was, since he'd drawn the line in their relationship, she really hadn't needed him at all. Not the way she'd once thought.

"Maybe I am. My life is just spinning out of control. But at the same time, I'm thinking clearly and trying to keep things in perspective."

He smiled at that. "Good."

She shrugged. "That's it? No words of advice?"

He brushed at his goatee with his fingers. "I don't think you need them. Not from me," he said at the same moment a solid arm slipped around Meg from behind.

"Am I interrupting?" Scott asked, an unusual edge to his voice.

"No. I was just telling Meg that pregnancy agrees with her," Dylan said smoothly, avoiding mentioning anything personal in their conversation. Scott wouldn't appreciate knowing they'd been talking about him, even in a roundabout way.

"Yes, it does." Scott squeezed her waist and pressed an unexpected kiss to her cheek. "I'm going to steal her away now," he informed Dylan, who stepped back immediately.

Meg narrowed her gaze, surprised there wasn't more pleasant conversation between the two men.

"Time to meet the rest of the clan," Scott said, leading her away from Dylan before she could manage a reply.

She spun out of his embrace. "What was that about?"

"Just—"

"Staking a claim? He's married to your sister, for God's sake."

Scott blew out a long breath. "And he's crazy about her. I know. Shit."

She narrowed her gaze. "What is it?"

He grasped her hand and pulled her to an empty, small study, decorated in dark colors, a leopard carpet on the floor, and gold accessories on the built-in wooden shelves.

He pushed the door partially closed. "I don't know what that was. I saw you with Dylan, knew he was the only guy you were really in love with, and I went a little crazy."

Jealous? Scott had been jealous of Dylan? Her eyes opened wide at his admission. "Dylan and I haven't been together since high school," Meg said, speaking softly because no way did she want anyone overhearing.

"Yeah, well, before me, he was the one you turned to for everything. And that wasn't all that long ago."

Meg searched for the words to explain, knowing it wouldn't be easy. "A few short months ago, I would have sworn Dylan and I were just friends. That he was my best friend and I was his."

"And now?" he asked, his jaw tight.

"Now I can look back and say my need for Dylan wasn't healthy. It wasn't a two-sided friendship. I was . . . clingy, needy, and to be honest, it embarrasses me." She refused to duck from Scott's heated gaze. He needed to hear this, and she needed to say it.

She reached up and stroked his cheek, wanting to ease his distress. She felt the rasp of razor stubble beneath her fingers and loved the feel of his skin against hers.

"And that's why you're so afraid of leaning on anyone?"

"Partly. I don't want to be that person who can't take care of herself."

She also didn't want to fall apart when this thing between them ended. Even before she understood his feelings on marriage and family, she'd worried that she wasn't enough to make him stay. Or worse, that she would come to be too much of a burden and drive him away. None of that mattered now. He was going no matter what.

"Scott?" a female voice called out. "Olivia told me you were here, and I want to meet Meg . . . There you are!" A pretty woman with long dark hair walked in, stopping short. "Oh, sorry! I didn't mean to interrupt a private conversation."

"No, come in," Meg said brightly. "Are you Avery?"

The other woman nodded. "Hi, Scott." She pecked him on the cheek. "It's great to meet you," she said, turning to Meg. "Olivia has told me so much about you. We have to all get together for girls' night. I can drink, and you two pregnant women can watch me drown my sorrows," she said, following up with an obviously forced smile.

"Av, are you okay?"

"I'm great!"

Even Meg knew her words were forced and wondered what was bothering her.

"I'd love to chat and get to know you, but Mom said it's dinnertime, so we need to go into the dining room." Avery spun around and walked out of the room.

"What's going on with her?" Meg asked Scott.

He groaned. "I think it has something to do with an old boyfriend." Scott explained that Grey Kingston of the band Tangled Royal was Avery's high school boyfriend. "He left her to go find fame and fortune, which he did. According to Olivia, he called her last time he was in town, and they got together. Nobody knows what happened, but she's been . . . off ever since."

"Scott! Dinner!" someone called.

He shot Meg a wry grin. "Let's go find out what my mother's big news is."

Meg had to hand it to Emma, she had a flair for the dramatic, ignoring her children's questions throughout dinner and holding her news for after dessert.

"So I'm sure you all wonder why I asked you to come here tonight," Emma finally said.

"Been wondering, Mom," Avery said.

"I think I know," Olivia said next with a grin.

"Not playing twenty questions," Ian muttered to his sisters. "Let's hear it."

"Well, Michael wanted to be here, but he had a work emergency, which is just as well because I wanted to talk to all of you alone."

Meg squirmed in her seat, feeling very much like an outsider. As if sensing her emotions, Scott reached for her beneath the table, his hand coming to rest on her thigh, squeezing lightly. The act calmed her, then immediately spiked her pulse, but she forced herself to focus on his mother's words.

"Michael asked me to marry him, and I said yes."

The women around the table squealed, called out congratulations, and Emma's daughters jumped up to hug her. The men, Scott and his brothers in particular, sat in stunned silence. Which was what Meg sensed had had Emma so concerned. And why she was glad her fiancé hadn't been able to make this family dinner.

Meg immediately slid her hand over Scott's, giving him silent support, as she knew he'd been dreading something like this. Having never met Michael, she couldn't judge Emma's taste in men or why her sons were so concerned.

"Isn't this a little soon?" Ian spoke up first, his dark tone silencing the women's excitement.

Emma turned her gaze toward her oldest son. "Funny you should ask that. Michael and I have been together now . . . for about as long as you and Riley," she said pointedly. "And my granddaughter is asleep in a crib upstairs. Any other objections?" she asked, her voice strong.

But the wobble of her chin and the sheen of tears in her eyes told a whole different story. She might be a grown woman, but she desperately wanted her family's approval. Meg didn't blame her. Though she didn't know what it was like to have such a large family, with everyone having differing opinions and feelings, Meg envied this group their closeness.

"He's a nice guy, but do you have to marry him?" Scott asked. "It's just so permanent, and what if things don't work out?"

"Are you saying you don't believe in marriage anymore?" Olivia asked her brother.

"Goddammit, Liv, this isn't about me," Scott snapped back.

That was too close to the conversation they'd had about his feelings on family, and Meg slipped lower into her chair. She didn't know how many gut-punching reminders she could take.

"He's good to her," Olivia said to Ian, but the sweep of her gaze encompassed all her brothers. "You've all seen it. What do you want? For Mom to be alone for the rest of her life? Dad's not. He's off doing what's best for him. He always has. Why does he deserve to get what he wants out of life with Savannah but Mom doesn't?" She wrapped an arm around her mother's shoulder.

"Okay, everyone, stop. Right now," Emma said. "I called you all here to give you the courtesy of letting you know. I wasn't asking your permission. I'd like it if you could all be happy for me. If not, then at least shut up about it." Emma's voice cracked, and Scott jumped out of his seat to go to her, followed by Ian and Tyler, who'd sulked in silence.

"I guess it's just that no one's good enough," Scott said gruffly as he reached her. "I love you. Michael's a good guy. I'm happy for you."

Or he'd get there, Meg thought, her heart too wrapped up in his feelings and this family drama. She really needed to get out of here and breathe. Except leaving here meant going to Scott's house, not her own. She pulled in a shaky breath, watching as everyone now congratulated Emma and made their peace with her decision. Meg was the last to step up and offer her good wishes.

Then finally it was time to leave. Exhaustion beat at every bone in Meg's body. She couldn't wait to go to sleep.

Olivia caught up with Meg before she made it to the front door. "Are you okay?" Olivia asked.

"Why wouldn't I be? I feel bad that your family isn't all supportive of your mom, but I'm sure they'll get there."

Olivia smiled. "They will. The guys are . . . guys. But I'm talking about you."

"Nothing to worry about," Meg lied. No reason to involve his sister in her feelings for Scott.

"Okay, well, I wanted to know if you and Scott were up for dinner tomorrow night. You know, the four of us. I think it'd be fun."

Meg blinked, surprised. "Oh, umm . . . I don't know. Scott might be busy." Not that he tended to go out at night, but a couple's date when she and Scott weren't really in a formal relationship?

"I'm not busy, and dinner sounds good to me," Scott said, coming up behind her.

"Great!" Olivia said. "One of you call me in the morning, and we'll pick a place and time. I'm going to check on Mom."

Once they were in the truck headed home, Scott glanced at her, one hand resting on the steering wheel as he drove. "Any reason you were trying to avoid going out with them?" he asked, way too perceptive as usual.

She figured honesty was the best way to handle this. "For the same reason I'm trying to get you to see that I'm here for security reasons only. I know we're sleeping together, but that's because we can't seem to keep our hands off each other."

He grinned. "You've got that right."

She shook her head. "I just don't want to give your family the wrong impression," she said.

"And what impression would that be?" he asked.

She wondered why he was deliberately being so dense. "That we're a couple with any long-term potential," she said.

"Well, thank you for being so blunt. Now I know you're only in it for sex," he said, sounding grumpy and put out even though he was the one, more than her, who didn't believe in anything else.

She raised an eyebrow at that. "And you're not? Or are you lining up for labor, delivery, and daddy duty?"

When he didn't answer, she glanced out the passenger window and remained silent for the rest of the ride.

By the time they arrived at Scott's, neither one of them was up for much in the way of conversation—or anything else, for that matter. She washed up in his luxurious bathroom that was three times the size of her own and climbed into his bed.

Long after Scott pulled her into his arms and drifted off to sleep, Meg's thoughts were churning around in her head. As was Olivia's shouted question at Scott.

Are you saying you don't believe in marriage anymore? his sister had asked.

Or are you lining up for labor, delivery, and daddy duty?

She squeezed her eyes shut tight, wishing she didn't care about his refusal to answer either question.

chapter ten

SCOTT DRESSED FOR DINNER, LISTENING TO THE SOUND OF MEG GETTING READY IN his bathroom: the low hum of the blow-dryer and the small sounds of different jars and items being placed on the marble countertops. Sounds that were becoming all too familiar and comfortable. He hated how strained things were between them now. He missed the days when they could say and do anything without thought or consequence.

He buttoned his shirt, which he'd chosen because Emilio's was a nice restaurant. No T-shirts there. It was located near his half brother Alex's apartment in an out-of-the-way location. So as not to run into Alex and Madison and have them feel slighted, Scott had texted Alex and asked if the other couple wanted to join them, but they had other plans. Alex promised to get in touch, and they could do something another time. Scott refused to think about whether or not that time would come. Where Meg would be in a few short weeks.

She stepped out of the bathroom, and Scott sucked in a shallow breath at the sight of her. Her hair fell over one shoulder in soft waves, and her skin had burned slightly during her afternoon in the sun while he'd been holed up in his home office. Her cheeks were flushed pink, her brown eyes highlighted in a soft purple, her lips a lush shimmer he wanted to taste. Now.

She stared at him, her gaze hesitant after this afternoon's distance, and he didn't blame her.

"You look gorgeous," he said, breaking the silence and, he hoped, any tension.

He couldn't stop staring. She wore a one-piece white outfit that set off her tan, with flowing pants and a ruffled layer that cut straight across her lush chest. He didn't miss the fact that her breasts were getting bigger . . . and more sensitive.

Hell, all of her was more responsive, to his hands, his mouth, and yes, even his cock. Her body accepted him easily, clasping him in amazing heat and shattering more easily each time. At this point, he was willing to concede prowess to her hormones, he thought wryly, not that he was complaining in the least. He just wished the emotions between them weren't such a minefield, laden with unforeseen traps and triggers.

"Thank you," Meg said. Her gaze raked over him, and a soft smile pulled at her lips. "You look pretty good yourself."

He glanced at his black pants and white long-sleeve button-down and shrugged. "I shaved earlier."

She laughed and the sound lightened the mood. "Then that's it, I guess."

"Ready for dinner?"

"I'm starving," she said.

He frowned. "That's because you missed lunch."

"I had a shake a little while ago." She picked up a small straw purse. "All set," she told him.

He hooked his arm in hers and led her down to his truck. He helped her into the seat, ignoring the feel of her waist in his hands, swallowing a groan. He slammed her door shut and headed around to the driver's side.

The trip to Miami passed quickly, music on the radio, easy conversation between them. This was what he'd missed, he thought. Although they hadn't been together long, their first weeks had been so easy. Had he ever been with another woman who fit him so well? Thank goodness that thought hit just as he pulled up to the parking lot near Emilio's and he pulled down his window to deal with the attendant.

A few minutes later, they were seated across from Olivia and Dylan in the small Italian restaurant. Olivia had made a reservation, and Anna had reserved them a private table in the corner. His sister had already ordered sparkling water. Dylan and Scott passed on hard alcohol. They ordered quickly, Olivia asking Emilio to serve slowly so they had time to relax and talk.

Talk made Scott nervous, especially when his sister was involved, but Meg and Olivia had developed a close friendship in a short time, so he hoped the women would carry the more intense parts of conversation.

Scott knew exactly what had him on edge. Olivia was intuitive and would notice any problems. His sister had already warned him about hurting Meg, and looking back, Scott should have listened harder. Thought more. If Dylan got a whiff of tension tonight, he'd be in even more trouble.

To make matters worse, his sister couldn't be trusted not to dig into private, personal conversations better left alone. Especially when it came to his love life. Knowing how much Olivia cared about Meg, he could only hope she was smart tonight.

They started with football, a conversation that was always fun and easy, and segued into Scott's new position within Tyler's firm.

"I'm enjoying the freedom involved, catching up on client files and getting to know what everyone needs. It's been challenging on a whole different level," Scott explained.

"I bet," Dylan said. "It's great to do something you enjoy." As travel director for the Thunder, Dylan knew what he was talking about. The man loved his job. "Meg, how are things at school? Kids still keeping you on your toes?" Dylan asked.

And just like that, easy conversation ground to a halt.

"Umm, I—" Meg stammered.

"Meg is fine," Scott said, hoping to help Meg bypass the answer entirely.

"Actually I'm not. I'm on temporary leave," Meg said, going on to explain how the situation with her ex had escalated, leading to the principal strongly suggesting she take leave.

"Oh my God! Why didn't you say anything?" Olivia asked. "I'd have come over . . . called, something," she said, offering all the support she could.

"I'm going to kill the bastard," Dylan said, his hands curling into fists.

"Well, get in line, because when *I* find him, he's going to wish he'd never been born." Though Scott appreciated Dylan backing Meg, when it came to protecting her, *he* wanted that job and didn't mind letting the other man know it.

Olivia studied him, eyes narrowed, and Scott swallowed a curse.

"I don't want anyone confronting Mike for me. He's dangerous," Meg said. "But I'm meeting with his parents on Wednesday."

"*We're* meeting with his parents," Scott reminded her.

Meg raised an eyebrow. "I was going to discuss that with you in the morning. I think it's better if I go alone. Rick will keep an eye on me."

Scott tensed, clenching his jaw and wondering when things had spiraled out of his control. "We'll talk about it when we're alone," he said, well aware of Dylan's and Olivia's intense stares, taking in every word and action that Meg and Scott made.

"Well, regardless, I'm not worried about meeting with them anymore. Luke said the background check turned up all good things. Lydia and Walter seem to be rational, decent people. They support children's charities and—"

"What the hell do you know about what Luke found?" Scott asked her. Everything about Meg's case was supposed to be his domain. Luke had no right to jump in with answers Scott had planned to give her, and he'd intended to have this conversation in the morning before the lunch meeting.

Meg merely shrugged, ignoring his sharp tone. "Luke called. *He* filled me in."

"I was going to tell you everything. There just hasn't been time."

Dylan braced his arms on the table. "Meggie, I can't imagine one good thing about the people who raised that asshole," he said skeptically.

At the old nickname Dylan called her, Scott's jaw locked in place.

"Actually, it's not what you think," Meg said to Dylan. "The Ashtons adopted Mike when he was a baby. I didn't know that. He also had fetal alcohol syndrome, so there's that component too. I suppose I can't necessarily blame them for how Mike turned out. There's definitely something to genetics."

She trembled as she spoke, and Scott could guess where her mind had gone. His anger fled in the face of her obvious fears. He knew for sure what she was thinking.

"Don't think that way." He settled his hand over hers, hoping to comfort her. "Your baby will be fine, even with that bastard's genes. He has *you*." And a deep-seated longing arose inside him, because he wanted to claim that position in the baby's life too.

Shit. He was in so much trouble.

"Meg, are you okay?" Olivia asked softly.

Scott glanced her way.

Her eyes looked suspiciously damp. "Actually, I'm going to go to the ladies' room. Excuse me."

Scott rose as she stood and headed for the other side of the restaurant.

He lowered himself back into his seat.

"Scott, what the hell is going on?" Olivia asked.

"I'd like an answer to that too," Dylan said.

Emilio walked over with food in his hands, and Olivia waved him away. "A few minutes, please?"

The older man nodded.

"Talk fast, big brother," she muttered.

"Shit. Everything was fine until I told her about Leah."

Olivia glanced at Dylan. "His ex-wife. I told you about her," she said.

Dylan nodded. "What about her?" he asked, his tone chilly.

"It's not about her, it's about what she did. Before her, I didn't want kids. When she got pregnant, I got excited. Invested. I really wanted to be a father. But she never came around, and instead of talking about it with me, she had an abortion. Just like that, everything I'd dreamed about was gone." He snapped his fingers in the air. "Telling Meg reminded me of the pain, and I said something stupid."

Dylan narrowed his gaze.

In for a penny, Scott thought. "I said, the whole family thing is for suckers, and happily ever after only happens in fairy tales." He ducked his head and groaned. "I pretty much put the last nail in the coffin of whatever was happening between us."

"So explain that you don't feel that way anymore!" Olivia glanced over her shoulder, but there was no sign of Meg yet.

"What if I do?"

"Excuse me?" his sister asked, sounding appalled.

"Look, Liv," he said, ignoring Dylan because he really couldn't deal with the other man at the moment. "I love her, okay? What if I let myself get involved with her and the baby, and then we wrap things up with her stalker ex and she doesn't need me anymore? She can pick up and move out, and that's it. Everything gone again. Except this time, I don't know if I'd get over it."

His sister's jaw had gone slack. "You love her?"

Scott couldn't believe he'd said it out loud either. Hell, he hadn't admitted it to himself before now. But what else was this driving need to be with her, to protect her, to get so involved in her life that she wouldn't want to leave?

"Yeah, I do."

"Then man up," Dylan said.

Scott clenched his hands beneath the table. "What the fuck do you know about me or my life?" he asked the other man. "Just because you are or were Meg's best friend doesn't give you the right to tell me what to do."

Dylan's hand came down on the table hard. Olivia jumped, then wrapped her fingers around his hand. "Stop it, and listen. Both of you."

She turned to Scott. "I, of all people, know how hard it is to get over the pain in your past."

His sister had lost a baby when she was young, been betrayed by both that baby's father and their own parent. So yes, Olivia understood better than most.

"But the risk is so worth it," she said, glancing at her husband, her eyes shining with love. "Dylan stuck by me. He never gave up on me. On us. And because of that, I was able to come around and believe that I deserved a future that included kids . . . and a good man," she said, her voice thick and full of emotion.

His sister's words wrapped around him, making sense not because of their logic but due to the fact that she'd experienced the same feelings of loss. She'd closed herself off to more. And she'd come out the other side because she'd been brave.

"Look, man. You knew Meg was pregnant when you started this thing. Are you really going to bail now because it's getting real?"

"Dylan," Olivia said, warning him to shut up with her tone.

"What? It's the truth," Dylan muttered.

"He gets what I said, don't you?" his sister asked him.

Scott met Olivia's gaze and nodded, because he did. Olivia had done what he would have thought was impossible and gotten through to him. Dylan was right. He had to man up. Not necessarily throw Meg's life into further turmoil by dumping his feelings on her in the middle of her current nightmare, but he had to stop waffling. He'd told her from the beginning he was all in.

Then he'd turned around and backed off when messy emotions had gotten involved. Shame on him, he thought.

"Here she comes," Olivia said softly.

Scott looked from his sister to Dylan. "I heard you. Both of you," he said, rising to his feet as Meg approached the table.

He held out her chair so she could sit, and Emilio returned with their food. The rest of the meal passed with general conversation. Scott was ready to get Meg home and fix things between them as best he could. The rest would come with time. He hoped.

Meg walked out of the restaurant and headed for the parking garage. The balmy air settled on her shoulders, too humid for comfort. She glanced at Scott, who seemed . . . calmer somehow. Which she didn't understand, considering how intense so much of the conversation had been.

"Would it be okay if we stopped by my apartment on the way home?" she asked. They weren't too far from her place, so it wasn't out of the way. "I need more comfortable clothes since I'm not going to be working, and while I'm there, I can grab my mail."

"Not a problem."

He braced his hand on the small of her back as they walked, and she did her best not to visibly react to his warm touch. Even if her body responded to him, would always respond to him, her brain was sending out warning signals to keep her emotional distance.

"I should have told you what I knew about the Ashtons," he said, surprising her. "I just figured you needed time to breathe before we jumped into that again on Wednesday."

She smiled grimly. "And you didn't know Luke was going to tell me first, which pissed you off."

"It's not that," he said, too quickly.

She deliberately cleared her throat, giving him a chance to change his mind.

"Okay, it's that," he said, obviously caught. "It's just . . . I wanted to be the one to tell you."

They paused outside the garage where they'd parked. "But you didn't. You decided to wait. We've talked about this already. You can't keep making decisions about what I need to know and when."

"You're right." He tilted his head, looking into her eyes as he spoke.

"I am?"

"But you have to admit we've had a lot of different emotional topics going on. I can't always know what's best or get it right."

She sighed, and the weight on her shoulders eased a little. "I'll give you that." Nothing between them was simple. Or easy. Not anymore.

His hand slid from her back to her hip, and he turned her to face him. "Don't give up on me," he said in a thick tone, his eyes a darker navy than she could remember seeing them, his expression serious. "I know I've given you reason not to trust me. I came on strong, and then I pulled back . . . but that's over now."

She shook her head, not understanding. But her heart beat faster inside her chest.

"You've been great," she told him honestly. "You stepped up when nobody else did. You're making sure both me and my baby are safe. I'm grateful."

His hand tightened on her waist. "I don't want your gratitude, baby."

Her heart tripped at his use of the word in *that* tone. He sounded more like the Scott who'd pushed his way into her life and promised he'd never leave and less like the man who'd pulled away emotionally.

She ran her tongue over her lips, gratified when his eyes followed the movement. "What do you want?"

"You," he said gruffly, pulling her against him and kissing her hard.

If he was trying to make a point, he did it well, his tongue swiping over her lips, demanding entry she willingly gave. As he consumed her mouth, he held her hard against his hips, her body well aware of his hard length pressing into her. Excitement and yearning filled her veins, a liquid pulsing desire that spoke of true need and longing for this man. She kissed him back with everything she had, ignoring the warnings that tried to intrude.

Suddenly a loud car horn sounded, and she jumped back. "Get a room!" a man yelled out the window of a car that had pulled up the ramp of the parking garage. She and Scott were blocking the driver from leaving.

Certain she was blushing, she stepped to the side and waved. "Sorry," she called toward the car's open window as Scott joined her, laughing.

They didn't discuss the moment outside the garage or the words he'd spoken, and Meg was grateful. Her head was spinning as it was, and she needed time to unwind and just *be*, something Scott seemed to sense.

Once they arrived at her apartment, they stopped at the mailboxes downstairs, and she pulled out the stack of letters and a bulky soft package that barely fit into the box.

Scott waited while she packed up a few more casual tops and other things she'd forgotten before rejoining him. "I'm just going to look through the mail here, so I only take what I need. I have my checkbook so I can mail out any bills I don't do online."

"Take your time."

She sorted junk mail from bills, tossing the former into the trash. Her eye caught on the package, and she picked it up, looking for a return address. "Huh."

"What is it?" Scott asked.

"I don't know." She grabbed scissors from a drawer in the kitchen and cut straight across the top. She turned it upside down and shrieked as a small baby doll, the head separated from the body, fell onto the table.

Meg stared, unable to believe what she was seeing.

"Holy shit," Scott muttered. "Don't touch it." He grabbed her and pulled her back, away from the doll.

Shaking, Meg glanced up at him. "He's lost his mind," she whispered.

"He's not going to get near you or the baby," he promised, wrapping his arm around her and leading her away from the counter and the offending package. "Let me just call someone to come pick this up and dust for prints. I don't expect to turn up anything, but maybe we'll get lucky."

Meg didn't reply. She couldn't. She was too nauseous and scared to even try. This time, a friend of Scott's from the force arrived, not a cop he didn't know. The man took more interest in Meg and her case, and they processed the doll for evidence, but like Scott, he didn't hold out much hope for prints.

Through it all, Scott held her hand or wrapped her in his protective embrace, and she didn't think it made her weak to accept his comfort. Mike wanted to kill her baby. No way would she let it happen. Neither, she believed, would Scott, and that was the only thing that kept her marginally sane.

A very long while later, they returned to Scott's house. She still didn't speak, and he didn't push, which she appreciated. His steady presence was all she needed.

He locked up the house and set the alarm before joining her in the bedroom. She'd already washed up, changed into a nightie, and climbed into bed. Scott slid in beside her, pulling her tight against his hard body, holding her until she fell into a fitful sleep.

The beginning of the week passed slowly, the damned baby doll never far from her thoughts. Scott offered to stay home with her, but she insisted he go to work and get used to his new job and let the guys see him pulling his weight as boss. He needed to do that for himself and for Tyler, and Meg didn't want to grow to rely on him any more than she already did. The house was alarmed, Rick sat outside, and Meg was as safe as possible. For now.

By the time Wednesday arrived, Meg was edgy from a combination of boredom and angry frustration. Mike had made her a prisoner in Scott's house, unable to live her life, and she resented him for that. The Ashtons had invited Meg to meet at their Palm Beach country club. She explained she was bringing Scott as her friend and as her bodyguard because she wanted them to understand just how serious a threat their son posed to her and her baby. She pressed her hand against her growing belly protectively, nervous now that she had to leave the safety of the house.

She dressed in a pair of knit leggings and a matching top, a gray-and-white outfit that was true maternity wear. It seemed as if her small belly had popped overnight, her baby making its presence well and truly known. A flutter of excitement filled her along with a healthy dose of trepidation. The thought of a baby was way different than the reality, and now she'd get a feel for how Scott would react when he noticed her body's changes.

He'd asked her not to give up on him, and she'd felt the intensity and seriousness in his tone and his actions. Ever since Sunday night, he'd been back to the Scott who'd barreled his way into her life and made her the center of his world. She just didn't know if it would last, and she didn't need the added emotional stress.

Scott drove them north to Palm Beach, where the Ashtons lived, and the long ride passed in tense silence. The tension wasn't between her and Scott, however; it was Meg's nerves that had completely overtaken her. It didn't help when they pulled up to the front of the club, an imposing structure with white pillars and lush palm trees surrounding the building. She felt way out of her league.

Valets were waiting to take their car. Scott accepted the ticket before walking around the car, toward her. He always took her breath away, and today was no different. He'd showered and shaved, so not only did he look good, he smelled delicious, his musky scent calling to her body and arousing her despite the time and place.

He'd dressed up in a pair of black slacks and a pale-blue long-sleeve button-down dress shirt. Blue was clearly his favorite color, and it had quickly become hers because of how the color set off his gorgeous eyes. He also wore a black sport jacket, his holstered gun hidden at his side. Though she hated the idea of the weapon, she felt so much better knowing he was with her and armed. She didn't want to think the older couple would set her up by bringing Mike, but anything was possible. Mike was tracking her or following her somehow, and today's meeting wouldn't go unnoticed. Her stomach flipped painfully at the thought.

"Are you okay? You didn't say a word on the drive up," Scott said, his big hand cupping her elbow as he joined her.

"No," she said honestly. "But I have to do this." She pulled in a deep breath of air.

"Well, you're not alone." He pressed his forehead to hers, the gesture both tender and intimate, and her entire body flooded with warmth and heat.

"I know." She pulled back and managed a smile to reassure him. "Let's get this over with."

He studied her face, as if making sure she really was ready, before nodding. "Okay."

A little while later, introductions complete, they were seated at a small round table, facing the older couple. Lydia seemed nervous, which ironically put Meg more at ease.

"Thank you for meeting with us," Walter said. He had gray hair and, now that she allowed herself to really look at him, kind eyes.

Meg swallowed hard. "You're welcome."

Lydia leaned forward in her seat. "How are you feeling?" she asked Meg.

"I'm fine. I was pretty lucky early on. The morning sickness wasn't that bad, and now I'm feeling good."

The older woman nodded. "That's good." She paused before speaking. "I wanted so badly to carry a child." She smiled, but her eyes appeared sad. "It wasn't meant to be for us, but we were lucky enough to be able to adopt."

Meg didn't know what to say, so she remained silent. Beside her but beneath the table, Scott reached over and clasped her hand in his. He always knew when to offer silent support, as if he could read her mind or her moods.

"I've always been hands-on with children's charities, and it made sense to me to adopt a baby that everyone else might not would want." Lydia wrapped her heavily jeweled fingers around a cup of hot tea, as if needing the warmth. "Mike had fetal alcohol effects," she explained. "We didn't know what the impact would be on him long term, but we thought we were equipped to handle it."

As if sensing she needed his strength, Walter reached over and took his wife's hand away from the cup, covering it with his own. Meg watched them, surprised. She hadn't expected a loving couple, and both her heart and her mind told her this wasn't a performance for her sake. The affection between them was real.

"I take it Mike was . . . more than you anticipated?" Meg asked gently.

Lydia's eyes filled with tears, and she nodded. "He didn't have the physical problems sometimes associated with a mother who drinks, but he had the behavioral issues. As time went on, things got worse. And with the inherited addictive tendencies, when he started drinking at a young age and hanging out with the wrong kids . . ." She shook her head. "We tried counseling, outpatient treatment, inpatient treatment . . ." She trailed off, her voice catching.

"I had no idea," Meg said. "When I met Mike, I didn't notice anything wrong. He was working construction. I met his friends . . . There were no warning signs. Until he lost his job, and then he changed."

She recalled that night, the first display of temper, and she shuddered. He hadn't hit her then. In fact, he'd never laid a hand on her until she'd told him about the baby, but the sudden shift in his mood had been terrifying.

"Losing a job is something that happens often, I'm sorry to say," Walter said.

"He did get another one quickly, so I didn't think much of it. Except he was laid off pretty fast from there too." Meg took a sip of water. "He used to say you wouldn't help him because he wouldn't be the person you wanted him to be, that your expectations were too high. Then again, he found my expectations too high, and all I wanted him to do was pay his share of the rent and come home at night instead of partying with his friends."

Scott stiffened beside her, clearly not happy with the replaying of her past.

"It's not your fault," Walter said. "My son is good at manipulative behavior and getting what he wants from people." He met his wife's gaze with a sad nod.

"This is all well and good, but we need to figure out how to get Mike to back off and leave Meg alone. He's threatened to *help* her get rid of the baby, and he just sent a beheaded doll as a warning in the mail," Scott said, his angry tone reflecting his frustration.

"Oh my. I'm so sorry." Lydia shook her head, unable to meet Meg's gaze. "What can we do?"

"From what Mike has said, this is all about money. Just assure him that if he signs the papers relinquishing his rights to the baby, you won't cut him off. That will take the edge off his anger and get him to back off and leave Meg alone."

Meg knew it wasn't a guarantee, but she agreed with Scott that it might be a start.

"I'm sorry but we can't," Walter said.

chapter eleven

"CAN'T? OR WON'T?" Scott asked the older man, disappointed for Meg's sake that the last twenty minutes of understanding and kindness had still led to disappointment.

"Scott—" Meg said in warning.

"No, he's entitled to his opinion. We've heard it all before," Walter said.

"Have you ever dealt with an addict?" Lydia asked.

Meg shook her head.

"Well, it's simple. We can't enable Mike in order to ensure good behavior. It doesn't work, it won't last, and in the end, more trouble will come down the road. You're asking me to keep paying him, which will only feed his addiction. And I promise you, it won't keep you safe," Walter explained, and in that moment, he appeared older than he had on first meeting. When speaking of his son's problems, the lines in his face, the extreme sadness, were more pronounced.

"Meg, it's not that we don't want to help, it's that we've had almost thirty years of experience raising him, the last I-don't-know-how-many years being taught how to deal with addictive behavior," Lydia said, her imploring stare on Meg's as she spoke.

"Then what do you suggest?" Scott asked, well and truly pissed off.

"Unfortunately, I don't have a suggestion, and I know that's not what you want to hear." Walter met Scott's gaze. "If you need money to help keep the mother of my grandchild safe, just say the word—"

"Thanks, but I've got this," he said too harshly.

Meg squeezed his leg beneath the table. Scott took the hint, but he didn't need it. He wanted to be offended by the offer . . . but he wasn't. He also wanted to dislike these people because of who their son was . . . and couldn't. He wouldn't want to be judged by his father. He couldn't do the same to this couple.

"Meg, I meant what I said when I came to see you at school. I'd like to be part of the baby's life. But I'd like to get to know you too. We have time before the baby is born. You can get to know me . . . us," Lydia said. "You can decide for yourself once you know us better."

Scott felt Meg's shock in the stiffness of her body. "I'd like that," she said softly.

He understood. She had nobody in the way of family. Not like he did. These people were offering her and, by extension, her child, a bond she was lacking. Scott wanted that for her. Just like he wanted her to think of his mother and siblings as her family too. But first, he had to get her to accept him as a permanent part of her life.

With the difficult discussions behind them, they ate and talked about neutral subjects. They asked Meg about her childhood, where she'd gone to college, and learned more about her in general. He watched as she slowly opened up to them, something he knew from personal experience she didn't do easily.

By the time the meal ended, Meg had relaxed, and Scott had a better handle on the Ashtons. He could honestly say he was comfortable with Meg spending time in their company, not that she needed his permission, he thought wryly.

They walked out the front entrance into the warm sunshine. Scott glanced around, seeing only two valets in green jackets and a taxicab idling not far from where the men would bring his truck.

"Thank you so much for coming. It was a pleasure getting to know you," Lydia said to Meg, pulling her into an embrace.

Meg hugged the woman, patting her back awkwardly, but in her expression, Scott could see the hope of acceptance, of family. It was everything Scott wanted for her, and he, too, prayed the couple lived up to the promise.

Walter stepped closer, grasping Meg's hand in his. "You're a lovely young woman."

She blushed, that pink flush Scott liked seeing on her cheeks. "Thank you."

"Traitors!"

The shouted word startled everyone.

Scott spun as a man strode forward from the yellow taxi. Meg turned fast, her expression turning to one of horror. "Mike," she whispered at the same moment Scott recognized him.

The man wore dirty clothes, his hair hadn't been washed in too long, and his eyes were bloodshot from drugs or alcohol.

"Mike?" Lydia gasped, her face turning pale.

And Walter, who still held Meg's hand, stared in shock at his son—who had a small revolver in his hand.

Scott reached for and raised his gun without thinking twice, training the weapon on Mike Ashton.

"How could you choose that bitch over me?" Mike asked, the hand holding the gun shaking uncontrollably.

"Calm down, son," Walter said, dropping Meg's hand and holding his up in the air. "You're my child. Nothing changes that," he said, speaking slowly and calmly.

"Except that baby." Eyes wild, Mike swung the gun toward Meg and lunged forward, shooting as he moved.

On instinct, Scott fired at Mike, diving for Meg at the same time. Walter was closer and threw Meg to the ground, but his shocked scream told Scott he'd taken the bullet meant for Meg.

"Call 911," Scott shouted to one of the valets who had ducked behind the small desk where he worked. "And keep everyone else away!"

Scott immediately spun toward Meg, calling her name.

"Fine," she called out.

Scott began breathing again, everything around them happening at warp speed.

Crying, Lydia rolled her husband off of Meg while Scott kept his gun trained on Mike, who lay groaning on the ground. Blood spread through the man's shirt, but it looked like the original injury was in the upper right shoulder, a result of Scott's preoccupation with getting Meg out of harm's way.

Mike flinched, moving his good arm, and Scott kicked the man's gun farther away, in case the asshole thought he had a chance of getting to the weapon.

"Come on, honey. Talk to me," Lydia said to her husband.

"I'm okay." Walter spoke in a weak voice. "Just my damn arm."

Scott let out a relieved breath that Walter's injury wasn't life threatening. From the corner of his eye, Scott saw Meg rise to her feet, while at the same time, the sound of sirens cut into the silence.

Without warning, Meg barreled into him, wrapping her arms around him tight. "Oh my God, I was so scared."

Her voice sounded muffled in his shirt, her tears dampening the fabric, and his heart clenched inside his chest. The same heart he'd thought had closed up for good only a short month ago.

"Join the club, baby. If this bastard had shot you, and I was a few feet away and didn't stop him . . ." He couldn't finish the thought, nausea filling him at the notion. "How's Walter?"

"Hurting, but I think he's okay."

Two police cars and an ambulance screeched to a halt. The men in blue surrounded Scott, and he placed both weapons on the ground, kicking them toward the police. Though it took a while with Scott no longer being in possession of a badge, the police eventually sorted out the facts.

Mike had been hit in the upper shoulder, and the paramedics quickly stabilized him, then loaded him into the ambulance for the trip to the hospital. With a police escort. He'd soon be read his rights and booked.

Another set of paramedics worked on Walter.

Lydia stepped back to give them room. She headed straight for Scott, her face streaked with tears.

Scott drew a breath before facing the woman whose son he had shot. "Mrs. Ashton . . ."

"Walter and I just had to say thank you."

"What?" Scott asked, confused.

The older woman stepped forward and hugged Scott tight, taking him completely off guard. "You didn't kill my son. Thank you."

"Mrs. Ashton!" a paramedic called out. "We need to go."

She eased back. "You two take care. I'll be in touch."

"Bye," Meg whispered.

"Good luck," Scott said to her retreating back before turning to Meg. Makeup smudged beneath her eyes, tears stained her cheeks, but her brown eyes sparkled with life, and that was all Scott cared about.

"She's right. You didn't kill him."

"Don't give me so much credit." He hated to burst her bubble or perception of him, but it couldn't be helped. "In the split second I had, I aimed dead center, but I was trying to get to you at the same time, and the shot went wide."

She sucked in a surprised gasp. "Well, then things work out the way they're supposed to. I'd hate for you to have Mike's death on your conscience. And I wouldn't want it on mine either."

It wouldn't have been either of their faults, but he wasn't going to argue with her. He brushed her hair off her face and tipped her chin up. "I said I'd keep you safe, and that was too damned close for comfort."

She nodded. "He can't walk away from this, right? It's attempted murder, right? He's going to jail?"

"He sure as hell is."

She closed her eyes and sighed. "Thank God. It's over."

It sure as hell was, Scott thought, pulling her close, breathing in the fragrant scent of her hair. Mike's reign of terror was over. And so was Meg's need to remain with Scott. In his house, in his arms, and in his life.

In a daze, Meg walked into Scott's house. She headed straight for the master bathroom and began stripping off her clothes piece by piece, shedding the memories along with the shirt that was covered in Walter Ashton's blood. He'd thrown himself over her, putting himself in front of a bullet to save Meg's life from a shot *Mike* had fired.

Mike, who she'd cared for, if not loved. Mike, who'd fathered her child. With shaking hands, she turned on the water, hoping the heat of the shower would warm the chill that spread through her from inside and out. She stuck her hand into the spray, testing the temperature before stepping inside.

"You didn't waste a second," Scott said, joining her in the bathroom.

She glanced at him through the see-through enclosure, watching his eyes heat up as he took in her naked body.

"I had to get out of those clothes." Her voice cracked, and she turned away, stepping under the hot spray to wash away her tears before he could see.

The sound of the shower door opening and closing drew her attention, and then Scott was there. He pulled her into his arms and held her tight as she cried, letting out all the pent-up emotion of the last few weeks and the hell Mike had caused. She hadn't really let herself fall apart, and now that the adrenaline rush had ebbed, she sobbed without holding back.

When she'd finally cried herself out, she became aware of Scott's body, his hard muscles, hair-roughened skin, and the gentle yet protective way he held her close. One hand stroked her hair, the other wrapped around her waist as he waited for her to pull herself together.

Once she was ready, she drew a deep breath and glanced up at him. "Thank you. I needed that."

His smile didn't reach his eyes. "I hope that's the last time you cry over that bastard."

She managed a nod. "Me too." She tipped her head up and tried to clean up her face, knowing her makeup had to be dripping down her cheeks.

"Here. Let me." Scott pulled a washcloth from a towel bar and wiped beneath her eyes, gently cleaning her up.

She didn't have the strength to be embarrassed and let him do what he wanted.

"There. All set," he said.

She gave him a shaky smile. "Thank you."

"My *pleasure*." His low voice and tone had an entirely different meaning, and her body perked up, suddenly awake and aware of him as a man. A very sexy man she desired with every fiber of her being.

Without speaking, he reached over and picked up a bar of soap, then proceeded to lather up his hands before kneeling at her feet. He placed the bar of soap on the floor beside him and cupped her ankle in his big hands.

She glanced down at his dark hair, his sexy pose, and her nipples peaked with desire, her breasts suddenly heavy, her pussy throbbing with need.

"What are you doing?" she asked thickly.

He glanced up, his eyes as dark as she'd ever seen them. "Taking care of you," he said, then bent to his task.

He soaped her skin, starting at her feet and moving upward, massaging her muscles with tender care. First he pressed his thumbs into her calves, slicked his hands up behind her knees—an erogenous zone she hadn't known she possessed—before graduating to her thighs. His talented fingers reached higher quickly, and she sucked in a breath as he slid his thumbs along the crease between her thigh and her slick outer folds.

She grasped on to his shoulders and held on, fingers digging into his skin as he soaped around her sex, fingers easing over her nearly bare mound but never touching where she needed him most. She arched her hips forward. He chuckled, low and deep, pausing only to soap up his hands again and keep moving, up her belly, over her breasts, paying special attention there but not stopping in his quest to clean her completely.

It was as if he understood how fragile today had made her feel, how out of control and afraid, and he was here to help her rinse off all traces of the horrific experience.

He slicked his hands over her shoulders, down her arms, threading their fingers together almost symbolically, his heavy-lidded, aroused gaze meeting hers. That's when it dawned on her.

Scott wasn't speaking. There was no dirty talk. No sexy descriptions of what he was going to do to her. No teasing comments about how many times he planned to make her come. Instead, there was an intensity and seriousness to his touch and his expression she'd never seen before.

It was as if he were memorizing every second, every bit of her because now that the danger had passed, this was their last time together. And though she knew it to be true, the pain of that thought lanced through her heart.

There was so much unspoken in the steamy bathroom and between them, but she couldn't bring herself to think beyond the here and now. All she wanted was to feel, and Scott was so capable of making her do that. He unhooked the handheld shower sprayer and rinsed her off, gliding his fingers over the soap, pushing the foam off her skin, helping the soft sprinkling of water do its job.

Once she was clean, he knelt before her once more. Her sex clenched in anticipation, but his next move was so much different than she expected. So much . . . more.

He braced his hands on her hips and leaned close, pressing his lips to her now slightly visible belly. Her throat swelled, her heart filled, and intense feelings of longing swept through her, rendering her unable to think, let alone speak. He glanced up long enough to meet her gaze, to hold on, to force her to look into his eyes, which were glittering with the same raw emotion pulsing through her.

He rose and slammed his hand against the faucet, shutting off the water, then opened the shower door and guided her to the floor mat. He wrapped her in a towel and gently patted her dry, keeping her wrapped and warm. He grabbed another towel and dried himself. He dropped his towel to the floor and tugged hers off, too, before sweeping her into his arms.

She wrapped her arms around his neck and held on, nuzzling her cheek against his, breathing in the warm, clean scent of his skin. She never thought she'd have even this much with any man, and Scott Dare exceeded all her dreams and expectations.

Even now, as he carried her determinedly into the bedroom and placed her in the center of his large bed, he was her white knight. She withheld her smile at the thought, knowing he wouldn't like it.

Moving over her, he bracketed her between his thighs, pinning her pelvis to the mattress with his naked body as he stared into her eyes.

"You've been quiet," she said, needing to break the silence, to know what was going on in his head even if she didn't want to hear.

"I'm not sure you want to know," he said, his jaw tight.

She had a hard time looking past his bronzed, muscular chest, which was just begging for her touch.

"Probably not," she agreed. "But we're going to have to deal with it sooner or later." Not that she could concentrate at all with his hard, hot sex throbbing against hers.

"Yes, we are." He lifted his hips and slid his cock over her damp sex.

She closed her eyes, and sparks flickered behind her lids at the erotic feel of him gliding against her. She whimpered and bent her knees, wanting him to take her hard and deep.

"No, Meg. Look at me."

She forced herself to meet his determined gaze. "I know you don't want to rely on me. That you need to stand on your own, and I respect that." He leaned over and touched his forehead to hers before looking into her eyes once more. "I respect *you*."

She swallowed hard, waiting for his next words.

"And know this," he continued. "I'll always give you what you need, even if it's not what I want."

"What do *you* want?" she asked.

He shook his head, his lips lifting slightly. "I can't believe you have to ask. I want you, Meg. I *love you*."

The words echoed inside her head, as if she were hearing them for the very first time ever. And in a way, she was. Nobody who'd said them to her in the past had meant them. Not the way Scott so clearly did. She'd never known her father, and she couldn't remember ever hearing those three words from her mother. And come on, *Let me move in, Meg. You know I love you* wasn't the same as this heartfelt declaration.

She'd never forget hearing Scott say it now, and her eyes filled with tears. "I love you too."

"Thank God." Scott felt the sheen of perspiration on his forehead and lower back. Sheer nerves. He'd never been so scared as when he'd taken that leap, waiting to hear if she felt the same way. He might not get to keep her now, but he wouldn't lose her forever. He had to believe that or he'd lose what was left of his mind.

He had more to say. So much more, but now wasn't the time. "I need to be inside you," he told her instead.

She smiled, laughing through tears. "That's my sweet-talking man."

Yeah, he was hers. Even if she moved out and insisted on doing things on her own, he'd be there until she came around. But that was talk for *after*.

He braced his hands on either side of her shoulders, flexed his hips, and drove home. Home being the only word crashing through his mind as he sheathed himself completely inside her warm, wet heat. He groaned as she cushioned him in her silken walls.

"Fuck," he muttered. "You feel so good." Beneath him, Meg arched her back, pulling him deeper when he hadn't thought it possible.

"I need to feel you everywhere," she said, her fingernails scraping against his scalp.

He groaned and began to move, thrusting in and out, totally in tune to her every sigh, moan, and shift of her body. And though his orgasm was building fast, it was obvious hers was as well, her breathing coming more rapidly, the tugs on his hair more urgent.

She wrapped her legs around his waist, locking him against her body, taking what she needed from him as they drove each other toward an explosive climax. Heat and fire sizzled up his spine, his balls drawing up tight, the need to come warring with the desire to wait for her to tip over first.

"Oh God, Scott, love you," she cried out at the moment she peaked and fell, her slick walls clasping him tight and sending him spiraling out of control as he came.

"Oh fuck, Meg, love you," he said, his hips slamming into hers, his hot come filling her. *Love you*, he thought. *Don't leave me*, came next. But with everything in him, he knew that she would.

A while later, they lay in his big bed, the silence surrounding them almost painful. Meg curled into his side, one hand on his chest, her naked body pressing against his. He savored the warmth and the feel of her wrapped up in him.

"I have to leave," she said softly, her tears dripping onto his bare chest.

The words hurt as much, if not more, than he'd expected. "Yeah, I know. But I have to tell you a few things before you do."

She sniffed and nodded.

His throat hurt, but he forced out the words. "If you're leaving because at any point I convinced you that I don't want a family or the fucking fairy tale I said doesn't exist, that's just not true anymore."

She stiffened, and he used her shock to his advantage, pulling himself over her, staring into her beautiful face.

"Dare I ask what changed your mind?" she asked.

The answer was easy. "You did. I can't live without you, and I don't want to. I love you. I am going to love that baby, and I want us to be a family." The words, once out, felt freeing. "I mean that. I don't want you to leave. I want you to stay here, with me. But if you don't stay, make sure it's for the right reasons."

"Scott—"

He silenced her with a long kiss, losing himself in her sweetness before pulling back. "Go because you need to prove to yourself, that you can get by without a man. Without me. But know that I'll be here waiting when you're ready to fight for us."

She cupped his face and ran her hands over his clean-shaven cheeks. "I love you too. And you're saying everything I ever wanted to hear."

"But you're leaving." He braced himself for the final slam.

In her big brown eyes, Scott saw all the hurt and pain he himself was feeling.

She nodded. "Like you said, I have to prove to myself I can be an adult and not the needy woman who chose a man, any man, as long as she wasn't alone."

He was so damned surprised she didn't know herself yet. Didn't see herself the way he did, as a strong, self-sufficient, woman capable of raising a baby alone. But she didn't have to.

"Okay," he said, forcing himself to roll to the side, off of her lush body. He felt the chill deep in his bones. "I'm not going to stop you or beg you to stay."

She bit down on her trembling lower lip, her eyes still damp. "You're not?"

He shook his head, his clenched fists the only outward sign of how difficult this was for him. But inside, he was dying. "I told you, I'll always give you what you need. So if you need to go, go."

Scott didn't have a plan. He didn't know what he'd do or how he'd get her back. Instead, he breathed in deeply, searching for a sense of calm he didn't feel, only to inhale the musky scent of sex and Meg.

Meg drove herself home, and Scott didn't argue. She didn't know whether to laugh or cry at the fact that she totally missed him telling her what he wanted her to do. It wasn't that she'd always listen, more that his insistences told her he was thinking about her, her welfare, and that he cared. Like he cared enough to let her pack up her things and move out.

Idiot, a very large part of her brain told her. Who leaves a man who loves her with everything he has? Who walks away from the best thing that ever happened to her? Apparently, she realized as she strode into the apartment she called home, the empty apartment that no longer felt like home, Meg wasn't finished making stupid, wrong, bad-for-her decisions.

Because as she unpacked her clothes and toiletries, she couldn't help but feel like she was in a strange place. A place she'd lived both with Mike and alone. And as she picked up the phone to order pizza, because she had no food in her pantry or refrigerator, she was forced to ask herself: Was being alone taking a stand? Who was she proving a point to? Not herself. She was miserable. She had a lump in her throat, her chest hurt, and she missed Scott like crazy. What was she accomplishing?

She sat alone at her kitchen table, a box of uneaten pizza in front of her, and she hated herself for her decision.

Her phone rang, and she dove for it on the first ring like a crazy person, but it wasn't Scott. It was Lydia Ashton.

"Hi, Lydia. How's Walter?" Meg asked. She'd called the hospital, but since she wasn't family, they wouldn't give her any information.

"He's doing well, thank you. In fact, they're releasing him as long as he promises to take it easy, and you can bet I'll make sure that he does," the other woman said, relief in her voice.

"I . . . I don't know how to thank him for what he did for me," Meg said.

"Don't worry, honey. He knows."

Meg sighed.

"There's something else I wanted to tell you. It's about Mike."

Meg stiffened but forced herself to remain calm and listen. "Yes?"

"Walter and I talked to Mike. We told him we would pay for his lawyer if he signed away his rights to the baby."

"What?" Meg asked startled.

"We explained that if he did, we'd hire a lawyer whose goal was to get him into a prison with treatment for addiction. If he doesn't sign the papers, he can go with a public defender and hope for the best," Lydia said, her voice cracking with emotion.

It was hard not to feel sorry for her as the mother of a man with serious issues. "Do you think he'll sign?" Meg asked.

"I do. He swore he would, because the thought of being left high and dry by us is more than he can handle. He realizes there is no situation that will give him access to money he can use to fuel his addiction. That should also help."

"Lydia, thank you," Meg said again. "I don't know what more to say." The couple had chosen their grandchild over their son, and Meg would be forever grateful. "I'd like to come visit when Walter is up to it."

"We'd love that," Lydia said. "We are looking forward to getting to know you."

Meg smiled. "I feel the same way."

"Good. And make sure that nice Scott Dare drives you. It's a long ride. You need to take care of yourself," Lydia reminded her.

A knot of emotion welled inside Meg at the sincere sound of affection in the woman's voice. She couldn't bring herself to explain why Scott wouldn't be with her or that she'd brought that on herself.

"Take care and we'll talk soon," Lydia said.

"Good-bye." Meg disconnected the call and placed her phone onto the kitchen table.

A glance told her there had been no missed calls or texts while she'd been on the phone. Why would there be? Scott had offered Meg everything she'd ever wanted. He told her he'd always give her what she wanted. And she'd basically informed him she wanted to be alone.

Brilliant, Meg.

She grabbed foil, wrapping the individual slices up and placing them in the freezer for another time. No way could she eat them now.

She turned to go into her bedroom and paused. Was she really going to do this? Continue on with a decision she'd made that, in her heart and soul, she knew was wrong for her?

Or was she going to correct it?

Scott appreciated his siblings more than anyone, but he really didn't want company. Unfortunately, Olivia had heard from Tyler about what had happened this morning with Mike. Olivia had called Scott, asking to speak to Meg. Which meant he'd had to tell his sister that Meg had gone home. And that had led to her arriving on his doorstep with Avery to check on him. Luckily for him, Olivia had left Dylan at home. Not so luckily, his sisters were in the mood to talk—at least, Olivia was.

"Give it time. Meg's been through a huge trauma. She needs to settle, you know?" Olivia propped her feet on a large ottoman in front of her chair in the family room.

"Meg made it clear what she wanted from day one. I just barreled forward, thinking I knew better," Scott muttered. And he'd had his heart gutted in the process.

Not that he was giving up. He'd just retreated in order to regroup. And though he hated to give his bossy sister credit for anything, she was right. He had to give Meg the space she needed.

He glanced over at Avery, who stared out the window beside her chair in pensive silence. He cocked his gaze her way and then met Olivia's eyes.

Olivia shrugged her shoulders, meaning she didn't know what was going on with Avery either.

"Listen, I appreciate you guys coming over, but I'm fine." Or he would be once they left and he could drown his sorrows in Jack. "I'm sure Dylan would rather have you home."

Olivia eyed him warily. "Are you sure?"

"Definitely." He rose from his seat.

"Come on, Avery. I'll drop you off on my way home," Olivia said.

Scott strode over to his youngest sister and grasped both her shoulders. "I want my bubbly sister back. If that means I have to kick some guitarist ass, I have no problem doing it."

Avery glanced up at him, an appreciative smile on her face. "It's a lot of things, all of which I'm dealing with. I promise. No need to get all big brother on Grey. Especially since he's a client."

Scott blinked in surprise. "You know that Lola Corbin hired us to handle the band's security?"

Avery grinned. "I know a lot of things that would surprise you," she said and patted his cheek. "Don't worry about me. Just figure out a way to get Meg back. I want you to be happy."

Scott's heart melted at that. He pulled her into a tight hug. "I won't let anyone hurt you, baby girl."

Avery squeezed him back. "And I love you for it."

He walked his sisters through the front hall. "Thanks for coming by, and drive safe," he said as he opened the door . . . and came face-to-face with the last person he expected to see.

"Meg!" Olivia exclaimed. "I'm so glad you're okay."

"Thank you." Meg glanced nervously at Scott as she replied.

"Hi, Meg. I'm glad you're out of danger too," Avery said.

"And we were just leaving," Olivia said, grasping Avery's hand and pulling her out the door.

God bless his sister for having the good sense to get out quickly, Scott thought, turning his attention to the woman at his doorstep.

"Hey," he said, his grateful gaze raking over her. Though he'd seen her a few hours ago, she looked more tired than he remembered, and he wanted to pull her into his arms and carry her off to bed.

Then he remembered he didn't have that right anymore.

"Did you forget something?" he asked, wondering why else she'd be here, even as he drank her in.

Her long legs peeked out beneath a tank top dress. No makeup on her pretty face. And those big brown eyes stared into his.

"Nope. I didn't forget anything."

"Then you're here because . . . ?" he asked, tamping down that elusive thing called hope.

"I came home."

He blinked, stunned. "You're . . ."

"Home. If you still want me, I mean." She bit into her lower lip. "I walked into my apartment, and I knew immediately I'd made a huge mistake. I was so wrapped up in thinking I had to stand on my own that I walked away from everything I wanted. Everything that was good and right in my life. And that's you. So I came back."

His heart started beating again. Damned if he'd realized it had stopped, but now that Meg was here, back . . . "For how long?" he asked.

"Forever if you'll have me. I want everything you said. You, me, this baby. I want to be a family, and I want *you*." She stepped forward, and he was there, pulling her into his arms and sealing his lips hard on hers.

Relief poured through Meg as he kissed her thoroughly, as if he'd never let her go. The entire drive over, she'd been afraid he'd changed his mind, that she'd pushed him to his limit, that he'd turn her away.

She threaded her fingers through his hair and kissed him back with everything she had. When they broke for air, she met his inky gaze. "I'm sorry."

He shook his head. "Don't apologize for what you needed, baby. You're here now, and we both know it's because you thought things through and you want to be."

"I do. I really do."

The sexy grin edging his lips was one she could look at all day and never get enough. "Okay then, but know this."

"Hmm?"

"I'm not letting you go. Ever." He lifted her into his arms, and she held on tight as he walked into the house and slammed the door closed behind them.

Continue this series with *Dare to Rock*.

DARE TO ROCK

NY Times Bestselling Author Carly Phillips turns up the heat in her newest sexy contemporary romance series, and introduces you to the Dare family... siblings shaped by a father's secrets and betrayal.

Avery Dare lives a quiet life in Miami as an online fashion/makeup video blogger. She has good friends, a close, large family and if her love life is lacking, she likes it that way. But when she receives an invitation to one of her ex's concerts along with an invitation to meet him back stage, she decides to take the risk... and comes face to face with the reality of his rock star lifestyle— the press, the crowds, and the half naked groupies.

At eighteen, Grey Kingston left everything he knew and loved behind to seek fame and fortune as a rock star, and he found it as the lead guitarist and singer for the band, Tangled Royal. Fans adore him, women throw themselves at him, and he can afford everything he couldn't growing up. Yet at the height of his career, he's ready to walk away and return home to a simpler life... and the woman he left behind, if he can convince her to give him another chance.

Except moving on isn't as easy as Grey would like. When Avery is threatened by a stalker, it becomes evident Grey's fans not only don't want him to retire, they don't want Avery in his life either. And Avery isn't sure she wants the pressures that are part of Grey's life... but she doesn't want to lose him again, either. Can their recently renewed love survive the fallout?

Want even more Carly books?

CARLY'S BOOKLIST by Series— visit:
http://smarturl.it/CarlyBooklist

Sign up for Carly's Newsletter:
http://smarturl.it/carlynews

Carly on Facebook:
facebook.com/CarlyPhillipsFanPage

Carly on Instagram:
instagram.com/carlyphillips

Dare to Love Series Reading Order:
Book 1: Dare to Love (Ian & Riley)
Book 2: Dare to Desire (Alex & Madison)
Book 3: Dare to Touch (Olivia & Dylan)
Book 4: Dare to Hold (Scott & Meg)
Book 5: Dare to Rock (Avery & Grey)
Book 6: Dare to Take (Tyler & Ella)
*each book can stand alone for your reading enjoyment

DARE NY Series (NY Dare Cousins) Reading Order:
Book 1: Dare to Surrender (Gabe & Isabelle)
Book 2: Dare to Submit (Decklan & Amanda)
Book 3: Dare to Seduce (Max & Lucy)
*The NY books are more erotic/hotter books

about the author

Carly Phillips is the *N.Y. Times* and *USA Today* Bestselling Author of over 50 sexy contemporary romance novels featuring hot men, strong women and the emotionally compelling stories her readers have come to expect and love. Carly's career spans over a decade and a half with various New York publishing houses, and she is now an Indie author who runs her own business and loves every exciting minute of her publishing journey. Carly is happily married to her college sweetheart, the mother of two nearly adult daughters and three crazy dogs (two wheaten terriers and one mutant Havanese) who star on her Facebook Fan Page and website. Carly loves social media and is always around to interact with her readers. You can find out more about Carly at www.carlyphillips.com.

wicked & devoted duet

wicked as sin

wicked ever after

SHAYLA BLACK

preface

If you HAVE NOT READ either the **Wicked Lovers** or **Devoted Lovers** series upon which the foundation of the Wicked & Devoted series is built, I've written these books so that you'll have no trouble jumping in and following along as I move forward. You will meet a host of new characters, and at the end of Wicked as Sin, if you're interested in getting to know them better, I've provided you a handy list of characters and their book titles. That's all you need to know in order to get started. I hope you enjoy your introduction to this new deep, delicious world!

If you HAVE READ the **Wicked Lovers** and/or **Devoted Lovers** series, let's talk about time. Real-world time and story-world time are not the same. The events of Wicked & Devoted kick off shortly BEFORE the events of *Falling in Deeper* (Wicked Lovers, book 11) and will carry through the same timeframes as *Holding on Tighter* (Wicked Lovers, book 12), then continue on through *Devoted to Pleasure* (Devoted Lovers, book 1), *Devoted to Wicked* (Devoted Lovers, book 1.5), and *Devoted to Love* (Devoted Lovers, book 2)—and beyond. This means, for instance, that while it's been years (in real-world time) since I created the stories of some of your favorite characters, only some months have passed in their world. But I promise you, there's a reason for this. Things are about to get mighty interesting…

I hope you enjoy your first foray into my Wicked & Devoted world.

Happy reading!
Shayla

wicked as sin

One-Mile & Brea: Part One

prologue

Sunday, January 11
Sunset, Louisiana

Finally, he had her cornered. He intended to tear down every last damn obstacle between him and Brea Bell.

Right now.

For months, she'd succumbed to fears, buried her head in the sand, even lied. He'd tried to be understanding and patient. He'd made mistakes, but damn it, he'd put her first, given her space, been the good guy.

Fuck that. Now that he'd fought his way here, she would see the real him.

One-Mile Walker slammed the door of his Jeep and turned all his focus on the modest white cottage with its vintage blue door. As he marched up the long concrete driveway, his heart pounded. He had a nasty idea how Brea's father would respond when he explained why he'd come. The man would slam the door in his face; no maybe about that. After all, he was the bad boy from a broken home who had defiled Reverend Bell's pretty, perfect daughter with unholy glee.

But One-Mile refused to let Brea go again. He'd make her father listen…somehow. Since punching the guy in the face was out of the question, he'd have to quell his brute-force instinct to fight dirty and instead employ polish, tact, and charm—all the qualities he possessed zero of.

Fuck. This was going to be a shit show.

Still, One-Mile refused to give up. He'd known uphill battles his whole life. What was one more?

Through the front window, he spotted the soft doe eyes that had haunted him since last summer. Though Brea was talking to an elderly couple, the moment she saw him approach her porch, her amber eyes went wide with shock.

Determination gripped One-Mile and squeezed his chest. By damned, she was going to listen, too.

He wasn't leaving without making her his.

As he mounted the first step toward her door, his cell phone rang. He would have ignored it if it hadn't been for two critical facts: His job often entailed saving the world as people knew it, and this particular chime he only heard when one of the men he respected most in this fucked-up world needed him during the grimmest of emergencies.

Of all the lousy timing…

He yanked the device from his pocket. "Walker here. Colonel?"

"Yeah."

Colonel Caleb Edgington was a retired, highly decorated military officer and a tough son of a bitch. One thing he wasn't prone to was drama, so that single foreboding syllable told One-Mile that whatever had prompted this call was dire.

He didn't bother with small talk, even though it had been months since they'd spoken, and he wondered how the man was enjoying both his fifties and his new wife, but they'd catch up later. Now, they had no time to waste.

"What can I do for you?" Since he owed Caleb a million times over, whatever the man needed One-Mile would make happen.

Caleb's sons might be his bosses these days...but as far as One-Mile was concerned, the jury was still out on that trio. Speaking of which, why wasn't Caleb calling those badasses?

One-Mile could only think of one answer. It was hardly comforting.

"Or should I just ask who I need to kill?"

A feminine gasp sent his gaze jerking to Brea, who now stood in the doorway, her rosy bow of a mouth gaping open in a perfect little O. She'd heard that. *Goddamn it to hell.* Yeah, she knew perfectly well what he was. But he'd managed to shock her repeatedly over the last six months.

"I'm not sure yet." Caleb sounded cautious in his ear. "I'm going to text you an address. Can you meet me there in fifteen minutes?"

For months, he'd been anticipating this exact moment with Brea. "Any chance it can wait an hour?"

"No. Every moment is critical."

Since Caleb would never say such things lightly, One-Mile didn't see that he had an option. "On my way."

He ended the call and pocketed the phone as he climbed onto the porch and gave Brea his full attention. He had so little time with her, but he'd damn sure get his point across before he went.

She stepped outside and shut the door behind her, swallowing nervously as she cast a furtive glance over her shoulder, through the big picture window. Was she hoping her father didn't see them?

"Pierce." Her whisper sounded closer to a hiss. "What are you doing here?"

He hated when anyone else used his given name, but Brea could call him whatever the hell she wanted as long as she let him in her life.

He peered down at her, considering how to answer. He'd had grand plans to lay his cards out on the table and do whatever he had to—talk, coax, hustle, schmooze—until she and her father both came around to his way of thinking. Now he only had time to cut to the chase. "You know what I want, pretty girl. I'm here for you. And when I come back, I won't take no for an answer."

chapter one

The previous year
Saturday, July 26

"You okay?" Cutter Bryant, her best friend and pseudo older brother, squeezed her hand as they stepped onto the back patio of his boss's home.

Brea Bell took in the chaotic summer party—the smoking barbecue, the loud music, the clinking beers, and male laughter booming from his fellow operatives at EM Security Management, none of whom seemed to have brought a date. She was the only woman in the yard, and suddenly every man seemed to turn and focus on her. "A little overwhelmed."

"I'm not surprised. It's hot as hellfire tonight, and there's a lot of testosterone here." He glanced at the handful of men clustered in conversation across the lawn.

"You tried to tell me."

"For your own good. But you're a stubborn thing. Always have been." He gave her an encouraging smile. "Try to have some fun, huh?"

She nodded. "Thanks for inviting me. Daddy has been encouraging me to get out of the house and spread my wings a little."

But he would never let her spend an evening out with a man he didn't know well and wholeheartedly approve of. Since Cutter had known her from birth, he was one of the few who fit into that category.

"You need to find your future, Bre-bee. It's time."

Cutter was right. She couldn't simply be the preacher's dutiful daughter, helping Daddy care for the residents of tiny Sunset, Louisiana, for the rest of her life. She and Cutter had talked about that more than once. Brea agreed…but she didn't know where to start. Since she enjoyed helping the folks in town look and feel their best, she'd gone to cosmetology school rather than college. Nothing she loved more than contributing, relieving, serving, and assisting others. Their happiness fed her own.

But lately, she'd been fighting a restlessness brewing inside her. A wildness, like the devil was whispering temptation in her ear. Brea didn't dare answer, no matter how alluring the siren call.

"It is." She tucked a strand of her long caramel hair behind her ear and peered Cutter's way. "So your teammates came alone tonight. Does that mean they're, um…single?"

"All of them, except the bosses." He slanted her a sideways glance. "You're not looking to get married right away, are you? There's more to life than that."

Sometimes his overprotective nature meant he treated her not just like the younger sister he'd never had, but a girl.

"Of course I know. But I'm almost twenty-two and I've been on exactly two dates in my life. I think I'm entitled to want male companionship."

"Yeah. I just don't know if this is the best place to look. These men are hardened warriors—special operators, spies, snipers... They have to leave unexpectedly at a moment's notice. They've seen things, done things..."

"You, too. But you're a defender. A protector. And you're perfectly wonderful. Some woman will be lucky to have you someday."

But it wouldn't be her. Her connection with Cutter was—and always had been—purely platonic. Neither of them wanted their relationship any other way.

"I'm not in any hurry to get married. But, contrary to what you say, I suspect you are. So..." He sighed. "I'll give you some background before I introduce you around. Remember, I told you that Caleb Edgington formed this team a few years back, then turned it over to his sons? Hunter, his older"—he pointed to the hard-jawed man grilling burgers—"is a former SEAL. He's married to Kata, who's probably in the kitchen with his brother's wife. Logan, his younger, is also a former SEAL. He's the guy at the cooler watching Tara, the redhead, through the window with that dirty leer."

Brea was relieved to learn she wasn't the only woman here. "And the others?"

"Hunter and Logan's stepbrother, Joaquin Muñoz, is former NSA. He's the tall one with his back to the fence in the circle of men across the yard. His wife, Bailey, is a ballerina, but she's on tour right now. Josiah Grant, the buff guy next to him, is former CIA. The other two, Zy and Trees, are tight. They served together in some government program I'm not privy to know about." Cutter rolled his eyes. "Trees' real name is Forest Scott but everyone calls him Trees because—"

"He's incredibly tall." Brea blinked. "Wow."

"Exactly. He's a cyber security specialist and he's exceptionally good at it. And his buddy Zy—"

"Looks a lot like Zac Efron. The grown-up version, not the Disney kid."

Cutter laughed. "Which is why he's nicknamed Zyron. His real name is Chase Garrett, but around here he doesn't answer to that. Besides being our class clown, he's our demolitions guy. He loves blowing stuff up."

"That's a little scary, but..." Brea let out a breath. She'd come here to get out of her sheltered bubble and meet people. "You should probably introduce me to everyone on your team."

Cutter hesitated. "Yeah. I'm just going to warn you... We're missing one, Pierce Walker. I don't know if the bastard will show tonight. He's a loner, and you're not missing much. But if he turns up, avoid him, you hear me? He's no good."

"All right." Cutter was a good judge of character, so she'd take his word on that.

"That's my girl." He smiled her way, then they stepped off the back patio together.

As they crossed the lawn, Brea clung to his hand. She'd always been shy around new people, men especially. Thankfully, every one of his teammates smiled as they approached. Josiah, whose voice told her he wasn't from around here, seemed nice. Zyron and Trees both had Southern gentlemen's manners, though charm rolled off Zy's tongue while Trees seemed content to let his pal do the talking.

No denying each of them was fit, sharp, interesting, and attractive. But none sparked her interest. Honestly, that was all right. Like Cutter had said, there was more to life than getting married. Still, she couldn't lie. She'd looked forward to being some man's wife since she was a little girl. Her friends had all left Sunset to pursue their ambitions of becoming doctors or actresses or teachers. And that was lovely—for them. Even if it sounded old-fashioned, Brea wanted a husband, kids, home, and happiness.

That wasn't too much to ask, right?

After some small talk, Cutter led her to Hunter and his brother, Logan, respectively. The elder brother flipped burgers with intent focus. Though he was perfectly polite, it was obvious Hunter was a doer, not a talker. Logan, on the other hand, oozed charm. He smiled, winked, and laughed, making up for all the conversation she hadn't had with his brother. But under his façade she sensed something relentless, something dark. In fact, she felt that undercurrent in all the men here, even Cutter. They'd seen atrocities, stockpiled secrets, even committed sins in the name of national security.

Undoubtedly, she'd be better off with someone simpler. She could smile and nod the rest of the night, happy to make the acquaintance of Cutter's co-workers, then figure out how to meet a nice accountant or a handsome professor with whom she might share her future.

She loitered for an hour with Kata and Tara in the kitchen, helping to prepare macaroni salad and bake cookies. They were lovely and witty and funny. Gritty and interesting, too. Stories of Kata's son and Tara's twin girls had her giggling.

Together, they brought the food outside and set everything on a big buffet table as Hunter yelled to all at the gathering, "Chow time. Come and get it!"

Before she and Cutter could grab a plate, Logan snagged his arm. "Bryant, can you give me a hand throwing more cold ones in the cooler?"

"Sure." He turned to her. "Why don't you get your plate? I'll join you in a few."

And sit with all these strangers by herself? "Actually, I need to use the ladies' room first. Meet you at the buffet table?"

With a nod, Cutter turned to help his boss, his smile a white flash in the setting sun. Why couldn't he have been more than a friend in her heart? He was perfect in so many ways, and falling for him would have made her life so much easier...

As the others filled their plates and settled at a giant picnic table on the back patio, Brea hustled inside and found the powder room. As she finished washing her hands, the doorbell rang. A glance out the big kitchen window proved no one else had heard a thing over the loud music and even louder conversation. Rather than disturb Hunter, Logan, or their wives, she headed to the front door.

When she pulled it open, Brea found a mountain of a man standing on the other side. He towered over her, his shoulders taking up most of the portal. Beefy, inked arms crossed over a midnight-blue shirt, stretched tightly across his imposing chest. He had shorn dark hair, an even closer cropped beard, black eyes that saw inside her soul in an instant, and a scowl that told her she'd better not mess with him. He looked like the devil. He smelled like sex and sin.

Her heart lurched, and she utterly lost her ability to think. "Hi."

"Hey."

His eyes didn't leave her face, but she had the distinct impression he'd already taken in every inch of her from head to toe. Brea couldn't repress her shudder.

He glanced beyond her shoulder, out the big window in the family room, which overlooked the backyard. "I'm here for the EM party. This Hunter Edgington's place?"

"Yes." She stepped back to let him in since she couldn't seem to find more words.

He shut the door behind him and stared down at her. "You got a name?"

She inched back…though some forbidden urge prompted her to scoot closer. "B-Brea."

"Yeah?" He stepped into her personal space, following her until she backed into a wall and blinked up at him. "That's a pretty name."

"Thank you," she said automatically. "I like your…" *Everything.* Each part of him was put together so perfectly, he made her heart beat like a mad, fluttery thing and her stomach tighten.

"My what?" A corner of his lips lifted into something she could almost call a grin.

"Shirt," she improvised.

Oh, could she sound any more ridiculous?

"Yeah?" He sounded amused.

"It's, um…a nice shade of blue."

He smiled, blindsiding her with the transformation of his face from desolate to dazzling.

"Good to know. I like your…" He scanned her up and down, his fathomless eyes traversing her slowly. "Dress. The lace is pretty, like you. Except…"

When he reached for her, one finger of his massive hand outstretched, her thoughts raced wildly. Would he touch her? Kiss her? Undress her? The way his eyes darkened told her all that—and more—had already crossed his mind.

Her heart thudded madly. "Except?"

He didn't answer with words, simply settled his fingers on her collarbone. The instant he touched her, their connection reverberated through her entire body, jolting and shuddering clear down to her toes. He glided one rough fingertip across her skin. Goose bumps erupted. Tingles spread. She reeled as he slid his digit under the thin strip of white lace draped over her shoulder and gave it a gentle tug.

Brea's eyes slid shut. She didn't know what he was doing to her or why, but if he wanted anything from her—anything at all—her answer was yes.

Then suddenly, his touch was gone. "Your strap was twisted."

He wasn't making a pass? No. But some forbidden part of her desperately wanted him to.

Embarrassed as all get-out, she sent him what she hoped was a blankly polite smile. "Thank you."

She expected him to release her then. Instead, he curled his fingers behind her shoulder and cupped it, drawing her closer. She could happily lose herself in his eyes. She ached to. Everything about him made her aware that he was a man... and that she'd never known the touch of one.

"You're a little thing."

"You're huge," she blurted, then blushed.

"You think?" He sent her a smug grin. "Or have you looked?"

Another rush of heat climbed to her cheeks. Did he mean what she thought? "Um, dinner just started, if you're hungry..."

"I am. But food can wait." His big, rough knuckles skimmed her cheek before he tucked a curl behind her ear. She barely managed to resist closing her eyes in pleasure. "Are you a friend of Kata's or Tara's?"

"Neither."

He paused. "Are you dating one of the other guys?"

"I..." She wasn't sure how to explain her relationship with Cutter.

"Brea!" She turned to find her best friend at the back door, his snarl warning the other man away. "Come here. Now, honey."

She jumped at the demand in his voice. He would never be so insistent... unless something was wrong. "O-okay." She faced the big, dark stranger again. "Excuse me."

For a second, he looked as if he might object. Something in her wanted him to, but he merely stepped back, his jaw set in a hard line.

Brea edged away. As soon as she reached Cutter's side, her breathing eased. Her nerves bled away. And when he curled a protective arm around her, she felt safe and sheltered.

But he didn't make her feel alive—not like the other man.

"Are you all right?"

Why was Cutter acting as if the newcomer might unleash terrible savagery on her in the foyer? "Of course."

He acknowledged her with an impatient nod. "Time to eat. Why don't you head on outside? I'll meet you at the buffet table."

And leave so he could berate the man for doing nothing but staring a little more than was truly polite and straightening her strap?

She shook her head. "I'd rather not go alone."

While Cutter weighed her words, Brea felt the stranger's stare all over her. She risked a glance his way. Sure enough, he hadn't peeled his eyes off her. He seemed especially fixated on Cutter's arm around her middle.

"Please. I'm famished." She added a pleading note Cutter had never been able to resist.

"In a minute. Before I go, I'm going to say something you won't like, Bre-bee. If you'd rather not hear, I suggest you either leave or don't listen."

She considered chastising him, but she knew Cutter too well. He intended to have words with this stranger. He wouldn't budge an inch until he did.

She let loose an impatient sigh. "Go on, then."

He turned to the other man with a killing glare. "Keep the fuck away from her, Walker."

Pierce Walker, the teammate Cutter had claimed was no good?

"Why?" the stranger challenged.

"She's mine."

Brea's eyes widened. *Cutter had not just made her sound like his girlfriend.*

Oh, but he had...

Pierce's eyes narrowed but he said nothing.

"Are we clear?" Cutter demanded.

"You want me to fuck the fuck off?"

"Yeah. I do."

"Too bad, Boy Scout." Pierce glared with contempt. "I don't take direction from you."

"I mean it. Stay the fuck away. Or else."

Before Brea could object that their language was horrible and that she didn't belong to anyone, Cutter swept her out the back door to the waiting feast. She glanced back. The dark stranger was still staring, the spine-tingling awareness she felt reflecting back in his hot black eyes.

She didn't know Pierce Walker, but one thing she didn't doubt? He intended to come after her.

"What the devil was that caveman bit about earlier?" Brea turned to Cutter in his big truck with a piqued glare. "You let everyone think I'm your girlfriend."

He had the good grace to wince. "Mostly Walker. I was protecting you."

"He was merely talking to me."

"While he undressed you with his eyes. I told you, he's no good."

Brea didn't understand. Nor did she feel like being the agreeable good girl she'd been her whole life. "He was perfectly pleasant until you confronted him."

"Bre-bee, you don't know him. I hate to be crass with you, but the man is only after you for a piece of ass. Besides being a lousy teammate, he's a douchebag. And I'm using exceptionally nice language for your sake. He takes unnecessary chances on the job, he doesn't listen to anyone, and he refuses to compromise."

She slanted him a glance. "You're no social butterfly yourself, and you've always been as stubborn as the day is long."

"But I would *never* put myself—or others—in an unnecessarily risky situation because I was arrogant enough to presume I was right."

"And he did?"

"He does it all the time." Cutter gripped the wheel like the memories alone chapped his hide.

"Is he usually right?"

"That's not the point—"

"Isn't it? You've always said people should fight for what they believe in."

"And they should. But how am I supposed to trust him as a teammate—with my life—when he won't stick to the plan?" He sighed. "Brea, look…he's not the marrying kind."

They'd just met, and she wasn't expecting a waltz down the aisle…but they had shared something—a moment—and she wasn't ready to let go yet. "You know that for a fact?"

"Well, I doubt when I saw him at Crawfish and Corsets off Highway Ninety last weekend, coming out of the back room with one of the female bartenders while zipping up his jeans and wearing a smile, that they'd been swapping Bible stories."

Brea swallowed down absurd jealousy she had no right to feel. "Cutter Edward Bryant, maybe you shouldn't be casting stones. You haven't been chaste your whole life, either."

He squirmed in his seat. "But I have relationships. I usually date women for a while before we take that step. I don't just nail random females in the back of a bar at one in the morning."

"No?" She raised a brow. "What were you doing there, then?"

"The whole team had gathered to play pool. Zy beat the hell—I mean, the heck—out of almost everyone. Since Walker isn't a team player, he decided to use his 'stick' for other activities."

"Maybe he just hasn't met the right woman yet."

"Are you thinking that's you?"

Cutter's tone made her sound incredibly naive, and it pricked her temper. She crossed her arms over her chest stubbornly. "How do you know I'm not?"

He sighed, looking as if he mentally groped for his patience. "Bre-bee, I love you. No matter what our blood says, you're my sister and I will protect you with my dying breath. If you want me to die early or go to prison for murder, you go ahead and take up with that man. Do you know he's a killer?"

"What do you mean? You killed people in Afghanistan."

"Combatants who wanted to end me simply because I was American. I wish I hadn't been put in that position, and I didn't relish a single one of their deaths. I'll even admit I haven't been without sin or blame since I went to work for EM. The job can force you to make snap judgments about whether or not the enemy feet away from you will really pull the trigger so you should pull yours first. I never do it without due consideration. But Walker? His sole job responsibility is to kill."

That couldn't be right. "What do you mean?"

Cutter nodded. "He's a well-trained military assassin who wants everyone to call him One-Mile because that's his way of bragging about his longest kill shot."

The news hit her like a punch to the chest. Yes, Pierce Walker had reeked of danger, but Cutter made him sound like a cold-blooded murderer. "His actions are not for us to judge. That's between him and God."

"But you need to know the truth. When Walker is given a mark, he doesn't ask questions. He doesn't feel compunction or remorse. He doesn't care about the blood on his hands, and if he touched you with them"—Cutter gripped the wheel so tightly his knuckles went white—"if he defiled you, I would have to kill him."

"I've never known you to dislike someone so intensely."

"That should tell you something." He stopped at a light and turned to pin her with a stare. "Promise me you won't ever tell him we're not a couple. That would be like waving a red cape in a bull's face. Promise me that when he comes sniffing around—and he will—that you'll have nothing to do with him."

Cutter's demand came from a place of caring. As far as he was concerned, her father wasn't worldly enough to protect her from men like Pierce Walker, so he would do it for Daddy. Brea wasn't worldly, either. She knew that. The instant, blinding attraction she'd experienced with Cutter's teammate had been unlike anything she'd ever felt. No wonder it had made her want him to be the right man for her.

But her feelings hardly meant he was.

"Brea, please," he pressed. "Promise me."

"All right." Cutter was probably right, and she tried not to be disappointed. But she already suspected she'd never feel as alive again as she had those handful of minutes with Pierce Walker. "I promise."

chapter two

Sunday, July 27

One-Mile did what he had been trained to do whenever he locked his sights on a target. He watched, studied, and dissected. He learned a mark's habits, weaknesses, and quirks. He traveled their haunts and memorized their stomping grounds. Then he figured out how and when to strike.

Except this time, he wasn't here for a kill.

During the EM shindig at Hunter's house last night, One-Mile had watched pretty Brea Bell. He hadn't spoken to her again. Cutter, the uptight prick, would have felt compelled to cut him off at the balls and start something. A team getting-to-know-you wasn't the place for strife. But neither his stare nor his thoughts had once strayed from the beautiful brunette. In those few hours, he'd discerned three important things: She was every bit as warmhearted as he'd first imagined. She was attracted to him, too. And most interesting, she was probably as passionate about her sex life with Cutter as she was about taking her trash to the curb.

As he'd watched Bryant lead her out to his truck and drive away, he had debated the wisdom of pursuing Brea. Then he'd decided fuck it. She deserved the orgasms her boyfriend wasn't giving her.

One-Mile couldn't put his finger on the reasons he wanted Brea so fiercely. She wasn't his type. Usually, he gravitated to blondes who liked to show off their tits, but he'd never encountered her sweet sort of allure. He wanted to see where this inexplicable desire led—and not merely as a fuck you to Cutter. Bryant could pound sand—or his own cock—for all One-Mile cared.

Which explained why he sat in his Jeep now, parked on Napoleon Avenue just before noon the following day, watching parishioners meander out of the little white church across the street and hoping for a glimpse of Brea.

She was one of the last to file out. Immediately, she fell into conversation with two elderly women before a little boy tugged on her skirt. When she bent and wrapped her arms around him, her smile was genuine and contagious. Then she slipped the imp a piece of candy from her purse and ruffled his hair in a motherly gesture that made the boy grin.

Thank fuck Cutter was nowhere in sight.

One-Mile was tempted to cross the street and plant himself in her personal space just to see recognition transform Brea's face—and make sure he hadn't misinterpreted her excitement when their eyes met.

But he could be patient, so he leashed the urge. The right moment would come. First, he needed facts.

"How deep are your ties to Bryant, pretty girl?" he muttered.

He'd stayed up half the night trying to figure that out, using search engines far more in-depth than Google. Within a few minutes he'd tracked down her vitals. Brea Felicity Bell. Her twenty-second birthday was next Thursday. She'd grown up in Sunset. Her mother had died from complications of childbirth. She'd been raised alone by her father, a local Baptist minister. She'd gotten good grades and never been in trouble. Apparently, everyone loved her. She currently worked as a hairdresser at a family-owned salon—the only one in Sunset. She'd grown up next door to Bryant and his family, but Cutter had moved to an unpublished address some while back. Brea wasn't shacking up with him, thank fuck.

Those facts told One-Mile everything and nothing. What did she look like first thing in the morning? What would she taste like under his tongue? What would she smell like after he'd freshly fucked her? He was hungry to know. But she intrigued him far more than mere sex would satisfy—a first for him. What made her smile? What made her cry? What made her mad? What made her heart melt? He needed to figure Brea out, and he'd never manage that simply by staring. He had to talk to her without Cutter or that church crowd surrounding her.

For the next twenty minutes, she weathered the summer heat, shaking hands, exchanging hugs, and listening to the people of her father's congregation, all with a patient smile and kind eyes. Something about her goodness was so compelling, probably because he'd never seen anything like it. He damn sure wasn't drawn in by her sack of a dress, which covered everything between her neck and her shins in a pale pink fabric sprinkled with gray and lavender flowers. She wore the silky light brown hair he ached to wrap around his hands in a loose bun that emphasized her delicate features and her slight build. She'd finished it off with a pair of sensible wedge sandals and a sheer wrap, presumably to combat the blast of air conditioning inside the church.

There was absolutely nothing sexy about Brea's appearance, yet everything about her made him harder than hell.

One-Mile made his living listening to his gut, and it was telling him there was something between him and this woman. So he didn't give a damn if she had a boyfriend. To hell with being polite. And fuck walking away.

Finally, a man he presumed was her father approached. After they exchanged a few words, she nodded. He cupped her shoulder and brushed a kiss across her cheek before disappearing inside the church again.

Then Brea headed for her little white Toyota. One-Mile already knew the make, model, license plate, and VIN, so he wasn't surprised when she hopped into the vehicle and pulled out of the lot. She drove right past him without so much as a glance in his direction. No surprise she didn't take stock of her surroundings. Why should she? She probably didn't have a care in the world, much less any enemies. She'd certainly never made her living by her gun, and he doubted anything ever happened in this sleepy town.

He was about to blow through Brea Bell's life and change it forever.

One-Mile turned his Jeep over and followed her down the road, then out of Sunset, south on I-49 toward Lafayette. On the outskirts of town, she pulled off. He followed at a discreet distance, though it wouldn't have mattered. She only looked in the rearview mirror when she changed lanes.

"Where are you going?" he mused aloud when she putt-putted down a bumpy two-lane road and pulled into an overwhelmingly brown strip mall that had seen better decades.

Was she stopping in for donuts? Or meeting someone, like Bryant, at the diner on the corner for lunch?

One-Mile pulled in and parked on the far side of the lot, near a barber shop, then watched as she bypassed all of those establishments in favor of the beauty supply on the end. She exited her car and locked it, then fished her phone out of her purse as she crossed the lot, not paying a lick of attention to her surroundings.

As long as he was around, she could have her head in the clouds. He'd keep her safe. But he'd be damned if he set foot in the foreign territory dominated by hair dye and nail polish. He'd rather clean a loaded gun.

As she disappeared inside, he rolled down his window, cut off his engine, then turned up Fall Out Boy. He tapped his thumb against his steering wheel to the beat of the music and stared at the glass door. As "Centuries" faded out and Radiohead's "Creep" filled his ears instead, he had to smile. Yeah, he felt a bit like a creep following Brea just to get a few minutes alone with her. All he needed now was Sting crooning "Every Breath You Take" to feel like a full-on stalker.

At somewhere near the ten-minute mark, instinct poked him between the shoulder blades. He rolled up his windows, then hopped from his Jeep. He'd no more navigated the lot and positioned himself against her car door, ankles crossed and arms folded over his chest, when she stepped out of the shop. Halfway across the lot, she looked up from the contents of her bag. Her gaze found his feet. He watched it climb his legs, his torso, his shoulders...and finally settle on his face.

As recognition dawned, Brea stopped where she stood. The bag fell from her fingers and onto the roasting asphalt. Surprise flared across her face. "Pierce."

He could imagine her whispering to him just like that when he shocked her in bed. The thought made him harder. "Brea."

"Did you...follow me here?" She scrambled to recover her purchases, looking anywhere but at him.

He debated on the best way to answer. But why lie? "Yeah. You knew I was coming for you. Can we talk?"

She looked around as if she was expecting someone. One of her girlfriends? Or a rescuer, maybe Bryant?

"I-I have to go."

"Five minutes."

She shook her head. "I can't stay. The heat... It's oppressive."

One-Mile couldn't argue. Since moving here, he'd quickly discovered that summer in Louisiana was like the crotch pit of hell. Today was particularly sweltering. But he also didn't think the sudden flush of her cheeks had much to do with the temperature. "Then let me take you to lunch. There's an air-conditioned diner right there."

"I can't."

"Is your father expecting you home?"

Brea frowned. "How would you know that?"

He ventured closer. "After last night, I learned more about you."

"You snooped?"

"Researched," he corrected.

"Why?"

"You want me to spell it out for you, pretty girl?"

"Please."

Her prim response did something perverse to his libido. He crooked his finger at her. "Come here, and I will."

She backed away with wide eyes. "I shouldn't be talking to you."

"Because?"

"Cutter made me promise I wouldn't."

One-Mile couldn't keep the cynical smirk off his face. So the good guy was afraid the bad boy would steal his woman? He ought to be. But One-Mile refused to make Bryant's tactical mistake and put Brea in the middle.

"I'm just looking for conversation."

Her eyes softened with regret. "I'm sorry."

Because she was the kind of woman who always kept her word. As much as her pushback frustrated One-Mile, he admired her conviction. "How about a little help, then? I moved here a few months back, and I don't know much about this corner of the state. You've lived around here your whole life. Insider information would be helpful."

"You didn't 'research' me and follow me here so I could be your walking Yelp."

He grinned. Brea might be sweet but that didn't mean she wasn't sharp.

"No. But I won't ask you for anything more. And regardless of what Bryant might have said, I would never hurt you."

Her full, rosy lips pursed. His cock jerked. The things he'd love to do to her mouth…

"What do you really want, Mr. Walker? Say it."

Since she'd asked for the truth… "You. Naked. Under me. Crying out in pleasure."

She sucked in a shuddering breath. "Why me? Why not the bartender you… connected with last weekend?"

Cutter would only tell her about that forgettable twenty minutes if he'd noticed, as One-Mile himself had, that Brea was attracted to him.

"Tell me you don't feel the pull between us."

Brea cut her gaze away and sank her teeth into that plush bottom lip.

"You do. I know you do." He edged closer. "Look at me."

She didn't. "I really need to go. Please don't follow me again. And don't pursue me. This"—she gestured between them—"won't work."

"Why?"

"We're different."

"Opposites attract."

She shook her head. "Too different."

"Meaning?"

"Sex could never be casual for me."

One-Mile believed that. "I suspect that, with you, sex would be anything but casual to me."

Brea sucked in a shaky breath. "Stop."

"What, trying to show you the options Cutter told you to ignore?"

Finally, she whipped an annoyed glare his way. "He doesn't tell me what to think."

"Good. You're smart enough to make up your own mind." He cocked his head. "Let me ask you a question."

"I've said no in every polite way possible, and we're done with this conversation, do you hear me?"

He did, but she wasn't listening to him, either. "Are you afraid of losing your boyfriend? Or worried you'll figure out he isn't flipping your switch and I can?"

"I'm not dignifying that question with an answer. Goodbye, Mr. Walker."

When she tried to walk around him, he planted himself in front of her again. "Tell me the truth, and I'll let you go."

She flashed him a surprisingly fierce expression. "I don't owe you anything."

"You don't owe *me* anything. But you owe it to yourself to be honest."

Then, because he couldn't stay in her way without pissing her off, One-Mile stepped aside, leaving her a straight path to her car. He'd rather stay and talk, even with the stifling midday sun beating down and the beads of sweat rolling down his back. But he'd given Brea food for thought. Hopefully, she'd thoroughly chew on it until he found another opportunity to talk to her.

She flashed him a wary glance, then made a beeline for her compact. As soon as she reached the door and gave the handle a tug, her phone rang, its chime clanging like church bells. She ripped into her purse for the device as she settled into the passenger's seat. "Hi, Daddy."

Her father. The preacher. Her only parent. Besides Cutter Bryant, he might be a major stumbling block...

"What?" Brea breathed in shock. "Oh, my gosh. How long ago? Where are they taking him?"

One-Mile's radar went off. Something was wrong.

"University. Yes, I-I know where that is. I'll be there as soon as I can. Did the paramedics say anything else?"

Shit. Had someone called an ambulance for her father?

"Okay. Th-thank you for letting me know." Brea turned and squeezed her eyes shut. Tears leaked from their corners. "I'll be there as quickly as I can."

She ended the call, visibly shaking as she tried to shove her phone back in her purse and set it in the passenger's seat. The thin strap snagged on the lace trim at her shoulder. When she nudged, the leather stubbornly resisted. Finally, she ignored the bag altogether and tried—twice—to insert her key in the ignition. But her fingers shook. Her keys jingled. She huffed in frustration.

One-Mile hated seeing her rattled.

He knelt in the open car door. "Hey. What's going on? I can help."

She looked a split second from bawling. "My d-dad collapsed at the church shortly after I left. Th-they think it's his heart. I have to go."

Third time was the charm because she finally managed to stick the key into the ignition, but her purse strap was still stuck. She grabbed at it with impatient fingers and yanked. The strap finally flopped off her shoulder but clung to the crook of her elbow. The bag itself fell to the passenger floorboard, dragging her forearm with it. The more she struggled, the more she looked ready to scream.

Touching her now was risky, but he'd rather she tell him to fuck off forever than have an accident in the twenty minutes it would take her to reach the hospital.

"Brea." He wrapped his hand around her fingers, still clutching the keys, and gave them a squeeze. "You're in no shape to drive. Let me take you."

She opened her mouth, an automatic refusal seemingly perched there. Instead, she pressed her lips together again. "You're right."

Relieved that she'd acquiesced, he helped her from the car, reaching in after her to retrieve her purse. He took the keys from her grasp, locked the compact, and guided her to his Jeep.

Once he had her buckled in and they were heading down the road, he slipped into problem-solving mode. "Has your father had any problems with his heart in the past?"

"No." And she looked completely stunned by the fact he was dealing with it now. "He's had high blood pressure for a few years, but he's controlled it with medication. I've tried to keep him on a heart-healthy diet, but he loves fried chicken and beignets and..." She shook her head as tears started streaming down her face. "The doctor told him his weight has been creeping up for a while, and he's more sedentary than he should be. I've encouraged him to walk with me or try one of my spin classes. Something. But lately he's been so busy and preoccupied. I thought it would pass. I should have insisted."

"You can't blame yourself. He's a grown-ass man, and you've gone above and beyond."

"No." She closed her eyes as guilty fear closed up her expression. "I do the grocery shopping, and I've indulged him more than I should, telling myself that once the summer cookouts were over and pieces of peach pie weren't so easy to come by that I'd make sure he ate healthier. But what if it's too late?"

One-Mile both understood and hated how much she worried, but her ability to love with her whole heart was obvious. Her body pinged with anxious devotion. The way she willed herself to be at her father's side this instant confirmed it.

He'd never had anyone love him like that. And he wanted it.

One hand gripped the wheel. The other he curled around hers. He was surprised—and thrilled as hell—when she grabbed his in return and squeezed.

"Wait and see what the doctors say."

She turned to him with big doe eyes that melted him. "I'm afraid."

"I know. But I'm here, whatever you need."

More tears fell down her cheeks. "He's all I've got. My mother died shortly after I was born."

"I read that last night. I'm sorry." He didn't know how any woman died in this day and age as a result of childbirth, and he wished like hell Brea hadn't lost her mom when she'd come into the world. Growing up without a mom sucked; he should know.

"I'll be all alone if…"

She didn't finish that sentence. One-Mile was glad for a lot of reasons, mostly because she didn't need to borrow more worry by assuming Reverend Bell would kick the bucket. But how interesting that she hadn't included Bryant in her someone-she's-got category…

"You won't. How old is your father?"

"Not quite fifty. He's still so young…"

For this kind of serious heart shit? "Yeah. That will work in his favor. And he's got you."

She tried to accept his words with a nod. "Along with his congregation. And God. The power of prayer is strong. I've seen it work. I need to pray for him and ask his parishioners to do the same."

"Absolutely." If that made her feel better, she should.

Brea nodded, then bowed her head. Her soft lips moved in silence. One-Mile couldn't resist sliding his gaze over her profile, sweeping from her crown, down the slope of her nose, past the stubborn point of her chin, and over the sweet swells of her breasts with his stare.

He wasn't proud of how hard that made him, but Brea flipped every one of his switches. He couldn't give up the chance to visually drink her in.

Suddenly, her lashes fluttered and she opened her eyes. "I feel better."

"Good." Prayer had never done squat for him, but if it centered her, then he was in favor.

"I should make some phone calls."

"Sure. We've got another ten minutes before we get there."

Absently, she nodded, then ripped into her purse to grab her phone. She called back the woman who had informed her of her father's collapse in the church. Jennifer Collins, the kind widow, had apparently agreed to ring some of the other long-time church members and start a prayer chain before coming to the hospital to start a vigil with Brea. Then she reached out to the associate pastor and asked him to field whatever community issues came her father's way for the foreseeable future. Finally, she dialed someone who wasn't answering the phone.

"That man…" She huffed in frustration.

"Cutter?" One-Mile ventured.

"He only answers about half the time. I swear I don't know what he's doing the other half."

Probably saving the world. That's who Cutter was and that was their job. But as far as One-Mile knew, there were no pressing cases at the moment, so he had to wonder if maybe Cutter was doing someone else. Cheating didn't seem like the overgrown Boy Scout's thing, but if he wasn't being faithful to Brea, One-Mile would have even less compunction about stealing her from the bastard.

He didn't offer up that commentary, however, just watched her dial someone else.

"Hi, Mama Sweeney. You seen Cutter today? He wasn't in church."

There was a long pause, then One-Mile heard the other woman speak, though he couldn't decipher her words.

But Brea's face fell. "Oh. Well…um, if you see him anytime soon, can you ask him to call me? It's urgent. Daddy's had an episode with his heart. I'm on my way to the emergency room at University Hospital right now."

From what he could tell, the woman on the other end of the line conveyed an appropriate amount of shock and worry, before promising to have Cutter call her as soon as he turned up.

Brea ended the conversation, looking tight-lipped. One-Mile bit back a million questions. Fuck Brea being none of his business. Right now, she felt alone in the world, and he intended to take care of her, hoist as much of her responsibility as she'd allow onto his shoulders. But she seemed a million miles away.

"You okay?" he asked as he exited the highway.

"Fine."

But she wasn't. Her mood had taken another downturn after she'd talked to Mama Sweeney, whoever that was.

One-Mile squeezed her hand. "If you need to talk, pretty girl, I'm listening."

She turned to him with a wrenching smile that nearly broke his heart. "Thank you."

But she didn't share her thoughts or give him her troubles, just sat taut and mute until they reached the emergency room.

The instant he parked his Jeep near the door, she shoved off her seat belt, grabbed her purse, and dashed toward the hospital. One-Mile jumped from the vehicle and ran after her, locking the doors behind him with a click of his fob. By the time he caught up to her, she'd already spoken to an attendant, who went to fetch someone who could tell her about her father's condition.

She clutched her hands together, looking as if she waited for the verbal equivalent of a mortal body blow.

Normally, he didn't think too much about other people's problems. Everyone had shit to deal with, and he didn't expect anyone to listen to him whine about his. But it ripped him up to see sweet Brea hurting this much.

"Take a deep breath," he encouraged as he slipped his arm around her petite shoulders.

It was impossible not to notice that she fit perfectly against him, her delicate frame just the right height to hold close.

"What if Daddy is—"

"Don't borrow trouble. Let's wait for someone to give us the update. In the meantime, stay strong."

"I'm trying. But when I imagine life without him, I don't feel strong..." She buried her face in his chest and began to sob softly.

Brea had sought *him* for comfort? Granted, everyone else here was a complete stranger. But to draw solace from him, she had to trust him on some gut level she hadn't yet admitted to herself.

Tamping down his triumph, One-Mile wrapped both arms around her and held her tight against him. "I got you for as long as you need."

That didn't turn out to be long at all. The doctor, a forty-something no-nonsense woman, came bustling down the hall moments later. "Ms. Bell?"

Her head snapped up from his chest. "Yes."

"I'm Dr. Gale, one of the cardiovascular surgeons here at the hospital. I—"

"Is he all right? Is he going to make it?" Every muscle in Brea's body tightened.

A patient reassurance crossed the doctor's face. "Your father is stable and conscious now, but—"

"Can I see him?"

She shook her head. "I'm afraid not yet. We're running some tests..."

The doctor went on, explaining the preacher's condition. The only words Brea seemed to hear were bypass surgery, probably in the next few hours. Gaping, she pressed a hand to her chest as her face went sheet white and she wobbled on her feet. One-Mile steadied her.

The doctor addressed him. "Is she prone to fainting? Has she eaten today?"

He had no fucking idea. "I'll take care of her."

The woman nodded grimly. "It's likely going to be a long day. She'll need her strength. We should be finished with all the tests in about an hour."

That gave him enough time to see to Brea since she was too worried about her father to even think of herself.

When the surgeon disappeared down the hall again, he turned Brea to face him. "Talk to me. Did you eat breakfast?"

"Oatmeal about six this morning." She blinked up at him. "What if he doesn't make it?"

The terror on her face hurt him. "The fact he's conscious and talking is a good sign. She wouldn't perform the surgery if she believed he'd never pull through. I know you're afraid—"

"You don't understand." She wrenched from him.

"Then help me."

As quickly as the fight had filled her, it left. "I'm sorry. I shouldn't yell. You're very kindly letting me lean on you."

"I'm also the only one around to hear your fears and frustration. So let me have it. I'm a tough guy. I can handle whatever you need to dish out."

She shook her head. "I'll be fine."

"You're like a bottle of soda someone shook up. I can see you bubbling under the surface. Yank the lid off and spew." He tried to smile to lighten the mood. "I'll help you clean up the mess when you're done."

"I don't let loose like that. Ever."

"Maybe you should, pretty girl."

He couldn't push her anymore if she wasn't ready…but someday she'd pop the top on all that repressed tension. Then, watch out. Brea with her hair down and her gloves off would be a sight. One-Mile hoped he was there for that.

Hell, he hoped he provoked it.

For now, he led her to the cafeteria, got her a sandwich and a salad, then encouraged her to eat.

"Thank you for staying with me," she said as she pushed away the rest of her turkey on wheat. "You didn't have to."

"I did." He would be here for her as long as she wanted him. Probably longer. She just didn't know that yet.

"You barely know me."

He shrugged. "I want to know more."

But now wasn't the time. In fact, his moments alone with her were likely ticking away. Soon, the parishioners, Mama Sweeney, and probably Cutter the asswipe would show up. Brea would feel obligated to give them her attention and support. Then he'd be in her way. He had to maximize his time with her now.

"Later," he added. "Focus on your dad today."

"You know it will never work between us."

"Besides the sex thing, which I already answered, why not?" One-Mile was expecting a lot of blah-blah and bullshit about Cutter and their budding love or whatever the fuck she thought they shared.

"I don't know you."

"We can fix that. I'm game. How about you?"

She shook her head. "I know what you do for a living."

She didn't like it, but she also didn't understand that he was doing the world a goddamn favor by offing scum. "Good. Then we won't have to have that awkward conversation. What else?"

"You scare me."

He had to give Brea credit; that was honest.

One-Mile took a risk and held her hand. "I said I'd never hurt you. I meant it."

She squirmed in her seat. "Not that kind of scare."

So he made her heart race and her female parts tingle, huh? And she'd never felt that before? Cutter must be a literal wet noodle in the sack, but that wasn't his issue. Getting her to see a future without the Boy Scout was.

He dragged his thumb back and forth across her so-soft palm. "It's the good kind of scare."

She didn't look convinced. "Are you this adamant with every woman you pursue?"

It was a fair question. "No. But I've never met anyone like you."

"You really don't know me."

"I know my gut tells me that I shouldn't let you get away."

"Pierce…"

"One-Mile. Pierce was my father."

"You say that like it's a bad thing."

It wasn't good, but she loved her dad, so she'd probably never comprehend the bleeding asshole his had been. "Having someone else's name can be like wearing a too-tight jacket."

She seemed to weigh his words. "At least it's a nice name. And you could make it your own. But I can't, in good conscience, call you something that celebrates another person's death."

Of course not. She only saw the loss of life, not the fact that if he hadn't pulled the trigger for that fateful one-mile shot, a terrorist had been prepared to blow up a marketplace filled with women and children simply because American servicemen had been there. Still, now wasn't the time to push her more.

"If Pierce makes you more comfortable, fine." He'd rather her call him Pierce than not call him at all.

"Why don't you and Cutter like each other?"

"Are you asking me questions to take your mind off your worries?"

She sent him a faint smile. "I might be."

Reading people could sometimes be the difference between life and death. "Try not to worry too much."

"I don't think I can stop it."

One-Mile palmed her crown, feeling the softness of her hair as he pulled her closer. "Think positive. You done here, pretty girl?"

She looked at her half-eaten sandwich and nodded. "We should get back to the ER."

He'd rather linger where it was unlikely anyone—especially Cutter—would find them, but Brea would feel better if she were closer to her father. "Let's go."

Sure, she could find her own way through the hospital, but he couldn't resist settling his palm on the small of her back and guiding her to the crowded room that smelled like antiseptic, puke, and fear. When they arrived, a tall man who looked like an older version of Cutter and a tiny woman who shared his eyes headed straight for Brea.

She bolted for the woman. "Mama Sweeney!"

"Oh, baby girl…" The older woman hugged her fiercely. "We're here for you and your daddy. Try not to fret."

"That means the world to me." Brea turned to the other man. "Thanks for coming, too, Cage."

One-Mile hung back, gritting his teeth as the other man folded her into his big arms.

"Of course," Cage assured. "I don't have to be back in Dallas and on duty until midnight. I'm sure my little brother will turn up long before then."

"Most likely." Brea's stilted smile didn't quite mask her worry.

"I left him a voicemail on our way over. But you know Cutter isn't the sort to disappear all night without a word. Of my two boys, he's the good one," Sweeney teased as she elbowed her older son.

Cage rolled his eyes. "You only think that because he's better at fooling you."

Brea's boyfriend had been out all night? And his family wasn't even trying to reassure her that Cutter hadn't danced the mattress tango with another woman?

Maybe they thought he was working. One-Mile knew better.

"Hush," Sweeney scolded Cage before she settled Brea into the nearest chair. "Honey, sit down before you fall down and tell us the latest from the doctor."

Brea did, looking alarmingly pale by the time she glanced his way. "Did I forget anything?"

"No."

Cage zipped a cautious stare his way. "We haven't met."

"Sorry." Brea jumped to her feet. "Cage, this is one of Cutter's peers, Pierce Walker."

"I prefer One-Mile." He stuck out his hand to Cutter's older brother.

As they shook hands, nothing on Cage's face said he'd heard the name before. "Good to meet you. Which branch did you serve?"

"Marines. Sniper."

Understanding dawned as Cage nodded. "Hence the nickname. Hell of a kill shot, man."

He'd rather not talk about it with Brea listening. "What do you do?"

"I'm a cop in Dallas."

It fit. Cage had that sharp, gritty edge he never saw on a salesman or an accountant. "Glad you could come before you have to get back for your shift."

"Always. She's like my sister." Cage stared him down. "You a friend of Cutter's?"

He and Bryant would become pals on the twelfth of never as hell was freezing over. "We just work together."

Cage's face closed up. Obviously, he'd read between the lines.

Brea tugged on Cage's sleeve. "You don't have any idea where Cutter is?"

"I don't. He dropped you home after the party, and we went out for a beer. I left the bar when they shouted last call. He stayed to, um…talk to some folks."

Folks who were female, no doubt. That lying motherfucker was covering his brother's ass. Was Brea too trusting to believe her boyfriend was cheating? One-Mile wanted to strangle Cutter. If Brea ever gave him a chance, he wouldn't dishonor her like that.

"I hope he's not hung over. I got concerned when he didn't show up for church this morning. I'd planned to go by his apartment after my errand, but then Jennifer Collins called…"

Cage slid into the seat beside her and gave her hand a squeeze. "He'll turn up."

Yeah, hopefully not smelling like skank. Oh, he'd love Cutter to do something stupid enough to prompt Brea to sever their relationship, but she didn't need the stress of finding out her boyfriend was a two-timing douche today.

She squeezed Cage's hand in return. "I know."

"Brea," a familiar deep voice called from the sliding double doors.

Speak of the devil…

As Cutter strode toward them, heads turned. Cage and Mama Sweeney looked relieved to see him.

Brea stood. "You made it."

"As soon as I got Mama's message." When Cutter reached her, he enfolded her in his arms, lifting her off the floor and against his body while she buried her face in his neck with a sob. "I saw you'd called. Why didn't you leave a message?"

"You might have been busy, and I didn't want to be a bother."

Was she kidding? She should expect her man to drop anything—everything—when she needed him. He sure as hell would if Brea belonged to him. Had Cutter given her a reason to think he'd put her last?

"Bre-bee, you're never a bother." He set her on her feet and cupped her face. "I'm always here for you. I always will be."

She gave him a shaky nod, rife with thanks.

That was it? She wasn't going to ask the bastard where he'd been all night and why he hadn't answered the phone until three o'clock in the afternoon?

No one else seemed to think it was odd, either. Sweeney hugged her son. Cage gave his brother a shoulder bump. Then they updated him about her dad's condition.

"I'll be praying for him," Cutter assured with a nod, then marched One-Mile's way, cutting a scathing look in his direction. "Why are you here?"

"She was in no shape to drive herself."

"You were with her when she got the call?" Cutter demanded, brow raised.

One-Mile didn't see the point of stating the obvious.

"Would y'all mind giving us a minute?" Cutter asked his family. "Maybe get me a cup of coffee. I could use one."

"Whatever you want, little brother. Let's go, Brea." Cage took her arm.

Brea twisted from his reach. "I'd rather stay."

Cutter scowled. "You don't need to hear this, Bre-bee."

"I'm not leaving. The doctor might return with an update."

"Let her stay, son," Sweeney implored.

"All right. But One-Mile and I are going to have a man-to-man talk." Cutter jerked his head toward the door. "What I have in mind is probably best said outside."

Did the fidiot think he was going to beat him up in the parking lot? It would be hilarious if he wasn't so annoying.

As Sweeney and Cage exited for the cafeteria, Brea propped her hands on her hips. "You will not speak a cross word to Pierce, do you hear me? He got me here in one piece. He fed me and took care of me and—"

"Ask yourself why he'd do all that," Cutter fired back. "It wasn't out of the goodness of his heart, Bre-Bee. I guarantee he's focused on the desperation behind his zipper."

One-Mile hated being run out by the prick, but the last thing Brea needed right now was to be in the middle of their bickering. "I'll just go, pretty girl. I wish your father the best."

"But—"

"It's fine," he cut into her objection, then pinned Cutter with a glare. "Bryant, maybe you should try getting your filthy mind out of the gutter."

As One-Mile headed for the exit, the asshole followed. "I have a few things to say before you go."

The moment they were out of Brea's earshot, he whirled on Cutter. "I'm not obligated to listen to your annoying-ass lecture, especially when it looks like you spent the night cheating on your girlfriend. So fuck off."

Bryant pointed a finger in his face. "Brea is off-limits to you, asshole."

"That's for her to decide. She's a grown woman."

"Who's too naive to know who you really are, so—hey!" the Boy Scout yelled. "Don't you walk away from me."

As he headed to his Jeep, One-Mile gave Cutter a one-fingered salute before he revved out of his parking spot and lurched toward the freeway, Brea Bell still on his mind.

Friday, August 8

Brea hustled up the walkway of the surprisingly well-kept mid-century modern home in Lafayette, questioning her sanity for the tenth time in as many minutes. Loud rock music throbbed behind the front door as she clutched the plastic food container in one hand. With the other she rang the bell, her fingers shaking—along with the rest of her body.

What the devil was she doing here? Courting danger. Pierce Walker was more man than she could handle. She was likely to get herself in over her head.

But Brea owed him her thanks. And, okay…she was dying to see him again.

What could five minutes alone with the man hurt?

Suddenly, the volume on the music dropped under a dull roar and heavy footfalls got louder as they headed her way. Then the door whipped open, and Pierce stood on the other side of the threshold, scowling.

He was covered in nothing but ink, body hair, and bulging muscle from the waist up. Well-washed jeans hung low on his hips. He dangled the neck of a half-empty beer in one hand. His bare feet were built like the rest of him—big and overwhelmingly masculine.

Brea sucked in a silent, shaking breath. "Hi."

"Brea." His scowl disappeared. "This is a surprise."

How was it possible that his eyes had been on her a handful of seconds and she somehow felt naked?

"Sorry to drop by. I-I just wanted to thank you." She held out the container to him.

He took the dish from her hands. "For what?"

As Pierce propped himself against the doorframe and stared, she nearly lost herself in his fathomless black eyes. She forced herself to blink, but her wayward gaze wandered down his body. A Marine crest tattoo covered his right pectoral. More dark ink enveloped both shoulders, emphasizing every ridge and swell of his sizable physique. Well-washed denim cupped the substantial bulge between his legs.

And she utterly forgot everything she'd planned to say.

"Brea?"

His deep voice jolted her. She jerked her gaze from places it didn't belong and cleared her throat. "Um…helping me get to the hospital the day Daddy collapsed. And for bringing my car to me afterward. It was very kind of you."

"No problem. How's he doing now?"

"Recovering. His surgery went well. Since you thoughtfully left me your contact information in my console, I meant to come sooner to tell you how much I appreciated your help, but I've been taking care of him. I finally got a few minutes, so I-I brought you these cookies. Since I didn't know what you liked, I baked a few different kinds…" She dropped her gaze to collect her thoughts and stop rambling, but her stare glued itself to him again, this time fixating on his ridiculously delineated twelve-pack abs. "But you don't look like you eat many."

He laughed. Pierce Walker was menacing when he scowled, but when he smiled he was stunning. Something wild and reckless quivered in her belly, urging her to put her hands on him, press herself against him, beg him to somehow stop this breathless, fluttery yearning she'd only ever felt with him.

"Because I don't have anyone baking me cookies." He peeled the lid off the top and peered down. "These look good."

"I baked the chocolate chip without nuts. I didn't know if you were allergic."

"I'm not."

"I also included checkerboard, cinnamon sugar, and gluten-free almond wafer."

"Thank you." He curled his fingers around her shoulder. They burned like a brand as he scooted her breathlessly close to his naked torso and locked the door behind them. "Why don't you come in and let me get you something to drink?"

"I shouldn't stay. I would never want to interrupt your…" Goodness, what *had* he been doing? It was a Friday night. Maybe he was getting ready to go out. Or heaven forbid, planning to stay in…with female company.

"Game of pool. You're not interrupting. Stay. Like a lot of things, it's a lot more fun when you're not playing alone." He winked.

His seemingly suggestive words sparked a reaction low in her belly. "I-I've never played."

He raised a dark brow. "Ever?"

"Daddy isn't much for games. My friends aren't, either."

"What about Cutter?"

She shrugged. "He's never shown any interest."

He sent her a stare that looked somewhere between stunned and dubious. "You sure? I've seen him play."

That didn't surprise Brea. Cutter had a whole life she barely knew about. "I'm sure he does, but not with me."

"I find that hard to believe."

Were they still talking about billiards? "Anyway, I won't keep you…"

"Don't go. One game." He wrapped his arm around her middle and ushered her deeper into his house. "What do you say?"

She risked a glance up at him. "You're sure I'm not in your way?"

"No. I'm thrilled as hell to have you here, pretty girl."

That low, deep declaration of his did something to her insides. Heat crawled up her cheeks. She ran her tongue across her suddenly dry lips. "O-one game, then."

"Let me get you a drink. Water? Tea? Beer?"

Brea shook her head. "Nothing. I also wanted to thank you for the thoughtful birthday gift you left me at the salon yesterday. I'm sorry I wasn't there, but I got it this morning. The wine was a lovely gesture."

He finished off his beer, then cocked his head at her. "You don't drink, do you?"

"Not much, but I'm looking forward to trying this." One of her fellow hairdressers who was a wine enthusiast had assured her it was a more than decent bottle.

Pierce led her deeper into his house. One wall was floor-to-ceiling windows. Movement outside hinted at trees in the yard, swaying in the dark. The adjacent wall was covered in white subway tile with dark grout. Over that he'd hung ten identically sized bright graphical pieces of art—skulls, poker cards, crossbones, masks, and the like—in two perfectly straight rows. Black modern furniture went with the vibe. A big vase of yellow daisies sat on top of a round, glass-top table, adding the lone homey touch. The living room was flanked by floating stairs with an angular steel railing that probably led to his bedroom. Beyond that lay a big pool table with a red felt top. His kitchen, with cabinets stained a warm, mid-tone brown, hugged the far wall.

The place seemed so him—vivid, sexy, contemporary, unexpected.

"This is really nice."

He smiled. "Thanks. I bought it a few months back. Gutted and rebuilt it."

That impressed her even more. "You did an amazing job."

Pierce grabbed a cookie from the plastic container and tossed it in his mouth. In fascination, she watched his sharp jaw work and his Adam's apple bob. Even the way he chewed dripped masculinity. It did something wicked to her when he closed his eyes.

"Hmm… Your cookies are delicious, pretty girl. I knew they would be."

The low dip in his voice nearly made her melt. "I like to bake them."

"I'm going to love eating them." He licked his full lips. "I'll do it all night if you let me."

He definitely wasn't talking about anything she whipped up in her kitchen.

She blushed. "Let me know when you run out. I'll be happy to make more." She turned for the door. "But I really should go."

He blocked her path. "You promised me one game, remember?"

"I don't know how."

"I'll teach you." He set the cookies and his empty beer aside, then sauntered closer. "Stay."

She probably shouldn't…but Brea couldn't resist. "All right."

Pierce gathered up the colorful balls on the table and racked them in a triangle, arranging each in numerical order. When he'd finished, he lifted the rack away, settled the plain white ball in front of the triangle's point, then grabbed a cue. "Do you know the object of the game?"

"To put your balls in your pockets?" When he laughed heartily, Brea realized her blunder. Her face seemed to heat to a thousand degrees. "I meant to shoot the balls you've chosen into their assigned—"

"I know what you meant. And you're mostly right." He grabbed the blue cube on the rim of the pool table and chalked the tip of the cue. "I'll explain along the way. Take this."

She wrapped her fingers around the stick he proffered in her direction. "Now what?"

"Bend over the table, behind the cue ball…"

Brea did, more than vaguely aware of her shorts creeping up her thighs, dangerously close to the under curve of her derrière, then glanced over her shoulder. "Like this?"

He tore his gaze away from her backside, then frowned. "Damn, you really are a little thing. You might have to stand on the tips of your toes to get your arms on the table for a good shot."

She did, feeling the muscles in her legs tighten and her butt lift in the air.

"Yeah." Pierce's voice sounded rough. "Like that."

Brea glanced back. She didn't want to notice that the bulge behind his jeans had grown…but she'd be lying if she said she didn't. The notion that a man like him found her attractive made her feel a little feverish and giddy.

The man is only after you for a piece of ass, Cutter had warned.

She straightened and turned—only to find him suddenly plastered against her body. She gasped, automatically setting her hands on his chest to put space between them. But he was like solid stone under her touch.

Pierce's hands dropped to her hips. "Would you rather do something besides play pool?"

Yes, please. "No. This is fine."

His fingers tightened on her. The heat of his touch penetrated the khaki twill of her shorts. Suddenly, she found it hard to breathe.

"Then turn and bend over the table again." He waited until she complied, and Brea was achingly aware of his body heat bracketing the backs of her thighs, of the sexual stirrings his closeness roused. "You're right-handed?"

"Um, yes."

"With that hand, hold the cue about five inches from the bottom. Now place it near your hip. Don't hold it so tight. You want to be relaxed but controlled. Good. Align your body with the cue ball. This will help your aim. Exactly. With your left hand, make a *V* with your thumb and index finger, like this." He demonstrated. "You'll balance the tip of the cue in that crevice."

Brea watched, acutely aware of the veins bulging in his forearms, the size of his hands, the length of his fingers, the hair dusting his knuckles.

Then he took hold of her hips again. "Spread your legs, pretty girl."

Her stomach tightened. "Why?"

"Your feet are too close together. You'll find it hard to stabilize when you take your shot. Go on. Yeah, just like that. Now lay the rest of the fingers of your left hand on the table and make a bridge for the *V* to rest on. You got it."

"Now what?" she asked.

Brea only half listened to his answer. She was excruciatingly aware of his body heat blistering her, of his hips packed against her backside as he leaned over and utterly surrounded her with his big body.

"That means you need to bend over a bit more."

"Oh," she breathed as she rushed to comply.

"Good. Now hold the cue steady and eye the ball. Like that." He sounded hoarse as his fingers gripped her tighter. Then he pressed his entire chest over her back and breathed against her neck. A shiver wracked her. "Hold still. Yeah. Now take your shot."

How the devil was she supposed to concentrate when he was all over her? When his musky scent swam in her head and she kept closing her eyes to drink him in? It was hard to concentrate on balancing the cue when her body kept urging her to press back into him with a moan.

But Brea did her best.

The tip of her stick barely poked the cue ball. The white orb rolled lazily across the table, made a polite clap with the first of the balls in the triangle, barely jostling them before rolling away.

"Not a bad first effort. Next time, put a little more force into it." He eased away, seemingly reluctant to put space between them.

"It was horrible." She straightened, and her hungry stare climbed him again. "Show me what I should have done?"

He hesitated, then set his pool cue aside. "You didn't come to play pool. Cutter made you promise not to talk to me, so why are you here?"

"To thank you."

"You could have left cookies for me at the office. But you came to my house. On a Friday night. With your hair curled and your makeup done, wearing pretty white lace." Pierce fingered the scooped neck of her top before he wrapped his hand around her neck and tilted her face up to meet his stare. "Look me in the eye and tell me why you're here."

"I don't know."

"Yes, you do. You're afraid to admit it."

Goodness, Pierce could see right through her.

She swallowed. "Terrified."

His fingers on the back of her neck tightened. "I'm more than happy to give you what you want, but you have to look me in the eye and say it out loud."

Brea dug her nails into his forearms, her heart pounding. "I don't understand."

"I won't settle for less than your enthusiastic consent when I take you to bed."

She gaped. "Don't you mean if?"

Abruptly, he released her. "If you really think it's still a question, you're bullshitting yourself. And we don't have a whole lot more to say."

"Wait. This is happening too fast." Brea looked up at him, not even sure what she was silently begging for.

But he knew. "I'm cutting to the chase, pretty girl. Let me tell you what isn't going to happen. I'm not going to seduce you. I'm not going to push or pressure or force you. You're coming to me because you want it. From me. And no one else."

"C-can't we get to know each other?"

Brea was grasping at straws. Pierce wasn't the sort of man who formed cute, benign friendships with girls. He had sex with women. Which meant he had no use for her.

As she'd feared, she was in way over her head.

"I'm sorry. That was a stupid question. I'll go." She looked away, humiliation blazing her cheeks as she charged for his front door.

Now if she could just manage to make it outside before her composure disintegrated...

Pierce grabbed her elbow and pulled her back. "It wasn't stupid. I want to know more about you than your body. But I know exactly where this attraction is heading. Whether you want to admit it or not, we'll wind up in bed. I'm just saying that I want your full consent when we get there. If you can't give me that when the time comes, say goodbye now."

Brea dragged in a deep breath. As far as he knew, she belonged to another man. Of course he would want her consent before anything happened between them. And she respected that he wanted a completely willing sexual partner.

That wasn't her.

She shook her head and backed away. "I shouldn't have come."

Brea whirled around and darted for the door again. She'd embarrassed herself enough.

Behind her, she heard Pierce give chase, his footsteps heavy as he spun her to face him. Brea expected him to pull her close, but she gasped when he shoved her back. Her spine made contact with the foyer wall. His hands spread on either side of her head. He pressed every inch of his body against her. Then he dipped his head as if he intended to kiss her here and now.

Brea's belly flipped with excitement. She gripped his bare shoulders, thrilled by his satiny skin over hard, steely muscle. Anticipation rolled through her as she tilted her head up to him and closed her eyes in surrender.

She wanted Pierce Walker's kiss so badly...

It never came.

Seconds later, Brea blinked, her lashes fluttering up until she focused on him. He studied her with a dissecting stare even as he pressed the hard length of his manhood against her belly. "I know you want me."

She looked away. "Let me go."

Pierce merely thrust his fingers in her hair and tugged until she had no choice but to look at him. "I want you, too, pretty girl. So fucking bad I can almost taste you. That's why I waited for you outside your church a week ago last Sunday.

That's why I followed you to Lafayette. That's why it's taking every bit of my restraint now not to kiss you."

"Why don't you?" She really wished he would.

"Because you have to be willing to admit what you want between us. Until that day…" He eased away with a shake of his head, then opened the door. "Unless it's an emergency, don't come back. If you do, Brea, you better be ready to confess that you want me—and me alone—to strip you down, get deep inside you, and give you every bit of pleasure I'm dying to."

Every cell in her body flashed hot. She gaped at him. Some wayward, wanton part of her ached to give in. She was a grown woman. She wasn't saving herself for marriage, just until sex meant something. If she spent the next hour with him, who would know? Or care? And why should it matter to anyone but them?

Before she could make up her mind, Pierce nudged her onto the porch. He cradled her face in his hands and lifted her face to him. Hope leaped. *Please God, let him have changed his mind.* But he merely pressed his lips to her forehead before shutting and locking the door between them with a final click.

chapter three

Thursday, August 14

"It's okay, Bre-bee. Don't be upset."

Through the open door of his boss's office, One-Mile heard Cutter's crooning tone. He risked a glance at Logan Edgington. How quickly could he wrap up this pointless chat with his boss and eavesdrop on the douche who didn't deserve his girlfriend? Because One-Mile hadn't stopped thinking about Brea Bell in the last six days. He didn't care if he had to fight dirty. He wasn't giving up on her.

"Uh-oh. I don't like your expression…" Logan grumbled.

One-Mile didn't give a shit.

"Tell me what you're thinking," his boss pressed.

"Gotta pee," he lied.

"Wait—"

One-Mile didn't. He dashed out the door to plaster himself against the wall, around the corner from where Bryant was having his low-voiced telephone conversation with Brea. Thank fuck that, despite a life spent around firearms, he still had superb hearing.

"You know your dad," Cutter murmured. "He's a perfectionist and he cares about the people of his congregation. Since he's recovering from surgery and can't handle his responsibilities without help, it makes him cranky. Besides, the doctors told you he might be irritable until they stabilized his meds."

"I know. I don't blame Daddy, just saying he's being difficult," Brea said on speakerphone. "I've been telling him for the past few years that he needs to rely on Tom more. He's the associate pastor, after all. And I think the stress of trying to do everything himself is one of the reasons Daddy had a heart attack. But when I pointed all that out, along with the fact that Tom wouldn't appreciate me taking over his duties, Daddy nearly blew a gasket."

Cutter sighed, sounding slightly impatient. "He's just not himself right now. It's not fair of him to put you in such an awkward position or force you to juggle your own job and his, but he's not being difficult on purpose. If it helps, I'll make a few phone calls, see if I can get the church van fixed before you need to pick everyone up for Sunday services. Will that free you up to run over to the Rutherfords' house this evening and pray with them? Shame about their son's overdose."

"Just awful. Aidan was only sixteen." Compassion filled her voice, along with real tears. "If you could find someone to fix the van, that would definitely give me more time to spend with those poor people. But I'm not stepping on Tom's toes. He's coming with me."

"I think he should. Stephanie Rutherford must be devastated."

Brea sniffled. "She loved Aidan so much. I want to give her and her husband all the comfort and fellowship I can."

Despite how frazzled and stretched thin Brea was, she was still worried about everyone else. She had such a big, beautiful heart. One-Mile ached for a chunk of it.

"Where's the van now?" Cutter asked.

"At the church, 'round back. Keys are in the glovebox. If you find a mechanic, can you leave me the bill in Daddy's office? I'll pick it up tonight after I drop Tom off."

"Sure thing. Just take a deep breath, Bre-bee. This will pass."

"Thanks. I know you're right. Hey, my three-thirty client just walked in. It's a cut and color, so I won't be able to answer for a bit if you have an update."

"Got it."

Cutter hung up. The SOB ended the call without a single romantic word. Hell, without even saying goodbye. No wonder Brea wasn't excited about their sex life. Hard to be thrilled about a cheating, dismissive asshat…

When he heard Cutter sigh and start across the tile floor, One-Mile peeled away from the wall and turned to head down the hall—only to find Logan right behind him.

His eavesdropping boss hustled them into his office and speared him with a vivid blue stare. "So it really is like that, huh? Damn it. Shut the door."

One-Mile hesitated, then complied. "Like what?"

"Dude, everyone saw how you looked at Brea during the party. You get that she's Cutter's, right?"

One-Mile shrugged. "He's wrong for her. And if he can't treat her well enough to hold on to her, that's his problem."

"You've got some giant balls. How serious are you about her?"

His feelings didn't much matter until he could figure out how invested she was in Cutter.

When Brea had delivered the cookies to his house last week, she hadn't withheld her consent because she wasn't feeling him. One-Mile knew that. Hell, her amber eyes had darkened with desire every time he even came close. His guess? She'd hesitated because of the Boy Scout. Did she think she was in love with Cutter?

"Serious enough to fight for her."

Logan sighed. "I was afraid you were going to say that. Your shit can't affect the team."

"I won't bring it to work if Bryant doesn't. But there's already no love lost between us."

"Yeah, you really pissed him off during that first mission in Mexico."

"He wasn't listening, and I didn't have the patience to stand around while he dithered and flapped his jaws. The fact that I was right and he hasn't gotten over it isn't my problem."

Logan sat back at his desk, arms crossed over his chest. "Jesus, you remind me of my brother."

Which was probably why he and Hunter butted heads. "Yeah?"

"He married Kata the night he met her, did you know that? He took one look at her, and he knew."

No shit? A few weeks ago, One-Mile wouldn't have understood. Today, he got it. "They happy?"

"Fucking as in love as I've ever seen. I knew with my wife right away, too. But we met in high school, and things got fucked up. I lost her for a few years. When we met up again, she was engaged to another guy."

Until now, Logan had never shared anything personal, but One-Mile wasn't too thick to grasp that the man was delivering some message.

"How long did that last after you found her again?"

"Not long." Logan tapped his thumb on his desk, clearly pondering his next words. "Especially after the asshole watched me go down on Tara…and I made sure he knew she enjoyed the hell out of it."

One-Mile grinned. "Damn, you shit-stirrer."

Logan shrugged. "We all gotta be good at something…"

"So…you get where I'm coming from with Brea?"

"That you don't give a shit about her relationship with Cutter? Yeah, but think hard. Is it really worth starting a shit storm if she's just a fuck? Or a way for you to provoke Cutter?"

"She's not." Even the intimation irritated One-Mile. "And I wouldn't put the time or effort into scheming something to piss off the Boy Scout when a simple fuck you would do."

"Fair enough." Logan stood. "That's not why I called you in here. I need the rest of your reports on the latest Mexico trip. We all hate paperwork, but we have to keep our documentation squeaky clean so Uncle Sam doesn't shut us down."

"It's done. I'll email the shit now."

"Good. Then get your ass out of my office and send Cutter in so I can have a nice, long chat with him about being prompt and thorough with his."

What was Edgington saying? "How long?"

"Probably long enough for you to go to Brea's rescue."

He'd never seen any of his bosses as potential bros. He worked for them. They gave orders, and he completed the dirtiest of the dirty missions on their behalf. End of story. But Logan was proving that he was all right. "Thanks, man."

As he turned and reached for the door, his boss called after him, "You're welcome. But if you make work ugly, I'll make your life hell."

That didn't scare One-Mile. He twisted around long enough to salute Logan, then hauled ass out of the office and headed to Sunset.

Mid-August was still hotter than fuck, and he wished he had some idea what was wrong with Brea's van, but he had a few hours to figure it out. Since he and machinery usually got along just fine, he hoped it wouldn't be too tough.

When he arrived at the church, a fiftyish woman who identified herself as

Mrs. Collins poked her head out...but didn't shake his hand. No surprise. He probably looked big and violent to her sheltered suburban eyes. He didn't give her his name, just said he'd come to fix the van for Brea. The woman nodded and disappeared inside.

About thirty minutes later, he figured out the vehicle was overheating and the likely culprit was a faulty water pump. He managed to run one down and get it installed way before the sun set. Then he knocked and let himself in the church's back door.

"Yes?" Mrs. Collins eyed him and his tattoos like he was the devil and if she let him too close, his sin might rub off on her.

But she was probably someone Brea knew and respected, so One-Mile made nice. "The van is fixed. Do you have a piece of paper so I can leave Brea a note?"

He'd rather text her, but she'd never given him her number. Sure, he had it. Finding her digits hadn't been hard. But he wanted her to *choose* to tell him.

"This way."

Mrs. Collins led him down a blessedly air-conditioned hallway that ended in a small office with white walls bare of everything except a cross. In the middle of the room sat a painfully neat desk. A plaque squatted front and center that read REVEREND JASPER P. BELL.

She retrieved a sheet of paper from the nearby printer and a pen from the top drawer. "There you go."

Mrs. Collins hovered awkwardly, watching him like she worried he might steal something. He tried not to roll his eyes. The truth was, he'd saved pretty much every penny Uncle Sam had ever paid him. Between that, his lucrative post-Marine contracts, and the money his granddad had left him, he'd managed to sock away a couple million dollars. He had zero interest in swiping the preacher's stapler.

"Thanks. How's the reverend doing since his surgery?"

Mrs. Collins looked surprised. "Brea told you about that?"

"Yeah." But he hadn't heard anything new in almost a week.

"Oh. Well, Reverend Bell is recovering nicely, thank you. Do you, um...know Brea?" Clearly, that possibility surprised her.

"We've met."

The woman relaxed. "Isn't she a doll? She's done an amazing job taking care of her father and keeping the church activities running while he's out."

That didn't surprise One-Mile. "Do you work here?"

"I just volunteer. I teach third-grade math at the elementary school down the street. But since Jasper's surgery, I've tried to step in and help more."

Probably because she wanted to be more than Jasper's parishioner. One-Mile could tell by the way her eyes lit up when she talked about the man.

Whatever. He'd rather hear about the preacher's pretty daughter. But—wild guess—probing Mrs. Collins about Brea's sex life with Cutter would get him booted from here.

Instead, he leaned over the desk, jotted a quick note explaining how he'd fixed the vehicle. Then he invited her to come by his place to pick up the plastic container she'd delivered her cookies in and stay for a round of pool…or whatever she wanted. "I'm sure she appreciates you. Got an envelope?"

He didn't need Mrs. Collins snooping.

"One minute." She disappeared around the corner and returned with a crisp white envelope.

He tucked the paper inside, sealed it, jotted Brea's name on the front, and left it on the desk. Then he nodded at Mrs. Collins and headed home, wondering when—or if—he'd see Brea.

Given her schedule, One-Mile didn't really expect any company soon.

But a couple of hours later, he was kicking back with a beer, eyeing the pool table where he'd taught her how to play so he could shamelessly rub up against her, when someone started pounding on his front door. He doubted Brea was the one demanding entry with a fist…which meant she probably hadn't been the one who read his note.

But he had a good idea who had.

Shit.

After racking his pool cue, he headed across the house and yanked the door open. Sure enough, Cutter Bryant stood on the other side, foaming mad, like a chihuahua with rabies.

"Damn it, I thought I'd taken the trash to the curb, but here you are…"

Cutter bared his teeth and shoved him back. At the unexpected push, One-Mile stumbled until he found his footing. Bryant marched in and slammed the door, then hurled his wadded-up note at his chest. One-Mile caught it reflexively.

"Listen to me, asshole. I'm only going to say this once more. Keep the fuck away from Brea. Stop talking to her, stop pursuing her, and stop writing trash like that to manipulate her into coming here so you can hook up with her."

Who the fuck did Cutter think he was, opening her mail, then barging into *his* house to start shit? Normally, he would beat the hell out of the asswipe…but that wouldn't win him any gold stars with Brea.

"Or what, you'll bore me to death?" He feigned a yawn. "I've already heard this speech, and I hate reruns. So get the fuck out."

Cutter didn't move. "You act big and bad, like you don't give a shit about anything. But I see through you. You're a gaping, know-it-all sphincter. And an insecure bully. Deep down, I think you feel powerless. Did your mommy not love you enough as a kid, Walker?"

Bryant couldn't know a damn thing about his mother, but it was still a low fucking blow, and it took all of One-Mile's restraint not to unleash his fury on the cockroach.

"Are you too much of a pussy to throw a punch? Is that why you're trying to hurt my feewings?" he snarked.

"Fuck you. Stay away from Brea. I mean it."

"You act like I'm going to hurt her. I fixed the van to *help* her. So get off my ass and get the hell out of my house."

Cutter didn't budge. "I'm serious. If you keep after Brea, you'll ruin her."

Dramatic much? "For what? I just want to get to know her."

The Boy Scout scoffed. "You want to take her to bed."

Of course he did. One-Mile refused to lie. But he wanted more than Brea's body. Still, he didn't owe Bryant any sort of answer. He'd only be giving the bastard more ammo.

"You think you have me all figured out. I'm the player who wants to sex up your girlfriend and break her heart. But you don't know a thing about me, asshole." He gave Cutter a shove backward. "And you're no fucking good for her yourself. You were too busy banging some girl you met in a bar the night before to be there for Brea when her dad collapsed. So I stepped in, you cheating douchebag. Get over it."

"I've explained that day to Brea. We're square, so where I was is none of your business."

Bullshit. Cutter was taking advantage of her goodness and spewing lies to cover his ass while he stepped out on her. Why should she settle for that, especially when One-Mile was more than happy to appreciate her—and only her?

"You're a selfish fucking prick for hanging on to her when you won't be faithful. What about her happiness? Her future? Or have you even thought past your dick?"

Cutter's jaw hardened as he spotted Brea's clean plastic container on the table in his foyer and snatched it up. "I don't have to justify myself to you. She's my concern, and I'll take care of her—always. But Brea is off-limits to you." He pointed a finger in One-Mile's face. "And if you step one more toe over the line, I swear I'll fucking kill you."

"Try it. We'll see who winds up dead."

Saturday, August 16

"Brea!" her father called across the house from his recliner.

"Coming, Daddy." She hustled into the living room with his cup of coffee, a piece of dry, multigrain toast, and his morning medicine, then set everything on the table beside him. "Eat up and take your pills."

She was surprised to see that he'd showered and shaved already, but not at all shocked by his sour expression. "Capsules of nonsense from a snake-oil salesman."

"No, medicine prescribed by one of the best heart surgeons in the state," Brea corrected. "Please take it. We don't want to put your heart at risk again."

She couldn't. The news that he had collapsed and that she'd nearly lost him had devastated her. Though Pierce following her shopping that day had rattled Brea, she thanked God he'd been there. She had been in no shape to drive herself to the hospital.

Daddy grumbled but sighed with resignation. "Fine. When you're done with your last client, I need you to run by the church and pick up my mail. If you get there by five, Tom will be meeting with the new youth group. Sit in on that session so you can tell me how he's doing. Then if you can head out to the Richards' farm… Apparently, Josette is having female surgery on Monday, and she's asked for someone from the church to pray with them."

"Tom should do it. That's his job, Daddy." And he'd let her know on the way home from the Rutherfords' place the other night that he'd appreciate her taking a step back.

Her father scowled. "He gives a decent sermon, but he hasn't learned how to compassionately connect with the community. You have. You know and love all these people. And you've got that gift of making everyone feel special."

Brea appreciated that but… "I have to work all day. If I sit through the youth meeting, then go to the Richards' farm for an hour or two, when will I eat? Plus, I'd planned to grocery shop and do some laundry tonight."

Well, she should…but she found herself resisting the urge to seek out Pierce instead. She'd heard nothing from him since he'd tried to teach her to play pool. Admittedly, she was a little disappointed. It was foolish, but she'd hoped he might ask her on a date.

Is he really the dinner-and-a-movie type?

She needed to clear him from her head. Seeking Pierce out, even to thank him with cookies, had been impulsive, reckless, and desperate—three things she'd never been with a man. But he filled her with such exciting, unexpected feelings. Forgetting him was impossible.

"You can do that after church tomorrow," her father insisted. "I know it's an imposition, but we have a duty to this town. I can't see to these people myself, and I raised you to think of others first. I need you, baby."

And there it was, the button he pushed ruthlessly anytime she resisted doing something he asked. It only worked because he was right. She would feel terrible if she put her needs above those around her. "I'll take care of everything."

He smiled. "That's my girl. So Cutter is taking you to breakfast before your first appointment this morning?"

"He is." And she felt a giddy, guilty excitement at being able to get out of the house and relax for an hour.

"You ought to marry that boy. His daddy was a drunk, and Sweeney was better off without Rod, but Cage and Cutter both turned out to be good boys. Cutter would take care of you, Brea."

He would, and they would both be miserable. "We're friends, Daddy. That's all."

"So you keep saying." He sighed. "Then I'll pray you find a righteous, God-fearing man who makes you happy."

Brea sighed. Her father didn't mean to sound either old-fashioned or judgmental, but she wasn't going to change him. "Thank you."

A knock put an end to their conversation. Brea hustled to the door and let Mrs. Collins in just as Daddy took his first bite of toast and downed one of his pills. "Good morning."

After some small talk, Jennifer sat on the ottoman at her father's feet and smiled when her father grumbled about LSU's first football game of the season still being another two weeks away. Thankfully, Cutter let himself in a moment later. Brea kissed her father's cheek and promised to check in before thanking Mrs. Collins for spending the day with him.

Forty minutes later, she found herself picking at her plate, dreading the two shampoo-and-sets on her schedule…and wondering again if Pierce had decided he wasn't interested in her after all.

"You've barely touched your waffle, Bre-bee."

Brea glanced up at Cutter and forced a smile. "That's not true. It's just a lot of food. Want the rest?"

"You know I don't eat that crap."

"But how do you choke down six eggs and a half a chicken for breakfast?"

"I'm a growing boy." He patted his flat stomach, which she knew was all abs. "And I need protein to keep up my strength."

"You're plenty strong," she said with a roll of her eyes. "Thanks again for getting me out of the house this morning."

"You're welcome. I figured you needed a break, and Jennifer Collins is all too happy to play nursemaid to your dad."

She swatted his arm. "You make it sound like they're engaging in hanky-panky."

Cutter shrugged. "It wouldn't surprise me. They both lost their spouses years ago, and I think they're sweet on each other."

"That hardly means they're having sex," Brea insisted in a low hiss. "Daddy had heart surgery less than three weeks ago, and they're not married."

"But if they were lovers, you'd forgive him, wouldn't you? He might be a preacher, but he's also a man."

What was Cutter getting at? "That's for God to judge, not me. But Daddy isn't the sort to commit carnal sins."

Her best friend leaned forward, elbows on the table. "You're twenty-two years old, and your mama died shortly after you were born. Do you really think he's gone more than two decades without sex because he's a man of God?"

Brea squirmed. "I try not to think of it at all."

"Yeah, I try not to think about who's been 'comforting' Mama since my dad ran off decades ago. But I'm telling you now, don't be shocked if your father is involved with someone. My money is on Mrs. Collins."

"That's absurd. She's just a very kind lady."

He scoffed and shook his head. "Bre-Bee, when you're confronted with things you don't know how to handle, you have a habit of burying your head in the sand. That won't always work."

"I don't like conflict," she defended. "How does it not upset you?"

"Sometimes it's a necessary evil."

Like his job, which she didn't like much, either. "I guess I should go. Gabrielle Brown is bringing her mama in this morning. They're both insisting on having a perm. Gabi swears those are coming back in style."

"She's got hair down to her ass."

"Backside," she corrected. "And you're right. So it's going to be a long day."

"Then let's get you to work."

Cutter stood, tossed a few bills on the table, then escorted her out of the restaurant. They were surrounded by familiar faces who stared, probably either wondering why the two of them weren't married or when they would be. Wouldn't they all be surprised to know that she'd never had a romantic thought about him...but she'd had more than a few lustful fantasies about the tattooed military assassin he worked with?

She waved to some of the townsfolk across the room, then stopped to admire Mrs. Jenkins's granddaughter, who had just turned four yesterday. Cutter urged her along, his hand on the small of her back, until they finally reached the sidewalk.

"I thought we'd never get out of there." He wriggled like he wore a too-tight sweater.

She laughed. "You like people as long as you're protecting them. Heaven forbid you have to talk to them."

He grinned. "You know me so well."

"All my life." She bumped shoulders with him. "That's why you're my best friend. What are you doing today?"

"Mama is working. Cage got off duty a few hours ago, so he's on his way back to town." He shrugged. "I might head back to Lafayette and run a few errands. You know, get ready to raise hell tonight."

"As much as you hide it from me, I know you're capable of that."

Cutter opened his mouth to say something. The revving of a motorcycle cut him off. Brea turned—and stopped in her tracks when she spotted a big man in a black helmet, leather jacket, well-worn jeans, and combat boots cruising toward them.

Instantly, tingles sizzled across every inch of her skin, awakening her aching nipples. They shocked her even more by pooling between her legs.

Brea couldn't see behind the man's glossy black visor, but he handled his bike with easy confidence. He stared in a way that told her she was his sole focus. She was magnetically drawn to him, as if her soul compelled her to follow his. Only one man had ever affected her that way, and every time she saw him, the feeling grew stronger.

Pierce Walker.

Was he in Sunset looking for her?

With his stare still glued to her, he revved his engine again and turned off Napoleon Avenue, heading left on Landry. She craned her head to watch until he disappeared behind the buildings and she couldn't hear his engine anymore.

"That son of a bitch," Cutter grumbled.

"Shush. He's only riding down the street."

Cutter gently guided her down the sidewalk, but she could feel rage pinging from him. "Walker is sniffing around you, Bre-Bee. He smells blood."

"What the devil does that mean?"

"You think he's a harmless kitten, that under all his BS he's got a good heart. That man is a hungry lion ready to eat, and you're the little rabbit he intends to sate his hunger with."

His intimation sent heat rolling through her. "You don't know that."

Cutter scoffed. "Yeah, I do. He's not even trying to hide it. You're just too nice to understand. He was pleasant at the EM party. He took you to the hospital when you needed help. He ate the cookies you baked him—"

"How did you know about those?"

"I didn't fix the church van. He did. But I intercepted the note he left you, 'inviting' you back to his place to pick up your container since he'd spent the evening 'eating your cookies.' I hope he meant your snickerdoodles and not your pussy."

"Cutter Edward Bryant!" He'd never spoken to her like that.

Still, a vision of Pierce, big and inked and naked, with his dark head between her bare thighs as she writhed in ecstasy, shot a bolt of fire through her bloodstream.

"I'm serious," Cutter growled. "He'd like to."

She knew. He hadn't kept that a secret. "Well, he never touched me, especially… there."

"And now he won't. I warned him away again. This time, I made sure he knows I mean it."

Brea stopped their stroll by putting her foot down. "Did you ask me what *I* wanted?"

"It's not him. You have better taste than that."

Admitting that she didn't would only start an argument. And why bother? Other than eyeing her on the street just now and supposedly fixing the church van, Pierce hadn't given her any real indication he was interested in more than sex. Besides, how could she introduce him to Daddy? Unless Pierce was willing to put a ring on her finger, that was impossible. But the notion seemed highly unlikely. He might give her a night of sin but never his last name. Time to stop indulging in this stupid fantasy that the bad boy wanted her for anything more than a fling.

Time to forget him.

Brea looked down the sidewalk. The door to the beauty shop opened. Rayleigh, the owner, stuck her head out and shot her an Instagram-ready brow.

"I've got to go. I'm sure Gabrielle and her mother are waiting for me. I'll see you later."

"Call me if you need someone to run you out to the Richards' place later."

Brea was tired just thinking about the twelve-plus-hour day in front of her. "Thanks."

Cutter leaned in and kissed her cheek. "I'm only trying to protect you."

She sighed. "I know."

After giving him the only smile she could manage, she headed inside the salon. Four hours, two perms, a shampoo-and-set, and a no-show later, she propped her feet on a vacant chair in the break room and waited for her next haircut. She was playing a crossword app on her phone when it rang. It was Cutter.

Brea almost didn't answer. He probably wanted to remind her of all the reasons Pierce wasn't right for her, and she wasn't in the mood.

But as her finger hovered over the decline button, something told her to answer. "Hi. What're you doing?"

He paused. His silence was somehow rife with tension. "Brea, I want you to listen to me carefully."

"What's wrong?"

Had he gone by to check on Daddy and found him collapsed again?

"I'm in a situation. I've always managed to make it out safely in the past…but I don't think this one will end that way. I'm sorry. I called to say goodbye."

chapter four

Brea's heart stopped. Her world came to a standstill. "What are you saying?"

But she knew. Cutter lived steeped in danger, and her worst fear, that something had finally proven stronger than him, had come true.

"Cage is on his way. Stay put. He'll explain. But—"

"No!"

"Don't make this harder," he barked, his voice gravelly with resolution and something she'd never heard in his voice—fear. "I've called the rest of my family and said my goodbyes. I love you, little sister. Take care—"

"Stop. There must be something you can do. This can't be happening. I don't..." *Know what I'll do without you.*

The words pressed on her chest, cutting off her breath and forcing out tears.

"I negotiated the release of a group of hostages. Saving fifteen lives at the price of one is a good deal. My end will be quick, and you'll go on. Live well." He let out a shuddering breath. "For me."

"Cutter, no. You can't just—"

But the line went dead. The reality that she'd probably never again talk to the brother of her heart slammed into her chest.

She believed in a benevolent God. Sure, bad things happened in this world... but why Cutter? Why now? Brea didn't understand anything about this—except that she had to do something to stop it. Surely, His will couldn't be so cruel as to let someone as wonderful as Cutter die for doing a good deed.

As she leapt to her feet, Rayleigh poked her head in the door. "Cage is here for you, honey. I think something is wrong."

"Cancel the rest of my appointments," she barked as she grabbed her purse and burst out of the break room.

"What's going on?" the woman called after her.

Brea didn't answer, just ran toward Cage, who waited near the entry, face somber. He wrapped his arms around her and squeezed her tight, as if he needed to give comfort as much as to receive it. She freely embraced him, but didn't want any consolation. She just wanted Cutter home safely.

"Tell me everything. Where is your brother? How did this happen?"

Cage glanced around. Brea followed suit and realized everyone in the salon was staring. There was nothing this small town loved more than gossip, the juicier the better.

She had lovingly nurtured this community all her life. She'd loved everyone openly and without reservation. Now they gawked like rapt bystanders, watching as if she and Cage were acting out a sensational TV spectacle.

She was being dramatic. Of course they wouldn't know what to say. She barely did. Still, their curious stares and pitying expressions irritated her.

"Let's talk in the car," Cage grumbled. "I need to get back to Mama."

She nodded feverishly, then sent Rayleigh an imploring glance. "I've got to go."

The woman's face softened. "I'll cancel everything for you."

Brea ran out the door, Cage hot on her heels. Thankfully, he'd found a spot at the curb and helped her into his truck.

As soon as he got behind the wheel, he faced her. "After you two had breakfast, Cutter stopped at the grocery store on his way home. A man was inside, threatening to kill his estranged wife. Some bystanders tried to help, but he pulled a gun. Most people ran to safety, but he shot the butcher simply to prove he meant business, then trapped fifteen people inside the store with him: four men, eight women—including his soon-to-be ex-wife—and three children. When Cutter pulled up, the police hadn't arrived yet and all hell was breaking loose. He intervened."

Of course. Not only did Cutter see it as his solemn duty to protect others, he'd negotiated hostage situations in the past. "So he arranged their release?"

"Everyone except the estranged wife. The gunman wasn't willing to let her go...at first."

But Cutter had worn the man down until he gave in and agreed to release the woman?

Brea turned to Cage with a gasp. "Cutter exchanged his life for hers, didn't he? That's why he was calling."

Cage nodded grimly as he started the truck. "He made the deal less than an hour ago. The gunman allowed him to say his final goodbyes to his family and relay his demands to the police."

"What does he want?" Not that it really mattered, but she had to know how much time Cutter had left.

"A black Camaro with a full tank of gas, ten thousand in unmarked bills, and two fifths of Jack Daniels."

The man didn't sound like he had his priorities straight. "Nothing else?"

As they stopped for the light at the corner near the salon, Cage pulled at the back of his neck. "No. The gunman knows he's already lost. That makes him reckless, stupid, and dangerous."

And Brea knew Cutter. Even if he died, he would be satisfied he'd won if all the hostages went free. "How long do the police have to deliver his demands?"

"Three hours. And thirty minutes of that have already passed."

Unless something happened, Cutter would be dead before the sun went down.

Dread gonged in her chest. "What are the police doing? Tell me they have some plan to catch this man before—"

"Cutter asked everyone not to intervene." Cage didn't sound happy. "Since he and the entire EM Security team are reserve officers, the police are honoring his wishes."

"What?" She'd ask if Cage was serious or Cutter was insane, but she knew the answer.

"I'm pissed, too. Fuck!" He took out his frustrations by beating the steering wheel with his big fist. "I'm sorry but…"

Brea waved away his apology. She'd never spoken that word in her life, but she'd sort of like to right now. "So the police are just going to let this happen?"

"They'll try to catch the guy when he leaves the store, but…pretty much."

"What about you? You could—"

"Step in? Don't you think I wish I could? Even if my brother hadn't asked me to stand down, I'm a cop in Dallas. I don't have any jurisdiction in Lafayette. If I went in there and killed that guy, I'd probably go to prison for murder." He shook his head in frustration. "My hands are tied."

She understood the laws and why they existed, but she couldn't accept giving up now. Thank goodness Cage had given her an idea. "Well, mine aren't. Take me to my car."

He shook his head. "Cutter told me to bring you to Mama to make sure you're safe and—"

"Let me go." When Cage hesitated, she pressed on. "If there's even the slimmest chance I can save your brother, don't you want me to try?"

"What do you have in mind?"

If she told him, he'd only waste time trying to talk her out of it. But Cutter wasn't the only one who could be sacrificial. "Please don't ask. I'd rather not lie to you."

"You can't go anywhere near that grocery store, you hear? You can't put yourself in danger."

She shook her head. "I won't. I promise."

The light turned green. Cage paused, then cursed as he slung an illegal U-turn in the middle of the street. He pulled into the parking lot behind the salon with a sigh. "If my brother makes it through this, he's going to kill me. And I don't care. If you can do anything…"

When he braked beside her compact, she laid a hand on his. "It's a slim possibility, but I'll do everything I can."

With that promise, she jumped out and slid into her little car, screeching out of the parking lot before Cage could maneuver his big truck around to follow her.

It should have taken her at least twenty minutes to reach Lafayette. She made it in twelve. Leaping out of the car and dashing up the walkway to the mid-century modern, she frantically rang the doorbell.

"Please be home." If not, she'd have to figure out a plan B, but that would take time she didn't have. *"Please* be home."

Suddenly, the door jerked open. Shirtless and scowling, Pierce Walker stood in the entryway, scrutinizing her with fierce black eyes. "What are you doing here?"

"I need your help. Please."

He hesitated, and she wondered if he would turn her away. Then finally, he stepped back and invited her in with a bob of his head. "Tell me what you need."

She rushed inside. "Cutter's in danger. He negotiated the release of some hostages from a gunman holding them at a nearby grocery store, but he wouldn't let his estranged wife go. So Cutter offered his life in exchange for hers. He's planning to kill Cutter in about two hours." Tears stung her eyes as she surged forward to grab his steely arms. "I know I'm asking for a lot. I know this isn't your fight. I know you don't like him. But I love him so much. Please… Please, save him. I'll do *anything*."

One-Mile stood over Brea's petite form, searching her big, pleading eyes. She was begging him—of all people—to save her boyfriend's life.

How fucked up is this?

"What makes you think I can do anything?"

"Aren't you a Lafayette PD reserve officer?"

He nodded. "But that means I have even less power to make things happen in this situation than a beat cop. I'm sure it's being handled—"

"Cutter told them all to stand down. Besides, I doubt any of their officers possess your…skill set."

Now he understood. *Oh, hell.*

One-Mile slammed the door behind Brea and crowded close. Her scent wafted across his senses and slammed into his brain. The soft sway of her breasts burned his chest with the rise and fall of every breath. His lust surged. Jesus, he ached to touch her, to fucking kiss her until she forgot Cutter Bryant had ever existed.

Fat chance.

"And you'll do anything if I save him, is that right?"

"Yes."

"So the pretty little preacher's daughter is offering to fuck me as payment to commit murder?"

She flinched but her stare didn't waver. "Yes."

Well, that answered his most burning question. She was so committed to Cutter that she would give a middle finger to her good-girl morals and do the nasty with a man who scared her in order to save the bastard's life.

Son of a bitch.

He'd deal with that later. But he only wanted Brea if she was wet and hot for him, not because she was martyring herself for another man. Even so, he hated to see her in distress. And she'd never forgive him if he didn't intervene. Caring at all probably made him a schmuck since she didn't give two shits about him. But he wouldn't shut off his internal compass for her or anyone, and it told him to move heaven and hell to keep Brea in his life. Besides, it wasn't as if he had any qualms about ending a scumbag who'd held innocents hostage. Plus, his bosses would either fire him or slit his throat—his money was on the latter—if he could have saved Cutter and hadn't.

Reality tasted really fucking bitter.

He managed not to slam his fist into the nearest wall. "I need a few minutes."

Without a word, he marched to the other side of the house, tore into his home office, then opened the gun safe bolted into the floor.

Brea tiptoed up behind him. Of course he knew. Not only could he hear her, his goddamn body was attuned to her. Every time she came within ten feet of him, his skin fried with lust. His dick got so fucking hard.

"Is that a yes?"

He yanked his MK-13 from where he'd nestled it, retrieved the scope and a tripod, then fished out a box of .300 Magnum rounds. From deeper in the closet, he retrieved a gun case and arranged everything inside, then shut the lid with a final click. "Why not? You want someone dead, pretty girl, I'm your man."

"You're angry." Brea's face said that troubled her.

He grabbed a long-sleeved camo T-shirt from the hanging rod above, thrust it over his head, and lied like a motherfucker. "Nope. Just putting on my game face."

Why tell her he was jealous? It served no purpose except to make him feel pitiful as fuck.

"I'm sorry." She laid a hand against his chest and looked up at him, her expression imploring him to understand. "I know I have no right to ask, but only you can help."

The shitty thing was, she was right. Sure, the Lafayette Police Department had a SWAT unit. Some of their officers had spent some time in the military. A couple had even served in war zones. But if someone was going to nail this guy from a few hundred yards away without alerting the perp while keeping the loss of civilian and LPD life to nil, he was the guy.

It just pissed him off that Brea was only eager to crawl into bed with him in order to save Bryant.

"That's why I'm on it. Stay here."

"Cage and Mama Sweeney are waiting for me back at—"

"No." He pinned her with a glare. "If you want this done, stay here."

She wrapped her arms around herself, but she nodded. "All right."

Fuck, he wasn't trying to scare her, but he also didn't need anyone except him and the cops to know what he had planned—if they even agreed to let him try.

"I'll be back." One-Mile turned for the door.

Brea grabbed his arm, folding one hand in his. "Please be careful."

Was she saying that because she actually cared or simply because she didn't want his blood on her conscience?

"The gunman will never know I'm there until I put a bullet in his brain."

She flinched but grabbed him tighter. "Will you keep me posted? I'll text you my number."

She really had no idea who she was dealing with. If she was never going to want him, maybe it was time to scare the hell out of her so she'd give him a wide berth. Because if he didn't get distance between them, he didn't know how much longer he could stop himself from tasting the sweet pink bow of her lips. And once he got his mouth on her…

Fuck.

One-Mile leaned into her personal space and braced himself against the doorjamb above her head, glaring down. "I already know it. I know everything about you because I made it my business. I'll call when there's something to say."

She swallowed and glanced up at him nervously. "Thank you."

He raised a brow. "You can thank me later."

By staying the hell away.

He left his bedroom and the house, dragging his phone out of his pocket as he launched himself into his Jeep. Time to compartmentalize all this destructive touchy-feely shit and get down to business. Which of his three bosses would listen without losing his head and pave the way for him to get busy?

One-Mile finally settled on Hunter, dialing the former SEAL's number as he turned down the main drag out of his neighborhood. Logan seemed to think he spoke the same language as his older brother. So far, he and the elder Edgington sibling had circled each other. Now he had to hope the younger Edgington hadn't been blowing smoke up his ass.

"What do you want, Walker? It's a Saturday. I'm spending it with my wife and son."

"Unfortunately, unhinged gunmen with an ax to grind don't work Monday through Friday. And your golden boy, Bryant, didn't waste any time playing the hero and offering himself up as the sacrificial lamb."

"What the…" Hunter sounded blazingly pissed as he swallowed a curse. "Kata, take the baby." After some rustling, heavy footsteps clapped across the hardwood floors. "That goddamn son of a bitch. How long do we have?"

"Less than two hours before time's up on the gunman's demands."

"And the shit hits the fan. Why the hell did the police clue you and not me?"

"They never said dick to me. Brea asked me to intervene."

"Fuck." A hundred questions hovered in his expletive, but to Hunter's credit, he didn't ask those now. He just cut to the chase. "You think there's a kill shot to get?"

"I'm on my way to find out. Can you make a few calls, take care of some red tape for me?"

Hunter hesitated. "I could try, but I know who will succeed."

One-Mile knew exactly who he meant. "Your dad."

"Bingo. Everyone respects the hell out of the colonel."

Since One-Mile was in that camp, too, he totally understood Hunter's reasoning. "Good thought. I'm heading to the scene. Let me know."

"I'll have my dad get in touch with you after he's reached out and touched the right people. Thank God he knows everyone in this damn town."

And was at the top of the good ol' boys' food chain.

"Thanks."

"I appreciate you intervening, especially when Brea's request puts you in an awkward-as-fuck position."

Did everyone fucking know he had a hard-on for her? "Your point?"

"Logan and I knew Cage in high school. I know you don't like Cutter much, but…rough childhood. His mom and his brother are good people."

And Cutter was also everyone's favorite at EM. "I got it. I'll take care of it."

Then he hung up. What more was there to say? He'd been tasked with saving the hero before he slunk back to the dark corners of humanity because no one liked to admit that people like him were a necessary evil.

When he reached the scene, the police had cordoned off all entrances to the strip mall that housed the grocery store. Caleb Edgington had apparently worked fast, because the beat cops keeping the parking lot secure let him through right away.

He didn't have to wander through the pandemonium to find the person in charge. A short, forty-something balding guy approached him, eyed him up and down, then stuck out his hand. "You must be Walker. I'm Major John Gaines, the precinct commander."

One-Mile shook his hand. "Tell me what you know."

"Sure. First, we're glad you came. Our SWAT unit is very qualified but…"

None with his credentials. "I'm sure they are."

"You're a little bit of a celebrity among the ranks. A one-mile kill shot is… Well, I don't need to tell you how rare that is."

Fewer than fifteen people in the world had ever actually managed one, but he wasn't here to discuss that. "Any further contact from Bryant or the gunman? Does he have a name?"

Gaines finally got the picture that he wasn't up for a trip down memory lane. "No additional communication. The gunman is Richard Schading. He and his wife, Emily, have been married four years. She's a checker here. Apparently, their relationship has been rocky, and she filed for divorce after he got fired from his last job. She's pregnant, and Richard is convinced another guy knocked her up. I think he went into the store with a murder-suicide plan. Mr. Bryant talked him out of it."

"Is the wife free now?" If he could talk to her, she could give him the scoop, especially her husband's habits and what he might be planning next.

"Not yet, just the others. Schading swears that once we meet his demands, he'll let her go."

So he was intending to use Bryant as a human shield in his getaway. And once they cleared the area, Brea's boyfriend would be a defenseless duck who'd get a quick bullet to the brain. It was also possible the gunman would kill both Cutter and the wife, then turn the gun on himself. Offenders like this were emotional, which made them as unpredictable as they were crazy.

"Where and how are you supposed to make good on his demands?"

"There's a back door. He wants us to leave the Camaro with a full tank of gas running there, money and the booze in the back seat before five."

One-Mile glanced at his phone. He had time, not a ton…but it would have to be enough. "I need to scope the area back there." He gave a visual sweep around the parking lot. "I'm assuming you have the building surrounded?"

"Yes, and we've advised him of that. We've also evacuated the rest of the businesses in this strip mall."

That was a plus. "Once I'm in position, you need to clear everyone out from behind the building."

"And leave you alone?" Gaines's scowl said that wasn't happening. "I don't think—"

"If Schading sees your men surrounding him with weapons drawn, we don't know how he'll respond. If he doesn't feel hemmed in and threatened, he'll be more predictable. And I'll stand a better chance of getting off a clean shot."

"What if you miss?"

"I don't. But if you think you've got this under control, I can leave."

Gaines gritted his teeth as they exchanged numbers. "When you're in place, give me the word. I'll tell everyone back there to clear out."

"Perfect."

The other man scowled. "You're every bit the arrogant asshole I heard you were."

As the precinct commander turned away, he heard a familiar laugh behind him. "Look at you, making friends wherever you go."

One-Mile couldn't not smile back as he turned to find Caleb Edgington. He stuck out his hand. "Good to see you, sir."

"You, too," the tall man with silvery temples said. "Don't mind Gaines. He has short-man's disease."

"I know his type."

"I'll soothe his little feelings," the colonel promised. "What are you thinking here?"

"I need to scout out back."

"Want me to walk it with you?"

"Yeah." He welcomed the colonel's seasoned opinion.

"Happy to." Caleb kept pace beside him as they used the nail salon beside the grocery store as a thruway to the back of the strip mall. "How have you been getting along with my sons since my retirement?"

One-Mile hesitated. "You want the truth?"

"I don't want bullshit."

Fair enough. "They're all right. But I hired on expecting to work for you."

"I know. I'm sorry that didn't happen."

"I get it. Things change. People move on."

"But you depended on me—all of you—and I let you down. That's bugged the hell out of me." He hesitated. "Did you know Bryant felt the same?"

"No."

"The evening after I delivered the news in our team meeting, he called to ream me a new asshole."

Finally, something he respected Bryant for. "I wanted to."

"I figured you would, so I kept you busy with another job." Caleb winked.

"Sly dog."

"I've learned a few tricks over the years, but give my sons a fair shake. They're all-around badasses and good men."

"Yes, but they're not you, sir."

"I appreciate that, but they'll win you over in time. I'm sure of it. They're just not used to handling someone who scares them."

None of them seemed to be shaking in his boots. "Come again?"

"Not literally, but you're a different breed than their SEAL teammates."

Those guys were like brothers. Hell, closer than family in some cases. Snipers like him tended to be loners. "You're saying they don't know how to relate."

"Logan is trying. Hunter and Joaquin are watching how you shake out. Bryant is easy for them to understand. He's damn good at what he does, and he has a noble streak a mile wide…"

While One-Mile himself was morally gray. "Got it."

"You don't. They know you're important. Special. They just don't know how to take you. And it's not like any of them are well known for their interpersonal skills."

One-Mile smiled. "So you're asking me to be patient?"

"I'd appreciate it. They only took over the business a few months ago. A lot of this is new for them, but especially someone like you."

One-Mile wasn't dumb; the colonel was buttering him up, but he understood the basic message. He wasn't a team player since that wasn't his role, and that made relating to him difficult. He also had a chip on his shoulder because Bryant had Brea, and he wanted her way more than he should. The colonel's sons were running a security firm, not overseeing a daytime drama. Hence, Logan's warning to keep his angst out of the office.

"I'm reserving judgment, doing my job, and keeping my nose clean. Speaking of which…" He scanned the alley behind the grocery store.

It looked typical. A lot of concrete, a couple of dumpsters, painted brick topped by a flat industrial roof. A retaining wall blocked off access to the street behind the strip mall. A residential development lay directly beyond that, leaving the gunman's easy path of escape an adjacent highway that led straight out of town. It also limited the places One-Mile could set up a shot in the immediate vicinity.

But across from the cookie-cutter neighborhood, he saw possibilities.

"Give me a minute."

At the colonel's nod, he jumped and grabbed the top of the eight-foot retaining wall, then hoisted himself up for a look-see over the whole vicinity. To his left, he saw a bank, but he didn't like the pitch of its roof or close proximity to the grocery store. If Schading was observant enough, he'd be spotted up there. Behind that stood a doctor's office, but that roofline was also too sloped to provide the proper stability for his setup. He could see rooflines beyond that but didn't know this part of town well enough to know what businesses they housed.

One-Mile whipped out his phone, found a satellite map, and answered his own question in the next thirty seconds.

He jumped down to join the colonel in the alley once more. "There's a two-story storage facility across the street about four buildings back. I'd like to set up there."

The colonel gawked over the wall at the building he'd indicated. "I won't ask you if you're crazy. I know the answer."

One-Mile shrugged. "Not the first time I've been accused of that."

"You know that's over a thousand feet away."

He nodded. "I've hit double that."

The colonel sighed, then slapped him on the back. "Which is why I hired you. I respect that you're not arrogant, just factual."

"I do my best, sir. Sure there's no chance you'll take over the business again?"

"The boys have already renamed it Edgington-Muñoz, so no. I'm out." He shrugged. "Carlotta and I have decided to travel instead. We're taking a cruise."

"I can't picture you at the buffet before shuffleboard."

The older man closed his eyes. "It sounds horrible, doesn't it? But still better than this high-stress, life-and-death shit." He clapped One-Mile on the back. "I'll talk to Gaines and get you on that roof. How long do you need to set up?"

"As much time as you can buy me. The good news is, I'll be shooting to the northeast, so Schading will have the sun in his eyes, not me. I need a weather report. Not the hotter-than-fuck part; I know that. But I could use a thorough wind forecast. I need to know if I can expect the current conditions to hold."

"Get your gear, and I'll have a chat with the powers that be. I'll meet you back at your Jeep in a few."

One-Mile headed back to his vehicle, struck by the stillness of what must be a typically busy parking lot. Beyond that, motorists rubbernecked, trying to see what all the fuss in the strip mall was about. Their lives went on as soon as the light turned green. Someone's was going to end today, and he would be the one pulling the trigger.

He just hoped Schading was the only person on the scene who met his end.

As much as One-Mile disliked Bryant, his squeaky-clean heroics, and his hold on Brea Bell, he didn't wish death on the guy. He'd tried to do the right thing, and One-Mile respected that. Besides, his passing would destroy the pretty preacher's daughter. And if she thought he was killing for any reason other than to please her, she was fooling herself.

It didn't take long for the colonel to approach, Gaines in tow.

The precinct commander eyed him. "You sure about that location?"

The guy who had never been a sniper was going to question his strategy? "It's the best balance between getting the right angle and being difficult for the gunman to spot."

"Our SWAT guys think we'd do better to put someone on the roof of the grocery store, so that when Schading walks out with the wife and Bryant, the car will be in front of him. He'll get distracted by his getaway and leave you a really easy shot from behind."

One-Mile shook his head. "Or he sees the obvious plan coming a mile away and looks on the roof, spots me, then kills someone to prove a goddamn point."

"That's the risk we take."

He shook his head. "Maybe that's the risk *you* take when you don't have someone who can hit this shot. But since I can and I'm probably the person he kills to make that point, I vote we do it my way."

"Let him do his job, John," the colonel encouraged in knowledgeable tones. "He's the best. I hired him myself."

Gaines cursed. "I need to make a few phone calls. We'll have to clear out as many civilians as we can."

One-Mile shrugged. "If that makes you feel better… I'm not going to miss and hit any of them, but if you're worried Schading will fire back, I promise he'll be dead before he even realizes he's taken a bullet."

"We'll see," the commander grumbled, then walked away.

"He's got to cover his ass. If anything goes wrong, the department could have the shit sued out of them, and the optics would be horrible around the community."

"Valid points." One-Mile wasn't used to worrying about shit like that, just about getting the damn job done.

"He'll come through."

Sure enough, fifteen minutes later, Gaines ambled back with a scowl. "You got your way. The police chief isn't thrilled, but he's on board. The bank is closing now. The doctor was having a staff meeting that he's wrapping up, and the light industrial offices behind that are already closed. The storage facility only has one employee on shift. He's scheduled to leave at five, so he's going to slide out early. You'll have a clear shot."

He could set up and get to work now. Best news he'd heard all day.

After that, shit happened quickly, which suited One-Mile just fine. To the police's credit, they cleared all traffic from the vicinity with minimal disruption. If Schading had any accomplices outside the store—and they'd seen no indication of that—it would simply appear as if all of these businesses had gone dark for the rest of the weekend. They'd also managed to block off the alley to the east and the street access, as if the city intended to bring in a road crew to fill some potholes.

Thirty minutes later, he'd set up his tripod, positioned his weapon, and gotten his scope in place. Then he did what snipers had to learn to do if they wanted to be any fucking good: he waited. He refined the shot, felt the wind and heaviness of the air, factored that into his mental calculations, then texted Caleb to let them know he was ready, along with a host of other instructions to make sure no one spooked Schading or blocked his shot.

Fifteen minutes later, a black Camaro rolled into the alley. The gunman hadn't left specific instructions about where and how he wanted the car positioned, other than to have it stocked with a full tank, money, and Tennessee whiskey. So One-Mile had been very detailed, and it looked as if the message had been communicated correctly when a uniformed officer left the running vehicle in the middle of the alley with the driver's side facing the retaining wall. Only the driver's door would be unlocked, which would force the gunman to walk around the car to escape. If he wanted to take Cutter as a hostage, Schading would either have to shove Bryant in first before he could take his seat or unlock the passenger door, escort Bryant to it, and force him in before finding his own seat. Either way, he'd be out in the open and vulnerable as fuck for far longer than One-Mile would need to get off a successful shot.

Not long after the officer left the Camaro idling, the grocery store's back door opened. Cutter was first to emerge, hands high in the air, blood dripping from his left temple. Schading was right behind him, gun in his grip as he jabbed Bryant in the back, prodding him forward. With his free hand, he gripped his wife by the hair and dragged her out behind him.

The woman trembled and cried, mascara running down her face. She was a little thing, with a hint of a baby bump. Schading yanked on Bryant's shirt, then turned back to shout at his wife. The terrified woman cowered and tried to make herself as small as possible. One-Mile felt really fucking sorry for her. Bryant must have had the same reaction, because he started talking, clearly trying to take the gunman's anger down twenty notches. The bad news was, while Brea's boy toy stood there and played the hero, he was shielding Schading from the shot One-Mile had painstakingly lined up.

Finally, the gunman shoved his wife to the ground. And because he was such a Prince Charming, he kicked her a couple of times. Cutter was clearly itching to use this distraction to launch more heroics. Not that he didn't understand Bryant's urge to punch this abusive asshole in the face, but the Boy Scout could help most by getting the fuck out of the way.

Schading's temper seemed to ratchet up as he waved the gun in his estranged wife's face. She shrank back and curled her arms around her belly protectively.

One-Mile would lose zero sleep over ending this douche.

He wrapped his finger around the trigger, triple-checked his sights, and held his breath…

Before he could pull the trigger, Bryant opened his mouth and started flapping his jaws again. Schading whirled, turning his crazy-eyed glare on Cutter, and charged toward him like an enraged bull. Then he shoved the gun against Bryant's bleeding temple and shouted something that looked expletive-filled.

Fuck, this was heating up too furiously and too fast. If he didn't act now, Schading might lose his shit, decide to take his wife hostage after all, and blow the head off his expendable tagalong, Cutter.

With a rapid mental ticktock in his head counting down the seconds, One-Mile realigned his shot, curled his finger a little tighter around the trigger…and squeezed.

chapter five

The crack of his shot resounded in his ears as the rifle kicked back, but he stayed with the scope and watched the bullet plant itself dead center in the middle of Schading's forehead. The would-be gunman crumpled to the concrete. Blood splattered onto the screaming woman behind him and pooled around his body.

Cutter whipped his gaze around, searching for the source of the shot. The Boy Scout couldn't see him, but he seemingly realized the ordeal was over and blew out a deep sigh of relief before turning his attention on the newly minted widow. More blood rolled down his temple as he bent and helped the shaking woman to her feet.

Cops rushed in from everywhere. A pair of EMTs followed with a gurney. Gaines marched in, the colonel by his side, followed by another guy who looked too bleak to be anything other than the coroner. Someone drove the still-idling car away.

One-Mile stood and stretched. The phone in his pocket buzzed with a message from Caleb Edgington that read Good job, Walker. He didn't reply. He hadn't done anything heroic or amazing, just taken out the trash.

What exactly did he tell Brea now? She'd be both relieved and horrified. Sure, she'd asked him for this…but it wouldn't take long for the reality to hit her that she'd begged him to kill a man. Then she'd probably tie herself in guilty knots. Would she even speak to him after that?

His thumbs hovered over the keyboard, but he didn't have a choice. With a grumble, he tapped in her number and typed out a message.

I'm done. Stay put.

Brea only wanted to know one thing.

Is Cutter all right?

As soon as the words appeared on One-Mile's screen, he cursed. Of course she wanted to know. She'd pleaded with him to save the son of a bitch's life because she loved him so much. Naturally, his fate was the first she'd ask about. He'd been an idiot to hope differently.

Fine, just a scratch or two.

Thank you.

For the update or for killing someone who had threatened her lover?

Shaking his head, One-Mile pocketed his phone. Time to blow this fucking shit show.

With short, sharp movements, he packed up his weapon and the rest of his equipment, then hopped in his Jeep and returned to the strip mall. When he arrived on the scene, Gaines sent him a businesslike nod. The colonel gave him a thumbs-up. The cops around him stared either in worship or terror.

Cutter jerked away from an attentive EMT applying pressure to his bleeding temple and scowled. "That was *your* kill shot?"

Why lie? "Yep."

"Why the hell did you get involved? I had the situation under control. I'd been talking to Richard for hours. I was just getting him to the point of admitting his impulsive plan wouldn't work and surrendering."

"Well, it didn't look that way when he pressed his barrel against your skull."

He rolled his eyes. "He hadn't yet pulled the trigger. I was less than three minutes from getting him to surrender."

"Or being dead, because he didn't look ready to raise a white flag to me. So stop bitching. It's done. He's dead. If you'd rather, next time I won't save your life. Hell, I wouldn't have this time except Brea begged me."

"What?" Cutter looked like his head was about to spin off into another dimension.

"She asked me to make sure you came home in one piece. I did. Now I'm leaving."

The colonel approached and clapped him on the back. "I'll take care of the red tape from here. We'll call you if we need anything, but Gaines and I both saw the whole thing. There shouldn't be too many questions."

One-Mile nodded. "Thanks."

Cutter was still sputtering. "Where is she?"

"My place." He just smiled. Yeah, it was a petty jab, but one that seemed to bug the hell out of Bryant.

"I'm coming with you to take her home."

"That's not a good idea." The colonel stepped in when the nearby EMT shook her head stubbornly. "Word is, you probably have a concussion. I think you should get checked out."

"I've had worse."

Caleb's affable expression fell away. "You're going to the hospital. My sons will insist. So am I. You won't be cleared to work until you do."

"Fine," Cutter muttered, then turned his back on the older man and glared One-Mile's way. "Why did Brea come to *you* for help?"

"You'll have to take that up with her." And One-Mile was done talking.

With a wave at the colonel, he turned and headed for his Jeep. Time to get back to the pretty preacher's daughter. Now that he'd done as she'd pleaded, was she expecting he'd demand her to pay up?

⚬⚭⚬

Brea paced the open length of Pierce's house from the kitchen to the front door and back again. As soon as she'd received his text that the gunman had been vanquished and Cutter had survived, she'd broken down and cried. Then she gathered herself and called Cutter's family to tell them he was alive. After his initial rush of relief, Cage began asking pointed questions about how she'd gotten that information and what exactly she had done to intervene. Brea forced a smile in her voice, then she did something she hadn't done since she was a child.

She lied.

"Nothing much."

Pierce had kept his end of their bargain. Now she had to be brave enough to repay him—with her body.

As she passed the kitchen table again, she grabbed the glass of water she'd poured herself hours ago and swallowed it down. She didn't drink alcohol much, but in that moment, she wished she'd sought out something stronger to fill her glass.

Still, intoxication wouldn't change the truth. She had promised Pierce Walker sex.

So tonight, she would give herself to him without regret. Tomorrow, she would repent for her sins. Afterward, their paths would never cross again.

The buzz of the automatic garage door snagged her attention, followed by the purr of an engine, signaling Pierce's return. Suddenly, Brea felt like a bunny trapped in a wolf's lair. Her hands went clammy. Her breath rattled in and out of her lungs. Her heart pounded like a wild thing.

She should have been terrified of crawling between the sheets with a man she barely knew. Sickened that he'd agreed to accept sex in exchange for a human life. Ashamed that she'd bartered away her virginity instead of saving it for a man she loved.

But when she thought of Pierce touching her, stripping her down, and covering her body with his, the flesh between her legs twisted with a shameful ache. She might lie to Cage about tonight to save face or to Cutter to spare him guilt, but she wouldn't lie to herself. She wanted Pierce Walker. Everything about him as a man that should repel her instead tempted the woman inside her.

Brea eased her empty glass onto the table and took a deep breath before she forced herself to approach the garage door. She folded her hands to steady herself, hoping Pierce wouldn't see her tremble.

The engine cut off. A car door slammed. Then he stepped inside the house—all six and a half feet of him—his big shoulders filling the doorway.

His black eyes fell on her immediately. "You're still here."

She nodded. "You told me to be."

Something passed across his face. Approval? Desire? Whatever it was, she felt the answering ping inside her.

"You okay?" he asked.

He had been the one to run headlong into danger. And unlike Cutter, Pierce hadn't ridden to the rescue out of the goodness of his heart. He'd done it because he wanted her—desperately enough to risk his safety, intensely enough to take another's life just to have her.

That made no sense to Brea. In a roomful of women, she was never the prettiest. Or the smartest. Forget the most gregarious, so she was never the most popular. She definitely wasn't the funniest or the sexiest or the most interesting. Why had Pierce agreed to something so perilous and horrific to have *her*?

"Other than some frazzled nerves, I'm fine." Another lie to mask her confusion, her desire. "What about you?"

He shrugged, his big body moving with stealthy grace. "Fine. If you didn't know, the EMTs took Cutter to the hospital for some tests, but he'll be all right."

"I heard. I called Cage shortly after I received your text. He said his brother rang before the medical team took him away. He and Sweeney are on their way over there. Cutter is going back for an MRI on his head before they stitch him up."

Pierce hesitated, then set his keys on the foyer table. He tucked his gun case on the floor underneath. "They're waiting for you, right? Go on."

He was letting her leave? Just like that? Without expecting anything in return? "But...I owe you. I'm prepared to give you what I promised."

He looked her up and down, then raised a brow at her. "No, you're not. And I don't want a martyr. Get out."

When Pierce brushed past her and headed for the kitchen, Brea whirled, frowning as she watched him pluck a tumbler from the cabinet. Her frown deepened when he filled it with whiskey and knocked it back in one swallow, ignoring her.

He'd not only given her a reprieve but seemingly released her from their deal altogether. She should be thrilled. She should be breathing a sigh of relief and running for the door. Instead, she felt shocked and disappointed. Angry, even.

What the devil was wrong with her?

It didn't matter. Cutter was at the hospital. Cage and Mama Sweeney were waiting. She should be beside them. They might need her moral support and prayers.

Still, she couldn't just leave without saying something. "I don't understand. You did something extraordinary for me today that I—"

"It's the same damn thing I did for Uncle Sam on the daily for eight years."

The math on that astounded her. He'd seriously killed that many enemy combatants? "But you were paid for your work. I owe you."

"Fuck that. I'm not your charity case, and I won't have you feeling guilty because you 'endured' my filthy hands all over you. Besides, I don't want the Boy Scout's leftovers. So get the hell out."

He poured another tumbler of whiskey and swallowed it back. Brea just stared. What was up with him? He pretended his kills didn't matter, as if he'd prefer to be alone and screw the rest of the world. But under all his bluster, she felt his hurt and loneliness. He was lost, wounded. And he had no one.

Except maybe her.

Brea softened. "Despite what you think, I committed tonight to you and I'm prepared to see this through. But if you don't want to have sex with me, then—"

"Oh, don't kid yourself." He slammed his glass on the table and stalked toward her on almost silent footfalls, spearing her where she stood. "Can you honestly say that you believe, for even a single second, that I'm not desperate to fuck you?"

Given everything he'd admitted the evening she'd brought him cookies? Given the way he was looking at her right now? "No."

"No," he confirmed. "I wanted you the second you opened the door at Edgington's house, skirt swishing and good-girl smile in place. I wanted you even after I knew you were Bryant's. Even when you refused to admit you want me, too. Hell, I even wanted you when you told me how much you love Cutter and offered me your body to save his life. I've imagined you, masturbated to thoughts of you, dreamed of you. So don't think, for one instant, that I've changed my mind."

His words stunned her. Brea's heart raced. "Why are you telling me this?"

"Because I'm being straight-up honest and I want the same from you. *That's* how you can repay me."

His demand terrified her…but she couldn't refuse. "A-all right."

"Good. Now we might get somewhere." Brea barely had time to grasp that he'd seen through her before he grabbed her arms and pulled her against his hard body. "I'm touching you. How does that make you feel?"

Heat radiated from him like a furnace, singeing all her exposed skin. She gasped. "Hot."

"And?" His nostrils flared. His eyes turned impossibly blacker.

When she tried to draw in a steadying breath, his scent filled her head instead. He smelled like musk. Like man. Like the most tempting sin. Her knees wobbled. Her eyes went wide. Her heart quaked.

And her whole body came alive.

What was it about Pierce Walker?

"That, right there." He pointed at her. "You want me, too, despite your better judgment. I see it all over your face. But you're still reluctant to admit it. You promised to stop lying."

Shame filled Brea. Her dishonesty was a selfish sin she wreaked on him to protect her pride. Pierce hadn't demanded that she give him her body, but she owed him her truth.

"You're right. I've thought of you, too," she whispered. "Even when Cutter told me to avoid you, even when I knew my father would never approve. And even when you scared me. I told myself none of what I'm feeling is logical or practical. But nothing has stopped my attraction to you."

"You're finally admitting you want me?"

Answering gave him the sort of power over her she could never take back... but her honor and his rough voice compelled her. "Yes. You make me ache in ways I shouldn't. In places I shouldn't. And I can't seem to stop."

Pierce grabbed her chin and lifted it. "What do you want from me?"

Did she dare answer him?

Brea bit her lip. "You already know."

"Spell it out." His fingers tightened. "I know what your eyes are telling me, pretty girl. But I want to hear you say it. Full consent."

This again? But why would he want that now...unless he intended to touch her?

"Pierce..." She tilted her head back, let her eyes slide shut again. "We shouldn't."

"Give me the words, pretty girl. I'm not asking for anything else."

What choice did she have? Sincerity was such a small price to pay him for saving her best friend's life.

Knowing she'd probably never be this close to Pierce again, Brea rose on her tiptoes and swayed against him, stealing a forbidden caress of her cheek against his hair-roughened one. "I want you to kiss me."

"I want that, too," Pierce groaned as he cupped her face, forcing her to meet his stare. "But I'm weak when it comes to resisting you. Don't say that again unless you actually mean it."

Something hot and twisted jolted through her body. "Or what?"

"Brea, I'm trying to do the right thing. When you look at me with those pleading eyes... And, fuck, your plump, pink mouth is so close, all I can think of are the indecent things I'm dying to do to it."

Probably the same things she'd secretly wanted him to do.

Her ache tightened. "What is this connection between us? I don't understand."

"Fuck if I know. I've never felt anything like it."

She hadn't imagined a yearning this strong was possible. It was bigger than her, and every time she tried to ignore it, the desire only grew.

Must be why folks call it temptation...

Brea searched his face, fighting her own impulse to touch him. And the fire in his black stare told her he knew it.

If she dared to repeat her desire, he'd be all over her. She wasn't sure she would have the will to resist him when he pushed her for everything she'd never given a man, then demanded more. But if she chose the coward's way out, she'd be lying, letting them both down, and leaving herself to forever wonder *what if.*

Which was really the bigger sin?

The truth was, Cutter didn't need her right now. His wounds weren't mortal. Even if he had a concussion, he would wake up tomorrow to live another day, secure in the knowledge that he was surrounded by community, family, and friends who loved him.

Who did Pierce have?

Tonight, he had her.

"I want you to kiss me," she whispered. "Now."

He tensed. "You're sure?"

"Yes."

"Even though it's wrong?"

According to Cutter, it was. Her father and God would concur, too. Pierce would probably break her heart in the end. Right now, none of that mattered more than giving him her honesty.

"Yes."

"Even though this could get out of control?"

"Yes."

"Brea. Baby…" Desire darkened his expression. "Don't say I didn't warn you."

Pierce's breaths came fast and harsh as he thrust his big hand in her hair, fisted the strands, and lowered his head.

She'd been kissed a few times, mostly by polite boys who hadn't taken things too far because they'd been afraid to incur the wrath of Reverend Bell or Cutter Bryant. Once, she'd made out on a bus ride home with a football player after a game in Baton Rouge. He'd kissed her with a lot of gusto and very little finesse before he'd tried to feel his way under her shirt. When she'd shoved away his wandering hands, he'd called her a prude and told his teammates she was a waste of time. Afterward, she'd felt angry, ashamed, and determined not to suck face with a boy again.

But the instant Pierce covered her mouth with his, she realized she'd never truly been kissed.

He pried her lips apart, surged inside, and touched her somewhere deeper than she'd ever felt. Sparks flared and zinged. Her skin stretched tight. Heat burst into a bonfire in her belly, awakening more of this dizzying need.

Brea threw her arms around Pierce, pressing her throbbing nipples against his chest in search of relief. He was hot and impossibly hard. Rubbing against him only increased her torment.

Their shirts were in the way. She needed his bare skin against hers. Ached for it. Craved it.

With an impatient fist, she tugged his camo T-shirt up his torso. The velvety skin and rigid muscle across his abdomen and ribs tempted her. She dug her fingers into his back, pulling him closer, feeling him deeper. It still wasn't enough.

At her touch, he groaned, twined their tongues together again, and reached behind his head. He interrupted their kiss just long enough to yank his shirt off and toss it to the floor.

She got a glimpse of his bare torso—big and hair-roughened, littered with tattoos and the scars of war, panting with desire—before he covered her mouth again and took her lips.

He seized her soul.

With shaking fingers, she braced herself on his steely shoulders and crashed into him, returning every jagged breath and stroke of his tongue as she curled her leg around his. As if he shared her desperation, he grabbed her thigh in his big hand and dragged it over his hip before backing her against the kitchen table and nudging her needy feminine flesh with his erection.

Pleasure spiked. Pierce swallowed her cries.

Under him, she wriggled, her blazing need burning through her misgivings and modesty. It demanded she get even closer, feel more of him—now.

Brea grabbed his steely biceps and writhed shamelessly. He ground his erection against the spot that made her wild for him. Pierce tore his mouth from their kiss, tossed his head back, and groaned out a curse.

Then he met her gaze. Instantly she knew if he'd been wearing gloves before, they were off now.

Good. She wanted to taste him, to feel him, to give herself to him.

She wanted to be his, even if it was for a night. Even if it was a sin. Even if she burned in hell for this desire. It couldn't be any worse than twisting in agony without him.

His hands took a rough plunge down her body, skirting dangerously close to the sides of her breasts before he filled his palms with her backside and lifted her off her feet. Her flip-flops fell to the floor as he set her on his kitchen table, spread her legs, and made himself at home in between. "Want your shirt off?"

"Yes."

Pierce gripped the hem of her floral tank and yanked it over her head. His stare fell on the skin he'd exposed. Beneath the lace-trimmed cups of her white bra, her nipples tightened and stabbed the modest cups. She shivered.

His rapacious black gaze skated down her bare belly, to the denim shorts clinging to her hips, to her bare feet with their painted pink toes. Then he settled his big palms around her hips and dragged her flush against him again. The sensations jolted her system. The longing between her legs torqued up, becoming pure torment.

"Pierce…"

"Jesus, pretty girl. You're perfect." He swept one hand across her abdomen, searing wherever he touched, before he dug his steely length right against her ache again. "Oh, fuck, yeah… You with me?"

Brea didn't hesitate. "Yes."

"You want more?"

"Yes."

"I want to suck those pretty nipples. What do you say to that?"

His demand sounded immoral. Wicked. Sublime. "Please."

"Tell me to take off your bra, pretty girl."

Her head was spinning. Her heart was chugging. She felt ready to burst into flames. "Take off my bra. Hurry."

Pinning her in place with his hungry gaze, Pierce lifted one hand to the strap bisecting her back and unfastened all three hooks in the blink of an eye.

Brea swallowed. This was happening. This was real. Pierce Walker was about to lay eyes on her naked breasts.

He let go. Her bra fell away.

His black eyes fastened on her, firmly affixing to her nipples. They drew up even tighter under his scrutiny, the tips so engorged they throbbed. "Fucking gorgeous."

His words made Brea blush. But she wanted more than his praise; she wanted relief from this endless ache.

She wound her arms around his neck and arched, flattening herself against his muscled torso. The jolt of his skin directly on hers was electric. She gasped at the new, foreign sensations.

"You feel so damn good," he groaned.

"You feel better."

But the skin-to-skin contact wasn't enough to satisfy her. She wriggled again, needing something more.

Pierce eased away, gaze fastened on her breasts again, as his fingers crept up her torso. "Tell me to touch them."

"Please." She prayed that would end her torment. "Touch them now."

She hadn't even finished speaking before he had her breasts in his scorching palms. He cradled them, testing their weight, squeezing. Then he swept the sensitive crests with his thumbs.

Tingles spread throughout her body. She hissed in pleasure and arched closer to Pierce, shoving herself deeper into his grip—and under his spell—silently begging for more.

"Like that?"

"Yes," she gasped.

"Want more?"

"Please." His touch made her need more insistent.

She feared only one thing would end it.

With a devilish smile, he flicked his thumbs across her nipples, bending the peaks—and her—to his will. Heat flared from the tops of her breasts to the tips of her toes, then zipped between her legs, twisting into a greedy, destructive inferno.

"I want your nipples on my tongue. Tell me to suck them."

His suggestion made her flare even hotter. And if he took her breasts in his mouth, he'd only destroy her that much faster.

Brea couldn't bring herself to care anymore.

"Yes." She clawed at him. "Please."

He skimmed his knuckles along the side of one of her mounds, back and forth, moving ever closer to her aching peak. "Please what?"

She knew why he kept prompting her with these questions, but she wished he'd stop. She didn't want to think, didn't want to consider every step down this road paved with lust and sin. But he was determined that she not only allow him to join her but *invite* him down the path of ruination with her.

"Please suck my nipples, then take off my shorts and lead me upstairs. Do whatever will make this ache go away. I need it. I need you. I consent."

⁓

Shock pinged through One-Mile. He'd fantasized. He'd hoped. But he hadn't truly believed Brea Bell would agree to let him spend the night inside her. "You're sure?"

"You can end this agony, right?"

"You bet I can, pretty girl." But given the chemistry between them, he had a sneaking suspicion the ache would only come back stronger, over and over again.

In fact, he was betting on it.

"Then yes," she groaned as she tried to wriggle off the table. "Hurry."

He would because he was dying to be inside her, but no fucking way would he let her go until they were both thoroughly satisfied. And maybe not even then.

One-Mile crowded her back onto the flat surface, then scooped her pert little ass in his hands again, crushing her against every hot inch of his body. Then he laid her out and swooped in for another unrestrained kiss. Just like the first time he tasted her, the instant her honey-sweet flavor hit his tongue, she ramped up his hunger.

He dove deep into her mouth, driven by the need to take all she gave. Brea melted, arms around his neck, drawing him closer as she writhed artlessly beneath him. He rocked against her, grinding where he ached to penetrate her.

His desire for her became a searing, infinite need. One-Mile ate at her mouth, hell-bent on imprinting himself on Brea Bell forever. He tried to slow his roll, not overwhelm her. Hell, he tried to let her breathe.

Not happening. Her every touch and little whimper only jacked him up more.

He jerked back, chest heaving as he sucked in air. Beneath him, Brea looked stunned and blinking, her rosy, swollen lips gaping in surprise. *He* had put that look on her face, and it made One-Mile harder than he'd ever been. He gripped her thighs and tried like hell to think. Because if he didn't find some goddamn self-control, he'd strip her where she lay and fuck her until she screamed.

"Do you need to tell anyone you'll be unavailable for a while?" The last fucking thing he wanted was to be interrupted, especially by annoying-as-fuck Bryant.

"No," she breathed. "My dad is playing cards tonight with friends. I doubt the hospital will release Cutter before morning. But I'll turn it off just in case."

The hitch and shiver in her voice torqued up his arousal.

"Do that."

"You have to let me up."

Reluctantly, he did, never taking his rapt gaze off of her as she pulled the device from her purse. She checked it…then silenced it.

Finally, she was his…at least for the night.

And the fact that she would rather spend it getting orgasms from him instead of holding her convalescing boyfriend's hand said that, while parts of her heart might still be with Cutter, the rest of her wanted only him.

One-Mile could work with that. He had every intention of blowing Brea's doors off in bed. Given her good-girl mentality, he'd bet Cutter had been her first—and only—lover. He hated that she'd given her innocence to the prick, but he would happily provide her a point of comparison. And since Brea was the sort of woman whose body followed her heart, if he did this right, she would soon be waving *adios* to the bastard for good.

When she swayed toward him again, he dragged her against his body and lifted her. "Wrap your arms and legs around me."

She didn't hesitate to sling her thighs around his hips and grip his shoulders, then squirm to get closer. He groaned. Goddamn it, despite how tiny she was, they were going to fit together perfectly when they fucked.

He grappled for the patience to at least get her clothes off before he ruthlessly impaled her.

With his hands full of her ass, he charged for the stairs. When she skimmed her lips across his bare shoulder and started kissing her way up his neck, his gait turned to a run.

"You're playing with fire," he warned.

"I already know you're going to burn me."

Her whisper shuddered down his spine. No doubt she'd leave him some blisters of her own. If she didn't realize that, she was either delusional or totally unaware of her own appeal.

Climbing the stairs took for-fucking-ever. When he finally reached the landing, he was out of breath—not from exertion but from his weeping cock rubbing the molten heat between her legs. When she sank her teeth into his shoulder, then lapped at the spot with her little tongue, he was damn near ready to crawl out of his skin.

"Brea…"

"Hmm… You have this hint of salt. I want to know if the rest of you tastes like that."

At the image of her mouth all over him, One-Mile picked up his pace toward his bedroom, melting with lust. It was taking so fucking long to get down the hallway. If he didn't get there quickly, he'd shove her against the nearest wall and get inside her just to give them both some goddamn relief.

"You can put your mouth anywhere you want on me, pretty girl. Just wait until we get to the fucking bed."

She lifted her wide gaze his way, wearing a hint of a smile. "You sound impatient."

"You think?"

When he grumbled, her smile widened. "So I get to you?"

"After one look, I wanted you. But after one kiss, I knew I'd do anything to have you."

The smile slid off her face. "Why?"

"We're about to find out." He bent and laid her flat across his rumpled sheets. "Let's take our chemistry for a spin."

One-Mile didn't give her a second to rethink or regroup. He covered her body with his and dove into her mouth, praying the balm of her kiss could soothe the rough edges of his agony. Beneath him, she parted her legs as if him sliding between them was the most natural thing in the world. It fucking felt that way when he notched his cock against her pussy again, which he hoped like hell was wet enough to take him. She cried out under him, her nails already digging into his skin like a kneading kitten's.

Brea tore her lips from his with a gasp. "Pierce…"

"You asked me to suck your nipples."

"Yes."

Craving a taste of her, One-Mile cradled one of her breasts in his palm and dragged his tongue over its tight crest.

Yeah, he'd held bigger tits, but none as sweet as hers. This was a pair he could be happy with for the rest of his life—symmetrical, bouncy and round, slightly heavier at the bottom, but still delicate, like her. Her rosy-brown nipples tempted the fuck out of him. They were small and taut, and he wanted to suck the sugary little buttons until she melted for him.

After his first lick, both her peaks swelled to stab the air—pretty, pouting, begging. He turned his mouth to the other and pinched the first, gratified when she arched toward him, as if she was surrendering these luscious little tips to him entirely.

Greedily, he wrapped his lips around the closest one, sucking it deep. He reveled in the toss of her head as she dug her nails into his back again.

"Oh… My…" she panted. "Yes."

One-Mile wasn't up for conversation, but he loved hearing her stream-of-pleasure babble. So he drew her deeper into his mouth, swirled his tongue around the captive crest, then released her slowly, teeth nipping gently along the way.

"Please…" She curled her fingers into his short hair and pulled him closer. "More."

He didn't argue, just switched breasts. This nipple looked as earnest and engorged as the first. With his thumb and fingers, he plucked at the peak he'd just popped from his mouth. Then he engulfed the other, pulling it ruthlessly between his lips, tonguing it, then gently biting, pecking, gripping.

He kept at her, first one breast, followed by the other, until he reduced Brea to incoherent animal sounds and she twisted in agony beneath him.

"How's that ache now?" he murmured as he dragged his lips up her neck to nip at her lobe.

"Do something. I need…" She bit her lip and stared with helpless eyes. "I need you."

One-Mile was only too happy to oblige. Sure, he'd love to take a leisurely tour of her body, get his hands wherever she had curves, and let his mouth linger anywhere she might taste good. That would have to wait until round two. Right now, he didn't think either of them could stand another second of him not being inside her.

Jesus, his cock ached. Brea was like a fever; he was fucking sweating with need for her. He had to take her. Possess her. Own her.

As he shucked his constraining pants and kicked them aside, Brea propped herself up on her elbows and stared, her eyes wide, her mouth hanging open. How should he interpret that fucking expression? She gaped as if she'd never seen a man's cock, but she must have. She'd been with Cutter for years, and he was no monk.

"Pretty girl?" He knelt on the bed and leaned over her.

She jerked her stare to his face, blinked, then dragged him down for a drugging kiss. "I'm here. Yes. Hurry."

No fucking way he would deny her anything.

As he crushed her swollen lips beneath his, One-Mile tore into the button at the waist of her shorts. Next, he yanked down her zipper. He tugged the denim and her underwear away all at once, jerking them down her thighs. Later, he'd take a gander at whatever pretty, lacy shit she'd worn that would undoubtedly tempt the hell out of him. Right now… He dropped his stare to the one place on her body that would no doubt seduce him most.

Oh, sweet pussy.

Soft and pink, hiding shyly behind a tuft of dark hair. And so fucking wet.

His mouth watered, and he dropped between her legs, bending them, then tossing them over his shoulders as quickly as he could. "I'm so fucking hungry."

"Pierce…oh—"

She stopped talking the instant he filled his mouth with her succulent flesh. The tart-sweet flavor of her teased his tongue as he explored her folds and valleys. She was lush and ripe—like a fucking fantasy. He ate at her ravenously, wondering if he'd ever get enough.

Under him, she cried out, head thrashing from side to side. Her thighs suddenly tightened around his head. Her fingers thrust into his hair as she began scratching at his scalp. Her little moans became high-pitched pleas that reverberated in his ears and messed with his restraint.

Fuck, he loved heaping pleasure on her.

One-Mile pushed her thighs wider, dragged his tongue up her center again, and let out a gruff groan as she gushed into his mouth. The clit he took between his lips was engorged and hard as hell. God, he'd love to mouth-fuck her half the night, but she wasn't going to last. And neither was his nagging cock. If he didn't get inside Brea soon, the fucker would drill a hole in his mattress to find relief.

Under his insistent tongue, her hips wriggled. Her harsh breaths filled the room. Her cries grew louder. He could fucking smell her—under his nose, on his lips, all over his sheets. It made him hungrier. Fair or not, he demanded more from her.

Reluctantly, he released her thighs to clamp his fingers around her hips so he could use his grip to press her onto his tongue. Every fucking time he lapped her up, she gave him more sweet cream. She was making him crazy. Goddamn hysterically insane. He was always in control, always aware of everyone and everything around him, threats assessed, escape routes mapped. Right now, his fucking house could burn down but he wouldn't give a shit about that or the danger until she fucking came on his tongue.

When her clit swelled even more and began to quiver as it turned to steel, One-Mile knew he had her.

Yeah. Oh, fuck, yeah. Give. It. To. Me.

As if she read his mind, Brea did, exploding with her next gasping breath as she stiffened and tossed her head back with an ear-piercing scream that made her entire body quiver and jolt.

Into his mouth, she pulsed and flowed. He plunged his tongue into her so he could feel the hard clamp of her body throbbing with the ecstasy he gave her.

He licked her through the pinnacle, making sure she rode every euphoric moment that twisted on and on until her body went limp, leaving Brea to gulp in recovering breaths of air. Smiling, One-Mile licked his lips as he climbed up her body.

Slowly, her lashes fluttered open. She blinked up at him, her eyes so golden they looked molten. Her stare was like a battering ram to his solar plexus. With just a look, she staggered him, knocked the breath from him.

Bullshit. She destroyed him.

"You good?" he managed to get out.

Her lips curled into a little smile. "Ahhhmazing. Can you make me feel like that again?"

He was already on fire, but her words poured gasoline over the blaze. Fuck waiting another second. "Right now, pretty girl. Right the fuck now."

His entire body buzzed with need as he took his cock in hand and fit it against her snug opening. He stared, forcing her wide eyes to meet his as he began to rock and thrust inside her, slowly shoving his tip past her swollen flesh.

Jesus, she was so fucking tight.

One-Mile eased out, rooted to her opening again, then pushed harder. She gasped in a catch of breath that had him freezing in place. She sounded as if she was in pain. He would have sworn he felt something inside her give way—almost as if it…broke.

What the fuck?

Before he could ask, the force of his next mindless thrust sent him delving deep. He tumbled inside her unimpeded, until he was blessedly submerged balls deep.

Dear God...

Her scalding heat surrounded him in a feeling unlike anything he'd ever experienced. An involuntary shudder wracked his body. Holy fuck. This woman was going to burn him the fuck alive. Right now, all he could think was how badly he ached for the flames.

He'd process these last few moments—how he felt and what it meant—then they'd talk. But later. Much fucking later.

Now was for making Brea scream his name.

"Oh, damn, pretty girl..."

When he looked down, he was surprised to find her eyes screwed shut tight.

"It hurts," she whimpered.

Fuck, the last thing he'd ever want to do was cause her pain. He had to find the control to be gentler—somehow. She'd had a massive orgasm, and while she was swollen he'd battered into her like a damn blunt-force object. He owed it to her to make her feel good.

But his goal was to give her so much fucking pleasure that she'd never want to spend another minute naked with Cutter Bryant.

"I'm sorry," he crooned. "I'll slow down. No more pain."

Slowly, she relaxed around him. "Really?"

"None. I promise." To prove it, he stroked softly into her, down, down, until his crest nudged her cervix.

Oh, holy hell...

"That's better," she sighed breathlessly.

"Yeah?" He kissed her overheated cheeks, swiped his thumb across the perspiration at her temple.

She nodded. "That feels...good."

Fuck, did it ever. He thrust a bit faster, still watching her face for any sign of discomfort. Thankfully, nothing but soft excitement filled her face. And when her lashes lifted from her cheeks, opening his view to the windows of her soul once more? Yeah, his cock nagged and ached for relief, but the vise in his chest squeezed even harder. Her expression played hell with his self-control.

Those fiery golden eyes of hers said that, at least for now, she totally belonged to him.

His fingers on her hips tightened. He tried so fucking hard to hold back and stay in control of his rhythm, but his body was done waiting.

His thrusts picked up pace. "A little or a lot?"

"A little." She writhed under him, moving with him as he slid in and out of her like melted butter. Then she tightened with a cry. Her gaze bounced up to his in shock a second before she liquified under him with a moan. "Oh. No, a lot."

So he'd found her sweet spot. *Fuck, yes.* "More?"

She clarified her incoherent sob with a wholehearted bob of her head.

One-Mile took that as a hell yes.

He tucked his hands under her ass and lifted her closer, tilting and opening her wider to penetrate her deeper. The shift didn't just give him access to the most untouched corners of her body but put him in direct contact with her still-sensitive clit.

As soon as he did, she gasped and shuddered, her stare going wide with both shock and a hundred silent questions.

He just smiled as he settled into a quick tempo. She'd figure it out—pretty quickly if her reaction was any indication.

There was something so unbearably intimate about staring into her eyes as he fucked her. Every emotion, every thought, every shred of bliss? He saw them all. One-Mile swore he wasn't reading just her body but her mind. And she was telling him that she couldn't hold out much longer.

"Pierce!" She clamped down on him.

He filled her faster and ground down on her clit just to help things along, because goddamn it, he'd held back for her as long as he could. Everything inside him was poised and screaming at him to let go of his restraint and fucking explode.

Hell of a time to remember that he'd monumentally screwed up and—for the first time ever—forgotten a condom.

He didn't care. Whatever happened next? Yeah. Bring it. He didn't need anything more than this moment, right now, to know that Brea Bell belonged to him. Whatever she had with Bryant was history.

He'd make sure of that.

If there were consequences from tonight…the timing might not be optimal, but the end result suited him just fine.

Beneath him, Brea suddenly went wild, rocking with him, nails in his back, lips on his neck, her cries in his ear. Then he felt feel her cunt clenching, her breath stopping, the air stilling, and the need building in his heavy balls bursting.

Teeth bared, he growled as his restraint broke. He shoved his way inside her with a dozen rapid-fire thrusts that had his headboard beating the wall—and Brea clenching on him as she let loose a shrill shriek of ecstasy and shuddered wildly under him.

Jesus. Holy hell. Fuck, fuck, fuck… But no self-talk could stop the overwhelming wall of rapture. It flattened him, undid him, turned him around, twisted him, then spit him back out. After long, mind-blowing moments, he finally found the other side of ecstasy, gasped for air, and tried to process what the fuck had happened. He felt different. He felt changed.

He felt like hers.

Under him, she heaved a sigh, lips parted, eyes closed. The tension in her body eased, except the occasional pulse of her pretty pussy around his softening cock.

She blinked up at him, clearly stunned. "Oh…my goodness."

That was her version of *holy fuck*, and it made him laugh. He slicked back the damp hair clinging to her forehead and cheeks. "Yeah, you could say that."

"I had no idea…"

Cutter must be a real deadbeat in the sack. No wonder she was here instead of with him. Keeping her might be even easier than he'd imagined. With chemistry like theirs, it would be years—hell, maybe a lifetime—before they got enough of each other.

"How do you feel, pretty girl?"

The smile that curled up her pouty mouth was almost self-conscious. It matched her still-flaming cheeks. "Happy. Like I'm floating. Best feeling ever."

One-Mile laughed, stupidly thrilled. Whether she knew it or not, she'd just admitted that was the best sex of her life. The fact that she loved being with him and wanted more only made him feel on top of the world. This was Christmas in August—but better. Unless he missed his guess, it wouldn't take much to make sure he could unwrap her every single day.

"It is." He laid a soft kiss on her lips. "It was amazing."

"Yeah…"

Her voice still had that dreamy quality when he reluctantly withdrew. She winced, biting her lip and clearly holding in a cry. Shit. Had he somehow hurt her?

"What's wrong?"

But the words had no more left his mouth when he sat back on his knees and looked down.

Blood.

One-Mile already knew from having his mouth all over Brea that she wasn't in the middle of her period.

The moment he'd pushed his way into her slammed back through his brain. The tightness. The feeling of something giving way. Her admission that it had hurt.

The obvious occurred to him, but…how was that possible? From his research, it seemed she'd been Cutter's girlfriend for years—at least based on her barely used social media accounts. The asshole had taken her to her prom. He'd held her hand and posed for a dozen pictures during her high school graduation. He'd been her first haircut when she'd finished beauty school.

If she had been anyone else, One-Mile would have dismissed even the small chance that she'd been innocent when he'd carried her up to his bedroom less than an hour ago. But this was Brea. She was a preacher's daughter. She was a good girl to the core.

Oh, shit. Maybe Cutter hadn't been cheating on her the night before her father's heart attack as much as getting some relief because he really was a Boy Scout who had agreed to wait for Brea until marriage.

At least that might have been his plan until One-Mile had barged in and ruined her. *Oh, holy fuck.*

"Brea…" He forced her to meet his stare. "You promised me the truth tonight, so be fucking honest. Were you a virgin?"

chapter six

BREA GAPED. SHE CROSSED PROTECTIVE ARMS OVER HER BREASTS. SELF-PRESERVATION warred with her innate desire to be honest. But the way Pierce kept staring tied her tongue. Thinking seemed impossible. She wished she could crawl inside her skin and hide.

He'd figured out she was a virgin. Was he mad? Shocked? Dismayed? Did he feel guilty? Responsible? Disgusted?

Those possibilities had her eyes stinging with mortifying tears. Why couldn't she stop feeling so horribly vulnerable?

Brea bolted up from the bed and scanned the room for her clothes. "I already answered your questions."

"I have more."

She shook her head. "I'm sorry. I have to go."

Pierce stood, utterly naked and unconcerned, and prowled toward her with narrowed eyes. "So…what? Now that we've fucked, you're done being honest?"

She flinched at his question. "Please. That's enough."

"If you're measuring honesty, it's never going to be 'enough.'"

Finally, she found her panties and snatched them up, doing her best not to stare at his big, naked body. "I meant that I don't appreciate your language and I don't owe you my personal information."

"As the guy who unwittingly took your virginity, I disagree. By the way, isn't lying a sin?"

"Yes." Technically, so was having sex outside of wedlock. She would have a lot to repent for after tonight. "But I was merely asking you to drop the subject and respect my privacy."

He scoffed. "Since I've had my dick deep inside you, I think we're past privacy."

Brea managed to step into her underwear, but it didn't make her feel less naked under his black stare. "I'm leaving."

Her dratted bra was nowhere to be found. Where the devil had he tossed it?

A blip of a memory flashed through her brain of Pierce stripping it off of her downstairs…just before she'd begged him to touch her breasts. What had she been thinking?

Nothing—beyond him easing the unrelenting ache inside her.

"Stay." He gripped her arm. "We need to talk."

Pierce spoke like he wanted to have a serious conversation…but his stare caressed her nipples, still tight and tingling from his attention. His penis began rising again.

An answering desire stirred between her legs.

She ignored it, plucking up her shorts and slapping them over her breasts. "No, we don't."

If she stayed, she feared they wouldn't spend much time talking.

"Since you were a virgin, even if you'd rather not admit that, I'm assuming you're not on birth control."

She froze. She'd had no reason to be on birth control. And he hadn't used a condom.

Brea's mouth fell open on a silent gasp. She staggered back. How had she been so careless?

Pierce's grip was the only thing that kept her from falling. "That's what I thought. Where are you in your cycle?"

She couldn't think beyond her dismay. "Pierce, please… I have to go."

"Not until we figure out how likely you are to get pregnant." His grip tightened. "Refusing to talk won't solve anything."

You have a habit of burying your head in the sand. That won't always work… Cutter's warning drifted through her head. He was right, but she wasn't ready to face the stark reality of her choice and its potentially monumental consequences.

"Please stop talking. And let go." She yanked her arm from his grip.

He released her so abruptly she stumbled back—only to get another eyeful of him in his head-to-toe naked glory.

Heat flared through her.

Brea had never imagined being blasphemous enough to think that God had a sadistic streak. But why else would He make the only man she'd ever found irresistible be the one her friends, family, and community would never approve of?

Biting her lip to hold in a cry, she turned away and dashed down the stairs.

Pierce followed, his heavy footfalls sounding determined not to let her get far. "You didn't ask, but I'm clean. I've never had sex with anyone else without a condom."

Of course she hadn't thought he'd been pure, but when she imagined him being as intimate with another woman as he'd been with her, jealousy twisted a knife in Brea's chest. Her stomach turned in a sick grind. Her eyes stung again.

She had to get out of here.

Brea dashed down the stairs and darted to the kitchen, plucking up her bra and shirt as she crossed the room to her purse. Pierce was right behind her, his breath hot on the back of her neck.

"Stop running, damn it, and talk to me. We'll work through it."

She whirled on him, the tears she'd been trying to hold back spilling like hot acid down her burning cheeks. "I've given you everything I offered you in exchange for Cutter's life. Now we're even. I need to go."

His eyes narrowed. "You're kidding yourself if you think the only reason you let me take you to bed was to save your boyfriend's life. I made no secret of the fact I wanted you. But you fucking wanted me, too. Woman up and own it."

He was right, just like she knew she should be honest with him about her relationship with Cutter. But when he looked at her, Brea felt more exposed than she had when he'd stripped her naked and penetrated her.

"There's nothing left to talk about."

"Bullshit. You're afraid. I get it. But this fucking wedge of distance you're driving between us right now isn't helping." He stalked toward her.

Brea juggled her clothes and her purse in her hands, backing up for every step he prowled closer. "Stop."

"Not when you're upset." He wrenched the items from her grasp and tossed everything on the kitchen table. Then he lifted her off her feet and carried her to the sofa, plopping down on the nearest cushion. He settled her over his lap, facing him so she straddled his hips. His big hands swept up her back, urging her head onto his shoulder. "Talk or cry or whatever you need. I'm here."

The sincerity in his voice told Brea he really would be there for her…but he was too close for her to breathe, much less rub two thoughts together. A terrible awareness consumed her—of his big arms around her, his warm breath in her ear, his hard, naked chest flattening her sensitive nipples, and his heart chugging in time with hers.

As if he felt their connection, too, his penis hardened even more, surging between them, nudging where her ache swirled and thickened.

"Pierce…" Brea meant to pull away.

Instead, she found herself writhing against him.

"I'm trying to be a good guy, pretty girl, but if you keep that up, I'm going to fuck you again," he groaned. "In thirty seconds—or less."

Fresh need tightened between her legs. Brea's head told her that would be terrible. But her body loved the notion, heating and softening all at once, arching to get even closer.

Pierce cursed, then lifted her breasts in his massive palms and sucked one nipple into his mouth. She gasped…and her protest faded into a wail of pleasure.

Why was she resisting him? The damage was already done. She was no longer a virgin. They had already had unprotected sex. Would another few minutes of sin really matter?

Of course she was rationalizing, but when Pierce tongued her sensitive peaks, then sucked one deep into his mouth, she dug her nails into his shoulders and gave in. "Oh…"

As he moved to thumb her stiff crests again, he slid his tongue up her neck. "It's so right between us. Say something if you don't want more, but otherwise… All it takes to feel good is a little shift and"—he yanked the crotch of her panties out of his way slowly, giving her time to refuse him as he fisted his erection and adjusted her directly over his swollen head—"fuck…"

He gripped her hips and gave her a gentle push down. Gravity did the rest of his dirty work. Together, they destroyed her resistance. When she finally enveloped every inch of his hardness, she sank against him with a long, agonized gasp.

Having Pierce inside her, filling her so completely, shocked her even more than the first time.

"That's it," he growled in her ear. "You're not too sore?"

Brea felt a slight sting everywhere her flesh stretched to accommodate him, but this time it only hurt in a good way. "Not enough to stop."

He urged her up the length of his shaft, then urged her back down. "You like the bite?"

Beneath her, he lifted his hips, his erection scraping her swollen sex as he shoved inside her, prodding some nerve-rich spot deep.

"Yes," Brea hissed, her head falling back with a moan of surrender as her blood raced and her heart careened.

"Grab on to my shoulders. I'm going to fuck you until you can't think about anything but us."

She was already there.

A voice of caution in the back of her head tried to scream at her to stop, to consider whose daughter she was and what she was doing. But Pierce's raspy breaths and rough hands distracted her from anything resembling reason. His male musk swam in her head. He overwhelmed her. He intoxicated her.

He owned her.

As he shafted her up and down his length, her ache tightened, her pleasure multiplied, and her objections fell silent. All that remained were his long fingers encircling her, his big body driving under her, and his thick cock filling her. Brea found herself rocking with him, swaying and grinding, gasping and keening toward the pinnacle of pleasure he was already so close to giving her.

"You look fucking beautiful." He pinched her nipples, his grip tightening even after she sucked in a shocked breath of pained bliss. "Open your eyes. I want to watch you come."

Brea lifted her lashes slowly. Immediately, his black stare fused itself to her. The intensity of his arousal seared her. His cheeks flamed with it. His jaw clenched with it. His entire body tightened with it. The sight of him—along with the feelings surging between them—mesmerized her. Everything about him more than accelerated her desire. A connection she'd never felt with another human being overwhelmed her. It wasn't purely sexual, but it was as if, with some click, her soul attached itself to his.

It was shocking. It felt irrevocable.

Her hunger climbed. She ached to be even closer, craved her mouth on him. She needed him in every way a woman could touch a man.

With a cry, she fastened her lips over his. Pierce might have been physically underneath her, but he took charge, tangling his fingers in her hair, locking their mouths together, binding them in ways she'd never imagined. Brea couldn't help but melt as she ground down on him, stroke after frantic stroke.

Finally, he tore his lips from hers with a gasp, then grabbed her hips tighter, thrusting himself hard and deep and sure, as if she was his and he had every right to claim her in any way he liked. "Give it to me. Orgasm number three. I want it now."

She keened as she plunged down, taking him deeper than ever. The tension gathering in her belly and between her thighs coalesced, knotting up so tightly she panted, dug her nails into his bare shoulders, and unraveled with a scream.

"Yes. Oh, fuck…" His fingers bit into her as he rammed up one last time, teeth clenched, tendons in his neck flexing as ecstasy overtook him. "Brea!"

Together, they fell into the abyss, clinging, clutching, holding on for dear life. Pleasure threatened to drag her into an addicting, sublime darkness as she panted, her head lost in a dizzy sway she no longer had the will to fight.

This climax was shockingly stronger than the first two. And when she finally opened her eyes again, she found Pierce's inky stare locked on her. The feeling of falling into him unnerved her. The longer she studied him as they tried to catch their breath, the deeper she fell. Something about being with this man in this moment… She felt as if she'd somehow tied herself to him for all time.

Like he was her destiny.

Ridiculous. God had a plan for her. And as much as she was loath to leave Pierce's arms because this would probably be their last few moments alone, He wouldn't curse her to lose her heart to a man her family and community would shun, right?

Pierce pulled her in, kissing his way up her cleavage, her collarbone, her shoulder. "Stay tonight."

She shouldn't. She couldn't.

But she was so very tempted.

The truth was, her father would go to bed early because, even if he wasn't giving the service tomorrow, he would want to be well rested for his first Sunday back in the church since his surgery. Cutter wasn't leaving the hospital tonight. It was already past visiting hours, and he wouldn't expect to see her until he was officially discharged in the morning. So the two people most likely to care where she spent the night would have no idea she wasn't at home, tucked chastely in her bed.

This might be her only chance to stay with Pierce, indulge her need for him…and purge him from her system for good.

Still, she had one question. "Why?"

"Want me to keep being honest with you?"

"Please."

Pierce looked at her as if he never wanted to let her go. "I've never felt about a woman the way I do about you."

Brea's breath caught. A wave of pleasure washed over her. Another rush of it flushed her cheeks. "I'd have to be up really early."

"Any time I get with you is better than none."

His words softened her heart. She felt the same. It probably wasn't smart but… "I'll stay."

A smile stretched across his face, transforming him, before he nuzzled his face in her neck. "I'll make sure you don't regret it, pretty girl."

Normally, she'd suspect he meant something sexual. And she didn't think for one second that he'd keep his hands off her the rest of the night. In fact, she hoped he didn't since the thought of him inside of her again made her whole body flash hot, as if she wasn't already spent. As if he hadn't utterly satisfied her minutes ago. But something about the way he watched her or touched her—Brea couldn't exactly put her finger on it—convinced her he wasn't simply wanting to hook up again.

If she were honest, she wasn't staying strictly for the sex, either. She more than liked him, despite all the reasons she shouldn't. But everyone in her life behaved as if she was a girl; Pierce alone treated her like a woman. Didn't she deserve one night with a man who made her feel good?

Maybe Pierce wasn't her sin but her reward—albeit temporary—for always being everyone's dutiful friend and helpmate. And maybe she was fooling herself. Even so, Brea resolved to pack as much pleasure as she possibly could into this one night and leave tomorrow with no regrets.

She smiled. "Are you going to feed me before you take advantage of me again?"

"I could." He nuzzled her. "Or I could just chain you to my bed and fuck you all night."

That should not turn her on so much, but it sounded both forbidden and wonderful. "How about both? I can fry eggs in less than five minutes."

Pierce cradled her face, and the way he looked at her again—as if she meant the world to him—had her stomach flipping over and upside down with a giddiness that spread through her body. If she wasn't careful, she would fall for him.

He pressed a passionate kiss to her bruised lips, something slow, urgent, and thorough. Something that told her what the rest of her night was likely to be like. Something that excited her almost more than she could contain.

When he finally lifted his head, he brushed his thumb across her tingling lip. "As long as I get to watch you cook naked, hell yes."

Sunday, August 17

Predawn darkness surrounded Brea as she slowed her car and killed her headlights. She wished she could turn off her guilt half so easily after creeping from Pierce's bed and tiptoeing out of his house. What would he think when he woke to find her gone?

Nothing polite. He wouldn't care that people had expectations of her—that her father required her in the front row at church or that Cutter needed a nursemaid after his release from the hospital. He wanted her all to himself. And if she could have been selfish for a bit longer, she would have stayed.

But that wasn't her reality. She had responsibilities and, unlike Pierce, she enjoyed people relying on her.

It was just frustratingly inconvenient today.

Shoving aside that reality, Brea brought her car to a complete stop in front of her house and let out an exhausted sigh. Since she didn't see any lights on inside, thank goodness, she figured Daddy must still be asleep. Hopefully, she could sneak in a shower and a power nap before they left for church.

Flushed and boneless, her whole body sensitive and beyond sated, she turned off the engine and eased from the seat. She winced against the soreness between her thighs, but the tingly, uncomfortable ache reminded her of Pierce. Of the best night of her life.

He'd kept her up half the night before he'd curled her against his big furnace of a body for a couple of hours of rest...only to awaken her again with his teeth in her shoulder and his heavy erection working its way back into her snug, swollen sex with a low male groan.

The memory nearly had Brea staggering against another bomb of desire detonating inside her. The urge to throw caution to the wind—to climb back into her car and return to Pierce—assailed her. She'd give almost anything to jump into his arms again and stay for good.

That was a lovely fantasy. Maybe if she wasn't a dutiful small-town preacher's daughter and he wasn't an outsider who killed for a living, they could find some way to be together. But all the what-ifs and wishes in the world weren't going to change reality.

They were doomed.

She had given Pierce her virginity more to satisfy her own desires than to save Cutter, and she would have to both atone to God for her sin and live with her actions. But right now...she didn't regret a thing.

Brea eased her car door shut, slung her purse over her shoulder, then, shoes in hand, crept toward her house.

"I never thought I'd see you doing the walk of shame."

That all-too-familiar voice made her heart drop.

She whirled. "Cutter..."

Brow raised, he sauntered in her direction, eyeing her up and down as if he had no idea who she was anymore. Shame rolled through her, but she beat it back. Who was he to judge? He wasn't her father or God. She might not have needed to give herself to Pierce Walker to save him, but she'd offered. Her heart had been in the right place...even if the rest of her had been far less altruistic.

"Listen. I can—"

"Explain?" he cut in sharply.

At the rebuke in his voice, she pressed her lips together mutely. He'd already grasped the situation. Nothing she could say, short of lying, would convince him of anything less than the truth. And she saw no point in compounding her sin with a falsehood.

"Help you home. I didn't think you'd already be released from the hospital, and I'm sure you shouldn't be out of bed. Why are you?"

He drew closer and clutched her arm. Even though the shadows hid the disapproval in his expression, Brea could feel it. "Been too 'busy' to look at your phone?"

She'd turned it off last night, and Pierce had kept her far too busy to even think about turning it back on. "Sorry."

"I called. Repeatedly. Until three this morning. Then I sent Cage out to find you. But you weren't home. You weren't at the church. You weren't at the hospital, either. Then I remembered that bastard Walker telling me—after he served as the shooter's judge, jury, and executioner—that you were at his house. That you were *waiting* for him there. And sure enough, that's where my brother found your car about an hour ago. And since there's no way you and Walker were having a deep, existential conversation in the middle of the night, I checked myself out against doctor's orders and had Cage drop me off at my truck so I could come after you." Cutter clutched both of her shoulders and dragged her under the nearby streetlamp in time to see a guilty flush crawl up her face. "Dear God. What the fuck did Walker do to you?"

She winced, both at his shout and his choice of slurs. "Please lower your voice and calm down."

"Calm down? I worried he took advantage of your naiveté. That he seduced you but..." Cutter's grip tightened, along with his mouth, which flattened into a grim line that promised retribution. "He left his mark all over you. You reek of him. Your cheeks are whisker burned. Your lips are bruised and swollen. He fucking *ravaged* you." The tightness in his voice told Brea that notion pained him. "Son of a bitch. He said you begged him to intervene on my behalf."

Had he really thought she wouldn't? "I-I was terrified for you."

"Not as afraid as I've been for you. I knew damn well what he wanted the moment he laid eyes on you." A scathing, cynical stare twisted his face. "He demanded you give it to him, didn't he?"

She shook her head and tried to think of some way to explain that wouldn't make him even angrier. "That's not what happened."

He clenched his jaw, turning deadly still. "Shit. Then it's worse than I thought. Because now that I see what he's done to you, the only other way I'll believe you spent a night in his bed was if he forced you. By all that's holy, I swear I'm going to kill him."

"Don't. You can't. He—"

"Don't try to sugarcoat what that motherfucker did to you."

Cutter only used that language around her when he was beyond furious. He underscored that fact by curling up his fist, rolling a growl up from his chest, and punching her driver's-side window.

Brea jumped and started—then blinked in horror when he reared back to do it again, as if he wasn't satisfied that the glass hadn't shattered the first time.

"Stop." She grabbed his elbow and hauled back with all her might.

He whipped a furious stare on her, then snarled out another curse as he shook out his hand. "You shouldn't have gone to Walker on my behalf. You promised me you'd stay away."

"You needed me, and I—"

"He's dangerous. I hope you fucking get that now."

"Cutter, please. Listen…"

"No. I know you. I know you sacrificed yourself for me. And I know what you're doing right now. Don't you dare try to make me feel less guilty."

"I'm not. I'm telling you that—"

"It wasn't too bad?" he scoffed. "A conversation with the asshole is torture. I can't imagine how you endured a whole night with him fucking on top of you." He clenched his hands into fists again with a guttural grunt. "I would have gotten myself out of the situation. And if I couldn't have, it wasn't worth whatever he put you through. I don't even want to think about how much he bent you to his will—and hurt you—without wanting to kill him."

The longer she let Cutter linger on this subject, the angrier he would become. And he wasn't calm enough yet to hear that Pierce hadn't forced her to do anything. He might not be for a while.

"It's over. Right now, I'm worried about you. You should never have left against doctor's orders. You have a nasty concussion. Don't break your hand, too. You need rest. I'm so thankful you're alive. Please don't worry me more."

"I'm fine. I'm taking you to the hospital to get a rape kit."

She blanched. "No."

"You're going to let him get away with defiling you?" His incredulous stare curdled her stomach.

"He's not getting away with anything. I'm focused on you right now. I'm worried about *you*. Nothing else matters."

Cutter raked a hand through his hair, angry knuckles reddening. "You can't expect me to let this go, Bre-bee. I understand why you might not want to tell everyone in Sunset or even your father. I don't agree because this isn't your shame. But I understand."

"You don't understand at all. Let it go."

"Are you fucking crazy?"

"Keep it down, bro," Cage hissed as he made his way down the driveway to join them on the sidewalk. "You're going to wake up the whole neighborhood if you don't."

Cutter whirled on his brother. "I'm supposed to be calm when Walker fucking raped her?"

"Don't say that. You don't understand," Brea insisted.

"Oh, I understand perfectly." Her best friend looked murderous.

She turned to Cage with an imploring gaze.

The older Bryant brother nodded. "Bro, you're not supposed to be out of bed. And you're definitely not supposed to be driving." He plucked the truck keys from Cutter's grip. "Today isn't the day to fight this battle."

Cutter looked gutted. "You're taking her side?"

"I'm taking yours," Cage insisted. "That pain pill should be kicking in about now… The one that warns against operating heavy machinery or an automobile."

Cutter clutched his head. "We can't let Walker get away with this. He needs to die."

Brea groped for her patience. "He did nothing wrong."

But one look at Cutter's face told her that he'd never believe her. He saw her as a little girl. He would never believe she had chosen to have sex with a man who wasn't her husband, especially someone he held such a low opinion of. If burying her head in the sand was sometimes her downfall, Cutter's was being stubbornly blind. He didn't want the truth, so it didn't exist.

"He did everything wrong," Cutter growled. "And you let him take whatever he wanted from you to save my miserable ass. I will never forgive myself."

Before she could say another word, he pivoted toward his mother's house and marched for the front door, leaving her alone with Cage. His expression was more measured, equal parts righteous anger and curiosity. "Want to talk about it?"

Brea shook her head. She loved Cage like family, but she'd never been as close to him as she was to Cutter. The last thing she wanted to do was share her personal life with more people or bring anyone else into this strife. "I don't, except to say that your brother is wrong."

"Walker didn't rape you?"

"No. Not at all."

"That fits. You might be pious and soft-spoken, but if he'd hurt you, then you would have said so."

"Thank you for being rational."

"Cutter will be, too. Eventually. I hope." He winced. "Right now, he's just angry."

"Your brother is so stubborn. We both know he may never change his mind."

"Without a significant slap upside the head? Maybe not," Cage conceded. "Anything I can do to help until then?"

"Get him back to the doctor. He shouldn't return to work until he's been medically cleared."

"I'll do my best. I need to be back on the road to Dallas. My shift was supposed to start about…now."

Brea closed her eyes as more guilt enveloped her. No, she hadn't called Cage and demanded that he spend half the night looking for her. Cutter had done that. But if she'd looked at her phone sooner or checked in or reached out... "I'm sorry."

He shrugged. "I could use the extra day off. I'm going to escort Mama to church this morning. Then I'll be heading down the road. You should probably take a shower before your father wakes up. I know you don't wear makeup often, but you might want to put on some today."

She blushed again. "Are the marks that obvious?"

He grimaced and pulled at the back of his neck. "Afraid so. I don't have a particular beef with Walker. I don't even know him. But I know you. So I know the guilt is probably eating you up inside. And if you exchanged your body for my brother's safety, I regret whatever you had to endure, but I'll forever be grateful that Cutter is alive today."

Then Cage was gone.

Brea swallowed, standing stock-still until she heard the soft thump of their front door closing.

God, she didn't even know what to feel anymore. Guilty, yes. Sorry? Some of that, too. Exhaustion, worry, uncertainty. Somewhere in there, shock that the world felt so different in some ways but exactly the same in others. Still, under it all, giddiness prevailed. Pierce Walker had more than touched her. He had stolen a piece of her heart. And rather than wring her hands and wonder how on earth she'd ever get it back, all she could do was wonder if—no, how—she could spend the night in his arms again.

chapter seven

Tuesday, August 19

One-Mile started Tuesday in a foul mood. Over forty-eight hours had passed since he'd last pressed his lips to Brea's—while buried deep in the sweetest, snuggest cunt he'd ever felt. Then he'd awakened alone. After cursing a blue streak, he'd tried repeatedly to reach her.

Calls and texts on Sunday morning went unanswered. Fine. He'd figured she was sleeping or, better yet, breaking up with that asshole Bryant. But a few hours later, he'd rolled up to the little white house of worship her father preached at and, from his Jeep across the street, he'd seen her talking to a group of middle-aged moms. Cutter had been fucking glued to her side, his arm wrapped around her waist as if he owned her.

Brea hadn't objected, simply curled up against him as if she was where she wanted to be.

The sight had been a punch in the gut.

After that, his mood had rolled downhill.

By Monday morning, he'd been itching for a fight. Since he'd promised Logan he wouldn't bring their shit into the office, One-Mile had been more than prepared to beat the shit out of the asshole in the parking lot. But the Boy Scout had been a no-show. Normally, he would have relished a day without the insufferable bastard. Not today.

Later, he'd learned the bosses had insisted Bryant get medically cleared before he darkened their door again. Whatever. All One-Mile had cared about was the fact that Brea still hadn't responded to him.

This morning she finally had—texting him four brief words.
I need some space.

That told him where he stood. Brea had enjoyed her night of fun with the bad boy and was now kicking him to the curb. He should just say *fuck it* and do his damnedest to forget her. But he already knew he'd fail.

Besides, two and two wasn't adding up. Brea hadn't merely fucked him to save her boyfriend. If she had, she would never have given him her virginity or let him take her repeatedly Saturday night. She would never have kissed him with such innocent gusto. She would never have moaned so uninhibitedly every time her pleasure climbed. She would never have screamed so loudly when her climaxes hit. She would never have clung to him while she slept like a baby. She'd wanted *him*. Her needing space now? That was either Bryant breathing suspicion down her neck or her good-girl guilt barking. Maybe both.

He was going to call bullshit—and call her bluff.

Once he'd tracked her down, he'd coax, cajole, or seduce her into listening to his pitch to leave her boyfriend—who had never treated her like a woman. Then she could move in with him. Sure, it was fast. Yes, he was probably crazy. One-Mile expected obstacles. But he wasn't wrong about them. Brea Bell was his. The more he thought about it, the more his gut told him that was true.

Cutter was nothing more than a speed bump.

One-Mile slammed the door of his truck and locked it before shoving his way into EM Security Management's offices. Just inside the lobby, their pretty blond receptionist, Tessa Lawrence, sat at the front desk, doing her best to ignore Zyron. But the big lug had perched his ass on the edge of her desk to flirt shamelessly, despite the fact their bosses had a strict policy against fraternization and the woman didn't seem inclined to say yes. Even now, Tessa looked pale and nervous as she focused on her computer screen, typing away as if Zy didn't exist. But he didn't take the hint, instead asking her out—yet again—in low, suggestive tones while flashing his Hollywood smile.

Dumb ass. Her baby was only a few months old, and her ex-boyfriend's desertion only a few weeks older than that. The last thing a woman like Tessa was looking for was some asshole to nail her.

As he passed them, Zy scowled—the nonverbal equivalent of *get the fuck away from my woman.* One-Mile held up a hand. His fellow operative was welcome to fall flat on his face all day with the cute receptionist. He wasn't interested in any woman except Brea.

When he reached the dark corner of the building that housed his desk, One-Mile slumped into his chair and booted up his computer, eyeing the avalanche of unread messages dropping into his inbox. Updates on hotspots around the world. Information that might affect current and upcoming cases. Forensic reports on incidents they'd wrapped. Miscellaneous shit about new toys the bosses had acquired. Paperwork reminders. And on and on…

His mood went from dark to black as hell.

Why hadn't Brea told Bryant to fuck off? Did she love the stupid Boy Scout, in spite of the fact he didn't light her fire? Or had things changed? Now that she was no longer a virgin, had she and Cutter decided to screw waiting for marriage and fucked?

The thought made One-Mile homicidal.

He launched himself to his feet and headed for the coffeepot, wondering if Bryant would show up today. As he rounded the corner, he picked up a clean mug from the shelf and looked up.

Speak of the SOB…

"I want to talk to you."

Cutter barely glanced away from the java he poured. "Fuck off."

Maybe the asshole didn't understand. "It's about Brea."

Bryant slammed the pot back onto the brewer. "You're never touching her again, so whatever happened over the weekend? Forget it and move on. She's going to."

Was the Boy Scout bullshitting him? "You and me. Outside."

"Not happening. I've already been warned against drama in the office. Since I can't kick the ass of my esteemed fellow operative"—Cutter raised a sarcastic brow—"I want you the fuck out of my sight."

With that, he turned away and slunk back to his desk on the far side of the adjacent conference room.

One-Mile had had enough—and he knew how to fix this.

He whirled around, in search of Logan. But when he entered the boss's office, it wasn't the younger Edgington he found. Instead, a completely unfamiliar man stood there. He was somewhere around thirty, had some awesome ink and a don't-fuck-with-me vibe.

Logan hustled up behind him, bitching about some computer virus or another.

"Stone, this is Pierce," Logan said to the other guy.

One-Mile looked the stranger up and down. Were they hiring him? He looked badass enough to fit with the crew. More importantly, he didn't look like a snitch, a douche, or another Boy Scout.

He nodded toward Stone. "I prefer One-Mile."

Logan sighed. "One-Mile, then. He's our resident sniper. Rather than his given name, he prefers to be known by his longest kill shot. God save me from big egos."

It had nothing to do with his ego and everything to do with hating his father, but he didn't owe anyone that explanation.

Stone stuck out his hand. "Hey."

"Good to meet you." One-Mile shook it.

"Stone Sutter is a computer hacker extraordinaire. Jack Cole and the boys at Oracle are letting us borrow him to isolate a virus on the server, so don't open any email attachments."

"Not a problem," he told Logan. "I'd like to speak to you."

"What's up?"

"I can't work with Bryant. I quit." Now that he'd delivered his news, he was free to find Cutter and beat the ever-loving fuck out of him.

Before he could escape Logan's office, the former SEAL shut him down. "Nope. You can't. I've got a contract. You signed. We paid the bonus, and you cashed the check. End of conversation."

One-Mile halted. Fucking Logan throwing legalities in his face. Even worse, the bastard was right.

Naturally, Cutter chose that moment to stick his head in the door, glaring daggers. "Fucking douche."

He barely managed to refrain from violence. "The feeling is mutual."

"I told you no drama, so give it a rest, you two." Logan rolled his eyes. "If I can work with my older brother, you can get along enough to get your shit done."

Bryant raked a hand over his military-short hair and shook his head at Logan. "I will never trust him enough to be on an operational team with him again. If he wants to quit, I say good riddance."

Logan slammed a fist on his desk. "Cutter, I don't give a shit that Pierce slept with your girlfriend."

"One-Mile," he corrected through clenched teeth.

"Whatever." Logan waved a hand through the air.

"No! It's not whatever," Cutter insisted. "I can't work with Brea's rapist."

What? Had the dickhead convinced himself that the only way Brea would have ever been underneath him was unwillingly?

I got news for you, buddy, and it's all bad…

"I had her consent."

"You manipulated her so that she had no choice but to say yes." Cutter clenched his fists.

One-Mile glared at the cockroach, arms crossed over his chest. "If you wanted her that badly, you should have claimed her sometime between junior high and July. You had plenty of time. But it took you too long to find your dick. That's not my problem. She's mine now."

Cutter narrowed fierce eyes his way, glowering as if he'd lost his mind. "She's not even speaking to you, asshat."

He shrugged it off. "Misunderstanding."

"No, reality. Something you're clearly not familiar with. And if she fucking winds up pregnant—"

"That's enough," Logan shouted. "I don't care if you beat the hell out of one another after hours, but stop bringing your personal shit to work. If you can't, I'll lock you in a room together until you learn to get along or one of you kills the other. I don't care which at this point. Be professional and do your damn jobs."

Silence fell in the wake of Logan's verbal beatdown. Cutter swore and stomped away.

Despite Stone watching with rapt interest, One-Mile felt a stupid urge to explain, probably because if he was stuck in this job and his bosses despised him, the rest of his two years here would really suck. "I didn't rape her."

"Since she had to choose between saving her boyfriend's life and sleeping with you, I'd say you coerced her. It doesn't get much lower than that in my book. Now get the fuck out."

Goddamn it to hell. They'd bought into Cutter's version of events without talking to him. Even when he hadn't done anything wrong, he got labeled the bad guy. Whatever. He could set them straight, but he really didn't give two shits about their opinion of him as a human being.

"Roger that." One-Mile sent Logan a mock salute, nodded Stone's way, then marched the hell out, making a beeline for the coffeemaker.

Before he could pour his first jolt of liquid caffeine, the elder Edgington peeked his head around the corner. "I need you in my office."

One-Mile rolled his eyes. "One minute."

"Now." Hunter disappeared around the corner.

One-Mile sighed. Somehow, this place had already become asshole central, and Hunter looked like he had even more attitude than Logan. He definitely needed java to deal with this.

After his mug was full of steaming fortification, he dragged his ass to the elder Edgington's digs. Trees Scott slouched in one of the two office chairs yet somehow still towered over everyone.

"What's up?" he asked, staring at the other two.

"Shut the door," Hunter barked.

Frowning, One-Mile complied, then when his boss gestured him to put his ass into the empty chair, he planted it beside Trees.

Hunter pressed his fingertips together, face taut. His voice dipped to something just above a murmur. "We have a mole."

"What?" One-Mile couldn't have heard that right. Fuck, if they accused him...

Hunter nodded. "Yeah. Someone inside this office. We've autopsied the most recent Mexico mission, trying to figure out what the fuck went wrong. Both of you thought on your feet and kept the whole thing from turning into a death trap. But I don't have to tell you how close it was. Somehow, the Tierra Caliente thugs not only knew we were coming in but when and where, too. Trees, if you hadn't hauled Zy out of there when something felt wrong—"

"We'd be dead," said the tall man.

"Exactly. Same with you and Bryant." Hunter nodded his way. "Logan, Joaquin, and I all talked to the colonel about this. We're in agreement that someone on the inside must have fed the cartel information, so we're trusting you two—and no one else—to help us figure out who."

Being on the good guys' team was an interesting turn of events.

One-Mile leaned in. "Uncle Sam hired us. No chance it was someone closer to Washington DC?"

Hunter shook his head. "We didn't tell them our exact plans. Sure, they knew we were going in, but not when, where, or how. Only our guys had those details."

So unless the cartel had guessed their multiple locations really fucking well—and what were the odds of that?—someone he worked with was a traitor.

The thought turned One-Mile's blood to ice. "What's the plan?"

"First, I have to take a step back and give you two a history lesson." Hunter sighed. "About eighteen months ago, Arnold Waxman, a wealthy doctor from Atlanta, hired the colonel to infiltrate the Guerrero region in Mexico and find his daughter, Kendra. She had traveled there with a group of doctors to give medial aid to the poor. They got caught in the crossfire when a couple of factions within the Tierra Caliente cartel started warring and they were taken hostage. Waxman paid the ransom, but Kendra wasn't released. That's when Logan, Dad, and I stepped in and discovered that another rival splinter gang, headed by Emilo Montilla, had overrun the first and taken the hostages. We located them, got in, then extracted Kendra, along with the rest of the survivors."

This was all news to One-Mile. But something must have gone to shit since because it definitely hadn't been their last trip to Guerrero. "Then what?"

"While Kendra was in captivity, she made friends with Valeria Montilla, Emilo's wife. She begged us to smuggle her out with the medical workers. She was pregnant and feared what would happen to her child if she stayed."

One-Mile let out a low whistle. "I know our friendly neighborhood drug lord didn't take that well."

"No."

"So we went to Guerrero a couple of months back...why?"

"Valeria hired us to rescue her sister. Emilo had been keeping her as bait."

"But everything went south," Trees pointed out. "Our mission failed, and we nearly died."

Hunter nodded. "Because of the mole."

"So we're going back in to retrieve Valeria's sister?"

The boss shook his head. "That's not a good idea until we figure out who within our organization turned against us. This mission is purely a screen to smoke out our rat. So you two will land in Acapulco and set up surveillance equipment together in a predetermined location. Trees, from there you'll drive out of the city and head inland to Taxco, where you'll set up surveillance in another location. Pierce, you'll head up the coast to Petalán."

"We're splitting up?" Trees raised a brow. "That's risky as fuck in a place like that."

"It's the fastest way to figure out who's selling us out." One-Mile shrugged. "If we don't, it's only a matter of time before we're caught unaware again. At least we'll be going into this with our eyes wide open." He turned back to Hunter. "So what are you telling everyone around here?"

"Each of the other three operatives will get a different cover story. We'll know who our mole is based on which location Tierra Caliente raids."

As ideas went, it wasn't foolproof. But they didn't have a lot of options, and he understood the rationale.

"We've only got a few suspects. Maybe we can discern our mole without all the cloak-and-dagger bullshit."

"And just so we're clear, Zy would never sell us out," Trees vowed.

How sweet. The tall dude was sticking up for his bestie. Based on what, a pinkie swear?

Still, Zy's family was loaded. He seemed less likely to betray his peers...but it wasn't impossible.

"Trees, I know you're convinced Zy is innocent," Hunter acknowledged, "but we can't assume anything. We have to rule everyone out before we know for sure what we're dealing with."

One-Mile considered the other two possibilities. Josiah Grant was former CIA, so he was more likely to have the international connections needed to stab his fellow operatives in the back. But was that really the surly loner's speed?

That left Cutter. The asshole had a hero complex…but was it possible appearances were deceiving? Just because he couldn't think of a reason Bryant would sell them out didn't mean he wouldn't. On the other hand, no matter how badly he wanted Cutter to be guilty, that didn't actually make him the culprit.

"When are we leaving?" he asked Hunter.

"Tonight."

Son of a bitch. Of all the terrible timing…

One-Mile bit back a groan. "Mission duration?"

With any luck, he'd be back in a few days, and his absence would only be a momentary setback with Brea. Hell, maybe this was for the best. She'd asked for space, and if he stayed in the same zip code, he'd be tempted to corner her, strip her naked, and remind her how good they were together.

"Couple of days, tops. You should head out before you and Cutter are tempted to commit murder on company property."

"Sounds like more fun than fucking with a cartel," Trees quipped.

Amen. But he didn't get that choice. Besides, if he killed Cutter, Brea would never forgive him. "I'm in."

"Listen, you can't tell anyone you're leaving or where you're going. Logan, Joaquin, and I will circulate your various locations after you've set up the surveillance equipment."

One-Mile rose. "Got it."

"Roger that." Trees stood, too.

"Both of you report here at twenty-one hundred. I'll be waiting with further instructions. That gives you about twelve hours to get your shit in order…just in case this doesn't go as planned."

Wednesday, August 20
Acapulco

Coastal Mexico in August was more humid than the ass crack of hell.

Trees downed the last of his beer as the sun set over the little seaside restaurant attached to their shithole motel in Acapulco. The few tourists vacationing here looked happy to disappear into their tequila. One-Mile shoveled in the last of his fish and scanned the area. Nothing out of the ordinary…but the back of his neck tingled and felt tight.

Like someone was watching.

He played it casual and glanced at his watch. "We should go. It will be easier to find our location before the sun sets."

Trees tossed a few bills on the table, then hoisted the duffel at his side as he stood. "Yep. Might as well get this shit over with."

One of the three remaining EM Security operatives—One-Mile didn't know which—had been told he and Trees were meeting a member of a rival faction tomorrow here in Acapulco who could help them bust inside Montilla's compound and free Valeria's sister. The second of the three operatives had been advised of a rendezvous in Taxco on Friday, while the last had been spoon-fed the bullshit about a clandestine meet-up in Petalán on Saturday night.

One-Mile was braced for trouble, but he had no idea when or where it would appear. The setup was making him twitchy.

He heaved a sigh as he paid his own bill and got to his feet. "Got the map?"

"Yep." Trees headed off the restaurant's terrace, toward the parking lot where they'd left their rental. "You been thinking about who's guilty?"

"Hard not to." But every one of the suspects had pros and cons.

"Any conclusions?"

"No." At least none he felt like sharing.

Trees eyed him. "You'd like Cutter to be guilty."

On some level, sure. But it would crush Brea. "I'd prefer not to have a traitor in our ranks at all."

"Same. I'm telling you, man. It's not Zy."

"We'll find out, I guess."

"The truth is, I can't picture any of these guys betraying us."

Maybe Trees just didn't want to. But One-Mile knew good men could be capable of bad things, given the right circumstances.

"And Joaquin felt the same," Trees added. "So did the colonel."

"Hmm." It was nice to know the elder Edgington believed in the motley crew he'd assembled shortly before his retirement...but that didn't change the fact they were in Mexico to hunt the snake slithering in their midst.

"Hey, when we're done with the first setup, do you want to head to the strip? Catch some pretty girls jiggling to some terrible music?"

That wasn't his speed. Besides, with every step he took, his dread kept sharpening. If he was feeling uneasy in broad daylight in the middle of a tourist area, visiting the city's seedy underbelly well after dark would only make him paranoid.

But another scan of the parking lot proved it devoid of people.

"Nah. Let's get the fuck out of here. I'm going to head north early in the morning, so I'd like to go to bed early."

"Fair enough." Trees nodded as they reached the car. "Hey, mind putting this in the trunk while I tie my shoe?"

One-Mile took the heavy duffel from the tall guy. "No sweat."

Trees popped the trunk with the fob and bent to his laces when One-Mile caught sight of a quintet of heavily armed men emerging from vehicles and behind trees at the perimeter of the parking lot and spreading out to surround them. They had the hardened look of cartel soldiers.

His blood ran cold. *Fuck.*

"Get in the car!" he shouted at Trees as he tossed the equipment into the gaping trunk and slammed it closed.

Trees whirled and caught sight of the foot soldiers charging at them, then dived into the front seat. One-Mile sprinted for the passenger door, weapon drawn, as Trees hit the button on the fob to unlock it, then shoved the key in the ignition. He turned the car over as One-Mile popped off a shot, hitting one thug square between the eyes just before he grabbed at the door handle—

Then someone tackled him from behind and forced him down to the gravel, trapping him under a heavy weight that smelled like sweat, testosterone, and gunpowder.

Blood roaring, One-Mile struggled for leverage so he could get off his belly and fight back. He'd learned to defend himself on the streets, goddamn it. He could get himself out of a scrape. But the bruiser on top of him had obviously learned to fight dirty, too, and countered every one of his moves.

He wasn't getting free from this.

"Go!" he managed to scream at Trees as the asshole sitting on top of him pounded his fingers into the crumbling asphalt and wrenched the weapon from his stinging hand.

His fellow operative hesitated for a split second, and he could feel Trees' indecision. Then the car peeled out and began to speed away. The other foot soldiers shot at the little white rental, but One-Mile watched it shudder out of the lot and jostle down the road, both glad Trees had gotten away…and terrified of what happened next.

"Not so tough without your backup now," the foot soldier spat, snorting and panting in his ear. "Are you, Walker?"

Oh, fuck. They knew who he was.

He was as good as dead.

At least Trees had gotten away. There was a chance—albeit a slim one—that his bosses could mount a rescue. The more likely scenario was that they'd recover his body. Someday…maybe. At least they'd know for sure that someone in their ranks was a backstabbing bastard who deserved to be purged.

"Fuck you." What the hell else could he say?

The pungent weight crushing his ribs laughed. "You will, no doubt, change your tune when you see what we have in store for you… But for now, it is best if you sleep."

The fat foot soldier on his back twisted to straddle him, then grabbed him by the hair before slamming his head against the pavement a few times. His skull exploded in pain. Blackness swam at the edges of his vision.

His last thought was of Brea. He wished like hell he had a few more stolen seconds alone with her. At least then he could tell her that he'd fallen hard for her.

chapter eight

Monday, September 8
Lafayette, Louisiana

Wringing her hands, Brea paced the too-familiar halls of University Hospital again. The first time she'd come here, it had been a sweltering summer afternoon. The birds had been singing and the flowers in full bloom. Pierce had been with her, patiently holding her hand and bolstering her while doctors tried to repair her father's heart.

Now, the weather had begun to cool. Football season was in full swing. The sky was pitch-black, except for a hazy moon hanging in the sky. The clock on the wall read two thirty-eight a.m., and the city outside the windows was almost eerily still. No one stood beside her, devoting himself to her moral support.

But her father's failing heart was the awful correlation.

She wished Pierce were here now. Since she'd started pacing the emergency room, she had talked herself out of calling him more than once. During her father's first episode this summer, his steadying force had been her bedrock. Without him now, she felt like she was in free fall. But it would be selfish to reach out to him after weeks of silence. After all, she was the one who had told him she needed space. He'd more than respected her wishes. Why should he come after she'd ignored him for so long?

"Brea!"

She whirled around to find Cutter jogging toward her. She dashed into his arms, grateful she was no longer alone.

But he wasn't Pierce.

At the thought, guilt filled her. Her best friend had come running after a mere phone call, despite the ridiculous hour, and she was grateful. She pushed thoughts of Pierce aside.

"Thank you for being here," she said against his chest. "I-I know it's late. I know you have to work—"

"Shh." He brushed her hair off her face and cradled her cheeks in his palms, forcing her gaze to his. "None of that matters. Tell me what happened. What have the doctors said?"

"I'm still waiting for news. I don't really know much. I was so tired that I went to bed after dinner. An unfamiliar crashing noise woke me up a little after midnight. I ran down the hall and found Daddy on the floor, struggling to breathe. I think he panicked and tried to call 911 but fell out of bed reaching for the phone. I couldn't lift him. He was in agony. I…" She pressed her hand to her mouth, trying to hold in useless tears, but the vision of her father pale and writhing and making inhuman sounds of pain haunted her. "I called an ambulance. I didn't know what else to do. I'm worried he's had another heart attack. He's barely recovered from the last surgery..."

"I know." Cutter held her tighter. "But don't lose hope. He's young. He's already dropped some weight and started exercising. You're putting good food in his system, and the repairs he's had on his heart will help the blood flow. I know you're praying."

"Of course." But she heard the squeak of fear in her voice, felt its burn singeing her veins. She wasn't ready to lose her father.

"Then you're doing all you can. Come sit down, Bre-bee. You look exhausted."

She'd just been tired lately. Not surprising. She had a history of being anemic, and she'd slacked off on taking her iron. "Don't worry about me. I just...have no idea what I'll do if Daddy isn't all right."

"You'll cross the bridge if you're pushed off of it, okay? In the meantime, have you called Tom? He should know that he'll probably need to take over for your father again."

"I was waiting until I knew something definitive. And until it wasn't the middle of the night. There's really nothing he can do now."

"Fair enough." He curled an arm around her. "Do you want some coffee?"

She shook her head. "I walked past the machine earlier. It needs a good cleaning. The smell of it turned my stomach."

Cutter led her over to a padded bench and sat her down. "I doubt you'd find anything appetizing right now."

"No," she confirmed, casting her worried glance to the double doors beyond the waiting area. "I don't know what's taking so long. I've been here nearly two hours. The paperwork kept me busy for a while, but..."

"You want information. I understand. But they'll fill you in once they have answers. For now, no news is good news."

She nodded, trying hard to believe that. "Talk to me about something else. Anything else. I need my mind off this or I'll just keep imagining the worst-case scenarios."

"Yeah. Um..." But Cutter shook his head blankly.

"You never said whether you're coming to the fall market at the church on Friday evening. We could still use a few volunteers to help us set up and break down."

He hesitated a few seconds too long. "I don't know. Brea, I need to tell you—"

"Ms. Bell?"

She turned to find a familiar woman in green scrubs. Her face looked grim. "Dr. Gale. I didn't realize you'd come in. How's Daddy?"

"That's why the attending physician called me. Your father is going to need more bypass work."

Her jaw dropped. Her heart fell. It wasn't the worst possible news…but it was close. "Why?"

"Back in July, the insurance company chose only to bypass the left anterior descending artery. They merely cleared us to stent the others with blockages, despite my recommendation otherwise. Since then, a blood clot has formed in his right coronary artery. We've just completed all the tests to confirm. Time is of the essence, so we're prepping now."

"You're doing the surgery this morning?" Her head told her that waiting any amount of time with a blood clot in Daddy's heart was incredibly dangerous. But all she could think about was her father going under anesthesia again for a risky procedure he might not survive.

What if she never got to say goodbye?

Dr. Gale's face softened as she took Brea's hand. "We don't have a choice."

Cutter slipped a supporting arm around her. "We understand. I know you'll keep us advised. When will you get started and how long do you expect the surgery to last?"

The surgeon glanced at the clock on the wall. "We'll be starting in the next thirty minutes. The surgery should last three to four hours, depending on complications. As soon as we know more, someone will speak with you."

"Thank you, Doctor," Brea managed to mumble, but she felt her legs crumpling beneath her as her head swirled in a dizzy spin.

"Whoa." Cutter caught her and helped her back to the bench, sitting her on his lap. "Are you okay, Bre-Bee?"

"Overwhelmed," she managed to say. "I can't believe this is happening again."

"You should call Mrs. Collins."

"I can't wake Jennifer up in the middle of the night."

Cutter gave her that patient expression he often flashed when he had to explain something she should already know. "You should. She's your father's…girlfriend, for lack of a better word."

He'd suggested that before, but she'd never seen any evidence of that.

"I…" She shook her head. "No."

He cleared his throat. "Yes. A few weeks back, when you went to that concert in New Orleans with the girls from the salon and stayed the night?"

"I remember."

Cutter was not about to say what she thought he would. *Please. Please…*

"You're going to make me say that she spent the night, are you?"

"She wouldn't." Brea shook her head in disbelief. "And Daddy wouldn't—"

"Yeah, he would. He's a man. They're both widowed. I'm sure they're lonely. I think they care about one another. It's not like they randomly hooked up after a swipe right on Tinder."

She winced. Cutter was right…but they were talking about her father. Having a sex life. She'd always viewed him as perfect, above reproach. She'd idolized him, worshipped him. To find out he was only human seemed both obvious and foolishly crushing.

Then again, she knew how tempting the flesh could be. Every single night, she held her finger over the screen of her iPhone, aching to press the button and call Pierce. She'd missed his gruff smile, his scent, his guttural grunts as he filled her, his unexpected tenderness, the rasp in his voice when he called her pretty girl…

"Hey." Cutter snapped his fingers. "Where did you go?"

Should she tell him everything? Brea had agonized over this a million times in the last month—and still had no answer. At first, she hadn't confessed her feelings for Pierce to Cutter because he'd been too angry to listen, and she'd been so sure that she and Pierce would never last. But as the days passed and the rugged sniper haunted her, as her body hungered and she'd begun to crave just having him near…

She realized she cared about him. Very much. And he'd given her way more space than she'd wanted or believed he would ever grant her.

It hurt.

But maybe now wasn't the time to mention it. She needed to stay focused on her father, and she sensed something weighing on Cutter, too.

"Thinking. Sorry." She tried to smile, despite the nagging worry about Daddy's health plaguing her.

Would the sunrise bring shining new hope for his recovery or cast a glaring light on her harsh new reality without him?

Cutter was right; she needed to be optimistic. The trick right now, when hope seemed razor thin, was to stay distracted. "You were saying something before Dr. Gale talked to us. You'll be someplace on Friday, other than the church's fall market?"

Cutter's face tightened. "I don't know if now is the time to talk about this."

"If it will keep me from fixating on my father, please."

He looked away with a grimace, then sighed. "I may be in Mexico come Friday. Walker went there almost three weeks ago on a mission. He was taken at gunpoint in a parking lot by a cartel. We might finally have a lead on his location. If it pans out, we'll be bugging out to extract him ASAP."

As soon as his words registered, Brea's heart—and her world—stopped. Panic ensued. Pierce had been abducted? The big, seemingly invincible warrior with the one-mile kill shot had been overpowered and taken prisoner? No. She couldn't picture it. Didn't want to. Couldn't stand it.

She heaved in a breath made more ragged by the crushing pain spreading through her chest. It wracked her system. Tears stung her eyes. Any calm she'd found since before Cutter entered the emergency room vanished.

"Oh, my… A-a cartel? Is he even…" She couldn't bring herself to finish that sentence. She could barely breathe past her distress.

He had to be alive. She *needed* him to be alive.

She squeezed her eyes shut. *Please, God, let him be all right.*

But what were the odds that an organization fueled by illegal drugs, money, and greed would keep a hostage alive for weeks?

"I don't know. We're hoping." But Cutter sounded grim. "The information we've collected is sketchy, and with every passing hour it's getting older. But it's more than we had to go on yesterday."

Brea clung to hope. She had to. If she let herself imagine where Pierce was and what he was enduring, she would melt down. "Why didn't you tell me sooner? I didn't know he was in danger. I didn't have any idea. I would have prayed for him or…"

Something. She would have done something. Honestly, anything. But what could a small-town hairdresser really do to save the man she cared for way more than she ought to from a cartel?

"I didn't want to bring him up after…you know, everything that happened. You did your best to save me, and you betrayed yourself to do it. I hate how much pain it caused you."

She shook her head. "It wasn't like that. He—"

"Don't." Cutter held up his hands. "Don't try to make me feel better. I don't deserve it."

The guilt was still eating him alive. "Don't ever think you're unworthy. There's no reason for that. And I don't regret a thing."

Brea didn't say more. Cutter wasn't ready to hear that some part of her heart belonged to Pierce and probably always would.

Cutter closed his eyes with a sigh. "As much as I hate to admit it, as much as I hate who he is and what he's done, he's saved my life twice. My bosses are absolutely losing their shit over this. I have to go. I have to help."

Even though he despised Pierce, Cutter insisted on being a part of his rescue. Because he was a good man.

"Please. Promise me you'll do whatever you can. Whatever you have to…" She grabbed Cutter's hands. "Bring him home."

He nodded. "I know how you feel about brutality and senseless death. Even if Walker's record is hardly spotless, you would never want more violence or wish anyone dead."

All of that was true…but hardly her rationale. She missed Pierce fiercely. Needed him. And she was sickeningly, painfully worried about him. Maybe she hadn't pictured a life with him—except occasionally, late at night when she missed him like mad. But it nearly killed her to imagine a world without him.

"Let me know as soon as you have any word. And you keep safe, you hear?"

"Yes, ma'am." He managed a smile for her. "Now call Mrs. Collins. I really think she'd want to be here."

It took all her will, but Brea managed to block out her terror and focus on mundane but important tasks. It turned out that Cutter was right. Jennifer didn't hesitate to jump out of bed, toss on her clothes, and drive through the black night. Tears sheened her eyes when she raced through the doors. The woman sobbed. Brea joined her as they clung together through the long wait for news.

But as the sun rose, Dr. Gale emerged from the operating room, looking both exhausted and triumphant, to tell the exhausted trio that her father had come through the surgery successfully. He was in recovery, had already regained consciousness, and was asking to see her.

Brea held back sobs as she thanked God for the miracle. Daddy would always have to watch his diet and weight, not to mention his cholesterol, but she was so grateful to Him for hearing her prayers and sparing her father.

But inside, she was quietly frantic with unrelenting worry—and shamefully ready to beg Him for one more favor. So as she was escorted back to her father's bedside, she closed her eyes and asked the Lord above for one more good deed.

Please, God, bring Pierce back to me whole and alive...

~

Thursday, September 11
Guerrero, Mexico—middle of nowhere

One-Mile had no idea what day it was or how long he'd been out. He pried open one swollen eye. He saw only bare concrete walls—thick and uninterrupted—without a window in sight. No surprise that he was alone.

He'd figured out a while back that he was being held underground. He knew that because the few times he'd been dragged outside, it had still been hot as hell, but the air on his skin now was almost chilly. Despite that, a wringing sweat covered his body. He trembled. His stomach cramped. His head felt as if it might explode.

Fuck, he needed to make some decisions.

He eyed the door. Sure, he should probably check it. But why? The damn thing had been bolted up tight each of the other four thousand five hundred ninety-two times he'd searched for some way to escape. No sense wasting more energy he might need to simply stay alive.

How much longer before someone came back and stuck a needle in his arm? He both craved and dreaded it. At least afterward he wouldn't feel the stabbing pain in his jaw or the throbbing of his knee. He wouldn't care that his back was in ribbons or that he could barely feel his fingers. No, once whatever shit they pumped his veins full of hit his system, he would fade off for...who knew how long? He'd awaken at some point, hungry, dehydrated, sweating, and wondering what fucking day it was.

Then someone would come in with a meal and a needle...and the cycle would start all over.

Unless they decided to "interrogate" him again. That was always a fab time. But no one had raised a whip or crowbar to him in a few highs. Unfortunately, that wasn't good news. If Emilo Montilla and his gang of assholes had given up on him divulging any useful information about Valeria's whereabouts, that made him expendable. Then they wouldn't bother beating him again. They'd just give him a double tap to the brain and toss his body into a shallow grave. He'd be buried somewhere in the goddamn desert on foreign soil. No one would ever know what the fuck had happened to him.

Would anyone even care?

Brea Bell—maybe. She alone might mourn.

Not that she loved him. He'd kissed her, even though she belonged to a teammate, because he couldn't stand not knowing the flavor of her mouth. He'd touched her because he hadn't possessed the self-control to leave her innocent. He'd worked his cock inside her again and again because he hadn't been able to tolerate an inch of space between them. Because he wanted her to be his.

Because he was pretty fucking sure he'd stupidly fallen in love with her.

Brea was gentle, kind. She would mourn him, if for no other reason than she believed in God, cherished the sanctity of life, and had the purest soul he'd ever had the privilege of knowing.

Of all his regrets—and he had plenty—he hated that he hadn't called her before he'd left on this mission and admitted exactly how he felt.

Now it was too late.

For a minute, he was tempted to pray to her God, but he didn't. He didn't really deserve God's mercy. Brea didn't know about his past, but God did…and that was probably why he'd end up dying in the middle of nowhere before they threw a little dirt on him and left him to become coyote shit.

On that cheerful note, he slumped back on the cot and closed his eyes, shivering against the chills and withdrawals. His sandpaper tongue stuck to the roof of his mouth. He swore he felt his ribs against his spine. And fuck, he needed to pee.

The next person who came into this room, he'd kill. Not that it would get him anywhere. Even without a weapon, he'd already offed a handful of them—until they'd started shackling his hands, bashing his kneecaps, and swinging fists at his jaw. They'd slowed him down, sure.

But unless he was dead, they couldn't stop him.

On his left, One-Mile heard the click of the lock. He swiveled his head, opened the one eye he could, and lay deceptively still, waiting to see who came through the door. That would tell him how much effort he'd need to exert to trip the thug du jour and stomp his larynx until the gunman suffocated.

But it wasn't some armed-to-the-teeth asshole who entered the room but a delicate Hispanic beauty who looked twenty, max. Her entire body trembled as, tray in hand, she cleared the door. Immediately, it shut—and locked—behind her. She jolted at the sound.

"Who are you?" The raspy slur of his voice barely sounded human.

She didn't look at him. Fuck, he probably should have saved his breath. Besides Montilla, only a handful of people in this shithole spoke English, and his Spanish sucked.

As she set the tray on the nearby table, she shook so hard the dishes rattled. She finally met his stare. Her brown eyes were wide and full of terror. "My name is Laila, Señor Walker. Emilo is my…um—how do you say?—my brother-in-law."

So she was Valeria's sister? The one the EM team had tried to rescue during their first mission, before they'd been ambushed?

"I am sorry," she rushed on. "I have not used my English in too long."

The guys who brought his meals usually had a face as attractive as a pug's ass and a wide sadistic streak, so sending in a pretty, unarmed female was definitely a new tactic.

He didn't trust it, but he played along. "Are you going to untie me so I can eat or feed me yourself?"

"I have been sent to feed you, see to your bath, and"—she swallowed hard—"any other comforts you may desire."

Her answer rolled around in his brain. Translation: drugging, starving, and beating him hadn't worked, so they were going to force this frightened woman to sex him up so he'd get happy enough to betray his bosses back home?

One-Mile nearly snorted at that bullshit. He would have—just before he set her straight—if he wasn't one-hundred percent sure Montilla and his thugs were listening in.

Instead, he played along…for now. "What do you have under that lid?"

Laila lifted the dome. "Water. Cold beer. Tortilla soup, refried beans, homemade flan…"

More than he'd eaten in one sitting since he'd been taken captive. And the food actually looked fresh for a change.

On the far side of the tray, he also caught sight of the needle with the drugs. "That my after-dinner cocktail?"

A guilty flush stole up her cheeks. "That is up to you."

Somehow, One-Mile didn't think she meant they'd pump him full of shit if he wanted it. But if he proved uncooperative… "I see. How about we eat first?"

"As you wish."

With a gentle hand, she helped him stand, then guided him to the room's lone chair. Patiently, she stood over him and fed a straw through his swollen lips, past his sore-ass jaw, and waited until he'd managed to swallow half the bottle. He eschewed the beer, slurped the soup down as she guided it—one slow spoonful at a time—into his barely open mouth, then fed him a few beans before finishing with some flan.

Since that was the most he'd eaten in weeks—or was it months now?—it didn't take much for him to get his fill. But consuming everything took a long damn time. He did his best to stay patient and use the time to figure out how he could benefit from this change of circumstance. Short of threatening a female half his size and trying to use her as a shield to fight his way out, he wasn't seeing it. Besides, Emilo wouldn't have sent her in here if she wasn't expendable.

Gently, Laila wiped his mouth with a napkin, then helped him to his feet. "Would you care for a shower now?"

"And a toilet?"

"Of course." She looked up at a camera in the corner of the room. Another internal door buzzed open, and she led him inside. It locked shut behind them. "I am allowed to untie your hands in this room."

He held them out and scanned the place. Sure, he'd been here before, but the memories were always hazy since the trips had come after the needle. But his captors had made certain there was nothing he could use as a weapon and no way to escape.

Slowly, she unwound the bindings from his hands. Blood rushed in, tingling and painful, as full circulation returned. Vaguely, he wondered…if he managed to find some way out of this hell, would he ever fully recover?

Why fucking care? It was unlikely he'd ever escape, so torturing himself with this train of thought was pointless.

For the first few days in captivity, he'd hoped the Edgingtons and Joaquin Muñoz would bust in here with the rest of the EM crew and save his sorry ass. But no. First, they probably had no idea where he was. Hell, he didn't, except that he was a long way from Acapulco. And second, why would they? It was no secret how much Cutter hated him. He'd thought for a while that maybe Logan liked him and Hunter trusted him somewhat…but they more or less thought he'd raped Brea, too. Why would they save him when it was easier to replace him?

When he'd been taken, Trees had driven away as quickly as possible—as he should have. But he hadn't fired a shot or come back with reinforcements. Zy was too busy chasing Tessa's skirt to care about much else these days. And Josiah…who knew where the guy fell? They didn't talk much.

One thing One-Mile did know? No one was coming to his rescue. He was going to have to work with Laila.

She allowed him a few minutes alone in the toilet, then started the shower while he washed his hands and brushed his teeth with the toothbrush she had helpfully provided.

When he'd finished, he pivoted to face her, assuming she'd step out while he washed himself.

Instead, she began disrobing.

He watched with a frown. This must be the "whatever he desired" portion of the evening.

No thanks.

One-Mile stayed her with a hand on her shoulder. "You don't have to get naked for me."

Relief stamped itself all over her face—but she kept stripping. "Yes, I do…"

Silently, he studied her as she peeled her dress from her body and draped it over a nearby counter. She'd worn nothing underneath. Shadows shrouded the feminine hollows of her body. Light clung to her curves. She was a beautiful woman…and she didn't do a damn thing for him.

Her breasts bobbed gently as she approached and helped him pull his shirt over his head. The movement hurt his back like a bitch. The wounds had finally scabbed over, but they'd likely leave scars—if he lived long enough for them to heal.

Then she reached for the button of his jeans.

One-Mile gripped her wrists to stop her. "Laila…"

"Shh." She pushed his hands away and continued on. "Let me. Please."

Her eyes begged. Since he didn't have much choice, he relented with a nod.

One-Mile stood motionless while Laila shoved his dirty, blood-stained jeans down his legs. He braced against the wall as he stepped out, now as naked as she was.

Then she took his hand and led him under the hot spray. He hissed and grimaced as the water pelted his healing skin. She merely pressed her body against his with a whisper. "The shower is the only place they cannot hear us."

So the girl wanted to escape. She had a plan and something to say to him. He was on board for that. It was a long shot…but any shot was more than he'd had ten minutes ago.

Smiling, he pulled her close, then bent to murmur in her ear. "Now what?"

"I want to be gone from here. I convinced Emilo that, if they let me see to you, I could seduce information from you."

One-Mile pretended to caress his way down her arm before he planted his hand on her hip. "I'm not telling you anything."

"I did not expect you to. I-I have begun sleeping with one of my brother-in-law's thugs, and I have been able to use his phone while he sleeps to sneak coded messages to my sister through a message board. I told her where we are and that Emilo is keeping you hostage. She said she would pass the information to the men who rescued her. Last night, she wrote back to say that a rescue mission is in place."

His heart started revving. He wanted to grill her. Hell, he was even half tempted to shake her by the shoulders and demand to know if she was telling the truth. But she glanced at the camera in the corner, then brushed her lips up his chest. Yeah, they were watching. So he caressed his way down her ass and nuzzled her neck. "When?"

She sent him a come-hither smile and sidled closer. "Tonight. About an hour."

That damn organ in his chest started chugging even harder. "Got a plan?"

There had to be a few dozen gunmen here, not to mention Emilo himself, who was fucking evil with the whip. Unless the Edgingtons and Muñoz were dropping in with some of Uncle Sam's boys, they were going to be incredibly outnumbered.

Her flirtation suddenly looked far more like a grimace. "You should pretend to attack me. I will scream. Emilo's men will come to my rescue…I think."

"You don't sound too sure."

"I am worth nothing to them. But Emilo wants Valeria back."

"Because he loves his wife?"

Laila scoffed. "No. He does not want her back as a lover. Why should he when he has so many whores willing to take his cock and his money? He flaunted them in my sister's face while she lived with him. He is a pig."

One-Mile didn't disagree. In fact, Laila had phrased things much nicer than he was inclined to.

"But he suspected Valeria was pregnant when she escaped, and he refuses to let his child go."

"What will he do if he manages to find her and the kid?"

"Punish her, make an example of her. He will kill her. She knows too much about his operations, and he fears she is already telling your government."

Probably.

"The child… If she gave birth to a son, Emilo will groom him to take his place in the organization. Perhaps if he is ruthless enough, he will survive. If she gave birth to a daughter, she will be raised a princess, then married off to another drug pusher who can increase Emilo's standing in the cartel. After that, she will have a miserable existence of sexual servitude and fear."

Laila was a realist, if nothing else.

He fisted his hands in her hair and sent her what the watching goons would interpret as a leer. "And you think Emilo is keeping you alive and well so he can use you as leverage against your sister?"

"Yes."

"You understand that if I attack you and they come to your rescue, we'll be separated. They'll beat the shit out of me, and I won't be in any position to help you."

She nodded, dragging her palms down his chest with what probably appeared to be a seductive scratch of her nails. "But quarters are cramped here, so they will take you outside to do it."

Where the rescue party could actually reach him…provided Emilo and his men didn't kill him first.

As plans went, it sucked. And it was a long shot. But any chance at freedom was better than no chance at all. "All right. What's your idea?"

She gave him a blank stare. "I have not thought beyond that."

One-Mile wasn't surprised. She was barely more than a girl. She wasn't a soldier, much less a tactician.

He reached for the bottle of shampoo and lathered his hair, while Laila grabbed the bar of soap and gave him a thorough scrub. "Any suggestions on how we kill the next forty-five minutes? Just a guess, but you don't want to fuck any more than I do."

"Emilo allowed one of his underlings to first rape me when I was fourteen. Sex is not something I do for enjoyment."

Every time she spoke, he hated Montilla and his violent band of assholes even more. "If I can do anything to make sure you get out alive, I will."

"Thank you." Her lips trembled.

He nodded. "How about you play along?"

"Of course. I am willing to try anything."

Yeah, he was, too—even getting the shit beat out of him again.

They lingered in the shower, pretending flirtation and sexual interest. Finally, he cut off the spray, dried them off with a towel, then carried Laila back to the cot, faking some sweet nothings in her ear.

Together, they fell into a naked heap on the cot with a forced laugh. He reached for the beer. She drank it while he held her on his lap, caressing her back and thighs.

"You're feeling drunk, aren't you?" he suggested in a low, almost unrecognizable mumble.

She pretended a giddy smile. "Maybe a little. Why does it matter? Are you thinking of taking advantage of me? I am far too small to fight off a big man like you."

Did that turn some guys on? Disgusting. "I have something else in mind. You're not going to fight me, are you?"

"Should I?" She batted her lashes. Fear gleamed in her eyes.

His gut cramped. They were both risking their lives. He didn't have any choice except to keep playing his part and push until the bad guys barged in to shut him down.

One-Mile dragged Laila closer, then reached behind her to grab the needle off the tray. "Someone else besides me should be high on this shit. And if I stick this into your veins, it won't be in me."

Her dark eyes flared, and he saw the exact moment she wondered if she'd made a mistake in trusting him. "That is enough to kill me."

"Oh, well," he quipped as he grabbed her arm. "Better you than me."

Then her fighting turned real—or if it wasn't, it was damn convincing. One-Mile didn't point out that if he'd really wanted to pump her full of drugs, he would have already done it, and she couldn't possibly have escaped him. Instead, he let her beat against him and empty the syringe into the air during the scuffle. After he ducked her attempt to punch him, she tried to knee him in the balls and kick his shins. He growled and snarled and pushed her against the wall, shaking her hard enough to jar her teeth as he growled empty threats her way.

She screamed. The tears came. She sent a pleading stare at the security camera.

He let that last a few good seconds before he picked her up, tossed her on the cot, then climbed on top of her.

Shouldn't be long now…

Right on cue, a group of underlings with automatic weapons and attitude lifted him off of her and hauled him to his feet, shouting things in Spanish he didn't understand. Then again, he didn't need to know the words to grasp that they wanted the pleasure of killing him.

Laila wrapped herself in the blanket on his cot and glared at him with accusing eyes as the goons prodded him into his filthy jeans, up the stairs, and out into the breezy desert night. Emilo Montilla was waiting, whip in one hand, crowbar in the other as they clapped him into the shackles drilled deep into the concrete wall of the bunker.

Fuck, this was going to hurt.

"You have been a pain in my ass. It is time we reminded you that you should play nice because *I* am in charge. But I will spare you if you tell me where to find my wife."

"Are you just stupid or is your memory that bad? I've already said a hundred times that I'm not telling you a fucking thing."

Emilo snarled, then opened his back again with a single lash of the whip. Fire burst across One-Mile's skin. He hissed and arched, but nothing stopped the agony until the drug lord backhanded the side of his face with the crowbar.

An instant after pain exploded in his head, One-Mile's world went black. If he ever opened his eyes again, he hoped he would be anywhere but here.

chapter nine

A BLAST JOLTED HIM BACK TO CONSCIOUSNESS WITH A GASP. GUNFIRE. POPS OF IT resounded all around him, along with scuffling and shouting. One-Mile lifted his cheek from the wall and tried to open his eyes. A floodlight beamed down into his face, blinding him. He flinched but couldn't escape.

What was happening, some fucking apocalypse? Maybe that meant the end was coming so his fuck ton of pain would finally stop.

Every bit of his body hurt as if someone had set him on fire. His jaw throbbed. His back sizzled. Something warm and liquid ran down his arms. He couldn't fucking move. With his remaining strength, he tried to rise from his knees, which felt as if someone had driven stakes through them. But he was shackled. He smelled blood.

He was pretty sure it was his own.

"Over here!"

The voice was male. American. Familiar. One-Mile's head hurt too damn much to place it. Friend or foe?

Did it matter anymore? Either way, he was going to die.

He slumped forward, pressing his overheated cheek against the cool wall, and closed his eyes.

A pair of amber eyes haunted him.

Brea.

"Find 'em?" asked that familiar voice again, this time closer. "Toss them to me." No sooner did a metal clink fill his ears than the man shouted, "Fuck!"

More gunfire filled the air with a rapid *rat-tat-tat*. One-Mile lifted a lid to find a shadow standing over him, clutching an automatic weapon, wearing an angel-of-death glower, and spraying bullets into the darkness beyond.

"Get him now. We've got to get the hell out of here!" another American voice called, even more familiar. "I'll cover you."

An Edgington?

"On it!" said the first man as he blocked the blinding light and jerked at his imprisoning shackles.

One-Mile squinted up to see who had come to his rescue.

Cutter.

What the fuck?

"We're going to get you out of here," Bryant vowed grimly.

Why? Sure, they were teammates, but why would Brea's boyfriend rescue *him*?

"Can't move. Leave me."

"I promised Brea I'd bring you home, and I'm going to live up to my word."

Suddenly, his wrists were free. He tried to steady himself and use the wall to stagger upright. But agony gouged his knees. And his left shoulder. Dizziness turned his pounding head around and upside down.

One-Mile slumped to the ground.

Was this where he'd die, face down in the mud, when he'd been on the verge of safety?

Fuck no. Not if Brea wanted him back. For her, he'd fight.

One-Mile planted a hand in the mud and grimaced as he mustered the last of his strength to climb to his knees, then cling to the wall and stumble to his feet.

Cutter was right there. "Let's go. You're in no fucking shape to walk." He shoved the automatic in One-Mile's hands. "Keep our backs clear."

Before he could figure out what Bryant had in mind, Cutter hoisted him onto his back. Then Logan was beside them, taking down Montilla's lackies and thugs, clearing a path forward.

More goons gave chase. Every fucking bone in One-Mile's body hurt, but the opportunity for some payback was too good to pass up. He saw one of Montilla's heavies grab Laila by the hair and toss her to the ground.

Fuck that. She'd suffered enough.

His hands were shaking. Seeing double would totally affect his aim, but he'd seen Laila's expression. She'd rather be dead than stay another minute in this hellhole.

But One-Mile didn't intend to miss.

He pulled the trigger. The kickback was a bitch, but the thug jerked and stumbled. Laila screamed.

The asshole fell to the ground.

Josiah was there to scoop her up and wrap her protectively against his chest. Hunter, weapon in hand, flanked his back, signaling everyone with a wave of his arm to get the hell out now.

The team made a mad dash into the desert for freedom. Cutter's every pounding footfall against the hard soil jarred him. He clutched the weapon and, through sheer will, watched as the floodlight he'd once been pinned under grew fainter and fainter in the distance.

He heard the whir of chopper blades nearby. Another undertow of dizziness threatened to pull him under. His strength gave out.

With suddenly limp fingers, he let go of the weapon. It clattered to the dirt.

Hunter scooped it up again, barking instructions. The cacophony scrambled his head; he couldn't hear a word. But Cutter flung him down inside the cockpit. One-Mile caught a glimpse of the rivets in the domed top before his vision blurred over and blackness closed in.

His last conscious thought was that he hoped he'd regain consciousness, and that he'd be looking into a pair of soft amber eyes if he did.

Friday, September 12
Louisiana

When her phone chirped with the ringtone she had assigned Cutter, Brea lurched up in bed. She glanced at the digital clock as she grabbed her cell off the nightstand. Three thirty-four a.m. At that hour, she didn't bother with hello. "Did you find Pierce?"

"Yeah." Cutter's voice sounded rough, grim. "It's not good, Bre-bee."

She shut her eyes as dread washed over her. She was almost afraid to ask what the cartel had done to Pierce. He'd been so big and vital, so larger-than-life. She couldn't imagine him any other way. Brea didn't want to harbor hate in her heart, but it festered and snarled for these savage people who pushed drugs on children and destroyed a man fighting for right.

But she dredged for her courage and asked what she was afraid to hear. "Is he still alive?"

"For now."

"Where is he?"

"New Orleans, at Tulane Medical Center. The entire team went in to retrieve Walker. We're all a little banged up, but we'll be walking out this afternoon. If he makes it the next twenty-four hours, he'll be down for a while."

Brea bit her lip, but nothing held in her tears. The arm she curled around herself didn't give her any comfort. She'd prayed and worried constantly since she'd learned he had been taken prisoner, but during the days and weeks before, when she hadn't reached out, contacted him, begged God to save him… Those ate at her. The guilt consumed her.

"I'm coming there."

But how could she do that? Her dad was recovering from another successful bypass surgery, which should keep his heart functioning for years to come, God willing. But he hadn't been home long. He still needed nearly round-the-clock care. She owed it to him to make sure he got his meds and ate healthy meals, to see to his responsibilities at the church and his comfort…

"Why?"

Cutter wanted to know the reason she'd traipse across the state to show mercy to her rapist. Brea wasn't wasting the time or energy to cut through his pigheadedness now. He wasn't ready to hear that she'd fallen for Pierce. He might be her best friend…but he didn't always understand her heart.

"He saved your life. For that alone, I'll be eternally grateful. And he has no one else." She defaulted to arguments he would understand. "And I show everyone Christian charity. It's not my place to judge who deserves it and who doesn't."

"But I know you." He sighed. "You won't want to see another human being nearly beaten to death."

Cutter's description made her catch her breath. She had to go to Pierce. Her father was getting stronger every day. If the remorse she felt for not reaching out to Pierce since she'd last seen him ate her up, how much worse would her regret be if he didn't pull through? Devastating. She needed to tell him that he'd touched her heart, that she would never forget him, and if God deemed it necessary, she would mourn him, bury him, and find some way to say goodbye.

"Please don't treat me like I'm fragile. He's endured this ordeal and fighting through all the resulting pain. It's nothing for me to come to him, hold his hand, and pray."

Cutter hesitated. "All right. Some of the others are heading up to Lafayette soon, but I'll wait for you here."

"I'll...call Jennifer. Hopefully, she'll be willing to come watch over Daddy."

"I have no doubt she will," he said wryly. "Ring me from the road. It'll be dark for most of your drive."

"I will."

Brea hesitated ending the call. Once she did, she would be severing the only line of information between her and Pierce. That scared her. The thought of him enduring such agony made her physically ache.

So often, she swallowed back tears in times of tumult or tragedy because she had to be the stalwart one. She almost always filled the role of someone's prayer partner, helpmate, or rock. Today, she couldn't hold in her sobs.

"Bre-bee..."

She sniffled and tried to quiet her tears. Between her father's relapse and Pierce's shocking captivity, she felt as if she'd been weepy all week. Knowing the man she'd fallen for might die was simply too much.

"I'll be fine. I promise." She hated lying to Cutter.

"You don't have to come here. Really."

"I do." She *needed* to be with Pierce. "I'll see you soon. Bye."

Brea ended the conversation before he tried to talk her out of coming again.

In under twenty minutes, she called Mrs. Collins, dressed, threw a few things in a bag—just in case—promised to call later, and hopped in her car. As she pulled out of the driveway, she waved at the widow who'd vowed to take excellent care of her father.

Then she sped down the road.

Brea hated driving in the middle of the night. Some of Louisiana's highways were a little narrow and a tad scary. A lot of it was over water, and she always had visions of accidentally driving off a bridge and into a swamp to become gator food. But now, she refused to let any of those fears stop her.

She would reach Pierce before dawn.

By the time she hit Lafayette's southern outskirts, her phone was ringing. She and Cutter chatted off and on for the next two hours. No change in Pierce's condition that Cutter knew of. He was in ICU. They were running tests. What he'd heard so far didn't sound promising.

"I need to prepare you," Cutter insisted. "His face is almost unrecognizable. But that's nothing compared to his back, which may have significant scarring. Those were the injuries I could see. I'm still waiting to hear about the rest. He's in surgery now. I don't know what for since none of us are family…"

Every muscle in Brea's body tightened as she tried to hold herself together. "Thanks for the update. How are you?"

"I'm fine. A few stitches aren't going to stop me for long."

"I'm grateful you're safe and relatively unharmed."

She ended the call, pleading the need to focus on the road. Just over an hour and a stop for coffee at a twenty-four-hour drive-thru later, she made it to Tulane Medical Center. Immediately, she tore into the parking garage, slung her compact into the first available spot, grabbed her phone, and ran as fast as her tired body would take her.

When she found her best friend in the emergency room's waiting area, her first two thoughts were that it looked like a larger, more crowded version of University's in Lafayette. The second was that Cutter, Hunter, and Joaquin all sat clustered together, seemingly big and out of place and obviously exhausted. She hadn't thought to bring them coffee and breakfast muffins or any of the other "nice" things she usually delivered in times of crisis. But she couldn't spare any regret as she dashed over to them.

"Any news?"

Hunter's and Joaquin's confusion showed as Cutter stood slowly, looking disheveled and weary, then wrapped his arms around her. "Other than he's out of surgery, no."

"No idea what they repaired? Or where they're taking him next? Or his long-term prognosis?"

"We're not family." And Hunter sounded bitter about that. "Logan has medical power of attorney documents back at the office. Once he gets there…"

Brea understood a patient's right to privacy, but right now Pierce needed people who cared about him. He needed her watching over him, holding his hand, advocating for him. He didn't need to be fighting for his life alone. "I'll be right back."

It took some polite asking, a bit of cajoling, and a whopping lie she didn't regret at all to convince his surgeon and the nurse in charge that Pierce had no one he considered family except her. Once they were on board, she finally got the lowdown on his condition and resulting surgery. What they told her was incredibly frightening to hear. It was beyond hard not to lose her composure. She also got permission for the others to see Pierce as soon as he came out of recovery. Suddenly, Hunter, Joaquin, and Cutter were really glad she'd come.

"The surgeon said he had broken ribs, which he can't do anything about. But Pierce had a punctured lung and some swelling of the brain, along with a broken jaw, sprained knees, and a dislocated shoulder. They also say he's going through some sort of detox."

"I think those fuckers addicted him to drugs," Hunter groused. "Pardon my language."

Brea shook her head. She had the urge to call those animals something even worse. "Speaking of...what happened to them?"

Their downturned expressions grew darker. "Emilo Montilla, the slimy bastard, got away. We took out a number of his cohorts. The *policia* were arriving to arrest even more as we pulled out. We also rescued a woman named Laila in the compound, who was instrumental in helping us arrange the rescue mission."

Brea didn't know anything about her or why she'd helped Pierce, but if she had contributed to saving his life, Brea wanted to shake the woman's hand.

"But Montilla seems to have disappeared somewhere into the desert. Poof..." Joaquin tossed his hands in the air.

That wasn't good news. She knew without being told that cartels were full of dangerous people with long memories. What were the odds they could give up on Pierce simply because his fellow operatives had rescued him and hauled him back to the States?

"How long until he's out of recovery?" Cutter asked. "Before they know what kind of permanent damage he'll sustain?"

She shook her head, resisting the pull of fresh tears. She shifted with nervous energy instead. "I'm hoping it's not much longer. The surgeon called the operation a success, but he has no idea at this point how much Pierce will eventually recover. The next twenty-four hours are critical, so I'm going to stay."

Cutter frowned. "In a motel?"

"Yes. I'll find one later."

He hesitated, then glanced Hunter's way, who nodded. "I'll stay with you."

"You don't have to. I appreciate you wanting to protect me, but I can do this." She needed to.

"I know." He sighed. "I forget sometimes how damn grown you are. I still remember being sixteen and scaring off the bullies in your third-grade class who pulled on your pigtails."

She managed a wobbly smile. "You did. But the only thing that scares me right now is Pierce's condition."

"That's why I'm going to stay. I can be as strong as you need me to be."

"You always are." She squeezed his hand in thanks.

Hunter and Joaquin stood, then the elder Edgington brother spoke. "We're going to head home for a spell. I'd like to see Kata and my son, get some decent sleep. Then I'll be back..."

"Your wife called me earlier, too, and said she'd like to see her brother." Joaquin pointed at himself. "And my wife is worried sick. Bailey wants me home."

"Go on," Cutter said. "If there's any change, I'll call you."

"You're a bigger man than me," Hunter said.

Brea wanted to correct him. Cutter had never been her boyfriend and Pierce hadn't raped her. But Joaquin quickly shook Cutter's hand, then nodded her way, before he lifted the duffel at his feet and headed out. Hunter did the same.

She sighed. Their opinions weren't important. Right now, she needed to focus all her energy on Pierce and his recovery.

But the hours waiting for news dragged on. She refused breakfast, choosing instead to pace and pray and worry how she would cope if the worst happened. For possibly the first time in her life, Cutter was unable to soothe or console her.

Finally, at ten a.m., a nurse sought them out. "Ms. Bell? Your fiancé is out of recovery and back in his room. He's not conscious yet, but visiting hours have begun, so you're welcome to sit with him."

Relief filled her. She snatched her purse up from her abandoned seat. "Thank you. I'll follow you."

Cutter fell in behind her. "Fiancé?"

She shot him a glare over her shoulder and silently shushed him. Later, she'd take the time and energy to explain that was the only way the hospital staff had been willing to bend the rules. Now was about laying eyes on Pierce.

But nothing could have prepared Brea for the sight of him lying so bruised, half-starved, and lifeless in the sterile hospital bed. Both his eyes were black and swollen shut. Another massive hematoma covered the side of his head, which flared with a goose-egg-size knot and had been shaved to reveal an ugly, multicolored wound. The respirator covering his nose and mouth were the least of her concerns once she saw the stitches in various places on his scalp and the drain taking fluid from his brain to a bag near the bed. Bandages pinned his right arm in place and more surrounded both legs.

The sight of him so broken took Brea to her knees. "Pierce…"

Cutter was right there to pick her up and help her into the chair he rolled to One-Mile's bedside. He stood beside her, palming his face. "Jesus…"

"He's in bad shape," the nurse said. "If it had taken you and your friends even another hour to get him medical attention…"

The shake of the older woman's head said what Brea could see with her own two eyes. He would have died.

Brea pressed a hand over her mouth to silence her fear, anger, and grief. They wouldn't help him now. Only her love and her positive thoughts might.

It had been almost a month since she'd asked Pierce for space, but not a day had gone by that he hadn't crowded into her thoughts. Now she was ashamed for avoiding him, for assuming they had all the time in the world for her to sort out her feelings, for being too afraid of everyone else's reactions to open her heart to him.

That stopped now.

"What can I do?" she asked.

The nurse shrugged. "Sit with him. Hold his hand. Talk to him."

"Even though he can't hear me?"

"On some level, I think he can. He'll feel you. If there's a TV show he likes, play it. If there's a book he enjoys, read it to him. Pray for him."

"I will. Thank you."

It struck Brea that she knew Pierce on an almost painfully intimate level as a man—his scent, his kiss, his growl when he found pleasure—but she knew almost nothing about him as a person. She didn't know his TV preferences or reading habits. Did he have any food allergies? Weird quirks? She'd never asked about his past, his hopes, his concerns. They'd never discussed his politics, his religion, or his beliefs.

That realization left her feeling ashamed and distressed. She hadn't taken the time to learn him before allowing their incendiary chemical attraction to overwhelm her good sense. And now she might never have the chance to learn the real, true Pierce Walker.

Something else to mourn.

She reached for his big hand. It, too, was bruised. And battered. But she held it between hers and closed her eyes, feeling tears burn down her cheeks. "You're not alone anymore. I'm here."

No response. Not that she'd expected one. But she'd wanted it. She'd wanted the miracle. Some foolish part of her had hoped that she could heal him with her caring and her touch.

Cutter dropped a hand on her shoulder. "Don't lose faith."

He was right. This was the real world. The miracle would be Pierce surviving. She met his glance. "I'll keep praying."

"I've never known anyone with a bigger heart. I don't know everything he did to you—"

"Don't." She couldn't talk about that night with Cutter. "Not now."

He held up his hands. "I won't. But your capacity to forgive is humbling."

Pierce had done nothing that required forgiveness, and she didn't want to waste the energy defending him now when he needed her more. "It isn't."

Because she hadn't forgiven herself for being human, for being weak in the face of temptation. But in some ways, she'd cast Pierce into the role of her personal Satan. It had been so easy to believe he'd lured her with his attention, his masculinity, his sexuality. He might have seduced her…but she had let him. And deep down, she'd blamed him. He had taken her breath away. He had overwhelmed her.

It had been so unfair. Pierce hadn't done anything except be himself. Acknowledging that painful truth made her want to cry. She needed to accept the blame for her own actions—and not let well-meaning people like Cutter and Daddy tell her she was too good to be at fault.

She would also have to decide what—if anything—came next for her and Pierce.

But the days of turning her back on him simply because she didn't have the strength to confront her own moral fragility were over.

"Would you mind leaving me alone with him?"

Cutter hesitated. "Are you sure?"

That she was ready to handle this, no. But she needed to. "Yes."

"All right. I'll, um, get us a motel room and wait there until I hear from you."

She nodded absently, then scanned him. "Are you okay to drive?"

"Yeah. And I'll be one-hundred percent after some food, a shower, and a nap."

"Thank you." She fished her car keys out of her purse and handed them over. "I'll call you when I'm ready to leave."

"All right." He pressed a kiss to the top of her head. "Bye."

"Bye," she called after him. As the sound of his footfalls grew fainter, she took Pierce's hand again and let her tears fall. "I came as quickly as I could. Oh, Pierce... My gosh. I can't even imagine how much you've suffered. You're probably not aware I'm here, and it's not much, but I'll stay by your side. I'll hold your hand. Together, we'll do everything we can to make sure you pull through."

Hours passed. She prayed and prayed. Nurses came in to check his vitals, draw blood, and change his sheets. She flipped channels on the TV until she found a sports station she hoped he might like. The shadows coming through the windows lengthened. She'd nodded off in her chair once or twice but awakened with his hand still in hers.

Early in the evening, the doctor came by to check on him. He glanced at Pierce's chart, studied his progress, then ordered more tests. As the orderlies took him away, she squeezed his hand, then glanced at the clock. It was nearly six in the evening. She hadn't eaten all day.

After a quick call to Cutter, he picked her up and took her to a nearby diner, where she devoured everything on her plate. At the motel room, she took a shower, then fell onto one of the two beds for a long nap. Cutter grumbled when she asked him to take her back to the hospital alone, but he did it.

When she arrived, it was late. The hospital was noticeably quieter. She was grateful the doctor had given her permission to stay as long as she liked.

She turned off the sports channel and turned on some of her favorite music, setting the device on the table close to Pierce. "I don't know how you feel about Coldplay, but if we're going to get along, you have to at least be willing to tolerate them."

Silence, except for Chris Martin's vocals.

She sat and stared.

Nothing.

Dang it, she had to stop hoping for the miracle.

"It feels strange not to have been at the church's market tonight. It's one of my favorite things to organize every year. I usually find a lot of Christmas presents there, you know. Well, you don't know, but I do." When she tried to imagine big, bad Pierce wandering around all the little handcrafted items that interested and fascinated her, she smiled. "It might not be your thing. But if we're going to get along, you might have to tolerate that, too."

She took his hand and squeezed it again. "When you wake up—not if, because I'm determined you will—we have a lot to talk about. And the first thing I want to tell you is how much I missed you."

Tears stung her eyes and trembled on her lashes.

As they began to fall, he twitched in her grip...almost as if he was trying to squeeze her hand in return.

Her heart leapt to her throat. She watched him, blinking, holding her breath, almost afraid to hope. "Pierce?"

He turned his head toward her voice and tried to open his eyes. "Brea..."

Wednesday, October 15

One-Mile glanced at his phone. It was after seven in the evening. Brea was usually here by now. He'd memorized her schedule—hell, her every move—in the weeks since he'd been released from the hospital.

He texted her. She didn't answer.

Fuck.

A solid dozen of his worst what-if scenarios—everything from a car accident to violence to her quitting him—rolled through his head. Panic crowded in. He sucked in a rough breath to cool his anxiety. Brea was a good driver. The likelihood of anyone shooting up the small-town salon where she worked was slim. And she would never turn her back on anyone without a word, much less the man for whom she'd been a savior for the last month.

After he'd awakened in the hospital in New Orleans, Brea had maintained her vigil at his bedside for the next two days. Cutter stayed glued to her, but by unspoken agreement, they'd kept the peace, in part for her. The other part... Well, he'd saved Bryant's life in the past, and now the Boy Scout had saved his.

They were square.

Everyone had encouraged him to talk about his time in Mexico. His bosses and his team claimed they'd come to visit, but he knew the drill. They mostly wanted tactical information—how many men, what kind of operation, who were the key players. Brea had simply encouraged him to share his experiences with her. One-Mile had declined. First, he hadn't seen much that would be helpful. Second, he didn't want to traumatize Brea any more than she already was.

Since his release nearly a month ago, his condition had improved day over day. He and Brea had settled into a rhythm. She came every night after work to puree him some dinner, tidy up his house, and do an occasional load of laundry. They talked—at least as much as he could with his jaw wired shut—mostly about his physical therapy and doctor's appointments, his frustration with lingering headaches, short-term memory losses, and periodic exhaustion. She empathized, always doing her best to maintain a cheerful front and positive outlook. Yes, he knew how far he had come in just over a month. But he was impatient to be one-hundred-percent healed.

When he could get her to talk about something other than him, Brea admitted how much she worried about her father's heart condition and fretted about organizing activities at the church. He sensed she had something else on her mind, but the few times he'd asked, she'd given him a false smile and changed the subject.

He had no fucking doubt he was in love with her…but he was clueless about where he stood. Trying to express himself beyond the superficial when he couldn't really enunciate was somewhere between grating and I-want-to-punch-a-fucking-wall frustrating. For multiple reasons, it was hard to ask why she'd stayed by his side and done everything to help him over the last month. Because she had feelings for him? Or because she just felt sorry for him?

The idea of being her pity project made him sick.

So did the knowledge that she was still with Cutter.

During her bedside vigil in New Orleans, he'd figured out that she spent her days with him…and her nights in a nearby motel room with Bryant. If he'd had any doubt before that the two had "taken their relationship to the next level," he didn't anymore. Sure, Brea might have refused to fuck her boyfriend while giving most of her waking attention to the guy who had popped her cherry. But realistically, if the tables had been turned, One-Mile would have been all over Brea every chance he got. He couldn't be in the room with that woman and not crave her. But he would have wanted to remind her that, no matter how much attention she paid to another man, she belonged to him.

He glanced at his phone again. Seven-fifteen. He tried to quell his rising panic. Hair took a while to color and curl and whatever else she did, right? She wouldn't have put this much care and compassion into helping him recover if he didn't mean *something* to her. Or was he desperate enough to bullshit himself?

Fuck if he knew. He had never had more than the standard ten-minute haircut. And he'd never tried to have a real relationship with a woman. Until he could fucking talk, he still couldn't.

Eight days. That's how much longer his jaw would be wired shut. That's how long he had to wait before he could open his mouth well enough to tell Brea how he felt, kiss her senseless…and hope she reciprocated.

He hoped like hell that she loved him—at least a little—too.

A gentle knock sounded at the door. Brea.

Thank fuck.

Excitement replaced anxiety. His heart started revving, just like it did every time he saw her.

Usually, she let herself in the house. Early in his convalescence, it had taken every bit of strength he possessed simply to get out of bed. Walking downstairs to open the door had been almost impossible and wiped him out for hours. So he'd given her a key. Tonight, despite nagging fatigue and needing a shower he feared would sap him even more, he let her in himself.

"Hey." He settled for greeting her with a nod, but he'd give anything to lay his lips over hers, get her underneath him, and convince her to ditch Cutter.

She sent him a wry smile and an eye roll as she stepped into the foyer. "Sorry I'm late, and I couldn't text you back while I was driving. My last appointment was a mess. Mrs. Goodwin thinks her husband is having an affair, and nothing I said would convince her that hair extensions weren't the answer to her marital woes."

It wasn't funny…but it kind of was. "You did them?"

"No. That takes *hours*, and I didn't have the product there. So I colored and curled her…and listened to her talk about buying new lingerie. She scheduled the extensions for next week."

"Eat something?" He shut the door behind her.

With a wrinkle of her nose, she shook her head. "My stomach is unsettled again today. Just…not hungry. What about you? Yogurt? Soup? Smoothie? Did that protein powder you ordered come in?"

He'd love to take her out to dinner, where they could eat together, talk, hold hands, and eye-fuck as they counted the seconds until they were alone. But he kept running into the limitations of his body…and the unspoken hesitation he kept feeling from her.

"Yeah. Surprise me." The short answers his broken jaw forced him to give were pissing him off, too.

"Okay. Any laundry?"

"I did it." At the surprise in her expression, he scowled. "You aren't my maid."

"No, but that's a lot for you to tackle. You should be resting. I'm here to help…"

He fucking didn't want her pity. "I got it."

When she reared back, he cursed. He must have been growlier than normal. But he felt like a volcano building and building. Every day he woke up, he ran face-first into all the things he still couldn't do—talk normally, pump serious iron, sleep without nightmares, resume his job, lay his heart on the line and tell Brea how he felt. And without that last part, sex wasn't happening. He wanted it. Ached for it. Two months was a long time without it, and she was right in front of him every day, somehow looking prettier and more womanly every time he set eyes on her. He thought about her, masturbated to fantasies of her.

He couldn't keep going like this.

"Sorry. I pushed today. I'm tired."

Her face softened as she set her purse down, gave his arm a gentle squeeze, then headed to his kitchen. Once there, she threw some juice, a protein drink, and vegetables into his blender. "And you're frustrated. I know you're used to being able to do anything and everything."

He retrieved the protein powder and set it on the counter beside her. Her hair smelled like some flowery fragrance he didn't have a name for, but it turned him the fuck on. "Yeah. Day felt long."

She paused while opening the canister and turned with wide eyes. "Oh, that's right. It was your first day without the home nurse. What was his name?"

One-Mile nodded, glad she'd remembered so he didn't have to explain while he felt like a cross between a ventriloquist and a drooler. "Stewart."

"Not too hard, I hope," she said as she scooped powder into the blender.

"No. Just more computer work."

Brea tried not to laugh. "I know how much you love that…"

"Not."

"Did you start making a dent in that Netflix list yet?"

One-Mile didn't have the heart to tell her no. She had painstakingly compiled that queue shortly after he'd been discharged from the hospital. He'd watched a few documentaries…but didn't remember much between the naps and the pain meds. In the past two weeks, he'd focused most of his effort and waking hours on rebuilding his strength and stamina.

So he'd started an exercise regimen, first walking, then running on his treadmill. Push-ups, pull-ups, biceps and triceps curls, planks—he pushed his body to the limit of the doctor's advice…and a little bit beyond—working harder every day. He'd also talked Josiah and Trees into giving him rides to the shooting range. He wanted to go back to work, so he had to stay sharp.

After all, he had a vendetta to settle.

"Got busy."

"Did you nap?"

"No." He'd resisted the urge, because once he resumed work, the bad guys weren't going to let him curl up with a blankie in the corner and check out for a couple of hours. And if he got tired enough, maybe he'd finally sleep a whole fucking night without waking up in a cold sweat.

She narrowed her eyes at him. "Did you work out again?"

Last Friday, she'd had a midday cancellation and dropped by to check on him, only to find him in his home gym pulling up on the bar attached to the door. She'd taken one look at him shirtless and dripping in sweat, swallowed hard, then blessed him out.

"Want me to lie to you?"

"Never." She sighed and started the blender. "If I thought it would do any good, I'd give you a tongue lashing."

"It won't." But he knew what he'd like her to do with that tongue.

She checked the consistency of his dinner, then, seemingly satisfied, poured it into the big plastic cup with its accompanying straw and handed it to him. "Is there anything the home nurse helped you with that you can't do yourself?"

"A shower."

Brea stilled before her stare drifted back to him. She studied him—up his legs, his abs, his chest…all the way to his face. Vaguely, One-Mile wondered whether she'd noticed behind his denim that he was hard as hell for her.

He sent her a lazy smile. "That a problem? You've already seen it all."

"Um…no problem."

Her breathless reply gave him hope. Despite his injuries, the passing of nearly two months, and however Cutter had fucking touched her, he still got to Brea. She hadn't forgotten the night she'd spent in his bed. It was all over her face.

"How can I help?" she asked.

Such a deliciously open-ended question. He almost hated to take advantage of her sweetness. He felt a teensy bit bad about trying to tempt her to cheat on her boyfriend again.

But not enough to stop.

He shrugged. "Pretty much everything. If I lose my balance and hit my head…"

"Oh…" She paled as if that possibility hadn't occurred to her. "That would be horrible."

"The neurologist said another concussion this soon could take me back to square one."

That was the truth. Not being able to shower without help…not so much. He'd been doing that for nearly three weeks. But if it took showing some skin to break down the walls between them, he was all for flashing her a full monty.

"O-okay." She nodded like she was working up her courage. "You drink your dinner. I'll, um…"

Busy yourself so you don't think too hard about seeing me naked? "You'll what?"

After a comically long moment, she sent him a stilted smile. "Find you some clean clothes. Maybe I'll change your sheets while I'm up there, too."

Perfect. "I'll be there in a few."

With a nod, she disappeared upstairs. Yeah, he felt a little guilty for stretching the truth. But he couldn't stand the bland politeness between them. If he wanted to know how she felt about him, he had to bust them out of it.

He also wondered how she would react to a body covered with a whole new litany of scars. His hair had grown back enough to disguise the ones on his scalp and the last of the yellowish bruising flaring from his temple, over his jaw. The bruising on his shoulder had almost healed. The tube they'd shoved between his ribs to help reinflate his lung was long gone, replaced by a red, puckered reminder. His back was still a network of scabs and discolorations. He'd never been anyone's definition of pretty, not with eyes like black holes, a long nose, and an aggressive jaw. Now he probably looked downright scary.

But so far Brea didn't seem afraid. He was calling that a win.

He did his best to slurp down dinner, then tiptoed upstairs. He found her in his bedroom being industrious and leaned against the doorjamb to watch her bend to tuck his sheets in place. Goddamn, she looked juicy, her hips seemingly a little rounder, her ass a little riper.

Fuck, he'd do anything to lay her across his mattress and muss up everything she'd just arranged.

"Need help?" he asked.

She turned, clearly startled. "No. Almost done."

One-Mile waited patiently while he enjoyed the view. She kept stealing clandestine glances at him. Did she want to know what he was thinking? Was she imagining him naked? Probably not, but a guy could dream.

Less than a minute later, she stood and squared her shoulders. Her face said she still worried about his condition, so she was trying to be completely appropriate and platonic.

Good luck with that, pretty girl.

"Where do we start? I'm assuming you can undress yourself?"

"Yep. Grab a towel from the linen closet in the hall and meet me in the bathroom."

Brea almost looked relieved he'd given her something else to do besides watch him strip. "Sure."

He winked her way, then headed to the bathroom and started the spray. Then he slid out of every stitch he'd worn—with the door wide open.

"I assume the blue one is okay. I—" She stopped in the doorway, blinking furiously as she stared at him. Her cheeks turned pink, her stare glued itself to his body, and her nipples went hard. "Oh, my goodness."

He just smiled. "Sorry for the, um…reaction. You do this to me."

Her gaze shifted down to his cock, standing tall and desperately ready to spend quality time with her.

Brea pressed her hand to her chest. "I…"

Clearly, she didn't know what to say. "You?"

"Ah…wanted to know if you need shampoo."

"Nope. But it might be a good idea for you to hold my hand while I climb in. You know, so I don't lose my balance on the wet tile."

"Right." Her voice trembled, but she still didn't move, just swallowed.

She was reluctant to touch him.

He backed off. "But if this is too much for you—"

"No," she assured him in a rush, then approached, hand outstretched. Her cheeks had gone red. "I just didn't expect to see you this…exposed."

She'd thought he'd be somehow less naked?

Wiping the smile off his face, he stepped into the walk-in shower, then released her hand. The hot water sluiced down his body, washing away grime and sweat. He groaned.

"Are you okay?" she asked. "Does something hurt?"

Brea was a carer. She worried about people, often more than herself. As he reached for the shampoo, he really looked at her face. The dark smudges he saw under her eyes worried him. He didn't remember seeing them before.

"Fine," he assured. "I'm better every day. What about you? Tired?"

"I am. I don't know why, just feeling run down lately. Suddenly, I want to nap all the time. It's got to be the change in seasons and the fact we've had such gloomy skies this week."

Maybe, but he didn't like it. As soon as he finished showering, he'd stop yanking her chain and take care of her for a change.

"Have you been sleeping?" she asked, changing the subject.

He lathered his hair, then grabbed the soap to scrub up his body.

Brea was still watching.

"Not much." Now that he was almost healed and getting good calories, he wasn't constantly exhausted. That was great during the day. At night? The fitful hours sucked.

"Are you still having nightmares?"

"Yeah." He turned his back on her, not eager to continue this conversational thread.

He'd been around other soldiers enough to know the symptoms of PTSD. He was a month out from his captivity. If the anxiety and bad dreams didn't ease soon, that therapist his bosses at EM Security Management had forced him to start videoconferencing with would put a label on him that might persuade everyone to bar him from action.

One-Mile wasn't having that shit.

"Do you want to talk about them?"

"No."

"Pierce…"

As he managed his final rinse, his half-formed plan to soap up his hard cock and stroke it for her went down the drain with the suds.

Fuck, he hated that the mood between them was dead.

"Don't worry." He cut off the water.

She handed him the towel. "Of course I'm going to worry. If I didn't, why else would I come see you every day?"

"Why do you?" he asked, wrapping the terry cloth around his waist.

A pretty flush that had nothing to do with the warm, humid bathroom rushed back to her cheeks. "Because you matter."

"To who? My bosses? The guys I work with?" He stepped from the shower, challenging her. "Or to you?"

She frowned. "Of course you matter to me. Now sit so I can put this ointment on your back."

One-Mile wanted to press her for more, but it was too many words to speak with his jaw wired shut. For now, he had to settle for the fact that he mattered to her in some way. He could build from that.

Instead, he bit back a surly growl and yanked the prescription tube from a nearby drawer, then handed it to her and lowered himself onto the closed lid of the commode.

Seconds later, she set the tube down on the adjacent counter and began to spread the thick antibiotic ointment across his back, focused on where Montilla's whip had opened his flesh repeatedly over his twenty-two days of hell. Her fingers glided over his skin in a delicate brush that made him shudder in pleasure.

God, he'd love to have her hands all over him…

"Your wounds are looking a lot better," she remarked. "The scabs are really healing over."

He grunted. He couldn't see his back, but he'd believe her.

"Do you have any vitamin E oil?"

Why would he? "No."

"I'll bring some tomorrow. It helps with scarring."

Honestly, he didn't care about that much, except the damage done to his ink, but… "Will you put it on for me?"

"Of course."

"I'd like that."

She lifted her hands off him and washed them in the nearby sink. "I laid some clothes out for you on your bed in case you were too tired. Can you manage from here?"

He nodded.

"I'll meet you downstairs."

"Thanks."

Thirty seconds later, he'd tossed on the sweats and T-shirt she'd folded nicely on his well-made bed he'd give anything to share with her tonight. Just being in the same room with her made him feel calmer, more centered. Whole.

Jesus, he sounded like a lovesick schmuck—and he didn't fucking care.

After finding a pair of tube socks, he slid into those and padded down the stairs. He stopped halfway down when he spotted Brea on his sofa, head propped up on her open palm, eyes closed.

She was asleep.

On soft footfalls, he made his way to her and sat. She awoke with a start as he pulled her onto his lap and curled her head onto his shoulder.

"W-what are you doing?"

"Showing you that you matter to me, too. Rest."

The starch left her body, and she melted against him, eyes closing again. "Just for a minute."

"Sure." He dropped a kiss onto her forehead.

She sighed, then her breathing evened out.

Suddenly, he was the happiest he'd been in what seemed like an eternity.

Without really trying, Brea had become his everything.

As she curled her legs against his side and cuddled closer, he started scheming ways to keep her with him forever.

chapter ten

Thursday, October 23

LESS THAN THIRTY MINUTES AFTER HER LAST CLIENT LEFT THE SALON, BREA RUSHED toward Pierce's front door, feeling almost giddy.

Today, his jaw had been unwired. Tonight, they would finally be able to talk.

For weeks, she'd purposely kept their conversations short since speaking had been both hard and frustrating for him. But as she'd left his house yesterday, his smoldering stare had promised he would have a lot to say tonight. So did she.

Brea couldn't wait.

She'd fallen in love with Pierce Walker. After their night together, she'd already been halfway there. But now? There was no denying her stalwart warrior held her whole heart in the palms of his big hands.

Looking back, she suspected she'd been head over heels from the start. Now she had the courage to admit it.

What happened next? She didn't know, but surely God had a plan. The gospel of John said, "A new commandment I give to you, that you love one another…" So whatever He had in store, she would follow her heart.

It wouldn't be easy. Cutter still disliked Pierce. Her father knew nothing about him except as Cutter's injured teammate who had needed her Christian charity. She and Pierce were from different worlds, and they were still getting to know each other. But she refused to lose faith. After all, Joseph and Job hadn't when presented with incredible trials. By comparison, this was nothing.

She and Pierce could make something work, right?

Brea hoped so…and prayed he felt something for her, too. Because her heart kept yearning for the fairy tale.

What if he didn't love her in return? Yes, he'd given her a hundred signs that he cared. He'd even admitted he'd never felt about a woman the way he felt about her. Had he meant that as romantically as it sounded?

He's not the marrying kind.

Cutter's assertion blazed through her memory. If her best friend was right, what did that make her to Pierce, simply a friend with benefits? Had she, in her naiveté, confused his desire for love?

Tonight, she'd find out.

As she stepped onto Pierce's porch, she fluffed her hair and double-checked her lipstick in her little compact's mirror. She'd chosen a berry shade that was a bit vampier than her usual nude pink. She'd taken extra care with the rest of her makeup, too.

After she tucked the compact away, she knocked softly and waited. When he didn't answer, she used her key to unlock the door. It was the first time since he'd come home from the hospital she'd hesitated to let herself into his personal space. Now that he was healed, he wouldn't need her every night. Would he even want to see her half so often?

As she tiptoed in, music filled his great room. Not his usual hard rock with screaming vocals, but a sexy R and B tune. Soft candles lit the space. And a profusion of white, pink, and red rose petals had been scattered in a trail across the dark hardwood floors.

Goodness, what was he up to?

"Pierce?"

"In here."

She followed the petals and the sound of his voice to find him standing in his dining room, wearing a blinding white dress shirt and distressed jeans. Light and shadows loved the angles of his sharp jaw—no longer wired shut—almost as much as she did. He looked so swoon-worthy, she got a little dizzy.

"You like it?" He gestured to the table beside him.

Until he pointed it out, she hadn't pried her gaze off him long enough to realize he had set it, much less elegantly.

Had he planned dinner to say thank you for helping him? To seduce her back into his bed now that he had healed enough for sex? Or did the gesture mean everything she hoped? "It's very nice."

"I hope you're hungry because I'm going to feed you for a change." He pulled out her chair. As she brushed past him to sit, he blocked her with his big body. "Wait. It's been so damn long. Are you going to let me kiss you, pretty girl?"

Brea didn't have to ask if he wanted to. His expression said he was desperate to get his mouth on hers.

That still doesn't make it love...

Despite that, she gave him the only answer she could. "Yes."

"Thank fuck." He took her face in his hands and bent to devour her mouth.

Her wildly racing heart stopped for an agonizing moment, then thudded furiously again. Eagerly, she pressed herself against him, barely noticing when her purse fell to the floor.

The rational part of her insisted they should talk first. But when Pierce sank inside her mouth, desire muted logic and muzzled her worries. She stopped caring about anything in that moment except being as close as possible to this man.

Suddenly, he pulled away with a groan.

She blinked up at him. "What's wrong?"

"Nothing. I promised to feed you, so I'm going to." He stepped aside and helped her into the chair. "And we can finally talk."

She was dying to know what he had on his mind, but his health came first. "Tell me what the doctors said."

"One second." He dashed into the kitchen and, with two mitts, took a pair of plates out of the oven. He set one before her. The other he dropped in front of his chair beside her, then eased into his seat.

Her eyes widened. "Lasagna, asparagus, and garlic bread? You remembered?"

"That they're some of your favorites, yeah."

"Thank you." Her heart fluttered. "That's incredibly thoughtful."

"It's not homemade since I can't cook for shit, but I asked around and heard this place had the best Italian food in town."

"It smells amazing." But after his kiss, her body was pinging with life. Food was the last thing on her mind.

"It's a small way to thank you. You came here to take care of me every day for nearly six weeks, even though you'd worked on your feet all day and your father is still recovering. Even though you were burning your candle at both ends and you were tired…"

Of course Pierce had noticed. Under his gruff exterior, he was kind. Brea tried not to be disappointed that he had planned this dinner merely to show his gratitude. He'd probably feel guilty if he knew her urge to nap often lasted all day. Or that, lately, her stomach rolled from the moment she got out of bed until long into the afternoon. But telling him served no purpose.

Tonight, she felt well enough to eat the yummy, cheesy pasta he had thoughtfully brought her, so she would. She'd push aside her stupid fantasies of a future with Pierce, too.

And now that he didn't need her anymore, when she left tonight she'd take a giant step back out of his life.

"My pleasure." She managed a smile.

"You were there for me every day," he finished. "That means more to me than I can tell you. So thanks."

"There was no place else I would have wanted to be." It was true.

She swallowed back the rest of her feelings. He didn't want them.

Pierce reached across the space between them to cup her cheek. "Being with you every day was *my* pleasure, pretty girl. Believe me."

She got lost in his eyes as tears stung her own. She was so utterly in love. And if he kept looking at her like that, she was going to stupidly blurt it out.

"Let's, um…get to eating, huh?" He sounded surprisingly rattled.

"Sure." She forced herself to bite into the tender pasta. The flavors burst on her tongue in a tangy surprise. "Oh, my gosh. This is really good."

"I'm glad." He shoveled in a forkful of chicken in a white wine sauce. "Hmm. I missed real food."

"No doubt." She took another bite and did her best to simply enjoy her time with him. Soon, she wouldn't see him much at all. "So tell me. What did your doctors say?"

"The neurologist went over my latest scan and gave me a clean bill of health.

It's hardly a shocker that I'm supposed to avoid more head trauma. But otherwise, he released me. The orthopedic surgeon studied the last films she took of my shoulder and knees. All good. I started exercising a little earlier than she'd recommended, but it actually ended up helping me build back my strength. It wasn't my first rodeo with the shoulder, so I knew how not to pull it out of whack again. She wants to see me in another month but told me I can go ahead and resume normal activity, including work."

Brea could see the relief on his face. She'd been worried his injuries were so extensive he'd be unable to come back, and he must have had moments of doubt, too. "That's great. Just make sure you take it easy for a while."

"I'll try." He leaned forward and studied her. "But it's not an easy job."

"I know." And she did from being around Cutter. What they did was dangerous and unpredictable. Just yesterday, her best friend had been sent to Dallas at the last minute to bodyguard an up-and-coming clothing designer with a stalker. Every time he left, she worried. She could only imagine how she would feel once Pierce resumed missions again. "And I know you're a tough guy, but you're only human."

"Don't tell the bad guys that." Pierce winked. "But the best appointment was with the oral surgeon. It feels great to have my jaw back."

"I can tell you're thrilled."

"Hell yeah. He's still stunned I didn't lose any teeth, which made the process easier." He smiled. "And no one can shut me up now."

"No one wants to."

He raised a black brow. Just like that, reality splashed cold water on her. Cutter would love to shut him up. Every time she turned around, he still seemed determined to come between them. He was convinced Pierce was no good for her.

She was so happy when they were alone together. Here, in his house, she and Pierce had shared some wonderful times just making small talk, performing domestic tasks, and curling up on the sofa. She sometimes pretended they could spend their lives that way. But the reminder that, even if Pierce ever fell for her, one of the most important people in her world would never approve ate her up.

And Cutter wasn't their only obstacle. Whatever he thought, he would convey to her father. Since Daddy had always trusted Cutter's judgment implicitly, once her best friend said that Pierce didn't deserve her, getting Daddy to hear her side of things would be difficult at best. Convincing him she was right would be even more challenging. Daddy didn't mean to be old-fashioned…but he was. Just like Cutter. Neither believed she was incapable of taking care of herself; they just didn't think she should have to.

"Well, I want to hear whatever you have to say," she corrected.

He gestured to her plate. "There's a lot. Hurry and get back to eating."

"I'm doing my best without making a mess," she pointed out, then sipped from her water glass.

"Shit. I got a bottle of wine. I forgot to open it…" He stood.

She laid her hand over his. "Don't. I have to drive. I'm good with water."

He sat with a sigh and reached for his own glass of *agua*. "You sure? I wanted everything to be perfect."

For what?

"It is. The music, the rose petals, the food." She gave him the best smile she could. "You didn't have to thank me for helping you, but this is very sweet."

"Just sweet?"

Their gazes connected. In his black eyes, she suddenly saw a lot more than gratitude. Everything inside her trembled. "Were you trying to make it romantic?"

"If you've got any doubts, pretty girl, I should have tried harder."

So he hadn't done all this merely to thank her? Pleasure rushed Brea. Her smile widened. Was it even a little bit possible that he loved her, too?

"How?" she breathed.

He leaned closer. "Maybe I should have been nicer."

"If you had, I would have wondered who you were and what you'd done with the real Pierce."

"Fair enough. Maybe I should have cooked your food myself."

"Even though you can't?"

"I didn't say it was a great idea."

She laughed. "Feeding me an inedible dinner wouldn't have done much to impress me."

"Yeah, screw it." He leaned closer. "Maybe I should have just kissed you longer."

Her breath caught. "Maybe you should have."

Pierce's eyes turned impossibly darker.

No, that wasn't love…but it sure felt like it.

Then he hooked his big hand behind her neck, tilted his head, and brought her in for a crushing kiss. The desire that had been simmering under the surface collided with the feelings she'd been hoarding in her heart. Together, they made her body ache for his touch, his caring, his possession.

As he slipped inside her mouth, his tongue sliding intimately against her own, she flashed with heat. She had missed this man desperately. Not seeing him for a month after their night together had been torture. She'd been so relieved when he'd been rescued, but even over the last long weeks of his recovery, during his lowest points and surliest moods, she'd begun to ache for him again in ways she knew many would call shameful. But the need was unrelenting and inescapable. She wanted him more than the first time. More than even yesterday.

Suddenly, he lifted free, heaving hot, harsh breaths. "Fuck."

Before she could even question why he'd stopped kissing her, he lifted her from her seat, strode to the other end of the table, then laid her across the cool, hard surface.

"I want you, pretty girl. I want to make love to you. I want to do this right."

He swallowed as he gripped her thighs, parted them, and stepped in between. "But I don't know how much more I can stand not being inside you. It's felt like an eternity."

"It's felt even longer than that." She didn't mean to utter her thoughts aloud, but she couldn't help it. Having Pierce so close rattled her.

"I've missed you so fucking much. I need you." He shoved her skirt up to her hips and stopped. Stared. Swallowed before he brushed his thumb up her sex, barely covered by sheer, pink silk panties. "Oh, Brea…"

Her womb clenched. Blood rushed between her legs. Moisture spilled to all the parts he caressed.

Her brain shut down.

With a whimper, she pushed her hips up to him in a desperate plea for more.

Their first night together, she'd been torn between what was right and what she'd wanted until the pleasure he'd dazzled her with silenced her misgivings. Tonight, she refused to think about anything except being close to him and feeling the ecstasy he heaped on her. Because her body burned for the satisfaction it seemed only he could give her. Because his captivity had reminded her that no one was guaranteed a tomorrow. Because she'd fallen in love with him and wanted to show him how she felt…even if she never spoke the words.

"God, I've missed you. You have the prettiest pussy," he whispered thickly as he bent to her. "Swollen, juicy…"

Pierce fastened his mouth over her, teeth nipping into the pad of her sex, tongue flattening against her clit as if her panties didn't exist. No, this still wasn't love, but need roared through her. She gripped the edge of the table to steady herself against the electrifying desire rolling through her.

"Pierce!"

"Say yes. Say you want me. Say you can't wait."

She didn't even hesitate. "Yes. I want you. Now."

With deft fingers, he unbuttoned his dress shirt and shrugged out of it. Then, with one hand, he draped it over the back of the nearby chair. With the other, he tugged her sweater up her abdomen. "Take it off."

Brea wanted it gone, too.

As she struggled to peel the V-neck over her head, Pierce shoved his big fingers under the elastic waistband of her underwear and yanked them down. The second he pulled them free and tossed them aside, he began petting her again where she ached most.

Finally, she wrestled off her sweater, but it didn't bring her any relief. Heat assailed her. Her feverish skin felt tight. If he didn't do something besides stoke this blaze, she would combust.

"Your tits look so fucking luscious," he rasped, his stare glued to her lace-clad breasts.

Under the black fire of his stare, her ache grew. Her nipples tightened and tingled. As if he now had mastery over her body, she arched, offering him her breasts. She parted her legs, giving him her sex.

"Brea. Baby..." His thumb delved between her slick folds to center on her sensitive bud. "I've dreamed of this. Why don't you remind me how pretty you look when you come?"

Everything was happening so quickly. Fierce need clawed its way past her remaining good-girl decorum, stomping all over her worry that he'd never return her feelings.

Maybe they didn't need to talk with words right now. Under this heady rise of ecstasy, she felt his caring in every touch.

As her heart gonged in her ears, her orgasm climbed in a hot rush, then crescendoed in a sharp slide up before peaking with a stunning shock of ecstasy. He unraveled her, and she imploded, bucking under him and keening until her throat burned.

"Yes." He panted, chest heaving. "Fuck."

Brea hated that word...except when he said it. Then, somehow, it ignited her. Because he was forbidden? Because when he said the word, it sounded like both an expletive and a need? Yes, and when he wrapped his raspy voice around that one blunt syllable, it sounded like praise. Like a benediction.

"I imagined you constantly," he went on. "After you said you needed space, I tried to tell myself that you couldn't have been as sexy as I remembered. But I was so fucking wrong." He brushed a kiss across her lips. "Memories of you got me through Mexico. You're everything to me."

Shock and hope sparked inside her. "Pierce, you mean so much—"

He grabbed a fistful of her hair and seized her mouth before she could finish. Brea didn't object, simply gave in to his urgency and opened herself to him, helpless to stop this new rise of desire.

Pierce tangled their tongues and slid deeper into her mouth, kissing her senseless—while managing to unfasten the clasps of her bra at her back. When the last hook gave way, he tore the garment from her body, took her breasts in his rough hands, and sucked desperately at her nipples. The pull multiplied the desire building again between her legs.

She wanted it. Craved him. But her breasts felt too tender. "Ouch."

He frowned. "Too rough?"

"A little."

"Tell me. Always tell me. I don't ever want to do anything in bed except make you feel good."

He eased off, licking, flicking, teasing. It drove Brea insane. The orgasm he'd given her so recently had somehow only left her achier and needier. Without him inside her, she felt hollow. Empty. Bereft.

She needed him to make her whole.

Brea wriggled to sit up as he kept at her nipples like a man too starved to stop.

But she persisted, nudging and shoving, until she finally got a breath of space in between them.

Then she tore into the fly of his jeans, ripping the button free and yanking down his zipper.

"Oh, pretty girl. Fuck... I can't wait anymore."

He shoved his pants down, nudged her to her back again, then aligned his crest at her opening. "Tell me this is mine."

"It's yours," she gasped.

"Tell me you're mine."

She met his stare. "I'm yours."

"And no one else's," he growled. "Don't you ever fucking forget that."

Brea nodded. It was all she could manage before he gripped her hips in his big hands and impaled her with his cock.

She gasped, back arching, as she went from clenching and empty to blessedly bursting full in seconds. "Just yours."

"Yes." He clutched her with rough fingers and pushed in deeper, setting a million nerve endings inside her on fire.

"More..."

Pierce hissed, teeth bared, as he set a steady rhythm. Her breasts bounced with every thrust. Her toes curled. Her clit swelled. But it wasn't enough.

She wrapped straining fingers around his thick, bunching shoulders. "Please. I need—"

"Me to fuck you harder?"

"Yes!" Even the promise had her body revving and tightening.

"Oh. I'm fucking dying"—he banged his way inside her with more force, prodding a spot that had her eyes flaring and her desire soaring—"to be inside this sweet, tight cunt and remind you that... You. Belong. To. Me."

"I do," she panted. "I always have."

He crushed her lips beneath his for a feverish press, then wrenched back with a gasp. Their stares collided. She fell into those twin black holes. There was no escape, especially when he grabbed her hair in one fist and pressed her closer. "From now on, no one else fucks you."

"Only you," she blurted as her tension gathered and her blood rushed. "Only ever you."

Pierce shoved himself deeper, then halted as he pushed his face against hers with a growl. "Ever?"

Her heart and her breath both ceased in that moment. "Just you."

"Why?"

She needed him to thrust inside her again too much to filter. "I'm in love with you."

His whole face softened as he withdrew, then plunged home again. "Oh, Brea... Baby. My pretty girl. I fucking love you so much. I've wanted to tell you..."

His words and his touch sent her heart soaring. "Really?"

Brea didn't get a chance to say more before he seized her mouth and slammed deep, filling her again and again. Breathless, clawing, desperate, she rocked under him, pressed against him, let herself be full of him. Her need rose to dizzying heights. She cried out, called his name. Legs wrapped around him, her nails in his back, she urged him on, more aroused by every growl and harsh breath he panted in her ear.

He grew impossibly harder inside her. His strokes lengthened, deepened. His fiery stare riveted her every bit as much as his insistent cock.

"You going to come for me again?" he asked.

"I'm close..." The ache swirled and churned just behind her clit, almost there.

He ground his pelvis against her, providing the extra friction she needed to completely unravel.

"Yes... Pierce!"

"Oh, fuck. That pussy. Baby!"

The force of his impaling cock sent her higher, robbing her of breath and thought. Vaguely, she was aware of the table shaking as his every thrust inched it across the hardwood floors. Then his body stiffened, his back bowed, and he gave a hoarse shout of ecstasy. A sudden gush of warmth filled her.

They'd forgotten a condom again.

She needed to see her doctor about birth control, because right or wrong, sin or not, she wasn't giving up the pleasure she shared with Pierce Walker. He owned her—heart and body.

And he loved her.

Rough breaths and damp skin aside, she smiled up at him. "That was better than dinner."

He smiled in return. "Way better. Want to finish the pasta now or..."

When he nodded toward the stairs, she didn't hesitate. "Definitely or."

"Hmm, you're perfect." Pierce kissed her, then eased free of her body before helping her off the table.

Brea stood on unsteady feet. "I'll put the food back in the oven."

"Great. I'll start the shower."

"Shower?"

His grin widened. "I want to clean you up before I dirty you again."

She bit her lip shyly. He had a wonderfully filthy mind. "That sounds good."

"I'm going for awesome. You can tell me later if I get there." He cradled her face in his hands. "I don't ever want to give you a reason to go to bed with anyone else."

She blushed. He must know she wouldn't. But his expression said otherwise.

Then again, she'd given him too many reasons to think she was still romantically involved with Cutter. She needed to sit him down and set him straight.

Promise me you won't ever tell him we're not a couple. That will be like waving a red cape in a bull's face.

"Don't keep me waiting." Pierce kissed her, then dashed up the stairs.

Brea covered their dishes, then schlepped them into the oven. Back in the dining room, she picked up their clothes and left them folded on the table. Then she headed up the stairs.

She heard the water running, but he hadn't turned on any lights. She stopped halfway down the shadowy hall. The air pinged with tension. "Pierce?"

Brea felt his body heat behind her an instant before he pressed himself into her back and plastered her, front first, against the wall.

He nuzzled his face in her neck. "You're still naked."

His breath made her shiver. Her own turned choppy. "Yes."

"Good. I like you that way." Pierce took her hands and tangled their fingers together. She had no idea what he was doing until he pressed her palms flat against the wall. "Keep them here." Then he shoved his feet between hers and nudged them apart. "I want you splayed out and helpless. You can't stop me from kissing your neck or playing with your pussy. I can rub against you, put my scent all over you, slide my dick inside you again."

And he could. Already she could feel him hard and prodding her backside.

A thick ache of desire she would have sworn moments ago would be impossible to feel replaced her languid satisfaction. "You're a very bad man."

"Who gets off defiling this very good girl."

As his lips trailed across her shoulder, his palms roamed down her ribs, curled in with her waist, then curved out to follow the shape of her hips. His fingers skimmed back and forth, dangerously close to where she ached.

"Pierce…"

"Pretty girl?"

"You're torturing me." Her head fell back to his shoulder, exposing her throat.

He took advantage of the vulnerable space she'd ceded, dragging his lips up her neck to whisper hotly in her ear. "You want me again?"

It was as if all Pierce had to do was touch her and her body went up in flames.

"Yes."

"Not until I can fuck you properly. I want you in my bed, all spread out—waiting and panting and mine."

When he took her hand and led her to the bathroom, she frowned. "You're mean."

"Poor baby…" He shot her a dark smile. "Don't worry. I won't make you wait more than an hour or two."

"What?" she screeched in protest, every inch of her skin already sizzling and tingling for him again.

He laughed as he eased her into the wide walk-in shower. As the warm water cascaded down her body, she moaned with a whole different kind of pleasure, then tilted her head back and let the spray drench her. When she opened her eyes, she found Pierce staring as if he'd never seen any sight sexier in his life.

Brea felt confident, like a vixen who could wrap her big man around her little finger. "Come here. Don't you want to be wet like me?"

"That's a dangerous question."

"Is it?" She raised a brow at him. "What are you going to do?"

His laugh was anything but reassuring. "You can't even begin to guess. I've had weeks to dream up the filthiest ways imaginable to make you scream. My list is long and obscene."

She shivered. If anyone had asked her before meeting Pierce what her sex life would be like ideally one day, she would have said things like loving, pleasant, considerate, and sensitive. But the need he inspired in her was carnal, almost animal. She couldn't *not* want him.

"Want to give me some hints?"

"When I'm enjoying tormenting you this much? No."

He reached for the bottle of shower gel on the nearby shelf and squirted a healthy dollop into his palm, then lathered up his hands. The stare he pinned her with then made her breath catch.

He soaped her shoulders, then he caressed his way back to cover her breasts. He paid gentle attention to her nipples until she dragged in a shuddering breath before he trailed his fingers down her abdomen. "Spread your legs so I can put my hands on your pussy."

That shouldn't turn her on as much as it did. But Brea was done questioning why she enjoyed him talking so dirty to her. Instead, she parted her thighs.

He covered her sensitive sex with one big palm, rubbing and working, circling and pressing until her breath turned more uneven. Her ache gathered and grew. Her knees nearly gave out as she melted into the wall.

Then Pierce swiped the shower head from its mechanism and set the spray against her throbbing flesh.

Brea let out a needy whimper and clutched his shoulders in a silent plea while he rinsed her good and clean with a smug smile.

That wasn't all right with her.

She grabbed the bottle of soap off the shelf, lathered up her hands, and rubbed him all over with a leisurely touch, starting at his chest and slowly working her way down toward the thick stalk of his cock. When she reached it, she skimmed around his erection, focused on his thighs, paid special attention to the scars at his knees, even soaped between his toes with her fingers.

When she glanced up, he'd gathered up the suds sliding down his body and was stroking himself, eyes flaring at the sight of her on her knees.

That gave her an idea.

She leaned to one side, letting the shower spray wash away the lather coating his body. Then she pressed kisses up his flank, to his hip, over to those notches low on either side of his hair-roughened abs. When he closed his eyes with a groan, she moved in.

And licked the swollen purple crest of his hard cock.

"Brea..." He sucked in a rough gasp and slid his fingers in her hair, nudging past her lips and onto her tongue. "Yes, pretty girl. Holy fucking shit..."

His girth stretched her lips and strained her jaw. But he tasted clean, if slightly salty. He smelled like soap and musk and him. She didn't know what she was doing, but there was something both intimate and primal about having the most private part of Pierce's body in her mouth. She'd never imagined she would like oral sex. Well, she'd loved it when he'd gone down on her, but this... It was heady, almost powerful, knowing how much she could affect him.

He let out a shuddering groan, then slowly pulled free. "Okay, you've persuaded me. We'll fuck now."

Brea laughed. He didn't mean that to be funny, and maybe she should have considered it downright crude. But she knew what Pierce meant. She felt it, too. He wanted to connect with her, be inside her.

She needed that so much.

"Glad you're seeing things my way."

Together, they dried off, sharing a towel and kisses before making their way to the bedroom. He flicked on the bedside lamp, bathing the room in a muted golden glow. Without a word, she took his hands, then lay back on the bed, bringing him down with her.

Pierce poised himself over her, cock in hand, crest pressed against her opening. "Did you mean it?"

"What?"

"That you love me?"

She'd never imagined this big warrior, who'd survived a cartel's torture, would look so afraid of her answer.

With a soft smile, she caressed his cheek and said the words with her eyes before they fell from her lips. "Yes."

His sigh of relief sent his whole body forward, onto her, into her. "Brea. My pretty girl..."

She exhaled, feeling complete as he filled her. "Did you mean it?"

Elbows braced on either side of her face, he cradled her cheeks as he worked a slow rhythm in and out of her pussy. "Yeah. You have no idea..."

Then they stopped talking with words and started communicating with their bodies.

By unspoken agreement, it was a long, slow avowal of their feelings. She'd never imagined Pierce could be so gentle, yet his touch held just as much passion. Brea soaked in all his attention and caring. She needed this. After tonight, she didn't know how she would do without it. They still had so many obstacles to navigate, but she tried not to let that daunt her. No, she didn't know when or how they would overcome their hurdles. She was only determined that they would.

Her need rose swiftly, a barely banked fire that he blazed back to life with his touch, his kisses, the sound of her name on his lips. Together, they climaxed, clinging to one another through lingering caresses and shuddering moans.

Then he curled his body around hers as if he'd never held anything more precious in his life. And she cried—for how much he'd suffered, for how renewed she felt in his arms, for how bumpy their road ahead would probably be.

"You okay?" he murmured, skimming her cheek with his knuckles.

"I will be. It's a lot. I'm used to being there for everyone else and only letting go of my emotions when I'm alone. But when I'm with you, I feel so safe and adored. And all my feelings just spill out."

His dark eyes swam with unshed tears. "I've never loved anyone in my life until you."

"No other woman?"

"No one, period. I've never said those three words to anyone but you."

"Except your parents."

Pierce stiffened. "My mother died when I was a baby."

They had that in common, and her heart went out to him. "I'm sorry. I didn't know. I know how that feels, though. Weren't you close to your dad?"

He hesitated a long time, choosing instead to kiss her face, brush his lips over hers, caress the hair from her forehead. Anything except answer her question.

"Pierce?"

He sighed and shifted. She could still feel him inside her, slowly softening, but he pressed in as if he didn't want to leave. "Pierce Senior died when I was fifteen. Since my father was a horrible human being, I'm glad he's gone. I hated him."

"You don't mean that."

"Yeah, I do. It's why I killed him."

The shock of his words had barely registered when his phone chimed with a siren-like peal.

"Fuck," he muttered, then eased free from her. He was gentle about that... not so gentle when he kicked the half-open bedroom door on his way down the stairs to retrieve the device.

Her brain was still replaying his words. Every part of her turned to ice.

Had he really just confessed to killing his father as a teenager out of hate?

Yes.

Why? She'd known he killed for a living, but he ended bad guys to make the world a better place, right? He didn't shoot anyone for sport.

But did that really make it okay? According to the way she'd been raised, no.

She'd conveniently swept his profession under the rug because she'd convinced herself she knew his heart. Even now, she was desperate to believe he had a compelling reason for taking his father's life...

Or had Cutter warned her away from One-Mile precisely because he was the sort of man who didn't need one?

Pierce had defied—no, laughed in the face of—multiple commandments. He had taken the Lord's name in vain and committed murder. Since he believed she belonged to Cutter, he didn't mind committing "adultery," either. And he definitely hadn't honored his father.

Still, she hated to think that Pierce was a bad man.

Because her heart would never let her fall for someone unworthy? Or because her devotion had made her blind to his faults?

Brea darted to her feet, grabbed the bath towel they'd shared, then ran down the stairs to her clothes, only to find Pierce standing beside the dining room table stark naked with the phone pressed to his ear.

"I'm in." He paused. "Yes, I'm sure. When and where?" He listened and nodded. "On my way."

He ended the call, then turned to her with regret, as if he had something unpleasant to say. As if he hadn't terrified and confused the devil out of her moments ago. "I have to leave."

"Where?" But deep down, she knew. She'd been through this with Cutter.

He palmed her shoulders. "I'm sorry. It's work."

A completely new fear ripped through her—that he'd come back bent and broken again. Or worse, in a pine box. "Already? You just got medically cleared today."

Pierce sighed grimly. "Emilo Montilla appeared in the US, not far from where his wife and her sister are staying in a safe house. We have to stop him." He turned and headed for the stairs, then paused.

When he cupped her face, she flinched.

He swore. "I dropped a lot on you about me and my dad. I swear there's an explanation. I'll tell you the whole ugly story when I get back. You'll understand."

But what kind of explanation would make what he'd done all right?

"I promise, Brea. For now...I love you. Please be here when I get home." He brushed a kiss over her frozen lips. "And say you'll move in with me."

wicked ever after

One-Mile & Brea: Part Two

chapter one

Thursday, October 23
Louisiana

Standing naked and numb, in the middle of the empty dining room, Brea Bell blinked. What had just happened?

She felt flattened. Her world had been shaken, turned inside out, upended every which way.

Pierce Walker did that to her.

While her body had still been glowing from the pleasure he'd heaped on her, everything had begun falling apart.

Now he was gone.

The second he had answered the unexpected ring of his phone, her lover had been replaced by pure warrior. Within minutes, he'd dressed, grabbed his bag, and disappeared on a dangerous mission to tangle with the drug lord who had nearly killed him mere weeks ago.

He'd left her terrified for his safety—and burning with so many questions.

She'd known he made his living as a sniper who killed bad guys and terrorists while keeping his fellow operatives safe. At least that's what she'd told herself.

I'm glad my father is gone. I hated him. It's why I killed him.

Until Pierce had uttered those words, she would never have thought him capable of murdering his father in cold blood. How could anyone kill their own flesh and blood? Brea couldn't fathom it, but Pierce had.

And he'd expressed no remorse.

Say you'll move in with me.

His soft, shocking demand just before he'd slipped out the door still rang in her ears. How did Pierce think she could do that without imploding her entire life? And how could she commit to any sort of future with him when she didn't know whether to believe he was the steadfast protector she'd come to know…or concede she'd fallen for a bad-boy fantasy who was good at manipulating her body?

Brea couldn't stay here. She needed to go home. She had to think.

Trembling, she dressed, then defaulted to familiar domestic tasks that calmed her mind. Soon, she'd silenced the music, boxed and stored their food in the refrigerator, and cleared the table. She also made Pierce's bed, trying not to remember just how good it had felt to be underneath him on these very sheets.

Some headstrong part of her wanted to linger, as if the secret to understanding him hid under his roof and she could absorb his truths if she simply remained. But that was her hopeful heart talking.

She had to start using her head.

As she retrieved her purse from the floor, she tucked the half-spilled contents back inside, then glanced at her phone. It was nearly midnight, and her father had texted to ask when she was coming home two hours ago.

On my way.

As soon as her reply was delivered, she darkened the device. Tears threatened to fall, but she stifled them. Once she was in her room, where no one would disturb her, she could start unpacking everything alone.

Brea flipped off lights all over Pierce's house and contemplated leaving his key on the table. But that would be a cowardly way to end their…whatever this was. She owed it to them both to hear his story. Then she'd decide if giving in to her heart and building a future with him was in her best interest.

How ironic. She'd knocked on Pierce's door a few hours ago, hoping they had a chance at a new beginning together. After tonight, she wasn't sure there'd be any coming back.

The silence as she headed through the inky night to Sunset felt heavy. The old her would have called Cutter and asked for his advice. But she already knew what he'd say. She didn't want any opinions now except her own.

When she pulled into her driveway, the house looked dark, except for the light Daddy kept on above the stove whenever she was late. Bless him…

Her fingers fumbled as she unlocked the door. She dead-bolted it behind her, then dashed to her room. In the dark, she dropped her purse on the desk to her left and shut herself inside before she fell across her bed and let her thoughts run free.

Who was this man, deep down, she'd given herself to? What had she done?

She'd fallen in love. She'd let herself believe she and Pierce could forge something lasting, despite their chasm of differences.

And she might have made a colossal mistake.

Brea grasped now why people called it heartache. Hers wrenched with uncertainty and pain. Sobs followed.

Behind her, the lamp on her nightstand suddenly flicked on.

She sat up with a gasp. Her father stood not two feet away, watching her with a disappointed stare.

"Brea." He never yelled. He never had to. His ability to emote, which made him so good behind the pulpit, also made him an amazingly effective parent.

She wiped the tears from her cheeks. "Daddy, what are you doing up? Do you need something?"

With a heavy sigh, he sat beside her and took her hand. "Just to talk to you. You've been the best daughter a man could have asked for, and I know you're a grown woman…"

Brea heard the "but" in his voice. Since she was a pleaser, the worst possible punishment had always been enduring her father's disapproval. "Daddy…"

"Let me finish. I know where you've been and what you've been doing." He frowned.

He'd found out about Pierce? Figured out they'd had sex?

Her heart stopped. "I can explain."

But what could she say to reassure him that wouldn't be a lie?

"You may think I'm naive or out of touch, and I realize almost no one saves themselves for marriage anymore."

She knew where this was going, and it wasn't fair. "Then why are you lecturing me? You're not waiting. I know about you and Jennifer Collins."

"I never said I was perfect. But there's a big difference. Jennifer and I have both been married. We lost our spouses because it was His will—my wife shortly after childbirth, her husband in war. We spent months getting to know each other. We started as friends. We've taken our relationship very slowly. We waited three years to take the step you have with this man you've known for…how long?"

By comparison, her answer would make her sound rash. "Not three years."

"Not even three months. I know your generation has a 'hookup' mentality, but—"

"It's not like that."

"All right," he conceded. "But the fact that I haven't met him—that he hasn't done me the courtesy or you the honor of even showing his face here—concerns me."

Of course Daddy would see it that way. "I didn't think I needed your permission to date someone. I'm an adult."

"You are, but I'm concerned. You haven't acted like yourself in weeks. You've been quiet. Secretive. Sometimes even evasive. I've been worried something was troubling you. So I asked Cutter. He expressed concern about your attachment to this fellow operative, whom he categorized as savage and unprincipled. Dangerous. Not good enough for you."

She wasn't sure what to think about Pierce right now, but she couldn't not defend him. "You don't know him, Daddy. Cutter is biased after they argued during a mission."

"Maybe. But do you know what this man does for a living?"

Her father was gentle. He condemned violence. Though Cutter and Pierce worked on the same team, her friend got a pass because he rescued hostages and often provided first-response medical attention to people in need. He protected those afflicted by war.

Pierce just killed.

"Yes."

And how would Daddy react if he ever found out Pierce not only executed others but had killed his own father?

"Then you understand why, in my eyes, he seems like a taker of virtue and lives. Brea, you falling for someone like this… It's not you."

"He's more than his job. And he saved Cutter's life."

"I'm grateful for that, but I fear he's twisted your naive heart to his advantage." He squeezed her hand. "Sweetheart, I'm not blaming you. I'm not surprised you weren't worldly or strong enough to resist. I just want you to open your eyes."

Brea reared back. Not worldly enough was fair. But strong? "I've taken care of you through two major surgeries while keeping your church activities rolling, handling your parishioners, and still doing my own job. I've always tried to make you proud. But if he's a mistake, Daddy, he's mine to make. I'll handle it."

"I know you've had a lot on your plate. And of course I'm proud of you. Like I said, I've been blessed with the best daughter I could have asked for. But this man—"

"Stop. I've resisted every other temptation. Maybe I didn't resist him because I'm not meant to."

He pressed his hands together, almost as if he prayed for her. "Has he ever discussed marriage?"

"No."

He'd talked about moving in… Something she couldn't do without bringing shame to her father, her church, and her upbringing.

Brea knew these were antiquated concepts to most people her age. Nearly everyone she'd met in cosmetology school thought she was nuts. They'd shunned her because she didn't want to drink at bars, swipe right, or spend her Saturday nights in bed with a stranger. She'd been okay with that—mostly because she'd never been tempted.

Pierce had changed everything.

If he had asked her yesterday to move in, she would have been hard-pressed not to say yes—even knowing she would have had to ask her father for forgiveness and her community for understanding. But for a man she *really* believed in, she would have risked everything.

Now she didn't know if Pierce was truly that man.

Despite her doubts, her heart didn't want to let him go. Most of her drive home, she'd tried to negotiate with herself and rationalize some way in which him killing his own father was okay. Other than self-defense, Brea couldn't think of a scenario.

"Is that why you were crying?"

It was tempting to tell Daddy what he wanted to hear, but compounding a sin with a lie wasn't right. "No. I was crying because I don't know if he and I can work it out."

"I'm sorry if he breaks your heart. Anything that hurts you hurts me. But I hope you'll make the best choice for your future." He took her shoulders in his grip. "If that's not with him, I promise you *will* heal. And someday, you'll find a man who loves you and wants to honor you with vows and his ring."

She understood what he was trying to say. But Pierce hadn't grown up a preacher's kid or steeped in a church. For most people her age, without her upbringing, moving in together was a vast commitment. He probably thought he'd shown her his devotion.

"I want to get married someday. Right now, I'm just trying to figure things out."

His face softened. "I know. And we all make mistakes. It's God's way of teaching us what we need to know. Your red eyes tell me this lesson has been hard for you."

"I hear the cautions you and Cutter are giving me, but my heart wants to believe he's the one."

His smile was full of understanding. "First love is like a fever. It sweeps through your whole body, and you feel so weak in the face of something so strong." He hesitated. "When I was seventeen, I knew what I wanted to be when I grew up. I'd already heard God's calling. But...so many of my friends had girlfriends. And they were having sex. It was fine, I told myself. Resisting temptation was a trial from God, so I stayed strong. Until I met a girl while working my summer job. We had a lot of fun dating in May. By the end of June, I suspected I was in love. Then things got heated. Over Fourth of July, her parents went on vacation and left her behind." He shrugged. "I was weak, and it wasn't my finest moment. I wasn't her first lover, but that didn't matter to me. I loved her. My parents found out what I'd done and they did something amazing for me."

"What?"

"They challenged me not to see her for a month."

Brea frowned. "Why?"

"My father told me that if it was truly love, then a month would change nothing. I would still be in love with her and she would be waiting for me. It was either that or they would take my car keys until school started in September."

"What happened?"

"I chose her and gave them my car keys. I thought walking to work in the heat and missing out on time with my friends would be a small hardship because she would be by my side. As it turned out, not so much. She wasn't as interested in being with me when I couldn't take her places. And by August, she'd found someone else and left me brokenhearted. I spent a miserable month wishing I'd taken my parents' alternative."

Brea understood. That girl clearly hadn't loved him at all.

"So I'm going to ask the same of you."

"Daddy, I'm twenty-two. I paid for my car. I'm not giving it up. Besides, I couldn't get to work without it."

He held up a hand. "That's not what I meant. I'm merely challenging you not to see him for a month so you can figure out how you feel. If he really loves you, he'll wait."

But Daddy's tone made it clear he was convinced Pierce would move on. Brea didn't know what to say.

"By the way, I met your mother four years later. I knew instantly she was the one. We both agreed to explore the sexual part of our relationship after we were married. My wedding night was one of the best of my life because I knew we'd made the right decision. I won't lie; that was a long wait, but so worth it."

Daddy was brilliant at persuading people to look at a situation through his lens. And he often made great points.

"I need to sleep on everything you've said." And she needed to hear what Pierce had to say before she could determine if she needed to fight for him…or let him go.

"Of course. We'll catch up on Saturday. I'm doing my first full day back in the office tomorrow, so I'm expecting a lot of crazy."

"Okay. Let's talk then."

He kissed her forehead. "No matter what, I love you."

"I love you, too."

"Just promise me you'll make decisions that add to *your* happiness before worrying about anyone else's."

"I will."

The following morning, Brea rolled over, stretched, and opened her eyes. Last night when she'd laid her head down, she would have sworn she was far too upset to do anything but toss and turn all night. Instead, the minute her head had hit the pillow, she'd all but fallen into a coma.

She glanced at her bedside clock. Eight thirty? Her first appointment was in an hour. Yikes!

Tossing off her covers, she sat up and bounded out of bed.

Instantly, a crash of nausea dropped her to her knees. She clutched her stomach and barely managed to crawl to the toilet before she lost the contents of her stomach.

Ugh. She must have picked up the stomach flu from one of her clients.

Early in her career as a hairdresser, she'd learned the hard way that the public was germ-filled. She'd been sicker that first year than she'd ever been.

When she'd finished retching, Brea flushed the toilet and lay back on the blessedly cold tile. She was going to have to call into work, darn it. After all the disruptions to her schedule these past few months, she really hated to lose the cash flow—or, potentially, her hard-earned clientele. But it wasn't like she could coif people while she was vomiting.

Brea took some deep breaths, trying to calm her rolling stomach. But the smell of her citrus-vanilla bath beads on the nearby tub stung her nose and revived her urge to throw up.

Seconds later, nausea forced her to pitch her head over the toilet again.

When she'd finished, she pinched her nose closed and picked up the offending box, dragging it—and herself—to the garage, where she dumped the bath beads in the trash to go out with Monday's pickup. The second she let herself back in the house, she sagged against the doorway with a groan.

What the heck was going on? She'd loved that scent since one of her middle school friends had given her those bath beads as a birthday gift. She had repurchased them over and over because they always brought her comfort and pleasure. So why had the smell suddenly made her sick? Well, sicker.

Scents had nothing to do with the stomach flu…

Instantly, a more terrifying reason for her smell sensitivity crowded her brain.

She raced across the house and grabbed her phone from its charger. The first thing she saw was a message from Pierce.

Made it to location. No sign of asshole yet. May be here a few days. I'll call when I can. See you when I get home.

Her relief that he was safe—at least for now—warred with her indecision about their future. But she shoved it aside to launch the app on which she charted her periods.

According to this, she hadn't had one since early August. November was a week away.

That couldn't be right. She couldn't possibly have missed *two* periods.

But she feared her memory wasn't faulty.

August, September, and October had been a whirlwind of craziness—Cutter's hostage standoff, Daddy's relapse and second surgery, Pierce's capture and recovery, keeping the church going, her business flowing… She vaguely remembered thinking earlier this month that she'd missed a period, but she hadn't been shocked, given all the stress she'd been under.

She hadn't really believed that in one night Pierce had gotten her pregnant.

But it was possible. She was tired all the time. Her breasts were tender. She was weepy. She craved sex. The signs were there; she simply hadn't put them together.

Brea sagged back to her bed, staring at the ceiling, and gaped. If she was pregnant…what was she going to do? If Daddy had been disappointed last night, he would be crushed by this news. And what would she tell Pierce? He'd asked her to be his live-in girlfriend, not have his children.

And what kind of father would he, a man who took lives, make?

Don't get ahead of yourself. One thing at a time.

First, she had to find out what she was dealing with.

Thanking goodness Daddy was already at the church, she brushed her teeth and called in sick to work. The receptionist, bless her, promised to contact all her clients and reschedule. Then Brea dragged on some sweatpants and a hoodie, mustered up her courage, shoved down more nausea, and drove to the drugstore.

As she sat in the parking lot at the little pharmacy around the corner, Mrs. Simmons, her first-grade teacher, walked out of the sliding double doors and waved her way. She watched Mr. Laiusta, one of her dad's parishioners, hop out of his car two spots down. Two guys she'd gone to high school with emerged, sodas and chips in hand, and eyed her through her windshield.

She couldn't possibly walk into that store and buy a pregnancy test. Someone would see her. And everyone in town would know her secret by the end of the day.

Swallowing down another wave of sickness, she backed out and drove to Lafayette. She was familiar with the drugstore near the hospital; she'd had some of Daddy's medicines filled there after he'd been discharged. No one at that location would know her. No one would care.

Even so, when she arrived, she braided her long hair, wound it on top of her head, then plucked one of Daddy's discarded ball caps from her backseat and pulled it low over her eyes.

It took her less than five minutes to purchase a pregnancy test. The bored forty-something woman behind the register didn't blink, just counted out her change and looked to the next customer in line.

Bag in hand, Brea froze in indecision near the door. Drive the twenty minutes home to take the test? What if Daddy's first day back at the church had proven overwhelming and he cut his day short to come home? Or what if she messed this test up and needed another one?

She couldn't risk it. Besides, she didn't want to wait any longer than necessary to learn the truth.

Head down, she slinked to the back of the store and found the ladies' room. Thankfully, it was a restroom for one. She shut and locked the door, then tore into the box and scanned the instructions.

As she washed her hands, they shook. Then she sat on the toilet with the test strip.

A wave of nausea swamped her again—a combination of her nerves and the sharp scent of the antiseptic cleanser. She swallowed back another urge to vomit as she finished administering the test. Then she set the strip on her plastic bag strewn across the counter and bent to wash her hands again.

She had to wait three minutes. It would be the longest one hundred eighty seconds of her life.

But as soon as she rinsed the soap and dried her hands, she glanced at the test strip.

Less than a minute had passed, and the result window was already displaying two solid pink lines.

Pregnant.

On a gut level, Brea had expected it, but she still found herself stunned. She looked at herself in the drugstore's grimy, water-splotched mirror. "What am I going to do?"

Her reflection had no reply.

She broke down and sobbed.

Everything in her life was about to change.

Why hadn't she insisted on a condom? Why hadn't he ever used one?

Maybe he just hadn't cared. After all, he wasn't the one pregnant now... He didn't have to pick up the pieces or face his community or raise his child alone.

The handle jiggled, then a light tap sounded at the door. "Someone in there?"

"Just a minute," she answered automatically, then gathered up the bag, box, and test before throwing them all in the garbage. Then she swiped away her tears, tried to plaster on a fake smile, and opened the door.

As she walked out, a woman with a baby on her shoulder and a diaper bag in hand gave her a little smile. "Thanks."

Then the door closed. Brea was alone, with the rest of her life stretching out, endless and terrifying, in front of her.

What was she going to do?

She slid her hand over her still-flat belly and exhaled. Apparently, she was going to have a baby.

But without hurting her father, jeopardizing her career, and tearing apart her community, how? And how would Pierce feel about this?

Mechanically, Brea eased into her car and headed back to Sunset. Traffic was light. She didn't remember the drive.

When she reached home, she parked and ran into the house. She tore off her clothes and slid back into her pajamas. The house was so quiet. She felt utterly alone—shocked and scared. Eventually, she'd have to get up and face her problems like an adult, and she knew her tears were pointless. But right now she needed to shed them, just like she needed reassurance that somehow, someway, everything would be all right.

She needed Cutter.

He was in Dallas, working. Normally, she would never call while he was on the job. But he would hear and understand her like no one else.

Brea grabbed her phone from the purse she'd discarded at the foot of her bed and dialed her best friend. Before he even answered, more tears sprang to her eyes.

"Hey, Bre-bee."

"C-Cutter, hi. I hate to call you…but I could use an ear."

"What's wrong?"

"This is probably a bad time, and I'm sorry. Really. But I don't know where else to turn."

"Slow down. It's okay. Tell me what's going on."

"I woke up this morning and I felt horrible. I didn't know what was wrong and then I… Ugh. I'm talking too much. But I'm afraid to just blurt everything. You're going to be mad. Everyone will be shocked. Daddy will be disappointed. I just"—her breaths came so quick and shallow that she feared hyperventilating—"don't know how to say this but…I think I'm pregnant."

"What?" he growled. "Have you seen a doctor?"

"No. I bought a test at a drugstore in Lafayette and took it in their bathroom. I'm still in shock. B-but I'm shaking and I can't stop crying. I don't know what to do."

"Make an appointment today. Find out for sure. If you're right, this isn't going to go away."

"I can't see Dr. Rawson. The first thing he'll do is tell my dad. I know he's not supposed to but…" She shook her head and tried to think of solutions instead of continuing to dump problems on him. "What about that clinic near your apartment?"

"Fine. Call there. But you need to see a doctor before you make any decisions. I'll go with you if you want. I'm home in a week. I promise not to confront Walker until then. But if you're right—"

"You can't say or do anything to him."

"The hell I can't."

"He doesn't know yet. He left on a mission last night, and I don't know when he'll be back. He's gone after the guy who held him captive in Mexico, so I don't even know if he'll return in one piece. I'm worried." She clutched the phone. "You have to promise me—"

"That when he shows his ugly face I won't kill him? I can't promise that."

"Cutter, you aren't helping."

"All right." His voice took a gentle turn. "I promise we'll figure this out. I'll take care of you. I always have. I always will. And I hate to do this to you now, but I have to go."

"Are you in a situation?"

"Client meeting."

She winced. "I'm sorry."

"No, I'm glad you called me. As soon as I'm free, we'll talk, okay?"

"Thanks."

The sudden silence in her ear told her that Cutter had ended the call. The sound was lonely and terrifying. And when she darkened her own device and tossed it on the bed, she lowered her head in her hands and started to cry again.

chapter two

Wednesday, October 29
Orlando, Florida

"YOU REALIZE THIS IS THE WORK OF OUR INTERNAL MOLE," Hunter Edgington said over the phone.

"I'd come to the same conclusion." One-Mile paced the small bedroom in the thoroughly average house located in Orlando, itching to get out. "Who else knew you'd stashed Valeria Montilla on the outskirts of St. Louis?"

"While she and her son lived there alone? Only Logan, Joaquin, and me. After we pulled Laila out of Montilla's Mexican compound when we rescued you? We had to make all those last-minute arrangements to get her to Valeria's, so the whole damn team knew."

"Which means we're back to square one trying to figure out who the fucking traitor is."

"For now," Hunter admitted. "But it appears you've relocated Valeria and her family to Florida without Montilla being any wiser."

At least something good had come out of this shit show. "Who on our team knows Valeria's new location?"

"Besides Logan and Joaquin? Just you."

"I suggest we keep it that way."

"That's the consensus here. The fewer people who know, the better."

"Yep." But it was bugging the shit out of One-Mile not to know who had tipped off Montilla about Valeria's St. Louis safe house. Which asshole on his team couldn't be trusted?

It was also bugging the shit out of him to be away from Brea.

When Hunter had called and said it was imperative he get to St. Louis and relocate Montilla's estranged wife from her no-longer-safe house before sunrise, One-Mile had just asked Brea to move in with him. The timing of the mission had sucked. He'd hated leaving her so abruptly, especially right after dumping his daddy bullshit on her with no explanation. But she loved him, and he loved her. Lives had been on the line.

So he'd left and caught a charter flight to St. Louis. By three thirty a.m., he'd been pounding on Valeria's door. Telling her that the feds had spotted her estranged husband in the area hadn't gone over well. Insisting the terrified woman pack up her infant son and her sister, along with whatever they could fit in his rented van so they could be gone before sunrise had been met with rants and tears. But she'd done it.

For the next two days, he'd driven two tense women and a fussy baby halfway across the country to this rental in Orlando—and safety. But One-Mile was still on edge.

He hadn't talked much to Brea in almost a week. He hadn't been worried at first. He'd been busy as hell until Sunday, and he'd known she spent that day with her dad and the church. But he'd only heard snippets from her on Monday and Tuesday. Yes, she'd locked his house up behind her. No, she wasn't angry that he'd had to leave. Of course she wanted to talk when he got home.

But there was something she wasn't saying. Something bothering her. He was itching to get home and address it.

"You haven't seen any sign of Montilla since you arrived, right?" Hunter asked.

"No." He'd been in Orlando over seventy-two hours. And he knew damn well they hadn't been followed. "I think the coast is clear. Do we have any idea where Montilla is now or if he's figured out his wife has relocated?"

"A few hours after you pulled out of St. Louis, he was spotted less than two miles from her safe house."

Closer than in previous sightings. But the asshole obviously hadn't known his estranged wife's location or he would have already torn the place apart. "But nothing since then?"

"No."

That gave One-Mile an idea. "Did he come with his entourage?"

"Since this is a personal thing, we think he's alone. He has been every time he's been spotted, according to the feds."

Perfect. "I want to go back to St. Louis and find him."

"By yourself?"

"Yeah."

"No. You need to stay with the client. If we were going to send you after him, we'd have someone watching your back."

One-Mile scoffed. "You sent me in with Trees last time. Look how well that worked out."

"Without a heads-up from him, we wouldn't have known you'd been captured for days."

"But how do you know he wasn't the one who set me up? I won't say his escape was convenient but…"

Hunter didn't have a comeback for that, which told One-Mile that possibility had crossed his mind.

"Let me try," he pressed again.

"It's too risky."

"Are you fucking kidding me? Risk is what we do. Once Montilla figures out that Valeria and his son are gone, he might slink back over the border and it will be a shitload harder to reach him. She will never be safe until that fucker is dead or behind bars. We can make that happen. *I* can take care of him. Just give me a green light."

"No. You want revenge, and that's not your mission. I won't have you going off on some crusade. You'll get your ass killed. You've barely been cleared to be back at work, and—"

"This is bullshit," One-Mile growled. "Why leave this son of a bitch on the loose?"

"Because it's the feds' responsibility to hunt Montilla and kill him like the animal he is—not yours. And because I said to stay there another few days to make sure Valeria is settled and safe. We were hired to transition her, period."

"I've done that."

"So finish the fucking job before you haul off on your own agenda."

One-Mile didn't like his pile-of-shit reasoning or his attitude.

"When can I come home? I have more doctors' appointments," he lied.

"Sunday."

That gave him four days to catch Montilla. If he succeeded, he'd be taking one more scumbag off his cartel throne and keeping Valeria's family safe. If he died… well, no one at EM Security Management would care.

But he hated leaving Brea behind.

He'd compartmentalized his concerns, but pacing his ten-by-ten cookie-cutter cage with nothing to do… It was hard not to wonder what was running through her head. Was she upset? Shocked? Or just swamped?

"Before you hang up, I got a question. Is Bryant in town?" And doing his best to smooth-talk Brea away from him?

"Cutter is still in Dallas. I expect him home Friday. This morning, he got a goddamn concussion. Someone whacked him in the back of the head while he was peeing."

It was so ridiculous, One-Mile would have laughed except he knew it would annoy Hunter. The good news was, Cutter horning in on his woman wasn't the reason for her distance. "Thanks. I'll be home Sunday."

"Call me if you spot Montilla anywhere in Orlando."

"Sure." But One-Mile's gut said the drug lord was still sniffing around St. Louis, trying to pick up his wife's scent. He wasn't letting that fucker go.

Hunter hung up. And One-Mile went back to pacing. How could he draw Montilla out? How could he get a jump on the sadistic asshole and stop his reign of violence? If One-Mile could get word to the drug lord about Valeria's former safe house, he would be waiting… But they weren't exactly pals, and he didn't know who Montilla might be connected to in St. Louis.

But they apparently had a mutual contact inside EM Security Management. Why not kill two motherfuckers with one missile?

Question was, who on his own team should he take aim at? He was only going to get one shot at this…

As much as One-Mile loathed the fucking Boy Scout, Cutter was too forthright and upstanding for this turncoat shit. That left Josiah, Zy, and Trees. Gut feeling?

This wasn't Josiah's speed. He kept his nose clean and kept to himself. Zy seemed too busy chasing their receptionist's skirt to pay attention to much else. Not that it had done him much good. Sure, Tessa stared at him like she might be interested in more than a friendly handshake, but they'd likely respected EM's zero-tolerance policy with regard to fraternization—at least so far.

One-Mile's money was on Trees. But he needed a test…and after a few minutes of scheming, he came up with a plan.

He dashed off an email asking Tessa to pass an attachment with the exact address and schematic of the St. Louis safe house to Trees. As a professional courtesy, of course, since they'd gone to Acapulco together. Naturally, he left out the part about it being abandoned. He'd also included a note that he'd debrief everyone else when he got back into town.

Like hell.

The communication would look more official going through the office, so Trees was more likely to take it at face value. Their efficient little receptionist would do as requested without asking questions. And Hunter wouldn't find out until later…if he found out at all.

This was a win-win. If Montilla turned up at Valeria's former address in the next few days, then he'd have a fucker to mete justice to *and* a two-timing rat to expose.

He'd deal accordingly.

But he had to jet back to St. Louis now. Tessa wouldn't forward that email until she came into the office at eight tomorrow morning. Which meant he'd likely see Montilla in twenty-four hours or less.

One-Mile intended to be ready.

After throwing all his belongings back into his duffel, he opened the door and prowled through the dusky shadows. Laila sat in front of the TV.

She glanced over at him, then down at the bag in his hand. "You're leaving."

He nodded. "Where's your sister?"

"Napping with the baby."

"I need you to listen to me. I'm going to St. Louis to track this motherfucker down."

Laila nodded solemnly, but he saw her relief. "Thank you. Will you kill him?"

"I'd like to." But the US government wanted Montilla. If he offed the drug lord on US soil for any reason other than self-defense, they'd crucify him and haul him off to jail. "At the very least, I'm going to get him off your back. Here's my number. If he turns up here, get out and call me immediately. Do you have a gun?"

"I am not supposed to."

Because she wasn't in the country legally. He shook his head. "That isn't what I asked. Do you have one?"

Finally, she nodded. "I keep it loaded. Because of the baby in the house, my sister is against it…"

"Keep it up high and keep the safety on. He hasn't started walking yet, so he shouldn't be able to find it and hurt himself. But never put it more than five feet from you. Never let the battery on your phone die. Watch everyone around you everywhere you go. Sleep with one eye open."

"I already do."

One-Mile wasn't surprised. After all the abuse she'd endured at Montilla's compound, she probably trusted no one.

His face softened. "You should start seeing a counselor."

She recoiled. "I would rather forget."

"You're not going to without help. I've been doing this long enough to know that." He didn't press any more. He wasn't here to harp on her. "If anything happens, especially if you see Montilla, call me. Day or night."

Laila nodded. "Thank you. I am glad you are the one who came to move us. It made me feel safe."

Because he'd had her naked and chosen not to touch her? Probably. He wished he could erase what those assholes had done to her.

"Take care."

Then he was gone. Once they had unpacked the rental, he'd returned the van, so he took a taxi straight to the airport and finagled a seat on the next flight, which left in less than two hours. After a layover, he would arrive in St. Louis in the wee hours of the morning.

While waiting for his plane to board, One-Mile stared at his phone again. Maybe he could catch Brea at the end of her workday. But when he dialed, no answer. Again. This time he didn't leave a message. He didn't want anyone to know where he was going.

With a curse, he hung up, then boarded the aircraft and decided he'd best catch a few hours' sleep.

Stopping the son of a bitch who'd nearly broken him—without his bosses figuring it out—wouldn't be easy, but he was determined. Once that was done, he'd go back to Lafayette, find Brea, explain his past and reassure her, then make her his for good.

Thursday, October 30
St. Louis

One-Mile arrived at the safe house just before one a.m. He doubted Montilla had gotten a message yet from EM's mole, but just in case, he perused the neighborhood. Quiet. Nothing out of the ordinary.

So he crept around the back of the house and let himself in with the key he'd pocketed the day they'd left.

He flipped on a few lights, figuring that if the place was being watched, it would look lived in.

A tornado would have had less impact on the interior. Valeria had only been able to pack for herself and her son what they could fit in a couple of suitcases. Laila hadn't struggled as much since she'd come with nothing and had acquired very little in a month. But Valeria had passed most of her pregnancy and all of her son's short life in this house. He knew leaving had been difficult.

Too bad this mission wasn't about putting everyone out of their misery and ending Montilla. One-Mile didn't bother lying to himself; he wanted revenge. And if the drug lord were no longer on this planet, his estranged wife could stop looking over her shoulder and fearing for her safety. Laila could finally breathe. Baby Jorge wouldn't be at risk of growing up without a mother.

But the scumbag wasn't worth losing his job or risking the wrath of his government. And Brea would be horrified if he intentionally added to his body count, rather than letting the wheels of justice do the job. So, he was going to be a good boy, even though he hated it.

He had a plan and a few hours to kill before Montilla likely showed. Right now was about fortifying this place and getting some rest.

The house didn't have an alarm system, and even if it had, it would have been some prefab piece of shit a guy like Montilla could easily skirt. So One-Mile got creative.

He opened the pantry and pulled out a dozen cans of soups and vegetables, then scanned the labels. Since airport food was barely edible, he'd skipped it. Now, he set aside some chili, opened the rest of the cans, and dumped their contents down the garbage disposal. Finally, he searched the house until he found a spool of twine and an icepick.

Not perfect, but he'd make it work.

While he heated the chili, he stabbed holes in the empty cans and tied them together. Then he attached a set to the handles of both the front and back doors. It wouldn't keep anyone out, but if an intruder tried to barge in while he slept, the cans rattling across the tile would serve as an early warning system. Finally, he checked all the windows in the house to ensure they were locked.

While he ate the chili, he scooped up the clothes Valeria had left strewn around and lamented having to leave behind. He tossed them in a big box he found in her closet, then emptied the rest of the baby's drawers in there, too. Since he had a little bit of space left, he included a couple of pacifiers and a few boxes of baby oatmeal, then taped it all up and shoved it in the back of the car she'd forgone. If he survived, he'd UPS her stuff to Florida. If he didn't…well, most of Valeria's things would already be packed for her. She wouldn't care about his fate.

As One-Mile took his last bite of chili, he glanced around. The place looked a bit more orderly, but tidying the shithole wasn't his concern. He needed sleep.

He found a roll of wide tape and some thumbtacks in Valeria's craft room, then stuck the heads of the wide pins to the tape and set a few strips in front of the door to Laila's bedroom. He'd sleep there since her room had multiple exit points.

Then he double-checked his weapon and drifted off in the dark corner of the house.

The night passed peacefully. So did most of the rest of the next day.

One-Mile ran out to grab some supplies, sent Valeria's box to Orlando because he was a nice guy, then returned to the house and started preparing for his uninvited visitor's arrival.

As evening came and went, his tension grew. If dawn came without an appearance from Montilla, he'd have to re-examine his supposition that Trees was the traitor. Until then, he'd operate on the premise that any intruder who wanted to steal stuff broke in during the day; anyone who wanted to kill crept in at night. And he'd act accordingly.

So after ignoring hordes of inconvenient trick-or-treaters, One-Mile turned off the interior lights just before midnight and stuffed pillows under the covers in Valeria's bed. He snatched an oblong throw pillow off the sofa and set it under one of the remaining baby blankets in the abandoned crib.

If Montilla came, he'd kill Valeria before he took the baby, but on the off chance he wanted to get a look at his son before he offed the boy's mother, One-Mile would be ready.

Until then…his thoughts turned to Brea. Nothing new from her today. Was she busy at work? Had her father had another relapse? Was she thinking about their last evening together? He wished he knew, but it was too late to disturb her now. And he had to keep focus.

Bathed in darkness and attuned to the still, One-Mile waited. If there was one thing a good sniper needed, it was patience. In the rest of his life, he hated waiting for anything. But when it came to ending scum bags, he could drag that shit out forever as long as it meant bagging his target.

Sure enough, a little after two a.m., he heard the jiggle of the handle at the back door. Figuring that was Montilla's most likely entry point, he'd taken the string of cans off the knob. No reason to let the enemy know he was onto him.

Instead, he melted into the shadows in the adjacent hall and peeked into the living room. After a little more rattling and a few clicks, the knob turned. The door swept open.

Montilla ducked in—alone.

He glanced at the baby swing and toys in the corner where Valeria had left them, then crept through the family room.

Wearing a ghost of a smile, Montilla tiptoed straight for the master bedroom—something he could only do if he knew the layout of the house. And he could only know that if Trees had passed on the schematic.

That motherfucker.

But he'd deal with the back-stabbing giant later. Now was all about taking off the head of the snake.

Once Montilla entered the bedroom, One-Mile slipped out of the shadows and crept across the floor toward him.

His heart revved. He gritted his teeth and put a chokehold on his fury. God, he'd love to raise his gun and double-tap the slimy son of a bitch. It sucked that he couldn't.

A few feet in front of him, the drug lord eased toward the bed, bare hands outstretched menacingly, then yanked back the blankets on the big bed. "Get ready to die, bitch!"

"Sorry. You get me instead." Before Montilla could whirl and attack, One-Mile smacked the drug lord on the head with the butt of his weapon. The sadistic bastard crumpled to the ground.

Time to take this fucker down a few notches…

Yes, he should just call the cops and wait for them to come arrest Montilla. But where was the fun in that?

Besides, he'd come so far and given the silent bird to so many people just to have a few minutes of quality time with this fucking asswipe. One-Mile intended to enjoy every moment.

He withdrew a blade from his pocket and cut off Montilla's shirt. Then, with a smile, he hogtied the son of a bitch—one of the many useful skills his granddad had taught him during his summers in Wyoming—and hauled him to the bathtub, setting him facedown. He closed the tub's stopper and flipped on the cold water.

Montilla came up howling and sputtering in the dark. "Son of a bitch! Who are you? What do you want?"

"Shut the fuck up and listen, Emilo. First, you're never getting your hands on Valeria or Laila again. I've made damn sure of that. Second, I owe you for the sparkling hospitality you showed me in Mexico."

"Walker?" When One-Mile flipped on the glaring overhead light, Montilla turned his head and met his gaze with a scowl. "Let me go, and I might allow you to live."

"I don't think so, you lying sack of shit. You almost killed me the first time. But I'm going to be a nice guy and show you a little mercy. Not much…but you'll live. I think. If not? Oops."

With a chuckle, he splashed water across Montilla's back, dipped the sponge-cushioned clamps of jumper cables under the tub's spray, then hauled the car battery he'd procured near his feet. Finally, he attached the cables to the top of the power source.

As he leaned in, Montilla's eyes went wide. "No!"

"Oh, yeah." He laid the wet sponges coursing with electric current against Montilla's ribs.

The asshole jolted, bowed, and screamed before he sniveled and begged.

After a satisfying series of uncontrolled twitches and a hint of burning flesh, One-Mile lifted the jumper cables away. "Are we clear?"

Montilla panted. "I will kill you."

"Those are big words for a guy with his wrists attached to his ankles behind his back. Besides, you're on US soil now, motherfucker. I'm sure the feds would be very interested in knowing your location…"

Montilla spit at him, his eyes full of fire and hate. "Killing is too good for you. I will capture your family and torture them slowly until they die like the pleading, whimpering dogs they are."

"Wow. That sounds really dramatic. I'll bet that threat usually works well—on other people. Me? Sorry. I don't have any family."

"Every man has a weakness. I will find those you hold dear and—"

One-Mile jabbed the wet jumper cables against his ribs again and listened to Montilla scream. "Shut up. Didn't anyone ever tell you that acting like a dick won't make yours bigger?"

After a few more seconds of uncontrollable jolting and hair burning, One-Mile retracted the cables.

Montilla panted as his body went limp—until he realized he was belly down and face first in a tub with the water level rising steadily.

"Turn it off!" the drug lord demanded.

"Because I'm a good guy, I'll show you more mercy than you showed me." One-Mile turned the water flow down but not off.

Montilla eyed the still-rising water. "Are you trying to drown me, you crazy bastard?"

"I'd be doing the world a favor, but no."

The drug lord ripped a murderous stare in his direction. "I will find those you love and make them suffer."

"Blah, blah, blah. If you can't shut the fuck up, I might have to rest my boot on your head for a few minutes. You know, with your face in the water. Just until you stop breathing."

Montilla jerked and cursed. "I heard that, when you were in the hospital, there was a pretty brunette who never left your bedside. My men said you were smitten."

One-Mile froze. Montilla's thugs had *seen* Brea?

He tried not to show any reaction. "She's not mine. Girlfriend of a teammate. I don't do permanent, and I don't believe in love."

Well, the old him hadn't. Brea had changed him.

"I don't believe you."

One-Mile scowled. "I don't care."

But he did. If Montilla's men had been watching, how much did they know about Brea? About the two of them together?

"I think you are lying. But perhaps I am mistaken." Montilla sneered. "After all, who would love you?"

"I could ask you the same. I know you took your wife from her little impoverished village at sixteen and forced her to marry you. Is it any wonder she left you the first chance she got?" Then he waved his hand in the air as he finally kicked off the water that had now risen to the prick's chin. "You know what? This conversation is boring me. I think it's time to put an end to this."

"You will not kill me." Montilla's sneer was full of bravado, but he didn't actually look convinced.

One-Mile picked up the thick lead pipe he'd found in the garage and thumped it against his palm. "Say nighty-night."

Then he swung and hit the asshole on the back of his head with just enough force to knock him temporarily unconscious. He drained the tub, carted the battery away, extracted the burner phone he'd procured earlier, and dialed the only number he had pre-programmed.

"St. Louis Police Department, Narcotics Division."

"Do you know who Emilo Montilla is?"

"Who is this?" the cop asked.

One-Mile didn't answer. "Do you know who I'm talking about?"

"Who doesn't?"

"Write this address down." He rattled the information off to the detective. "Montilla broke into that house. I put a stop to him. You'll find him facedown and unconscious in the tub. Hurry…"

"Who are you?"

One-Mile hung up and hauled ass out of the house, hopping into Valeria's abandoned car. He was already heading for the freeway when he heard the sirens.

One-Mile scrapped his plan to drive Valeria's car to her in Florida, then fly home on Sunday.

In case Montilla could somehow make good on his threat, he needed to warn Brea now. It couldn't wait.

Through the thick of night, he forced the little compact down the highway at speeds not intended for this small engine, refusing to stop for food or drink. The trip that should have taken over ten hours, he managed in less than eight.

At ten on Saturday morning, he screeched up in front of the preacher's house. He feared Brea would be at the salon, already doing someone's hair. But her car still sat in the driveway.

Thank fuck.

As he yanked the keys from the little import's ignition, the front door opened. He hauled ass up the walkway just as Brea emerged and headed for her vehicle, staring at her phone.

The sight of her alive and in one piece sent visceral relief sluicing through his body. He'd fucking missed her like he'd been gone for a year, not nine damn days. He visually inhaled her, but that only made him hungrier.

She'd dressed in a billowy gray sweater and black leggings he'd love to peel off her. She'd piled her hair in a haphazard knot. Even under the layers of makeup she didn't usually wear, she looked too pale. Almost sick.

Though he preferred her bare faced and bare assed, right now he was just so fucking glad to see her.

"Brea!"

Her head snapped up. When she spotted him, she stopped short and blinked. "Pierce, you're back. When did you—"

"Just now." He closed the remaining distance between them and took her shoulders. "Is your dad home?"

"No. He's at the church."

"Good." Without warning, One-Mile shoved her into the house, crowding her against the adjacent wall with his body, then locked the door. He stared out the glass opening. No one had followed him; he'd been watching. He breathed a sigh of relief.

It felt so good to be close to Brea, but he could only afford a few minutes with her right now. He had to keep his head. "I need to talk to you. It can't wait."

"Okay. I-I need to talk to you, too. There's something you should—"

"Let me go first." He didn't have the luxury of being polite.

Frustration bubbled. Why had he hopped on his high fucking horse and decided it was his responsibility to make sure Valeria lived so that Baby Jorge grew up with his mom?

You know the answer to that.

But why the hell hadn't he simply captured the drug lord and immediately called the police?

Because, dumb ass, you couldn't have your pound of flesh, so you insisted on stealing an ounce or two. Way to go.

Now, he was paying for his stupidity. No matter how much he ached for Brea, he couldn't be with her until he knew Montilla was behind bars for good—or dead.

"Listen, Brea. I hate like hell to do this, but something has happened." One-Mile tried not to terrify her. "I can't see you for a while."

"I know you just got back. This can wait. My weekends are always busy. In fact, I'm late for a client now, but—"

"It will be longer than a few days. I'm not sure how much. We could be talking months."

Shock crossed her face before she frowned. "What do you mean?"

How the hell could he drop the bomb on her that a dangerous drug lord wanted to kill her slowly and painfully? He couldn't without scaring the shit out of her. "Like I said, something's happened. It's complicated and it's my fault…but we need to take a step back." Fuck, he was bungling this. "What I'm trying to say is—"

"So you don't want me to move in?"

He did. He'd love to have her against him every night. But he would choose her safety over his happiness every fucking day. Explaining that was a scary, long-winded bitch.

He heard the tick-tick-ticking of time in his head. The second the Tierra Caliente organization talked to their captured drug lord, they would haul ass to Lafayette with revenge on their minds. He didn't worry about himself. If he died, he died.

But Brea couldn't be anywhere near him.

"Not now. I'll explain when I can but—"

"Actually, don't worry." Her face closed up. Her eyes filled with tears.

He tensed. "What does that mean?"

"I was going to say no anyway."

Seriously? He hadn't fucking seen that coming. The night he'd left, she'd claimed she loved him. Now suddenly she'd decided to give him a polite fuck off? Because she'd interpreted his words as a breakup…or because she genuinely didn't want him anymore? "Why?"

"Pierce, I'm a preacher's daughter. I can't shack up with a man, especially one my father has never met. The fact that shocks you tells me we weren't suited anyway."

That hadn't crossed his mind…and it should have. *Fuck.*

Looking ready to dissolve into tears, she shoved against him and edged toward the door. "I have to go."

Seriously, that was it? She was done talking? Pain spread through his chest and ice-picked through his veins.

One-Mile sucked at relationships. Did her hesitation have anything to do with his confession about his father? Probably, but he couldn't stay to fix it. He couldn't fucking risk her. "So do I, but we *will* talk about this later."

"What's the point?" Brea wrenched the door open.

Before she could flee, he slapped a big palm over her head and slammed it shut, locking them in again. He should let her go; he knew it. Instead, he stupidly backed her against the door and slanted his mouth over hers, ravaging her like he intended to tattoo her taste on his tongue.

After a little gasp, she grabbed him with desperate fingers, dragged him closer, and opened to him. He tasted her desperation as he sank deep and reveled in her softness. Their breaths merged. Her body clung.

Fuck, she felt like home.

Suddenly, she pushed him away and glared with accusing eyes. "Stop. You have your reasons for not wanting me to move in and—"

"Because while I was gone—"

"I don't care why you changed your mind or who you slept with or…whatever. My dad found out about us and asked me not to see you for a month. After thoughtful consideration, I think he may be right."

"What?" Why the fuck would she think that?

Because she didn't love him, after all?

"We were never going to work out. It's best if you don't come back." She shoved him away and wriggled out the door.

One-Mile watched, too stunned to stop her.

By the time he surged outside in pursuit, she had already climbed in her car. He bit back the urge to call out to her. What good would it do?

She thought it was over, and she would keep her distance. It was best...for now.

But the second this shit with Montilla got sorted, he would hunt her down and resolve everything. He'd explain. He'd even beg if he had to. And since she couldn't simply move in with him, he would propose. He loved her. He wanted to spend his life with her.

As soon as he figured out what the fuck had happened to change her mind.

One-Mile watched Brea drive away with a curse, vowing that he would set eyes—and every other part of him—on her again.

chapter three

Saturday, November 1
Louisiana

As everyone in the salon joked and laughed around her, Brea held in a sob. Pierce didn't want her anymore. Sure, he'd come up with an excuse, but the truth was he'd pushed her away. He'd lied. He had never loved her.

That reality pelted her brain in a litany through the long day of stilted smiles and prying clients.

It took all her will not to break down, but she refused to weep over a man who'd abruptly decided she wasn't enough for him.

Still, she couldn't stop turning their brief conversation over in her head.

If he no longer wanted or loved her, why had he rushed home to see her? And kissed her as if his life depended on it?

The man had always confused her.

As she swept the last of the hair from the floor and stored the broom, the chime on the empty salon's front door rang. She turned, hoping to see a friendly face.

Cutter appeared around the privacy partition dividing the front desk from the clients. "Hey, Bre-bee."

"You're back!" She ran to him.

He opened his arms and hugged her tight. "You okay?"

She clung gratefully. He'd always been her lifeline. "Tell me what happened to you. Your client got kidnapped? And you got a concussion?" She skimmed her fingertips across his face. "That's a nasty scrape on your cheek, but whatever gave you that bruise at your temple must have hurt like the dickens. And what about that long scratch on your chin?"

Cutter pulled back with a scowl. "I'll heal. But it wasn't my finest case. Thankfully, Jolie Quinn, my client, kept her head up. Her corporate security specialist, Heath, managed to save her. They both got out alive."

"Oh, thank goodness everyone is all right."

"I'm not going to lie. Wednesday was rough. I should have done better."

She laid a comforting hand on his shoulder. "I know you. I'm sure you did everything you could."

"Except pee with my back against the wall," he groused. "But how are you? Feeling any better?"

Brea glanced into the break room to make sure everyone had, in fact, left. Finding it empty, she returned to Cutter's side with a frown. "Not so good. Lots of nausea and exhaustion."

"Your text said your doctor appointment is Monday morning at eleven?"

She nodded. "Can you make it?"

"I'll be there."

"Thanks. And thanks for coming to see me. I could use a friend." Tears filled her eyes.

So much for her vow not to cry. But at the thought of never seeing Pierce again, hot drops scalded her cheeks.

"Hey, Bre-Bee, shh... I know you're worried. But don't borrow trouble until you've seen the obstetrician and—"

"P-Pierce broke up with me this morning."

"What?" His mouth pinched. His nostrils flared. His fists clenched. "Are you kidding me? You told him you were pregnant, and that motherfucker—"

"I didn't get to tell him. I don't know what happened…" She sniffled. "Before he left on a mission last Thursday, he told me he loved me. He asked me to move in with him. But when he showed up at my house this morning, he…"

She couldn't finish that sentence without falling apart.

"Dumped you. What reason did he give?"

"He didn't. He just said that something had come up and he couldn't see me anymore. But he seemed impatient. Or nervous. I'm not sure. And he talked to me like…he was already half out the door."

"Oh, Bre-bee." He caressed her back and held her as the tears she didn't want to shed fell freely. "I'm sorry."

"You warned me." She dragged in a deep breath and tried to stop blubbering. "B-but I'm so confused… When he told me he didn't want me to move in anymore, I told him it was impossible anyway and tried to leave. Then he grabbed me and kissed me like he didn't want to let me go."

"Don't look for logic where Walker is concerned. You gave yourself to him in good faith because you fell for him. He's just an asshole who played you. I hate that. And I hate him." He gritted his teeth. "But now, it's over. You have to move on. I'll kick his ass for you."

"You can't. That won't solve anything. I just don't know what I'm going to do if the doctor confirms I'm pregnant."

"Well, Pierce wasn't going to be much help as a father anyway, so don't bother giving two shits about him."

She couldn't put this on his shoulders. "Cutter…"

"Fine." He clenched his jaw, which told her he wanted to say something more but didn't to keep the peace. "I won't bad-mouth him anymore. But I'm right. He's gone, and you're better off. Don't worry. You know I've always taken care of you." He squeezed her shoulders. "I always will."

One-Mile ambled around his house, shaking his goddamn head. Everywhere he looked, he saw Brea. Clutching her cookies in his foyer. Bending over his pool table. Undressing in his dining room. Spreading her naked body across his bed.

And now she was gone—he feared for good.

Goddamn it, he felt like he'd taken a dull knife, jabbed it into his chest, and fucking gutted himself.

You always suspected you were all wrong for her. Good job proving it.

"Fuck off," he snarled at the voice in his head.

He glanced at the wall clock. A little after six. After driving all night, he should have been starving and exhausted. He should have consumed half his refrigerator and crashed until dusk. But no. He'd choked down an egg and a few crackers, taken a scalding shower, then tossed and turned in his pristinely made bed for a few hours.

Sleep hadn't come, not with his head turning and his guts rolling.

He opted for whiskey instead.

Bottle in hand, he screwed off the cap, planted himself in front of his massive-ass TV, and flipped through the college football games. But he didn't give a shit who won or lost.

Hell, he wasn't sure he'd ever really give a shit about anything again except losing Brea.

On that cheerful note, he chugged a good quarter of the bottle in one long swallow. If he was going to get completely trashed, why wait?

But as he lifted the bottle to his lips again, someone began pounding on his door.

His money was on Cutter.

By now Brea had probably told her daddy-approved boyfriend that he'd been an absolute asswipe to her. Cutter would come in, full of vitriol and swinging fists.

One-Mile welcomed it, and Cutter wouldn't hold back. With physical pain to focus on, maybe One-Mile could forget how much his breaking heart fucking hurt.

With a sigh, he lunged to his feet and headed toward the insistent knocking. "I know you came to beat the shit out of me. Don't say anything. Just do it, okay?" He wrenched the door open and reared back. "You're not Bryant."

Instead, all three of his bosses stood on his porch, looking somewhere between disgusted and pissed.

Clearly, this wasn't a social call.

Fuck.

"None of us is Bryant," Hunter drawled. "But I'll be more than happy to take you up on your invitation because you obviously need an ass kicking. Are you out of your fucking mind?"

So they had already heard about Montilla's capture? Bitchin'. "Yeah, I probably am. I should have just killed that son of a bitch for what he did to me, but when I had him in his wife's former safe house, I didn't pull the trigger. I just turned him over like a good little citizen. I thought that would make you happy. But you're clearly annoyed I didn't follow orders."

"Do you ever turn on the fucking news?" Logan challenged, looking ready to wring his neck.

Joaquin, who wasn't much of a talker, rolled his eyes with a grunt and grabbed the remote, flipping the channel to cable news.

The top-of-the-hour headline horrified him.

FIVE COPS DEAD, TWO INJURED IN ST. LOUIS POLICE DEPARTMENT ESCAPE.

Shock poured over him like a bucket of ice. "Son of a bitch."

"Montilla's thugs rolled in there, shot up the place, then took off with their boss—killing two more cops as they left just for the fun of it."

And every one of their deaths was on his head. One-Mile felt utterly sick as he sagged against the wall. "Oh, fuck."

"Yeah." Hunter swiped the bottle from his hand and slammed it on the coffee table. "So you better start giving us reasons not to kill you ourselves. Explain what the fuck you were thinking and why you didn't clue us in."

"And toss in a good rationale for we shouldn't fire your insubordinate ass, too," Logan chimed in.

Honestly, he couldn't think of a single one.

Joaquin grabbed his arm and shoved the cuff of his long-sleeved athletic shirt past his elbow, examining the underside of his forearm. Then he turned to the others. "No new tracks."

They thought he was still taking the drugs Montilla and his goons had addicted him to? And that it had led to his lapse in judgment?

One-Mile jerked free and exposed his other forearm. "Of course there are no fucking new tracks. But here. Examine this arm, too, so you can be really sure. But if you'd just asked me, I would have told you that once I went through detox in the hospital, I haven't had any other cravings. I wasn't high in St. Louis. I just fucked up."

"You got too involved." Joaquin turned an accusing glare on the Edgington brothers. "I told you he wasn't ready for an assignment."

"Bullshit," One-Mile defended. "You asked me to relocate Valeria and her family safely. I did that."

"Sure, then you totally ignored orders and went rogue. So don't fucking yell. You're lucky we're talking to you at all. You're a talented son of a bitch, but not irreplaceable. I wanted to kill you for this stupid-ass stunt." Joaquin pinned him with cold hazel eyes. His low voice was like a blade down One-Mile's spine. "I got voted down."

"Too bad," One-Mile quipped. That would have made everything so much easier... "Is Valeria still safe?"

Logan nodded. "No thanks to you. We've warned her. Thankfully, Jack Cole recommended a bodyguard in the area, who's with her now. She'll call if she needs us."

Thank God for that.

"Sit," Hunter demanded. "We're going to talk."

One-Mile flopped onto the sofa, grabbed his bottle, and took a long pull.

The elder Edgington grabbed the booze from his grip and sent him a narrow-eyed glare. "What the fuck? Jack Daniel's straight up at four in the afternoon? Did you trade booze for drugs as a way of dealing with the trauma from your last mission to Mexico?"

No, it was how he was coping with Brea's loss, but he didn't owe them that explanation. And he'd be goddamned if he let them slap a PTSD label on him, too. That was getting better…somewhat. But he refused to have that conversation now.

"Fuck you. It's been a long day, and I'm kicking back. Are you here for a mental health check, Mommy?"

"What. The fuck. Happened?" Hunter snarled.

Since they weren't going to go away, he started at the beginning, telling the others that he'd gotten Valeria, her son, and her sister out of St. Louis without a hitch. And that with too much time on his hands in Orlando, he'd started to think—about ways to pay back Montilla…and how to catch their mole.

"At least I've figured out who's betrayed us." One-Mile explained the email chain.

Logan leaned in. "You're sure?"

"Unless everyone else somehow got the memo…"

They all shook their heads.

"First I'm hearing of it." And Hunter didn't sound pleased.

"Then I'm positive. Trees is your asshole."

His trio of bosses looked at one another. "Why would he do that?"

None of them had an answer.

"Money?" One-Mile suggested. "Drugs? Blackmail?"

Logan stood, then looked at his brothers. "That other problem we talked about this morning?"

What did they mean?

Joaquin raised a dark brow. "You have an idea how to deal with it?"

"Yeah. Let me look into something." Logan headed for the door.

Hunter and Joaquin exchanged a glance before the quiet bastard shook his head. "That frightens me."

"Same. We're coming with you. And you—" Hunter scowled, then pointed a sharp finger in his direction—"don't do another fucking thing. You don't even fart without talking to us, am I clear?"

"Crystal."

"If you have contacts, start working them—quietly," Logan insisted from across the house. "Try to find out where Montilla is going and what he plans to do next. Try like your life depends on it."

But it wasn't his life that worried him; it was Brea's. It seemed likely Montilla or his goons would pay him a visit at some point. One-Mile couldn't give that son of a bitch any reason to look her way.

And as the trio left, he shoved the bottle aside, retrieved his laptop, and started calling everyone he knew.

This time, when he found Montilla, he wouldn't bother with any slap-and-tickle torture before an orderly arrest; he would just kill the bastard, possible repercussions be damned. At least Brea would be safe.

Nothing else mattered.

Monday, November 3

Brea walked out of the doctor's office at the clinic in Lafayette, feeling numb and stunned. Her life would never be the same.

Cutter rose to his feet in the empty waiting room and stared. But his grim face told her he expected her next words.

"I'm pregnant." Her whisper turned to a sob.

With a soft curse, he pulled her into his arms, stroking a big, comforting hand down her back. "Bre-bee…"

She sank against him and clung for comfort.

Except his two tours in Afghanistan, Cutter had been there for her since the day she was born. She had pictures of him, a gangly eight-year-old boy, holding her as an infant. She'd grown up next door to him. Though he had relocated to nearby Lafayette after returning from the Middle East, she saw him all the time. They spoke most every day. He had been her staple, her rock…and sometimes, her shield from the real world.

He couldn't shield her from this reality, but she'd never been more thankful for him than she was now.

"It's all right." He pulled back and cupped her face. "We'll handle it."

"How is it all right? You know what my father will do. What the town will say."

Brea feared her father having another heart attack because his only daughter had disappointed him so deeply. Without a husband, the town would gossip that she was a "fallen woman." Not everyone in Sunset was so narrow-minded, but being Preacher Bell's daughter, she was held to a higher standard. Once the news that she was "in trouble" spread, her living as a hairdresser would likely dry up. Then how would she support her baby?

Even if Pierce found out, she doubted that the man who had suddenly told her they needed to "take a step back" would care.

"Do you want to consider terminating the pregnancy?" Cutter asked softly.

She hadn't had much time to adjust to the idea that she would be a mother come May, and after her own mother's fate, giving birth scared her. But instinctively she slid a protective hand over her slightly bulging belly. "Heavens, no. I would never do that. I'm not judging. That choice might be all right for some but you know I wasn't raised that way."

Besides, if her being unwed and expecting would devastate Daddy, ending the pregnancy, if he ever found out, would be ten times worse.

"Understood. Let's grab a bite of lunch and talk." Cutter dropped a hand to the small of her back and led her toward the exit.

The front door's electronic chime sounded. Brea looked up to find a man she'd never seen entering the clinic. A stranger, thank goodness. If he'd been anyone from Sunset, her appointment here would have caused the kind of speculation and chin-wagging that kept the town's gossip mill churning for days.

It was only a matter of time before they knew her secret.

What was she going to do?

Outside, she shivered in the November chill. Brea wrapped her sweater around her shoulders as Cutter opened the passenger door. She hopped in his truck, her mind reeling in the silence.

Once he'd settled in the driver's seat, he tugged on his seat belt and started the vehicle. "What are you going to tell One-Mile?"

"Nothing." Thankfully, he didn't live in Sunset and wasn't connected to the town grapevine. So if and when he heard, she would be the one to fill him in. "You can't confront him about this, either."

"Look, he's a jackass and he'll make a lousy father, but—"

"I'm asking you to keep my secret." If he didn't want her, she refused to say anything that might guilt him into taking her back. "Please."

Cutter tossed his hands in the air. "I have to work with him."

"It's not as if you two voluntarily speak. All you have to do is not mention me."

"He'll ask me about you."

Maybe he had in the past, but Brea doubted he would anymore. "If my daddy finds out I got pregnant by a man who's never even taken me on a date, he'll disown me."

Cutter slanted her a chiding glance. Okay, maybe she was being dramatic. He wouldn't disown her…but he also might never forgive her. Daddy had been both her mother and father growing up. Not having him to guide her as she learned how to parent would be a devastating blow.

If she had Pierce's love and devotion, it would help to cushion the hit. But she didn't, and dwelling on his abandonment accomplished nothing. Wishing he'd come back was an even bigger waste of time.

Until her son or daughter was born, other than Cutter, she was alone.

"When are you finally going to tell me what happened between you two?"

She shook her head. The last thing she wanted to talk about now was the night she'd gotten pregnant, especially with Cutter. He would never understand. And he would blame himself. "Leave it."

"Be honest with me. Did Walker even bother to wear a condom?"

No, and that was just as much her fault as his. "Don't do this."

"At least tell me if he forced you—"

"No." She wished he would stop prying. "And I won't cry rape when it wasn't."

Her time with Pierce had been like a fantasy, all fireworks and grand passion. But now the time to pay the bill had come, and she alone was holding the check—with no way to pay except her grit and stubborn determination.

"Move to Lafayette." Cutter broke into her thoughts. "My apartment building has great security and good neighbors."

In theory, that sounded ideal. New town, new life—one close to Cutter. But she'd already thought through that possibility. "With Daddy's heart condition? I can't leave him."

"You wouldn't be far away."

"Too far for his circumstances. Besides, all my clients are in Sunset." And they'd likely desert her once the news got out. "I'd have to start my business over."

"You can move in with me until you get on your feet. I've got a spare bedroom."

She appreciated his sacrifice, but she hated to take over his home office—or any part of his life. He valued his privacy, just like she did. But he wouldn't care about that, so she had to phrase her refusal in a way he could understand.

"I can't live 'in sin' with you. You know that's what the town would say. The preacher's daughter and the town drunk's son shacking up. What a shame…"

He let out an exasperated sigh as he put the truck into drive. "Damn it, I wish those small-minded idiots would keep their mouths shut."

"You lived in Sunset most of your life. You know they won't."

Gritting his teeth, Cutter pulled away from the clinic. "Can I ask you a question? Was Pierce your first?"

Surely, he didn't think she slept around. Probably not, but they'd also never asked about one another's sex life. "Of course."

Cutter gripped the steering wheel like it was Pierce's neck. "We should get married."

Brea sucked in a breath. She'd always hoped someone would propose to her someday. But Cutter was the wrong man, and he wasn't offering because he was in love with her.

She swiped the tears from her stunned face. "Have you lost your ever-lovin' mind? I can't ask you to do that."

"You're not asking. I'm offering."

"It's sweet but—"

"You're out of options, Bre-bee. In order to keep the townsfolk and your father off your back *and* keep your baby, you need a husband."

He was right, and his offer meant the world to her, but… "I love you, Cutter. Like a brother. I don't think of you…that way."

He scowled. "I don't think of you that way, either. You're my sister in every way except blood. But we've stuck together through thick and thin. We've grown closer over the years because we both know what it's like to be the latch-key kid of a hardworking single parent. I don't want that for your baby. I doubt you do, either. So unless you want to find yourself cast out of Sunset altogether for trying to raise your child alone, I'm your best hope."

"What would you do if you married me?" She hated discussing such an indelicate topic, but he'd brought it up. "I don't go out of my way to hear gossip, but I can't always avoid it. I know you're a red-blooded man. I know you like women and you don't enjoy spending your nights alone. I can't give you…"

Sex.

Cutter winced. "I wouldn't ask you to."

Brea breathed a sigh of relief. He wasn't interested in getting naked and sweaty with her, either. Thank goodness.

But what would they do about intimacy? About the fact that, despite everything, her heart belonged to a man he despised?

She bit her lip. "I guess if we lived in Lafayette, and you were discreet…"

"What about you?" he asked. "What will you do when you need a man to touch—"

"Pray. Meditate. Garden. Work. I won't…" She couldn't imagine another man near her. Brea only ached for Pierce. Yes, giving in to him had created this mess, and if she ever saw him again she would have to guard against her foolish yearnings. But she already knew her heart would never belong to anyone else. "I'll be fine."

Cutter stopped at a red light and sent her a narrow-eyed glare. "There's something you're not telling me. Did Walker hurt you?"

How stunned would he be if she told him that Pierce had given her such sublime pleasure and made her feel so much like a woman that she'd never once thought of resisting? "Leave it, Cutter."

"I won't let that son of a bitch get away with what he's done. He took advantage of you. He caused you anguish. Goddamn it—"

"Don't take the Lord's name in vain," she snapped, mostly because it was something they generally agreed on.

"Figure of speech, Bre-bee. Stop derailing me. I want to know every way he harmed you so I can make him pay. Now."

She shrank back into her seat because he didn't really want the truth. "Doesn't it always hurt the first time?"

"Other than that, was he too rough? Did he bruise you? Use you too hard? Too often?" Cutter ground his teeth together.

Brea tried not to blush. Pierce had spent half that night inside her and he hadn't held back. And she'd loved it.

"Talk to me." He sounded exasperated. "Did he spank you or bind you or—"

"Stop." Those words sent images spinning through her head. Had Pierce wanted to do such things to her? How would they have felt? Why did she ache so badly to know? "Whatever he may or may not have done, I'm all right. I went to him for help and he did exactly what I asked. Nothing else matters."

At least as far as Cutter should be concerned.

He finally gave up his awkward questions. "All right. I won't pry. Just tell me what you want to do."

"I need to think. I suspected I was pregnant, but hearing the doctor confirm it was a shock."

"I know. My offer stands. Getting married will quell the gossip. We can spin the wedding as two friends who've realized they're in love."

"I hate lying to everyone…"

"I do, too. But the truth will ruin you and tear your father apart. There are no good options here, so we have to pick the best of a bad bunch."

Brea feared he was right. "How do we convince anyone that we're romantic?"

"One step at a time. Worry about you and the baby first. How many weeks along are—"

"Thirteen."

Certainly he could do the math. He knew exactly when she'd gone to Pierce. And there was no question he'd gotten her pregnant after the hostage standoff that hot August night.

That same math brought home the fact that, even if she and Cutter married today, the minute her baby was born, Sunset would be filled with speculation and innuendo. How much longer before her pregnancy showed? Right now, she was able to hide the developing bulge of her tummy…but how long would that last?

"Don't take too long to decide or people will figure it out."

"I know. Thank you. Do you have an assignment next week?"

"Yeah. Originally, Logan Edgington scheduled me to keep an eye out on a former FBI director who's coming to New Orleans for reasons I'm not supposed to know or care about. But he's rescheduled, so Jolie—you know, the clothing designer I worked for last week?"

"The one whose offices you were almost killed in?" She hated the thought of him going back there.

But wherever he went, the job was dangerous.

"You're overreacting. I got whacked in the head at the urinal." He rolled his eyes at himself. "Anyway, she asked me to go bodyguard some pampered celebrity friend of hers for a week or two in LA. But I'll be back for Thanksgiving. I think we should get married then."

Brea didn't want to make them both miserable, but she wasn't seeing many other options. "I would offer to divorce you after the baby is born but…"

She couldn't, at least until her father had passed. Even then, she felt squeamish about putting asunder that which God hath joined. But she would have to let Cutter go eventually. She couldn't keep him trapped in a loveless marriage for the rest of his life.

"We'll worry about that later. For now, think about what I've said."

She nodded. "Can we skip lunch? I'm not up to it."

Her energy levels had bounced back, but her morning sickness was still an everyday, all-day reality. And more than anything, Brea wanted to be alone.

Cutter looked hesitant, but he finally nodded.

When he reached the street on which they'd both grown up, he parked between their childhood homes and leaned across the cab of the truck to kiss her forehead.

She met him halfway and brought him in for a sisterly hug. "Thank you for everything."

"No, thank you. I hated to admit this to Walker, but I probably wouldn't be alive today if you hadn't persuaded him to help me. I know what that cost you." He sighed as if it pained him to admit that. "So let me take care of you in return."

None of this was his fault or his doing, but what other choice did she have? "We'll talk soon."

"Brea…"

With a shake of her head and a wave, she headed inside to think about her future and make plans—without Pierce.

chapter four

Thursday, November 13

BREA SAT ACROSS THE DINNER TABLE FROM HER FATHER, UNCOMFORTABLY AWARE OF his probing stare. "More mashed potatoes, Daddy?"

"You finish up the last few spoonfuls. I think you need it."

"I'm fine." She tried to keep calm, but Daddy had been asking gently loaded questions for the last few minutes and she was desperate to change the subject. "Tell me how Tom's new youth group is doing. Last time I had two minutes to rub together, he was really just getting it going. There seemed to be a lot of enthusiasm—"

"It's fine, and right now that's not my concern. We haven't spoken much since the morning you agreed to stop seeing that man. Has he contacted you?"

Daddy didn't mean to rub at her sore spot, but even thinking about Pierce made her ache. "No."

"Do you regret your decision?"

If Pierce had come home from his last-minute mission, adequately explained why he'd killed his father, embraced their coming baby, and vowed to love her for the rest of her life, Daddy would still have pressured her to give him up. But she would have refused for the man she loved.

Instead, except for that blistering kiss, Pierce hadn't been able to get away from her fast enough. And since then, he hadn't given her any indication that he'd missed her one bit.

Brea tried to tell herself that she was better off without him. Her heart wasn't listening.

"No."

With Cutter gone to California babysitting some starlet these past four days, she hadn't heard any secondhand news about what Pierce was doing at work or whether he'd asked about her. Whatever Cutter was up against in La La Land must be intense because it was unlike him not to text or call for days.

"Brea? Did you hear what I asked?"

She hadn't. "I'm sorry. Would you mind repeating it?"

"I asked if you're still in love with him."

Even if Pierce didn't love her; that's what Daddy meant. Of course she did, but that's not what he wanted to hear. "It doesn't matter. He's gone and I doubt he's coming back, so you got your wish."

Regret crossed her father's face. "I never wanted you to be brokenhearted, just for you to see this man as he really is."

"Can we talk about something else?" Or she would get angry at how little

Daddy understood her. Pierce's feelings not being genuine didn't make hers less real. She'd heal...eventually. But she was too raw for this conversation. "How's the prep for the Thanksgiving feast at the church going and what can I do to help?"

"It's fine, and I don't need you to do anything. Jennifer has things under control."

Brea reared back. "Jennifer? I've organized that every year since—"

"You were twelve, yes. But this year when the planning started, you seemed distracted." He frowned. "Honestly, I'm glad your last appointment this evening cancelled so we could talk. I'm worried about you."

She tried not to freeze up. "Other than being upset, I'm fine."

"Are you sure? You're looking awfully pale these days."

"Not surprising. My summer tan has definitely faded," she quipped.

"Seems like you're tired, too. All the time. Have you seen Dr. Rawson?"

"Daddy, he's a pediatrician." But Brea still saw him for most things because he was local and he knew her so well, and she was sidestepping the question.

"All right, then. Any other doctor you've been seeing?"

Had he somehow figured out that she'd met with the obstetrician in Lafayette that the clinic had recommended? She'd tried so hard to be discreet.

"I just neglected to take my vitamins for a few months, and you know how I get anemic. I'm back on them now." All true...but it felt like a tremendous lie.

"You've been in Lafayette a lot lately. Why?"

"Just trips to the beauty supply..." She struggled for more of the truth. "And since Cutter is out in Cali, I stopped by his place yesterday to make sure everything was all right."

Not that he'd asked her to, but after seeing the female doctor and talking about her baby—taking video as she'd heard the heartbeat for the first amazing time—being in any way near her best friend brought her comfort.

Daddy's eyes narrowed. "Is there anything you want to tell me?"

She hated lying to him. Eventually she would have to come clean about her pregnancy...but not until she'd decided her next course of action. Not until she felt sure her father's heart could take it. "No."

Daddy didn't look convinced. "I heard you up early this morning."

"Couldn't sleep." That was the truth. Morning sickness had jolted her from bed and sent her charging for the bathroom. She'd barely managed to get the door shut and land in front of the toilet before her stomach had given way.

"I thought I heard you throwing up."

Her heart started to pound. If he'd heard her retching, she wouldn't be able to talk him out of it. "I, um...got home late from the salon last night. I ate cereal for dinner, and I think our milk has gone bad."

He raised a graying brow. "Really? I had cereal this morning and I felt just fine."

"Huh." She shrugged. "Must have been something else. Maybe I caught a bug."

Daddy pushed his plate aside and leaned forward, elbows on the table. "Are you sure? I noticed you've been skipping breakfast a lot. This morning wasn't the first I've heard you throwing up."

Panic rose, and she tried to stamp it down. "Stress isn't good for my appetite or my stomach."

"What's got you worried?"

"Your health, Daddy. Always your health. Things are a little crazy at the salon and…and the holidays are coming up. And I've missed Cutter since he's gone."

Her father nodded like he heard every word she said—and he didn't believe a single one. "Listen to me, Brea Felicity. If there's something you want to tell me—"

"Cutter and I are thinking about getting married," she blurted to cut him off.

After ten days of thinking through her options, she didn't see many others that didn't lead to giving up her home and family. She'd eventually have to tell Daddy she was expecting, and he would undoubtedly do the math. Hopefully, his health would be more stable then so he could better weather the shock.

That stopped his questioning instantly. "He proposed?"

"Yes."

Her father frowned. "When?"

"A few days before he left for Cali. I've been thinking about it since."

"I thought you two were just friends."

"Well…" *Think fast…* "He hasn't met anyone else he'd like to marry, but he's thirty. He's ready to settle down."

"First I'm hearing of that."

"And the time I spent with the man I'd been seeing convinced me that you're right; no one else will ever be as good to me as Cutter. So we started talking about getting hitched."

"Do you want to be married to Cutter?"

Brea tried not to squirm in her seat. "We both think the time to be sensible has come. I just need to let him know that I'm saying yes."

If there was one thing Daddy appreciated, it was a well-measured response. This one would hopefully set him at ease.

To her surprise, he scowled. "I never meant to give you the impression you should marry for any reason other than love."

"I know, but Cutter and I both think getting married seems like the logical, adult choice."

"Hmm," Daddy mused. "How's that going to work?"

"What do you mean?"

"In Corinthians, Paul tells us one of the reasons for marriage is to avoid fornication. Cutter loves you, but not in a…carnal way. So if he's marrying you to avoid succumbing to temptation…"

"We both know there will be an…adjustment."

"A huge one."

She acknowledged her father with a nod. "Neither of us expects our feelings to morph overnight. But Genesis tells us that it's not good for man to be alone, so God made him a helpmate. In Cutter's case, that's me."

"He's been managing his own cooking and laundry for years. Why does he need a helpmate now?"

Brea dropped her silverware on her plate in frustration. The clatter lent her bravado. "What do you want, Daddy? We've decided to move forward together because we're both lonely, we trust each other, and it makes sense. I was hoping you'd be happy for me. There's no groom on the planet I can imagine you approving of more, yet you're *still* questioning me?"

He held up both hands. "You're right. I love Cutter like a son, and I hope he makes you happy. But your heart is tangled up elsewhere, and I want to be sure you're not making this decision to please me or Cutter—or anyone else—at your own expense."

Her problems were so much bigger than that. "We'll find ways to be happy together."

"I want that for you more than anything. And I don't mean to question you." He leaned forward. "You know the problem fathers have?"

She shook her head. "What?"

A faint smile crossed his face. "They never want to admit their little girls have grown up. And despite what you may think, I'm proud of you."

He wouldn't be proud of her if he knew this conversation was built on so many lies…

"Thanks, Daddy." Brea tried not to get choked up, but it was hopeless.

"Hey." He grabbed her hand and squeezed. "Don't cry. Weddings are a happy occasion. Once that boy comes back from California and asks me for your hand, we'll have a celebration."

"He will." They hadn't talked about it specifically, but Daddy wanting to give his blessing wouldn't surprise Cutter.

"So when's the big day? We have to start planning, after all."

"We haven't decided." But they couldn't afford to wait long.

"Well, I'm sure we'll get all the details worked out."

She nodded, but she couldn't stop feeling as if she wouldn't be planning her wedding so much as burying her future.

Friday, November 14

Brea gripped the toilet and retched again. Blasted morning sickness. She was nearly in week fifteen of her pregnancy. When the devil would it end?

This morning, she'd turned on her music in the bathroom, hoping it would disguise the sounds of her sickness, but Daddy was likely awake. What if he could hear her? How many more well-meaning lies would she have to tell him to keep her secret?

It was already too many.

After rising weakly from the floor, she flushed the toilet, washed her hands, and rinsed her mouth. The nausea wasn't done with her yet; she knew that from experience. But after so much upheaval, her body felt weak.

She stumbled back to bed and grabbed her phone off her nightstand along the way. Five forty a.m.

Tears stabbed at her eyes. It had been nearly two weeks since she'd seen Pierce. She so badly wanted to call him, hear his gruff voice, confess how much she missed him. Tell him she still loved him. In her fantasy, he would say he loved her, too. Then she would confess they were having a baby, and he would be so happy, apologize for everything, propose instantly, and sweep her away to their happily ever after.

Brea shook her head at her own absurdity. Pierce had played her, and she'd loved him so much—or at least the man she'd believed him to be—that she had let him.

Finally, she'd ripped off her rose-colored glasses and resolved to face her future with eyes wide open.

She scrolled up from Pierce's contact and dialed Cutter instead. She couldn't put this off anymore.

He answered on the third ring. "Bre-Bee? You okay?"

"Hi, Cutter." She could hear her own voice shaking, but she was determined to forge ahead.

"What's going on?"

"I haven't heard from you. Everything all right there? Your starlet a problem child?"

"No. Her situation is more complicated than I thought at first glance, but…" There was such a long pause, Brea wasn't sure he actually intended to finish his sentence. Finally, he sighed. "I'll figure it out."

Something was troubling him. Since he almost never let a case get to him, whatever he was dealing with in California must be deeply problematic. "You always do. But I'm worried about you. You sound so tired."

"Pacific time is two hours behind Central."

"Oh, my gosh." It wasn't even four in the morning there. "I'm so sorry. I always mess up time zones…"

"What's going on?"

In other words, why was she calling so early.

Though Cutter had offered to marry her, he probably wasn't braced to hear her accept in the middle of the night. On the other hand, she'd already awakened him, so why hang up now? "Daddy is suspicious. I'm scared."

"Tell me everything."

She paraphrased her conversation with her father over supper the previous night.

Cutter didn't sound at all surprised. "So you're still having morning sickness?"

"Like crazy. Sometimes it lasts until evening, then suddenly I'm ravenous and eat everything in sight. It's like my body isn't my own anymore." Same with her emotions. She'd read online that her hormones were irregular during pregnancy and might make her behavior unpredictable. That was certainly a nice way to put it.

"It's not."

He was right. And during her next appointment with the obstetrician in mid-December, the doctor had promised they would do an ultrasound to check the baby's progress—and reveal the gender if she wanted to know.

What would her life be like by then? Even though she'd called Cutter to start their future together, Brea still couldn't picture it.

Or maybe she was afraid to.

"Eventually your father is going to realize what's going on. He's going to *see* that your body is changing."

Cutter was right. Her bras were getting uncomfortably tight. So were her pants. Layers of billowy winter clothes would help disguise her pregnancy for the next couple of months, but come spring? Nothing would hide the fact she was carrying a child.

"I know. No matter what I do, I'm going to hurt someone. I've worried that I either have to risk my father with a heart condition or make a choice that goes against my moral code. And then there's you... I can't bear the thought of ruining your life."

"You have enough to worry about right now without worrying about me."

"But—"

"Brea, you're not going to have an abortion."

"No." Even if her religious upbringing didn't forbid it, her heart did. She wanted this baby.

"You're not going to tell your father that you hooked up with a guy you have no intention of marrying and got pregnant."

It was the truth, and that's what she should tell him, except... "What if the news kills Daddy?"

Maybe if she sat him down, braced him before she explained, made sure she had a phone and his medication nearby... Wasn't it worth a try? She loved him so much and hated being dishonest.

"Are you going to tell him you're planning to raise your baby on your own?" Cutter added.

And that was where she stumbled. Even if her father accepted the truth—that she'd bear the fruit of her love for Pierce come May—the town wouldn't.

To outsiders and city folk, Sunset probably seemed backward and small-minded. But Daddy loved it here. They both had deep roots. This was the only home she'd ever known. She'd already accepted that she'd lost Pierce. But she didn't know how she'd cope with losing everyone else she'd known all her life, too.

Brea hated adding more lies, but this plan would only work if she got ahead of the narrative, announced her engagement to Cutter, and convinced the townsfolk they were just another happy couple pledging their lives to each other. Of course, once she started showing and the baby came, everyone would deduce that she'd been expecting when they'd married. But they would assume Cutter had fathered the baby, and he'd never say otherwise. It would be a minor scandal, but they would weather it. Daddy could keep the town's respect, and she could keep her clients. Gossip would die as soon as the next drama hit town.

"And what if he disowns you?" Cutter went on.

Daddy wouldn't. She might have worried, but he wasn't a cruel man. Yes, he would be shocked and disappointed she'd gotten pregnant by a man he'd never met…but now that she thought about it, maybe he'd already guessed. And he still seemed to love her. God willing, he would love her child, too. They would get through this as a family.

"You know if he does, the folks in Sunset will do the same," Cutter went on. "We've covered all this. You either have to leave Sunset alone to raise the baby in secret or—"

"I'll marry you. I-if you'll still have me."

It was time to stop hiding her head in the sand and face the inevitable.

Brea had expected Cutter to be relieved that she'd finally seen reason. Or impatient that it had taken her so long to reach the logical conclusion. Instead, he paused.

His silence was rife with resignation.

"Of course, Bre-Bee. I'd be honored."

But he wouldn't, not at all. Clearly, he wished she'd made any other choice. But she didn't have a better one. If Daddy had noticed her off moods and behavior, there was a chance some of the ladies at the salon had as well. She had to act now for this plan to have any chance of working.

"Thank you. A-and like I said, I'll never infringe on your personal life. I want you to be as happy as you can in the midst of this mess. If you want children of your own, we'll figure something out. Artificial insemination or—"

"Let's not get ahead of ourselves. That's years away, and we'll address that if I get the urge. You just worry about you and the baby right now. Unless plans change, I'll be back early next week, and we'll go to the Justice of the Peace."

"We can't do that. Daddy will want to marry us."

He would insist, just like he would want the ceremony in his church—a big shindig the whole town would attend.

Cutter cursed softly under his breath. "How soon can you plan a wedding that doesn't look slapped together?"

"In Sunset? January sixth."

"That's too long. Your pregnancy will likely be showing by then."

"Maybe not, with the right dress. But everything is booked up with the holidays. Out of curiosity, I called Norma Kay and asked if she could cater food for an event in December. She said she promised her family she'd do pre-Christmas parties, then take a vacation until the first of the year. Who else in Sunset can do the event except Violet? She just had a hip replacement yesterday in Baton Rouge."

"Brea, you'll have to bend a little or run the risk of everyone finding out."

"If I bend a little, as you call it, people will guess that something's off right away."

"What if we took a cruise out of New Orleans and got married in the Caribbean, told your father and the rest of the town we eloped because we didn't want to wait? You've always said you wanted to sail to paradise. Everyone knows it."

That made her pause for a long moment. "Let me think about that. Maybe…maybe everyone would buy that. Can I let you know next week?"

"Yeah." There was that something heavy weighing him down again.

"Cutter, are you all right?"

He paused such a long time that dread twisted her. Finally, he sighed. "I, um…need to get something off my chest."

"Of course. What is it?"

Yes, she worried about her baby and her situation and how to save face in Sunset. But she loved him and worried about him, too. "I've been babbling on about my issues and haven't listened to yours. I'm sorry. Tell me."

"I need to make sure you can handle a marriage that isn't…romantic. If we do this, we either have to give it a genuine go or—"

"It's not possible." She couldn't be intimate with a man she considered her brother. Heck, she didn't think she could betray her heart and have sex with any man who wasn't Pierce.

"I don't think I can, either." He sighed again. "Bre-bee, I'm in love with someone."

Brea froze as his words registered and shock sank in. "Oh. Then of course you're not marrying me. I'll find another way to keep my baby and my life. Don't worry. Please. Marry the woman who has your heart. I want you to be so happy, Cutter. I want that for you more than anything."

"I can't. She's sweet and wonderful—but she has her own huge life that doesn't include me. I knew going in that she'd talk to me, go to bed with me, but…"

Since Cutter had never before mentioned being in love and he'd been uncharacteristically quiet these past few days, it seemed obvious he'd fallen for the actress he was guarding. "So, it's your starlet client? I'm sure she's very pretty."

"That's not why—"

"You don't have to say anything. And you don't have to make excuses. I understand. I really do, more than you know." Sometimes love just happened, whether a person wanted it or not. And once it took hold, there was no shaking it. "If you think there's no long-term chance between the two of you—"

"None."

The finality in that sad syllable made her heart hurt for him. Brea knew what it was like to love someone who would never love her back. "Then she doesn't know what a great husband she's missing out on, and it would be my distinct honor to be your wife."

A sad pause hung between them. "It's settled. You think about eloping, and we'll make a plan once I'm home next week."

"Okay." She'd already messed up her life. All Brea could do now was hope she didn't mess his up, too. "I'll do whatever I can to make sure you don't regret this."

In case any of Montilla's assholes had eyes on him, One-Mile hadn't had any contact with Brea since that shitty morning in her foyer thirteen fucking agonizing days ago. Being apart from her—her smile, her softness, her kiss—was driving him beyond batshit. He paced his cubicle at EM Security Management like it was a cage.

Since the clusterfuck of Montilla's breakout in St. Louis, the bosses had punished him with the shittiest assignments. Last week, he'd spent two days in New Orleans babysitting the son of a former president, now running for Senate. The former first son had received some vague death threats on social media shortly before attending a summit on responsibility in government. After giving a rousing speech about community and personal accountability, he'd rubbed elbows and shaken hands for two hours. Then the white-privilege poster boy had spent the rest of his Big-Easy stay balls deep in strippers while snorting perfect white lines of cocaine.

No wonder people hated politicians.

And that had been his most hard-core assignment lately. Logan had sent him off for "training" with a group of corporate security blowhards who fixated on firewalls in between hours of coma-inducing slideshows about gun safety—a class he could teach in his sleep. For three days, they had focused on things like safekeeping of records and, his personal favorite, maintaining a strict chain of command. The following day, Hunter had volunteered him for security at an all-day seniors' bingo tournament. And on Tuesday, he had worked a community parade.

He got it; he'd fucked up by subverting their authority and taking matters into his own hands. They didn't know he was already paying the worst possible price since he'd had to push away the woman he loved and didn't know when or how he'd ever win her back.

But he would—no matter what it took.

Cutter being gone to California was both a blessing and a curse. Great that the Boy Scout wasn't trying to cozy up to her. But terrible because Cutter wasn't there to protect her. So One-Mile hadn't dared to paint a target on her back by paying her even a speck of attention, no matter how tempting. Instead, he'd watched from a safe distance.

Someone had to.

Sometimes, he cruised around Sunset, driving "aimlessly" in case anyone was trailing him. He hadn't noticed Montilla's guys on his ass...but that didn't mean they weren't lurking. Thankfully, everything around the sleepy little town seemed normal. One-Mile took reassurance from that. Because news would spread through Sunset like wildfire if someone had done Brea harm. He would have overheard it during his "random" stop in the grocery store or his fill-up for gas just down the street from her father's church.

Since he didn't dare head to her little spot on the map every day, he'd taken to stalking Brea on social media, too—what little she had of it. She had an occasionally used Instagram account for posting clients' new hairdos or a very pretty sunrise. She only used her Facebook to help organize various church groups. The salon where she worked also had accounts on most social platforms, as did the church, so he'd focused on those, too.

He grabbed his phone off his desk to check the time. Quarter till five.

"Walker, got a minute?" Logan approached, looking grim.

"Sure." Fifteen of them. Then he was fleeing this corporate prison, thank fuck.

"In the conference room."

Logan ignored the brow One-Mile raised at him. Not the boss's office? Were they going to officially reprimand him? Or just fire him?

Son of a bitch...

With a sigh, he made his way down the hall to the lone conference room. He wasn't terribly surprised to see Joaquin and Hunter sitting there, waiting for him.

He stopped in the door. "So you waited until Friday afternoon just before quitting time to give me the ax?"

"Shut the door and sit down." Hunter's tone made it clear he had no patience for his attitude today.

Joaquin didn't bother speaking, just sent him that mean motherfucker face that told him the trio of badasses wouldn't hesitate to come down like a ton of bricks if he gave them shit.

Fine, he'd play along.

He shut the door and slid into the chair across the long table from the other three men. "Now that I've followed directions like a good boy, what do you want? If you're going to fire me, fucking do it."

Hunter snorted. "If it were up to me, you'd already be gone. Thank my brothers that you're still gainfully employed."

Fuck you. "So what's this little soirée about?"

Logan sighed. "We have good news and bad news."

"Give me the bad news."

"We didn't ask your preference," Hunter growled. "We're going to start with the good."

With a well-placed elbow, Logan shut his brother up. "Don't be an asshole."

"According to you, I *am* one."

"You are," Joaquin said with a little smile. "Now I know why God gave me two sisters growing up. I couldn't stand this fucking bickering."

"Hey," Hunter protested. "If you think your younger sister can't argue…"

That made Joaquin break out in a rare laugh. "Oh, I know she can. And I'll bet that makes for a really charming wife."

Hunter snorted. "Charming isn't the word I would use to describe Kata."

"I would since she's got you by the balls…"

One-Mile had heard enough. "The good news?"

"Right." Logan nodded. "We're going to cut you some slack. It wasn't a bad idea to pursue Montilla while he was still on US soil, but you shouldn't have done it behind our backs, risked the client, and gone in without backup."

"Over the last couple of weeks, you've been loud and clear about what I did wrong. I got the message, Dad."

"Goddamn it, I'm trying to be on your side. Why don't you close your mouth for a minute and fucking listen?"

As much as One-Mile didn't like it, Logan was right. He sighed. "Fine. I'm all ears."

"Great. Here's the thing: your decisions sucked…but your instincts were right. And we fucked up by not taking your idea more seriously when you called and proposed it."

"He means me," Hunter cut in. "And I still stand by my decision."

"You got outvoted on that, too," Joaquin put in slyly.

That was more honesty than One-Mile had expected. "So where do we go from here? I've beat all the bushes I can to track down that son of a bitch. Nothing. I'm sure he's back in Mexico."

"You can bet on it." Logan nodded. "Cartels don't run themselves… But I don't think he's going to give up on his son."

In Montilla's shoes, he wouldn't either. "Nope."

"If he picks up on Valeria's trail again, he'll be back."

"Absolutely," One-Mile agreed. "But this time he won't come alone."

"Agreed."

"And since he walked into a trap last time, he may not take more information from our mole. Ever prove it's Trees?"

"We're…working on it." Logan sighed. "Well, Zy is."

Were they out of their minds? "He is never going to believe his bestie is guilty of even a parking ticket, much less selling us out."

"No, I asked him to do whatever he could to prove his best friend *innocent*."

Okay, that made sense in a subversive way. Zy wouldn't lift a finger to dig up dirt on Trees, but he'd move heaven and earth to prove the guy was clean. "And how's that going?"

"Well…funny thing," Joaquin drawled.

"What he means is that Tessa and her situation are really distracting him."

"Situation?" A vague crutch-word like that could describe anything from a minor snafu to a catastrophic shit show.

"Apparently, her ex-boyfriend is sniffing around again. Zy isn't happy."

"She's giving the time of day to the asshole who got her pregnant and left?"

"Yep. I get that they have a kid together, but…" Logan's tone said he thought her decision sucked.

One-Mile agreed. Tessa deserved better. But since Zy was the one hard for her, it wasn't his problem. "So you think he's too busy with Tessa to investigate Trees?"

Logan shrugged. "Zy says he's working on it. We'll see what he comes back with."

One-Mile scoffed. Based on what he'd seen? "I wouldn't hold your breath."

His teammate would give his left nut to seduce their receptionist into some hot action between the sheets, but One-Mile doubted he'd succeeded. Even if he miraculously had, he'd keep it on the down low so neither of them got fired.

Hunter shot his younger brother an I-told-you-so glare. "See, Walker isn't stupid all the time."

"Gee, thanks."

The elder Edgington replied with a very dignified middle finger, but turned to Logan. "Seriously. We can't let this drag on."

"I know." Logan held up placating hands. "But give Zy a little more time."

Hunter rolled his eyes but sighed. "Fine."

"It might help things along if we plant more information," One-Mile suggested. "If we give tidbits to Trees that make it to Montilla, then we'll know. If not, we'll re-evaluate."

The bosses looked at one another. Hunter's expression said he'd already had this idea. Joaquin and Logan looked at one another behind his back, speaking some silent language. But he could tell from their faces that they were coming around to his way of thinking.

"All right. We'll try," Joaquin conceded. "Where do you want this paper trail to send Montilla? He knows the safe house in St. Louis is dead."

And he'd be hesitant about walking into a trap again. "Why not direct him to somewhere around here? That way, if Montilla shows and something goes south, the rest of the team is just a phone call away."

The trio appeared to think things over before Logan nodded. "We're going to need an address. I'll find someplace that's suitable."

"Once you have, Hunter can write something up and pass it to Trees," Joaquin added.

It wasn't a perfect plan, but a decent one. "I get to help take this motherfucker down, right?"

"Absolutely." Logan nodded. "That should be even better news to you."

"Oh, yeah." The only thing that would be a step up was dusting Montilla for good so he would finally be free to pursue Brea again. Yes, he knew the asshole had underlings, but Emilo's vendetta against Valeria wasn't their fight. In fact, it was likely someone would be grateful to him and the EM crew for offing the boss so they could fill his shoes and carry forth their drug-selling glory or whatever. "How soon do you think we can get started?"

"A couple of days. I'll keep you posted." Logan grimaced. "Now for the bad news…"

He'd almost forgotten about that, but since they clearly weren't going to fire him and they'd finally taken his balls out of their purse, One-Mile didn't see how bad it could possibly be. "Lay it on me."

Joaquin and Hunter both looked at Logan, who tossed up his hands with a scowl. "What the fuck? Why me?"

"You're the best with touchy-feely shit."

No, he wasn't. He sucked just as hard as the other two.

"Why would you think that?" Logan challenged.

Hunter and Joaquin exchanged a glance, then a smirk and a fist bump. "Okay, maybe you're not better, but you're the youngest so we're pulling rank. Tell him."

Logan gritted his teeth, clearly annoyed. "I hate you two. I'm so getting you back. When you least expect it—"

"Tell me what?" One-Mile demanded impatiently.

For a moment, no one said a word. Finally, Logan sighed. "Have you looked at your phone lately?"

"No." He unlocked it and glanced at his boss.

"I know there's no way you're not cyberstalking Brea. Open Facebook."

Those words jabbed fear in his gut as he launched it. "Why?"

"Cutter called us earlier. Don't forget; no dragging your drama to the office."

One-Mile opened his mouth to ask what the fuck was going on when he saw the announcement on the salon's Facebook page.

Congratulations to our stylist Brea Bell and her fiancé, Cutter Bryant, on their engagement last night. Wedding details to follow!

His blood turned to ice as he lurched to his feet, chair scraping the floor. "What the…?"

"Sit down, big guy," Logan tried to soothe. "Whatever you think you and Brea had? It's over."

"The fuck it is."

chapter five

It was just shy of five thirty in the afternoon when Brea heard a familiar male voice around the partition dividing the salon from the reception area. Over the whine of the blow dryer in her hand, she froze.

It couldn't be…

"My mother-in-law is driving in from San Antonio for Thanksgiving dinner," huffed the newly minted Mrs. Gale. "Michael says his mother is coming to help since I've never cooked a turkey on my own, but she stuck her fingers in our wedding every which way until I hardly recognized the ceremony I'd wanted. Of course she's going to try to run all over me in my new kitchen."

"Uh-huh." Normally, Brea would have found a diplomatic way to point out to the newcomer from Beaumont that Michael Gale had been a mama's boy most of his life and that wasn't likely to change. Instead, she found herself trying to hear the low exchange on the other side of the privacy wall.

There was the rumble of male again, a voice with just the right depth and the perfect amount of gravel. She tensed. It couldn't be Pierce. Why would he come here? Why would he seek her out now?

Unless he'd heard the news…

Suddenly, Rayleigh bustled around the divider, eyes wide, and headed straight for her. "Brea, you have a visitor. He's *very* insistent." Her mouth gaped open as she whispered, fanning herself. "And so hot."

Since all the ladies knew Cutter and he was still in Los Angeles, Rayleigh didn't mean him. Or Cage, either, though a couple of the other stylists had expressed their interest in the big cop.

Brea tried not to panic. "I'm finishing Mrs. Gale's hair."

The last thing she wanted was to have it out with Pierce in the middle of the salon. He probably wouldn't be shy about airing their laundry in public, and Brea couldn't afford to give the locals something other than her recent engagement to chew on.

"I tried to tell him that. He's not going away."

Shelby Gale patted her arm and stood. "It's all right. I could use a trip to the ladies' room and a coffee."

When her client disappeared down the salon's back hall, Brea pinned Rayleigh with a pointed stare. "I know what he wants and I don't want to see him."

"Why don't you tell me that yourself?"

Brea whipped around at the sound of Pierce's voice. She didn't know what stunned her more—the fact that every head in the place turned to watch this suddenly interesting exchange…or the feel of her heart seizing up at the sight of him so big and fierce and seething.

She did her best to ignore her forbidden thrill. "What are you doing here?"

Rayleigh melted into the background. The rest of the salon fell utterly silent. But no one looked away.

"Taking a big fucking risk to talk to you." With a glance over his shoulder, he looked at the partition blocking their view to the street, then faced her again. "I only came here because no one outside can see in."

The big wall had been designed so that passersby wouldn't catch a glimpse of their neighbors in foils or perm rods, but why did Pierce care? Clearly, discretion didn't mean a dang thing to him.

"I want answers." He glanced around as if suddenly realizing all eyes were on them. "Where can we talk more privately?"

She shook her head. "I can't right now."

And what was the point, anyway?

"Can't?" He raised a brow. "Or won't?"

Her heart pounded. "Both."

"We never finished dinner at my place, so you can either find us somewhere now or I'll think of a secluded spot to take you after your last client."

It was on the tip of her tongue to tell him that he was being an ass, but she had to quell gossip. Otherwise, as soon as people realized she was pregnant, there would be whispers that Cutter might not have fathered the baby after all.

"I'm sorry business didn't allow us to finish that conversation, and I would have liked to hear more about your ideas, but I'm afraid I've found another opportunity that suits me better."

"We both know it wasn't business that interrupted our 'discussion,' pretty girl."

Brea felt her face turn bright red. He might as well have announced to everyone that they'd had sex.

Clearly, Pierce wanted to know why she was marrying Cutter. He was determined to get answers today, never mind how much his presence would make her friends and neighbors chin-wag.

Brea didn't understand why he thought he had a right to demand anything after he'd been the one to break up with her, but if a few words would make him go away, then fine. Maybe she'd give him a piece of her mind, too.

And…okay, some foolish part of her ached to spend a few minutes alone with him.

"Rayleigh, can you finish up Mrs. Gale for me?" Thankfully, the salon owner's last client of the day had cancelled.

"Sure, honey. No one is in the break room, if y'all want to chat in there."

"We'll only be a minute."

As she turned away, mortification rolled over her. Every eye in the place followed as she led Pierce down the shadowy hall and opened the door on the right. As Rayleigh said, it was empty. The radio in the corner, with its volume turned down low, played a Carrie Underwood tune. The scents of hair dye and chemical cleansers filled the air. The queasiness she thought she'd overcome earlier rushed back.

She crossed her arms over her chest. But Pierce didn't do subtle. If he wanted to touch her, her silent barrier wouldn't keep him away. "What do you want?"

"You fucking agreed to marry Bryant?"

"Yes." She stood her ground. And the more she thought about it, the more she got mad. "Why do you care? You told me in no uncertain terms that you were taking a step back. Then you left my house as if your backside was on fire. Why do you think that entitles you to any explanations?"

"Less than a month ago, you said you were in love with me."

"Well, at least it took me nearly a whole month to change my mind. It only took you a week."

He gaped at her. "What? I never said I didn't love you. I asked you to move in with me, for fuck's sake. And you decided the right response was to get engaged to a man I know doesn't do a damn thing for you?"

Was he serious? If he still had feelings for her, why hadn't she seen or heard from him in nearly two weeks? Did he only want her as a convenience when he was in the mood? For a forbidden thrill when she belonged to someone else? Was that "love" to him?

Maybe they saw relationships so differently that his definition and hers would never align. Now that they were having a baby, she couldn't be with someone who showed up a couple of times a month and considered that devotion. Regardless of whatever Pierce was after, she could no longer afford to play his game. She had an unborn baby to protect.

"You're wrong. I love Cutter. I have all my life. We finally decided to make it official. There's nothing more to say."

Pierce used the hard slab of his body to propel her against the nearest wall, then slammed his big palms on either side of her head. "Did he take you to bed?"

She gasped at the contact. God, he was so close. His body heat. His scent. His eyes all over her... Everything about him rattled her. Tempted her. "That's none of your business."

"Is that what you think?" His black stare drilled down through her eyes like he could see all the way to her soul.

She forced herself to nod.

Every time the man got near her, fire scorched her veins. She went hot all over. Her heart thundered. Even now, Brea couldn't help arching closer as she panted and ached for his touch.

He grabbed her chin. His hot gaze sizzled its way to her mouth. Her eyes automatically fluttered shut in anticipation. Would his kiss be as all-consuming as she remembered?

"That invitation all over your face is so tempting, pretty girl. We need to talk more than we need to fuck...but I'll be happy to accommodate."

His sexy rasp nearly melted her. Why was she cursed to so completely crave a man who could destroy her?

When he reached for his zipper, she found her head. "No. Don't touch me."

"Why not? I'd bet every dime I own the Boy Scout still hasn't laid a single finger on you. So all I have to do is lift your pretty plaid skirt, rip off your panties, and prove that pussy is still mine..." He grabbed fistfuls of the hardy fabric and started gliding them up her thighs. "Just like you are."

She wrapped desperate fingers around his beefy forearms, nearly crying in need. "No, Pierce. Stop."

He might still have her heart, but he didn't want marriage and babies and all the things she yearned for. She couldn't let him back into her body just because he spoke the words he must know she wanted to hear.

His expression darkened. "You're not marrying him."

"Yes, I am."

He grabbed her left hand. "Without a ring?"

Brea blinked. She and Cutter hadn't even talked about that. When Pierce was this close and clouding her senses, everything inside her resisted the idea of wearing a symbol that proclaimed she belonged to anyone else. "A formality."

He cursed. "No. It's bullshit. I don't know what the fuck is going on, but I only left because I'm trying to keep you safe, not because I don't love you. And I'll be damned if I'll let you marry him the second my back is turned."

Pierce thought he'd been protecting her? "Safe from what?"

"My life is dangerous as fuck right now, and the less you know, the better." He glanced at the clock on the wall and cursed. "And I've been here too long. But this isn't over, pretty girl. *We* aren't over. And as soon as I put an end to this shit, you'll say yes to me." He grabbed her face and forced his gaze into hers. "I'll do whatever it takes to make sure of that."

Her heart seized up. Everything inside her wanted to throw herself against him and tell him she still loved him. But she didn't have the luxury of following her feelings anymore. "No. I'm getting married."

Pierce lowered his lips dangerously close to hers. "Not to him."

Suddenly, the door crashed in, and Cage stomped into the room, his prying stare bouncing between them. "Brea?"

"I'm fine." But her voice shook. Her head reeled. Her chest tightened.

"Good. Go ahead. Your client is leaving. And I have a few things to say to Walker."

Brea didn't want to leave, but every minute she spent alone with Pierce was another minute the town would gossip.

"Thanks." She eased away from him.

He grabbed her arm again. "I mean it, pretty girl. I'm coming back for you."

Cage broke Pierce's hold on her, and Brea seized the opportunity to leave…but she couldn't do it without looking back at him.

His face said he was dead serious; nothing would stop him from winning her back. And as she hustled out of the room, she feared all the way down to her soul that she wouldn't be strong enough to say no to him for long.

"Outside," Cage growled and grabbed his arm the second Brea left the room. "Let's go."

One-Mile jerked free. "Don't act like you're perp-walking me out of here, asshole. I've said what I came to say. Now I'm leaving."

But he hadn't gotten through to Brea. Worse, he couldn't stay any longer without putting her at risk.

God, everything between them had become a gaping clusterfuck. Why was she so goddamn hell-bent on marrying Bryant all of a sudden? Yeah, One-Mile got why she'd doubted his feelings. Telling her he loved her in one breath and that he'd killed dear ol' Dad the next probably didn't inspire her devotion. Insisting he needed to put distance between them the next time he saw her had jacked things up even more. But of course he still loved her. He'd fucking told her so.

It hadn't made a damn bit of difference to her…and that fact nearly gutted him.

I love Cutter. I have all my life.

One-Mile cursed under his breath. If that was true, then why the actual fuck had she once pledged her heart to him?

It didn't add up.

Maybe she'd accepted Bryant's proposal because he was her safe bet. Daddy's choice. The smart one who'd known better than to defile Brea before marriage or ask her to shack up.

Except…why would she say yes to Bryant now? Cutter was in another state, so it wasn't as if they had recently shared a romantic heart-to-heart—or even a hot night in the sack—during which he'd persuaded Brea to be his wife. Nope, the asshole had been in California for nearly a week, and she'd chosen *last night* to become the future Mrs. Bryant? Over the phone? When she didn't feel an ounce of passion for him? Brea couldn't fake that, and One-Mile knew her lush little body was still his. Every time she looked at him, that fact was all over her face. No, passion wasn't love…but she still wanted him. That fucking mattered.

Stifling a curse, he shouldered his way out of the little break room, then exited the back of the salon, into the mostly vacant lot. Not because he gave any fucks about the biddies in the beauty shop gawking at him but because he'd embarrassed Brea. He hadn't known how much that would disturb her until the damage had been done.

Besides, if he saw her again, he wasn't sure he could make himself walk away. For her safety, he had to. Hopefully, anyone from Montilla's organization who might be watching would think he'd tried to ditch them by ducking through the beauty shop. But coming here had been an impulsive, knee-jerk reaction. Fucking stupid. He had to lock down this emotional shit.

When the back door began to swing shut behind him, Cage knocked it open so hard it crashed into the opposing wall, then slammed home with a teeth-rattling thud. "I'm talking to you, fucker."

"I'm not obligated to listen."

"For Brea's sake, you should."

That made him pause and glance back over his shoulder. "Why?"

"I don't pretend to know everything that happened between you and that girl, but I can guess. The best thing you can do for her is to keep walking and let my brother handle things from here."

As long as he was breathing, Brea would never be Mrs. Bryant. "Why the fuck would you think that?"

Cage gaped at him like he was an idiot, before he rolled his eyes into some smug-ass, superior glare. "Did you grow up in a small town?"

"Nope." He was from San Diego, and with a million fucking horrible memories there, he hoped never to set foot in the city again.

"Then you don't understand. That stunt you just pulled? The town will talk about nothing else for days, maybe weeks. That's not good for Brea's reputation or her future. If you keep coming here, you'll only make things worse for her."

"All we did was talk."

Cage snorted. "You might as well have announced to the whole damn town that you've fucked her. I'd love to roast you for that, asshole, but Sunset has an ordinance that prevents me from burning trash."

Was his barb supposed to be clever? "Fuck you."

"No. Fuck *you*. You said you didn't force Brea into bed, but I've known that girl her whole life. And I think you're a liar."

"I don't care what you think." He and Brea knew the truth.

"You should, just like you should get over yourself and start giving a shit what everyone around her thinks. She is the preacher's only daughter. She's adored by this town. They look at her like she's one step away from the Virgin Mary. She's worked hard to maintain that spotless reputation. You might well have destroyed it in three minutes—and dragged her daddy through the mud with her."

"Because she's not a virgin anymore? None of them are, either."

"None of them are the reverend's kid. And you're not only an outsider, but you're obviously trouble."

"Because I don't dress like you? Or talk like you? Because I'm not one of you?"

"No, because your attitude is shitty, and you have a huge chip on your shoulder. God knows you don't give a rat's ass about anyone but yourself."

It was on the tip of his tongue to tell the prick that he loved Brea and had from the moment he'd set eyes on her. That he intended to fight for her until she was his. That he'd gladly give up his happiness—his life, even—to keep her safe. But he didn't see the point of wasting his breath and he refused to put a target on her back. "You don't know a damn thing about me."

"What did you think confronting her in front of God and everyone would accomplish?" Cage shook his head. "Fuck it. It's done now, and your stupid-ass stunt flopped. So why don't you do Brea a favor and steer clear? She's got a solid future mapped out now, no thanks to you. Stop trying to ruin it. I don't love that she roped my brother into mopping up your mess, but the very least you could do is leave them in fucking peace."

Only about half of Cage's bullshit made sense. "What does that mean?"

The other man's brow furrowed before his eyes widened with shock. Then he shut it all down. "Nothing. Forget it. I'm going to check on Brea."

When Cage made a beeline for the back door, One-Mile jerked him around by the elbow. "Not until you tell me what the fuck you meant by my 'mess.'"

The elder Bryant brother yanked free and sneered. "You're supposed to be the shit. You figure it out."

Then he disappeared inside the salon again, and One-Mile stood staring at the door.

What the fuck? Was this about Brea's reputation? Or something more?

Did everyone in this goddamn drama know something he didn't? It sure as hell felt that way. And if he wanted to keep her from marrying Cutter, he needed to figure it out—fast.

As Brea plastered on a false smile for Mr. Davidson and scheduled his two-week follow-up so he could maintain his precise banker's cut, she sensed Rayleigh hovering nearby. The woman had swept and cleaned every surface in the salon, despite the fact a crew came in overnight to do that, and her last customer had left hours ago. Brea could guess why.

Her boss wanted the scoop.

Exhaustion tugged at Brea. As her pregnancy progressed, heartburn was beginning to replace nausea. It especially gave her fits at night. Sleep didn't always come.

But that's not what had her on the brink of stupid tears now. Life as she'd always known it was tumbling down around her like a house of cards. Until lately, she hadn't realized how often or deftly Cutter or her father stepped in to bear the brunt of her difficulties—before she even realized they were doing it. Long before she ever asked for their help.

But now Cutter was gone, and she wasn't ready to confide in her father.

So her problems were hers alone. Despite feeling overwhelmed, she knew this self-reliance was good for her.

As kindly Mr. Davidson left with a wave, she locked up behind him with a tired sigh.

Rayleigh put an unexpected arm around her shoulders. "You look like you could use a friend, honey."

She had no idea. "It's been a long day."

"Uh-huh. And ever since you and that fine specimen of a man had words earlier, you've looked ready to cry."

Brea had felt that way, too. "I'm fine."

Rayleigh narrowed her expertly made-up eyes. "I know your daddy taught you that lying is a sin. I'm going to the Sundowner. It's a Friday night. Why don't you come with me?"

"My father is expecting me to make supper and—"

"Nope. He came by while you were mixing up Mrs. Stringer's color a bit ago. He and Jennifer Collins were heading to Josephine's for dinner, then to a movie, so you're free for a while. Grab your purse, and let's go."

She wondered if Daddy had already heard the gossip that a disreputable man, probably on his motorcycle, had barreled his way into the salon—complete with tattoos, loud mouth, and oozing sex appeal—demanding to talk to her and all but admitting they'd had sex.

This was Sunset. Of course he'd heard.

But the fact he was busy now was a guilty relief. And Rayleigh was right; she could use a friend.

"All right. I need to use the restroom and grab my coat."

"I'll meet you there. Since it's Friday night, tables will be at a premium. So I'm going down there to grab one. Lock up behind you," Rayleigh called out as she left.

Brea had never actually hung out in the bar, but she'd heard it got crowded just after quitting time at the start of the weekend.

After a quick trip to the toilet, she washed up, put on her coat to protect her from the sudden November chill, and tried not to think about Pierce.

What danger had he been talking about?

She turned off the lights and let herself out of the shop, securing the door behind her. Huddling into her coat, she bustled down the sidewalk, not surprised to see a few folks running from some shop along Napoleon Avenue to their cars, giving her a speculative side-eye.

Brea put her head down and pretended not to notice.

The wind caught her coat as she stepped into the Sundowner. The place was nothing to write home about. It was dark and dim, decorated with dartboards, beer signs, and a lot of men still carrying the sweat from their day's work.

Rayleigh waved at her from a table in a quiet corner. Brea headed her way.

They weren't exactly friends. The salon owner wasn't old enough to be her mother...but it was close.

Her boss had grown up in Sunset, but moved away when she'd quit college to say *I do*. Three years later, she'd decided that she didn't after all since her husband spent more time with his "work wife" than his legal one. So she'd moved back home and taken over the salon when her mother retired.

After slipping out of her coat, Brea eased into the chair. A glass of white wine sat waiting in front of her. "What's this for?"

"Besides a friend, you looked like you could use a drink, too."

"Thanks, but I'm okay."

"You're not, honey. A nip or two after the day you've had will make everything a little easier to bear."

She shook her head. "I-it's very sweet of you, but I have to drive to Lafayette."

"So we'll stay here for a bit. One glass won't hurt."

Brea searched for another excuse to decline the drink. "Well, I...um, have this headache—"

"No, you don't." Rayleigh slanted her a shrewd glance. "You're pregnant, aren't you?"

Brea froze, panic biting at her. "What makes you think that?"

"Well, you've been sick more than usual. I chalked it up to stress since you've been through a lot with your daddy the last few months. Your sudden engagement surprised me because I didn't think you were in love with Cutter, but I was willing to give you the benefit of the doubt and believe y'all were just private about your feelings. But I get it now; he's giving you his name. That man who demanded to see you today is your baby's father." The woman patted her hand. "It's okay. Your secret is safe with me."

"Rayleigh..." How could she possibly refute her boss when she was right?

"I know we've never been close, and you've clearly gone to great lengths to keep this secret. Your deer-in-the-headlights expression tells me you didn't expect me to figure it out. But I know one thing. Whoever that tall, dark, dangerous hunk of man is, you love him."

Brea closed her eyes. If Rayleigh had seen that, who else had? "It's complicated."

"It shouldn't be that complicated. He loves you, too."

"I thought so, but..."

"Listen, I've spent twenty years fixing hair, and I'm damn good at it. But there's one thing I'm better at, and that's reading people." She leaned closer. "You don't look pregnant now, but you will at some point. Even if you start wearing Cutter's ring, that man is going to know he's the one who got you pregnant, isn't he?"

She paled. Eventually, there would be no hiding it from anyone...especially Pierce.

"And once he figures that out, do you really think he's just going to give up? Walk away?"

Brea hadn't thought he'd care if she was pregnant—until today. "He said he wanted to take a step back. I thought it was over. I hadn't seen him in a while. But…"

"I'm guessing he made it clear pretty darn clear today that it's *not* over."

And then some.

She was so confused.

"Until he showed up, I never imagined he'd even want to see me again. I thought Cutter and I would announce the baby shortly after we got married and…" *Pierce would be long gone.*

"You'd planned to let the town gossip that you and Cutter had been fooling around and decided to get married once you were expecting?"

"Yes."

Rayleigh shook her head. "I have a feeling you're going to need another plan. When Mr. Studly realizes that's his baby you're having, he's not gonna go away quietly, honey."

On the one hand, she didn't see a single scenario in which the Pierce who had stormed into her salon today wasn't as possessive about his child as he was about her. But he was also the same stranger who'd seemingly walked out and confessed to killing his own father.

"I don't know what he'll do."

"Oh, I do. You're kidding yourself if you think you've seen the last of him. Why don't you tell him you're pregnant, honey?"

"I was going to the day he seemingly broke up with me."

"What about now?"

She and Cutter had made all these plans and announced their engagement. What would the town think?

Did any of that matter if she and Pierce could manage to work things out and he wanted a future with her? If she had to make a choice between appearances or happiness, she'd pick being ecstatic with Pierce every time.

But to get to that place, there were so many ifs in their way… If he truly loved her and believed in the same kind of abiding devotion she did. If he wanted to be a father to their baby. If she could explain everything to Daddy without triggering his delicate heart. If Pierce would be willing to ask him for her hand.

"I don't know." But she needed to tell Pierce about the baby. She owed him that much.

"Well, I'm around if you need anything."

"Thanks."

"Don't mention it, honey. Just be happy. I married the man I thought was 'safe' when I was young, and it turned into a disaster. The one who got away left for good…and I'm alone. I'm doing all right, but I look back and think about what might have been. And I wish I could do that summer over." She sighed. "Don't make my mistake."

Rayleigh made a good point. Hiding behind Cutter wasn't fair to either of them, especially since he was in love with his starlet. He didn't think it would work out, but for his sake, Brea prayed it would. He deserved to be happy. And weren't they both entitled to a chance at a future with the person who held their heart?

Yes.

"Thanks. I'm going to do some thinking." Brea needed a plan, and she'd rather not be scheming at home. After his date, her father would want to talk about town gossip, and she didn't want anyone influencing her decisions. She needed to decide her next step alone.

"Got someplace to go?"

"I should." She didn't think Cutter would mind if she spent a night or two at his place, and the silence would do her good.

"If it falls through or you need anything else, you have my number, honey."

"I appreciate it."

"Get a good night's sleep." Rayleigh clasped her hand across the table. "I'll see you in the morning."

One-Mile left Sunset in a really shitty mood. Brea wasn't marrying Bryant, and he needed to figure out how to convince her to his way of thinking fast. That meant using his brain and asking the right questions.

Mentally, he sifted through his options. They all sucked. As usual, he was on the outside. Yeah, his sparkling personality was probably to blame. He didn't go out of his way to make friends, never had. SEALs like Hunter and Logan formed bonds as deep as brothers with their teammates. One-Mile had always worked alone and that hadn't bothered him.

Until now.

As Led Zeppelin ground out "Kashmir" over his Jeep's speakers, his phone rang. He hoped Brea wanted to talk…but he was half expecting Cutter, itching to cuss him out. Instead, he saw Zy's name on his screen.

"What's up?" The hesitation on the other end started to worry him. "Zy?"

"Oh, fuck it. You free tonight?"

"What do you need?"

"I want to talk." He sighed. "About Trees."

Yeah, Zy probably wasn't happy that he'd accused his BFF of being a backstabber. "What's there to say?"

"I want to go over the evidence."

"All right. When and where?"

Zy rattled off the name of a sports bar downtown. "Can you meet me about nine?"

Not exactly the way One-Mile wanted to spend a Friday night, but… "I'll be there."

"Thanks."

Then the line went dead. One-Mile looked at the clock. He had two hours to kill. After grabbing a crusty sandwich at the deli near his house, he headed for his destination. The bosses had known about Cutter and Brea's engagement before he had. It stood to reason they knew more than they were letting on. But Joaquin had never spoken much to him. And currently, Hunter wasn't speaking to him at all. That left Logan, who wasn't thrilled with him…but was least likely to slam the door in his face.

When he rang the bell, he heard a commotion inside. A kid was crying. A woman's high-pitched exasperation cut through it. A man mumbled something as footsteps stomped toward the door.

A smile crept across One-Mile's face. Sometimes, he had trouble reconciling that fierce, brash Logan was a devoted husband to his high-school sweetheart and father of twin girls. His house must be loud and chaotic and nonstop responsibility.

But it wasn't Logan who yanked the door open. Instead, Caleb greeted him, one of his granddaughters cradled in a beefy arm.

"Sir. I didn't expect to see you here."

"Hi, Walker. You're actually coming at a good time. Here." He thrust the child into his arms. "See if you can get Macy in her high chair. I've got to round up Mandy."

Before he could object, the colonel turned away to chase another little one shrieking across the living room.

One-Mile peered down at the cherubic face of the girl in his arms. Her wide blue eyes, just like her father's, looked as startled as he felt. The swish of dark curls, her tiny button nose, and baby-powder scent made her seem so innocent. But the pout on her little mouth said trouble was brewing.

Sure enough, she belted out an ear-splitting wail and tried to lurch out of his arms.

He held her firmly and raced her to the kitchen. "Look, cutie, we're stuck with each other for a few minutes. Why don't you sit down and chill?"

But when he tried to maneuver her into her high chair, the little hellion bowed her back, kicked her legs, and howled like she was on fire.

One-Mile shook his head. "I see you have your daddy's temper."

Caleb entered with a laugh, holding another screaming bundle. "You have no idea. And she's the easy one. Mandy here is the real troublemaker. Aren't you, baby girl?"

She paused to grin at her grandfather and flash a pair of dimples, as if she liked the idea of being a rabble-rouser from hell. Macy watched. And when Caleb cooed at her, she mimicked her sister's angelic expression. Well, if he didn't count her crazy eyes.

Logan was going to hate his life in about fifteen years. One-Mile almost felt sorry for the bastard.

The colonel took advantage of that moment to put Mandy in her high chair and shove a cracker in her hand. One-Mile managed to do the same with Macy as the other man slammed a sippy cup full of water on each tray.

Finally, other than the sounds of babies munching and slurping, silence reigned.

Caleb sagged against the nearby kitchen counter. "Tonight reminds me why having babies is a young man's game."

One-Mile couldn't hold in a laugh. "You a little ragged, Grandpa?"

The colonel leveled him a quelling glare. "Well, this old man has two words for you. They start with an F and a you."

That only made him laugh harder. "You babysitting tonight so Logan and Tara could go out?"

That would suck…but that's the way his luck was running these days.

"No. If I'd willingly signed up for that insanity, I would have come prepared. This was a last-minute emergency." Caleb grabbed a couple of jars of baby food from the cabinet and a pair of tiny spoons from a drawer before swiping two bibs off the counter. "Logan thought it would be a great idea to test out the Razor scooter he bought—strictly for Tyler Murphy's boys, of course." His accompanying eye roll called bullshit on Logan's claim. "Did I mention there are three of them, all under the age of five?"

That made One-Mile grin. "So you're saying they didn't need one, and Logan took it out for a spin himself?"

"Yep." Caleb opened a jar of sweet potatoes and shoved it in his hand, along with a little spoon. "So about ten minutes later, Tara had to take him to the ER. He's got a broken finger, a sprained knee, and he's waiting for stitches." The older man bent to Mandy. "Sometimes I wonder about your daddy, princess. I think war scrambled his brains."

The little girl giggled and shrieked in happiness, flashing her dimples again. Her twin's expression was identical.

"Did Carlotta come with you?"

He nodded. "She's in the girls' room, trying to clean up the Chernobyl-like disaster of toys they made in three minutes flat. When my kids were young, I wasn't home a lot, so I missed most of this day-to-day craziness. When I was around, I'd take the boys outside with a ball and chase them to exhaustion. Kimber…" He shook his head. "She always wanted to have fashion shows and paint my nails—at least until the boys teased the girliness out of her. But I never knew how to entertain her, so I can only imagine these two are going to keep Logan on his toes for a couple of decades. Isn't that right, princesses?" he asked them with a big smile.

Clearly, the colonel loved his granddaughters.

"Hey, see if you can get Macy to eat, would you?" The older man shoved a jar of food in his hands.

One-Mile froze. "Sir, I don't… I've never fed a—"

"Baby? It's not rocket science. Put food on half the spoon and see if she'll eat it. Be prepared to wipe her mouth. Dodge if she starts spitting."

Those instructions weren't exactly comforting. He stared between the baby and the pureed sweet potatoes in his grip. Oh, fuck. He was going to suck at this.

But surprisingly, he didn't. Most of the jar, ten minutes, and a messy face later, Macy started to fuss when he tried to feed her another bite.

"She's done," Caleb said. "I think they both are. Thanks for the hand."

"You're welcome."

The colonel wiped off their sweet little faces and set them free to roam the house again, then turned to him. "I'm guessing you didn't come here for a crash course in parenting."

His mouth twitched. "No, sir."

"Anything I can help you with?"

As much as One-Mile liked the colonel and respected his opinion, it was doubtful he knew anything about Cutter and Brea's engagement. "Not unless you can explain a woman."

"No. God, I hope you weren't coming to Logan for advice."

"Information."

"Ah, well, I can't give you that, but it took me thirty years and two wives to learn the only skill that's saved my ass: listening. It sucks, but it's effective."

One-Mile sighed. "Yeah, I'd listen if she'd talk to me."

"Even in her silence, she's telling you something. You've just got to stop talking long enough to hear it."

With that bit of advice pinging through his brain, he shook the colonel's hand and headed to the sports bar Zy had suggested. Since he'd arrived a few minutes early, he grabbed a brew and waited.

The place was dark and narrow and decorated with tacky light fixtures emblazoned with beer brands' logos. A neon sign led patrons to the bathrooms with a bright yellow 2 pee. The place was filled with hipsters of all ages, but way more men than women. TVs lined every wall, playing all kinds of programs—everything from high school football games to tabloid entertainment shows.

One-Mile tuned them all out and ordered a Stella. When the bartender slid it across the scarred countertop, he paid, then took a long pull and started thinking.

Why would Brea suddenly decide to marry a man she claimed to love but wasn't hot for? And why would she choose the safe option when he was standing right in front of her? Yeah, he wasn't perfect. And if he had a do-over, he wouldn't charge into the salon like a fidiot and make the even stupider mistake of letting her crawl under his skin so much that he forgot to ask the most important question about her engagement.

Why?

So what had she said in her silence? She'd admitted she'd been hurt when he'd walked out that awful fucking morning he'd returned from St. Louis, but she hadn't said yes to Cutter then. Which meant she hadn't agreed to become the Boy Scout's fiancée simply out of spite. And One-Mile figured she hadn't done it merely to make him jealous…though he was. He knew it couldn't be for the sex. The two of them hadn't been having it a few weeks back. With Bryant out of town, they couldn't be having it now, despite the fact they were engaged. Even though she said she loved Cutter—which chapped his ass—he wasn't convinced she was *in* love with the guy. If she was, wouldn't she have agreed to marry the asshole long ago? Yeah, and she would never have fallen into his own bed once, much less again and again.

So Brea had a reason for this sudden engagement he just wasn't seeing.

Cage had mentioned his brother mopping up the "mess" he had supposedly made. The big cop hadn't been talking about her reputation, since he'd apparently just ruined that today. So what the hell had Cage meant?

One-Mile turned the question over in his brain for a few minutes while absently staring at the overhead TV. But he could only think of one.

Brea was pregnant.

"Hey, man."

A slap on the back had him spinning around to find Zy sliding onto the stool beside him and motioning the bartender for a brew.

One-Mile felt too frozen to nod back.

Had he actually fucking knocked Brea up?

That made sense in a way nothing else did.

Given Brea's upbringing, she'd be looking to get married ASAP so the good people of Sunset wouldn't think she was a "fallen woman" or some other antiquated notion. Every time he'd taken her to bed, he'd been too fucking impatient to wear a condom. Since she'd been a virgin, he doubted she'd been on the pill.

It all fit.

Oh, holy shit.

Had she conceived when he'd last taken her to bed three weeks ago? Would she even know yet? Granted, he was no expert, but One-Mile doubted it. That meant she'd conceived in August—three fucking *months* ago.

"You okay, man?" Zy asked, gripping the neck of his cold one. "You look shaken. Friday treating you all right?"

"Yeah," he managed to reply…but his head raced.

He pictured Brea in his bed, her belly rounding with their child. He imagined holding her hand while she birthed the life they'd created together. He envisioned feeding his own son or daughter sweet potatoes and looking into his or her cherubic face with a smile.

Everything inside him both roared in celebration and quaked in terror.

After the shithead example he'd grown up with, what did he know about being a father?

"Hell of a week, huh?" Zy prompted.

You could say that. "Yeah."

Why the fuck hadn't she told him?

Because she'd never intended him to be anything but a good time? No, that wasn't Brea. She didn't have a snooty or conniving bone in her body.

But after he'd seemingly walked away from her following his stupid-ass confrontation with Montilla, what had she felt were her options? Especially when she'd convinced herself he didn't love her anymore?

Cutter Bryant was her backup plan.

The question now was, how did he convince her to have faith again and choose him instead?

"Look, I know you're probably not thrilled that I want to grill you about why you decided Trees is the asshole around here but—"

"You hear that Cutter got engaged last night?"

Zy blinked at the abrupt change of subject. "Um…yeah. I overheard the bosses talking about it shortly after quitting time."

"Did they say why?"

"Cutter popped the question? No." Zy clapped his shoulder. "Look, I know you had a thing for the girl but—"

"Not anymore." He didn't dare tell anyone how he really felt about her, especially if she was having his baby. Time to compartmentalize his shit, get down to business, then figure out how to corner Brea again—alone—and wrest the fucking truth from her. "Never mind. Let's talk through the evidence."

Zy scowled at the abrupt change of subject. Then he shrugged. "I've talked to Trees about the night you were taken from the parking lot in Acapulco. He said you told him to leave."

"Yep. But I expected him to put up a little more of a fight, bring backup—something. He just drove off."

"What would you have done in his shoes?"

"Shot a motherfucker or two."

Zy scratched the side of his head as if he was scraping for patience. "You know his specialty is computers and tech. He doesn't have your gift with a gun. Pretty much no one does, man."

He'd had this same argument with Hunter while he'd still been in the hospital. Maybe they were right. But something still felt off.

"Okay, but he didn't come back or call anyone for hours, did he?"

"You didn't realize your food had been drugged?"

Is that what Zy thought? "Why do you say that?"

"Trees made it to the parking lot of the police station about a mile away and passed out. Some cop woke him up, like, ten hours later. He didn't even remember driving there. I assumed you'd figured out that you'd been drugged, too."

Was it even true or just Zy covering for his bestie? "Since they beat my fucking skull in and I passed out, I didn't get that chance. Why didn't Trees tell me himself?"

"He's felt so fucking bad about what happened to you, man… He didn't know what to say."

Maybe. And maybe it was all bullshit. But if Brea was really pregnant and planning to marry Cutter so she'd have a father for his baby, he couldn't care about EM Security's internal mole now or wait for Montilla to come to a fabricated local safe house.

He was going to have to wrest his future back now. He was going to have to take the fight to the drug lord.

"Well, if you can prove Trees innocent, then I've got no hard feelings. If you can't, tell your pal to keep looking over his shoulder. Someday, I'll be there."

That pissed Zy off. "Wanting your pound of flesh?"

"Wouldn't you?"

Zy couldn't say no without making himself a liar. "I get it. But I'm telling you, it's not Trees."

"Are you convinced it's not him because you have a shred of proof or because you don't want him to be guilty?"

"Stop being an asshole. Trees and I go way back. I know because I *know*."

One-Mile sneered. He'd seen people sell their own family out for a buck. Exchanging a co-worker no one liked for a pile of cash was nothing to lots of folks. And if that resulted in the death of the drug lord's wife, too bad.

"Sure. Whatever. I've got to go." He stood.

Zy grabbed his arm. "I'm not done fucking talking to you."

He glared down at the thick fingers wrapped around his arm, then back into Zy's angry blue eyes. "What are you looking for here? You want me to believe Trees is innocent because you said so? I don't work that way."

The Efron lookalike released him and sighed as he sank onto his stool again. "I just want you to listen."

This fucking game was annoying him, but the guy wasn't going to let it go. "For shits and giggles, let's say you're right. Trees is a choirboy. But we have an internal mole, no question. It's not me or any of the bosses. We *know* that. It can't be Josiah or Cutter. Neither of them had the memo with the address and schematic of Valeria's house in St. Louis. I passed that on to Trees to see what would happen. Then I waited. And what do you know? Company came, ready to kill. If it's not your pal, who do you think is the guilty fuck?"

Zy fell silent for a long moment. "Maybe someone hacked his email."

"Maybe you're grasping at straws."

"No, I'm looking at every potential possibility to explain what happened. But let's be real. If you hadn't decided to go all cowboy on us, Montilla's crew would never have killed a handful of cops and he would never have gotten away."

Yeah, that had been his life for the last two weeks. It would fuck his future, too, if he couldn't make everything right. "Don't deflect blame. I know what I did. But even if I snuff Montilla, we'll still have a mole who will be susceptible to the next son of a bitch who comes through with a pile of cash and a desire to shut us down."

"I know. But I'm telling you, man, it's not Trees."

This argument was going nowhere.

"There's no evidence his email was hacked." And no one else on EM's payroll One-Mile hadn't already considered, except… "What about Tessa? She's the only other person I sent Valeria's address and home schematic to. Maybe she passed it on to Montilla."

Zy recoiled. "What? No. Hell no. How would she have ever met a monster like him anyway?"

One-Mile shrugged. "Maybe he found her."

"You're wrong. She's too sweet to sell anyone out."

"You only think that because you're fucking her."

"Fuck you! I'm not. When it comes to the bosses' nonfraternization policy, I have not stepped one toe over the line."

One-Mile wasn't sure whether to believe him. Yeah, it was possible Zy had never touched the pretty blonde. But even if he hadn't fucked her physically, he'd done it mentally at least a thousand times.

Elbow on the bar, One-Mile leaned in. "Listen, either your best friend or your girl is our traitor. You better figure it out before the blind spots in your vision cost someone around here their life. And now I'm leaving."

Zy snarled a curse, jaw clenched, and cast a furious glance away. Then he froze. "Holy shit. What is this?"

One-Mile followed the other guy's line of vision and glanced at the TV. He nearly rolled his eyes in disgust at the tabloid program on the screen. Why should he give a shit that very famous bombshell Shealyn West was kissing some random dick who clearly wasn't her co-star and reported off-screen lover, Tower Trent? Except…this wasn't a scene from a TV show and it wasn't a mere press of lips. It was a full-on, ravenous invasion of her mouth as the mystery man wedged her against a car with his body and tongue-fucked her ruthlessly.

One-Mile peered closer at the profile of the man steeped in shadow on the screen. Even if he hadn't known whose body his teammate was supposed to be guarding, a glance told him exactly who that random dick was.

Cutter Bryant.

"Son of a bitch…"

"You're seeing this, too, right?"

Yeah. "Impossible to miss."

"We both know who that is. I'm not hallucinating?"

"Nope." It was fucking obvious.

"Lucky bastard. Damn…" Zy muttered. "But I feel sorry for his new fiancée. He's never looked at Brea like he wanted to do *that* to her."

Because Cutter didn't. And Brea didn't want him to. This was just more evidence to support his theory that their engagement was one-hundred percent fucking fake.

"Oh, I feel sorry for her, too." Because One-Mile was determined that, no matter how ugly the truth was, they were going to have it out tonight. "Bye."

"Where you going?" Zy called after him.

He didn't answer, just walked out the door.

chapter
six

One-Mile drove around Brea's neighborhood a few times. Nothing suspicious, so a couple of blocks from her house, he parked the SUV he'd borrowed from Caleb to make sure he evaded any possible tail of Montilla's, then ran for her house.

Her white compact wasn't outside.

It was one o'clock in the morning. Cutter was in California sucking face with a TV star, so where could she fucking be? Montilla couldn't have zoned in on her already, right?

That possibility made him break out in a cold sweat.

The cottage she shared with her dad was dark. Around the back of the house, he found a window unlocked and took a chance the preacher had never bothered retrofitting this old, small-town place with an alarm system. Sure enough, when he raised the pane, no shrieking pealed to alert the whole street—or the cops—that he was breaking in.

He eased onto the hardwoods inside and closed the window behind him. On silent footfalls, he crept through the house. Without a floor plan, he wasn't sure which direction he'd find Brea's room.

His first trek took him to the master. Empty. That didn't surprise One-Mile much. He thought he'd seen Brea's father's practical brown sedan parked at a house a few blocks over. Jennifer Collins's place? That was his guess. At this time of night, that probably meant the preacher was banging the lonely widow…

So where was Brea?

Through the dark, he doubled back to the living room to investigate the other side of the house. Behind the last door, he found another tidy bedroom. It had to be hers. It, too, was empty. Since her room wasn't visible from the street, he flipped on a small desk lamp and gave it a visual scan.

The walls were a pale lavender. A simple white quilt covered the bed, accented by gray sheets with little white flowers. She'd tossed a purple and gray throw at the bottom, over the simple white footboard. The furniture looked like a relic from her childhood. An area rug that matched her walls warmed the floor beside her bed. On the other side, gray curtains that matched her sheets gaped wide open, overlooking their small but meticulous backyard.

The room looked like Brea. Smelled like her.

But where the fuck was the woman herself?

Her absence prompted more questions. It incited panic. He wanted some goddamn answers.

He booted up the computer sitting on her desk. While he waited, he prowled through her drawers to see if she kept a calendar or list of appointments.

Maybe he should feel guilty about invading her privacy. He didn't. This was about her safety, his sanity, and their future. Scruples weren't going to fix any of that shit.

His search dredged up only notes from her beauty school days, a small stack of bills with due dates written neatly on the front, and a few pictures of years gone by, mostly of her and Boy Scout Bryant.

With a scowl, One-Mile replaced everything where he'd found it, then did a quick dive through her dresser across the room. He found prenatal vitamins under a stack of her very modest underwear—and had to tell his suddenly pounding heart to take a rest. Not every woman who took these horse pills was actually pregnant. She might have them merely because her body needed a major supplement.

He felt behind the dresser and found a gap in the cardboard backing, toward the bottom. Tucked inside was a large envelope with the name and address of an ob-gyn in Lafayette, along with a reminder card for an appointment a month from now. More circumstantial evidence, not proof. After all, women often saw a doctor for female-related things at least once a year.

The rest of the room netted nothing except to give him a sense of what her life within these four walls was like. She'd been coddled, adored, and sheltered. She'd grown up quiet and dutiful and kind.

As far as One-Mile could tell, falling into bed with him was the only time she'd ever done anything her father would disapprove of.

For her to defy what she'd been raised to believe, what would her feelings for you have to be?

Unless he missed his guess, she'd loved him. Since she wasn't flighty, he'd bet some part of her still did. But she'd gotten spooked when he'd told her they needed to take a step back.

More and more, Brea being pregnant fit. He just needed to find her to confirm.

After righting the rest of her room, he sat at her desk. Her computer wasn't password protected, so with the touch of a button, he was in. He did a quick prowl through her emails, but they netted nothing of interest. Ditto with her electronic calendar. But one other icon in the dock along the bottom stuck out.

He clicked the green circle. Up popped the app to locate her phone. *Bingo.*

Seconds later, the system prompted him for a password. Shit.

He clicked until he found a list of her passwords. The one to find her device was dangphone1. With a grim twist of his lips, he typed it in.

Within seconds, he had her location. An apartment building on the north end of Lafayette. Why the fuck was she wherever this was?

One-Mile zeroed in until he had an address, then he cross-referenced that with her contacts.

Cutter's place. Why would she go to the Boy Scout's apartment in the middle of the night? It wasn't for a booty call since the son of a bitch wasn't there.

One-Mile jotted the address and was about to shut down the device when another icon caught his attention. Pictures. They were worth a thousand words, right? Maybe they would tell him something…

She hadn't snapped any images since Friday morning. The last few were of a client's freshly auburned hair with a cascade of reddish curls down her back. That's it. The afternoon before was more along a similar theme.

Yesterday morning, however, she'd taken a forty-two-second video. It seemingly started on a small, sterile room. A doctor's office?

He clicked on the clip.

"You ready?" The camera reflected a young, professional blonde in her early thirties, dressed in a pair of pastel scrubs.

"I think so." That was Brea, and she sounded nervous.

"This is going to be cold."

The camera jiggled and jostled for a second until it panned down to Brea's belly. She'd pulled her leggings down to her hips and lifted her T-shirt up above her ribs.

And he saw the slight bulge that hadn't been there before.

One-Mile's entire body pinged electric. She *was* pregnant—and not just a few weeks. He'd fucking been right.

Heart racing and palms sweating, he watched as the blonde in the video smeared some clear gel all over Brea's little bump, then set a rounded implement low on her belly.

A crackling noise filled the air, followed by a sound that seemed like something in a vacuum. Then…he heard it, a faint but rapid *whoosh, whoosh, whoosh*.

His breath stopped.

"Is that it?" Brea sounded on the verge of tears.

"Yes, that's your baby's heartbeat. He or she sounds strong."

"Oh, my gosh." Brea sniffled, then fell silent and listened.

That soft sound was the best fucking thing he'd ever heard. That was *his* son or daughter, conceived with the woman he loved.

"Amazing," Brea breathed, her voice catching on emotion. "Wow…"

The electronic heartbeat filled his ears for a few precious moments more, strong and reaffirming his will to claim all that belonged to him.

Then the video ended.

One-Mile played it again. He wanted to memorize every sight and sound. He wished like fuck he'd been there with Brea, holding her hand as they'd listened to their baby's heartbeat together.

All too soon, the video quit, jolting him back to her empty bedroom.

With a curse, One-Mile texted the clip to himself, then deleted the electronic trail. Next, he shut down her computer and stood.

Resolution burned in his veins.

He'd had plenty of reason to fight for Brea before. But now that she was having his baby? He would stop at nothing, burn down the world—whatever it took—to remove the obstacles between them until he called her his for good.

One-Mile tucked himself in the shadows outside Cutter's door less than twenty minutes later, the visible puffs his breaths created in the chill the only sign he was there at all.

Just before he'd trekked up to the apartment's second floor, he'd spotted a white compact in an assigned spot, double-checked the VIN matched Brea's, and continued up.

She was at Cutter's tonight for a reason. Since her father wasn't home, she hadn't run here simply to be alone. One-Mile had to wonder if she was avoiding him.

I've got news for you, pretty girl, and it's all bad...

Fuck giving her the opportunity not to answer the door. She was not wriggling out of his grasp tonight. He would do whatever necessary to extract the goddamn truth from her.

From an earlier glance down the side of the building, he knew every second-story apartment had a balcony. Cutter had chosen his unit well; it was the most defensible of the bunch. No one could reach his second-story terrace without equipment.

Good thing that, even though One-Mile had never been a Boy Scout, he always came prepared.

After a quick dash back to his Jeep, he found what he needed. Then he hustled back to Cutter's door and tossed a grappling hook over to the nearby balcony. He secured his end of the rope to the landing's wrought-iron railing, tested it with a strong tug, then climbed over. Dangling from the line, he worked his way, hand over hand, toward the jutting ledge.

Less than a minute later, he stood facing French doors that led to a darkened room, probably the master. Would he find Brea asleep in that bastard's bed?

Not surprisingly, the door was locked, but if no one had ever installed a deadbolt... French doors were notoriously easy to breach. And God knew he'd never been a saint.

After a little jimmying and a swipe of a plastic card later, a click told him that lock wouldn't be an impediment anymore. He worked the rope free so that no passersby would spot his means into the unit, coiled it, and secured it to the side of his belt.

Then he walked into the apartment.

He smelled Brea before he saw her. But she wasn't in the rumpled king-size bed in the master. A touch to the warm sheets told him she'd been here recently, though.

Her purse sat in the nearby chair, with her skirt and sweater draped neatly over its back. A small duffel perched on the carpet beside it, next to her shoes.

She was definitely here.

Through the crack in the door, he saw a faint sliver of light flicker on. He peeked into the rest of the smallish, shadowy apartment. On the far side of the unit, a lone pale bulb above the stove illuminated its burners and cast a halo of light into the rest of the kitchen.

In the middle stood Brea.

The sight of her, barefoot with her long, loose hair flowing to her waist, was a sucker punch to his chest. His whole body went taut. His temper flared.

She'd had the chance to tell him about his baby when they'd been alone at the salon a few hours ago. She fucking hadn't. Had she ever intended to tell him? Or had she simply planned to pass off his kid to the rest of the world as Cutter's?

Brea stepped toward the refrigerator. The hem of her thin nightgown skimmed her slender thighs. She looked small and vulnerable. Fuckable. He was angry as hell, but not even fury stopped desire from scalding his veins. Nothing did, goddamn it. Anytime he and Brea were in the same room, he wanted her. But when she was half-dressed and alone, like now? All he could think about was stripping her down, then penetrating and fucking her until she clung to him. Until she screamed. Until she admitted that she only wanted him.

Until she confessed that she was still in love with him.

One-Mile yanked on his mental leash. He'd come here with objectives. Prying the truth out of her came first. After that… Well, he saw no reason not to press Brea underneath him until she understood she was at his very dubious mercy. Then he'd happily prove her will to resist him was all show.

And he'd confess, too. He had no problem being brutally honest about the fact that, when it came to Brea Bell, he had no defenses.

One-Mile crept out of the bedroom and trekked across the dark living room, never taking his eyes off her. She tugged on the refrigerator door and ducked inside to grab a glass. After a few swallows, she turned, giving him her profile as she yawned and stretched.

The gleam of the nearby light penetrated her sheer nightgown. He caught sight of the small but unmistakable bump of her belly.

More proof that Brea was pregnant and that baby was his.

Two urges hit him at once. To stamp his claim on her and their child, yes. That, he'd expected. But he hadn't anticipated the extra kick of lust impacting his system at the sight of her rounding and fertile. He wanted his hands on her, his fucking mouth all over her, his dick everywhere inside her. He wanted her to understand she belonged to him—now, always, and forever.

Brea shut the refrigerator door, then leaned over to extinguish the bulb above the stove. A split second before the room went dark, she caught sight of him. Their gazes connected. Her eyes flared. The cup slipped from her hand.

As blackness fell, the sounds of glass shattering filled the air.

"Pierce?" she gasped.

Was she surprised he'd found her or spooked that he'd broken into Cutter's lair to reach her? Either way, the raw panic in her trembling voice was unmistakable.

If she didn't know yet that he intended to screw up all her wedding plans, she should.

"Don't move." Crossing the tile floor, he reached the stove and flipped on the light once more, shards of shattered glass crunching under the thick soles of his combat boots.

Brea blinked at him, pale and shaking. "W-what are you doing here?"

He prowled toward her. "Did you really think you and I were done?"

"What, talking?"

An ugly smile curled up the corners of his mouth. "To start."

She shook her head and tried to back away. "No."

"Don't move." One-Mile plucked her off her feet and lifted her against his chest.

She squealed. "Stop. Put me down. What are you doing?"

To start? "Making sure you don't slice up your feet."

As he walked back over the broken glass and carried her across the apartment, she steadied herself by looping her arms around his neck. "How did you find me? And how did you get inside?"

One-Mile lifted a sharp brow at her. "You should have figured out by now that nothing will keep me from you."

She hesitated, rosy lips parted as if she meant to speak...but she didn't have a comeback. "What do you want?"

"To make a few things clear. First, you're marrying Bryant over my dead fucking body." As he stormed into the bedroom, he thought of her wearing the Boy Scout's ring and warming this very bed. Rage bubbled in One-Mile's veins.

He kicked the door shut behind him. Darkness enveloped them.

She trembled. "Pierce—"

"I'm not done." When he reached the mattress, he laid her down, feet dangling off the side, and flipped on the nightstand lamp as he straddled her, caging her flat. Then he reached for her nightgown.

"What are you doing?"

"I want to see."

Confusion settled between her brows. "See what?"

"Your body." He shoved the thin cotton up her thighs, over her hips, and dragged it halfway above her belly—before the hem trapped under her refused to stretch any more.

"Don't!" She shoved his hands away. "I'm not getting naked for you."

"I'm not looking for a cheap thrill."

"Then what—"

"I'll give you one chance to be honest with me." He held up a finger and pressed his relentless gaze down on her. "One, pretty girl. Are you pregnant?"

Her eyes went wide. She paled. The panic he'd heard in her voice earlier spread across her face. "W-why would you think that?"

One-Mile tamped down his frustration. He'd scared her by walking away. He hadn't given her the reassurances she'd needed. Fine. He accepted responsibility for that. But he'd be damned if he left here before she admitted the truth.

"I'm not playing twenty questions. Yes or no?"

She sent him a defiant lift of her chin. "Why do you care?"

"Don't yank my chain. Are you pregnant?"

"Pierce..."

"Answer me," he snarled.

"Yes." Anger tightened her lips even as tears trembled on her lashes. "Yes, I'm pregnant. Now you know."

He let out a rough breath. Since she was finally talking, maybe they'd get somewhere. "Oh, I already knew. Just like I know the answer to this question, but I want to hear it from your mouth. Who fathered that baby?"

She pressed her lips together. "Does it really matter to you?"

"You fucking better believe it does. Who?" He grabbed her shoulders. "Tell me."

Brea trembled in his grip. "You. There's only ever been you."

So he'd been right. And she might have accepted Bryant's proposal, but she hadn't taken his cock.

Even as One-Mile's triumph roared, he saw her fear. Was she afraid of him? Or of facing everything without him? Either way, he'd reassure her...eventually.

"That's right. It's *my* baby. You got pregnant that first night, didn't you? Back in August?"

She nodded. "But I only found out for sure a little over a week ago."

Everything about the way she answered told him that she'd believed he was gone from her life and she'd panicked. So she'd turned to Cutter.

"I want to see." With a growl, One-Mile lifted her off the mattress with one hand and gave the gown a savage yank with the other, dragging the cotton up her belly and over her breasts. Since she wouldn't be needing that tonight, he sent it sailing across the room. Same with her panties, so seconds later he tore those off, too.

Then he dropped her back to the sheets and stared.

Her hips had begun to round out. The slight bulge of her belly wasn't as pronounced lying down, but her tits were heavier and riper, her nipples seemingly darker. They were definitely calling his name as he cupped them in his hands and felt the change in their weight.

"Oh, pretty girl…" He could barely fucking breathe as he swept his thumb over her crest. Then he dragged his palm down the slight curve of her abdomen. The gravity of the moment felt a million times heavier than air. He couldn't drag enough into his lungs. Instead, they worked like a bellows as he cataloged the changes pregnancy had wrought on her body. "So beautiful."

Fuck, he couldn't stop touching her. And like every other time he did, his most primal urges compelled him to get close to her, touch and claim her. Never let her go. Seeing her pregnant twisted his impulses into biological imperatives. He could not walk away from her now and live.

"My body is changing."

It was, and he was loving it. "We have a lot to talk about, and we'll get to all that. But I need you. So bad."

One-Mile dragged his lips over the swells of her breasts, then worked his way down the valley in between before lifting one heavy globe to his waiting mouth and sucking her nipple inside.

"Pierce." Her breathy cry said she'd missed him and needed the hell out of him, too. "Why are you doing this to me?"

"What, touching you? Reminding you how good we are together? Want me to stop?" He circled her begging bud with his tongue before sucking it deep again. "Do you, baby?"

Under him, she wriggled, hips shifting. He knew the smell of her arousal; it was burned into his brain. It scented the air now, filling his nostrils, driving him to the edge of his restraint.

As he turned his attention to the other taut tip, nipping with his teeth, her lashes fluttered shut. "No."

"No, don't touch you? Or no, don't stop?"

She opened her eyes, glowing golden with desire as she bit her lip and arched closer. Her breaths turned fast and harsh. She gripped his shoulders, her little nails digging into him. Yeah, she was fighting it…and she was losing.

"Tell me, pretty girl. What do you want?" He punctuated the question with a long pull on her pert nipple.

Brea dragged in a sharp gasp. "Oh!"

He watched her pulse beat wildly at her neck. Beneath him, her legs drifted apart, the beautifully welcoming gesture unconscious.

One-Mile fused his stare with hers, took another drag on the hard peaks of her tits, then threw a fucking party at the throaty moan that slipped from her lips.

Brea may not have said yes yet…but she clearly didn't have the resolve to refuse him with a no.

He could work with that, especially since he didn't mind playing dirty.

"I'm going to keep touching you until you tell me to stop," he challenged as he pinched her nipple and skimmed his lips up her neck. When he felt her pulse pound under his lips, he bit gently, reveling in her gasping response. "Got anything to say?"

She shook her head, then pressed it back into the pillow, offering him her throat.

He just smiled. "That's what I thought."

Need surging, he kissed his way up the smooth, vulnerable column before covering her mouth. He didn't have to part her lips with his own; she was already open to him. Waiting for him. He raked her shy tongue with his, tasting the tart hint of the lemonade she'd been drinking mixed with a heady something so Brea. A shudder zipped down his spine.

Jesus, this woman slayed him.

She wrapped her arms even tighter around him as another feminine moan slipped free. Then she cocked her head to encourage his kiss and slowly began to give herself over. But he was a greedy bastard. He wanted more. He wanted her to surrender faster—like right fucking now.

One-Mile reached under her head to grab a fistful of hair at her crown and angled her face to his satisfaction. He jerked her even closer. His tongue slid even deeper.

She met him stroke for stroke. Her next moan pinged off the walls. Her kiss grew wild.

He greedily took all she offered and still demanded more.

What was it about this woman? He'd gotten an early start on his sex life, thanks to his degenerate dad. Wherever the military had taken him around the world, he'd fucked hard, well, and often. He didn't have any trouble going online or walking into a bar and finding someone willing to shuck her clothes and spread her legs. So why was it that the minute he'd met the preacher's pretty virginal daughter, every other female had ceased to exist for him?

Brea was kind and sweet. She put others first. She was too delicate to be sexy in the way he used to prefer, but Brea and her shy sensuality lured him like no one else. She was somehow both sheltered and smart. Quiet but stubborn. One of a kind. But none of that explained why she'd hooked him with a glance.

That big heart of hers did.

She'd seemingly looked at him in Hunter Edgington's open doorway and given him some untouched chunk of it that he'd been desperate to have. Cutter warning him away had meant nothing since Brea spent the rest of that barbecue sending him curious glances from under her long lashes. He'd tattooed her timid, pink-cheeked smiles into his memory. They'd kept him hard well into the next day.

From the instant he'd met her, he'd known he could pleasure the hell out of her. But for reasons he hadn't been able to explain, he didn't simply want to bang her. When he'd driven her to the hospital after her father's first heart attack and she'd clung to him for comfort, he'd understood then what else she needed—besides toe-curling sex—that he could give her in return: security. So he'd held her in his arms and resolved to make her world better.

When she'd clung to him and cried, Brea had sealed her fate.

She was his.

Since he knew shit about relationships, it was no surprise he was doing everything ass-backwards. He'd taken her to bed before he'd taken her out. He'd gotten her pregnant before he put a ring on her finger. The situation wasn't optimal, but he'd work with it and fix it all eventually.

Right now, he had to make sure she knew exactly in whose arms—and whose bed—she belonged.

"Pierce..." she panted.

"I'm not going anywhere. You got a yes or no for me yet?"

"Just kiss me again."

"If I do that, pretty girl, I'm going to get inside you and fuck you hard. All night. I won't stop. If you're going to say no, say it now."

Her breathing stuttered. Her thoughts churned.

Then she licked her lips. And finally, buttoned-up Brea closed her eyes and offered him her pretty pink mouth, swollen with sin. That was an invitation he couldn't turn down.

He grabbed her chin. "Last chance. You saying yes?"

Brea's heart beat wildly as she blinked up at Pierce. The air was thick, tense, silent except for their rasping breaths as he waited for her answer.

She hesitated. She shouldn't consent. She shouldn't want him.

Even if Cutter didn't love or desire her, he would be disappointed that she was weak to the sins of Pierce's flesh, especially during their engagement. Then again, he wasn't in love with her, and she doubted he was spending his nights in California alone. And it wasn't as if she could get more pregnant.

Her father would be dismayed that she hadn't kept her promise to distance herself from Pierce for even two weeks, much less a whole month. But unlike Daddy's high school girlfriend, the man she loved hadn't left her because he'd gotten bored and wandered into the arms of another. Not even close. The minute he'd learned about her engagement to Cutter, he'd come after her—hard. And he clearly wasn't letting up.

Because he still loved her?

"C'mon, pretty girl. What's it going to be?"

She shivered, just like she did every time he called her that.

Was she being stupid? Impulsive? She'd let him undress her and touch her. And Brea couldn't be less than honest with herself. Even if they'd resolved nothing, she ached for Pierce. She wanted him.

"Heaven help me, but I can't say no to you."

"Yeah?" His fingers bit into her jaw as a dark smile crawled across his mouth.

He laved his way up her neck and guided her lips under his again. "Then get ready to scream."

Before she could so much as whimper, he took her lips with a muffled groan, tasting potent and wicked and wonderful. The moment she yielded her mouth to him, he tightened his grip, demanding she give him more.

Right or wrong, sin or not, Pierce was exactly where she wanted him.

Brea clutched his steely shoulders under his black formfitting shirt and let her fingers roam his strong, broad back. Then she wriggled and swayed to entice him closer as she lost herself in his dizzying kiss.

Everything about him made her feel female—sensual, adored, vulnerable. Every time he came near her, her skin awakened and her heart raced. She ached. Even now, she was acutely aware of his shirt sliding slickly over her sensitive nipples. The rough cotton canvas of his khakis abraded the insides of her thighs. She wrapped her leg around his calf and slid her toes against the thick leather of his combat boots as she lifted her hips in entreaty.

"Fuck," he growled as he ground his thick erection right where she needed him most. "Every time I get my hands on you, all my good intentions go out the window."

She knew exactly what he meant. Until he'd barged into the beauty shop, she'd meant to put him out of her life and walk the straight-and-narrow for her baby's sake. That meant marrying Cutter. That meant giving up on love. But every time she found herself near Pierce Walker, she got weak and all her good intentions ended up paving her road to hell.

He toed off his boots, fisted his shirt at his nape and tore it free, then dropped his hands to his fly. As he unbuttoned his pants, his knuckles brushed the aching bud between her legs. She let out a breathy, pleading groan.

He focused his black eyes on her, then raked merciless fingers through her folds. "Oh, fuck. You're wet and swollen."

Approval roughened his voice. Pleasure jolted her.

But when he settled his thumb over her throbbing button and rubbed, bliss became wrenching torment. Her breathing turned choppy. She bit her lip to hold in a cry. "You do that to me."

"I'm not even a little bit sorry. You arouse the hell out of me, too, baby. When I look at you, every shred of IQ I have rushes down to my cock. I don't care that you make me stupid. I'll do anything to fuck you."

That shouldn't warm her or make her feel so wanted. But it did. She loved his single-minded focus on her pleasure.

No, he hadn't talked about tomorrow or being a part of his baby's life or anything remotely practical. But when he slid a pair of his big fingers inside her and rubbed at a sensitive spot, her eyes widened, her breath hitched, and she let go of everything except her undeniable attachment to this man who literally held her in the palm of his hand.

"Pierce. Oh! That feels so…"

"Good?" he murmured against her ear. "Yeah, that's it. Grind on my fingers. I love to make you hot and watch all your good-girl decorum give way to begging, leg-spreading need."

He had the filthiest mouth—and she'd never imagined she would like that in a man. But on Pierce, she loved it.

When she was in his arms, she barely recognized herself. He seemed to know exactly where, when, and how to touch her. He understood her body far better than she did. He'd introduced her to a part of herself she hadn't known existed. She couldn't unknow it now. She didn't want to.

"How do you do this to me?" Brea clung as her need gathered, thickened, sharpened.

"Do what? Ramp you up? Make you pant? Remind you that you're *mine?*"

"Yes," she said into his skin as she opened her lips over the hard cap of his shoulder.

His salty musk pervaded her nose and revved her heart as his maleness glazed her tongue. Her need kindled hotter. She laved him again before nipping his hard flesh with her teeth.

He tossed his head back with a hiss and shoved his digits even deeper. "Oh, yeah… Sink your teeth into me, pretty girl. Fuck. Take what's yours. Show me you're as hungry as this little pussy tightening on my fingers."

His words speared her with savage need. She bit down again, this time sinking her teeth into the muscle between his shoulder and neck. Then she sucked frantically.

Pierce went taut with a growl. "If you keep it up, I'm going to shove every inch of my cock deep and fuck you now."

"Please." Her body jolted and pinged. Her blood raced. Her restless, hollow desperation for the climax he'd dragged her to the edge of made her claw at him in silent demand.

Brea couldn't remember ever wanting him more. She bit at the strong tendons in his neck again, wishing she could imprint his taste on her tongue. In response, he manipulated that so-sensitive spot between her thighs until her ache for him felt boundless, ceaseless.

"Pierce!" she gasped in a writhing plea.

"You want more?"

Why was he even asking? She whimpered in answer, squeezing her eyes shut as she twisted and bucked, seeking that last bit of sensation she needed to find ecstasy.

He pulled back. "Don't be stubborn. You want to come? All it takes is one word. Just say yes."

Brea could no longer think of a single reason to say no. Even if their future was uncertain, she still loved him. She always would.

Maybe tonight would be the beginning of something new for them. Or maybe it would be the last time she ever touched him. Either way, she wanted to give herself over to him completely so she could savor and hoard every moment they had together.

"Yes." She pressed her lips along his jaw before settling her mouth under his. "Always yes."

"Thank fuck. I've missed you so much."

"I've missed you, too." Her body clenched. Her heart panged. Her eyes stung. "Don't leave me again."

With one hand, he cupped her cheek and forced her stare to his. With the other, his thumb still swirled where she ached most. "Shh, pretty girl. I never want to."

His solemn expression had Brea clutching him tighter. "Hurry. I need you."

"How? Tell me."

"Inside me." *And with me. Always.*

His fingertips rubbed and prodded inside her again. "Oh, I am."

"No." She groped for his zipper and yanked it down, then wrapped her greedy hand around his hot, pulsing shaft with a squeeze. "This. Inside me. Now."

Agonized pleasure tightened his face as he growled, "Spell it out. Tell me exactly what you want."

Brea pulled on his thick erection again, stroking the veins, cataloging the velvet skin over his steely length. "You know."

"Yeah, but I want to hear you say it. C'mon…"

"Fuck me," Brea whispered.

She had never spoken that word in her life. It was both horrifying and freeing.

And ultimately rewarding.

"Oh, hell," Pierce groaned as he kicked off his pants. Within seconds, he'd curled his big hands around her backside and fitted his crest against her clutching opening. Then he went still.

"You're speaking my language, pretty girl. I'm going to fuck you so hard." With a harsh forward thrust, he made good on his threat, breaching her to the hilt and slamming the headboard against the wall. "But I'm also going to make love to you until you *know* you have my heart."

Brea's breath caught. "You've always had mine."

Pierce drew back and captured her gaze before he thrust inside her again, penetrating her clear to her soul.

Then, when he was fully seated again, he surprised her by rolling to his back and spreading her out on top of him, chest to chest, slanting his mouth under hers for a breath-stealing kiss. Brea fell into him even more, drowning as he plunged up into her. She rocked to meet him, shocked by the sensations of her skin dragging over his and his erection scraping all the nerve endings inside her.

"Your cheeks are flushing." He shot her a cocky grin.

It was no secret Pierce got off on undoing her.

She licked her lips. "Your eyes are getting darker."

"Shit, I have to watch you." She didn't even have time to sputter a question before he sat her up on his erection, bent his knees, and rammed up into her with dizzying force.

Her head slid back with a long moan as her breasts bounced, her breathing hitched, and her sex clenched greedily.

"Oh, look at you. My pretty, pregnant girl getting fucked..."

Pierce unraveled her with every heartbeat, every moment, every word. Brea scratched and gasped for the climax swelling inside her. She ached for him almost as much as she wanted this pleasure to go on forever.

He caught her breasts in his big hands and squeezed, thumbing her nipples, sending her spiraling up even more. "Are they still tender?"

"Sometimes."

He gentled immediately. "Better?"

She nodded, closing her eyes on a ragged sigh. "Every time you touch me, it's so good."

"Yeah?" he moaned, then cupped the small bulge of her belly. "God, I love the way your body is changing."

"Really?" When she looked in a mirror lately, she felt so self-conscious.

"You have no idea what you do to me. So sexy. I was desperate to fuck you before, but now...you'll have to push me off you, and even then I'm never going to stop."

Brea never wanted him to.

He grabbed her hips, shoved her down harder, hurtling her even faster toward climax. They fell into a rhythm, hard and deep, staring into each other's eyes as the sensations clawed higher. He dragged his thumb across her clit, ripping through the last of her composure. She ground down on him and dug her nails into his shoulders as her blood roared and converged. Her body seized up. She struggled for her next breath as she jolted and let out an anguished cry.

This climax was going to roll over her and redefine ecstasy for her. Like the man himself, it terrified and thrilled her at once.

"Pierce!"

Suddenly, he rolled her to her back once more, took her legs into the crooks of his elbows, and careened into her over and over, each lunge punctuated by a hiss of seething breath. "I feel you. Oh, fuck. Yes... Give it to me."

She'd been unable to deny him anything from the moment they'd met. Nothing was different now.

Orgasm exploded, rocking through her body. Above her, Pierce fucked her furiously through the pinnacle, shaking the entire bed and banging the headboard against the wall as an involuntary scream tore from her.

A throat-wrenching growl rumbled from his chest as he hardened impossibly inside her. Then his whole body shuddered as he released, too, shaking her all the way to the overwhelming end.

As they quieted and softened together, the world fell away, leaving only panting breaths, their inexplicably deep connection, and the sweet remnants of pleasure.

Brea sagged against Pierce, struggling to catch her breath and desperate never to let him go. "What happens now?"

"I tell you I love you."

She'd doubted that so many times during their days and weeks apart. But now, as he stared into her eyes, she couldn't deny his truth. "I love you, too."

He smoothed stray curls away from her face, then cradled her cheek. "So let's talk—at least until I can't stand that I'm not fucking you. That means we'll have to hurry because we've got a lot of ground to cover."

Brea lay beside him and rose up on her elbow, her long hair playing peekaboo with her lush tits and pretty berry nipples. One-Mile stared and tried like hell not to be distracted.

"All right. Let's talk." A little smile pulled at her lips. "Quickly. I don't know how long I'll be able to stand being without you, either."

He couldn't resist kissing her. "I've created a monster."

Her smile widened. "And now you have to deal with me. Poor you."

"Yeah. It's a real hardship." He winked, then he sobered. "Were you ever going to tell me you're pregnant?"

"I was trying to the morning you said we needed to take a step back. After that…" Guilt flashed in her eyes.

She hadn't seen the point. She hadn't thought he'd care.

Fuck. "So because you thought I'd 'broken up' with you, you ran to Cutter and got yourself a fiancé?"

"I didn't see any other choice. I couldn't risk upsetting Daddy, and not just because I hate to disappoint him, though that played a role, I admit. But his health…"

If her father had suffered another heart attack after that shocking news, he might not have survived.

One-Mile hated it, but… "I get that."

"I also didn't want to take a chance that the church or the town would turn its back on me. It may sound silly in this day and age, but that's why being a single mother was never an option. My reputation affects Daddy, too, not to mention my business. I rely on the good opinion of the folks in Sunset. If I don't have it, I don't have any clients."

And no way to make a living.

One-Mile scrubbed a hand down his face. He'd created a catastrophic clusterfuck with his stupid, impulsive need to feed Montilla his balls, along with a healthy dose of humiliation. *Goddamn it.* "So Cutter stepped in to 'save' you?"

"Yes."

But why would he do that? Until One-Mile had seen the video of his fellow operator with Shealyn West, he'd assumed the bastard had feelings for Brea and had moved in while she was vulnerable to secure his position in her life. But if that wasn't true, what the fuck was going on?

"I mean, we knew there still would have been scandal," Brea went on. "We talked about tying the knot the first week of January, but I'm having this baby in early May. People were going to do the math, but they would have 'forgiven' us since they've known us our whole lives. If they found out I'd been with you, though…"

A stranger. An outsider. A defiler of innocence. A foul-mouthed killer. They would have condemned her.

Who did they think they were to pass judgment?

"I get that, too. But it pisses me off."

"Honestly, Cutter didn't want this, either. But what else could I do?"

And given Montilla's vow of revenge, their options still sucked. But One-Mile refused to let her go. "Listen, whatever you think happened between us, Brea, I didn't walk away because I wanted to. Leaving you that morning killed me. You're mine, and that's our baby. I don't want you marrying Bryant. He's not in love with you."

"I know." She looked suddenly sheepish. "He never has been. I love him, but I'm not *in* love with him, either."

He froze. "But you've been together for years."

Bryant had called Brea his. The son of a bitch had warned him away at every turn.

On the other hand, he'd never seen them kiss, much less passionately. The Boy Scout had never looked at her like he couldn't wait to get her in the sack. Until their night together, she'd been a virgin.

"No." She sighed. "He's my best friend. The older brother I never had. But we've never been a couple."

Was she fucking serious? "Then why did he let everyone at EM believe you're his girlfriend?"

"To protect me."

"From who?" But One-Mile knew the answer.

She winced. "You."

He stifled a frustrated groan. "Why didn't you tell me sooner, pretty girl?"

"Honestly?" She bit her lip. "He made me promise I never would."

Of course the overprotective bastard had… One-Mile wanted to be pissed that Brea had waited months to be straight with him. But he had to focus on the bigger picture. Tonight she'd broken her promise to a man she'd known and trusted all her life. What did that say about where her loyalties lay now?

The satisfaction he got from that realization more than outweighed his anger.

"Now that I know the truth, you're definitely not marrying him."

"I don't think it would work out anyway. The morning he and I officially got engaged, he told me he's in love with someone else. I'm happy for him... except he doesn't think they have any future together."

One-Mile mulled his options, but stupid lies and well-meaning half-truths had landed them in this pile of shit. He saw no point in being anything other than straight-up with Brea from now on. Besides, she should know what was going on.

"I don't know. Have you seen this?" One-Mile rummaged on the floor for his pants, then pulled out his phone, Googled the clip of Shealyn West's scandalous kiss with her "mystery lover," and held it up.

"Seen what?" But as Brea watched, her eyes widened steadily. "Oh. Oh, my goodness. That's the actress from *Hot Southern Nights*. And Cutter!" She pressed a shocked hand to her chest. "Obviously, he feels a great deal for her."

Besides a raging hard-on? Yeah, seeing it again, One-Mile believed more than Bryant's dick was involved.

It would probably end badly for the schmuck. If the famous actress moved on, she'd rip out Cutter's heart in the process. One-Mile didn't envy him that.

Yet despite falling for the blonde bombshell, Bryant had been willing to sacrifice himself and his future to protect Brea. As much as One-Mile hated admitting it, he respected the guy for that.

"The press is calling him her 'mystery lover.' They haven't identified him yet?" Brea asked.

"So far, no. If they do, it will get ugly."

"I'm sure. But if Shealyn West makes him happy, I hope they can work it out somehow. Cutter deserves happiness. Besides, he would be miserable in the chaste marriage we agreed to. I told him I was okay with him finding pleasure wherever and with whomever he could as long as he was discreet, but I could tell he didn't like it. He's the kind of man who will take his vows seriously."

One-Mile respected that, too. But he had other questions. "What were you going to do for sex in this marriage?"

She looked at him with earnest eyes. "After you, I didn't want anyone else."

Damn it. This woman was perfect. He had to yank on his mental leash to resist kissing her. If he didn't, he'd only end up inside her again. And he still had a whole lot of explaining to do.

"I don't want anyone else, either. Just you. I want to live with you and raise our baby with you. But I've got to deal with Montilla so you two"—he slid a hand over her belly—"can be safe."

"What do you mean 'deal with'?"

"Kill him."

Her eyes went soft and wide with terror. "No! You can't."

"I don't have a choice. It's my job. But I'm not going to lie; I'll relish snuffing this son of a bitch. No one threatens what's mine and lives."

"Can't someone else bring him to justice? The Mexican police, the DEA, the—"

"No." He hated to burst her naive bubble, but justice had nothing to do with this now. It was personal. And it would be a fight to the death. "He threatened me. He'll come after anyone I care about. That's why, the morning I came home from St. Louis, I told you we needed to take a step back."

He explained his run-in with Montilla in Valeria's abandoned safe house. She listened quietly, shock and fear twisting her delicate features. He did his best to hold and soothe her.

"Oh, my goodness."

"That's an awfully nice way of putting how dangerous this asshole is. That morning I 'walked away,' I only meant to protect you. I thought you'd be safer in the dark, and I'm so fucking sorry I caused this mess. I hate like hell that I hurt you."

"You had good intentions. We both kept secrets, hid things…" She cupped his cheek. "Let's not do that anymore."

He lifted her hand and kissed her palm. "From now on, I'm your open book, pretty girl. Anything you want to know, just ask."

She hesitated, thoughts clearly whirling before she sighed. "We never talked about what you did to your father."

"Oh, fuck." He hadn't given that shitbag two thoughts since the night he'd asked her to move in with him, but she clearly had. As close to her own dad as she was, his admission would definitely have rubbed her wrong. "It's not what you think."

"Was it self-defense?"

He'd love to say yes and see relief slide across her face, but he refused to lie. "No. It's…complicated. But I did what I thought was right and I'd make the same choice again. I'll explain right now if you really want me to, but I'll be honest. I'd rather not waste tonight talking about someone so toxic. I'd rather make sure you're as safe as you can be while I'm gone. But it's your call."

Brea hesitated, then shook her head. "What happened between you and your father is something we'll have to address, but it's not important until after Montilla. Nothing is, really."

Yep. If there was an after.

"Exactly." One-Mile loved that she understood what was really important. "I'm working on a plan. I need some intel. I have to devise a strategy. I should have more information in a couple of days. But my first priority is you. As much as I hate you even pretending to be engaged to Cutter, it's a great cover. So unless he breaks things off, don't end it. Anyone guesses about the baby? Let them think that's his, too. It sucks, but if people believe you're with him, Montilla won't have any reason to suspect you're mine."

A little frown burrowed between her brows. "I hadn't thought of that, but it makes sense."

"So keep talking about the wedding, say you're excited, put something on social media. Be as public as possible about your engagement to him."

"All right. But if the paparazzi learns Cutter's identity, won't that cast negative attention on me?"

"Yeah." And the backlash was likely to be brutal. Still, unless push came to shove, he didn't want to worry her about that. "That's not a bad thing, either. It will suck. The press is nothing but leeches. But Montilla operates in shadows. *If* he somehow manages to figure out your engagement to Cutter isn't real, you'd have so much light on you he wouldn't dare come after you."

At least for a while, hopefully long enough for One-Mile to figure out how to end him.

Her expression told him she hated the idea. "I'm not used to being the center of attention. It makes me anxious. But you're probably right."

"You'll be fine."

"What do I tell Cutter about the engagement?"

"I'll handle that."

Brea looked at him as if he'd lost his mind. "He's far more likely to listen to me than you."

"But he and I speak the same language. Even if we don't get along, we both understand what's most important."

"Me?"

"First and foremost." He wrapped his arm around her waist and dragged her closer, pressing her naked body against his. "I'm going to do everything I can to keep you safe, I promise."

Her big amber eyes were filled with worry. "I know, but—"

"Shh." He pressed a soft kiss to her lips. "No buts. This situation…it is what it is. But I'm going to take care of you."

"Certainly I can do more to help than smile and pretend to stay engaged."

He wanted to assure her that she didn't need to lift a finger because he didn't want to scare her. But it was more important that he didn't leave her defenseless.

"Yeah. Start self-defense classes and basic firearms training today. Get a concealed carry permit. Don't wait."

"I-I don't know if I could shoot someone."

He raised a brow. "If they were going to kill you and the baby?"

Her face hardened. "I'd have to."

"And you'd succeed." He palmed his phone again, then scrolled through his contacts and forwarded one to her. "Call this number before you leave for work. That's Matt. He's a good guy; he owes me. I'll let him know you need a security system in your house ASAP. You tell him when he can come install it."

Brea's phone dinged from across the room, but she frowned down at his screen. "Area code 307. Where is that?"

"Wyoming. I spent my summers there with my grandpa. I've known Matt most of my life. He'll fly down here. He'll hook your house up with the best equipment available. He'll take care of it for me."

"What do I tell Daddy? We've never had a crime problem here in Sunset. Heck, half the time he forgets to lock our doors and windows."

"I know." He snorted. "I went there before I came here."

She scowled. "Since I wasn't there, how did you figure out I'd come to Cutter's?"

"Really want to know?"

Her eyes narrowed. "Why do I have the feeling you're about to scare me?"

"Terrify might be more accurate."

"Oh, my gosh. What did you do?"

"Well, since your dad is at Mrs. Collins's house, or he was at one this morning, I—"

"Doing what?" The truth seemed to dawn on her. "Oh, you think they're…"

"Fucking. Absolutely. But I found an unlocked window, searched your bedroom, broke into your computer—"

"What?" Her eyes widened. "That's…stalking."

"Occupational hazard." He shrugged. "I also found the video you took of the baby's heartbeat and sent it to myself. Damn, pretty girl, that hit me hard. I'm not too macho to admit it. I just hate like hell I wasn't there with you to hear it."

Her face softened. "I wish you'd been there. It was so humbling to actually hear the life growing inside of me that you and I created together. I barely made it out of the doctor's office and to my car before I started sobbing."

One-Mile brought her closer, loving her soft heart. "Yeah? What else did the doctor say?"

"Everything looks normal. She's pleased with my weight, blood pressure, and measurements so far."

"So it's been a normal pregnancy?"

She wrinkled her nose. "Normal…but hellacious. Now that I'm in my second trimester, I'm not tired all the time, so that makes me happy. And the constant nausea has finally tapered off. I don't know why it's called morning sickness when it usually lasts until dinner. And now I have heartburn at night, which makes it harder to sleep. But I'm changing my diet and building more breaks into my schedule so I can have the healthiest baby possible."

Regret clutched his chest as he held her closer. He dusted kisses across her forehead, silently apologizing for the fact she was going through this pregnancy alone. It sucked that he couldn't see her, soothe her, or share the baby's progress with her every day. "I'm sorry there have been some shitty parts, but I love that you're pregnant. And I'm thrilled you're doing well. In fact"—he swept her hair behind her shoulders, exposing her luscious breasts as he rolled her to her back, settled himself between her legs, and eased inside her so slowly Brea arched and groaned—"I want to compliment you on a job well done in the most personal way I know how. Orgasms work for you?"

When he pressed in to the hilt, she closed her eyes and groaned. "Please…"

"You're welcome. I intend to be thorough and make sure you know just how much I appreciate you." He covered her lips with his and fucked her mouth slow and deep, just the way he fucked her body.

But with every deep, grinding, back-clawing thrust inside her, One-Mile swore that if he was still alive after dealing with Montilla, he'd wrap Brea in his arms, claim his place beside her, and make her feel both safe and well pleasured for the rest of her life.

chapter seven

One-Mile kissed Brea's forehead as she slept. Then he dressed, swept up the broken glass in the kitchen so she didn't cut herself, and reluctantly let himself out of Bryant's apartment before the sun rose. He locked it behind him with a sigh of utter satisfaction.

Damn, he'd enjoyed corrupting Brea. For a good girl, she fucked like she was bad to the core. But that big, pure heart of hers he'd always wanted was undeniably his.

He was the luckiest bastard on the planet.

Or he would be if he could make his Montilla problem go away—once and for all. From a foreign country, this asshole was ruling his life. No more. He had a baby coming, and if he didn't kill this motherfucker before the day Brea and Cutter were scheduled to tie the knot, the life he wanted might be out of his reach forever.

He hopped into his Jeep and withdrew his phone from his pocket, then shot off a text to Logan. His boss probably wouldn't be up, but what the hell.

Shit has changed, so I'm taking my fight to Montilla. Don't know when I'll be back. Fire me if you want.

The phone rang immediately. Not surprisingly, it was Logan.

One-Mile answered as he started his Jeep. "Yeah?"

"Are you out of your fucking mind?"

"Good morning to you, too," he quipped as he backed out of the parking spot and turned onto the empty street.

"Don't yank my chain, you son of a bitch. I had a really shitty evening and—"

"Yeah, I stopped by your place last night and talked to your dad. I guess I won't be getting you a Razor scooter for Christmas."

"Ha ha. I don't need a fucking comedian. I do not have the time or the energy. Cutter is in California sucking face—"

"With Shealyn West. Zy and I saw last night."

"So did most of the world. Thank God the press hasn't identified him yet."

"Yet. Too bad that, instead of protecting the client, the Boy Scout thought his assignment on the West Coast would be a great time to work on his safe-sex badge."

"Don't be an asshole."

One-Mile was wrung out and worried. He had the fight of his life on his hands, so Logan's shit just set him off. "You want to talk about an asshole? Look in the mirror. I've fucking had enough of this. You don't like my attitude? Fine.

I don't get along with the guys or act like a team member? Who gives a fuck? It doesn't affect my job performance. Except my screw-up in St. Louis, which I've taken full responsibility for, I've done everything you've ever asked. I almost died for this job. But I've never been irresponsible enough to fuck a client, much less a high-profile one like Shealyn West. So next time you want to bitch at me, why don't you worry less about what I've said and think more about what I've done."

Logan was silent for a long moment. "You're right. My brothers and I don't like that you're a maverick or that you don't take orders for shit. Every time I've tried to toss you an olive branch, you seem inclined to gnaw off my whole arm. But you've never let me down."

That was a big admission coming from the hottest head among his bosses. It took One-Mile's anger down a few notches. "Did choking those words out hurt as much as I think it did?"

"More, you motherfucker." Logan chuffed. "So what's your terrible plan?"

"I'm going to Mexico. I'm done letting Montilla fuck up my life indefinitely. I don't know how long it will take, but I'm not coming back until one of us is dead."

"Jesus, Walker. He almost killed you the first time and—"

"You think I don't remember that?" He scoffed. "But this time, I'm doing things my way. I'm going to slip into the country, figure out where he is, how to get to him, then put a bullet in his head when he least expects it."

"That's murder."

"Oh, don't give me that shit." One-Mile clutched his phone, wanting to punch someone. "If I'd followed my instinct the first time, he'd already be dead. But we're valuing the poor, victimized drug pusher above innocents now? Think about how many lives I can save by ending his. Valeria's, for sure. I won't let her die. Her son needs her."

He'd also be saving Brea's and his baby's. And as far as he was concerned, that more than justified offing the soulless, homicidal tyrant.

"Legally, that's wrong." Logan sighed. "Realistically, that's valid."

"I'm not doing this on your dime or your time, so if I get caught and there's blowback, disavow me. Say I've gone rogue or crazy. Whatever saves your ass."

"Don't make me do that. I'm worried about more than saving EM. I just… Why do this now?"

"I've got someone to protect and something to fight for."

Logan didn't speak right away, and One-Mile could all but hear the wheels in his head turning. "You're worried Montilla is coming after someone? The only person besides yourself you give two shits about is Brea."

He considered letting his boss think whatever he wanted, but if Montilla brought the fight here while he was gone and Cutter was still too busy losing his dick inside the blond actress to protect Brea, he'd rather have someone watching her back. "She can't protect herself from him."

"Why would Montilla come after her? She's engaged to Cutter."

"It's bullshit. And if his fling with Shealyn West goes public, it won't take long for the whole fucking world to figure that out. Montilla's goons saw her at the hospital holding my hand. If I piss him off enough, he'll hunt her down. So I can't afford to miss." One-Mile weighed his next words, but Brea's protection was far more important than her reputation. "It won't be much longer before her pregnancy shows."

"Her… Oh, son of a bitch. That's not Cutter's baby, is it?"

"No. He's never touched her. But I can't have any sort of life with her or our child as long as that fucking drug lord is still breathing hot air down my neck."

Logan's sigh was rife with frustration. "You're putting me in a really shitty position."

"Maybe, but what would you have done in my shoes? If he had threatened Tara?"

"Whatever I had to do. Hell, I would have pulled the moon out of the sky and moved mountains."

"Exactly." And One-Mile was done with the argument. "Listen, I need a favor. If I don't come back, liquidate everything I own and give Brea every dime. And whatever happens, don't let her anywhere near my fucking funeral."

Logan hesitated, but he didn't argue, just caved. "All right. You'll have to come to the office on Monday morning and sign papers to that effect—"

"Will do. Then, as soon as I talk to Cutter, I'm leaving. When does his flight land on Monday?"

"Oh, come on. Leave it be, man. You got the girl. She's having your baby. You won."

"I'm not after a blue ribbon in our pissing contest. I need to talk to him, convince him to watch Brea while I'm gone. I know he probably wouldn't lift a finger to help me, but he'd give his life for her. I just hope it doesn't come to that."

"I hate this fucking plan." But Logan's tone said he understood.

"Thanks." One-Mile hesitated, then figured he'd be honest with Logan in case he didn't come back. "For what it's worth, you're more like your dad than I first thought. See you on Monday."

A faint pinging noise jolted her from sleep. Brea opened her eyes and stared at the clock. Just after three in the morning. *What the devil?*

She was about to decide she'd imagined it and curl up in her blankets when she heard the sound again.

Frowning, she sat up and turned toward the noise.

She found Pierce lifting her formerly locked bedroom window and stepping inside.

Was he crazy?

"What are you doing here? My dad is home! How did you open that?" she whispered furiously as she rose to him, glancing at her bedroom door to make sure she'd closed it before crawling into bed.

Thank goodness she had. Still, if Daddy was having another sleepless night, it would be a miracle if he didn't hear them.

"We've got problems, pretty girl. Cutter has been identified by the press. His name is everywhere." He extracted his phone, tapped the screen, and shoved the device in her hands. "So is yours...as his pregnant fiancée."

Shock banged her chest. The air left her lungs in a terrible rush. "What?"

She glanced down at some tabloid's Twitter feed to find a picture of her and Cutter taken at the live nativity last Christmas, which had been posted on the church's Instagram page. He'd draped an arm around her shoulders, and she'd been smiling up at him. Brea remembered that moment. They'd been laughing that Mr. Carlson had volunteered to play one of the wise men, but couldn't stay awake. There'd been nothing romantic about it. This trashy post painted her as the jilted girlfriend. A small-town object of pity Cutter had tossed over for the hot TV star. The comments were even more wretched and biting.

Dizziness and nausea assailed her. Brea reached out to brace herself.

Pierce was there to support her.

"Oh, my gosh. How did this happen?" *And what am I going to do?*

"Apparently, Tower Trent got jealous that Shealyn, his supposed girlfriend, was stepping out on him with her bodyguard and blabbed Cutter's name."

So the star had destroyed her privacy without a second thought? "But how did the press find out I'm pregnant? The only people in the world who know are you, Cutter, my doctor." She closed her eyes. "And Rayleigh."

"Who?"

"The woman who owns the salon. Last Friday, she guessed. I didn't think fast enough on my feet. And I really needed a friend... I should have known better. She loves to gossip." But Brea had never seen the woman pass on secrets, just chew on general knowledge. And she'd seemed so sincere. It was possible that if Rayleigh had guessed, someone else in the salon had, too. That wasn't what was really important now. "Oh, no... If everyone on Twitter knows I'm pregnant, it won't be long before Daddy does, too."

"Yeah. This timing couldn't fucking be worse. I'm sorry." He took her hands and drew her closer, holding her against his body. "I leave for Mexico tonight."

Shock ripped the air from her lunch. Dread gonged in her stomach. "Already?"

"Yeah. I wish like hell I'd had time to meet your dad first. Explain us. But now...there's no way. Reporters and gossips will start flocking here soon. I can't be seen anywhere near you. It could be weeks before the media swarm dies down. Besides, this shit with Montilla can't wait."

"I know you're right, but..." Pierce leaving terrified her.

Brea had thought they would have more days and nights together...in case she needed to store up memories for a future without him. Some foolish part of her had even hoped that Emilo Montilla would forget about all this and move on. But unless someone put that man in the ground, Pierce never would. Every moment he stayed here with her in Louisiana was another moment the brutal drug lord might be planning his revenge, so it was another moment Pierce would sneak through her window in the middle of the night instead of living openly as her man and the father of their baby.

Until Montilla was gone, they had no future.

Brea wrapped her arms around Pierce. "I'm so afraid."

"You're going to be fine, pretty girl. Your daddy loves you. Yeah, he might be disappointed. He might lecture you or be angry with you. He might wish you'd made different choices. But he'll stand by you."

He thought Daddy's anger was her first concern? "I know that."

Funny, when she'd realized she was pregnant, she'd done so much hand-wringing about disappointing her father. She still worried about triggering another heart incident, and she'd need to manage that. But her fears about being Sunset's "hussy" or losing all her clients? In the face of everything else, they hardly mattered now. If the people in this town didn't like her or her life choices, they could go hang.

"I'm worried about *you*. Montilla is dangerous. He almost—"

"I'm going to do everything possible to come back in one piece. This time, I have the element of surprise, and I'm not playing by anyone's rules except my own." He cupped her face. "War is my business. Every time I'm on the job, I know it might be my last day. So I'm careful. I take precautions. But if I don't come back, I'm still going to take care of you. You'll have everything you need."

Brea's insides froze in terror. "Except you."

Pierce shrugged those big shoulders of his.

He was trying to be responsible, and Brea did her best to appreciate that. But when she thought about living the rest of her life and raising their child without him, she couldn't.

"Don't go." She latched on to him even tighter. "Let's leave here. Go someplace where he can't find us and—"

"I'm not looking over our shoulders for the rest of our lives. I've never run away from a fight, and I won't put you or the baby at risk. I've got to do this. If it ends well, we'll start our lives together. Focus on that while I'm gone, pretty girl."

Brea tried not to lose her composure, but everything was happening so fast. And once he left here, she might never see him again. "How long will it take?"

"To kill Montilla? Might be a few days. Might be a few months. I need to find him, figure out a way to get close enough to observe him, learn his patterns, discern when and where he's vulnerable...and it's going to be a bitch. He likes to hunker down in compounds with lots of armed guards. He's not light on the surveillance. Since he threatened me and mine, he knows I'm coming. I doubt he'll make the mistake of spending much time alone."

"Can't you take someone with you to watch your back? Josiah or Zyron or… Cutter is due home in a few hours. He'd go—"

"No."

The finality in his answer stabbed her with foreboding.

His heartbeat, loud and steady, filled her ears as tears spilled down her cheeks. Why couldn't this bittersweet moment last forever? "You're one man against a cartel. Don't do this."

"It's what I'm trained to do. Please don't worry."

That was like asking her not to blink or to breathe. Or to love him. "I'll try, but—"

"You're strong. You can do it, pretty girl." He cradled her face and wiped her tears away. "Do you want to spend the rest of our time together crying or feeling good?"

It would be so easy to lose herself in her fears, but if he was going into battle for them, for their future, he needed her comfort. He needed to know without a doubt that she loved him. He needed to be sure he had something to live for.

And she needed to press his body against hers—tattoo that feeling onto her heart—and memorize him.

"Love me," Brea murmured. "I want to love you."

"Good answer." He reached around to drag her nightgown up her backside.

Then with a seductive slide of his palm over her hip, he whisked the cotton up her body and flung it across the room. She tugged at his shirt, pulling it over his head as he bent to help her out of her modest white panties. The instant she stood naked in front of him, he removed the gun from the holster at his waistband with one hand and reached between her legs with the other. When he set the weapon on her nightstand with a soft thump, she gave a startled jump.

"What's wrong, baby?" Pierce cupped her possessively and skimmed his lips up to her ear. "Tell me. As much as I want to lift you onto the bed and fuck you, something made you tense. If you're worried about your dad, I'll make sure he won't hear us."

Brea didn't know how he'd manage that since she was prone to screaming whenever Pierce touched her, but that wasn't what worried her. "I was just thinking there's never been a gun in my house."

"I don't go anywhere without one, especially now."

He was being practical, and she had to stop being squeamish. The world wasn't full of good people, rainbows, sunshine, and glitter. Monsters like Montilla existed. She'd seen what he was capable of. The worst possible thing would be for him to find Pierce unarmed. If that happened, history would repeat itself, but worse. Pierce wouldn't survive Montilla's captivity a second time.

"I'm glad. I want you to be safe. And I should get used to the idea of defending myself in case I have to."

He nodded before he brushed his lips over hers. "It would make me feel so much fucking better if you would."

She nodded. "I've also never had sex in this house."

"Oh, I know. And I'm going to fix that but good."

Despite everything, anticipation wound a hot trail through her. "Want to know something? I've never even had an orgasm here."

Pierce raised a dark brow. "You don't masturbate?"

"Of course not."

"C'mon. You never rubbed one out in the morning? Your fingers haven't done any walking late at night? You must own something that requires batteries…"

"No. I always thought self-pleasure was a sin." And the few forbidden times she'd put her hand down there experimentally, she'd been so self-conscious she'd stopped long before climax.

He slanted her a downright dubious stare. "Who convinced you of that?"

"It's the way I was raised. Corinthians tells us: 'Or do you not know that your body is a temple of the Holy Spirit who is in you, whom you have from God, and that you are not your own?'"

Pierce scoffed. "Since it's attached to my body, it's mine. Think of masturbation as self-maintenance."

"How do you figure that?"

"Isn't everyone happier after an orgasm? Granted, giving yourself one isn't as much fun, but in a pinch…" He shrugged. "And I'd feel a lot better if I knew you were making yourself feel good while I'm gone."

She tsked at him. "You're kidding. You want me to…"

"Get yourself off?" He bulldozed forward, backing her onto the bed, then followed her down. He draped half of his enormous body on top of her, his big palm still unerringly covering her sex. "Hell yeah."

Her breath caught. "Why?"

"Couple of reasons. I'm hoping that good self-maintenance means you're less likely to look at another stiff dick and wonder if his would make you happy."

"I would never think that. I love you. I only want you."

"Uh-huh." He started to rub her mound in slow, seductive circles. "But I also like to see you smile."

Her breath caught. "You make me smile."

"But if I'm not here, I want you to be as happy as you can be." He plucked her hand from his shoulder and settled it over her damp folds. "Let me see you thrill the hell out of yourself."

She stiffened. Touching herself was already foreign, but having him watch her, too… Brea risked a glance up at him as she tried to inch away.

His stare was patient, his grip firm. "Do it for me."

He wasn't budging until she'd learned this "skill." She wasn't sure why it was important to him until she realized Pierce was trying to make sure she could take care of herself as much as possible in his absence. Like the gun safety classes he'd insisted on, which started tomorrow. Like the self-defense sessions she'd found at a church in Lafayette over the next four Monday nights. Like his friend Matt, who would be here on Thursday.

This was one more way Pierce was doing his utmost to make sure she would be all right without him.

Brea tried not to think of the ramifications and focused instead on the moment. "You really do this?"

"If there's no other alternative, yep. It's basically a public service. Otherwise, I can be a surly son of a bitch."

She rolled her eyes. "You're surly, anyway."

"All right. Surlier. Since no one wants a cranky Brea"—he pressed her palm back over her sex and covered it with his hand, guiding her to rub and stroke herself—"show me you can put yourself in a good mood."

Normally, she would have balked. Resisted at least. Maybe in time she would have felt more comfortable sinning so utterly in front of Pierce… But time was the one thing they didn't have. He wanted her to do this, and she wanted to show him that she was strong enough and brave enough to handle whatever came next.

"All right."

He rolled beside her and propped his head on his palm like he was settling in to enjoy the show. "I'm looking forward to this, but I can already tell I won't be able to keep my hands off of you."

As if to prove his point, Pierce cupped her breasts and thumbed her nipples as she strummed the sensitive button between her thighs.

A jolt of sensation spiked through her belly. Because he was watching her? Because, thanks to Pierce, her body now knew what it felt like to orgasm? Either way, she mimicked the circular, teasing motions he'd used to arouse her in the past.

"That's it," he murmured against the side of her breast as he pinched her sensitive nipple. "You look so fucking hot. I'm putting this in my spank bank, for sure."

His assertion was so unapologetic it was almost funny. But it was also sexy as heck. He found her alluring. He wanted her enough to imagine her while he touched himself.

Right or wrong, that sparked her desire even higher.

She met his fathomless stare. Black could seem so cold. Forbidding and impersonal. Menacing, even. But Pierce's eyes gleamed as they scorched her with his heat. Her breath caught. Her skin tightened. Her heart banged against her ribs. Her spine twisted. Her ache grew.

She slid her eyes shut and moaned for him.

"Yeah." He grabbed one of her thighs and dragged it wide so he could get a better view. "Oh, fuck, baby. That's pretty."

Brea could feel his unblinking stare on her *there*, where her fingers met her needy flesh and she craved him most. Her hips began to move and lift in rhythm with her stroke. "Pierce…"

He dragged his tongue over her nipple, then smoothed a hand down her belly. "I'm so here for this. Watching you is the best torture. Rub that clit."

She did, dragging her slick fingers across her flesh. Pleasure mounted until she no longer felt self-conscious with his stare on her. Instead, she felt empowered. Free. Suddenly, she understood that her body wasn't shameful. That nothing done in the expression of love should be a sin. She still loved God…but she loved Pierce, too. Those two things weren't mutually exclusive, and her body wouldn't have been made for pleasure if she wasn't meant to give and receive it.

"I feel it coming," she gasped out. "It's big."

"Yeah, it is." His stare turned impossibly hotter as he plucked her nipple in his mouth, look a long, decadent drag, then clamped it between his thumb and fingers. "I can tell. Your fingers are moving faster. Your skin is flushing. Your pulse is pounding at your neck. You look so hot."

"Oh." Her heart echoed and gonged between her ears as the nub under her fingers swelled and hardened more. "Oh!"

"Just like that. Tease yourself now. Lighten your stroke. Really slow. Yeah," he encouraged. "Wait for it…"

Brea did—and gasped as a wave of hot, greedy need scalded her a moment later. She bit her lip, but nothing stopped her little whine of need.

"I fucking smell you now. It's taking everything inside me not to put my head between your thighs and eat your pussy mercilessly."

"Pierce?"

"Baby?"

"You're not helping…"

He laughed. "Sure, I am."

With a hot stroke of his tongue, he laved her nipples again, first the one closest, before he leaned over her body to inhale the other in his mouth and drag it tormentingly deep.

Against her will, she cried out. Her back arched. Her hips bucked. Arousal licked her in an unrelenting firestorm. She was so close… "Help. Please."

"You don't need me, pretty girl. You got this. But I'm right here, watching every fucking second of you. Give yourself all the pleasure you can. For me." He kissed his way up to her ear to whisper, "After you come, I'll fuck you like a bad girl and make you feel so good."

That shouldn't turn her on even more. But everything about Pierce thrilled her. It was as if he could see into her psyche and soul. Somehow, he always fed them perfectly with every bit of himself so she felt whole and wonderful.

"Pierce!" Brea couldn't stop herself from rubbing faster and harder as she imagined him pinning her with his big, hair-roughened body and filling her until she felt stretched, achy, and complete.

That was all it took.

Her need surged. She dragged in a sharp breath and blinked up at him in shock as blood rushed to fill her nipples and engorge her pussy. It lit a fire under every inch of her skin in between.

As ecstasy burst inside her, he smothered her scream with his kiss, encouraging her without a word to milk her orgasm for every last sensation. Yes, it felt amazing to know exactly where and how to touch her body in order to elicit this response, but she was also stunned by how unfettered she felt in not only giving herself pleasure but in doing it to please him.

As she shuddered and jerked all the way through her climax, Pierce made love to her mouth ruthlessly, filling his hands with her breasts as he guided her in a gentle crash back to her body.

The moment she sighed in repletion, she opened her eyes to find him unzipping and shoving his pants down. Then he plucked her hand from between her trembling thighs.

"Mine." He sucked her wet fingers into his mouth with a groan as he made a space for himself between her legs.

Brea opened herself in invitation to him. "Yes…"

The word had barely left his lips before he plunged his thick erection into her tight, still-clenching opening. Brea arched to adjust to the burn of his tunneling girth. She was still wriggling to accommodate all of him when he clamped onto her hips, bit her shoulder to muffle his groan, and started pumping in deep, furious strokes.

Brea felt his animal need in every thrust. It lit her body up again. The orgasm she'd thought was on the soft downhill slide to repletion suddenly regathered and soared her toward stinging bliss once more.

She dug her fingers into his back, wrapped her legs around his pistoning hips, and clung as if this might be the last time she felt him.

Because it might be.

"It's fucking cold outside, and your pussy is like July, baby. Everything about you makes me hot. Always has."

She rocked her hips with his. "The first time I looked at you I wanted you."

"It was all over your face. If Cutter hadn't busted us apart, I was going to shove you in the nearest closet and put my mouth all over you until you said yes." He punctuated his statement by dragging his lips along her shoulder, then nipping at her lobe. "And the first time I got inside you, I knew you were the last woman I was ever going to fuck."

His words weren't romantic, yet they made her swoon. "I've never wanted anyone but you."

"When you say shit like that, I can't hold out. God, I love to fuck you. This is gonna go fast. After watching you get yourself off…" He grabbed her hair and forced her gaze to his. "And now being inside you? You fucking own me. Give me your mouth."

He had always owned her, too.

Brea tilted her lips under his. Pierce took them fiercely, tongue raking inside, teeth nipping at her as he drove her higher and higher. His demand lit her up—powerful, charged with fire, inescapable.

Suddenly, he wrenched his mouth free with a groan, changed the angle of his stroke to deliver lightning to her clit. He worked her rhythmically—hard, steady, unrelenting.

"Pierce!"

"Here. With you. Fuck. Kiss me and let go."

She was trembling, on the edge, and beyond happy to comply.

Brea's lips collided with his again. When he nudged her mouth open farther, she stroked against his tongue in a frantic kiss while he panted and thrust.

Then his stare bored down into her. "Come for me."

His growled command ignited her until she couldn't do anything but comply.

He slammed deep again, jostling her clit as he scraped a sensitive bundle of nerves inside her. Pleasure swelled and seized her body. While a scream worked its way up her throat, he pressed his palm over her mouth, absorbing her cries as she launched into dark, soaring pleasure.

Above her, he sucked at her shoulder, stiffening. His long, hoarse cry against her skin resounded in her ears as they rode the pinnacle of ecstasy together and, as one, sighed in satisfaction.

Dreamy, dizzying moments later, he melted against her and nuzzled his face in her neck. She stroked his back with her palms, legs still wrapped tightly around him. Brea tried to stay in the moment, but without the bliss blinding her to everything except Pierce's touch, reality crashed in.

She burst into tears. "I'm so worried."

"Pretty girl…no," he crooned in soft concern. "I hate to see you like this."

That made her cling tighter. "You're everything to me. I don't want you to go."

"If I had a choice…"

But he didn't. Brea knew that.

"You're only putting yourself at risk for me." She dropped a hand to her stomach. "For us."

"Yeah. To me, nothing matters more. This started over a job. And even after everything Montilla did to me, I was willing to let it go and to let the police handle it. But he's making it personal because I'm keeping him from his son. Since killing me won't get him what he wants, he's determined to take a loved one from me."

"So you can suffer the way he has?"

"Whether I squeal or suffer, he's won. Montilla is determined and he's dangerous. And he won't stop. My only option is to put him in the ground."

"I know." He'd explained that once, but logic didn't make her feel any less scared.

"Don't worry too much, pretty girl. I'm just taking out the trash."

"Don't be flippant."

"I got this. You and the little one just hang tight. I'll do my best to return soon." He eased from her body and gathered her into his arms. "Have you thought about any baby names?"

He was telling her what she wanted to hear and changing the subject to keep her from dwelling on the worst-case scenario. It killed Brea, but she put on a brave face because she believed in Pierce. If anyone could end Montilla, he could. Still, his question snaked pain through her chest. They both knew that if they didn't have this conversation now, they might never have the chance.

She sniffed back tears. "Do you have any suggestions?"

He shook his head. "I've barely had time to get used to the idea you're pregnant. Tell me the ones you've been considering."

"If it's a girl... My mom's name was Lavinia, Liv for short. Since that's a mouthful, maybe Olivia?"

"That's pretty. My mom was Rose. That might be a nice middle name." He stroked her hair and kissed her gently. "What do you think?"

Brea tried not to sob at the thought that he might be long dead before his son or daughter was ever born. "I love that. And if it's a boy, I was thinking Pierce Jasper, for you and my dad."

"I'm touched, but I'm not worth naming him after. Why don't you—"

"I think you are. I think you're the best thing that ever happened to me. You didn't wrap me up and tell me I was too young or fragile for the world. You've encouraged me to be strong. You've taught me pleasure and love and..." The dam broke on her sobs. They wracked her whole body, and she couldn't stem their tide. "I don't know what I'm going to do with you gone."

Especially if you never come back.

"Hey...shh. You're going to be great. You're signed up to learn what you need to know. Get every ounce of knowledge about home security from Matt when he comes. He'll help you. So will Cutter. Lean on your dad. Everyone else? Fuck them. If they want to pass judgment, they should start by looking in a mirror. Focus on a healthy you and a healthy baby. The rest...we'll take care of all that together as soon as I get back."

She prayed more than anything that would be possible, but what was one man in the face of a murderous drug lord and his army?

"I will." She sniffled.

"Oh, pretty girl. Don't ever gamble. You have a terrible poker face." He held her closer. "I'm here if you need to cry."

"I'm so afraid. I'm trying to be brave for you, but..."

"I know, baby." He cradled her cheek and brushed a kiss across her lips. "You can lean on me as much as you want right now. I got you."

"I've got you, too." She clutched him tight. "I need you to know that."

Pierce looked inside her as much as he looked at her, as if he saw the real, deep-down her. "I do."

Brea wished she could lose herself in his arms forever. "I love you."

Something on his face changed. His expression opened, and for the first time, she felt the vulnerability under his strength. "The night I met you at the EM barbecue, I wasn't looking for anything except brownie points from the bosses for making an appearance. When I left there, I already knew you'd change my life forever. I love you. No matter what happens, never forget that."

Brea nodded as she wiped away hot new tears. "I won't."

Pierce eased from the bed and bent to kiss her again. "Neither will I."

Her heart clutched as she watched him dress. She bit back the urge to promise him that if he didn't come back, she would raise their baby to know his or her father was an amazing man, a fierce warrior who loved them with his whole heart, and had made the ultimate sacrifice to protect them. But she didn't want Pierce to think she didn't believe in him. She didn't want to jinx him, either. So she swallowed her worries and slipped back into her nightgown and panties. She felt a chill without his arms around her, his skin blanketing hers, his flesh heating her, and his heart beating against hers.

Would she ever really be warm again?

"You're really leaving tonight?"

"Yeah. From here, I'm heading to the office to tie up some loose ends. And this is important: If I don't make it back, go see Logan. He'll have all my paperwork and he'll know what to do."

"Pierce…" Her voice cracked. "Don't say—"

"I'm being practical. It's all right. He'll make sure you and the baby are taken care of. Then after I'm done at the office, I'll be heading to DFW for my flight later."

"Where are you going?"

He hesitated. "After I land, that's something I'll have to figure out."

"But you must have some idea…"

"No. And even if I did, you're safer without that information."

He was leaving her no way to find him—on purpose. She understood, but it made her angry. "Don't do this. Please."

Pierce sighed. "We've been over this."

They had, and she was only making things harder. Brea took a deep breath and clutched him as close as she could while pressing his big palm to her belly. "We'll miss you."

"Oh, pretty girl, I already miss you and the baby so much."

"Will you think of us?"

He settled his lips on hers for a soft kiss. "I won't think of anything else. But I don't want you to focus on me, just worry about you and the baby. If things go my way, I'll be back for you two. I'll meet your father and explain everything."

"Then we'll live the rest of our lives?"

"Yeah. That's what I want."

"Do you, really?"

"More than anything, Brea Felicity Bell." He took her hands and stared into her eyes. "I do."

His words rang with the solemnity of a wedding vow, and she felt his commitment all the way to her soul. "Pierce Jackson Walker, I do, too."

They sealed their impromptu vow with a lingering kiss that Brea wished would go on forever.

But an unexpected tap on the door cut it short. The clock in her line of vision said it wasn't even five a.m.

"Brea?" Her dad's voice had her eyes widening in panic.

He never knocked this early.

Pierce gripped her shoulders and whispered, "It's okay. I'm going. I'm leaving my phone behind, so I'll be underground for a while."

She tried not to cry again even as she clung to him, wishing she could melt into him and become one with him. "You haven't even left and I'm terrified."

"I know." He kissed her forehead. "But I'll do everything in my power to come back."

"If you don't?" She barely managed to get the words out.

"Be happy and don't forget I love you."

"I love you, too," she sobbed. "Pierce..."

"Shh. Take care of you both." He dropped his hand to her belly.

"Brea?" Daddy asked a bit more loudly through the closed door. "Who are you talking to?"

"J-just a minute."

She didn't dare speak another word to Pierce. Instead, he pressed his lips to hers, lingered through a few short heartbeats, then eased away with a caress. She was still clutching his hand when he climbed out the window, looking back at her with a black-eyed stare full of longing she'd never forget—as if he meant to memorize her.

Then he was gone.

With her heart wrenching and clutching, she tried to stem the tide of her tears as she smoothed her hair, tossed on a robe, padded to the door, and pulled it open.

Daddy stood in the portal, his phone in hand. He raked her body up and down, focusing on her middle. A frown furrowed his brows. "We need to talk."

Her heart stopped. He'd read the gossip. He knew she was pregnant.

It had become an ingrained habit to conceal her relationship with Pierce, along with the life that had resulted from it. But she was tired of hiding her love. She wasn't going to keep acting as if she was ashamed. Yes, she'd be cautious about Daddy's heart, have her phone ready and an aspirin nearby. But she was done burying her head in the sand.

Pierce was facing their obstacles head on. It was time for her to do the same.

"All right."

"I've made a pot of coffee. Why don't you get dressed and come to the kitchen?"

After a quick few minutes with her toothbrush, she dragged on some yoga pants and a baggy T-shirt with shaking hands. Everything else in her closet was getting too tight. Once she'd donned fuzzy socks and pulled her hair back, she padded out to the kitchen, grabbed the bottle of aspirin, took a deep breath, and met her father's gaze. "You want to ask me if I'm pregnant."

He looked taken aback by her directness. "Yes."

"I'll save you the breath. I am. I'm sorry if that disappoints you—"

"It's not Cutter's, is it? You're pregnant by the man who left you."

"Pierce. That's his name. Yes, the baby is his, and I love him. He didn't leave me, Daddy. In fact, he was just here to explain how he intends to keep me safe. His job is dangerous and—"

"Now that you're expecting, his most important job is to take care of you. And he's…where? It seems as if he's shirking his responsibility."

She got mad on Pierce's behalf. "You don't get it. He's leaving tonight, alone, to hunt down a man the whole world views as a criminal. For me. And all he's asked me to do is wait here and continue pretending I'm engaged to Cutter so I don't become a target. Pierce is risking his life in the hopes the three of us can have a future together, but we both know full well he may never come back. And he still didn't hesitate for an instant to put his life on the line for us." She cradled her belly as her tears fell. "So don't lecture me about his lack of responsibility. And don't tell me that what I've done is an affront or a sin to you. I love you, Daddy, but this is my life. And Pierce is *my* choice. I love him."

He came closer, his expression placating. "I appreciate that he wants to keep you safe, but if he can't be here and provide for you, maybe his nobility is misplaced."

"I can provide for myself and the baby. I'm not worried about that. But I fell in love with Pierce because he's so larger-than-life. He's a warrior and a protector. I can't ask him to be someone else just because I'm pregnant."

"Have you thought at all about your reputation, your standing in the community, your livelihood, your—"

"I've been worried about those things since the moment I found out I was pregnant. I wish now I had that time back to focus on what really matters."

"This man?"

"Yes. Pierce loves me, Daddy. More than anything."

"Cutter doesn't like him at all."

"I can't help that. And I know none of my choices are making anyone's lives easier. But you've always said you want me to be happy. Every moment I'm with Pierce, I'm ecstatic. He understands me. He encourages me." She caressed her stomach. "I'm glad that, no matter what, I'll always have a part of him."

He sighed, clearly wanting to understand but struggling. "He impregnated you without marrying you. Has he even proposed?"

"It's not really important anymore. I refuse to care what other people think." She glanced at his phone. "I've seen what the world is saying about me right now, and it's horrible. But I know the truth. The gossip will blow over once the paparazzi finds a new scandal. Our love and our baby? That's forever. And if it's too much for you to accept, I understand. I'll move out if you'd like me to."

"No." He looked shocked. "No. I would never force you to go. You're my daughter."

"No matter what, I always will be. And I'd rather not leave, because I'm worried about your health—"

"Oh, honey... I'm worried about yours. You'll be going through childbirth. Your mother—"

"I know." Mama's tragic death had crossed her mind. There was no way it couldn't. "But I have to have faith. Don't you always preach that? Medicine is better now. I'm strong. My will to live so I can raise my son or daughter will see me through. I owe it to my child. And I owe it to Pierce."

Daddy looked at her, blinking hard in confusion. "You really aren't a little girl anymore."

"Because I'm pregnant?"

He shook his head. "Because you're not hiding or leaning on me the way you used to. You're a woman who knows what she wants in life now. I realize I've been overprotective. Cutter has been just as bad. Together, we smothered you so much that we kept you from growing."

"You can thank Pierce for the change in me. He made me *see*. He made me a woman, and I don't mean that figuratively. He forced me to look at myself and face hard realities. And for us to have any kind of future, I have to drown out all the judgment, the disappointment, and the whispers. I know that I may have to start my business over. I know I may no longer be welcome in everyone's good graces. But I know who *I* am. And none of their opinions matter more than that and Pierce's love."

He stared at her for the longest time. "Wow. I'm proud of you."

Brea had never expected that, and it made her heart light up. "Thank God. Do you know what would make me happy?"

"What?"

"*You* being happy. I think you've had your life on hold for fear of upsetting my status quo. Stop that. If you want to marry Jennifer Collins, then propose to her."

A guilty smile flitted across his face. "I've been thinking about that since my first heart attack. I didn't do it at first because I didn't know if or when I'd get better. Then...you seemed to be going through something, so I was afraid to rock the boat. But I'd love to have Jennifer as my wife. It's past time."

Brea smiled, happy that her dad had finally found a partner and helpmate after over two decades alone. "It is. I also want you to promise me that if Pierce makes it back, you'll welcome him as a part of my life."

Daddy sucked in a breath. "You're asking for a lot since I don't know this man."

"You have a big heart. I know you'll come through." Brea did her best to smile for him. "But I'll warn you now, he probably hasn't spent a day of his life in church and he has one of the foulest mouths I've ever encountered. Sometimes I want to shake my head at that man, even as I say a prayer for him. But his heart is pure. He's a good man, so put whatever Cutter told you out of your head and judge him for yourself."

"You're right. I owe you that much. I hope he's everything you want and that he makes you happy for the rest of your life."

"Me, too, Daddy." She sighed, worry for his safety already crushing her. "Me, too."

At DFW Airport, Cutter stepped through the revolving door from the terminal located on the far side of the bag claim, falling in inconspicuously with a group of students as he slung a duffel over one shoulder and pulled a ball cap low, his sunglasses firmly in place. One-Mile probably wouldn't have recognized him if he hadn't known the guy's walk—though hampered by a bullet that had grazed his thigh mere hours ago—and the other man's watchfulness, which came from their sort of training.

A few press types clustered around the terminal exit closest to the flight's assigned baggage carousel, waiting for their prey. One-Mile just shook his head at them as he peeled away from the wall and followed.

When Brea's bestie reached the sliding double doors that led outside, a gust of northern wind swept in to tug at his cap. Dressed in jeans and a short-sleeve gray T-shirt, the other guy grimaced against the chill of the mid-forty-degree weather.

"You're not in sunny LA anymore, Boy Scout."

Cutter whirled, caught sight of him, then huffed in irritation. "What the fuck are you doing here, Walker?"

"Is that him?" A woman's voice sounded about twenty feet behind them.

"Right height. Right build," answered the man with her, holding a camera and shoving a portable microphone in her hand. "I think so."

As they darted for Cutter, the rest of the paparazzi contingency caught on to the fervor and started running in their direction, too.

"I came to take you to your car. Or I can leave you here with them to figure it out. Your call."

"Cutter, did you shoot Shealyn West's boyfriend in a jealous rage?" shouted one reporter dashing in his direction.

"Were you so violent because she'd kicked you to the curb?" another demanded, sprinting toward them.

"Word is you were shot, too. Who pulled the trigger?" asked yet another, quickly closing in. "What is the extent of your injuries?"

With a snarl, Cutter turned to him. "Fine. I'll ride with you."

"Smart man."

"Asshole."

One-Mile laughed. "You're welcome. I'm parked in the garage across the street. Give me your bag."

Bryant gripped it tighter. "I got it."

"Oh, so you can lug it and outrun that crowd chasing you after someone took a hunk out of your thigh a few hours ago? Fine by me."

Cutter thrust the duffel at him. "Let's go."

One-Mile shouldered the bag and jetted to his Jeep, unlocking it with his fob just before he wrenched the door open, dumped Bryant's bag, and hopped in, the reporters mere seconds behind. The second Cutter's ass hit the passenger's seat, One-Mile screeched out of his parking spot and surged toward daylight.

"Why are you here?"

Normally, One-Mile appreciated people who didn't waste his time with blah-blah-blah bullshit. In this instance…he'd spent his six-hour drive from Lafayette trying to figure out what the hell to say. If asking the Boy Scout for a favor had only been for his benefit, he would have skipped the whole thing. But this was for Brea, and he wasn't letting Cutter leave this Jeep before he agreed to protect her.

"I know we're never going to be pals, but—"

"You think?" Cutter snorted. "If I had my choice, I'd do the world a favor and kill you. I told you never to put your hands on Brea—"

"I'm in love with her. There was no way we weren't going to happen. Do I know I'm not good enough for her? Sure. I'll spend every day I have left on this earth trying to be worthy of her. But I'm not giving her up—not for you, her dad, or anyone else. And before you cast stones and tell me I should never have touched her, I'd be willing to bet the bosses told you to keep your hands off Shealyn West. But you didn't listen; you took her to bed anyway. Why?"

"Shut your damn mouth."

"Because you're in love with her. Just like I love Brea."

"You love her so much you raped her?"

This again? "Did she tell you that? Or did you convince yourself I must have because you couldn't imagine any other way in which Brea willingly let me take her to bed?"

"Shut up."

"No. I made love to her because I'm in love with her, the same way you're in love with Shealyn. That's why you got sloppy and thumbed your nose at every protocol we've ever been given. Because there was no force on earth that was going to keep you from her. Tell me I'm wrong; I dare you." He raised a brow. "I'll wait while you find the balls to lie to my face."

"It's none of your business. I don't want to hear another word."

"Are you salty because Brea is pregnant?"

Cutter whipped a furious glare at him.

One-Mile merged with traffic around the terminal. "Yeah, I know, just like I know you two are friends, not lovers. She told me everything."

"Son of a bitch." Bryant beat at the dashboard. "It wasn't enough for you to plow through her virtue and ruin her future. You had to knock her up and break her heart and—"

"That's why I'm here. I never meant to hurt her, and now shit is going down. You and I need to talk."

The guy pressed his forehead into the heel of his palm, looking somewhere between bitter and exhausted. "You know, it's been a really long, shitty day. I don't need you piling on with your problems. You made them; you clean them up."

"Something wrong beyond you being shot at?" He glanced down at Cutter's thigh. "That hurt like a bitch yet?"

"The local is still working. It's a surface wound. Just needed a stitch or two." Bryant waved it away. "But I've already had to defuse a threat to Shealyn's life today by putting a bullet between someone's eyes, so I'm not in the mood for you."

One-Mile downshifted. He'd charged into this conversation with Cutter, guns blazing, knowing only the sensationalized tabloid outline of the events the other guy had endured this morning.

"That sucks."

"Sucks? It scared the shit out of me. Shealyn was seconds away from—"

Death.

One-Mile knew why Cutter refused to finish that sentence. When he pictured Brea in that same position, it both terrified and enraged him. He'd be homicidal, too. No wonder Bryant was in a crappy-ass mood. "I'm sorry, man. I can only imagine…"

"The scene was pandemonium. Bullets flying everywhere. And it was barely past sunrise. So yeah, it's been a damn long day."

"Then you had to deal with the questioning and the paperwork…"

"The hospital, the doctors, and"—Cutter thumbed behind him in the vague direction of the terminal—"the press."

Together, it had created an all-around shit show.

"I'm surprised you flew home instead of staying with Shealyn. She must have been shaken by all this, too." If someone had threatened Brea, he wouldn't have let her out of his arms for days.

Cutter turned a scathing glare his way. "Don't play dumb. I know you saw this coming, asshole. Everyone did. It's over."

"What happened?"

"Oh, please… You don't care."

For himself? No. But Brea did. Bryant being happy would make her happy. And since her happiness was his priority, he swallowed back his snarly reply. "When the press ran with this story about Brea being your pregnant fiancée, did Shealyn really believe that?"

Bryant clenched his jaw. "Every word. She didn't even want to hear my side of things."

"Fuck. She, of all people, should know the press is full of liars peddling clickbait."

"Yeah, but she had a rough childhood. Trust is hard for her, and I knew that. I fucked up. I should have told her about Brea when we started getting personal, but I thought she'd never see me as anything other than a fling. God, if I could go back two days and change everything..." He shook his head, regret tightening his face. "But it's done. The only bright spot is that I finally figured out who her blackmailer was and made it back to her house before it was too late."

"Saving her life didn't count for anything?"

He shook his head. "Why should it? I was just doing my job. The reality that I'll never spend another minute with the woman I love, except watching her on the little screen in my living room, is hitting me. Can we skip this heart-to-heart? Just take me back to my car."

"Where is it?" He felt kind of bad that he had to lean on the Boy Scout when he was clearly fighting his way through fire. But with Brea's safety at stake, he couldn't afford to back down.

"Long-term lot on the north side of the airport. Turn here." Cutter pointed.

"On it." One-Mile complied. "So you're home for good?"

"Yep. And after the way I fucked up that op, I'll be shocked if Hunter doesn't lead the charge to fire me. He's pissed."

He snorted. "If it's any consolation, I've weathered that storm. You'll be fine."

Cutter shrugged like he didn't care. Not surprising since he obviously felt as if his heart had been ripped out. "Whatever. You didn't come here to hear my sad-sack problems. So why did you drive all this way?"

"For Brea. I'm flying to Mexico tonight. I need your help to keep her safe." He explained the situation with Montilla, along with his plan.

Bryant swore under his breath. "Are you crazy? That's a suicide mission."

He'd put the best spin possible on his scheme for Brea, but he couldn't bullshit Cutter. "Probably. I maybe have a one-in-ten chance of walking out of this alive."

"Then why do it?"

"Because there's no damn life I want to live anymore without her and our baby in the center of it. Either I make us whole and safe or I'm out of the picture and she goes on."

"I'll go with you."

Cutter was offering to risk his life? Yeah, probably for Brea's sake. But it still shocked One-Mile. "Thanks, but I need you to watch over her. Keep pretending you're engaged to her. Pretend the baby is yours. And if I don't make it back, do what you've done all her life and take care of her."

"By marrying her?"

He tried not to seize up. "I know it's not your first choice. It's definitely not mine. But if you have to…"

"You hate me and yet you're trusting me?"

He shrugged. "You hate me, too. But I know you love her like you'd love a sister. You'll keep her out of harm's way. I rewrote my will and life insurance policies this morning. Logan has all the paperwork. Everything I own goes to her. So even if she doesn't have me, she'll have money. Just protect her from Montilla. If you can, keep the town from ripping her to shreds. And don't let her fall apart."

Thankfully, Bryant didn't hesitate. "I'll always do everything I can to protect her."

"Her dad probably knows by now that she's pregnant."

"Fuck. He'll know it's not mine."

Worry twisted One-Mile's guts. "Is there any chance he'll disown her? She didn't seem to think so, but…"

"She's been worried about it, but no. He loves her too much."

He let out a sigh of relief. "Good. If Brea has both of you, she should be set, no matter what."

"And maybe this is a good thing. She's needed to stand her ground with her daddy for a long time. Now that she has a reason to, I'm hoping she will." Cutter grimaced at the bright sunlight slanting in through the windshield as the car veered slightly west, toward the setting sun. "What's next?"

"I'm catching a private flight to Mexico City in a couple of hours. From there, I'll put out feelers to locate Montilla. I've got some cash to throw around and a few favors I can call in. That should help."

"Exit here. I'm parked in the lot on the right."

One-Mile followed his directions and quickly pulled up beside Cutter's truck. "Here you go."

Bryant climbed out of his Jeep and grabbed his duffel from the back. "It's no secret I don't like you and that I don't like what you've done to Brea. But I respect the hell out of what you're doing to keep her safe. I'll do my part, no worries. For her sake, I'll hope you come back. Good luck, man."

Then Cutter was gone.

One-Mile watched the guy start his vehicle and head out of the lot before he steered back to the airport for the most important—and dangerous—mission of his life.

Brea barely slept that night. By now, Pierce would be in Mexico. Since he'd left his phone behind to make sure no one could track it, she couldn't call or text him one last time. In fact, he'd told her to go on, live her life, and be happy.

She didn't know how she would without him, but he had made her promise, so she had to try. Besides, if she wanted to keep herself and the baby safe, she had to act as if her heart belonged to Cutter.

And to maintain her sanity today, she'd had to turn off her cell. Until she'd done that, it hadn't stopped ringing with requests for comment and infuriating *gotcha* questions.

With a tired sigh, she emerged from her house. Her white compact was surrounded by a small crowd of strangers with cameras and portable microphones.

She marched to her car, glad for the chill that made wearing a big, concealing poncho necessary. "No comment."

"What do you think about your fiancé cheating with one of the hottest stars in Hollywood?" one man barked at her.

"Rumor has it you and Cutter are continuing with your wedding plans. Because you're pregnant? Or because Shealyn West dumped him?"

Another woman thrust a mic in her face. "How awful do you feel knowing that your fiancé took a more beautiful woman to bed?"

Ouch. Still, Brea refused to rise to the bait.

"I said no comment. Now please move." She nudged the annoying reporters aside and slid into her car, then drove off with a sigh.

But matters were hardly better at the salon.

When she arrived, she slipped in through the back, only to find twenty people crammed into the salon's little waiting area at the front, some familiar, most not.

Rayleigh met her with wide eyes and a long-suffering sigh. "I'm glad you're here, honey, but are you sure you want to be?"

"Do you need me to leave?" The reporters would disappear if she did.

"No," the salon owner assured. "Just pointing out today might be tough."

"I'm not letting rabble like them mess with my life. I've got a full day of clients, and I intend to keep my appointments." She hesitated. "Unless they've cancelled."

"No one has. If anything, strangers have called asking if you have any availability this week." Her boss dropped her voice to a whisper. "And last Friday, your mysterious man friend made an appointment with you for tonight."

Brea had seen that. Pierce had probably intended to confront her before he'd gotten impatient and hunted her down at Cutter's.

When she'd seen his appointment on the books, she'd been somewhere between annoyed and worried as hell. Now, it was all she could do not to cry at the thought Pierce wouldn't be coming through those doors tonight. He might never come around again.

"You can cancel that. He's gone. If there's someone on the waiting list, maybe Joy could call whoever's first to see if they want that six o'clock?"

Rayleigh frowned in concern and hustled her firmly behind the partition dividing them from the foyer. "What do you mean gone?"

Brea didn't dare answer honestly. For all she knew, Rayleigh was the reason the world knew she was expecting. She didn't want to think her own boss would sell her out...but it wasn't impossible.

"Absent. No longer here. Not someone I'll be seeing today."

"Honey, that man loves you. He—"

"He hates Cutter, whom I'm still marrying. I won't be in the middle of their vendetta anymore." It wasn't a total lie...but it was definitely misdirection. "I'm putting him out of my head, the same way I'm sure he's put me out of his."

At least she hoped he was focused on Montilla and not spending any of his energy worrying about her.

"All right." Rayleigh didn't look like she believed a word, but she didn't argue anymore. "I'll have Joy call the first person on the list. Your ten a.m. isn't here yet. Do you want to take this time to make a statement to the press? If you do, it's possible these folks will leave."

Brea didn't want to...but she understood Rayleigh's point. "I'll make a brief one."

With that, Brea stopped into the back room, tucked her purse away, applied a tinted lip balm, then took a deep breath. She had to be convincing. Her life—and her baby's—might depend on it.

The moment she walked around the partition, she saw the crowd had grown in the last few minutes. Rayleigh was trying to shoo and wrangle them out the door. Most simply ignored her and shouted questions.

Brea grabbed the step stool Joy kept behind the counter so that all five-feet-nothing of her could reach the top shelf of the products they sold, climbed on the top rung, and cleared her throat.

Instantly, the room fell silent. "I'm Brea Bell and I'll be making this one and only statement. I won't be taking any questions afterward, so please listen carefully. As you know, Cutter Bryant is my fiancé. We've already discussed his recent time in California protecting Shealyn West. I know the story beyond the salacious gossip and I'm satisfied with his explanation. We will be pressing forward with our wedding. We hope you understand our desire for privacy as we look forward to our future. That's all."

En masse, the reporters started shouting questions—all prying, indelicate, and as titillatingly phrased as possible. Brea ignored them when her first appointment of the day squeezed through the door with a confused frown. "What's going on here?"

Brea glared at the tabloid press with disdain. "Nothing important, Marcie. Go on back and we'll talk about what you'd like to do with your hair."

The forty-something woman nodded, then inched through the throng before finally making her way behind the partition to the empty salon.

Satisfied that her client was no worse for the wear, she addressed the press again. "If you don't have an appointment today, you'll need to wait outside. If anyone is unwilling to do that, we'll be forced to call the sheriff."

Then Brea stepped off the stool, folded it up, propped it back in the corner, and disappeared behind the partition.

Thankfully, most of the rest of the day was far less dramatic. After the press camped outside, clients came and went, most offering her a smile, a sympathetic ear, or an encouraging pep talk. They expressed excitement that she and Cutter were finally getting married and having a baby. Some even asked if they could help.

Today had proven folks in Sunset had bigger hearts than she'd thought, and she felt almost sheepish that she'd imagined differently.

At least until five o'clock. Then Theresa Wood arrived, all scrutinizing green eyes and gray roots concealed by an updo that showed off her faux platinum ends. Brea sighed. She'd always suspected the woman didn't like her. Why the divorcée continued to make appointments with her, given their mutually unspoken enmity, was anyone's guess.

"How are you today, Mrs. Wood?"

The fiftyish woman leaned around the partition to stare out the plate-glass windows at the reporters clogging the sidewalk, then turned back to her with a judgmental smirk. "A damn sight better than you, I'd say."

Brea pasted on a smile like she didn't have a care in the world as she dismantled the woman's updo. No way would she let Mrs. Wood dig those artificial claws into her hide. "I'm fine, thanks for asking. Your roots definitely need attention. Let's head on over to the shampoo bowl. I think you need a good clarifying shampoo before we get started."

The older woman made her way to an empty chair and plopped down. "How are you coping with this mess, girl? I know you're not used to being quite so...popular. And now to hear that your man has been cheating? You poor thing."

Maybe Mrs. Wood was being genuine...but her tone didn't sound that way.

Brea tried not to grit her teeth as she wet the woman's wiry hair and lathered it up. "Not at all. Cutter and I are closer than ever. Wedding plans are chugging along. I'll be having this baby next year. Life couldn't be grander."

"I told those silly reporters as much when they accosted me outside of Jasmine's after my grocery shopping on Sunday afternoon, asking a million questions about y'all."

"Oh?" Brea rinsed the suds from the woman's hair and tried not to lose her cool.

"Yeah, they seemed all kinds of interested in how happy you were, how close you were. I was surprised they didn't ask me a thing about the baby." She raised a platinum brow, her smile just shy of superior. "So I made sure they knew about it."

This old viper had speculated to the press about her pregnancy? Blabbed it without any proof, then preached it like gospel?

Rayleigh whirled around from her nearby station and pinned the older woman with a glare. "Why would you have done that, Theresa? You didn't know for certain Brea was pregnant."

The woman scoffed. "Of course I did. When I was in here six weeks ago for my last touch-up, the poor girl looked positively green. She all but ran to the bathroom. I had to use the facilities after her, and given the stench it seemed fairly obvious she'd been vomiting. I just put two and two together."

"She might have been sick, too. You didn't know," Rayleigh fumed. "And yet you spread rumors to internet gossip rags?"

Mrs. Wood shrugged a bony shoulder. "I was right, so I don't know why you're all bent out of shape. Far as I can tell, she's still Sunset's sweetheart and no worse for the wear."

Brea shut off the water and wrapped a towel around the woman's head so tightly Mrs. Wood winced. "My private life is being bandied about by all of Hollywood and half the country. I'm on internet gossip sites and trashy tabloid TV. They've made me into an object of pity and ridicule. My name and my child will forever be attached to a scandal I had nothing to do with. And you have the right to say I'm no worse for the wear?"

"Goodness, I didn't mean to upset you." Mrs. Wood bristled.

"Let's not pretend you thought of me at all," Brea blurted, then realized Pierce was rubbing off on her.

Saying what was on her mind really was ridiculously freeing.

The older woman sat up in the chair, gaping. "That's not true, honey. I just—"

"I'm not your honey and I don't like liars." She skimmed a glance over the clock on the wall. "You know, it seems I don't have time to do your hair after all. So sorry. Maybe someone else in the salon would like to finish Mrs. Wood?"

None of the other five stylists said a single word.

"Or not." Brea flashed a saccharine smile at the older woman. "Sorry."

"You can't leave me like this. I can't walk out of this salon with wet hair. Everyone will see me."

"You're not worried about 'everyone.' You just wanted to be pretty before you drove on out to the Rodeway on the north side of Lafayette to shag Pam Goodwin's husband," Rayleigh spouted.

Brea gaped. Had Mrs. Goodwin been right about her husband's affair after all? Never mind why the man would pick someone ten years older. Brea knew well the heart couldn't help who it wanted. But she couldn't fathom why the elementary school principal would choose someone so vile when his wife was such a doll.

"That is not true." Mrs. Wood stamped her foot. "You take that back right now."

"I will not." Rayleigh crossed her arms over her chest. "I know full well you've been sinning with that man for the past two years. I saw you two coming out of that motel myself."

Holy cow. Since she was single, Mrs. Wood might be entitled to have sex with whomever she wanted, but that didn't make it okay for her to help a married man commit adultery. Brea wouldn't tell Mrs. Wood how to live; Lord knew she had sins of her own. But that didn't mean she had to continue dealing with the woman.

"Liar!"

Rayleigh was a lot of things, including a gossip. One thing she'd never been? A liar.

Brea calmly dried her hands on a nearby towel. "I'm afraid I'll no longer be fixing your hair. I suggest you find another stylist."

"In fact, why don't you find another salon? You're no longer welcome here, Theresa," Rayleigh said. "Buh-bye."

The rest of the salon erupted in applause. Not surprising, Brea supposed. No one liked the woman anyway, but when Mrs. Wood huffed her way outside, Brea was astonished that the small crowd remaining—hairdressers and clients alike—rushed over to her with hugs and smiles, all congratulating her for standing up to that horrible woman. She blinked at Rayleigh in confusion.

Her boss laughed. "You've been too nice to her for too long. We all have for your sake, but now that you've grown a spine and cut her loose..."

Was that how they'd all seen her? Spineless?

Brea winced. She supposed it might appear as if she had been. She'd meant to be polite, give others the benefit of the doubt, turn the other cheek as a good Christian should. But some people simply stopped deserving chances. Telling them so felt wonderfully liberating.

Yet another way Pierce had rubbed off on her. And honestly, that made her happy.

"Thanks, y'all. I'll try not to take on any more disagreeable clients."

"We'd appreciate that," said Li Na, a gorgeous Chinese stylist with purple streaks and swagger, as she winked.

Impulsively, Brea hugged her. "My pleasure."

When she turned, Rayleigh waited, arms outstretched.

Brea embraced her boss. "I'm sorry about my attitude earlier."

"For suspecting me of telling the world your secret? It's all right. In your shoes, I probably would have suspected me, too. But I'm on your side."

"I appreciate that more than you know."

As the others returned to their clients and blow dryers started whining again, Rayleigh pulled her aside. "You looked so sad when you came in. I didn't have Joy schedule you a six o'clock. I had her call Cutter. I thought you could use a friend."

Thank goodness he was back in town, though she hadn't seen him. "I really could. Thank you."

"It's all right. Let me know if you need anything else." Then she dropped her voice. "But I still think that hot mysterious man will come back for you."

If he can, he will. But Brea just smiled. "I owe you."

The woman waved her away. "You don't owe me anything. Just know I'm here for you."

Brea disappeared into the back room with her phone for a bit to call Daddy and check on him. Thankfully, the church had been mostly quiet today. As she hung up and muted her phone again, the door opened.

"Bre-bee."

She shoved her phone on the nearby table and leapt to her feet to run to her best friend, who looked tired and sad as heck. "Cutter."

He scooped her up in his arms and held her close. "You okay?"

"I'm all right. How are you?"

"I'm sorry about everything." He pulled free to study her with solemn eyes. "I never imagined my choices would impact your life so horribly. One minute I was guarding Shealyn's body, and the next the feelings neither of us expected were front-page news. I knew she was a public figure…but I didn't think anyone would care about me, much less the people in my life…"

"I would have assumed the same thing. Don't worry about me. It really is all right."

"How did your father take the news?"

"About the baby? Better than expected. It was good to finally be honest with him, and I realize I should have found the courage to do it a long time ago." She sent him a little smile. "You told me once that I had a habit of burying my head in the sand. I didn't like hearing it, but you were telling me the truth. I was afraid to pull my head out, but I finally did."

"And he didn't disown you, did he?"

Brea shook her head. "No, that was my irrational fear about disappointing him talking. He knows the baby isn't yours."

"I figured. He's always suspected our relationship isn't like that." Cutter pulled at his neck. "Walker picked me up at the airport yesterday afternoon so we could talk."

Her breath caught. She hoped like heck they hadn't come to blows. "About what?"

"Me watching over you. For all his faults, he truly does care about you. He wants us to continue with our engagement as if we're going to marry."

"Are you all right with that?"

Cutter shrugged. "It doesn't make me any difference."

He tried to hide his feelings, but Brea knew him too well for that. "She broke your heart, didn't she?"

After a long pause, he finally cracked. "Yeah."

Brea gathered him into her arms. "I'm so sorry. I don't know anyone more deserving of love and happiness. She doesn't know what she's missing out on."

"She never will, and I'm at least half to blame." He sighed. "Let's talk about something else. Has it been too crazy—"

"No. I won't let you bury your head—or in this case, your heart—in the sand. I'd like to march outside and tell all those reporters we were never really engaged, and this isn't your baby."

"You can't," he growled out.

"I know. And I feel horrible that I'm placing my welfare above your happiness."

"If you didn't, I'd be angry as hell."

"If I weren't pregnant, I wouldn't care. I'd use those reporters to speak directly to Shealyn West."

"It wouldn't matter. She's past listening." He frowned down at her. "But who is this defiant, opinionated little thing I'm talking to now?"

That made her laugh. "You can thank Pierce."

Cutter scoffed. "If you're getting mouthy, I don't know if it's thanking him I'll be doing."

She took his teasing in stride. "Well, too bad. This is me now. You're going to have to deal with it."

"You know I'm happy to, Bre-bee."

"You want to talk about her?"

"No. Forty-eight hours ago, we were trying to figure out how to defy odds and make it work. Now…it's done because I screwed up." He sighed. "It was probably just a stupid-ass fantasy anyway."

"I'm sorry." Brea gnawed at her lip. "I hate to ask, but… I don't suppose you'd be willing to find Pierce in Mexico and help him."

"I already offered. He doesn't want me. He doesn't want anyone." Cutter shrugged. "And I respect him for not wanting to take others down with him."

Everything inside her froze, then started to ache. "Do you think he'll make it out of this alive? Is there any chance?"

Cutter hesitated, then shook his head. "You're a woman now, and I won't candy-coat it for you. No. He's probably not coming back. I think we press on with our January wedding. If he somehow beats the odds and proves me wrong, I'll step aside and let him take my place as your husband. Otherwise…I think you and I better figure out how to spend our futures together, without the people we love."

chapter eight

Saturday, December 13
One month later

A MONTH—FUCKING GONE. AND ONE-MILE HAD STEPPED ONTO US SOIL AT DFW Airport less than two hours ago with one top-of-mind focus: seeing Brea ASAP.

Since he was in desperate times, that called for desperate measures. After yesterday's shit show, his situation had leapfrogged over merely wretched and landed squarely in last-gasp, holy-fuck land. He needed to regroup—fast. But he'd never imagined he'd be doing it in this swanky suburban mansion.

When he'd exited the plane, the invite to this shindig, along with Cutter's RSVP plus one, had been sitting in his inbox. That had made his decision for him. Normally, he hated gatherings like this, but if Brea was here, a mere forty-five minutes away, instead of in Louisiana, a distant six hours east, he'd attend the fucking party with bells on.

So he ambled into Callie Mackenzie's massive kitchen, decked out with festive holiday decorations, feeling severely out of place. As he scoured the room for Brea, cheerful party conversations fell to whispers, then died to a hush. Everyone glanced around, trying to pinpoint the source of the unrest, including Cutter Bryant, who stood alone.

One-Mile wasn't shocked when all eyes fell on him.

Surprise!

He knew a lot of the people at this upscale Christmas party. Half were EM Security employees and their dates, as well as the operatives and significant others from their sister firm, Oracle. Clearly, no one had expected him to show.

Jack Cole, Deke Trenton, and the Oracle gang knew *of* him. Likely they'd heard he was a lowlife, a rapist, a horrible human being, and all that jazz. He really didn't give two shits. Since the EM guys all thought he was in Mexico, they looked at him as if they'd seen a ghost. And in some ways, One-Mile felt as if he'd been dead since he'd left a month ago. But that wasn't important. Right now, he needed to have a few critical conversations. And lay eyes on Brea.

Where the hell was she?

When he gave the room another visual sweep, he still didn't see her. She should be here as Cutter's date, but the Boy Scout looked stag. What the hell? Hadn't she come? Was something wrong?

His agitation—and his blood pressure—ratcheted up.

Cutter met his probing stare. One-Mile glared, trying not to resent the guy…

but failed. It wasn't Bryant's fault that he was free to spend most of his time with Brea while One-Mile had to hide in the hole he'd dug for himself that was looking more and more like a grave.

Bryant's contempt flared back at him from across the room as if he'd sent it via flamethrower. So much for their truce. Sure, they'd come to an understanding last month that Brea and her safety mattered above all else…but that didn't mean they would ever be pals.

The one thing that saved One-Mile's sanity? Cutter didn't appear worried, look guilty, or seem as if he was in mourning. Hopefully that meant Brea was all right, simply absent for some benign reason. But he intended to find out pronto.

Before he could cross the room to interrogate the SOB, Logan's wife, Tara, and Callie Mackenzie appeared in front of him with cautious smiles, as if they worried he might bare his teeth and attack.

"Welcome, Mr. Walker." The brunette flashed him her hostess smile, blue eyes bright with welcome.

He didn't really believe it, but he gave her points for trying. "Thank you, Mrs. Mackenzie." He glanced at Logan's pretty redheaded wife. "Mrs. Edgington."

"Glad you could make it," Tara said.

Despite that whopping lie and what he suspected was their disquiet at being so near him, Callie threaded her arm through his. Instantly, he felt daggers in his back, and they weren't Cutter's. A glance over his shoulder proved both her husband, former FBI agent Sean Mackenzie, and her Dominant lover, Mitchell Thorpe, scrutinized his every move.

"Don't pay attention to them," Callie encouraged as she guided him to a bursting table. "They're always overprotective. Most everyone has already eaten, but the buffet is still out, so please make yourself a plate. Let me know if you need anything else."

What he needed was Brea, but Callie and Tara weren't who he needed to ask. Still, he tried not to look like an absolute bastard.

Tara handed him a napkin and some plastic utensils. "Would you like a beer?"

He'd love one, but he had to maintain a clear head tonight. "Just water, if you don't mind."

"Coming right up." The redhead shimmied her way toward the refrigerator.

One-Mile put a few things on his plate so he didn't look as if he had zero interest in this party. But the warm, catered chow beat the hell out of everything he'd hunted and scrounged in Mexico. His stomach rumbled. So he dug in.

As he shoveled dinner into his mouth, One-Mile took in the rest of the scene. In one corner, Trees stood alone, staring at Zy, who leaned over Tessa with a smile that broadcast the fact he'd love to eat her whole. The pretty blonde receptionist stared back at him like a sugar addict gazing longingly at a lush cake with a dollop of pure-orgasm frosting. If they weren't fucking yet…it was only a matter of time. Josiah crowded next to Stone and some of the Oracle guys, engaged in an animated conversation.

Logan took the opportunity to sidle up to him. "You back?"

Besides Brea, here was the other person he needed to talk to. Might as well get it over with. "Temporarily, but—"

"I haven't heard from you in a fucking month. Want to fill me in?"

Before he could, Hunter and Joaquin joined their conversation, glaring daggers.

"You can't come to work, but you can show up to a Christmas party?" Hunter challenged.

Oh, fuck you. He didn't have the patience for this. "We all know how much I love social occasions, especially when it involves your sparkling company."

The older Edgington replied with a snarl and an obscene finger gesture.

"What's going on in Mexico?" Joaquin asked, trying to be the voice of reason. "Is it done? Is Montilla dead?"

One-Mile prepared to launch into his rehearsed speech when, out of the corner of his eye, he caught Cutter waving to the small crowd. Did the asshole think he was leaving?

"I'll catch y'all later. Merry Christmas." Then Bryant turned, extending a hand toward their host. "Thanks for everything, Sean. Your wife did an amazing job. I had a great time."

One-Mile shoved his half-eaten plate of food aside. If the Boy Scout was heading out, he damn well intended to follow.

He wouldn't rest until he knew Brea was all right.

"Can you stay for three more minutes?" Sean asked Cutter. "Callie hosted this party for a reason."

Cutter hesitated, then caved. "Sure."

When Tara returned with his bottle of water, One-Mile thanked her and released the breath he'd been holding. Callie gave a heartfelt speech about everyone in the room being a member of the family the Mackenzie-Thorpe trio had chosen.

"Hear, hear!" The party guests raised their glasses before hugs began all around.

One-Mile knew he wasn't included in that group, and he tried not to care. Would it be nice to have a circle of tight-knit friends? Maybe. He'd never had such a thing. But for Brea's sake? Yeah. Some of the unconventional relationships like Callie, Sean, and Thorpe's, not to mention the freak flags everyone in this group openly flew, would shock his pretty girl. But once she got past that, she would love their close sense of community.

If fate decided that she should spend her life with Bryant, she'd get it.

People hugged and guys slapped each other on the back. The happiness in the room was palpable. He tried to shove down his resentment and envy. All these men were sure of their futures, secure in the knowledge they would spend the rest of their days with the woman they loved.

One-Mile hated that he might have to let his girl marry another man. But for her safety, he would stand back and let her—no matter how much it killed him.

Hell, the odds weren't good that he'd even be alive by then.

Speaking of which, he didn't have any time to lose.

When Cutter headed for the exit again, One-Mile tossed his half-empty plate into the bin, then turned to Logan. "I need to talk to you. I have to regroup, and I need a hookup on more supplies, but I'll have to call you later."

"What? No, goddamn it. You owe us some fucking answers," Logan shouted.

But One-Mile was already across the room, trying to block Bryant from leaving. As he barreled closer, the Boy Scout stiffened.

Former British MI5 agent Heath Powell stopped a conversation with his wife mid-sentence and grabbed Cutter's arm. "Let it go, you two."

One-Mile reached them and glared at Powell. "This has nothing to do with you."

"It's fine," Cutter assured. "I've got to go anyway. Great to see you, Heath. Let's get together soon."

Powell nodded but he clearly wasn't buying Bryant's *aw-shucks* bullshit. "You have my number."

One-Mile watched from the corner as Cutter circled the kitchen shaking hands, hugging some of the women, then finally brushing a kiss across Callie's cheek before heading down the long hallway—straight for the exit.

Did this asshole seriously think he was leaving without telling him where Brea was and if she was all right?

"Hey, fucker! You're not marrying Brea." There. He'd said what every other person at this party expected him to. Bonus, it should get Bryant's attention.

But no. The Boy Scout simply slammed the front door between them.

Maybe he could have been less flippant…but what the hell? Weren't they both on Team Save-Brea anymore?

They had to be. Cutter might be a lot of asswipe, but he'd never let anything happen to her.

If you want a different response, maybe you should be less of a flaming asshole.

Blaming his month of isolation and frustration, he jerked the door open and followed outside—just in time to watch Cutter peel away from the curb. One-Mile chased him down the sidewalk to no avail, cursing a blue streak.

Fuck. He'd screwed the pooch. Now what?

Reluctantly, he whipped out his phone, which he'd retrieved from his Jeep earlier, and dialed Cutter's number.

The asshole answered on the first ring. "What were all the growls and death stares about?"

Who the fuck cared? "Where's Brea?"

"At my apartment. Her day at the salon ran long, and she was too tired to come to the party."

"But she's otherwise all right?"

"Yeah. Everything's good. Pregnancy is all fine." Cutter hesitated. "She's even doing a lot better with her dad."

That made him damn glad on her behalf.

"Great. Thanks." One-Mile jogged down the street toward his Jeep. "Sorry for being a douche back there."

"You mean you're sorry for being you?"

"I don't want to do this with you, man."

"Fine." Cutter sighed. "Did you come to the party all the way from Mexico just to see her?"

"More or less."

"Is Montilla dead?"

"No. Long story. I'm following you back to your place. I need to see her."

Hold her. Kiss her. Love her.

One-Mile needed that so fucking bad.

"You don't know where I live."

Um…I've fucked Brea in your bed. "I'll figure it out."

"I'm still not convinced you're good for her."

"That's not your decision."

He had more questions, but he'd far rather talk to Brea herself than the Boy Scout, so he hung up and hunkered down for a long drive.

The trip back to Lafayette was long and dark and seemed to last forever. He stopped once for strong coffee but otherwise caught up to Cutter quickly and maintained his position on the guy's back bumper for the majority of the ride.

As they drew closer, his palms turned damp. Would Brea be happy to see him? Would she welcome him, even though he hadn't yet slayed her beast? Or had her feelings for him changed?

One-Mile tried to compartmentalize his worries as he parked a few spots down from Cutter, locked his Jeep behind him, then trailed the Boy Scout across the lot and up the steps to the front door, all the while wondering what Brea would do when she saw him. Welcome him with open arms…or say that she'd realized he was a bad bet and decided to move on?

Brea set aside the pregnancy book she'd been reading, then rose and stretched with a forlorn sigh.

Every time she was in Cutter's kitchen, she remembered the night she'd spent here with Pierce. The way he'd stood across the darkened apartment with righteous fury and lust burning in his eyes. The moment he'd swept her off her feet—literally—before he'd worshipped her pregnant belly, then ravaged her to boneless satisfaction all night.

And now he was gone.

For the millionth time, Brea wondered how he was faring and if he'd made any progress in ending Montilla's threats. But as the days dragged into weeks, which had now become a month, she couldn't stop herself from wondering if he was even alive.

Since it hurt too much to believe he wasn't, she bowed her head and prayed to God for mercy, for some sign that Pierce was well.

As she lifted her head and swiped at the tears slowly rolling down her face, a light knock rapped on the front door. She glanced at the clock and froze. Past ten thirty. If Cutter had returned from Callie Mackenzie's Christmas party, he would have simply let himself in. So who was dropping in to visit unexpectedly at this late hour?

In Pierce's absence, Cutter had drilled situational awareness into her head. She'd learned a lot from her gun safety and self-defense classes, which made her feel more prepared to handle a potential threat. But Pierce's friend Matt had been a blunt-force eye-opener. After spending an incredibly patient nine hours with her, installing her new home security system and showing her how to use it, he'd stuck around to ensure she understood the skills everyone else had taught her. At the end of the day, he'd given her his number, said he had a few weeks of free time coming, and that he'd be staying in Louisiana both to keep an eye on her and to avoid returning to Wyoming, where he'd freeze his balls off.

Since then, he'd checked in regularly. He'd promised he could come running if she ever needed him. And he'd be beyond infuriated now if she didn't raise a red flag, especially when Cutter was probably on the freeway, potentially hours away.

She shot off a quick text to Matt. I'm alone at Cutter's. Someone's knocking on the door. I'm going to peek through the peephole.

Instantly, he replied. Gun handy?

Yes.

Let me know who's there. I can be at your location in ten.

Thanks.

He was a very good friend to Pierce.

She darkened her phone and shoved it in the hidden pocket of her yoga pants. Then she made her way to the door and set the Beretta sat on the hall table, just beyond her fingertips, accessible if necessary, before she peered out the peephole.

A woman stood under the circle of the porch light, wearing a blue peacoat, head-to-toe black, and high-heeled boots. She looked familiar but… No. It couldn't be. Yet the longer Brea looked, the more she was convinced that she was right.

Gaping, she pulled open the door and stared.

"Brea?" the stunning blonde asked.

"Mercy me. Shealyn West?"

The woman nodded sheepishly. "Hi. Is, um…Cutter here?"

Wow, the famous actress was really standing on his porch. But this wasn't the time to be star struck. The woman had broken his heart. True…but she had also traveled here from Los Angeles, found Cutter's apartment, and knocked on his door late on a Saturday night for a reason. Brea intended to find out why. If the blonde had ventured here simply to stamp all over his heart again, she'd stop Shealyn cold.

"No. I expect him soon, though. Come on in." She stepped back, inviting the woman inside.

"That's all right. I can come back when he's available."

"No, really. Come in. I think you and I should talk first. He hasn't said a lot about what happened in California." *Just enough to make me madder than a wet hen at you.* "I know what the press said, of course."

"Half of that isn't true." Shealyn took a tentative step inside and looked around.

It probably wasn't anything like her fancy digs in California, but it was homey and comfortable, and the woman better not have come here to judge. Thankfully, nothing on her face indicated she was.

Brea shut and locked the door. "I figured the rumor that you and Tower Trent had never had a relationship was hogwash."

Shealyn clutched her purse nervously. "Actually, that's true. It was good PR for the show, and we were friends. I meant the bit about the secret lesbian fling Jessica and I supposedly had that led to her jealous rage."

"I didn't even give that tripe the time of day. But I know whatever happened between you and Cutter changed him." *Let her stew on that…* "Coffee? Iced tea?"

"Tea, please. Sweet?"

"Is there any other kind?"

"Not in my book."

Darn it all, despite Shealyn being a star and a heartbreaker, there was something down-to-earth about her. She was likable. Seemingly sweet. Girl-next-door, like her image. Could she really be the sort of woman who took pleasure in ripping out a good man's heart?

"So you really are a Southern girl… Please, sit." Brea waved her to a little round table adjacent to the kitchen as she headed for the refrigerator. "Since I just made a pitcher for Cutter before lunch, the tea is fresh."

As Shealyn slid into a chair, Brea sent Matt a clandestine text that all was well, then turned back to the starlet, who was biting her lip, looking both uncomfortable and uncertain.

Wondering what was on the woman's mind, Brea poured the glass of tea and set it with a coaster in front of her.

"Thank you," Shealyn murmured, stare lingering on her hand.

Looking for an engagement ring? Brea frowned as she slid into the opposite chair, tucking one foot under her thigh. "You're welcome. I wish I could have some. But too much caffeine and sugar isn't good for the baby."

Shealyn's smile faltered into a wince of pain. "Congratulations. You and Cutter must be very excited. I'm happy for you two."

The actress said the right words, but her talent in front of a camera was failing her miserably in real life. Shealyn looked anything but thrilled.

Suddenly, the puzzle pieces fell into place.

Brea scowled. "He didn't tell you, did he?"

"Tell me what?"

She crossed her arms over her chest. "Of course he didn't. That stubborn, stubborn man. Ugh! You don't know why he and I are planning this wedding, do you?"

"I presumed it was because you loved each other and were excited about your coming child."

It was all Brea could do not to shake her head in frustration and call Cutter screaming. "Would a man madly in love with a woman and looking forward to starting a family with her give his heart to someone else? Scratch that. Some men might. Would Cutter do that?"

"The man I thought I knew? I've been trying to reconcile that in my head."

"He would never do that. Ever since he stood next to my daddy the day I was born, he's been the big brother I never had. It's a long story, but when I got pregnant, Cutter blamed himself because I got close to my baby's father while trying to help him escape a hostage situation."

Shealyn blinked, looking utterly stunned. "You mean...the baby isn't Cutter's?"

"Heavens, no. We've never..." Brea shook her head. "Ever. He really is like my brother. Anyway, I worked up the nerve to see a doctor right before Cutter went to California to protect you. When we found out for sure I was pregnant, he proposed so I wouldn't have to face my daddy—he's the local preacher—and admit my sin as a fallen woman. I'm sure that sounds silly in this day and age."

"No. I'm from a small town, too."

"So you understand why that thought terrified me. Heck, at the time I was more than a little afraid of the man who got me pregnant, too. Pierce is... overwhelming. Cutter kept threatening to kill him, but it was my fault. I knew I needed to be honest, face him and my father—"

"You're saying Cutter offered to sacrifice his future for you?"

"Exactly."

"My question sounded rude. I-I'm sorry."

"No, it's the truth. And I was such a coward that I agreed to let him." That was an oversimplified version of events, but the rest was too personal and painful. And Shealyn didn't need the details in order to forgive Cutter so he could move on. Or hopefully decide she loved him and wanted to spend her future with him.

The blonde reached across the table and took Brea's hand. "I'm sure he understands."

"It's Cutter, so of course he does. But I should tan his hide for not explaining our 'engagement' the moment he realized he was in love with you. I'm not surprised he didn't, though. He wouldn't have spilled my secret to anyone without a—pardon my French—damn good reason. And he would never have put his own happiness above my fears." She huffed. "I'm going to have some words with that man."

Shealyn stared for a very long time, clearly mulling everything over and making some decisions. "Thank you for explaining. It's none of my business, and I hate to just barge in or ruin your plans—"

"Do you love Cutter?"

"With all my heart." Shealyn's face said that, without him, the organ beating in her chest was broken.

Brea smiled big. "Then you just muck up every last plan. I could never make him happy, but I think you can. And no one deserves it more." If Pierce came back to her, he might be furious that Cutter had started a future with Shealyn, but Brea could still pretend she wasn't One-Mile's girl without having Cutter in her life. "He has always had a chip on his shoulder about being the town drunk's kid. But he's so much more than that."

"Except for my grandfather, he's the best man I've ever met. You really don't mind if I steal him from you?"

Was she kidding? Brea probably wasn't going to get her own happy ending, but if Cutter could have his with the woman he loved, she'd be thrilled.

"So you can make my best friend ecstatically happy? Goodness, no. My life has gone to heck in a handbasket, but that's my own doing. Even so, I can't tie Cutter down. Just…if you're going to take him back to California, let him visit every so often. My baby will need an uncle."

Shealyn smiled. "Of course. I'd never try to keep him from seeing you two. And I'm sure—"

The jiggling of the lock startled Brea. At the sound, Shealyn fell silent and stood, nervously wringing her hands.

Seconds later, the door opened and Cutter walked in, palming his keys. He walked in—then stopped in mid-stride. Brea watched his stare climb up Shealyn's body and saw their gazes lock. His expression twisted with pain and need. The air between them sizzled. She felt their mutual longing like a physical pang.

It was obvious Cutter loved Shealyn with every ounce of his being.

"What are you doing here?" He sounded as if someone had stolen the breath from his chest.

Shealyn lifted her chin. "I came to talk to you."

"And that's my cue to leave." They needed privacy, and she'd only be in their way. "Shealyn, it was lovely to meet you. I'm glad we've had this chance to talk."

"Me, too." The actress smiled and hugged her. "Thank you."

Brea had a feeling they'd eventually be friends. But for now, Cutter scowled in confusion, so she sidled closer and wrapped her arms around him. "You two talk. Be happy. Don't worry about me. Tomorrow, we can discuss what idiots we've been. Then we'll figure out the best way to let everyone know the wedding is off."

Shock spread across his face. "You're good with ending it?"

"Absolutely." From the sound of his voice, it seemed Cutter had been contemplating breaking off their engagement, too. For her safety, he'd remained her fiancé longer than he should have, and she loved him for it. But now he needed to follow his heart. "I only had to see you and Shealyn look at each other once. I would never stand in the way of love."

Brea kissed his cheek, swiped her gun off the table, grabbed her pregnancy book, then shoved everything in her purse. She wriggled into her tennis shoes by the door, then grabbed her keys.

"Um, Brea… Before you go, I should tell you—"

"We'll talk about it tomorrow. You have someone way more important than me who needs you right now. Bye." With a little wave, she backed out of the door and shut it, leaving them in privacy.

As the door clicked closed, she sighed. Hopefully they would work everything out and live happily ever after.

Brea feared she wasn't going to.

"Hi, pretty girl," a wonderfully familiar, dark voice rasped inches from her ear.

With a gasp, she whirled.

Pierce?

There he stood just beyond the circle of the porch light.

Her world stopped. Her heart thundered. A two-ton weight of relief hit her. "You're alive!"

"Yeah."

But there was something different about him… He had an edge she'd never seen. It wasn't just the dark clothes hanging from his leaner frame or the thick beard he wore over his sunken cheeks. It was more than the determination gleaming in his hungry black eyes as he visually inhaled her. The difference was danger. He reeked of it. Its intensity pinged off him.

"And you're really here?"

"For now. God, you look beautiful." Pierce clenched his fists at his sides, as if he was desperate to touch her…but didn't.

Brea bridged the chasm between them and threw herself against him, wrapping him in her arms.

Pierce groaned as he pressed every inch of her against his hard body, clutching her so tightly she could barely breathe. "I needed to see you, baby. So bad."

Brea had a million questions, but she held back as he buried his face in her neck and breathed her in as if he'd never let her go. She clung to him in return, fisting his shirt and pressing kisses along his razor-sharp jaw as stinging tears gathered in her eyes. He'd lost sleep and lost weight. Concern rose.

Her phone buzzing in her purse shuttled her questions and dashed the moment.

"That better not be Cutter." Pierce scowled.

She doubted that very much as she reached for her device. "It's Matt. He's staying at your place."

"He's still in town?"

"You haven't spoken to him?"

He cupped her face in his big, rough hands. "Pretty girl, if I was going to take the risk of talking to anyone, it would have been you."

The way he stared down into her eyes, as if he ached to possess her body by taking her soul, made Brea shiver. "Are you going to kiss me?"

It wasn't the question she should be asking, but they'd get to everything else. This mattered most now.

"Here?" He shook his head. "No."

Didn't he want to? "Why?"

"It's been a long month alone. The minute I put my mouth on you, I'm going to want to bury my cock inside you. And here isn't a good place for that."

His bluntness made Brea laugh. "No, here isn't a good place at all. I guess I don't have to worry that you don't want me anymore."

"Oh, baby… If I could have stopped wanting you, I would have saved you from me a long time ago."

"Then I would have missed out on the best thing that ever happened to me."

"Damn it, you're making resisting you hard. Literally." Pierce grimaced as if he was trying to focus. "Why is Matt still in town? Did something happen?"

"No. He said he's taking a vacation. The weather is supposedly better here."

"No supposedly about it."

"He might have mentioned his…um, nether regions appreciating a break from a Wyoming winter."

"Only you would describe a man's balls that way." The smile that creased his face now, just like the first one he'd ever flashed her, transformed him. She'd forgotten how brutally masculinely beautiful he was.

"I'm polite."

"To a fault," he teased. "You're adorable."

She smiled. "I suspect Matt thought I was helpless, so he stayed around because you weren't here."

His smile widened. "That's Matt. He's a good son of a bitch."

A gust of wind surged and blew. Despite Pierce's big body, she found herself shivering in the December chill.

He wrapped his arms around her again. "Where's your coat?"

"I don't have one. It was warmer when I left my house this morning." At Pierce's frown of displeasure, she tsked. "Don't pass judgment. Where's yours?"

"I'm not cold. You heading home?"

"I was planning to."

"Did Cutter tell you I was here? I followed him back from the party."

"You went?"

"Thinking you'd be there, yeah."

Now she regretted that she'd begged off. Then again, if she'd gone, she would have both blubbered all over Pierce and thrown herself at him in front of everyone. Still, she hated that she'd lost even a minute with him. "I'm sorry."

He shrugged. "I wanted to surprise you."

"You did." The tears that had teetered on her lashes fell as she cupped his cheek. She warmed when he kissed her palm. "Seeing you is the best surprise ever. Cutter didn't say anything because he had an unexpected visitor waiting inside for him." She dropped her voice. "Shealyn West."

"Holy shit. Yeah?"

"I think she came to claim her man. So our 'engagement' is off."

Pierce instantly looked as if he wanted to punch something, namely Cutter's face. "Goddamn it!"

"Don't say that. I'll still be safe without the lie." She sent him a disapproving scowl. "I let your F-bombs slide, but…"

"Fine. I'll try to watch my tongue," he groused. "Let's get you home."

He wrapped an arm around her and led her down the steps, toward the parking lot.

She frowned. "Daddy will be there."

"Then that's not going to work."

"I know. It's awkward you two haven't met yet."

"I'm not so worried about that." Pierce scratched at his scruffy beard. "I'd be happy to rectify that after a shower."

Did he imagine her father would be pleased to meet the man who'd gotten his daughter pregnant at something near midnight while danger all but dripped from him? Was he crazy? Yes…and that was part of his bad-boy appeal.

"Daddy is probably in bed, so I don't think that's an option. What are you worried about?"

"That he'll hear you screaming and come busting down your bedroom door while I've got my head between your legs. That would be an awkward-as-fuck first meeting."

She felt her cheeks heat. "You weren't worried about the sounds I made before you left for Mexico."

"Extenuating circumstances."

Brea had to smile. "How about I come to your house?"

"Only if you leave your car here and let me drive."

So that none of Montilla's spies would see her car at his house, Brea supposed. "That's fine."

He led her down the stairs, pulling her with him into the shadows, then guiding her through the pitch-gray cold until they reached his Jeep. "Do you think someone has been following you? That they're watching us now?"

"Not likely. But I'm not taking chances."

He tucked her into the vehicle, then ran around and bounced into the driver's seat, pulling out of the lot with a watchful scan of his surroundings.

Something had spooked him. And knowing Pierce, the minute they really got alone, he would start seducing her...and she wouldn't be able to think enough to ask questions.

"What's going on?"

He didn't even try to put her off. "When I got to Mexico, it didn't take long to track Montilla to a new compound. I observed him for about two weeks. I got a good handle on his schedule, his habits, the compound's weaknesses. Then I found an insider willing to betray his boss for cash, so I paid the bastard for answers and access. I had a fucking plan ready to roll. But the stupid son of a bitch started throwing around his extra cash in town a few nights back. Questions flew. The next morning, Montilla put a gun to his head in front of everyone, demanding answers. I'm presuming he talked. I could tell he blubbered. Then Montilla blew his brains out and sent everyone in the compound searching for me." He let out a shuddering breath. "I tried to get back to my rental car in town a few miles away, but they'd already found it and torched it. I spent eight days hiding in the desert before I sneaked into Mexico City, where I could disappear."

Brea's heart stopped. She reached for his hand, gripping it desperately. "Stop this. Stop it now. Forget him. Don't go back. We'll leave here and—"

"I can't." Pierce scanned the mostly empty roads and made a right. "He's not going to give up until he finds us. So I've got to find him first."

"But if something happens to you..." Pain wracked her chest just thinking about it.

"Then he won't come after you. You'll be safe because if I'm gone, he'll have won. The only reason he wants you now is to hurt me. But I'm going to end him. I'm not going to put you in that fucking position."

Brea wanted to scream that she didn't understand...but she did. She wanted to rail at the horror and unfairness. But that wouldn't change anything.

"So how long are you here?"

"I've got a flight back at oh-five-hundred on Monday."

Her breath froze. She tried to swallow down her tears, because he needed her to be strong, but her fear fused with her hormones. She started to sob.

"Baby, no. Don't waste tears on me."

"Stop saying that! I love you. For a month, I didn't know if you were alive. I didn't know if you were coming back. In barely thirty hours, you're leaving again and—"

"Shh." He stroked her crown with his big hand. "We have the rest of the weekend. I'm sorry I'll miss your doctor's appointment on Monday."

Appointment? It took Brea a moment to remember... "How did you know I have an appointment with my ob-gyn?"

He hesitated, as if he was looking for the best spin on the truth. "I might have found the paperwork when I was searching your room the night I realized you were pregnant and made a note about the date and time."

Brea wasn't even surprised. In fact, she was almost touched.

"I'd planned to be home for that. Of course, I'd planned for Montilla to be decomposing by now, too." He sounded bitter that the drug lord wasn't.

"The baby's gender reveal is Monday."

He frowned as he took her hand. "Damn it. I'm so fucking sorry I won't be there, but your safety is more important."

She couldn't pretend she wasn't disappointed. "I'm sorry, too."

"I need you to put your head in my lap now."

Was he suggesting... "Pierce, I've missed you, but I'm not doing *that* to you while you're driving."

Despite the heavy pall of angst and sadness, he laughed as he approached the red light outside his neighborhood. "I'm not asking you to suck my cock, pretty girl. At least not yet." He sent her an unexpected grin. "But you should hide so that if any of Montilla's goons are watching my house, they see me, not you."

"Isn't that dangerous, too? Won't they kill you now that they know you're hunting him?"

"Not here. Not in secret. Montilla is arrogant. The way he deals with his enemies is mostly for show. When he had me captive, he only beat me in front of people. As I observed him over the last few weeks, he only raped and murdered with an audience. It doesn't suit him to sneak here and snuff me in the dead of night. I've become an official thorn in his side, and he'd want to make a public example of me. Since he can't, what he really wants is to get his hands on you because then I'll either tell him where to find Valeria and his son to save you or suffer horribly as you die."

Brea didn't understand these violent people and their twisted games, but she grasped that Pierce knew far better how to keep her and their baby safe.

Trembling, she scooted to her right and settled her head on his thigh. She felt his heat, smelled his male musk. Took in more of the danger dripping off him into her nostrils. Despite everything, it stirred her.

Then again, Pierce always did.

Instantly, he laid a protective hand on her head. "Just until we pull into my garage."

"Okay."

"Thanks for trusting me."

"Always." She breathed him in again.

"But if you're motivated to make me feel good while you're down there, I won't object."

"Pierce…" Her body ran hot at the thought. The notion might be reckless, but it was tempting. And they had so little time together before he had to leave…

"What? It's been a long month without you."

She craned her head to look up at him in the dark. "No pretty señoritas?"

He shook his head. "Like it or not, I'm all yours. And in less than five minutes, I'm going to strip you bare and prove it."

Her body tightened. Her womb clenched. She pressed her thighs together in longing.

Brea got bold and cupped the obvious bulge through his jeans.

He let out something between a curse and a groan as he got harder under her palm. "Baby… Fuck, I've missed you."

She'd missed him so, so much.

Finally, his thigh below her cheek tensed, and the Jeep shot forward. He drove like a madman through his neighborhood, slinging left, then right, then left again before coming to an abrupt halt. He reached up, and the mechanical purr of the garage door opener resounded above them. He pulled into the garage and hit the button again. She lifted her head.

Matt stood in the door between the garage and the house, weapon drawn, wearing a mean scowl. When he caught sight of them, he lowered the gun with a sigh and tucked it away. "Hey! I didn't expect to see you, man. When did you get back to the States?"

"Earlier today," Pierce said as he hopped out of the Jeep and shook Matt's hand.

As Brea eased out on the other side and inched around the front of the truck, Matt whipped off his cowboy hat and shared a bro hug with Pierce. She approached, and the man's angular face softened as he wrapped an arm around her, giving her a friendly squeeze.

"Hey, little thing. How you doing? Who was at Cutter's door, this one?" Matt thumbed in Pierce's direction.

"No. You wouldn't believe me if I told you."

"Get your fucking hands off my woman," Pierce growled good-naturedly… mostly.

Brea giggled as Matt released her and held up his hands. "Just being friendly, man."

"Find another woman to be 'friendly' with. I'm going to go get friendly with my woman now. We'll talk later."

Was he kidding? He'd all but announced they would be having sex. Her face flamed hot. "Pierce!"

"What? Matt knows I haven't seen you in a month, so he knows where I'll be spending the night."

She blushed. "It's impolite to talk about the bedroom."

"That's one way of putting it. A lot nicer, too."

Matt burst out laughing.

Brea frowned. There was a grand joke, and she clearly didn't get it. "What other way is there to put it?"

"Inside you." Matt tried to wipe the smile off his face—and failed miserably. "That's what One-Mile meant."

"You're a fucking mind reader." Pierce fist-bumped him before he wrapped an arm around her and swung her off her feet, against his chest, ignoring both her red cheeks and her surprised squeak. "You mind holding down the fort, man?"

"As long as you lovebirds keep it down. I don't need to be reminded of what I'm not getting in this town."

Pierce pushed his way through the door and emerged into the foyer, killing the nearby lights with his elbow and throwing the space into shadow. "Probably not going to happen. You're better off turning up the TV."

"Yeah?" Matt laughed uproariously and winked her way. "I wouldn't have taken you for a screamer, little thing."

She gaped at them, her face broiling with embarrassment. "I... You..."

Pierce chuckled. "Have I ever told you that you're perfect and I love you just the way you are?"

Brea closed her mouth. When he said stuff like that, it was hard to be angry.

And when he took her upstairs, into his dark bedroom, and slowly pulled off her clothes, worshipping her with his sure caresses and soft strokes of his tongue, she forgot that Matt and every other person in the world existed, because, for her, there was only Pierce.

chapter nine

Friday, January 9
One month later
Outskirts of Mexico City

ONE-MILE PULLED HIS HOODIE OVER HIS FACE AND BOWED HIS HEAD AGAINST THE pelting rain. Normally this part of the globe was a sweltering cesspool of humidity and humanity, but Mexico City—like a lot of the world—was recovering from a hectic Christmas and a raucous New Year's. He'd missed both of those at home, and he hoped Brea understood. But Montilla and his band of thugs hadn't taken a week or two off to celebrate the holidays. The average citizen, however, seemed to be partied out. Most of the tourists had emptied from the streets and seemingly gone back to their responsible, desk-jockey lives. So tonight, he walked a largely uninhabited route to his destination, his breaths forming white puffs in the unusual chill.

After nearly another fucking month in this shithole, tonight was hopefully the night Montilla would die.

One-Mile gave the son of a bitch credit. While he'd gone back to the States and weaponed up, thinking he'd have to declare open war to snuff Montilla, the weasel had gone deep into hiding. He'd changed locations, doubled security, increased surveillance, restricted those coming in and out to a few trusted lackeys, varied his schedule, and generally made this mission fucking impossible—except for one appointment he never missed.

One-Mile didn't intend to miss, either. He only had one shot.

Finally, he made his way from the dark, dirty street into the mostly empty hotel. It was a terrible dive in the middle of an even worse slum, but if Montilla died from a kill shot he fired here, this place would rate five fucking stars in his book.

The stucco walls had probably been white decades ago and a row of scarred windows faced a street known for violence. He'd slept in worse, and the idea of unguarded slumber in a real bed after weeks of catnaps on the cold ground was damn appealing. But if all went well, he would only be here a handful of hours. Then he'd be on a plane back to the States. Back to Brea and their baby. And on to his future.

If it didn't go well, he'd be captured, tortured, and killed.

One-Mile glanced at his watch. Just after seven p.m. Time to set up was running out.

He checked in, bribing the front desk clerk with extra cash to forego the ID requirement. Within two minutes, he walked up the darkened stairs to the third floor, key in hand, and entered the room he'd requested.

Last week when he'd followed Montilla into this slum, he'd scoped out this motel, walked it inside and out, figuring out exactly which room he needed to finish this job—and this asshole. The unit he'd chosen had a big window with unfettered views inside the building across the street. It also had direct access to the interior stairwell that led either down to the multiple exits in the lobby or up to the roof. And bonus, if he had to go up to avoid detection, he could climb to the adjacent parking garage from the top of the hotel, disappear into the alley behind, and be gone in under a minute.

Escape routes weren't a problem…unless he fucked up.

Glad for his water-repellant backpack and the plastic tarp he'd wrapped his gun case in before he'd tucked it inside, he set up his MK on its tripod at the window, attached the scope, and focused on the front of the run-down gray-brick business across the street, pinpointing a second-story opening. This week, a redhead half Montilla's age waited for him, pacing.

After double-checking his equipment and perfecting his angle, One-Mile opened the old-fashioned window, heedless of the damp chill. The downpour had dried up to an occasional spit. Even better, the hotel's external light above seemed to have burned out, leaving him in charcoal shadows.

Breathing through an adrenaline rush and his pounding heartbeat, he hunkered behind his scope and set in to wait.

He was ready.

At precisely nine p.m., the girl across the street suddenly jerked and reluctantly opened her door. And what do you know? Montilla walked inside, right on time, as he had every other week, sporting a lascivious leer and a boner.

Only a lowlife drug lord worth millions would come to a slum for a ten-dollar teenage prostitute. *Depraved fuck.*

Montilla didn't say anything before pulling off her T-shirt. Since she wasn't wearing a bra, her small breasts popped free. Then he pushed her down to the bed, lifted her skirt, and spread her legs before shrugging out of his water-beaded jacket.

The redhead closed her eyes, bracing herself, as his hand dropped to his zipper and he yanked it down.

Maybe he could have let Montilla have one final good time before he bit the dust, but One-Mile knew people had always thought of him as an asshole. Why break form now? After what Montilla had put him through, he gave zero fucks about robbing this son of a bitch of one last orgasm, one last chance to cheat on his wife, and one last opportunity to take advantage of someone smaller, weaker, and poorer than him. Pity the fucker would never know what hit him, but getting the satisfaction of his face being the last thing this lowlife saw was Hollywood shit.

His job now boiled down to aligning his shot and pulling the fucking trigger.

That's murder, Logan reminded in his head.

Fuck him. If his boss couldn't see that the world would be much safer without this violent, drug-manufacturing rapist roaming it, then he'd definitely lost his edge.

As far as One-Mile was concerned, he was performing a fucking public service. Sure, he'd be saving Brea; that was his first priority. But he'd have a clean conscience when he left here because this girl would have one less john and Baby Jorge would have the chance to grow up with his mother.

Too bad no one had helped his own mom before it was too late.

At the memory, his anger spiked. His heartbeat surged. He breathed, trying to calm it while Montilla dropped his pants around his ankles. But One-Mile's palms were unusually clammy. His hands shook. He couldn't fucking compartmentalize this mission like he had all the others. He wasn't killing this asshole for his unit or his country. This was personal. If he made this kill shot, months of fucking torment and worry would be over. He could finally go home, meet Brea's daddy, wait for their baby, and love him or her forever. That was more than enough incentive for him.

But first, he had to fucking focus on the actions—which he'd performed hundreds of times—not the stakes. If he thought about the consequences for fucking up, he'd never succeed.

Dragging in one more breath, One-Mile forcibly cleared his mind to steady himself and froze, hyper-focused. He didn't blink or hesitate. And he definitely didn't let Montilla climb on top of the girl. He merely curled his finger around the trigger and squeezed.

Through the scope, he watched the asshole for the pure thrill, but he didn't need to wait the fraction of a second it took for the bullet to plow into the fucker's temple to know he'd hit his mark. It was done.

Montilla was finally dead.

As the drug lord crumpled to the ground and the redhead screamed, One-Mile closed the window and packed up his equipment with an economy of movement, hurrying without rushing. When he was done, he slung everything on his back, wiped every surface he'd touched clean, pulled his hoodie over his face again, and trotted down to the lobby. As if he didn't have a care in the world, he bypassed the people scurrying and clustering around the bordello, ducked out the hotel's back entrance, then disappeared down an alley and into the rain once again driving.

He didn't mind getting drenched now. Tomorrow, there would be sunlight because tomorrow there would be Brea.

Saturday, January 10
Comfort, Texas

Brea dabbed at her happy tears as she watched Cutter dance with his new bride. After a touching ceremony in Shealyn's grandparents' barn that seemed so quintessentially small-town Texas, they clung together under fairy lights and swayed to Ed

Sheeran, blocking out the rest of the world inside their bubble of happiness. It was probably a good skill since the press continued to hound them. But for this moment they looked ecstatic.

Hard to believe that, after their two-week Maui honeymoon at the Sunshine Coast Bed-and-Breakfast, Cutter would be moving to California with his new wife.

Brea was both happy for her best friend and beyond sad that he'd be leaving her. It added an extra pall over her despair.

Nearly a month had passed since she'd last seen or heard from Pierce.

This morning, a news report had claimed Emilo Montilla had been shot dead last night in a bordello in Mexico City by an unknown assailant. After hearing the report, she'd brimmed with hope. While Brea wouldn't celebrate any person's death…she didn't mourn the drug lord's loss. All day, she'd waited for a call or message from Pierce that he was coming home safely to her.

But the hours had dragged by without any word. By afternoon, worry had set in. As preparations for the wedding continued and the guys from EM Security had rolled in before the ceremony, she'd asked Logan if he'd heard from Pierce. He'd given her a regretful shake of his head and a few well-meaning words. By sundown, her worry had contorted into thick dread.

A man like Montilla probably had a lot of enemies. His death didn't mean Pierce had been the one to kill him. Someone else could easily have ended the terrible man's reign of terror…while her man lay rotting in an underground compound or a shallow grave somewhere.

Brea tried to shake off all the destructive what-ifs and worries, but it was useless. If Pierce hadn't surfaced in the twenty-four hours since Montilla's death, she feared there was an awful reason.

She dabbed at more tears.

"You okay?" Cage asked, slipping a brotherly arm around her.

She tried to smile. "Sure. How about you? I know you were expecting to see Karis here."

"Yeah." He sounded down.

"Do you know why she didn't come?"

Cage sent a sideways glance to Karis's sister, Jolie Powell, who stood with her husband Heath. "They said she suddenly caught a cold."

"And you don't believe that?"

"It's possible…but no," he grumbled.

Gossip said Cage and Karis had rung in the New Year together—naked, tequila-soaked, and oblivious to their screams and groans keeping the neighbors awake. She'd been aloof since.

Cage was a good guy, and Karis would be a fool to pass him up.

Brea tried to give him an encouraging smile. "I doubt she's avoiding you."

"I know she is. She's made that perfectly clear."

"Why?"

He shrugged. "Can we talk about something else?"

"Sure." Brea scrambled for a topic. "Ever think you'd have a TV star for a sister-in-law?"

"No. Honestly, it's kind of weird. I got off shift a few days back and some reporter was waiting at my truck, asking my opinion about my brother's upcoming wedding, the bride, their future…and climate change."

Brea managed to laugh. "I'll bet you've perfected the 'no comment' response by now. I sure have. Not that what I say matters. Even when I've corrected them, those tabloid rags are determined to push the story that I'm Cutter's something on the side."

"Of course. It's juicier if he's marrying one of *People*'s Most Beautiful People while flaunting his pretty baby mama under her nose."

She grimaced. "They're all liars."

"Can't deny that. Listen, I know you're used to having my brother around, but I'm going to take care of you after he's gone. I'll be farther away but—"

"You don't have to." Brea placed a hand over the little swell of her belly covered by her burgundy chiffon bridesmaid dress. "We'll be fine. Everyone seems to forget that I'm a grown woman. But I'll keep reminding y'all. Even Daddy is coming around."

"You're going to have a little one soon, probably alone and—"

"Don't say that." It was likely true, but Brea wasn't ready to accept it.

"Honey, Walker isn't here. And I don't think he's coming back."

"He is. He has to be." But her reaction was more of a knee-jerk than a conviction.

"Maybe. If he's able. But besides the fact he's an absolute douche, I have to be honest. A mission like that has wiped out squads of soldiers, even taken out most of a SEAL team. He's one sniper alone."

"Stop!" She jerked away and fought a rise of more tears. Cage wasn't saying anything she didn't know, but she didn't need to be reminded that Pierce's survival chances were slim—and dwindling by the hour. "I'm clinging to hope right now. Please don't take it from me."

"Okay. I'm sorry. I just want you to know that, after Cutter is gone, I'll be around as much as I can."

Cage meant to be helpful, and she had snapped at him. "I'm sorry, too. I'm just really worried about Pierce. Constantly. I know the odds aren't good, but if anyone could survive and succeed, it's him."

Every day, she'd prayed. Every night, she'd cried. Now all she could do was try to beat back despair and hold on to hope. Pierce had returned once. If there were such a thing as miracles, maybe he could pull off one again.

Suddenly, she heard a commotion on the opposite side of the tent. Cage frowned and whipped his gaze around, looking over the crowd, toward the ruckus. His eyes went wide. "Holy shit."

"What?" Brea really resented being so short. No matter how she stood on her tiptoes and craned to peer around everyone, all she saw was the crowd's backs.

"Speak of the devil."

Which devil? On this earth, she only knew one...

Hope gripped her chest. "Pierce?"

"You shouldn't be here, Walker." Brea vaguely recognized Josiah Grant's voice.

That was all the confirmation Brea needed. Astonishment closed her throat as she turned to tug on Cage's sleeve. "Oh, my gosh, he's really here? Can you see him?"

"Yeah. Somehow, he slipped past all our security and waltzed right the hell in. I'll be damned..."

Thank God!

All Brea could hear was her own heartbeat roaring in her ears as she held in a jubilant cry and dashed through the thick crowd. She didn't care if she was rude or that she bumped into Jennifer Lawrence's back, spilling the woman's drink. She only cared about reaching Pierce.

"Fuck off." That voice—a dark, sure rasp that always held a note of irritation...except when he talked to her.

Definitely Pierce. She'd never heard anything so wonderful.

Her heart lifted. Joy soared. She pressed even quicker through the throng toward him.

"Now isn't the time. Cutter doesn't need this tonight." Josiah again, clearly trying to keep the peace. "He just got married."

"I don't give a shit about him," Pierce growled as he yanked free from Josiah's hold. "Where's—" Suddenly, their eyes met. He breathed her name. "Brea..."

She gaped, speechless. Montilla was dead, and Pierce was really, really here. They were free!

As people around her parted to clear her path, Brea's feet took her forward. She stopped short of Pierce, trembling. She couldn't stop staring.

He looked even leaner and more dangerous than he had in December. His burning black eyes sat deep in their sockets as he looked her over, his stare lingering on her middle. She wrapped her hands around their baby. His thick beard was back. He was horribly out of place in a black T-shirt and camo pants. But the sight of him brought her to tears.

"Brea?" he boomed over the residual chatter and music. She was vaguely aware of heads turning and people whispering. He didn't seem to care. His sole focus was on her.

Her throat closed up, and her voice caught. "Pierce..."

Never breaking their stare, he tossed a chair out of the path between them and charged toward her. Brea's eyes widened as he backed her against the nearby buffet table with his big body. "I need to talk to you, pretty girl. It won't wait."

The torment on his face ripped at Brea's heart. Was something wrong? She looked around for privacy so they could talk, but all she saw was a crowd of curious bystanders. "No. Not here. Please."

Josiah shoved his way between them with a no-means-no speech all over his face and gave Pierce a push just as Cutter approached, expression hard. "You weren't invited, asshole."

Pierce tore his gaze from her to scowl at him. "You're married now, and Brea is mine. That's *my* baby she's carrying. So. Back. The. Fuck. Off."

"Hey, looks like she doesn't want your company tonight, big guy," Josiah cajoled. "Turn around, get in your Jeep, and head to Lafayette."

Darn it all, Josiah had no idea what she wanted, much less how badly she wanted to touch Pierce. He was working off old gossip. She'd venture most people here were. And she appreciated that Josiah meant to protect her, but this was ridiculous. "No. It's—"

"Like hell," Pierce growled, then settled his weighty stare on her again. "I've waited weeks for this."

They both had.

After more squabbling Brea ignored, Cutter's bride approached, holding out her hand to Pierce. "Shealyn West. Well, Bryant now. Pierce, Brea is dealing with a lot. She will talk to you when she's ready. I know she wants to. She just needs a little more space and a bit more time to decide what to do."

What?

Brea hadn't spilled the details of her relationship with Pierce to the actress. Apparently, Cutter had respected her privacy, too. Either that or Shealyn had been too busy planning their wedding over the last four weeks while flying back and forth between big-city LA and small-town middle-Texas to get the 411. Either way, she wished all the well-meaning people who didn't understand what was going on would simply shut up.

Pierce took Shealyn's hand with a scowl. "What is there to decide? She's going to marry me."

Marry? Brea's breath caught. Had he really just said that? Pierce had never used that word…yet he spoke like it was a forgone conclusion.

Shealyn cocked her head as if trying to make him see reason. "You can't force her—"

"It's okay. I'll talk to him." Brea placated the woman. It would take far longer to explain, and it was none of anyone's business. Still, she struggled to keep a silly grin off her face. *Marry?* "We're drawing attention, and the last thing I want is for you to stop your festivities for me. Go. Enjoy your honeymoon. I'll be fine."

Cutter looked reluctant. "I won't leave you when you need me."

"Yes." She took his hand and squeezed it. "You will. You and your wife have two amazing weeks in paradise at the most beautiful little bed-and-breakfast in Maui, ignoring the rest of the world, including me. I'll talk to Pierce. Josiah and

Logan are nearby, just in case." She wouldn't need them, but it seemed to make everyone feel better if she had "bodyguards."

"Are you sure?" Cutter still looked reluctant to leave her.

He needed to stop being overprotective.

"Really." She hugged him. "I'll text you later." At that point, she lost all patience for everyone's well-meaning interference. "Excuse us."

People mercifully backed off. Pierce didn't waste any time taking her hand in his. He felt so warm and big and alive. It was all she could do not to cry tears of joy.

Then he dropped to his knees and placed a hand on her belly, cradling their baby. Around them, the small crowd gasped. She ignored everyone else as he touched her with such tenderness. Then there was no stopping the tears from welling in her eyes.

"Come on," Shealyn murmured to Cutter. "Let's give them some privacy and get started on our married life."

"All right, sweetheart," Cutter conceded. "Brea, call if you need anything at all."

Nodding absently, she fisted a trembling hand at her side, trying so hard not to throw herself against Pierce in a sobbing puddle, ask him a million questions, and make him promise he'd never leave her again.

He settled her into a chair and crouched in front of her, his hands in hers. "You okay, baby?"

She nodded. "Are *you*?"

"Yeah. Don't cry. I'm fine. I promise."

She pressed a hand to her mouth to hold in a sob, but it was useless. "Another month with no word from you… It scared me so much. Then I heard this morning that Montilla is dead. Is it true?"

He nodded. "I killed him last night and I started making my way back to you as soon as the deed was done."

"So it really is over?"

"Yeah. I'm home for good," he promised. "We can finally be together without you being in danger, and I don't give a fuck who knows. No, I hope everyone knows. I'm here to finally make you mine."

Relief crashed through her. Happiness flooded in, destroying the last of her composure. Tears fell in earnest.

He cupped her shoulders and pressed his forehead to hers. "That shouldn't make you sad."

She shook her head. "It makes me so happy. But I was scared. I didn't know what I was going to do if you didn't come back and—"

"Shh. You've got nothing to worry about." He gave her belly another stroke. "Neither does the baby. Everything okay?"

She nodded. "Fine."

"Boy or girl?"

She'd kept the gender of their baby to herself, wanting him to be the first person she told yet so afraid she'd never get the chance. Now she was bursting to deliver the news, but… "Not with an audience. I'd rather tell you and you alone."

He glanced around at the wedding guests still gathered, pretending to be interested in the reception, but too close to be paying attention to anything but them.

"I'd like that."

"All right. I have to have a glucose screening next week. You can come with me to that."

He tensed. "There a problem?"

"I don't know. The test is standard. I get woozy when I forget to eat, so…" She shrugged. "But I'm otherwise okay."

"Forget to eat?" He raised a brow. "You won't be doing that anymore. Do you feel okay now? Do you need food?"

He'd been in a foreign country for the better part of two months, dodging thugs and criminals as he plotted to single-handedly take down the overlord of a drug cell, and he wanted to know if she'd eaten? "Josiah brought me a snack after the ceremony, and I nibbled a little more during dinner. I just…haven't been able to eat today for worrying about you."

He cupped her face. "I love that you think of me, but don't ever worry about me. My job from here on out is to take care of you."

Brea didn't think she would ever stop worrying about him, but the white lie would make him feel better. "Okay."

Then he stood and hooked a finger under her chin. She blinked up as she followed his penetrating gaze. He stared down at her with something dark and dirty in his eyes. She shivered.

"It's been a fucking month since I've touched you, and I'm dying to show you how much I appreciate you in that sexy-as-hell dress—"

"Sexy?" It covered her from her shoulders to her shins.

"Oh, yeah." His thumb brushed her lower lip. "I'm looking straight down and I can see your lush tits. And it shows how much your baby bump has grown. But I need to see it naked. Touch it. Just like I need your pussy, too. And I need to fuck you so I can remind you that you're mine forever. I need you now. Where can we go?"

Brea's heart started thudding. Everything inside her tightened and tingled with desire. But she had one concern. "Everyone is already gossiping about us. If I leave with you, they'll know exactly what we'll be doing, and I'd rather not give them more fodder."

Pierce shook his head, but he wore a fond smile. "Always the good preacher's daughter."

Warmth climbed up her cheeks. "Not always. You know that."

"Yeah, you're a bad, bad girl when I fuck you." He was breathing heavily now, and his entire body had gone hard. "I'll give you a thirty-second head start to find us some privacy around here. If you don't, I'll haul you onto the next available surface, shove your skirt up, and prove how much I've missed you. And I will give zero fucks about who watches."

The warmth in her cheeks turned scalding, and she tsked at him. "You wouldn't."

He raised a challenging brow that dared her to try him. "I'm going to start counting now."

Oh, goodness. He really would.

Brea jumped up and dashed through the crowd, past a frowning Josiah, then out of the tent.

Running across the dusty yard and up the driveway, she tore into the empty house and slammed the door behind her, panting all the while. She wasn't sure where to go next. She'd only stepped inside long enough to get dressed and have her hair fixed. But she was excited. She was eager. And she was so wet. Pierce had always thrilled her. No use denying it.

Through the big window in the living room, she watched him march from the tent, his face full of resolution, and hop into his Jeep before he fired it up and skidded out in the dirt. Then he hit the paved road with a squeal.

Her heart dropped. He was leaving? Why? Where was he going?

Brea stood rooted in place. Had she misunderstood? Had someone tossed him off the property after she'd left? After everything he'd done so they could be together, she knew he wouldn't simply walk away.

But one minute turned into two, then into five. After that, she had to face the truth. For some reason, he'd gone.

She bowed her head and tried not to succumb to confusion and more tears. Both were useless.

"How attached are you to that dress?" His voice suddenly rumbled in her ear and his hot breath spilled down her neck.

She gasped and whirled to face him. "How did you get in without me hearing you?"

"You really don't know what I'm capable of. But you will." He eyed her up and down. "Make a case to save the dress now or it's toast."

Would he really rip her out of it? That had her panting. "I don't care about it at all."

She had another change of clothes upstairs.

His smile was filthy. "Perfect. Anyone else in the house?"

She hadn't thought to check. "I-I don't know."

Pierce cursed under his breath. "Oh, well. I don't care anyway."

He lifted her and carried her up the stairs, kicking in the door to the first bedroom at the top and flipping on the light switch, illuminating the soft recessed lighting overhead. The walls were gray except for one, which was decorated with a big photographic mural of a pink rose. He set her down on a black-and-white geometric rug, less than a foot from a rumpled bed. Since she'd changed in here earlier, her bag sat in the corner.

She'd barely found her footing when she heard fabric rip and felt a draft of cold air rush along her back. Suddenly, he spun her around, jerked on the sleeves, then tore her bra away. Less than ten seconds, and she was bare from the waist up.

If she helped, she could get the other half naked in less time.

"Holy shit." Pierce groaned as he cupped her breasts in his big palms. The feel of him cradling her was electric. She needed to be naked faster.

As she reached behind her middle to untie her sash, he dipped his head, seized her lips, and tasted her tongue. Just as she lost herself in the purely masculine flavor of his kiss, he jerked away and bent to her breasts. "Fuck, you have the prettiest nipples. I could suck them all day and still want them in my mouth more."

She'd feared she would never see him again, so having his hands on her and his dirty words filling her head felt more like a fantasy than reality. But he was here with her. For her.

Never in a million years had she imagined she would fall in love with a man like Pierce. Over the last month, insidious fears had forced her to imagine her life without him.

It had nearly killed her.

He laved her nipples. Her back arched. All thought stopped.

"Please…"

"Hmm, you beg so pretty in that sweet little voice." His tongue circled the other bud before he dragged it deep into her mouth, eliciting a moan that rushed from her lips and dipped straight between her legs.

"Pierce!"

He didn't answer, simply kept plundering her nipples, alternating them into his mouth, against his tongue, as he yanked at the zipper near the small of her back, holding up the rest of her dress. After it fell with a quiet hiss, the flouncy fabric began to slide down her thighs. Pierce gave it another brute-force shove. It puddled around her ankles, leaving her in nothing but her kitten heels and her plain cotton underwear.

"Step out." He held out his hand, his gaze utterly fixed on her belly.

When she did as he demanded, he tossed the dress to the other side of the bedroom—never taking his eyes off her. Then he grabbed a fistful of his T-shirt behind his neck and shucked it off. He was so shredded now that every muscle stood out, hard and delineated.

Brea couldn't keep her hands off him.

As she brushed her fingertips over his steely pecs, he caught her wrists. "Don't. If you touch me, my restraint won't last."

She blinked up at him, falling into those black eyes she wanted to lose herself in forever. "I don't need your restraint. I just need you."

He groaned and shoved her back onto the bed, his body big and hair-roughened and smelling like man covering hers. "And I need you, pretty girl. So fucking much. My life meant shit before you." He dropped his hand to her belly and knelt between her legs. "And this one. Boy or girl?"

Brea lay back on the mussed bed, her eyes misty and full of love, her lips softly pouting, her breasts ripe. He'd never seen her look so beautiful, and his cock was screaming at him for relief. But One-Mile palmed her belly and waited for her answer, breath held.

A primal urge way beyond sex filled his veins. Because he could finally *see* that she was pregnant? Unlike the last time he'd laid eyes on her, there was no denying it now. He couldn't stop touching her bump, couldn't resist the need to press his lips against their child. The baby was months from birth, and he already loved their little one. Would gladly lay down his life to keep him or her safe.

That blew his mind. He'd never wanted to ever become a father. After a shitty role model like his, what sort of lousy-ass excuse for a dad would he be? He'd always refused to put a kid through the hell he'd endured to find out. But somehow, learning that Brea was pregnant had changed everything. And during his long two months in Mexico hunting that violent motherfucker Montilla, thoughts of Brea and their baby—of their future—had fueled him when nights were long and cold, when food was scarce, when he felt so fucking lonely he'd wanted to scream.

Looking at her now, he was more than ready to conquer his fears and slay his demons.

"You going to keep me in suspense?"

Tears filled her eyes as she laid her palm over his, linking their fingers. "We're having a boy."

Those four words crashed into his chest like a battering ram, stealing his breath. "Yeah?"

"A son." She sniffled. "During the ultrasound, he looked so amazing. I got to see his face. He had his thumb in his mouth. His little eyes were closed, then he wrinkled his nose and…he was beyond precious."

Jesus, One-Mile wished he'd been there. Montilla had taken so much from him, including the chance to see his son for himself, and he hated the asshole's guts for it. But that SOB would never take anything from him again.

"Oh, pretty girl. He sounds amazing."

"And he's strong like you. Just this morning I felt him kick for the first time, like he knew you were coming for him. I was lying in bed, half asleep, then…I felt him. It's not like anything I can describe." The tears in her amber eyes pooled and threatened to fall. "I rubbed him and he did it again. It filled my heart."

Their son. The notion was a fucking marvel, but hearing her talk about the baby and feeling him growing inside her... Even her description bulldozed his heart.

One-Mile couldn't speak. He hadn't cried since he was five, but he felt his throat begin to close up and his eyes sting.

"Having you here filled it even more." Her words cracked.

"Oh, pretty girl." He held her closer and tried his best to keep himself together. "I can't wait to hold him."

"Me, too."

"You don't know how much I missed you..."

"I do. Love me?" Brea pleaded, her eyes so earnest.

"There's no way you can stop me," he quipped, trying to lighten the mood.

A watery smile crossed her face. "There never has been."

"That won't change. Take those off." He pointed to her underwear. They were the only thing keeping him from Brea, and he wanted them gone. "Show me your pussy."

With a catch of her breath, she nodded, then pushed them down her hips. He hooked his fingers inside the elastic to help, dragging them down her thighs, exposing her puffy cunt as he kissed his way over her belly. Then he peeled the white cotton away, impatiently tossing her fancy footwear with it.

"You don't like the shoes? I thought men had a fetish for sexy heels."

He scoffed. "I'm not evolved enough for that. I'm always going to prefer you barefoot and pregnant. In fact, I like it so much I want to keep you this way for a while."

A pink flush stole up her cheeks as she laughed. "It's a good thing I like children."

"You're going to be a great mom."

Something pensive crossed her face. "I hope. I didn't have one, so I'm not really sure how to be one."

"I already know you're going to be the best."

She bit her lip. "I'm worried about childbirth."

"I'll be there. I won't let anything happen." One-Mile was painfully aware that he could handle many crises, get them out of tons of scrapes. But medical emergencies, especially involving babies, were way beyond his area of expertise. And if he lost Brea, he would never forgive himself.

She nodded bravely. "I keep telling myself it's going to be fine."

"It will." He had to believe that.

Or he would go completely batshit insane.

The best way to help her from borrowing tomorrow's trouble and forget the last terrible two months was to give her something to focus on now. God knew he didn't merely want her. His heart had become a slave to hers the minute he'd touched her.

One-Mile rose back up her body, but her splayed thighs and her pussy in between were too much temptation to resist. He pressed his lips to the inside of her knee, then worked his way up as he cupped her hip and positioned his shoulders between her legs.

"Pierce…"

"Oh, this pussy." He breathed against it, and she shuddered in his grip. "Baby, I dreamed about you."

She twisted under him, arching, unconsciously spreading wider for him. He dragged his tongue up her thigh, let his fingers graze the soft curls above her secrets, then took a little nip at her hip bone. Her cry gratified him.

"You're already wet for me."

Brea nodded frantically. "Every time you come near me, I ache. I always have."

He skimmed his thumb over her clit, toying with her. "I like you aching for me. But not when I'm gone. Did you use the skills I taught you before I left last time? Did you put your fingers in your pussy and make yourself feel good?"

Her head fell back against the pillow, her brown hair spreading out across the sheets. "Yes."

God, he would have loved to have seen that. "More than once?"

"Yes." She writhed.

"Good girl. Want me to make you feel good now?"

"Yes," she moaned. "But I want to make you feel good, too."

"Don't worry, pretty girl, you will." He dropped a kiss on her plump mound.

Funny, when he'd been a kid, his old man had always warned him against being led around by his dick. He'd railed about the evils of women, especially when he'd been deep into his Crown and Coke. But One-Mile didn't mind at all that his world seemed to revolve now around this one woman and her pussy. She was his life. His pleasure would come from her. His children would be birthed from her.

This pussy was his, just like she was.

With a hungry hum, he raked his tongue up her juicy slit, gratified when she bent her knees wider for him as he continued kissing his way up her body. He lingered on her belly, letting her know that he loved her and he loved their son. Then he wended his way back to her breasts, curling his tongue around them as he pressed a pair of fingers inside her and teased her distended clit with his thumb.

Her body went taut. He could see her heartbeat throbbing at her neck and her fair skin flushing with arousal. She wouldn't last long. Neither would he.

"This is the first night of the rest of our lives," he murmured against her skin. "I want to spend it inside you."

"Yes," she whispered, lifting her head to kiss him.

Her mouth was a distraction he'd never regret. No matter what he was doing or where he was going, if she offered him this mouth, he was going to take it.

One-Mile nipped at her soft lower lip, then slid inside. She tasted as sweet as the wedding cake she'd eaten earlier. He moaned, drowned, and happily lost himself as she put her arms around him. Then she urged him onto his back.

To humor her, he rolled to a prone position. "Want something, pretty girl?"

She nodded. "You always give me pleasure from head to toe. I want to do the same to you."

He folded his hands under his head with a wicked grin. "You want to touch me? You go right ahead."

"Anywhere?"

"Everywhere. It's all yours…"

"It better be, mister." She shot him a playful grin.

He smirked back as she bent and slid her pouty lips across his jawline, breathed on his neck, then nipped at his ear before she whispered, "When I touched myself, all I could think of was you. The thumbs grazing my nipples were yours. My fingertips gliding down my skin were yours, too. And when I stroked myself…"

The cocky grin slid off his face. "You thought of me when you touched your clit?"

"Every time."

Her purr in his ear, coupled with her touch skimming his torso like the most elusive tease, made him shudder. "Yeah?"

"Yes. And I sometimes lay in bed at night, fantasizing about of all the ways I'd touch you if you came back to me."

"All of them?" He swallowed hard.

"Over and over." She pinched his nipple.

He sucked in a breath, feeling a jolt of pleasure all through his body. "Oh, baby. You're not my shy thing anymore."

She shook her head, the satisfied female grin she wore a temptation in itself. "Between your seduction and the pregnancy hormones, you've created a monster."

Hot damn. "Show me."

Her smile merely widened, then she dragged her lips down to his pecs, nipping at the flat discs of his nipples as her teasing fingers swirled around his abs, played in his navel, then toyed with the button on his pants. "You're overdressed."

Holy shit, she was raising his blood pressure. "Couldn't agree more."

One-Mile shucked everything he wore in record time. His cock ached for her, and he resisted the urge to lead her hand down. He wanted to see how bold she would get on her own because he was definitely enjoying this. Not that it would last. He loved seducing his pretty girl and making her blush too much to give that up.

"Think I won't show you?" Her smile was almost smug as she bent her head and flattened her tongue across his nipples. At the same time, her fingers stopped their idle wandering and wrapped around his cock with a squeeze.

One-Mile hissed at the dual jolts of sensation, then muttered a thick curse when her thumb skimmed over the sensitive head in a barely there brush and her fist bumped the ridge under his crown.

Holy fuck, where did she learn that?

He moaned. "Pretty girl?"

"Yes?" She toyed with his nipple and stroked his shaft in long, slow glides, dallying with all his most sensitive spots and acting as if she had all night to torment him.

Touching her had aroused him enough to start his heart revving and his blood pumping. But this? If she didn't fucking stop soon, he'd embarrass himself. "It's been a month. Why don't you let me—"

"You said I could touch you everywhere because it's all mine."

And he'd meant it...when he'd thought she would be shy and cautious, and therefore merciful. But not this siren all but floating on top of him, her mouth drifting to torment his other taut nipple before she started meandering down.

He sucked in a breath. "Oh, baby..."

Brea lifted her head, licked her lips, and smiled again. "That sounds almost like begging."

It felt almost like begging. "I left you alone too long. Let me make you feel good."

"You left to protect me. Let me show you how much I love you for it."

When she kept pressing butterfly kisses down his abdomen, punctuating each by dragging her tongue along the ridges of his muscles as she kept sliding lower, he nearly jackknifed up, rolled her to her back, and shoved his face in her pussy.

But he didn't...yet.

"What did you have in mind?" he finally panted out.

"I want to show you that when I'm hungry, you're my favorite snack..." She breathed over the head of his cock.

One-Mile gasped and shoved his hands in her hair. "I'm getting that. Oh, hell. Yeah..."

She licked her way up his shaft, then glanced at him. She might be an angel, but she had the devil in her eyes tonight. "Good."

Then she stopped talking...and he stopped fighting. Instead, as her lips pursed around him, he sank back into the bed with a long groan and closed his eyes. He wouldn't be able to hold out long like this, but he'd warned her...

"Hmm." She licked him like a lollipop, alternating long strokes and hard sucks.

He tensed, need coursing through his body like someone had supercharged his veins with lightning. A thick ache gathered, and her hand dropping to fondle his heavy balls didn't help his struggle in the least.

"How about a little mercy?"

"No."

He tightened his grip on her hair and meant to lift her mouth from his cock so he could take over again. Instead, he ended up showing her the exact pace he craved.

She took to giving him pleasure like she'd been born to bestow it, catching on to every silent cue he gave her. Soon, he was tensing, panting, thrashing under her slow, heavenly mouth as desire built and morphed into full-blown demand.

Shit, shit, shit. Brea had taken him right to the edge. He gritted his teeth to stave off the need, but she just kept coming at him with her soft, relentless determination.

As much as he'd love to go off now, he wanted to be *with* her.

"That's enough." He lifted her off of him with a growl, rolling her over again. He splayed his big body over hers so she couldn't move. "I want you so fucking bad, but not like this. Not now."

She licked her lips again and sent him a little pout. If she was trying to torment him, it was working. "It didn't feel good?"

"You know it did, and I will let you suck me raw later if you want, but that's not what I dreamed about when I made love to you in my mind over this last month."

"What did you dream of?"

"First, you need to catch up with me." He rose over her on his hands and knees.

"Catch up?"

He grasped her thighs in his hands and shoved them wider. "You need to be on the edge of orgasm, too. But I'm not a nice guy, so I may just make you scream instead."

Before she could reply, he dove for her pussy, parted her delicate folds with his thumbs, and lapped her from her soaked opening to her hard clit. Teasing him had clearly aroused her. *Good to know.*

Under him, she cried out and twisted. He leaned in, settling more of his weight over her.

"I dreamed of this, too." He swirled his tongue around her, shoving his fingers inside her, then nipped at her tender bud with his teeth. When her little yelp morphed into a moan, he gave her a dark smile. "I dreamed of making you take every dirty thing I'm desperate to give you."

And then he stopped talking because he didn't want another fucking thing to interfere with him consuming her. Sweet and tart and clean, everything about her flavor was so Brea. He wanted to bottle it. He wanted to bathe in it. He wanted it on his tongue always.

He wasn't gentle and he wasn't slow as he ramped her up until her cheeks turned red and her fingernails dug tiny pinpoints of pain into him. And still he didn't let up, just kept devouring her until she squirmed and squealed and finally begged.

"Please, please, *please…*"

When he felt her clit pulse and she tugged on his hair, pulling him deeper into her pussy, she was finally aching the way he was. One-Mile jerked free from her hold and eclipsed her body with his as he aligned his crest at her opening.

He pushed his way deep with one savage thrust.

Brea's eyes widened. She cried out and arched, need clearly surging—just like his. "Pierce!"

"Want me to fuck you?" he growled in her ear, filling her frantically, trying to get as close to her as possible.

"Yes."

"Need me to fuck you?"

"Yes."

"Ache for me to fuck you for the rest of your life?"

Her eyes met his, looking so molten and hot. "Yes."

"Marry me." It wasn't a question.

"Really?"

"Marry me."

"Yes." Her voice hitched as she half moaned.

His heart stopped. "You mean it? You'll marry me?"

"Yes!" She tossed her head back, eyes closing as she rocked and gyrated under him. "Yes…"

He pressed his lips over hers and dove as deeply into her mouth as he plowed into her body. She accepted all of him and gave him every bit of herself in return. One-Mile reveled in the fact that there were finally no walls between them and no part of her that wasn't utterly his. He didn't stop giving her every bit of his desire and devotion until she clung to him—lips, arms, legs, pussy—as if she knew only he could make her whole.

"Brea?" he gritted out as he ground into her. He couldn't hold out anymore. "Baby?"

"I'm here. I need…" She gasped as her whole body suddenly clamped down and stiffened. "Yes!"

The instant he felt her pulsing around him, One-Mile lost it, emptying himself into her, giving zero fucks that he had irrevocably given her his heart and soul and tomorrows. There was no one else he'd ever share any of those with except Brea.

As he collapsed on top of her, breathless and drained, his heart roared and his head swam. But he smiled. "If you think I fucking love you now, wait until you're my wife."

"I love you." She gave him a spent little grin as she peppered breathy kisses all over his face. "I love you so much."

"That's something else I dreamed of in that godforsaken desert." He brushed the soft waves of her hair away from her damp, flushed face. "Coming back and putting a ring on your finger."

Her shy smile somehow torqued his just-sated desire back up. "I can't wait for that…but we have a lot of things to work out first."

"Like what?"

"Well, we have decisions to make like when and where to get married, not to mention where should we live and—"

"ASAP. You pick. And my place."

"Okay. That's fine. But"—she winced—"there's something you have to do first. Well, two things."

One-Mile sighed in contentment as he sifted through his thoughts. Then he realized at least one shit pile she probably wanted to talk about. "I owe you an explanation about my father."

"That's one, yes."

He tried not to stiffen. He'd opened that Pandora's box of crap and he owed her the truth. "All right. And the second?"

"You have to meet my dad and ask him for my hand."

Somehow, he'd suspected she was going to say that. What if the man refused to give them his blessing? One-Mile wasn't sure, but whatever it took, whatever he had to do, he couldn't take no for an answer.

An hour after Sunday services, Brea floated on cloud nine as she chatted with some of Daddy's parishioners who had come to their house from the seniors' Bible study group for a luncheon. After a nice honey ham and potato salad, she'd cleared the dishes away and fired up the coffeepot. But a couple of the ladies bustled into the kitchen to join her.

"Can I get you something, Mrs. Rogers? Mrs. Lloyd?"

"No, dear." Betty Rogers bustled closer, the string of pearls around her neck gleaming as brightly as her blue eyes. "We're here to help you."

Emma Lloyd nodded and reached for the coffee pot, despite her arthritis. "You should be sitting more. Don't want to get too tired before the baby comes."

She smiled at them both. Contrary to her fears, most of the members of the church had been lovely and accepting since learning that she was pregnant. All those fears about disappointing everyone and running off Daddy's parishioners had been unfounded. Sure, a few seemed a tad dismayed, but mostly that Cutter had married someone else, rather than taking care of the girl he'd gotten "in trouble." No matter how many times she'd conveyed this baby wasn't Cutter's, they chose to believe the tabloids. A couple of them even confessed to being addicted to TMZ. Go figure.

Hopefully they would believe her once she and Pierce finally made everything official.

Marry me.

Brea was so giddy, so ready to openly and officially be his fiancée.

"I appreciate the help, ladies, but I'm fine."

"You might be, but I saw a devastatingly handsome man parking a black Jeep just down the street and striding up here like he means business. Sound like anyone you know?" Mrs. Rogers asked with a wink.

Pierce had come here to talk to her father? Already? Today? Now?

Suddenly, Jennifer Collins raced into the kitchen. "I think you should come quickly."

"So I've heard. Where is Daddy?" This might be a disaster waiting to happen. Her father meeting her baby's daddy for the first time was definitely going to be somewhere between tense and contentious. But in front of a good chunk of the church?

As much as she hated it, she had to stall Pierce.

"You two start the coffee," Brea said to the elderly ladies, then turned to her father's fiancée, who was already planning a June wedding. "Keep Daddy away from the door. For now. They need to meet but…"

"This isn't the best time," Jennifer agreed with a nod. "It's why I came to find you. Jasper is still in his study with the 'boys' talking football, but that won't last."

"Keep them busy if you can. Thank you."

Then Brea darted out of the kitchen and into the living room to intercept Pierce.

"Do you have a minute, dear?" Mrs. Benson stopped her with a gentle hand on her arm. Her husband stood beside her with a hand to his belly. "I think Tom needs some antacids, and I'm afraid I don't have any more in my purse."

Of all the terrible times…

"I've got some." Emma Lloyd came to her rescue, digging through her little blue clutch.

She turned to the woman and mouthed a big *thank you* before hustling toward the door again.

Until last night, she hadn't dared to dream of a day Pierce would knock on her door and ask Daddy for her hand. But since telling him last night that he needed to if he wanted to marry her, he'd wasted no time.

When she reached the window, she spotted Pierce outside. Her eyes widened in shock. He was wearing an actual suit with a legitimate tie. *Oh, dear goodness.* Not only was he trying to win her father over by looking downright respectable, she had no doubt he was making the extra effort for her sake. For their sake.

She loved him all the more for it.

Not only that, he looked incredibly hot in a charcoal suit, a black shirt, and a pale gray tie. What were the chances everyone would give them privacy so she could strip him down, climb him, and ride him like the stud he was?

Blushing at the thought, she rushed toward the door as he mounted the first step up to her porch.

Suddenly, he stopped and yanked his phone from his pocket. "Walker here. Colonel?"

Brea could hear his clear, deep voice just outside.

Who was this colonel? What did he want?

"What can I do for you, sir?" Pierce asked as Brea pulled the door open. "Or should I just ask who I need to kill?"

She gasped. He'd just gotten home, and already someone needed his skill set again? She knew that was his job and that it would never be easy, but it was a Sunday and they hadn't had a moment's peace in months...

Pierce winced, looking like he'd love to curse but refrained for her sake. "Any chance it can wait an hour?"

Brea blinked. She needed more than an hour with him. Just the conversation with Daddy would probably take half the afternoon, but for her to get her fill of his company after so long apart... It wasn't possible.

The annoyance in his expression deepened. "On my way."

With a sigh, he ended the call and pocketed the phone as he climbed the last step onto the porch. Something somber crossed his face as she stepped outside and shut the door behind her, swallowing nervously as she cast a furtive glance through the window to see if Daddy was barreling down on them. Thankfully, Jennifer seemed to be keeping him occupied.

"Pierce," she whispered. "What are you doing here?"

"You know what I want, pretty girl. I'm here for you. And when I come back, I won't take no for an answer."

She shivered at the hot determination in his tone. "All right. But can you tell me where you're going already?"

"A meeting. In town. I don't know how long I'll be until I assess the situation."

"Situation?"

"The colonel—Hunter and Logan's father—needs me. It's urgent. I owe him so many favors... I know this is really shi—I mean, lousy timing. But I *am* coming back. I'll always come back to you."

"Maybe tonight?" She looked over her shoulder again to see several of the older ladies staring at them out the window and fanning themselves with their hands. She tried not to laugh. "We won't have the seniors' Bible study here then."

He looked up and finally seemed to comprehend the attention they were getting. "Gotcha. Tonight. I'll, um, text first. But you know why I'm coming."

She couldn't wipe the smile off her face. "Yes."

"Good. That's the answer I want to hear when I come back." He winked. "Got a time in mind?"

"Seven?"

"Perfect. See you then." Clearly not caring what anyone saw or anyone thought, Pierce leaned in to kiss her. He lingered as if he wanted to press for more, but he pulled away reluctantly. Then, with a little salute, he headed down the street and hopped into his Jeep.

Jennifer rushed outside. "Isn't he the man who fixed the church van when it was broken?"

"Yes," Brea breathed. "He did that for me."

"He cleans up awfully nice."

"He does." She sighed. He dirtied up awfully nice, too. But she kept that to herself.

"You're in love."

She smiled. "Definitely."

Mrs. Lloyd bustled out next. "That is one fine, strutting rooster you've got there."

Mrs. Rogers was right behind her. "Indeed. You're a lucky lady, Ms. Bell."

"Believe me, I know." Brea grinned.

And hopefully by this time tomorrow, everyone would know that she would soon be Mrs. Walker.

chapter ten

SON OF A BITCH. One-Mile parked his Jeep in front of the address Caleb Edgington had given him and scowled. What the hell was this place?

The colonel stepped outside, face grim. "You're late."

"I didn't know you were way the fuck out here. I was up in Sunset."

The older man grunted. "Thanks for coming. You clean up good. What's with the suit? You go to church?"

"No. I was supposed to be proposing to my girl right now."

Caleb had the good grace to wince. "Shit. Sorry. I wouldn't have called—"

"If it wasn't an emergency, I know. What's up?"

He nodded. "Come on in."

One-Mile stepped inside a building that looked like part of a light industrial complex circa 1977. But inside, everything was modern as fuck. Banks of computers lined two walls. A tall metal table scattered with folders and papers dominated the space in the middle. Clustered around one monitor stood two men, one with dark hair that held a little bit of salt, the other with short blond stubble. He didn't immediately recognize either. They both turned.

"This is Jack Cole."

Co-founder of their sister firm, Oracle, former Army Ranger, and all-around badass. One-Mile had heard a lot about this tough son of a bitch. He'd met the man in passing, along with his pretty redheaded wife, Morgan. He didn't know much more about Jack, but if the man was here, too, whatever shit was going down was serious.

One-Mile stuck out his hand. "It's an honor."

Jack cocked his head. "The honor is mine. You're amazing, from what I hear."

"Thank you."

"And this is Trevor Forsythe. He's new to Jack's team. Former FBI. Hell of an investigator."

Well, that explained the pale haircut that was between boot camp and banker. But there was something familiar about him besides the name…

The other guy stared and nodded, a little frown deepening between his brows that seemed to hold recognition, too.

"Jock Strap?" One-Mile asked.

Instantly, the guy started laughing. "Serial Killer?"

"Yeah."

The colonel scowled in confusion. "You know each other?"

He let Trevor answer since the guy had always liked hearing himself talk. "We, um...went to the same high school."

Jack smirked. "I'm guessing you didn't like each other much, based on your nicknames."

One-Mile looked at Forsythe and shrugged. "We didn't actually know each other well. It was more that I didn't appreciate arrogant jocks like him plowing through all the best pussy at school."

"And Walker seemed like an antisocial loner fixated on guns. I worried he'd pull a Columbine. In fact, he was probably the only guy in the whole school who scared me. Didn't you end up screwing my senior prom date?"

Hell, he'd nearly forgotten about her. "Hillary? Yeah. Twice. Once right before you picked her up for the dance."

"See?" Forsythe gestured to him with a chuckle. "Asshole."

The colonel slapped him on the back. "Most will tell you not much has changed except that his fixation with guns paid off. He's one of the best snipers the Marines ever trained."

That was high praise coming from the colonel.

One-Mile smiled. "A few things are different, though. I won't try to mack on your girl. I've got one of my own."

"So I heard. Good for you. I don't have one and I don't want one."

As soon as Forsythe unloaded that verbal turd in the conversational punchbowl, everyone fell silent. Since he'd made the mistake of saying the too-honest thing many times before, One-Mile nodded. "I get you, man." Then he turned to the colonel. "So what's up? Why are we wherever the hell we are?"

"We've got trouble. I've kept this place because my wife's ex owned it. Long story, but it makes me happy that I've turned his personal porn hub into my soldier cave. But I didn't bring you here for a tour. It's Valeria Montilla."

"Is she mad I offed her husband?" Honestly, One-Mile thought she'd be relieved as hell.

Forsythe swiveled a stunned glance at him. "That was *your* kill shot? It had to be a thousand yards."

"A little less, actually."

The colonel clapped him on the shoulder. "There's a reason everyone calls him One-Mile."

"That's amazing, man. Seriously. I need lessons."

Bullshit. The FBI had a gun culture. Any agent had to be pretty fucking good with his firearms to make it, and Forsythe had never been a slouch at anything. "What brings you here from San Diego?"

"Change of pace."

Closed subject. One-Mile recognized that instantly.

"You?" Forsythe asked.

"Working for this guy." One-Mile gestured to the colonel. "Until he decided to go soft and retire on me."

"Well, you can't say your life has been dull since I left," Caleb pointed out.

"Nope. But I'm glad to be home now."

"Don't get too comfortable."

Oh, hell. "What's going on? Valeria Montilla really shouldn't be pissed that I shot the asshole she married."

"Hell no." The colonel shook his head. "She seemed far more upset by the sudden move to Florida. She hates it and she's clammed up. Her sister has been cooperating with the DEA and other agencies, telling them all she knows about the cartel, and Laila's information is a lot fresher, but…"

Good for Laila. It wouldn't change anything those motherfucking misogynists and rapists had done to her, but if she could get any measure of revenge, One-Mile applauded it. "What's the problem?"

Caleb sighed. "I think Valeria is afraid. Someone in the Tierra Caliente cartel is threatening us if we don't hand her over."

Yeah, drug cartels didn't like their secrets spilled. But if they wanted to stop hemorrhaging information, why weren't they interested in Laila? Maybe they just didn't know yet.

One-Mile snorted. "Bring it on. I've been fighting them for months, and so far the body count is them zero, me one."

"That was my attitude until this turned up at my house this morning." The colonel dug into his pocket and pulled out a tube of lipstick, of all things, then reached across the table to open a large envelope. He withdrew a piece of paper and a photo, then slid both under his nose.

RETURN VALERIA OR WE WILL TAKE THE WOMAN THIS BELONGS TO.

A glance at the photo showed the original team who had smuggled Emilo Montilla's wife out of Mexico. Caleb, Hunter, Logan, Joaquin, and a guy he didn't recognize.

"Who's this?"

"Blaze Beckham. Mercenary. Best at what he does, so I hired him for this extraction. A month later, he went to Africa to fight with some insurgents. I haven't heard from him since. And as far as I know, he has no woman to target."

"What do you think all this means?" Jack asked him, expression carefully blank.

One-Mile hated to say it, but at this point wasn't he stating the obvious? "Someone higher up the Tierra Caliente food chain than dear departed Emilo wants Valeria back. If we don't surrender her, they won't come after us; they'll come after one of our women."

"That was my takeaway, too." The colonel's voice said that confirmation gave him no thrill.

"But why?"

The colonel shrugged. "I don't know. None of this makes any sense. Not this note. Not this tube of lipstick… It's not their usual way of doing business."

It wasn't. "Any idea who it belongs to?"

The older man shook his head. "It's not Carlotta's. That's all I know. I hate to ask around and scare the shit out of everyone. Maybe it's strictly symbolic?"

Of a woman in general? Drug cartels weren't the figurative type. "I doubt that."

"We need to figure this out so I can start locking people down. That's why you're here. We don't know exactly which asshole in the cartel sent this message or why they want Valeria back so badly. That already puts us at a disadvantage. But it worries me a lot more that we can't pinpoint which of our women they're gunning for."

"Kata, Tara, or Bailey, you mean?"

Caleb winced. "One of them is my best guess, yeah. Which is why I haven't told Hunter, Logan, or Joaquin yet."

They would all lose their shit. "Understood."

"Since it seems the cartel wants revenge on the team that originally extracted Valeria from Mexico and none of you were involved, Morgan and Brea seemingly aren't in their crosshairs. That's why I asked you here. And with EM having an unresolved mole problem…"

While One-Mile had already proved he wasn't said mole… "What do you need me to do, sir?"

"You're in?"

"Yeah. But it would be better if you didn't send me back to Mexico right away—"

"No. The first thing we need to do is figure out which motherfucker we're dealing with and who their target is. Give it some thought this afternoon. I'll call you later tonight so we can discuss. Everyone is due at my house in an hour for a family get-together, so they'll be safe that long. Just keep this between us until I'm ready to say something."

"I understand. We'll figure this out, neutralize the threat, and protect your family." While keeping Valeria sheltered. After everything she'd been through with Montilla, she and her son deserved that.

"Thanks. I'll be in touch."

One-Mile nodded at the colonel, then shook hands with Jack Cole. Admittedly the guy hadn't said much…but he had a weird feeling the cagey Cajun was actually running the show. Then he sent Forsythe a head bob. "See you around."

As he turned for the door, eager to get back to Brea, the other guy jogged to catch up. "Hey. I know exactly one person here. You. Got time for a beer? We could talk shop."

He peered at the late-afternoon sun. Brea had said to come back tonight. How long did seniors' Bible study last? Since he had no flipping clue, he shrugged. "Why the hell not?"

Forsythe flashed him a movie-star smile. "You turned out all right, Serial Killer."

"Verdict is still out on you, Jock Strap," he teased.

Trevor laughed. "So where do you get a decent beer in this swamp?"

"Follow me."

One-Mile hopped in his Jeep and waited for the other guy to follow in what seemed like his rented sedan. All the while, questions kept niggling at him. Was Valeria safe in Florida? Who had taken over Emilo Montilla's splinter faction of the Tierra Caliente cartel after his death? And why would the organization suddenly get desperate enough to threaten innocent women days after one of their bosses had bit a bullet?

Brea breathed into the blessed silence filling the house. Finally, the never-ending Bible study luncheon had concluded and people headed out. Jennifer and Daddy decided to go to a nearby Mexican food place for an early dinner. They'd invited her along, but they needed time alone, too. With all her father's heart issues, which thankfully seemed to be stabilizing, they'd been through some tough times.

Besides, this gave her an opportunity to fix her face before Pierce returned to ask Daddy for her hand. She was nervous as all get-out.

What if he said no? His blessing wasn't a given...

Then she'd have to chart her own path. It would be nice if Daddy accepted her choice of husband and gave his approval. If he refused, it would break her heart to defy her father, but for Pierce—for their love—she would.

As she finished up the dishes from this afternoon's luncheon and started the dishwasher, her phone rang. When she scanned the screen, she smiled. It did her heart good to see Pierce's name pop up. For months, she'd tried not to wonder if she would ever see it again.

"Hi." She sounded as giddy as she felt.

"Hi yourself. I was having a beer with a guy I know from way back and I was about to grab a bite out when I realized I've never actually taken you on a date. How about dinner, pretty girl?"

Brea giggled. "We really did everything completely out of order."

"It's my fault. Feel free to blame me."

She knew she'd had a hand in all this, too, but she liked to tease him. "Careful, or I'll decide everything in our married life will be your fault."

"It probably will be." As she laughed, he pressed her. "But seriously, dinner?"

"Sure."

They decided to try out a new bar and grill that had a little bit of everything on their menu.

"Want me to pick you up?"

"Where are you now?" she asked.

"Sitting at their bar."

Was he silly? "Then there's no point in you coming all the way back here. I'll just meet you there. It shouldn't take me more than twenty minutes."

"Okay, that gives me time to run a quick errand down the street and grab a table."

Brea grabbed her purse and her car keys. "See you shortly."

"Can't wait."

She hung up, texted her father that she'd be back by seven and to please be home, then she hopped into her car. When she arrived at the restaurant, Pierce stood waiting for her inside the foyer.

A giant smile crossed her face when their eyes met. "Hi."

How amazing would it be to come home to his face every day? To wake up to his face every morning? To peer into his face every time he made love to her? Her smile widened, and she knew she probably looked sappy and lovesick. She didn't care.

Pierce had changed her life.

He was even less shy about showing everyone his feelings. He simply pulled her into his arms and dropped a long kiss on her mouth that was so passionate her toes curled inside her espadrilles.

He gave her tongue one last stroke and reluctantly pulled away. "Hi. I wanted to do that earlier, on your front porch. But with all the ladies looking on…"

"Probably not the best idea," she agreed.

A hostess cleared her throat. "Your table is ready. If you'll follow me…"

Pierce stepped back to let Brea go first, like a good gentleman. She ignored the gaping of a sad Hispanic woman who had just walked in and trailed the hostess through the dim restaurant. He dropped his hot palm on the small of her back all the way to a booth in one dark corner. She sat and slid in on one side. Instead of sitting on the other, Pierce plopped next to her, nudging her almost against the wall, his big body pressed against hers from shoulder to knee.

She shivered. "What are you doing?"

"Being as close as possible so I can kiss you whenever I want. And touch your pussy. That's important, too." He winked.

Fire scalded her blood, battling her embarrassment. "You can't do that here."

"Why not? I'll keep it under the table. No one but us will know. Well, unless you scream."

With him touching her, chances were high that she would. Brea blushed.

It was impossible to tell from his grin if he was serious.

"Do I have to set ground rules? No touching my private parts in public."

"Ah, c'mon. I probably won't get to touch you later tonight. Don't take one of my favorite toys from me."

"My girl bits are not a toy."

"But I love to play with them." His black eyes danced as he leaned in to brush kisses along her neck. And then he dropped a hand on her thigh.

Apparently he was serious.

"Welcome. My name is Miles. I'll be your waiter tonight." He poured them both glasses of water. "What can I get you?"

Neither of them had looked at the menu, but they quickly scanned it and ordered their meals. Miles jotted everything down, grabbed them both iced tea, then left, promising to have their drinks and food up quickly.

"So how was your meeting?" she asked.

"Not good." He grew pensive. "The world I live in is dangerous."

Worry twisted Brea's belly. "I know."

"Sometimes the innocent get dragged into it."

"I'm not surprised."

"I worry about you."

She didn't like the sound of that. "Is there something you need to tell me?"

"You're not in any danger I'm aware of." He sighed. "At least not this time. But I can't promise it won't happen in the future, and I need you to decide if that's something you can really handle."

Brea had already thought this through. "I'll be fine." When he opened his mouth to rebut her, she carried on. "You made sure I learned skills that would keep me safe. I'm way better prepared than I was before I met you. Situational awareness. Assessing threats, looking for potential weapons, as well as devising distractions and exit strategies. I think in a pinch I'd have a fighting chance."

He looked impressed. "You have been paying attention. Carrying your Beretta?"

"Not right now. It wasn't necessary in my house during seniors' Bible study. And I forgot to pick it up before I left."

He scowled. "You have a permit to carry, so you should keep your weapon with you. You have to be prepared."

"Are you armed right now?" She hadn't seen a weapon on him anywhere.

"Always. Promise me."

She nodded. "It's going to take a change in mindset. I've mostly been in hair salons and the church—"

"Anyone can walk into either and start shooting. Better prepared than dead."

"Point taken. I'll start carrying it Tuesday when I go back to the salon." But the concern in his surprisingly on-edge tone made her frown. "Is someone being threatened?"

He hesitated. "Yeah. After I talk to your father tonight and hopefully get his blessing, I have another meeting. We've got to start figuring some shit out. I may be bodyguarding until this gets sorted."

The thought rattled her. But if he could walk away relatively unscathed after two months hunting a cartel boss in Mexico, she had to believe he'd be okay now. "I understand."

"Listen, at the first sign of anything suspicious, don't wait for trouble. Get ahold of me. I would rather you overreact than brush something off, only to realize too late that you're in danger."

Brea nodded. It was a completely odd way of living to her, and she knew the transition wouldn't be easy. She definitely hated bringing her baby into danger. But she would do anything to keep him safe and knew Pierce would, too.

"Good." He brushed a soft kiss over her mouth like he couldn't stand not touching her. "No more depressing shit right now. Let's talk about this wedding. What do you want?"

"Something simple in the church. Just friends and family." She dropped a hand to her belly. "Something hopefully before the baby comes."

He nodded. "I was hoping we could make it happen next weekend."

His impatience was cute, and she had to grin. "Probably more like next month. These things take planning, and I'd like Cutter to be back from his honeymoon." She tsked at him. "Don't look at me like that. He's still my best friend."

"Who did everything possible to come between us."

"I know. And I'm not happy with him. He meant well, but he knows better now. He won't come between us ever again. Nothing can except death." As soon as the words left her mouth, she shivered.

As if he sensed her fear, Pierce tossed his arm around her. "And I won't let that happen anytime in the next seventy years. You're going to have to get used to me."

"Is that a threat?" She poked her finger into his ribs.

Her grabbed her fingers and kissed them. "It's a promise."

After another soft kiss, Miles returned with their food and refilled their drinks. Pierce had ordered a gargantuan hamburger overflowing with Swiss and mushrooms and dripping juice.

When the waiter set her plate of smoked fried chicken in front of her, her eyes widened. "That's huge."

"Better start eating," he quipped. "Before I get hungry for something else.

He dropped his hand to her thigh again, fingers inching up.

She slapped his knuckles. "Stop that."

Pierce laughed and dug into his burger. She made her way through as much of her chicken as possible, but it was hopeless. Even eating for two she couldn't possibly consume this much food.

Miles came back and asked about dessert. They both shook their heads, then Pierce paid the bill.

"Wait here. I need to hit the head."

Brea couldn't not giggle. She was so used to her father and his far more delicate way of expressing that bodily need. "I'm going to go ahead and go." She glanced at her phone. "It's already six fifteen. Daddy will be back home, and I think tonight will go better if you give me a few minutes to talk to him before you knock on the door."

His face said he didn't like it, but he understood.

"Fine. And after that, I'm climbing out of this monkey suit." He pulled uncomfortably at his collar.

She winked. "I'll even help you."

He leaned in to give her a lingering kiss. "I'll absolutely let you. See you in less than an hour."

"See you then."

"I love you."

"I love you." Brea pressed another kiss on his lips, then backed away, waving when he finally headed to the bathroom.

As she made her way to the front door, the Hispanic woman who had entered just after them stood and fell in behind her. Brea looked over her shoulder at the woman pulling a tissue from her purse.

When the stranger looked up, she realized they were about the same age. The woman had the most beautiful black hair…and the saddest red-rimmed eyes. She'd definitely been crying. Brea's heart went out.

"I'm sorry to intrude. I just… Are you all right?"

She looked startled and shook her head. "No. I… I am very sad. I lost my brother this week."

It took Brea a minute to understand around the woman's thick accent, but the second her meaning hit, Brea hurt for her. She was clearly grieving. And angry. Not a surprise since anger was one of the stages of grief.

"I'm so sorry."

The brunette shook her head. "I-I am the one who is sorry. I do not know why I told you. You have a kind face. But my problems are not yours."

When the woman walked around her and pushed out the door, Brea followed. "It's all right. You should never apologize for your grief. You have my condolences for your terrible loss. If you ever need a welcoming community or just an opportunity to pray with people who will understand, my father is the reverend of a church in Sunset, just up the road."

The stranger dabbed at her eyes, then tucked the tissue back in her purse. "Thank you. I am very sorry for this."

Before Brea could question the woman, she pointed a gun in Brea's direction. "My brother is dead, and your man is the one who killed him. Come with me now or I will shoot you."

chapter eleven

One-Mile sauntered through the dimly lit restaurant toward the exit with a roll of his eyes. He would have already been in his Jeep and gone if one of the waitresses hadn't spotted him leaving alone, tried to rub up against him, batted her lashes so fast he was shocked she hadn't taken flight, and pressed her phone number in his hand.

He tossed it into the trash bin behind the hostess stand, not giving two shits if she saw. Despite her obvious cleavage and musky perfume, he wasn't interested in the least.

The only woman he wanted was Brea Bell.

They'd been through so fucking much together. Ups, down, miscommunications, lies, injuries, separations, saboteurs like Cutter, and hell, even a whole damn town. He'd had to fight her family, her religion, her perception, and her fears... But he'd soldiered on because she belonged in his home, in his bed, wearing his ring, and carrying his babies.

Now the only thing that stood between him and that future was for one man to say yes.

One-Mile didn't delude himself. That blessing, if he got it, would be hard-won. In fact, winning Preacher Bell over might be the hardest battle he'd ever fought because he couldn't use his fists or pull out his firearm. He had to use his words and be persuasive. And he didn't know what to say except that he loved Brea and wanted to take care of her for the rest of their lives.

With his thoughts running in circles, he pushed his way out of the restaurant to head for his Jeep so he could make the drive to Sunset, then do or say whatever necessary until Jasper Bell gave his consent. The sound of screeching tires to his right caught his attention. He turned and saw a sight that stopped him cold.

A black SUV hauled ass out of the parking lot—with Brea's panicked face plastered against the back window.

Fucking son of a bitch...

Fear crashed through his system and tried to freeze him, but he shoved that shit into a mental compartment and locked it down as best he could. Then he breathed and forced himself to remember his training.

Still, his heart revved furiously as he yanked his keys from his pocket, unlocked his Jeep with a press of his jittery thumb, then dove behind the wheel, peeling out in hot pursuit.

The black SUV had disappeared around a curve. Goddamn it, he'd been so fucking focused on Brea that he'd only caught part of the license plate, and that wouldn't help much if the vehicle had been stolen.

One-Mile careened around the bend in the road, his thoughts churning. Who would abduct her now? Why? It might be random...but he doubted it.

Was the tube of lipstick the colonel had received this morning somehow meant to be a warning for him, too? One-Mile didn't see how it added up, but he couldn't untangle that shit now.

When he reached the intersection, the black SUV was gone and he'd missed the light. Nor did he see it in the thick fall of traffic.

Fuck. Left or right? North or south? He had to decide quickly.

Following a hunch, he got in the left-hand turn lane to go south. Traffic was heavier in that direction because the majority of town lay that way. If this motherfucking abductor wanted to blend, he would head downtown.

Seconds dragged on, and he imagined all the horrible things a monster could do to his gentle pretty girl. He started to fidget and crawl out of his skin.

"Fuck the red light."

One-Mile dodged between cars crossing the intersection legally, managed to turn, and tore down the street. His blood boiled. His rage seethed. He tried to quell the panic and think.

He hadn't seen her purse scattered or lying abandoned in the parking lot. If she still had it, that meant she had her phone. That probably wouldn't last long. The kidnapper would know she could be traced and ditch the device—leaving him without a clue where to find Brea.

He had to get his hands on her computer and track her cell phone ASAP, but he didn't dare head away from her and waste time off the road.

He needed help.

"Who the fuck can I call?" Not Cutter; on his honeymoon. Not Cage; probably in Dallas. He didn't know her father's number. He didn't know how to contact anyone else in her life.

He banged a fist on his steering wheel.

Motherfucker, there must be someone.

He yanked his phone from his pocket and dialed Matt, who answered on the first ring. "Hey, man. What's up?"

"Someone took Brea." He described the incident as he merged over one lane and scanned the cars around him.

"What do you need me to do?"

"Where are you?"

"Down by the airport, looking at a bike."

South end of town. "Great. Get on the highway and head north. Look for a black Escalade with a license plate that begins with *W*-eight. If you see it, follow and call me."

"You got it. Call the police?"

"Not yet. They'll want to interview me before they put out a BOLO."

"And you can't wait around for that. I'll call you if I find anything." Matt hesitated. "She's a good girl, and she doesn't deserve this."

"It's my fault." Self-loathing clawed through One-Mile.

"You don't know that. We'll find her."

Before it was too late, he hoped. "Thanks."

He needed another hand. Since he had just exchanged numbers with Forsythe, and the guy was supposedly a top-notch investigator, One-Mile hoped that would work for him today. He pressed the button for Trevor's contact.

The guy answered on the first ring. "Hey! Decide you like me after all?"

"I've got an emergency."

All hint of teasing disappeared. "What do you need?"

One-Mile thought of an easy half-dozen people he could have Forsythe track down—her father, the man's fiancée, her boss. He didn't trust any of them to stay cool in crisis. "Where are you?"

"On I-49, north end of town. Need me to head back south?"

Jesus, what a lucky break. "No. Head to Sunset. It's the next town you'll come to. I'll text you an address. Go around the back, head into the bedroom window on the southwest corner of the house. On the desk, you'll find a computer—"

"Hold it, Serial Killer. I can't just break into someone's bedroom for you."

"It's my fucking girlfriend's. She's been kidnapped. She's still got her phone, and her computer can trace it."

"Oh, shit. All right. Stepping on it. Any idea who took her?"

"No." And that bugged the shit out of him. "But if they're any good, you know she won't have her phone for long."

"She won't. I'm actually almost to Sunset. Someone said rent out here was cheap."

Probably. "Call me once you're in her room. I'll help you into her computer. Oh, and her dad might be home, so don't get caught."

"If I get arrested, you're bailing my ass out."

"Yeah."

"Hey, man. We'll find her."

One-Mile fucking hoped so.

They hung up, and he stopped at a red light. It was a major intersection, and he looked all around, hoping against hope to spot the Escalade. But it was getting dark now. It looked like rain might fall.

He had no fucking idea how he was going to cope if he didn't find Brea in time.

Fuck no! They had been through too much for their love to end this way. He would use everything he'd ever learned and exert every bit of his will to save her. For now, he could best serve her by shutting down the goddamn fear.

Working to keep his calm, he texted Brea's address to Jock Strap. The guy replied with a thumbs-up. The light turned green, so he followed the stream of traffic.

Would the kidnapper be looking to get Brea out of town or hunker down nearby to force on her whatever sick shit was in his head? He didn't know. He just knew he needed to move mountains to save her.

Plucking up the phone again, he dialed the colonel, who answered immediately. "Got something already?"

"A problem." He explained the situation.

Caleb cursed. "What do you want me to do?"

"Call your buddies at the police department. I didn't make any friends over there during Cutter's hostage standoff at the grocery store, so—"

"You only pissed Gaines off. Most everyone else thinks you're a fucking hero."

If he was the ultimate cause of Brea's death, then no. He'd deserve to rot in hell.

"I need you to get them to issue a BOLO, have squad cars out looking, check any traffic cams, follow up on leads people might phone in. But I can't sit still and talk to them now."

"I'll take care of it."

One-Mile let out a breath. "Think this has anything to do with that tube of lipstick you got?"

"Maybe…but my gut says no. You weren't a part of that original mission, and these people would prefer to have Valeria back without incident. Taking someone before we've even had time to act doesn't fit that MO."

"True." And that made him feel better—to a point. "But this may be revenge for Emilo's death."

"My sources down there say that shit show he ran is in chaos now. There's some infighting about which of his lackeys will take over, but word has it that the big boss intends to step in and appoint someone."

"El Padrino?"

"Yep."

It seemed unusual that the organization's kingpin would stoop to care about Emilo's scrap of territory, but maybe it had been more important than he'd thought. "Think someone bucking for the job is using Brea to get to me so he can prove how effective and brutal he is?"

"It's possible…but unlikely. Once El Padrino gets involved, no one down there so much as breathes without his consent."

Not usually, no. That calmed One-Mile a little more. If the cartel had Brea, he knew what would happen and how bad it would be. But if Tierra Caliente wasn't involved…

"Have any idea who else might have your girl?"

"None." He had enemies, sure. But unless they'd just been waiting for him to reveal his Achilles' heel, One-Mile didn't see it.

"Keep looking. You'll figure it out or find a clue. Something... Need me to send the boys out to help find Brea?"

Meaning his bosses. Since he'd mostly pissed them off left, right, and center, he doubted they'd do much to help him. "If they're willing."

"I'll get them on it."

"Thanks."

There wasn't much more to say, so after Caleb promised to check in if he learned anything new, they hung up.

One-Mile continued to drive around. He saw black SUVs, but not Escalades. The one he did spot, he followed to a residential district, only to realize four kids sat in the back and the license plate didn't match.

He pounded his steering wheel again. Goddamn it, he was chasing a needle in a haystack. Brea could be anywhere by now. She could already be out of town. Hell, she could even be on a plane out of the country, depending on who had her and what their resources were.

But under the panic, his gut told him this was about him—not her—and they wouldn't take her anywhere until they put the screws to him.

A minute later, the phone rang. He glanced at the display and picked it up. "Jock Strap?"

"I'm in. Her computer is up," he whispered. "Her dad is in the living room pacing, so I'm trying to be extra fucking quiet. What's her password?"

One-Mile recited it, hoping like hell she hadn't changed it in the last two months since he'd hacked into her machine.

"I'm in. It's locating. I'm fucking shocked they haven't ditched the phone or turned off location services. Amateurs?"

Maybe. And that would be a huge fucking relief. "Anything?"

Trevor didn't answer for a long moment. The silence seemed to stretch so thin he would have sworn it would snap. He tapped his thumb on the steering wheel and drove too fast back out of the residential part of town, closer to the highway.

"Okay, her phone is still on the grid. Her last location is somewhere on Highway 353. What's out there?"

"It's the road to the lake...and not much else." It made no sense, but One-Mile still floored it in that direction.

"What do you want me to do?"

"Hit refresh. See if the phone is still moving and in which direction."

"Yeah."

One-Mile heard him tapping a key and waited. "You haven't overheard her dad say anything about receiving a ransom, have you?"

"No. Earlier, he was talking to someone on the phone about meeting you. He didn't sound excited."

Why would the preacher be? From her father's perspective, he had ruined, impregnated, and jeopardized the man's daughter. Fuck, even if he got Brea back, he'd be lucky if Preacher Bell ever spoke to him. And One-Mile didn't blame him one bit.

But that wouldn't stop him. Nothing—not this kidnapper, not her father, not her best friend or the whole damn town—was going to keep him from making Brea his.

Except death.

"Shit."

One-Mile snapped back to the conversation. "What?"

"Either your girl is heading into an area without cell signal or the location services just got turned off. I'm now getting an old location. But I got enough of an update to see that they're going east."

His heart stopped. His stomach plummeted. The one surefire way he had to help her was gone. "Fuck. Now get the hell out of there. And thanks."

"Are you sure? Is her dad expecting her home? Will he call the police if she doesn't show?"

He was and he might. "Good point."

"Want me to fill him in?"

One-Mile weighed the pros and cons, then decided he didn't have much choice. "Yeah. Thanks again. He's got a heart condition. Try to keep him calm."

"Sure. I don't know you well, man. But you're doing every fucking thing you can."

He just hoped it was enough. "Call me if he becomes a problem."

Jock Strap just laughed. "The FBI taught me how to sidestep direct questions and difficult conversations. You do you. I got this."

"Thanks again. I owe you."

"Knowing me, I'll need it someday."

They hung up, then he called Matt. "What you got?"

One-Mile gave him the location update. "Know where that is?"

"Vaguely. I'll figure it out. Headed that way now."

Maybe they could run this kidnapper down. He had to hope so.

He rang the colonel again next.

"I'm in touch with the police," Caleb said. "They're going to issue a BOLO in the next few minutes. They'll get cruisers looking. Traffic cams are a no-go without a warrant."

"Thanks." Then he updated Caleb on the location of Brea's phone. Thankfully the man knew exactly where the road was. "I'll pass that on. I also know a guy who runs a swamp tour out there. Crazier than a rat, but observant and suspicious. I'll ask him to poke around."

They ended the call as the last of the sun disappeared below the horizon. Now that he couldn't do anything but drive and hope for the best, more worry crept in. He tried to tell himself that even if Brea wasn't armed, she wasn't stupid. She knew self-defense. She knew to look for weaknesses and escape paths.

But he couldn't deny that she'd also never had to put that knowledge to real-life use. People often panicked. And there was no way she could get too physical with a kidnapper. Besides being petite and peaceful, she was nearly six months pregnant.

A trek down the road from its origin to its end didn't net anything concrete. Next, he'd start trying some of the ramshackle buildings he'd seen off the side of the road. If that didn't give him any results, he'd investigate the narrow two-lane roads that shot off of 353. Yeah, the abductor might have taken the road to its end and turned onto 314, but hell, that mostly led to nowhere.

One-Mile hoped he was making the right decisions. It wasn't just his life or his future hanging in the balance. So many people would suffer if he failed Brea. Cutter, her father, all of Sunset…and their son, who might never know life. He swallowed grief and guilt down and vowed to keep searching. But as seven p.m. became eight, then nine and ten, he stopped looking at the clock. His phone wasn't ringing, goddamn it. And he hated to assume the worst, but his hope began to dim. And as the time inched toward two a.m. and he was forced to stop for gas, he hung his head in the front seat of his Jeep and cried.

Brea's shoulders ached from her hands being zip-tied behind her back for hours. She shifted on the hard metal chair in the abandoned repair shop and studied the woman who had abducted her. Clara, she called herself when she muttered out loud. She clearly hadn't thought this plan through. Brea suspected the woman's grief had overwhelmed her mental state, because she'd been acting frantic and half-crazy for hours.

Clara's bony fingers gripped Brea's phone. She wished she could snatch it back, at least long enough to tell everyone where she was and that she was all right. She hated to think about Pierce and Daddy both worried sick. Instead, the woman clutched the device in her hand and paced.

"I simply have to call that *cabrón* and lure him in. His number is here." She held up Brea's cell. "Why am I waiting?"

Seemingly to find her courage.

Brea was trying to hang on to hers. The good news was, Clara Montilla appeared to be working alone. She'd seen no hint of accomplices or heavies or anyone else who wished her harm. Apparently the cartel wasn't helping with this rash plan, nor did she act like she was accustomed to committing violence. Brea clung to those small comforts.

"All I have to do is ring him and tell him I have his *puta*," Clara went on. "He will come. Then I will shoot him, and my brother will be avenged."

That thought terrified Brea, but she refused to let that happen without a fight. "It won't be that easy."

The woman whirled on her. "You think I do not know that? Your man has slaughtered many for the sake of his government, his paycheck, and his pride." She spit on the ground at Brea's feet. "He is a macho pig."

And her brother had been an angel? Brea glared but kept her sarcasm to herself.

"He is also dangerous," Clara went on. "I know this."

Brea played on Clara's obvious fears. "And Pierce won't go down without a fight I'm not sure you're ready for."

Clara's lip quivered. Her fear morphed into terror, but she tried to play it off. "The gun is the great equalizer. I can fell any man with the pull of a trigger."

Brea couldn't refute her except to make one point. "Pierce can kill you from a mile away."

"Not in the dark. Now shut up! And do not speak again."

Brea was afraid to push the woman any further, so she tried another tactic. "Could I have more water, please?"

Something guilty flashed across Clara's face. "You have but to ask. I do not wish you or your baby harm."

The woman assured Brea of that often, even as she rampaged about getting her revenge. And no matter how many times Brea had argued that ending Pierce's life wouldn't bring her brother back, Clara didn't want to hear it.

After the woman set her phone on the nearby counter—so close yet so far away—then lifted the bottle to her lips, Brea took a few sips. When she was finished, Clara set the bottle aside.

They couldn't go on all night this way. She had to do something.

"I also need to use the bathroom."

Clara let out a sigh of irritation. "Fine, but do not try to be clever." She fumbled in her purse for her gun and pointed it in her direction. "I would rather not shoot you, but I will."

Brea nodded. So the woman had said before. Clara was unstable enough to pull the trigger. Her emotions were a roller coaster—fear gave way to tears, then fits of anger, which morphed back into fear. Grief had made her behavior erratic and unstable. As the hours went on and the woman grew weary, she seemed more unhinged. Brea feared Emilo's sister would lose her ability to think rationally and shoot her in panic.

It was now or never.

"I understand."

Clara approached with an industrial-size box cutter and the zip-tie holding her wrists behind the back of the chair suddenly gave way. Brea's shoulders screamed as she rolled them and rose to her feet. The woman escorted her to the bathroom with the barrel of her gun poking her spine. Brea tried to ignore it and let herself into the small, dirty space.

She wasn't sure where they were exactly. In some sort of repair shop, though seemingly not for cars, close to the lake. There were chains abandoned on the concrete floors, bays where a few scattered tools still sat, darkened lights everywhere, and a rusting trailer or two.

As Brea took care of business, she was dejected to realize the bathroom had no window. It was a long shot that she could have crawled out, given her growing belly, but it would have been worth a try. She was going to have to find another way out. Clearly, Pierce had no idea where she was or he would already be here.

The stricken look on his face when he'd seen her in the window as Clara drove away haunted her. He must be worried. He probably blamed himself. He'd likely do anything and everything to save her.

Brea hoped it didn't come to that.

As she flushed the toilet, her mind raced. She managed to find some hand soap under the sink and washed up. Maybe when she let herself out of the bathroom, Clara would be elsewhere and she would have an opportunity to sneak through the vast darkness of this seemingly abandoned place, then out into the night. Or she could lead the woman on a chase in the grounds around the building, then double back for her phone. Something.

But when she opened the door, Clara waited there, gun pointed in her face. "Back to your chair."

No. She was done with this. Done being this woman's victim. Done being afraid. Maybe this wouldn't turn out well, but if she let Clara run the show, nothing would.

Time to act.

"All right," she murmured.

Clara took a step back to allow her out of the bathroom. Brea pretended to trip, then stumble into the woman. Clara yelped. Brea half expected to feel a bullet penetrate her, and she squeezed her eyes shut. But nothing. Emilo's sister fell, her backside hitting the concrete with a thud. Brea landed on top of her, reaching for the gun as it fell out of the woman's hand and skated across the hard cement. She leapt to her feet as quickly as her pregnant belly allowed and reached for the weapon, only a few yards away.

Suddenly, the woman's hand closed around her ankle like a vise, and Brea felt herself falling. She managed to catch herself with her hands. Pain radiated up her wrists, all the way past her elbows and to her shoulders, but she managed to keep her weight off her baby bump, roll to her knees, and find her feet again.

"Bitch." Clara shoved past her and scrambled on the ground for the gun.

No way was she going to win that fight now. With her, Clara had been polite, almost gentle. But she wouldn't make that mistake again.

So now Brea had to be smarter.

She ran into the darkest part of the massive building, shoving tools onto the ground and rattling chains. The deafening sounds magnified by the echo in the cavernous room masked her footsteps as she ran to a blessed door she saw on the far wall, unlocked it, and hurtled outside.

A bullet pinged off the doorframe inches to her left.

Brea bit her lip to hold in a cry of fear and ducked, scrambling along the side of the building. Run into the adjacent swamp or double back for her phone?

The creatures in the swamp could be every bit as deadly and unpredictable as Clara. Brea didn't know where she was or what, if anything else, was around. She needed her cell.

Creeping through overgrown foliage, she tiptoed her way back to the front of the building and the main office where Clara had been keeping her, praying the phone still sat there. As she reached the entrance, she spotted a rusty tire iron someone had propped against the dilapidated wood and snagged it. That wouldn't protect her like a gun, but it would provide a last line of defense. She had to keep thinking ahead—and think positive.

Behind her, she heard Clara's loud footsteps and her angry grunts. The little beam of the flashlight from her phone gave her away.

Brea ducked into the office, grabbed her phone from the counter, then disappeared into the body of the warehouse again, hoping that since Clara had just searched there, she wouldn't double back to scour the place again.

She unlocked her phone with trembling hands. Her first instinct was to call Pierce or the police—someone. But Clara wasn't far behind. She'd hear. So Brea searched her settings, turned on her location services, silenced the device, then opened her messages. She dashed one off to Pierce.

Location turned on. I'm okay. One woman. No accomplices. Emilo's sister. She's crazy.

Seconds later, she received a reply. **In the area. On my way. Don't move. Bringing help.**

Brea breathed a sigh of relief. Pierce was coming. She would be okay. Someone would cart Clara away. Except for Emilo's sister, everyone would hopefully live happily ever after.

If she could reach the main road in front and escape this crazy woman, maybe her wishes would come true.

Brea pocketed her phone and glanced behind to make sure Clara wasn't following. Nothing. She didn't know where the woman had gone, but as long as Clara couldn't find her, Brea didn't care.

When she turned and stood to make her way to the main road and to freedom, she rounded the corner—and came face to face with her assailant. Clara's face was pinched and harsh as she stomped closer. Brea didn't dare run; she had zero doubt the woman would shoot her.

"Bitch." She pressed the barrel of the gun to her head and glanced at the tire iron in her hands. "Drop it."

A quick mental calculation told Brea that Clara could get a shot off way before she could ever swing the heavy metal bar to strike her. With a sigh, Brea tossed it a few feet away, onto the concrete.

"What did you do?"

"N-nothing." Brea tried to be brave, but her voice shook. Her whole body trembled. Her heart threatened to beat out of her chest.

Please, please don't let this be the end.

"Liar."

She had to come up with some version of the truth that would allow Pierce time to get here. "Really. I was trying to find the road to escape, b-but I got turned around. Please. I don't want to die." Tears pricked her eyes as she wrapped her hands around her belly. "My baby…"

Clara's mouth pinched even more as she wrapped a cruel fist in Brea's hair. "Come with me."

If she did, would she be as good as dead?

Brea didn't have the opportunity to make that decision. She heard the hum of a vehicle approaching soft, lights off. It stopped. The door opened.

Clara turned to her, eyes flaring. "Who did you call, *puta*?"

Tell her or lie?

"Who did you call?" she hissed as she yanked on her hair.

A cry slipped past Brea's throat, and the woman clenched the gun tighter, looking ready to explode in fury.

Using her ponytail, Clara dragged her around the corner of the warehouse and peeked. Brea saw no one, heard nothing, but she sensed Pierce. She felt him in the electricity in the air, in the sudden calm that came over her. He was here; he would keep her safe.

But who would keep him safe in return?

Brea clammed up. The woman didn't want her dead, so hopefully she could buy a little time until Pierce's backup arrived. She'd managed to put the unstable woman off this long. She could do it a bit longer.

"It doesn't matter," she answered finally. "This won't end well. Nothing you're doing will bring Emilo back."

Clara whipped around, hate in her eyes. "But I will avenge him. His bitch of a wife got pregnant before she abandoned and betrayed him. Then your brutal American sniper ended him ignominiously in some seedy part of town. And no one has done a thing about it. I know what my brother did for a living. I know he was no saint. But he was *my* brother. And I loved him. Since no one else in his organization intends to seize retribution, I will."

"Then what? Even if you succeed in killing Pierce, do you think he doesn't have friends? Do you think they or the police will let you walk free?"

Clara turned bleak eyes her way. "I will have turned the gun on myself long before then. I have nothing more to live for."

As her terrible words sank in, the woman seemingly reached a decision and gave her hair another savage tug, dragging her to the front of the abandoned building and into the circle of weak yellow light spilling through the front door. Then she slung Brea in front of her and pressed the gun to her temple.

Brea's heart revved uncontrollably. Fear made her body tremble and her legs unsteady. *God, please don't let it end like this…*

"Walker!" Clara called into the darkness. "If you want your woman to live, come toward me, toss down your weapons, and surrender."

"No!" Brea shouted.

"Shut up, *puta*." The woman yanked viciously on her hair again and pressed the gun so hard against her temple, Brea cried out in pain.

"Let her go," Pierce called from the darkness, his voice booming across the feet separating them. Then he walked into the stream of light, gun in hand, still wearing his suit.

Brea gasped. "Don't do this."

Other than a glance to assess that she was okay, Pierce didn't acknowledge her. "If you let Brea go, I'll toss this down and do whatever you want."

"You can't. No!" Brea pleaded. "It's a trap."

"I don't trust you," Clara hissed. "You must surrender before I let her go."

"If I do, what assurance do I have you'll actually release her?"

"If you don't, what assurance do I have you won't simply kill me and walk away?"

He shrugged. "You don't except that I'm a man of my word."

"You are a man who kills," she hissed. "You have no honor. Until now, I have not killed your woman because I have no strife with her, and I do not like to think of killing children before they are born. But I will. Right now."

"She won't," Brea argued.

"Shut up!" Clara said as she covered her mouth with a sweaty palm. "Will you surrender or watch your woman and child die before your eyes?"

Pierce dragged in a deep breath, shook his head in regret, then met Clara's gaze. "What do you want me to do?"

That was it? He was giving up? Sacrificing his life for hers? Pierce had felled enemy combatants and torn through armies, and he was going to simply let this unhinged woman put a bullet in his brain?

Brea struggled and squealed—to no avail.

"Toss your gun over there." Clara pointed toward the swampy darkness, away from the warehouse. "Far away."

Pierce didn't hesitate, just chucked it into the abyss. "Now what?"

"That pole over there. I prepared it for you." Clara gestured with a bob of her head. "Go. There are handcuffs on the ground. Put your arms around the pole and cuff yourself to it."

No matter how she screeched or struggled, Pierce did exactly as he was told, and the click of the handcuffs as he doomed himself to death was a stab to her heart.

Horror swept through her. It couldn't end this way. She would not let it, damn it.

She tried to catch Pierce's gaze, but he seemed to look right through her. "Now let her go."

Clara released her hair and removed the gun from her temple, then gave her a shove that almost sent her stumbling to her knees. "Leave."

Hell no. Somehow, someway, she was going to get them out of this. "Let me at least say goodbye."

If she could get close to Pierce, maybe they could devise something…

"I did not have the chance to say goodbye to my brother," Clara quipped.

Brea didn't point out that she hadn't been having Emilo's baby because it wouldn't work. She needed an appeal to Clara's heartstrings that she could grasp. "And doesn't that feel cruel to you? I've done nothing to you, so why hurt me even more when you're already taking the person I love most in this world?"

Tears fell down her cheeks, and Brea hoped they would move Clara to give her at least a few precious seconds.

The woman let out a noisy sigh. "Fine. One minute. Then you will leave. And look on the bright side. Walker is already dressed for his funeral."

Brea shook as she ran across the property toward Pierce and wrapped her arms around him. The moment felt so surreal. This couldn't be happening. This wasn't how their future should end.

"Why are you letting her win?"

"Because nothing is more important to me than you. Matt and a guy named Trevor are both on their way, but they won't get here in time."

"Then I'll stop her," she whispered so softly only he could hear. "Tell me what to do."

"To save me?" He shrugged like it didn't matter, but his black eyes pleaded. "Don't. Save you. Save our son."

"Please don't give up." Her voice cracked. "Please."

"Turn around and walk away. My end won't hurt, and you'll be fine. Go."

"No." She wasn't usually obstinate, but now? This moment? Brea was digging in her heels and not giving up. "Help me get you free or I'll stand between you and her bullet."

Pierce glared. "This isn't the time for you to get stubborn."

"I think it's the perfect time."

"What is the problem?" Clara called across the twenty feet separating them. "If you are not going to kiss and say your tearful goodbyes, then I would like to shoot him now. I have been waiting for days."

"Not yet," Brea pleaded.

Clara's face went cold. "Kiss him and leave."

She had to come up with some excuse…

"I have no way to do that. I don't know where I am. I have no car…" Brea gave Clara a shrug. "I'm sure he has keys in his pocket. Can I get them?"

"Hurry up."

"What are you doing?" he growled.

"Saving your ass." Brea breathed heavily and caught his gaze. "Where are your keys?"

"Front right pocket."

Brea rounded his body and, with shaking hands, withdrew the fob, then shot him a desperate glance. "Keep her talking. Buy yourself two minutes and I think I can get us forever."

"I won't risk you."

The baby chose that moment to kick, and she rounded the pole with tears in her eyes and pressed her belly against his hand. "Do you feel that?"

A moment later, the baby kicked again. Pierce's eyes widened. He stared at her with wonder. "That's our son."

"Yes. He's worth fighting for. I don't want to live without you. I love you. We need you."

She pressed herself against his side again and stood on her tiptoes as he leaned down to kiss her, then drink the tears from her cheeks.

"I love you," he whispered.

But that didn't mean he'd changed his mind.

"Help me to help us. Please. Don't give up."

After a moment's hesitation, Brea felt his subtle nod. Then he whispered against her temple, "Glock behind my seat. No safety. A lot of recoil."

"I won't let you down," she promised.

"You never could."

"That's enough!" Clara screamed. "You have the keys. Walk away and don't stop. If you do, you'll be next."

Even though she and Pierce had a plan, she was loath to leave him. What if Clara refused to be drawn into conversation? What if, the second Brea ran for the Jeep, the crazy woman pulled the trigger? What if she made it back in time…but missed? She'd only get one chance to save Pierce. Clara wouldn't be stupid enough to allow her a second.

Brea stood on her tiptoes and kissed Pierce for what she prayed wouldn't be the final time. "No matter what, I love you. I didn't know who I was or what I was supposed to do with my life until I met you."

"Same, pretty girl," he whispered. "Do your best, and if it doesn't work—"

"Shh. I'll make it work. You taught me to be strong and stand up for what I want. That's what I'm going to do."

Brea pressed her lips to his, then cuddled to him as close as she could, feeling the quick but steady beat of his heart. Then she raised her head, stepped away, and set off to save her man.

"Are you finally leaving?" Clara snapped.

Brea held up Pierce's keys with a nod. "I'll be gone in two minutes."

"Good riddance." As she walked away, Clara went on. "Look, Walker. Your woman is leaving you to die. You will depart this earth knowing you are nothing to her." The woman laughed. "No one deserves it more."

As soon as Brea left the circle of the light, she ran. Her pulse throbbed and adrenaline ripped fire through her veins. She wasn't exactly sure where Pierce had parked his Jeep, but it couldn't be far, probably near the road.

Dragging her phone from her pocket, she turned on the flashlight. The Jeep sat dark and silent a few feet away. Brea dashed to it, yanking the back door open and fumbling around in the pocket behind the driver's seat.

Her fingers found the cool metal of the Glock, and she wrenched it free. Then she darted back for the repair shop, crouched and on her tiptoes. Brea hadn't heard anything that sounded like a gunshot yet, and she counted her blessings, even as she counted the seconds. Pierce was clever enough to keep her talking…but Clara craved blood now.

When Brea reached the edge of the light, she found Pierce standing taut with his arms around the wide pole, wrists still cuffed. Clara hissed something in his ear. He merely shook his head once, but didn't acknowledge her in any other way. If he knew Brea was back to save him, she saw no indication of that.

Clara stomped her feet, her face red with fury. "You killed him! Say you're sorry."

Pierce pressed his lips together mutely, refusing to say a word.

The woman shoved the gun against his head. "Say you're sorry. Now!"

"You want me to lie?"

Brea's eyes widened. Was he crazy?

With trembling hands, she raised the gun and aimed at Clara, then she hesitated. She'd only had a few weeks' practice with a firearm. She'd never shot this gun. Fear coursed through her veins. Her hands shook. What if she missed? What if she hit Pierce instead?

Clara screeched in rage. The sound gave Brea goose bumps. Her heartbeat roared in her ears, nearly drowning out everything else.

"Say. You are. Sorry," the woman demanded. "Or I will kill you where you stand."

"You're going to anyway."

"I hate you!" Her voice got higher; her hand shook more erratically. "You killed my only brother. The only person who loved me and took care of me."

Her finger curled around the trigger. Pierce didn't respond at all.

Clara bared her teeth. "I want you to die."

She meant that.

Brea's heart leapt to her throat. She'd never thought she could willfully kill anyone, no matter the circumstance. The good girl in her who loved family, God, and all His living things had never imagined that she would intentionally snuff out anyone. But in that moment, she realized she fucking would. Yes, she might hit Pierce, but if she didn't try, he *would* die. It was that simple.

She swallowed, sent a quick prayer up, then aimed. Her heart beat so fast now it inhibited her breathing and threatened to choke her. Her palms sweated. Her entire body trembled. But she focused on everything she'd learned and took a deep breath.

Then she pulled the trigger.

The recoil nearly sent her tumbling back. An instant later, Clara jolted and glanced down at the red stain blooming from her left shoulder. Then she started searching beyond the circle of light. "Bitch! I will definitely kill your man now."

No, she wouldn't.

Brea risked creeping a few steps closer as Clara made her way back to Pierce. She held her breath, dredged up her courage, and fired again. This time she was prepared for the kickback and managed to stay steadier on her feet.

A second scream ripped through the air, this one filled with pain. Clara looked down at the stain forming on her yellow sweater two inches closer to her heart. Blood drained from her face. She stumbled back. "No."

Brea tried to stay strong. She didn't speak; it would give away her hiding spot in the shadows. She didn't argue her perspective; Clara had already made up her mind. She simply waited to see what the woman would do—fight to the death or surrender. She prayed for the latter.

"No," Clara repeated, her voice sounding more like a gurgle. "He dies before me."

Despite weaving unsteadily, she raised her weapon in Pierce's direction. Brea tried to fire first, but Clara's shot resounded in the air a split second sooner. Thankfully, she missed.

Brea didn't.

The third bullet lodged in the middle of Clara's chest. She stumbled, then crumpled to the ground, prone and unmoving.

"Pierce!" Brea cried out as she ran across the yard toward him. "Are you all right?"

"Fine. Check her first," he barked.

Brea wanted to touch him more than anything, but the urgency in his voice reached through her trembling relief. "For what?"

"Kick the gun out of her hand, then see if she's breathing."

Brea did. No heartbeat. No exhalations. "I-I think she's dead."

Oh, God. She'd killed someone?

Behind her, someone clapped. She whirled to find Matt walking toward her. "I just caught the end of that. You did good, little thing."

"Did I?" Now that it was over, she felt overwhelmed and dizzy. She felt like throwing up.

Yes, she had killed someone. She had aimed a gun and pulled the trigger on another human being. It was horrible. The shock. The guilt. She wanted to cry.

But what would have happened if she hadn't?

"Catch her," Pierce shouted.

Brea heard his voice as if through a narrowing tunnel. The edges of her vision went black. She fell back.

Matt was right there to swing her up in his arms. "You're okay."

"I don't feel so good. And Pierce…"

"Take some deep breaths. He's fine. Let's go cut him loose."

"Got it," said another voice.

Matt whirled, and Brea caught sight of a tall man with a blond crew cut and a badass vibe.

"I'm Trevor," the newcomer said with a friendly head bob as he tucked away the gun in his hand. "You must be Walker's girl."

She nodded. "B-Brea."

"I'm Matt. Got a handcuff key?"

He nodded. "On it."

Brea gripped Matt's shirt as her head cleared. Her body shook as the adrenaline began to bleed from her veins, but she needed to get to Pierce now that she wasn't going to faint. At least she didn't think so. "You can put me down."

"You sure?" Matt raised a brow at her.

She squirmed. "I need Pierce."

"And he needs you." Matt set her on her feet, not letting go until she proved she was steady. "He's a lucky bastard."

There was someone out there for Matt, but Brea swallowed back the sentiment. Her first priority was to reach the man she loved.

As she strove to keep her balance, Trevor unlocked the handcuffs. They fell away. Pierce was free.

He didn't spare his friend even a glance. That black stare of his locked onto her, and he sprinted across the space separating them. Brea picked up her pace, too, willing her dizziness away. Her one and only thought was to reach him, touch him, be held by him.

Forever.

Tears streamed down her cheeks as she launched herself at him. Pierce caught her and held her tighter than he ever had.

Relief hit her like a two-by-four. Her legs gave out. Sobs took over.

"Shh." He pushed her hair from her face and searched her as if he couldn't look his fill. "You okay, baby?"

She nodded, but her tears kept falling.

Pierce was there to comfort her. "The first time you take a life is hard. I'm so sorry…"

Brea shook her head. She would recover from having to end Clara. She would never have survived if Pierce hadn't. "I'm just grateful we're both alive. I'm grateful you're all right and still with me and—"

"Always, pretty girl. From now until you take your last breath, I will always be with you."

chapter twelve

One-Mile rubbed his sweaty hands together, swallowed, then lifted his fist and did one of the most terrifying things in his life.

He knocked on Preacher Bell's quaint blue front door.

If this didn't go well, he was fucked.

Interminable moments passed before he heard footsteps across the hardwood floor, then the door swung open. The preacher stood expectantly with a blank expression. He was just shy of medium height and medium build with kind eyes and a guarded smile. One-Mile felt as if he eclipsed the man.

"Yes?"

This was it. Now or never. Make or break.

Time to find your manners, asshole. You remember those?

Blowing out a breath, he stuck out his hand. "Hi, sir. We haven't met yet, which is a mistake I'm here to rectify. Pierce Walker."

The instant he spoke his name, the preacher's face closed up. The man eyed him from the collar of his leather jacket to the tattoos peeking above the buttons of his shirt and down to the hard tips of his combat boots.

Fuck. The suit that had gotten ruined last night would have gone over far better.

Reverend Bell gave his hand a cautious shake. "It's good you came. This face-to-face is long overdue."

"I know. I'm sorry. Since Brea is on her way home with her car—"

"I know where my daughter is. I didn't last night, however," the man reminded sharply, arms crossed over his casual gray V-neck sweater.

And he was squarely to blame for that.

Yeah, this wasn't going to go well.

One-Mile nodded, doing his best not to let the preacher's hostility unnerve him. After spending most of the night panicking about his daughter's safety, he was entitled to be rattled. "Yes, sir. I'm sorry about that. But I'd like to talk through a few things before she arrives. Man to man."

The reverend considered him, then finally stepped aside with a nod. "Come in. I won't pretend to be excited that you're a part of my daughter's life. You stripped her innocence, used her, disgraced her, left her, put her in danger—"

"None of that was my intention, and I intend to take care of her from here."

Brea's father scowled and waved him onto the sofa in the homey living room. As One-Mile sat, the preacher lowered himself into an easy chair a few feet away, then cocked his head. "I'm willing to concede there are two sides to every story. I only know bits and pieces. If you think I've got it wrong, tell me yours."

"Both Brea and I will basically tell you the same story. We met and—"

"I doubt it's the same. She's in love with you."

Did her father think he wasn't mad about Brea in return? "I'm in love with her more."

That seemed to take Preacher Bell aback. "Then clearly, I don't understand what's happening. But I know what's troubling me. In today's day and age, things like tradition, marriage, and the family unit seem old-fashioned and unimportant to many—"

"Not to me. I want those things." He just needed a chance to prove that he could make Brea happy.

"I'm glad to hear that. I grew up in a house filled with faith, love, and constancy. I tried to give Brea the same after her mother passed away. She deserves that in the future."

"She does. You did an amazing job, sir. I love everything about her, especially her enormous heart. I've never known anyone as kind and compassionate."

The man's mouth twisted. "She was always that way—until she met you. Now she's secretive and willful and—"

"No, she's private. And with all due respect, she's not willful; she's an adult who shouldn't need your permission to live her life. She's become so self-aware and strong. After last night, I know she'll fight when she has to."

"Before you, she never needed to. She had never been in danger."

One-Mile couldn't refute that, so he didn't try. "I know you've always protected her. I respect that. But I promise you, I would lay down my life for her."

"I heard you tried last night." The reverend pressed his lips together. "So did you come here to tell me how you see my daughter?"

He didn't want to make enemies with this man. Brea was the one who would suffer most, and he'd do anything to avoid hurting her. "No. I came to introduce myself, clear the air, and talk about the future."

"You're very direct."

"In my line of work, I have to be."

"I don't approve of your line of work. It should be up to God to decide when someone's time is up."

One-Mile didn't want to get in a theological argument with the preacher; he'd lose. But he needed the man to understand his world.

"As a society, we've organized for war. We recognize that some enemy combatants target innocents as leverage. When these combatants become an eminent threat, someone with the will and the backbone is tasked with putting down the threat. I'm that someone. It's a responsibility I take seriously. I have to live with the blood on my hands and the deaths on my conscience. But I *can* bear it to keep people like you, your fiancée, and Brea unharmed." He raised a brow at the man. "Could you handle that responsibility?"

Reverend Bell was mute, his expression considering. Then he sighed. "No."

"Without people like me, how many more lives would we grieve?"

"Even one is too many," the man admitted, though his tone said he didn't like the logic or One-Mile's job.

"You don't condemn Brea for ending Clara Montilla last night to save me, herself, and our baby, do you?"

"No." He shook his head. "She did what she had to."

At least they saw eye-to-eye on something. "I've come today because I want you to know that I love Brea more than anything. I never expected someone like her in my life. She stole my heart the moment I laid eyes on her. Nothing and no one has ever been more important to me. It was never my intention to disgrace her, you, or your church. I didn't intend to get her pregnant, but I won't say I'm sorry for it. I am sorry, however, that things outside of my control kept me from meeting you sooner and assuring you that I want to make Brea my wife and raise our family together. So I've come to ask for your blessing."

Brea's father was silent for so long One-Mile started to sweat. But he forced himself to remain still, regulate his breathing, mute his panic, and meet the man's direct gaze.

"I know nothing about you, your character, your family, or your faith. How can you expect me to simply hand over my only daughter, whom I love with all my heart, to a stranger?"

One-Mile had thought about this. "I could answer in one of two ways. Strictly being matter of fact? I'm here as a favor to you. I'll do or say whatever it takes to make Brea my wife. I will never stop, never tire, and never give up. I want a life with love and laughter, compassion, and a reason to come home after what often feels like war. Brea wants that, too. With me. If you make her choose…not to be harsh, but you won't win. So I'm here apologizing and willing to get down on one knee to ask for her hand. Mostly for her sake. But for yours, too."

The preacher didn't like that answer. "And if I refuse, would you take her from me?"

"Do you want her to deny what's in her heart so she doesn't leave you?"

His face tightened. "Don't manipulate me."

One-Mile held up his hands. "I'm just being honest. The other way of looking at this is, I want to pay you my respects. You've raised a remarkable woman. I admire and love Brea with my whole heart. As the man who wants to share her life, it's my responsibility to ensure she has whatever she needs or desires." He withdrew his phone, opened to his photos, and set the device in her father's hands. "I own my home in Lafayette outright. The next ten pictures encompass the exterior and interior. She can redecorate however she wants."

The man flipped through the pictures with vague consideration but said nothing.

"The next two pictures are screenshots of my bank balance and investment portfolio."

Reverend Bell kept flipping, his brows rising when he scanned the images that proved his seven-figure worth. "You've clearly saved."

"Virtually everything. I inherited some, and I've invested well."

"She doesn't care about money."

One-Mile knew that. "She's never even asked how much money I have, and I've never mentioned it. But I'm offering you proof that I can take care of her for your peace of mind."

"Materially, you can far better than I have."

And that obviously didn't hold much weight with the good preacher. "I also understand Brea well enough to grasp that she values harmony. Cutter and I will have to bury the hatchet. He's pissed at me for breaking protocol on a mission because I sensed a trap and I was right. But I'll apologize, swallow my pride, and be the bigger man because I know what he means to her."

Brea's father nodded, his expression slightly less guarded. "A great deal. He always has."

"That brings me to you. If we can't get along, she'll never be happy. That's not something I can live with. So what do you need from me to make sure there's no wedge between us? Name it. If it's within my power, it's yours."

"I don't suppose you'd be willing to walk away and let her find someone else?"

"Who does that benefit? Not me. Not Brea. Definitely not our son—"

"Son?" He pressed his lips together. "I didn't even know she was having a boy."

That tore Brea's dad apart, and One-Mile softened. "She wanted to tell me first. We're thrilled. I hope you can be, too."

The man sighed. "My grandson will need a positive male role model growing up."

"My son will need *me*." Despite having no one to emulate, One-Mile would do his absolute fucking best to be a good dad. "If you think past your anger, my leaving wouldn't benefit you in the long run, either. If you managed to guilt Brea into cutting me loose, she'd eventually resent you for it."

Reverend Bell exhaled deeply and closed his eyes in defeat. "I know."

At least he was man enough to admit it. "We'd like to start our lives together, sir."

"Jasper."

That was a good sign, right? "Jasper, the only thing keeping us apart now is you."

The man said nothing, but his face told One-Mile he saw the ugly truth for himself. "I'll bet you're a real bastard at work."

He smiled. "So I'm told."

"If someone had lined up a thousand men and told me that my daughter's chosen mate was among them, you're the last one I would have picked."

"If it's any consolation, she took me completely by surprise, too." Since he was finally getting somewhere, One-Mile inched forward on the sofa. "I know we're not off to a good start. But you and I want the same thing: a happy Brea. Will you work with me?"

Before Jasper could answer, the door crashed open, and Brea ran in, her long brown waves tumbling around her. On autopilot, One-Mile stood. Like every other time he set eyes on her, his heart thumped. But today, emotion clogged his throat. She was almost his. And she looked so beautiful he couldn't stop staring.

Vaguely, he was aware of Jasper watching him.

"Hi, pretty girl," One-Mile managed to scratch out.

Her gaze fell on them and her eyes flared wide. "You're here already?"

Her father got to his feet. Together, they approached her. One-Mile hung back.

"We're just talking, sweetheart." The preacher kissed her cheek and squeezed her as if he feared losing her. "Why don't you join us?"

She looked nervous, her flustered gaze darting back and forth between them as if she'd half expected an argument or violence. "Sure." She took in the empty table between them. "Before I sit down, coffee? Tea?" She sent him an apologetic glance. "We don't have anything harder."

He waved her off. "I'm fine."

"Nothing for me," her father said.

"O-okay." She set her purse and keys down, then sank to the sofa beside her father. "What did I miss?"

"Pierce was apologizing that we hadn't met previously."

"And?" Brea glanced tensely between them, as if she was braced for conflict.

"Like your dad said, we're talking."

"He asked me for your hand."

A smile crept across her face as she reached out, slipping her palm in his own. "And?"

"We're talking about that, too. But before he answers, I need to say something." One-Mile took a deep breath. "You need to know everything before you decide if you truly want to marry me."

She stilled. "You're going to tell me about your father?"

He nodded, his gut in knots. "I won't lie. I've avoided this because I didn't want you to look at me like a monster."

"Pierce, I already know—"

"You don't." He turned to Jasper. "I want you to hear this, sir, because I fully admit I'm far from perfect. But if you give your consent, I want you to know exactly the son-in-law you'll be getting. I want your blessing to be real." He grimaced. "And I only want to say this once."

The preacher nodded, his expression neutral, but his demeanor said it would probably be a cold day in hell.

Yeah, he'd figured. The man thought he was a lunatic with bloodlust coursing in his veins. That there was a nonstop circus of violence in his head. That he fed his soul by stealing the life from others. Baring his past wasn't going to help.

But he had to do this for Brea.

"Your daughter knows I was fifteen when I killed my father. She doesn't know the circumstances."

Brea, bless her big heart, gripped his hand tighter. "I want to hear it all. I'll be here for you, no matter what you say."

One-Mile wasn't so sure about that. She wasn't equipped to understand his father's brand of filthy depravity. Nor was the preacher. But she deserved to know who and what she was getting in a husband. To keep her, he would gladly rip open every old wound and gouge out his fucking soul.

And he prayed this wasn't the last time she looked at him with love in her eyes.

He squeezed her dainty hand one last time, then let go. They would either succeed or fail based on the next five minutes. "My mom died when I was a baby."

Brea nodded. "We've talked about having that in common."

The information had been more for Jasper's edification than hers. But he went on. "Growing up, it was just me and my dad, except the summers I spent in Wyoming with my grandpa. If not for him, I probably would have ended up a sociopath. Because from the time I was about four, I knew something was wrong. Not just because I didn't have a mom like the other kids. But because I spent a lot of my time alone."

Brea frowned. "You mean without him or…"

"Alone. He eked out a living by fixing cars in the freestanding garage he built in our yard. Hell of a mechanic. I got maybe a tenth of his aptitude there. He could fix anything. He modified guns on the side, too."

"Is that where you learned to shoot?"

"The basics."

One-Mile blew out another breath. He was nervous as fuck. Already he could tell this story would be a jumbled-ass mess. He'd never told it. Hell, he avoided thinking about it.

"The rest"—he shrugged—"I picked up here and there. It's not important. But my dad was always violent."

Brea held her breath. "Abusive?"

He shook his head. "Not like that. Not when I was a little kid. He had a crappy temper. I knew when to run and hide. We had a lot of walls with holes in them."

Brea flinched. Her father shifted in his seat uncomfortably.

Shit. He was just getting warmed up. "But he didn't hit me. Mostly Dad was antisocial. He worked alone. He didn't have friends. We didn't know anyone in town. People who tried to be neighborly or lend a helping hand, he rebuffed."

Jasper raised a brow. "Cutter said you do the same at work."

He pulled at the back of his neck. "Yeah. Old habit. I should probably break it. Anyway, he'd work all day…and often go out all night. It wasn't uncommon for me to wake up at three a.m. and be alone."

"He just left you?" Brea looked horrified. "A young child? By yourself?"

"He told me I was a little soldier and to man up. So I did. He was gruff, but it wasn't awful…until one of two things happened. He got drunk or he got laid. One inevitably led to the other. But whenever he got a girlfriend and she moved in, that's when he became a real prick. If there was one thing my father was, it was a misogynist. God, he hated women. He wanted them, too. And he hated himself for wanting them. He never had the money for hookers. Everyone would have been happier if he had."

"That's horrible! Why would you say that?" Brea sounded shocked. "It's so dirty and impersonal and—"

"Yeah, but it would have been less destructive. When he had a girlfriend, he had a pattern… He'd be alone for a few weeks, maybe a few months. Then he'd get the itch. He'd go out, get drunk, and come home with some woman. If he liked her opening-night 'audition,' he'd ask her to move in a week or two later. Most of them were all right. A few got freaked out by the idea of being a replacement mommy or something, so they didn't stay long. Dad resented the hell out of me then. He never held back on all the things that were my fault. I'd made my mom fat and I'd made her sad. And I'd definitely been the reason she left us. That's what he told me. Eventually, I found out he lied."

"Oh, Pierce…" Brea took his hand again, her big heart opening to spill compassion for him. She was willing to give him everything inside her, and he motherfucking hated to take from her, but right now he needed her fortitude.

So he held her tight and squeezed…then let her go. He had miles to go before he could earn her touch again. "The women who didn't seem to mind that Dad had a kid wore out their welcome eventually. Then they'd run into Dad's temper. And his fists would come out. It was never pretty."

Brea looked horrified. "You saw him beat his girlfriends?"

"More than once. I knew it was wrong, but I was just a kid, so I couldn't stop it. But Dad was like a powder keg. I always knew when the explosion was coming, and I tried to tell them every damn time. Most didn't listen."

"How did he not get arrested?"

"He did a few times. But most of the women just left battered and never came back. Maybe they were ashamed. I don't know." He let out a breath. This was so fucking hard. "After they'd gone, I was usually sad. They were often the women who really tried. They read me bedtime stories and cooked. They were almost like a mom. It was nice while it lasted."

"Pierce…"

He didn't look at Brea. "It wasn't all bad. My grandpa kept me normal and sane. Those summers with my mom's dad…they were everything. He taught me about normalcy, self-discipline and control, anger management. And watching him with my grandma until she died of cancer taught me about love." He shook his head, wishing like hell he could stop here. "I dreaded fall, hated every time Grandpa put me on a plane back home."

"Did you ever ask your dad if you could just stay?"

"Sure. I was about eight. Matt and I were best friends. I loved the ranch. I liked the people and the big open spaces. But Dad said if I had too much of my grandparents coddling me that I'd turn into a pussy. I stopped asking because I knew if I didn't, he'd never let me go again." He turned to Jasper. "Sorry. I know my language sucks."

"Brea forewarned me." The preacher didn't sound amused…but he didn't sound hostile anymore. He was listening.

One-Mile could work with that.

"When I came home, Dad usually had a new woman. He liked them young; most were barely eighteen. It wasn't so creepy when I was little because Dad wasn't much older than they were. But by the time I was a teenager, he was in his thirties…" When both Brea and her dad grimaced, One-Mile had little hope the rest of this would go well. "The real shit started when puberty hit me. I shot up quick and I was built big. I had a full beard before I was fifteen. Most people thought I was a grown man, especially Dad's girlfriends. He started introducing me as his little brother because otherwise I made him look old. And the girls started coming on to me."

She pressed a hand to her chest. "You didn't."

Jesus, he didn't want to continue.

"I did. A lot." He closed his eyes because if he saw her disappointment, he didn't know if he could get out the ugliest parts. "I'm not going to candy-coat and I'm not going to lie. It was a lot like having my own live-in girlfriend. I was probably the only freshman in high school nailing a pretty girl every night."

Her mouth dropped open. "Did your dad know?"

"Oh, yeah. He condoned it. Said it would make me a man." He wouldn't tell her about his first time now. He'd been thirteen and trembling when his father had shoved Katie, his then-girlfriend, into his room and announced that he was going out drinking. He'd told Katie to put her pussy to good use and left. She'd wanted to please the asshole. They both had. So they'd fucked.

"He doesn't sound like a good person or a good father. I pray for you," Jasper offered.

One-Mile had never been one to ask for divine assistance, but if it brought him any absolution, he'd take it. "Thank you."

"What happened?"

He hated the way Brea's voice shook and he wanted to reach out, touch her. He didn't dare until he got this out and unless she said she wanted his touch again. "The summer before I turned sixteen, I got a girlfriend of my own. Allie was twenty. I'd lied and told her I was her age. Dad saw me out with her the night before I left for Wyoming that summer, but I brushed it off. They'd said a polite hello and that was it. But I didn't hear from Allie much over the next few months. Then again, I was busy. She had a job. I hoped it was fine…but I worried what I'd find when I got home. I never imagined she was shacking up with my dad."

Brea's jaw dropped. "He was sleeping with your girlfriend?"

"He didn't think I would mind sharing since he'd never been stingy. But I was pissed. Even before I left, I knew Allie and I were doomed because she would eventually figure out I'd lied about my age. But she was nice. I'd hoped we could make something for a while." One-Mile shook his head. "When I got home from Wyoming, she told me she was in love."

"With your father? How?"

He shrugged. "In retrospect, I think she had self-esteem issues. He treated her as crappy as she expected to be treated. I tried to suck it up and not be too pissed off. But I resented the hell out of him every time I watched them kiss and every time I heard them going at it in the next room. Since some of his other girlfriends, as they were leaving, had made the mistake of telling him they preferred me, I think he secretly liked the fact he'd taken Allie away. Made him feel superior and more manly."

"That's horrible." Brea searched his face like she was trying to understand. "But I hope that isn't why you killed him."

"No. I just wanted to punch the shit out of him, but I didn't. Allie wasn't right for me and she'd made her choice. To avoid the two of them, I started going out a lot. Drinking, getting high, racing cars. I should have died a hundred times at least."

"God must have been looking out for you," Jasper said.

"You're probably right." One-Mile didn't see another explanation. "I have no idea why."

Except so that he could grow up and love Brea. She was his purpose in life. His mission.

"Anyway, about a month after school started, I came home one night late. I could hear Allie screaming from down the street. I went running and I burst in to see my dad beating the fuck out of her. I thought at first it was because he'd had his fill of her, and I cursed myself for being so absent that I hadn't seen it coming. But I quickly figured out that she'd broken Dad's one cardinal rule: never get knocked up."

Brea gasped. "Did your father know she was pregnant?"

"Yeah. That's why he was beating her, punching her stomach over and over. I screamed at him to stop. He wouldn't. I fought him, got in a few punches. But he was meaner. He clocked me good. I stumbled out and called the police, but they were at least ten minutes away. I didn't think Allie's baby would last that long. Hell, I doubted she would either." He swallowed. "I went and got a gun."

"Oh, my gosh." Brea paled.

"I fucking demanded he stop. I thought if I threatened him he would. But he didn't. He just called her a dirty slut, said he didn't want any more brats, whether they were his...or mine. He told her he was going to deal with her the way he'd dealt with my mom. Then he put his hands around her neck and squeezed."

"D-did he...kill your mother?" Brea looked horrified.

One-Mile didn't blame her. "Yeah. And he admitted that like he was proud. So when Allie started choking and turning blue, I knew he'd do it again."

"So you killed him," Jasper finished quietly.

"Yeah." His fucking voice broke.

"Oh…" Brea wrapped her small hands around his. "He didn't leave you much choice."

Dad hadn't.

But One-Mile sometimes worried he wasn't any better. He had killed so many, taken their blood and ended their lives. Despite that, Brea, with her pure heart, comforted him, stroking his knuckles as tears ran down her cheeks. He knew she wasn't crying for Allie or her father. She was crying for him.

Tears stung his eyes, too. He blinked and clenched his jaw and tried not to fucking lose it.

"What happened?"

After he'd cried like a baby? "My grandpa came down. He stayed for a few months, but then he got sick and passed away. I barely managed to drive him back to Wyoming in time. Then…I was alone."

"You were just a kid."

"Sixteen. But honestly, I'd been alone most of my life. Allie lost her baby, but she did me a favor. She convinced the courts that she'd been the closest thing I'd had to a mother, and because I was a problem child, they were more than happy to let her take custody of me. But it was just on paper. She moved back in with her parents, and I lived at home off Grandpa's money until I graduated. When I turned eighteen I sold everything, invested it all, and joined the Marines. You know the rest."

Then he clutched her hands, terrified he'd see condemnation or disgust in her eyes. Instead, she rose and threw herself against him, pressing her cheek to his chest and wrapping her arms around him as if she meant to heal every one of his hurts with her love and devotion.

One-Mile couldn't hold back. He enveloped her, relief flooding him until he nearly went weak-kneed—and he lost all sense of composure. He didn't know what he'd done to deserve this woman, but he'd wake up every day and do his best to be worthy of her.

"Pretty girl, don't cry, especially for me." He stroked her head. "Your tears hurt too much."

"Oh, Pierce… I can't believe how horribly you've suffered."

"It was all a long time ago… It's okay."

"It's not. You've suffered even since I've met you. I'm so, so sorry," she sobbed. "I wish I could take it all away and make it better. I wish—"

"You do, baby. You have from the very moment you let me into your life." He kissed the top of her head and looked over her, at Jasper.

Compassion softened the man's kind face. Acceptance filled his eyes that brimmed with tears. "You survived hell, and the fact you did whatever it took to save someone smaller and weaker tells me a lot about who you are. God forgives all. I can't do any less. You have my blessing...son." The man swallowed thickly and stuck out his hand. "Take care of her."

One-Mile's chest twisted as he shook it. "Yes, sir. Thank you. I will."

The preacher might never like him, but the man understood that he would love Brea every moment of every day because no other woman would ever have any part of his heart. Jasper knew he would protect her and their children to his dying breath.

For now, that was enough.

Brea raised her head from his chest and looked up at him with big golden eyes full of love. "I want to make the rest of your life so happy."

"Yeah?" He reached into his pocket and pulled out the little box he'd stashed there. Then he opened it to reveal the simple, winking solitaire. "You could do that by marrying me. Still want to?"

He'd never imagined he would ever do something as traditional as get down on one knee to propose, but for Brea he'd go to any lengths to prove how much he loved her.

"Yes." She nodded furiously as more tears fell. "Yes!"

With his heart soaring, he slid the ring on her finger, brushed the moisture from her cheeks, and pressed a resounding kiss on her lips. "Thank God. I can't wait. Can we get married on Saturday?"

She laughed. "No, but we will soon. Because I can't wait, either. There's nothing I want more than to spend the rest of my life with you."

"You *are* my life. I love you, pretty girl."

epilogue

Monday, January 26

Feeling like he might crawl out of his skin, Zyron paced the reception area of EM Security Management. Thank fuck he was finally home. The last two weeks he'd spent in Speck-on-a-Map, Texas, had been fourteen days too many. The good news: Their mission there was over. Cutter's wedding to Shealyn West had gone off mostly without a hitch and the creepy-as-fuck cult down the road had been shut down in a hail of yeehaw and gunfire. The bad news: His wholly dependable fellow operator, Josiah Grant, had fallen for Shealyn's sister, Maggie, gotten the girl, and decided to stay behind. Now the organization had a new guy to break in, the fucking small-town deputy from Maggie's hometown. Zy snorted. In a team full of SEALs, Green Berets, and other elite warriors, he didn't see this Rosco P. Coltrane working out. Yeah, Kane Preston had some military experience and he'd seemed all right, but c'mon… At least the hazing would be fun. But the worst news: He was going through withdrawals because he hadn't seen his sweet confection of female, Tessa Lawrence, since leaving on assignment.

Now it was Monday morning, and she was late.

Was something wrong?

Logan Edgington approached him, black coffee in hand. "You have a desk."

He did—way in the back and around the corner where he couldn't see Tess walk through the front door. Logan knew it. But Zy didn't dare admit that aloud. EM Security Management had a strict nonfraternization clause. No dating or physical relationships with co-workers. Violating the policy was grounds for job termination. The whole thing would have been funny as fuck since the company was mostly straight-as-an-arrow males…except that it had screwed him from doing more than stare at Tessa and stroking his dick raw to filthy, dirty thoughts of her.

And Logan knew that, too.

"Waiting to say hey to the new guy," Zy lied.

Logan shot him a dubious stare over the rim of his mug. "Sure, you are. Lucky for you, Kane is already here, finishing up some paperwork with Joaquin. I'll take you right to him since you're so eager to shake his hand."

Bastard. His boss was calling his bluff. "What the fuck do you want?"

"A sit-down. Conference room. Five minutes. Come with less attitude. We've got a mission for you."

He'd just gotten back, goddamn it. Yeah, yeah… This was his life, and he'd signed up for this job. He was often gone for weeks at a time with almost no advance warning. But his gut was twitching about Tess. Before he'd gone, something had upset her. She'd freaked out and clammed up. Stopped talking. Started avoiding him. He wanted answers.

But he'd have to get them later.

Zy didn't bother to swallow down his sarcasm. "Can't wait."

"Don't worry. You're going to love this mission," Logan assured with an evil grin. "Right before you hate it."

Then the son of a bitch disappeared.

What the fuck did that mean? He didn't have time to figure it out before the door behind him opened.

Zy turned. And there she was, his gorgeous bundle of blonde, all big green eyes, lush mouth, and tits for days. He'd missed her Southern sass and bless-your-hearts. Jesus, the sight of her after two miserable weeks away had his breath catching and his body pinging.

Yeah, he had it bad for Tess…and every fucking person on this team knew it.

She dumped her keys in her little pink clutch and looked up. She stopped mid-stride when their gazes locked. Her breath caught on a soft gasp. The heavens fucking parted; he felt it.

Why did he have to be fixated on the one woman he couldn't have?

She sent him a breathless smile. "You're back!"

Zy wanted to touch her so damn bad—and he didn't dare. Not only would he get fired but he'd been assured he would never work in this "town" again, as the saying went.

He'd wanted Tess for ten agonizing months. Seeing her almost every day and never having her felt like ten years of torture…and a decade of foreplay.

"Got back last night," he managed to say past the knot in his throat. "You okay?"

Another smile, this one less genuine. "Fine."

"Baby okay?"

Adoration softened her eyes. "She's fine. Walking everywhere now. I can hardly keep up."

"What about—"

"Let's go, Garrett," Hunter Edgington called out as he made his way to the conference room. "Shit's hitting the fan and time's wasting."

Zy gritted his teeth. "Got to go. Lunch later?"

Her smile disappeared. Her gaze fell. "You know we shouldn't. After what happened last time—"

"Nothing happened." Absolutely fucking nothing—no matter how badly he'd wished otherwise.

"Okay, almost happened," she whispered. "You're splitting hairs."

"I'm being factual."

But she was right. He'd been close to saying fuck it all and kissing her senseless until she'd lost her clothes.

Tessa sent him a pleading expression. "This job pays better than everything else. I need it."

As a single mom with an undependable ex, she probably did. And if he hadn't burned a million bridges and come here to start over, he might not have needed this job so badly, too.

Fuck.

"I know. I just want to talk to you. I won't..." *Touch you, try to seduce you, tell you all the lascivious ways I'm dying to make you scream.* He cleared his throat. "I'll be a gentleman. Please. I just missed your voice."

Didn't he sound pathetic?

She sighed like she couldn't refuse him. Fuck, he wished that was true.

"A-all right."

"I'll come around about noon."

Tessa smiled at him again, this one so real and pure he wanted to lose himself in it. "Looking forward to it."

"Now, Garrett," Joaquin Muñoz growled as he stuck his head around the corner. "For fuck's sake..."

"Go," she encouraged. "Whatever it is seems important."

It did, and that didn't bode well for a peaceful Monday.

"If something comes up, I'll let you know," Zy promised, then stomped down the hall, hung a left, and barreled into the conference room, trying not to snarl. "I'm here. What's up?"

None of his bosses spoke. After the rush and hurry, now they were all silent?

Whatever. Zy studied the new guy. Around six foot and built broad with an obvious hard-on for bodybuilding, he had piercing dark eyes, a black mustache, and a watchful mien.

"You met Kane Preston?" Hunter offered.

"Briefly." While all the shit had been going down with the creepy cult, the deputy had been cleaning up the absent sheriff's mess.

"Josiah highly recommended him, said he'd done an excellent job the last couple of years in Comfort."

Kane stuck out his hand. "But I was looking to make a change. Some folks call me Scout. But as long as you don't call me motherfucker, I'll probably answer."

Zy clapped his hand in the other guy's. "I'm Chase Garrett. Most people around here just call me Zyron."

"Good to see you."

"Got everything you need now?" Joaquin asked the former deputy.

"I do," Kane replied. "I'll go make myself useful."

"Perfect," Logan said to the guy's wide, retreating back. The minute he'd gone, his boss turned an annoyed gaze his way. "Shut the door. We need to talk."

Sighing, Zy did, then took his seat in the nearest chair, across the table from Logan. "What's up?"

"We need to get to the bottom of some shit. Up until now, the only people who knew the location of Valeria Montilla's new safe house were the three of us and One-Mile. At least until last night."

Zy froze. Valeria and her sister, Laila, had been through hell. Valeria's husband, Emilo, was finally dead, but his thugs and that criminal bunch from his splinter offshoot of the cartel had wreaked absolute destruction on those women's lives.

"What happened?"

"Someone broke into their new digs in Orlando. Valeria was at a concert, thankfully. But Laila stayed behind to babysit her nephew. She and Baby Jorge barely escaped with their lives. We have to relocate them now."

"You need me to go?" He hated to pack another fucking suitcase, but to save them from being snuffed and slaughtered, he gladly would—no questions asked.

"No. We're sending Kane and Trees today to bring them back here."

Hunter jumped in. "A couple months ago, we started working on a plan to relocate Valeria and her family nearby, then shit happened…"

Over the last few months? Yeah, had it ever.

"And you've got everything in place now?" Zy asked.

He nodded. "We'll be watching their new safe house ourselves. But we worry it's for nothing until you figure out who our fucking mole is. If it's not Trees, we need you to prove it *now*."

He tried to keep a leash on his temper. "I know you all have a boner to blame him, but he isn't guilty."

Hunter sent him a cutting glare. "Forgive me if we're not willing to just take your word about your bestie."

"I've spent two fucking months digging. I've seen zero evidence he's leaked even a drop of urine out of this place, much less critical secrets. Seriously, I took him with me to Comfort so we could isolate him, just like you insisted. We slept in the same bunkhouse. I dug through his phone. Unless he was shitting or showering, I watched him. He's done nothing, and I don't know what you want as proof that he's innocent."

The trio fell silent and exchanged glances.

Hunter raised a brow. "Here's what we know. It's not the three of us. It's not One-Mile. It's not you, Cutter, or Josiah. That leaves Trees."

"Or…" Logan cut in before Zy could push back, "Tessa."

It was all he could do not to punch the asshole. "No. Fuck no. She's the goddamn receptionist. She doesn't have access to those secrets."

"We didn't think so either. But now we're rethinking."

"This is bullshit."

"Shut up and listen," Joaquin growled. "We've eliminated every other possibility. It's either your bestie or your girl."

"She's not my girl," he objected automatically.

Logan rolled his eyes. "Oh, please. We all know you're one bad decision away from breaking your contract...unless you already have and there's something you want to tell us?"

"I haven't touched her."

The three of them exchanged another glance, then seemed to come to some silent conclusion he wasn't privy to.

"Then here's the deal: You've got two weeks to figure out which one of them is guilty or we're letting them both go."

"What?"

Hunter picked up where his brother left off. "We made it easier for you by sending Trees out of town for a week. Invent a reason you need to stay at his place while he's gone. Search it from top to bottom. If he's got dirt, you need to hand it the fuck over."

"He doesn't." Zy knew he kept repeating that, but Trees wouldn't stab him—or anyone else—in the back like that.

"Now you get to find out for sure...at the same time you investigate Tessa."

Were they insane? "How? You sending her out of town, too?"

"Nope." Logan reached behind him and plucked a file folder off his credenza, then whipped out a small pile of papers held together by a staple. He flipped a few pages, drew a giant X on one, then jotted something in the margin. He passed it to his brothers next. Each of them also scribbled on the side. Finally, Logan shoved the document back in the folder and slid it down the table to him. "You're welcome."

Zy opened the folder and found his employment contract inside. The nonfraternization clause had been crossed out. All three of them had initialed.

They had removed the restrictions keeping him from pursuing Tessa? Even the goddamn idea made his skin tingle.

When he looked up, Logan smiled. "Yes, you're now free to fuck her. Congratulations. But you better think with something other than your dick."

Too late. His dick was already having a party...and his conscience was choking on guilt. The only way to get close to her was to deceive her?

"No." He couldn't do that to Tessa.

Joaquin shrugged. "Told you we should have just fired Trees and Tess and been done with it."

It took everything he had not to jump out of his seat and tell them to go fuck themselves. "Neither of them deserves that."

"No?" Hunter shrugged. "Then prove it."

Over the past ten months, he'd seen the three of them push, shove, and maneuver some of his fellow operators into tight spaces and corners to get what they wanted. Zy had always been careful to keep his nose clean, so he'd never had it happen to him. He'd even wondered if the rumors were an exaggeration. But no.

They really were manipulative motherfuckers.

"Tessa won't touch me. She needs this job."

Joaquin flashed him a rare smile. "I'm going to take her aside this morning and present her with a new contract. Better sick pay and vacation, tighter non-disclosure...and no nonfraternization clause. She'll sign. Then you're both off the hook."

Goddamn it. Their coercion pissed him off. But the thought of touching Tess while proving she'd done nothing wrong? "Fine. I'm in."

"We know." Logan sounded like an arrogant prick. "You've got two weeks. Get a move on."

He clenched his jaw against some choice words that would probably get him fired and stood. As he marched for the door, it crashed open. In walked a man he hadn't imagined he'd see in this office ever again.

Caleb Edgington looked shell-shocked, like he'd collided with panic and run face-first into death.

What the fuck was wrong? "Colonel, sir?"

Hunter and Logan both stood. Joaquin, not far behind, rose with a frown.

"Dad?" Hunter approached him.

The older man swallowed. "Your sister..."

Sudden tension gripped the room.

"What's wrong with Kimber?" Logan scowled.

"I received a threat a couple of weeks ago. It wasn't specific, just a tube of lipstick and a warning to hand over Valeria Montilla before they took whoever the tube belonged to. I didn't know who—" Emotion choked off the colonel's words. He pressed his fist to his lips, grasping for the fortitude to finish delivering the bad news.

Zy stood in shock, his gut twisting. The man's only daughter, Hunter and Logan's sister...

Another guy came in behind the colonel—big, blond, badass, and totally pissed off. Deke Trenton, Kimber's husband. "She's gone. She dropped the kids off at preschool, then made a trip to the grocery store...and didn't come home. A courier delivered this thirty minutes ago."

They all crowded around as he whipped out a picture of Kimber, her auburn hair tangled, her big eyes red rimmed, with a gag over her mouth, her hands tied behind her back, and a gun to her head.

Oh, holy shit.

"We'll get her back." Despite having gone ghostly pale, Hunter found his voice. "We'll do whatever it takes—"

"You're fucking right we will," Deke spat. "I want my kitten back. Jack and the rest of the Oracle team are at our offices strategizing. Any help you can spare..."

"You'll have it," Hunter promised. "We need to lock down the rest of the wives and kids."

"Fast," the colonel managed. "Before it's too late."

The older man ducked out, looking as if he could barely keep himself together.

Deke didn't look much calmer. "Thanks for whatever you can do."

"Fuck that, she's our sister. We'll devote day and night to saving her."

Kimber's husband nodded, then he was gone. Silence prevailed for a protracted moment. Then Hunter swallowed, collecting himself first. He turned to ice in an instant. Logan lived up to his fiery temper, grabbing an eraser from the nearest whiteboard then throwing it violently. His empty coffee mug followed next, shattering against the wall.

Before he could toss anything else, Joaquin stepped in. "We don't have time."

"I know. I fucking know. Goddamn son of a bitch!"

Hunter and Joaquin raced out the door, already strategizing to keep all the others in their family safe. Logan fumed, trying to gather himself, his lungs working like a bellows.

"I'll come with you," Zy offered. "I'll devote all my energy—"

"No. This shit is centered around Valeria Montilla. Trees and Kane are going to protect and relocate her pronto—and we'll be monitoring every step. But none of that will mean shit if you can't figure out our mole. Two fucking weeks—max—or they're both off the fucking payroll and we bury them professionally. If you fail, we'll do the same to your fucking ass, too."

Logan tore out of the conference room, slamming the door behind him. After some shouting in the hall and more door slamming in the distance, the office fell silent.

Two weeks? Zy cursed. He had to start planning and setting some wheels in motion now—or they were all fucked.

When the woman he loves becomes the enemy, he'll seduce her for the truth.
Zyron and Tessa, part one—next in the Wicked & Devoted series.

WICKED AS LIES
Zyron and Tessa, Part One
Wicked & Devoted, Book 3
By Shayla Black
February 9, 2021!

Thank you for joining me in the new Wicked & Devoted world. In case you didn't know, this cast of characters started in my Wicked Lovers world, continued into my Devoted Lovers series, and have collided here. Between Wicked as Sin and Wicked Ever After, you've read about a few other characters who may interest you. I've already told some of their stories. Others are still to come. Below is a guide in case you'd like to read more from this cast, listed in order of release:

Wicked Lovers

Wicked Ties
Jack Cole (and Morgan O'Malley)
She didn't know what she wanted…until he made her beg for it.

Decadent
Deke Trenton (and Kimber Edgington)
The boss' innocent daughter. A forbidden favor he can't refuse…

Surrender to Me
Hunter Edgington (and Katalina Muñoz)
A secret fantasy. An uncontrollable obsession. A forever love?

Belong to Me
Logan Edgington (and Tara Jacobs)
He's got everything under control until he falls for his first love…again.

Mine to Hold
Tyler Murphy (Delaney Catalano)
His best friend's ex. A night he can't forget. A secret that could destroy them both.

Wicked All the Way
Caleb Edgington (and Carlotta Muñoz Buckley)
Could their second chance be their first real love?

His to Take
Joaquin Muñoz (and Bailey Benson)
Giving into her dark stranger might be the most delicious danger of all…

Falling in Deeper
Stone Sutter (and Lily Taylor)
Will her terrifying past threaten their passionate future?

Holding on Tighter
Heath Powell (and Jolie Quinn)
Mixing business with pleasure can be a dangerous proposition…

Devoted Lovers

Devoted to Pleasure
Cutter Bryant (and Shealyn West)
A bodyguard should never fall for his client…but she's too tempting to refuse.

Devoted to Wicked
Cage Bryant (and Karis Quinn)
Will the one-night stand she tried to forget seduce her into a second chance?

Devoted to Love
Josiah Grant (and Magnolia West)
He was sent to guard her body…but he's determined to steal her heart.

As the Wicked & Devoted world continues to collide and explode, you'll see more titles with other characters you know and love. So stay tuned for books about:

Zyron (Chase Garrett)
Trees (Forest Scott)
And more!

I have *so* much in store for you on this wild, wicked ride!

Happy reading!

Shayla

also by
SHAYLA BLACK

CONTEMPORARY ROMANCE

MORE THAN WORDS

More Than Want You
More Than Need You
More Than Love You
More Than Crave You
More Than Tempt You
More Than Pleasure You (novella)
More Than Dare You
More Than Protect You (novella)
Coming Soon:
More Than Hate You (Summer 2021)

WICKED & DEVOTED

Wicked as Sin
Wicked Ever After
Coming Soon:
Wicked as Lies (February 9, 2021)
Wicked and True (March 16, 2021)

THE WICKED LOVERS (Complete Series)
Wicked Ties
Decadent
Delicious
Surrender to Me
Belong to Me
Wicked to Love (novella)
Mine to Hold
Wicked All the Way (novella)
Ours to Love
Wicked All Night (novella)
Forever Wicked (novella)
Theirs to Cherish
His to Take
Pure Wicked (novella)
Wicked for You
Falling in Deeper
Dirty Wicked (novella)
A Very Wicked Christmas (short)
Holding on Tighter

THE DEVOTED LOVERS (Complete Series)
Devoted to Pleasure
Devoted to Wicked (novella)
Devoted to Love

THE PERFECT GENTLEMEN (Complete Series)
(by Shayla Black and Lexi Blake)

Scandal Never Sleeps
Seduction in Session
Big Easy Temptation
Smoke and Sin
At the Pleasure of the President

MASTERS OF MÉNAGE
(by Shayla Black and Lexi Blake)

Their Virgin Captive
Their Virgin's Secret
Their Virgin Concubine
Their Virgin Princess
Their Virgin Hostage
Their Virgin Secretary
Their Virgin Mistress

DOMS OF HER LIFE
(by Shayla Black, Jenna Jacob, and Isabella LaPearl)

Raine Falling Collection (Complete)
One Dom To Love
The Young And The Submissive
The Bold and The Dominant
The Edge of Dominance

Heavenly Rising Collection
The Choice
The Chase
Coming Soon:
The Commitment (2021)

FORBIDDEN CONFESSIONS (Sexy Shorts)
Seducing the Innocent
Seducing the Bride
Seducing the Stranger
Seducing the Enemy
Coming Soon:
Seduced by the Bodyguard (October 22, 2020)

SEXY STANDALONES
Naughty Little Secret
Watch Me
Dirty and Dangerous
Her Fantasy Men (Four Play Anthology)
A Perfect Match

THE HOPE SERIES
Misadventures of a Backup Bride
Misadventures with My Ex
Coming Soon:
Untitled (Summer 2021)

SEXY CAPERS (Complete Series)
Bound And Determined
Strip Search
Arresting Desire (Hot In Handcuffs Anthology)

HISTORICAL ROMANCE STANDALONES
The Lady And The Dragon
One Wicked Night

STRICTLY SERIES (Complete Victorian Duet)
Strictly Seduction
Strictly Forbidden

BROTHERS IN ARMS (Complete Medieval Trilogy)
His Lady Bride
His Stolen Bride
His Rebel Bride

about the author

LET'S GET TO KNOW EACH OTHER!

ABOUT ME:

Shayla Black is the *New York Times* and *USA Today* bestselling author of roughly eighty novels. For twenty years, she's written contemporary, erotic, paranormal, and historical romances via traditional, independent, foreign, and audio publishers. Her books have sold millions of copies and been published in a dozen languages.

Raised an only child, Shayla occupied herself with lots of daydreaming, much to the chagrin of her teachers. In college, she found her love for reading and realized that she could have a career publishing the stories spinning in her imagination. Though she graduated with a degree in Marketing/Advertising and embarked on a stint in corporate America to pay the bills, she abandoned all that to be with her characters full-time.

Shayla currently lives in North Texas with her wonderfully supportive husband and daughter, as well as two spoiled tabbies. In her "free" time, she enjoys reality TV, reading, and listening to an eclectic blend of music.

Tell me more about YOU by connecting with me via the links below.

Text Alerts
To receive sale and new release alerts to your phone, text SHAYLA to 24587.

www.shaylablack.com
Reading order, Book Boyfriend sorter, FAQs, excerpts, audio clips, and more!

VIP Reader Newsletter: bit.ly/NLSNLBM
Exclusive content, new release alerts, cover reveals, free books!

Facebook Book Beauties Chat Group
www.facebook.com/groups/ShaylaBlacksBookBeauties
Interact with me! Wine Wednesday LIVE video weekly. Fun, community, and chatter.

Facebook Author Page: www.facebook.com/ShaylaBlackAuthor
News, teasers, announcements, weekly romance release lists…

BookBub: www.bookbub.com/authors/shayla-black
Be the first to learn about my sales!

Instagram: www.instagram.com/ShaylaBlack
See what I'm up to in pictures!

Goodreads: www.goodreads.com/author/show/20983.Shayla_Black
Keep track of your reads and mark my next book TBR so you don't forget!

Pinterest: www.pinterest.com/shaylablacksb
Juicy teasers and other fun about your fave Shayla Black books!

YouTube: www.youtube.com/channel/UCFM7RZF38CqBlr6YG3a4mRQ
Book trailers, videos, and more coming…

If you enjoyed this book, please review/recommend it. That means the world to me!